BAEL
-OF KING'S BLOOD-

Book One
Of
THE DARK LINEAGE

P. R. CARTWRIGHT

This is a work of fiction. Names, characters, organizations, places, events, and incidents are either products of the author's imagination or are used fictitiously.

Text copyright © 2020 by Peter Roy Cartwright. All rights reserved.

No part of this book may be reproduced, or stored in a retrieval system, or transmitted in any form or by means, electronic, mechanical, photocopying, recording, or otherwise, without express written permission of the publisher.

Bael: Of King's Blood is dedicated with much love to my lifelong friend **John Bryson**.

Who sadly passed away during the Covid19 pandemic.

Table of Contents

ACKNOWLEDGMENTS..1
MAPS...2
PROLOGUE..4

1. WOLF..21
2. HUNTER...28
3. CAILEAN-AMBUSH-WEAVING...................44
4. MUTE..69
5. FATHER'S GRIEF...79
6. TRAINING DAY..84
7. THE OLD CRONE..96
8. THE HUNT - BLACK WOLF - THE BEAR..124
9. SONS AND DAUGHTERS............................137
10. SHARED SECRETS.......................................156
11. THE WEAVING - GATES OF LIFE AND
    DEATH..168
12. RAIDERS..178
13. THE WEAVING-THE FIGHT-THE RUNE
    STONE..183
14. ALONG THE EMPEROR ROAD...................190
15. THE FAIR-THE FIGHT-THE TREE-THE
    PLAN...207
16. THE BEGINNING TO THE END OF ALL
    THINGS..240
17. TERRIBLE THINGS......................................251
18. THE EMPEROR ROAD (part two)................270

19. AFTERMATH..277
20. THE STRANGER..292
21. AMBUSH..301
22. CAPE OF STORMS......................................306
23. NEGLECTED ALLIES.................................315
24. THE RETURN...332
25. THE RESCUE-THE PACK..........................341
26. RECONING...354
27. HUNTER-CRAB GIRL-WEAVING...............361
28. OLD CRONE...387
29. JACK'AND - SEVERED HAND – TORAN..398
30. TROUBLING MESSAGE.............................408
31. CAILEAN - THE ORPHANS.......................412
32. A PROMICE REVISITED............................422
33. AN INTRUDER...425
34. KOVAL - TYRNA - THE VISITOR...............427
35. TROUBLING REVELATION.......................433
36. LESSIEN – AN UNEXPECTED THREAT....441
37. PORT OF THENEN – SLAVERS WAREHOUSE………………………………….....452
38. THE CORPSE...462
39. SLAVE MARKET...469
40. WAYCREST – WITCH.................................478
41. DREAM WEAVERS.....................................492
42. TO KILL A SISTER......................................504
43. AN INJUSTICE-SERVED............................518
44. THE DELIVERY – KILLER'S GOOD FORTUNE..523
45. A DESTINY UNFORSEEN..........................530
46. AND SO, IT BEGINS...................................545
47. CRIMSON RIVER...576

48. THE FORGE – A FRIEND'S GRIEF..............576
49. A CALLING..580
50. THE LAKE-A POWER REALIZED...............584
51. THE KEEP-AN AWAKENING......................591
52. ALL THAT REMAINS....................................616
53. LAMIA – A DAUGHTER - THE VISIT.........631
54. PREPERATIONS...640
55. THE CITY OF THE FALLS - A
    WARNING – A QUEEN.................................649
56. THE WEAVING AND THE NIGHT-
    MARE..664
57. THE JOURNEY BEGINS...............................668

EPILOGUE VUL-SARH - THE VOID...................678
ABOUT THE AUTHOR...681

Acknowledgments.

My thanks to my family for all their support. To Ulla, Chandra and friends for proof reading the final draft. And a special thanks to my Daughter Danielle and my son Christian whose patience and support helped me immensely during the final stages of the book. It has been a long and worthwhile journey. Thankyou all, I couldn't have done this without you.

ENDLESS OCEAN
Frostlands
Frozen Fangs
Icefall
Icefall Bay
WHITE OCEAN
NORTHERN
TERRITORIES
Crystal Lake
Fairwald
Sea of Souls
Dorford
Mischank
Bay of Bones
Blackbarrow
Forest of Mere
THE MIDDENS
CALADUR
Dark Pines
Shimmerin Deep
Coral Sisters
Fallow Town
Aldricch
Belmere
Waycrest
Waycrest River
Blackwood
Eastern
Expanse
EASTFALL
WESTFALL
Farroch Lake
Kings Wood
Stonehaven
East Emperor Rd
Dalehaven
Goldmill
Coalforge
Calan River
Freehaven
Jade Isles
Cape of Storms
To the Western and White isles
Free Islands

WHITE OCEAN
Alari
FROSTFIRE
THE GREAT EASTERN EXPANSE
Aerondel
WINTER'S VALE
THE BOUNDLESS SEA
MYTHRIA
Saphire Isles
BAY OF ISLANDS
MISTHAL
Isle of Wolves
Clorien
To the Emperor Rd
GREAT DIVIDE
Shadow isles
Forbidden Forest
Thalos
SHADOWLANDS

PROLOGUE

COMING OF THE WOLF

Foretold by our ancestors, of an age long before the birth of our kind: A Prophesy. Written in blood at the Battle of Sith-Ilyan by the Scribes of The Ancients....
They said. He would enter our lives an outcast of ignorance. Neither one nor the other yet stronger than both and through him the power of those Ancients would be unleashed....
A beacon of Light in a Darkness born of Malice....
And from the Chaos and Death will come LIFE.

LIFE

The fresh smell of rain on leaves greeted the two warriors as they approached the battered door of the Old Huntsman's cabin. Kor-yllion the Elder King knew this was no place for his daughter to bear child. But it had been seeded of *Man*; and though he loved his daughter dearly he could not allow the coming of this abomination to take place on Elven soil.

Inside, the cabin was a place of gloom and menacing shadows, where dust motes danced in what little light the two shuttered windows surrendered. Against the far wall, flames from a freshly made fire licked the bottom of a small iron cauldron, boiling whatever concoction lay within.

The door opened. The two Elders entered the room and removed their wet fur rimmed coats. Uncharacteristically the King turned for a friend's reassurance, there was none for the Shaman loved the child within as if she were his own. What was to follow weighed heavily on his conscience, for as much as his lifelong friend was a just and honest leader, he was also a rigid purveyor of Elder Law; a Law which would see a mother exiled forever from her kind and a new-born abandoned to chance where death was almost certain.

Shouldering this burden, the King's head Shaman Kor-aviel made his way across the sparsely furnished room, to where the Queen and her entourage were tending to her daughter Elleriel as best they could. Her screams of agony as she rolled around on the cot bed confirmed the Shaman's deepest fears: though both Elder and Human looked similar of appearance they had vastly different constitutions and without his help both mother and child would surely perish.

Barely able to lift her head the Princess looked to the door where the King stood alone; and though almost too weak to talk she made one last desperate attempt to find a father now lost to her.

"Please father, find forgiveness in your heart for my child is innocent. If fault has to be laid on anyone's shoulders then let it be mine and deal with me as you must, but please, please allow my child the right to life?" Hope faded as only silence followed. She waited a moment before laying back her head.

"I love you father." She murmured, as she watched the face of a father change to that of King and Leader of the High Elders of Erendor. But as he turned to leave his face softened and quietly so no other ears could hear he said.

"I love you to my child."

Before he could get through the door Melia his sister, a tall dark-haired beauty stormed across the room grabbed his arm and dragged him outside. The Shaman paid no heed to this; his focus was on the task at hand.

"Please, if you wish to save the life of your daughter and her child I would have you all leave, there is little else you can do here," he said to Lessien the Queen, his tone firm yet compassionate. Nervously, before following his instruction she gently took the Shaman's hand, her anguish plain to see.

"I know what my husband feels compelled to do, but please, please don't leave their fate to beliefs you know to be questionable. You love her as you would your own, I know this. Do not let outdated tradition cloud sense born of wisdom."

The Elder squeezed her hand.

"I will do what I can but you must leave as time is short."

The Queen kissed her daughter on the cheek and whispered in her ear.

"I love you with all my heart, you must trust in Koraviel now."

"I love you too."

Reluctantly, Lessien moved away from the bed and turned for one last look before exiting the room.

Elleriel watched helplessly as the Elder Shaman prepared himself. The day's sadness had dulled his bright green eyes, he seemed not at all the Elder she remembered; one who would tell stories of Heroes past that fired the wild imaginings of a small Princess.

Using every ounce of his considerable skills, Koraviel whispered an incantation, leaving the young Princess in a semi-conscious state while he readied himself for the ordeal ahead. From the pain she was suffering it was obvious the baby had turned, leaving him with only one option: he removed a sleek curved dagger from his belt, its ornate hilt inlaid with ancient runes. Carefully, he poured a strange green liquid along its blade from a small glass phial he placed on the bed earlier. Speaking in the Old tongue he removed the excess liquid with a torn piece of linen. Slowly the beautifully forged blade began to shimmer in gossamer like blue light. With steady hand, he cut a large split in the Princess's sweat soaked birthing gown, exposing her swollen stomach. He paused for a moment making sure she was still in a comforted state, and then slowly he drew the blade from her navel downwards, the flesh parting like petals of a flower. Considering the size of such an incision there was little blood, the blade of the knife cauterizing the wound as it cut. His fears were confirmed, the child had turned, but even worse the life cord had wrapped around the babe's neck cutting off its air supply. Quickly he cut the cord and removed the baby from the open womb, laying its lifeless body on a nest of cloths he had placed on the table. Touching its still chest with two of his fingers, he sensed but the tiniest flicker of life; a heartbeat so faint no ordinary hand could detect it. He closed his eyes and focused all of his life-giving energy through those two fingers. At first it looked as if nothing was happening, then slowly the skin's blue grey veneer of near death turned to a wonderful blush colour and without warning the room was filled with the cry of LIFE.

***

Melia the King's sister was in no mood for pleasantries, she knew all too well what her brother was capable of: she'd had the misfortune to witness his misguided, moralistic judgement once before, on their brother. A brother she had loved dearly. She squared up to the King, no longer able to contain her anger she said.

"There has to be another way, you must know this…. Her blood runs through your veins… Have you no conscience?"

"You grieve me dear sister, that you see me void of such feeling that would let me undo these passing events. The law is there to protect our kind from the corruption of impure blood, a law which has worked until this day for thousands of years," he replied, more hurt than angry.

As she stared at him her face softened slightly.

"The preaching's of the old ways blind you my brother. What you consider to be a folly of the young is really the wind of change; a change that neither you, I, nor any of the Elders will be able to stop and though you wish not to believe it, humans have strengths we are foolish to ignore."

The King's shoulders dropped as if in defeat, but he quickly regained his composure and just as the Queen appeared in the doorway, he took his sister's hand in his.

"I am duty bound to honour our ancient laws even if they take me on a different path to that of my heart."

"Then you are a fool driven by stubborn arrogance my brother," she replied, as she tore her hand from his. Shocked by the sheer venom behind her words his features hardened.

"I do not take pleasure in any of this, but this is the way it has to be, and I will hear no more about the matter."

Melia pulled away in temper and headed for a group of the King's elite guard who stood sentinel at the forest's edge. Before she had walked ten paces down the worn cobbled path the Queen called out to her.

"Please Melia, wait. You can't rush away before the child is born; you will never forgive yourself."

"I have to, I will not lay witness to such hypocrisy. Go, you are needed back there, I will be fine. Now go, please," she insisted. Then cries of a new-born emanated from within the cabin. It was a sound that would tear at the heart of any mother and though she wanted to leave she could not; this was not a time for selfish thought, so she followed the Queen back into the cabin.

***

The weeks that followed saw mother and baby grow stronger by the day. The Queen, Melia, and Kor-aviel made frequent visitations supplying fresh food, clothing and whatever comfort they could offer. But the day Elleriel was dreading had finally arrived.

She was sat on the banks of the fast-running brook at the back of the cabin, watching butterflies' flit from flower to flower, while her baby was content to just soak up the warmth from an early morning sun. The ground began to tremble slightly as eight Elven warriors approached on horseback, led by the unmistakeable figure of the Shaman, Kor-aviel. Bravely, she stood up and put herself between them and her child; the real fear of being separated was now beginning to consume her, leaving her shaking in a way she had never experienced before and though an Elder could shed no tears her eyes cried out in utter despair.

The Shaman dismounted and left his and the spare horse with the captain of the guard. He approached the grieving Princess with nervous trepidation, but before he could utter a word the young Princess rushed towards him.

"Please you cannot do this. You are like an uncle to me," she said, in desperation, almost collapsing into Kor-aviel's chest. "There has to be something you can do to convince my father that this is wrong."

The Shaman rested his hand on the back of her head to comfort her as best he could.

"There is a hope, my child. What I am about to tell you will seem strange. But in time all will become clear, this I promise."

Elleriel lifted her head from his chest.

"What do you mean?" She asked.

The Shaman locked eyes with her.

"Pick up your child and follow me, and do exactly as I say."

"What are you going to do"? She asked. *Weren't you supposed to take my child and leave it in the woods for whatever fate would befall it?* She thought, not daring to speak the words out loud.

"Do you trust me?" He whispered.

"Yes," she replied, filled with half a hope.

He waved for the Elder captain and the rest of the guard to join them. He took Elleriel by the hand.

"You must go with the captain and begin your journey to Mythria and the Isle of the Lost."

"But what of my child?"

"You must trust me otherwise all will be for naught," he urged.

She nodded her understanding, then reluctantly gave her babe over to the Shaman. She mounted her horse and followed the guard into the forest. For a moment, she turned back for one last look before they disappeared amongst the trees.

It took a full month of hard riding with stops at several Elven settlements and outposts to reach the Isle. Elleriel never uttered a word the whole journey. Being parted like that from her child had placed her in a living nightmare, which, for such a disciplined mind was beyond unbearable. Hate for her kind was such an empty emotion but that was the very emotion which consumed her, every time her father entered her thoughts. The single ray of light in her darkness came from those parting words of the Shaman. She had to trust him; it was her only hope.

The group were met at the shores by the envoy to the King, a tall, lean, official looking Elder, dressed from head to toe in finest Elven silk with the Emblem of a Wolf emblazoned across his chest. He approached the young princess with the grace of his office and bowed his head, a courtesy only shown to someone of high calling.

"My name is Mitore-ly, my Princess. You grace us with your presence, please follow me," he said, sporting a smile as smug as it was insincere. She nodded her head in reply and followed him to the waiting boat. *You speak as if I had a choice in this matter*, she thought, *words as false as your smile.*

It was large for a row boat; fourteen crewmen steered the vessel towards the Isle, their muscles rippling with every stroke of oars that were shaped like leaves; the hull made from larger versions of those very same leaves, to finish both fore and aft with the head of a *Dire Wolf.* The Princess was seated next to the Envoy on a bench at the back of the vessel; not a word passed between them for the rest of the journey.

Elleriel took this opportunity to look around at the breath-taking scenery that surrounded them. The Isle they were heading for lay at the centre of the largest lake she had ever seen. Her mother had told her stories about this place; of the Lake surrounded on all sides by snow-capped mountains, its waters originating from three huge glaciers whose icy rivers sped far into the distance. An Isle, cloaked in mystery, a mystery only known by a chosen few.

The only port of entrance from the lake was a small harbour, shaped like a crescent moon; one long jetty moored several similar vessels to the one she occupied. Elleriel shifted in her seat nervously as the boat pulled into its mooring. The envoy helped her to her feet and escorted her ashore.

They were greeted by a young Elven warrior the likes of which she had never before seen. He was shorter by a head than most males of her kind, black shoulder length hair with a streak of silver grey, framed a strong unnervingly handsome face with eyes that shone like radiant Sapphires. He approached the princess, flanked on either side by two huge Dire Wolves.

"I hope you had a comfortable journey my lady," he said, with a smile that could lighten the heart.

"As comfortable as one could expect I suppose," she replied, sarcastically.

"Well, we cannot ask for more than that, can we now?"

She looked nervously at the Wolves as he gestured for her to follow him.

"Please, do not be afraid they will not harm you," he said, running his hands down the back of the Wolves necks.

The Wolf King watched from his balcony high in the West Tower as his son approached the structure; the Princess and the wolves following close behind. He coughed a little, clearing his throat he turned to his unexpected guest.

"Your daughter approaches, it is time for you to leave before your presence here is discovered," he said, making no attempt at hiding his contempt for his old ally. Kor-yllion looked down as the group below disappeared into the lower reaches of the tower, his demeanour rigid and unforgiving.

"There is one more thing I have to see done before I leave… so I shall stay until then."

"As you wish, but please stay here, I will have my own personal ward tend to your needs. He is very discrete," the Wolf King replied.

"Thank you for your courtesy."

The Wolf King nodded his head as acknowledgment for the tiniest hint of civility his Royal guest had afforded him, then left to greet the new arrival in the great Throne Room at the base of the Tower.

The throne was more like a wooden canopy than a seat for a king; it was cut from the trunk of the Emperor tree, a giant of the forest beyond, ornate carvings of leaf and flowers swept around and over the seat culminating in the huge carving of a Wolf's head. The Wolf Lord relaxed onto the dark red cushion as the massive doors at the opposite end of the hall creaked open. Two of his elite guard led the Princess and her escorts towards him, passing between imposing wooden statues of Elven Heroes past. On reaching the lower steps in front of the throne the two huge wolves moved either side of their Alpha lord. He shifted forward to stroke the beasts before addressing his beautiful guest.

"I hope your journey here has not troubled you too much little princess?" He asked. His voice deep but surprisingly compassionate. She couldn't look at him, only anger and uncertainty filled her heart, leaving room for little else; so, she just stared at the floor affording her captors the courtesies their positions demanded.

"You speak to me as if I were your guest. Yet, is this just not a play on words on this Isle of secrets? Am I mistaken? Or is it not a prison without walls?"

The Wolf Lord set his gaze to the warrior by her side, totally ignoring her previous comments.

"My son, it is obvious our guest is tired from her travels. Show her to her quarters. We can talk later when she is rested."

"Yes father," the young warrior replied.

Feeling a little uncomfortable by his father's rather indifferent attitude toward their guest, the Prince bowed and gestured for the Princess to follow him to her room.

As they turned to leave, the Wolf King stood up and made one final comment before exiting the Throne room himself by another door.

"Please treat my house as if it were your own, feel free to wander as your curiosity demands."

This time she returned the discourtesy by not replying, an act of defiance that brought a smile to the face of his son as he led her through the Hall.

Three mornings passed without the Princess uttering a word; her only visitor other than a maiden of service was the young Warrior Prince. Whom, it could be said, was more than a little intrigued by the beautiful newcomer. Though, had she looked from her balcony each of the three following nights, she would have seen a huge Black Dire Wolf with a unique Silver-Grey Streak running down its neck, staring up at her room under cover of the weeping willow by the bridge.

Although outward appearances suggested otherwise, she actually found herself looking forward to the Prince's visits. He had been leaving her pastries from the Royal kitchens as peace offerings of sorts, without success; until the afternoon of the fourth day.

As usual he arrived with his parcel of offerings, but instead of wallowing in her misery, he found her sitting by a stream close to a bridge overlooking a waterfall at the back of the grounds. This was the first time he had seen her show interest in anything around her. She looked mesmerised by the wolf cubs as they played their feral games around the grounds.

He approached her with trepidation, expecting the same cold empty response he had received on previous attempts at communication. But this time she stood up to receive his gift willingly, though her jade green eyes still remained full of question.

"Please may I join you?" He asked, half expecting a refusal.

She nodded yes and sat down to eat the Elven fancy, wrapped so neatly in the fine leaf of the Mountain Willow. The young Prince sat beside her and began to eat one of the offerings himself. What was left he threw to a singing bluebird that had landed just a few feet infront of the Princess. As brave as you like, it pecked at the morsel and then flew off holding a large piece in its dark blue beak.

This simple kindness made her relax slightly, she peaked quickly sideways looking at the handsome profile of her strange host, then quickly turned away as he looked to speak to her.

"I cannot imagine how difficult it must be, finding yourself separated from your family and friends like this, without explanation," he said, carefully avoiding the matter of her daughter. "But when you are ready to speak with my father and his council, things will be made clear to you, this I promise."

For a moment she paused, then stood up and looked across the grounds at the fast running waters of the fall.

"Please, I only wish to know what is going on here? Why would my father send me to such a place? And I find the silence surrounding the whereabouts of my child both heartless and unbearable."

The Prince shuffled about uncomfortably, for no matter how much he sympathized with her plight, he dare not break silence on such matters, not before his father had spoken with her first.

"I wish I could give you the answers you seek. These you must acquire from my father. All I can do is assure you that you are safe here amongst us and that things will be made clearer in time, but for now you must trust me."

Those words brought back memories of the last time she saw her child, when Kor-aviel uttered the very same.

"Then I am ready to meet with your father." Before she could finish, a ward of the Royal Court crossed the bridge and walked up to them. Addressing his Lord, he bowed graciously.

"Sire, you asked me to inform you when the boat arrived."

"I did," he replied, "and?"

"It docks as we speak."

The words brought a smile of relief to the Prince's face.

"My lady there is something you must see; now some of your questions will be answered."

She stared at him puzzled.

"What do you mean?"

"Please follow me all will become clear." Without saying another word, he headed across the bridge towards the harbour; a bemused Princess close behind.

Kor-aviel stepped onto the jetty, Melia close behind holding a swaddle of fine silk wrappings close to her breast. As the three figures approached, she disembarked carefully from the boat and waited as her niece broke away from the group and ran as fast as she could towards her. Breathless and silenced in disbelief by what now faced her, the Princess threw her arms around the old Shaman kissing him over and over. Then turning towards Melia like the weight of the world had just fallen from her shoulders, she took hold of the bundle covering her child, first, taking in its scent before kissing its little rose blushed cheeks. Melia hugged them both tightly, not wanting to let them go.

Elleriel looked at both her Kin folk with a warmth and love she feared had abandoned her and said.

"I am lost for words. I will never forget what you have done for me this day. I love you both dearly."

Before either could reply the Prince quietly intervened.

"Please I must ask you all to follow me and join my father in the Great Hall."

Unable to contain herself, Melia was the first to respond.

"We will follow, my young Lord, there are things we all need to discuss, so please lead on."

As the group made their way back to the Palace, the Princess noticed the odd shaped building resembling a Wolf's head seated high on a small tree covered Island, connected by a league long causeway from the Palace's West gate.

The young warrior noticed her curiosity and prepared himself for a question, but it never came, as her attentions turned immediately back to the beautiful bundle in her arms.

High above out of sight Kor-yllion watched from the balcony as his daughter and all her followers walked towards the Tower. He was joined momentarily by the Wolf King, who addressed him with some urgency.

"I think your time here has come to an end. You should leave now by the stairway in the eastern wing."

"You were able to persuade Kor-aviel to change my mind and see, not just my daughter, but my granddaughter also brought to this Island of yours." Koryllion said. "I only hope I do not come to regret my decision."

The Wolf Lord couldn't hide his surprise as the Elder King left by the door leading to the rear of the Tower; in the millennia they had known one another he had never known Kor-Yllion to reverse a judgement of such magnitude. But he had and only time would reveal the truth. Now it was time to answer questions.

***

After learning of her fate and that of her daughter, the Princess was traumatised. She paced up and down her room, periodically stepping out onto her balcony to stare at the strange Wolf Head building she spotted earlier. The Ritual, she was told, would be painless, as both mother and child would be rendered unconscious through some sort of mind control. But there was no consolation in any of this. By nights end they would both be transformed and there was nothing she could do about it. She held her baby daughter close to her chest, mumbling words of disbelief, that anyone who loved her could be party to such a life changing event. That Kor-aviel and Melia were part of this conspiracy, made it all the more intolerable.

After her meeting with the Wolf King, Elleriel stormed back to her room crying. Melia thought it best to leave her alone for a while and though Kor-aviel felt otherwise, her feminine intuition won out.

Sometime later there was a knock on the door. The Princess kept quiet hoping that whoever it was would just go away, then Melia's head appeared.

"Go away, I don't want to talk to you, any of you," Elleriel sobbed.

Both Kor-aviel and her aunt stepped into the room neither sure what to say, because in reality there was nothing they could do to change the outcome.

Melia made the first move. She eased the baby from Elleriel's arms and took hold of her niece's hand.

"Come. Sit beside me," she whispered, sitting on the side of the bed.

Kor-aviel felt awkward. Keeping quiet he sat down on the other side of the Princess and put his arm around her. Elleriel buried her head into his chest, her tears soaking into his robes. He kissed the top of her head and pulled her tight against him.

"There, there," he said, feeling the tension in her body relax a little.

Melia stroked the back of her hand, trying to think of what to say. But before she could utter a word.

"You can't let them do this to us, it is grotesque," Elleriel said. "Please, you have to stop this madness. I can't bear it."

"I know it all seems beyond imagining, but there is no other way. There is a curse on this Island and all who reside here and before long the transformation would happen anyway, and without the ritual your child would certainly die," Melia added.

"Please, I am begging you. Take us from this place."

"We can't. Powers beyond your understanding are in play. And if this ritual doesn't take place then everyone we know and love will perish. And all we have built for thousands of years will be lost forever." Kor-aviel lifted Elleriel's head off his chest and turned her to face him. She could see he looked sad. "I know none of this makes any sense, but in time you will see the truth and I promise, we will not abandon you after the change."

Elleriel stopped crying and seemed to surrender to the inevitability of it all. She took back her baby and cuddled her lovingly. And for a while they all just sat together in comfort of one another without another word passing between them.

***

The Wolf Prince addressed his father as he stood looking towards the Wolf's head building the Princess had noticed earlier.

"Father. When it is time for the *changing,* I would like to accompany the Princess and her child and be there for them throughout the ceremony."

"I am afraid that is not possible my son, the head Summoner would not allow it."

"He would if you told him to father."

The King pondered with idea for a moment. *Why are you so intent on attending a ritual that for all time has been performed solely by the Summoners?* He thought.

"Why my son? Why should I allow such a request?" The King asked.

"I am not sure; all I know is I share a bond with Elleriel that I have shared with no other."

"Well, I would be foolish to ignore your gift of foresight my son, so I will see what can be done."

"Thank you, father."

With this the King left his son on the balcony. The young warrior looked first to the Island then to the balcony where Elleriel sat cradling her baby. A feeling came over him, a feeling that the strange bond he felt with their new guest had somehow changed something within him forever.

***

Years have passed since the Princess and her daughter stepped foot on the Isle, but now it was time.

The King of Wolves looked down at the Changeling Dire Wolf and her Daughter, a beautiful young Wolf with eyes of liquid gold. He knew, for the Prophesy to be realized, a Prophesy written in blood at the Battle of Sith-llyan, the young Wolf must make the perilous journey to the Realm of Men.

1
WOLF

"How did it ever come to this? I look upon the battlefield, filled with a sadness no man should ever have to bear. The bodies of the fallen so great in number I can hardly see the ground beneath them. Friends I have known all their lives lost forever in a sea of blood. It seems like a life time ago now, in the place where it all began; Serenity. What a strange name for a place that would birth a legend, who's journey foretold, would be written in the blood of so many. Serenity: a clearing in a forest, a cabin in a clearing, blessed with a peacefulness that birthed its name. How fitting then, that where it all began it now ends."

In the distance a winter sun dropped behind the Taelyn Mountains, their jagged snow-capped peaks stabbing at the clouds like the teeth of some giant beast. Thundering through the valley Kor-yllion the King led the Elder search party along the snow-covered trail to the point where the river entered the forest. Reining in his mount he leapt from the saddle to take a closer look at the tracks they had been following for the past few days. Kor-aviel his head Shaman pulled up shortly after, spinning his horse around to face the rest of the party; it was a signal for the King's Elite to spread out and form a protective cauldron around their leader. Before dismounting himself, the shaman scoured the area ahead looking down at the broken snow waiting for it to reveal its secrets. It was obvious from the markings in the snow that something had caused the riders to group together.

Kor-yllion stood up and looked around the surrounding area. The same Wolf tracks which had been following this group along the trail, had spread out, forming a protective circle; the Elder leader knew this wasn't a circle of threat, instead, these were beasts protecting their masters, but from what? His friend and Shaman moved to his side; he paused for a moment and listened. A haunting silence hung over the frozen landscape, the type of silence which befalls the land when nature herself is witness to something truly terrible.

"We must proceed with caution Sire. Something is not right here…listen?" The Shaman urged.

Kor-yllion looked up at the sky.

"It is just the wind," he replied.

"That is my point, what has happened to the sound of birds, and the chattering's of the forest? It is as if all the voices of nature have been sucked out of the very air." Looking concerned the King walked across the trodden snow to where both sets of tracks broke away from one another, heading in the direction of the forest. He spotted strange black shapes dotted about further up the road, but it was too far for him to make any sense of them, so he waved over his Captain.

Oromar was powerfully built for an Elder, broader by half than any other member of the King's Elite guard he was renowned for his hawk like vision; his birth gift from a magic that had permeated in their realm since the time of the ancients. A gift that was different for all High Elders, a gift chosen from the very essence of nature herself. He broke ranks and rode up to his leader, his beautiful black war horse snorting and cantering sideways as if it too sensed trouble ahead.

"My Lord?"

"Captain…Please tell me what you see on the road ahead," Kor-yllion said pointing towards the black shapes in the distance. Oromar rose from the saddle and focused on the shapes: It was almost dark as the last of the sunlight melted away behind the mountains, but there was enough of it for him to confirm the nagging fear that had chipped away at him the moment they set foot on that place.

"Sire I…I cannot say for certain, with the onset of darkness coming upon us, but," he paused.

"Please, what is it?" the Shaman asked, fearing inside what he believed the answer would be.

"It looks like horses and riders…" again he paused awkwardly. Kor-yllion saw the pain in his captain's face which only further fuelled his own misgivings.

"What about the horses and riders?"

"It looks like they are all dead my Lord," the Captain replied, reluctantly. The King looked to his friend and then without uttering a word mounted his stallion, spinning it around.

"We must move with caut…." Before the Shaman could finish, his leader had kicked his steed into a full gallop.

"Follow him, now! The Gods only know what he is riding into," the Shaman ordered.

The captain responded instantly, rallying his troops into action.

As he got closer to the fallen riders Kor-yllion noticed the change in the air around him; it was the smell you get in a violent storm, more than fresh – charged. Then, even in the dimmed light he recognised the deep red spatters that peppered the snow; a bloody precursor to the horrors that followed. He pulled hard on the reins causing his horse to rear up on its hind legs. Lying in a pool of blood was the torn carcass of a huge Dire Wolf, it was obvious to the King that this was the Alpha and was probably the first to die. It wasn't long before the rest of his group had joined him and for the first time they saw a leader torn with anguish, for they knew all too well what this meant to him. Kor-aviel pulled alongside his friend and dismounted.

"Sire I will search for her here," he said, before turning to the Captain. "You will escort the King, take half of the guard, I will take the rest with me."

"Yes, my Lord," Oromar nodded, turning his horse in instant response. The King had already started to ride towards the fallen riders, but his guards were close behind and closing fast in a protective 'V' formation.

Meanwhile Kor-aviel and his group went from carcass to carcass, some ripped apart beyond recognition. But they hadn't found what they were looking for and now the search was further hampered by the fall of night: cold, black and uninviting the road ahead was barely lit by the silver light of a perfect full moon.

The Shaman and his followers thundered towards the King and his group, who were already searching through gruesome remains of both horse and rider that littered the ground at the edge of the forest. The Shaman watched as his leader went from body to body with ever increasing urgency until he came upon a female lying face down in the snow. Even at this distance he recognised the dress and colours of the Royal family. He rushed over to the King who had already begun to turn over the body. Approaching from behind he couldn't see the victims face but he knew it was her; Melia the King's sister.

Kor-yllion, unaware of his friend's comforting hand on his shoulder, dropped his head in grief, strangling the scream he could not allow to get out. The

Shaman removed his hand and moved around to look upon the body. After the initial shock of seeing a friend dead he realized there was something different about this and some others amongst the Elven corpses. There was only a little blood; the bodies were intact but their faces. *What could have done this?* He thought. It was as if their very life force had been sucked out of them, leaving their faces like a mask twisted and screaming as they tried to hold onto that final breath. The Shaman looked towards the darkness behind the trees ahead, it felt as if they were being watched, and he could not understand why his magically enhanced intuition hadn't uncovered any of the mystery surrounding these tragic events.

The King leaned forward and kissed his sister lovingly on the forehead. His friend helped him to his feet, then raising his head the Shaman closed his eyes in deep concentration.

"My Lord the evil…it is gone. But there is something else, another presence." At first the King did not realize the gravity of what had just been said so torn by grief was he, but slowly its significance became clear.

"Did you find the Wolf?" he asked, as Kor-aviel moved towards a large bush just inside the forest perimeter.

The Shaman's feet crunched through the snow drift which had gathered like a wall of ice around the base of the bush. Pushing back the branches it was the sight he had hoped for.

"Sire, she is here."

The Captain joined his leader, leaving his warriors on high alert. They both approached the Shaman and looked beneath the overhanging bush. Even in the moonlit darkness they could see hidden and alive a large young Dire Wolf. A sense of relief swept through the group. The King dropped on one knee and caringly stroked the beast's neck running his hand along its side until he felt the sticky warmth of a bloody open wound, claw marks of the wolf's attacker. Kor-aviel already aware of the animal's grave condition responded immediately. Placing his hand on his friend's shoulder he squeezed gently.

"I must tend to that wound before it is too late," he urged.

The King moved beside his Captain, who had tried his best to comfort his grieving leader; a skill set that had not been part of his martial training, but he did his best, and the King knew this.

Kor-aviel touched the beast's chest; its breathing was laboured and shallow. Then he slid his hand towards its neck where a large black Rune stone hung as a protective ward against whatever evil had befallen that place. The Shaman knew the black stone was the sole reason the beast was still holding onto life, even if it was but a thread.

The Wolf watched every move understanding every word that was spoken by its helpers. It turned its gaze to the King as he addressed his friend the Shaman tending her wound.

"Will she live?" Kor-yllion asked, nervous of the answer. No answer came, but as the Shaman tried to remove the stone from around her neck, she lifted her massive head in a weak endeavour to aid him with his task.

She lay limp, hardly able to move as Kor-aviel laid his hands over the wound and listened as her helper spoke a language only known to the Elders. Suddenly a black putrid mist began to seep from rendered flesh causing the Shaman to slump back weakened by the ordeal. She closed her eyes as consciousness left her; a temporary respite from the pain that burned in every nerve of her body.

Most of the pain dissipated through whatever magic was used. The Captain lifted the weakened Shaman to his feet, the King feeling helpless as his friend fought to keep the beast alive.

"Will she live?" Kor-yllion pressed, trying to hold back the anger that welled inside. This time his friend afforded him a reply.

"Her life hangs in the balance. I have done all I can to remove the evil from the wound, but I fear some still resides within her."

"But will she live?" The King asked, still waiting for a finite answer.

"For now, but we must get her to safety. There is nothing more I can do; her fate lies in her own strength. She must embrace the power she was born to wield, a power yet unproven." The Shaman paused for a moment and gazed deeply into his friend's eyes.

"Even though you do not wish it my lord, it is time we took her to Hunter. Her life and her destiny lie with him; I fear it was always going to be this way." And in those jade green eyes he saw his answer.

2
HUNTER

A white veil of mist hugged the ground as the last of the snow melted under the warmth of an early spring sun. Bael stepped out from the trees; freshly killed game slung over his shoulder. He followed the path at the back of his lodge until he reached his skinning hut, a small timber building open on one side with a thick wooden table at its centre. He placed his bow on a stand and hung two pheasants on meat hooks suspended from the roof; he did the same with two of the four rabbits, before skinning the two remaining. Even though he lived alone Bael prided himself on being a good cook, from whom he got such culinary skills, he had no idea: his mother had died at his birth and what clouded memories he had of his father he doubted he was the source. Pausing for a moment he looked across to the large custom-built wooden pen off to his right, there was no movement, so he carried on preparing the meat. From a bucket by the side of the table he removed an iron spit rod and impaled both rabbits with it. Throwing the rod over his shoulder he picked up some root vegetables and entered the lodge by the back door.

It wasn't long before the smell of cooked meat filled the room as the rabbits' spit roasted nicely on the open fire. In the meantime, he removed several types of herb and dried leaves from boxes by the window and placed them by the vegetables. After dicing sweet potatoes, turnips and suede, he dropped them into a small cauldron of boiling water, then sprinkled both rabbits with some of the herbs. He cooked them a little longer before removing one from the spit and placing it on the table near the window. Carefully he crushed the dried leaves with a small mortar and pestle, then dusted the cooked rabbit with the ground mixture. *That should do it*, he thought as he turned the meat over making sure he had covered it properly. He let it stand for a moment to cool before taking it outside to the compound at the back of the lodge. Bending down in front of the strong wooden bars he held out his hand, dangling the rabbit inside the pen.

"Here eat this, it will help you regain your strength," he said, his voice gentle but commanding.

The huge Dire Wolf opened its eyes and stared at its captor. Bael could see, she was still cautious, even though he had shown her nothing but kindness during the two weeks she had been in his care. Two weeks that saw him sit night after night by the pen talking to her; allowing her to get used to his scent and his kindly intentions.

Slowly and with considerable discomfort she rose to her feet and edged her way across the pen to accept the roasted gift. She dropped to the ground right in-front of Bael and began licking the herbs off the rabbit's flesh before devouring it in a couple of bites: it was as if she knew the herbs impregnating the meat contained special healing properties.

Hunter moved to the side a little to get a clear view of the Wolf's wound. He was pleased to see it had healed considerably over the weeks she had been with him; in-fact it was quite the miracle she could even stand let alone walk to him like she did. The poisons that had entered her body still seeped through the poultice covering the wound; a concoction of his making consisting of various crushed roots suspended in the gooey sap of the Arosetta tree. He stood up and smiled at the beast.

"You heal well my friend, but you have some way to go yet before you are strong enough to hunt again," he whispered, half expecting the animal to understand. As he walked away the Wolf lifted her head slightly, her round golden eyes following his every step; a sound of contentment rolled around in her throat, for she understood every word.

As the night drew in, Bael changed out of his hunting clothes, freshened himself up, threw on a black leather jerkin and headed into town.

***

Vena, the shapely madam of the only whorehouse in the region was stood in the doorway plying her trade, when she spotted one of the few clients, she serviced herself. She knew him as Hunter as did most of the town; his real name forgotten or ignored for the one fuelled by his reputation with bow and blade. The streets had no lighting other than what little came from the houses, even so his strong muscular silhouette and long black pony tail left her in no doubt who it was: She pushed back her shoulders and stood a little taller as he passed.

"Not seen yer in town for a while Hunter," she said, throwing back her hair seductively.

"Been missin' me 'ave yer?" Bael carried on walking down the narrow alley without responding to her jibes. Angered by his indifference Vena stepped out of the doorway and shouted after him.

"Well suit yer'self-big man…your loss aye?"

From the end of the alley he entered the town square; passing market vendors as they packed up for the day. The Rogue Bear Tavern lay straight ahead of him, but first he had to pass the square's fountain where Sylda the baker's wife counted her day's takings.

"You off to the tavern then Hunter?" She quizzed, as he passed her in a futile attempt to elude her gaze.

Keeping his head down Bael carried on walking but Sylda wasn't having any of it. *You're not ignoring me mister,* she thought, shouting after him.

"Well, if you see that good for nothin' husband of mine, tell him the bread won't bake itself and if he thinks I am going to fuckin' bake it, well he knows the answer to that one."

Bael waved a hand in acknowledgement but had no intention of passing along any such message. Still not content she bellowed.

"Tell that slippery old bastard if he isn't out 'ere before I finish counting this money I will come in there, cut off 'is balls and drag his sorry ass back to the shop myself."

Bael wanted to ignore her completely but theirs was the best bread in town, so he waved, more out of courtesy than intent.

The Rogue Bear Tavern was one of the oldest establishments in Stonehaven, being built not long after Farroth Keep; its clientele then almost exclusively militia men and guards from the fortress. Bael never tired of the smell of aged wood, ale and burnt candle wax that welcomed him as he stepped into the old interior. Oak beams taken from ancient Galleys supported ceilings bowed with age and Elm candelabras whose candles filled the room in a rich orange glow. As usual the imposing figure of Dogran the Innkeep was behind the bar chatting to some of the regulars; his beautiful daughter Emma by his side busy serving a chubby olive-skinned man dressed like a merchant. Bael headed straight for her knowing that his presence would almost certainly agitate the burly Innkeep; their relationship fiery to say the least.

Emma smiled as Hunter slipped in next to the merchant at the bar, a smile which hadn't gone unnoticed by her father. The merchant was no stranger to Hunter either and the troubles which shadowed him; so, he picked up his drink and joined the group of regulars talking to Dogran.

The group welcomed the chubby merchant then carried on chatting.

"Strange one that Hunter," the merchant whispered.

Dogran never one to miss an opportunity shouted across the bar.

"Still have a way with folks I see, Hunter."

Emma glared at her father.

"Father," she scowled, embarrassed by his sarcasm. "I am sorry about that, it was totally uncalled for," she said, turning to Bael who seemed completely unfazed by it all.

"You don't need to apologize for your father. He has his reasons."

Emma was surprised at his response.

"Well, I think it was out of order… Anyway, what will it be?"

"A mug of ale," he replied, his voice low and penetrating.

"Try this, brewed by the Monks, best in the land," she said, filling the tankard from the barrel at the end of the bar. Bael tried to give her coin for the drink, but Emma refused payment giving him the drink on the house to make up for her father's untimely sarcasm. He accepted the offer with his usual economy of words before Emma moved along the counter to serve someone else.

Dogran seized on this window of opportunity to speak with Hunter, out of earshot of his daughter.

"Now listen, we want no trouble in here tonight... Understand?"

Hunter ignored the comment and carried on drinking. Dogran, aware his daughter was approaching, stood up straight and moved back to his regulars at the other end of the bar.

"Not seen you around here for a while?" she said smiling.

"That's because the last time he was here he near parted a man's jaw from his face," Dogran interrupted. The baker Jered who'd just placed his order couldn't ignore what he'd just heard.

"Yes, but let's have it right Dogran, you cantankerous old bull, the man was an animal, a drifter itching for a fight... And that's just what he got and let's face it *he* challenged Hunter."

Dogran wasn't amused by the baker's interruption but he let it lie. Emma scowled. Her father knew that look and knew it was time to back off; he loved his daughter dearly and though he disagreed with her, in the end he would always put her feelings first. Bael not being good with small talk responded coolly, ignoring Dogran's interruption.

"Been busy – nothin' more."

Emma never one to give up, carried on.

"Hear you caught a wolf?"

"Did you now?" He stared into her deep brown eyes and carried on drinking. Emma felt a little uncomfortable with his unwillingness to elaborate; she had known Hunter for some time now but she just couldn't read him. Yet there was something she saw in him, something she saw in those vivid blue eyes the very first time they met; something her father either had not seen or did not want to see...*Kindness.*

***

Bael sat alone at a table in a corner alcove just people watching. It had been a long time since he had spent two consecutive nights at the tavern, and though no-one would have guessed, Hunter was flattered by the young barmaid's attention. Dogran as usual was entertaining some locals with his typical barkeep humour while Emma served the tables. The place was pretty busy for mid-week. Jered was avoiding his wife again supping heartily with his friends. *Some men never learn,* Bael thought finishing his ale, half expecting the baker's wife to storm in, grab her husband by the ear and yank him back to the shop.

The table which had drawn his attention though, from the moment he entered the room, was one by the stairs where four rough neck strangers were becoming more and more animated. Bael moved his chair so the table legs wouldn't pose as an obstruction just in case he needed to move quickly; he had this innate ability to sense when trouble was brewing and he was rarely wrong. He was so preoccupied with the strangers he didn't notice Emma approach.

"We are honoured. I can't remember the last time you graced us with your presence two nights running," Emma quipped, her smile warm and welcoming.

Bael could feel Dogran's eyes burning a hole in his side, the barkeep had followed his daughters every step the moment he spotted her intent.

"So, what brings you back in town so soon?" She asked with genuine interest.

Never one for small talk, her directness made him strangely uncomfortable; he'd been alone for so long, the art of conversing with the fairer sex was not one of his stronger points and strangely, he couldn't remember when it ever was.

"I just wanted a drink, nothing more," he replied, staring at the tankard in his hands.

She couldn't hide the disappointment she felt in his cool reply.

"Well, if that's all you're here for, can I get you another?"

He handed her the empty tankard; aware of the change in her body language.

"Please," he replied.

As she turned to leave, one of the strangers with a patch over his eye stood up and began banging his mug on the table.

"Hey! Serving wench. What does a man have to do to get a drink in this place?" he said virtually belching out his words. The others at the table began laughing like idiots; it was obvious that he was the leader of the group. Emma had plenty of experience dealing with drunken fools like these and wouldn't let them ruin the night for others.

"I'm on my way," she replied.

Bael grabbed her hand.

"Ignore them," he said concerned.

"Why, anyone would think you were worried about me Hunter." Her smile returning. "Don't worry. I can handle fools like these." With that she headed for the four drunkards who were becoming increasingly troublesome. Before she had moved more than two paces her father's booming voice filled the room.

"Emma come here."

She was inwardly relieved as the sound of friendly chatter faded with the increasing tension.

Dogran poured four fresh tankards of ale; Emma arrived back behind the counter.

"You carry on serving here. I'll see to those fools."

"Right father… but please be careful."

"I'll be fine; you just carry on." The big man picked up the tankards. When he reached the four by the stairs, he placed the drinks in the centre of the table and leant forward.

"This is your last. Now drink up and leave."

One Eye pulled his drink towards himself spilling half of it on the table.

"We don't take kindly to threats," he said menacingly. "We will go when we're good and fuckin' ready."

Dogran rested his massive hands on the table.

"I don't care how you take it…. I have asked you nicely this time the next won't be so nice."

Bael knew what was coming: The four strangers had become less vocal but more menacing in their behaviour. He could see they were talking about Emma who was busy serving Jered and his friends only two tables from their own. He watched, as they followed her every move sniggering like a bunch of mischievous children.

Emma had to pass the table on her way back to the bar; the scrawniest of the bunch with long matted black hair waited until she was alongside him, then grabbed her dragging her onto his lap. Bael felt his muscles tense as Emma shook herself free of the thug's grip. But the man was quick and pulled her back onto his lap, his grip stronger than his skinny appearance would suggest.

"Now that's no way to treat a customer is it my pretty?" He said, spraying her face with saliva.

She tried to pull herself free, but he held tight abusing her with a slobbering kiss. Pumped with adrenalin she broke free of his wiry fingers and slapped him hard across the face. The thug swore; lashing out he sent her careering across the floor. Before he could get to his feet Bael was upon him. Grabbing the thug's head, he smashed it into the edge of the table breaking the villain's nose. For a moment, the group sat stunned by the speed and ferocity of the attack but within seconds' One Eye lunged at Bael, cursing. Bael was too quick hitting the villain with a thundering uppercut sending him sprawling across the table into the other two. Just out of Hunters line of sight the scrawny one was back on his feet; with knife drawn he'd gathered his senses and was about to attack when - Boom! Dogran's cudgel hit him square in the gut. Jered grabbed Emma pulling her to safety whilst a few of the regulars rallied behind her father. Bael held the scrawny one in a neck lock. Then Dogran grabbed One-Eye by the throat.

"Ever show your face around 'ere again scum and I'll make sure you meet your maker… Now out, the lot-o-yer."

Outnumbered, the gang gathered themselves mumbling and cursing to one another as they left. Then surprisingly Dogran turned on Bael.

"You an' all Hunter, you are nothin' but trouble."

Bael knew, as did everyone else what was really going on with the barkeep; so he offered no resistance and left without uttering a word. Emma was furious.

Now, more angry than shaken, she squared up to her father.

"Why would you do that? I don't understand. He was only trying to help."

Although non-to fond of Hunter himself Jered couldn't stand idly by when his friend as big as he was spoke unjustly.

"She's right Dogran, if it wasn't for Hunter who knows…" Before he could finish Dogran cut him short.

"I didn't need his help, I had everything under control."

"I know but…"

"No buts, the man courts trouble. Never seen anyone itchin' for a fight more than that one," Dogran interrupted, in no mood for criticism no matter how well intentioned.

"You are wrong father and you know it," Emma said ignoring her father's reasoning.

***

Dogran locked up for the night. It had been a trying day; the trouble with Hunter and the four brigands had left him drained. He put out the last of the candles, removed the day's takings from the draw behind the bar then made his way to the living quarters at the rear of the Inn.

Emma sat staring into the flames of a roaring fire with Raga the old black war hound cuddled around her feet. Dogran could see from her posture that she was still angry with him over Hunter. She turned to look at him as he made his way over to the large rocking chair in-front of the hearth, but as he sat down, she turned away, her face stern and reddened by the heat. On seeing its master approach, the dog jumped up, its docked tail wagging excitedly. Dogran leant forward and began stroking the beast; it licked the back of his hand then dropped to the floor by his feet. The last thing he wanted at the end of the day was an argument with his daughter. He'd never meant to offend or embarrass her earlier, but he had and he knew he would pay for it. She was headstrong like her mother and in the glow of the fire was her living double.

"Come on smile… Why the long face?" He asked.

"You were wrong tonight father. Hunter was only trying to help me."

"Listen to me. If it had been anyone else I would have praised such chivalry, but…"

"But what? I understand your grievance with him is sometimes justified, but not this time father."

Dogran kept quiet, letting her vent her frustration without his usual fatherly interruptions.

The heat from the fire had dried her skin, so she slid back to the edge of the rug where Raga slept blissfully unaware of the tension in the room. She didn't want to argue either, but she couldn't shake her anger.

"If you were honest with yourself father you would agree – from the day Hunter arrived amongst us he has always been made to feel like an outsider. Most of the town have only ever treated him with suspicion and ignorant prejudice."

Again, Dogran thought it was like watching her mother. The way her nose would pucker when she was annoyed, her eyes wide and unflinching and lips full and always smiling: a smile that so often masked her true feelings. She was a living reminder of what he had lost.

"I have seen many a fighting man in my time. Hard men… But I have yet to see one who fights like this one," he said caringly.

"But in all the time he has lived amongst us, few in this town have ever tried to get to know him," Emma replied.

"I know enough… The blade he carries. There is nothing like it in these parts. The only time I have ever seen the like, was in the Pit Arenas way up North. So, the question I ask myself is – why would a simple huntsman carry such a weapon?"

Emma could see her father wasn't going to budge on the matter, so she stood ready to retire to her sleeping quarters.

"You always told me; we should never judge a person on first impressions. You said that hidden in everyone are the reasons for whom and what they are. Yet you won't give Hunter a chance. You have judged him as have many others in this town, yet you know little about him."

Dogran dropped his gaze for a moment and stared into the smouldering embers. He couldn't deny there was truth in his daughter's words but that still didn't quell the feelings of anxiety he felt every time she displayed her obvious affection for the man.

"You have been like this ever since mother died. If I show as much as a grain of interest in a man you become this defensive overbearing father."

At the mention of her mother's death Dogran's face softened. A sadness washed over him and for once, this self-assured imposing figure of a man looked vulnerable. Emma faltered. She hadn't meant to use the passing of her mother as an argumentative weapon like this: she was only a child when her mother passed, but she knew the words would hurt her father and they did, which left her filled with shame.

"I'm so sorry father. Please forgive me, I had no right mentioning mother in that way. I know you mean well, but I am no longer the little girl who sat on your knee listening to tales of Goblins and Fae folk," she said smiling nervously.

Dogran rose from the chair, slid his feet from under Raga, then wrapped his arms around her drawing her into his massive chest.

"You have wisdom beyond your years my sweet," he said kissing the top of her head.

She tucked her head under his chin and hugged him tightly; her anger melting away as she did so. She always knew inside that he was just trying to protect her; it had been no easy task raising a daughter in a tavern where boisterous banter could so quickly turn to violence. But it was a task he had undertaken all the years of her life without complaint or regret and she loved him dearly for it.

"Please father - give him a chance… I can see it in his eyes. Hiding behind the wall he puts around himself is a good heart," Emma said, affectionately kissing her father on the cheek.

He held her back at arm's length and gently sat her down.

"What I am about to tell you I have shared with no other, but I feel it will go some way in explaining my behaviour," Dogran said quietly.

For a moment, he stared at a sword and shield that hung on the wall over the fire; his daughter following his gaze.

"Before you were born I served as Sergeant at Arms in the King's skirmishers. We were given orders to enter the Northern Territories with fifty thousand of the King's finest, in an attempt to purge the land of a barbarism that saw men pitched against one another in Arenas of brutal combat: pits of horror where women who had done nothing more than speak against their King were raped and worse by creatures that should not be of this world. All for the pleasure of the masses, corrupted by a leader who found such savagery a way of life. In the main we succeeded, driving the despot King and his hardened followers into the frozen wastes beyond the Rift. But sickness and a lack of natural resources left our King with no other option but to abandon our final goal."

Dogran paused for a moment gathering his thoughts.

"Please. Go on father."

"I'm sorry. Yes, our goal was to rout out this vile King and bring him to justice rough or otherwise and in so doing free the land of his brutal oppression. Sadly, we had to compromise. We were able to close or demolish most of these cesspits, but much further north a few survived and in time flourished: one in particular was rumoured to be the grandest of them all where the best of the fighters could even earn their freedom. We just didn't have the manpower to reach such places let alone lay siege to them, so we had to be satisfied with the things we had achieved, though what it has done for the people in the long term is questionable…. The day we closed the last of the Pits before our return home, I heard talk amongst the locals of a fighter in the Great Arena who was fast becoming a Legend: it was said this warrior fought alongside his father, something the people had never seen before. They called him - The Ghost. People called him by this name because of the bird that fought to protect him, as white as a ghost they said. They feared it was a demon, so fierce was it in combat, a white Hawk with eyes as red as fire…. It's not an image that is easily cast from one's thoughts; so, when Hunter entered our lives all those years ago in the company of such a creature, it set me to thinking."

Dogran paused again; he could see his daughter's cheeks had flushed, not as before from the fire but from a questioning uncertainty.

"But surely father, Hunter cannot be the man you speak of? He is too young to be him," she said with nervous reservation.

"I know my sweet. I know it cannot be. But I am not a believer of coincidence, yet such as it is the alternative would seem impossible. And I know the one thing Hunter is not, is a liar. The few times I have questioned him about his past I have never felt his reply was the product of a lie."

Emma stood up, she was glad to share such a moment with her father and was a little more understanding of his reasoning. But Hunter? With Hunter, she was now left with a nagging doubt that chipped away at her sense of reason. She kissed her father once more then straightened the goat rug she had been sitting on, before retiring to her bed.

"I will try to be more understanding of Hunter… You have my word."

Dogran watched her leave, but though he meant every word he still couldn't stop thinking there was more to Hunter than any of them realized, and it filled him with a father's concern. He knew the measure of a man, but this man was a mystery. It was hard to tell; Hunter was often unshaven and sported a beard but from the day he entered the community some ten years ago Dogran could swear he hadn't aged a day.

3

CAILEAN-AMBUSH-WEAVING

Cailean's room was by far the brightest in the Keep, its stark grey walls lifted by bursts of colour from freshly picked flowers and heavy woollen tapestries depicting periods in the Keeps history. She loved the spicy scent of ground ginger, cinnamon and thyme which she had her maid place in bowls by the window so their exotic aroma could be carried on the wind to fill the room.

Against her father's wishes she readied herself for a trip into town to pick up the gown she had commissioned for the forthcoming feast. Her uncle the King was to pay her father a visit of state, a visit that was making him apprehensive and prone to more than his usual mood swings. She suspected there was more to this brotherly reunion than she was being told; as this would be the first time in five years the Keep had entertained such an event.

While Jiney her handmaiden searched for her hooded cape in the next room, Cailean wandered out onto the stone balcony overlooking the long bridge and the Town beyond. She filled her lungs with fresh summer air and stared into a blue cloudless sky. A flock of brightly coloured Mallards came into view on course for the cool waters of the Lake below. For a moment she followed their flight, the greens, blues and reds of their feathers glistened in the bright sunlight. Then out of nowhere a white streak plummeted from above taking out one of the trailing birds. The duck died instantly its neck broken from the impact. It took Cailean's breath away as a white Hawk plunged after the falling bird grabbing it in its razor-sharp talons just before it hit the water. The sight of the duck being carried away by its ghostly attacker infuriated the young lady of the Keep. It wasn't the first time she had seen the Hawk; she had heard rumours about some loner in the town who owned such a strange creature.

There was a knock at the door; Jiney entered the room carrying her green cape. The young mistress stretched out her arms allowing Jiney to place the cloak over her shoulders and secure it with a large copper broach.

"There," Jiney said, "all done."

Cailean smiled, grabbed her friend's hand and led her outside onto the balcony.

"I saw that white hawk again. That damnable thing just killed another bird... How can someone own such an obvious affront to nature like that?"

"I don't know my lady," Jiney replied.

"Someday I would like to meet this loner the people talk about and give him a piece of my mind."

"Yes, my lady, I'm sure you will... but we have more pressing matters... your shoes mam, which would you like to wear?"

"Well, my father demands I dress appropriately, so I must choose the simple leather ankle boots. They shouldn't be too fancy for a visit to town, now should they?" She said sarcastically.

"I suppose it's for your own good my lady. Naturally Lord Farroth worries about you. There are people in the town jealous of your position, who might see you to harm."

"I'm sure I won't be recognized with this hood covering my face," she said pulling it over her head, casting her face in shadow. "Anyway, aren't you supposed to agree with *me* -not my father?"

"Sometimes my lady," she replied cryptically. "We should go now, the guards are waiting for us in the courtyard, as you insist on walking into town."

"Then we shall keep them waiting no longer."

***

Cailean and her entourage entered the town square from the main street and stopped outside a small stone cottage. Light was fading as the last of the market venders finished for the day. She couldn't help but notice the fiery red hair of the baker who was being slapped across the back of his head by a stout fowl mouthed woman who cursed him with every step.

"The poor man. Why does he put up with that? I've never heard such filth spill from a woman's lips like that," Cailean said to her maid.

"It's the baker mam. I believe his visits to the tavern have become more frequent of late and his wife is none too pleased."

"After hearing what just came out of her mouth, who could blame the man."

"I suppose," Jiney replied.

Cailean shook her head then instructed her guards to stand sentry outside whilst she and Jiney entered the cottage of the town's dressmaker.

The main living area was small but cosy with minimal furniture, but enough to be comfortable; a stone fire place large for a room of that size was surrounded by a tailor's tools. The elderly couple who greeted Cailean into their home, made clothes for town's folk and gentry alike. They had been forewarned of the high-born visit, giving them time to prepare the beautiful gown they had designed and tailored for the rumoured Royal feast.

Cailean pulled back her hood, prompting the obligatory curtsey and bow from the elderly couple.

"Please that isn't necessary," Cailean said.

"Mam," replied the portly old woman struggling to straighten her sciatic back.

"I have your gown finished, if you would like to try it on?"

"Please," she said excitedly.

"My young lady if you could follow me then," the tailor's wife said, leading her into the sleeping quarters.

The dress was stretched out on the bed in all its regal splendour its deep blue silk highlighted with rich gold embroidery and an ornate red sash.

"I will leave you to try it on my lady."

"Thank you it looks wonderful," Cailean replied. It wasn't long before she emerged from the changing area to a universal gasp of approval.

"You look beautiful," Jiney said, as her mistress gave them all a twirl displaying the dress's faultless cut.

The tailor asked her to give him another spin whilst he checked that everything was to his liking; satisfied he smiled.

"The fit is perfect, as your young friend here said, you look beautiful my lady."

"Thank you, your work is exquisite," Cailean replied, making her way into the other room to change.

"It has been an honour my lady… it's not every day one gets a visit from the King and for such occasion one must look their best," the old tailor said. It didn't take long for Cailean to change and have the dress wrapped ready to take.

The guards were waiting patiently as Cailean and Jiney emerged from the cottage: Jiney carrying the dress in plain wrappings so as not to draw unnecessary attention. Cailean very rarely got an opportunity to wander freely about town. So, against her father's wishes she took it upon herself to stroll over to the fountain in the centre of the square. The guards shadowed her every move, they too had been ordered to dress as ordinary townsfolk; the swords hanging from their wastes the only evidence that they were anything more. The water in the fountain felt cold against the humid early evening air. Cailean swished her fingers around playfully flicking water at Jiney. As she looked up she couldn't help but notice the tall dark-haired stranger pass by the other side of the fountain on his way to an alley where four rough looking thugs loitered suspiciously. Pulling her hand out of the water she turned to Jiney.

"Who is that?" She asked.

The maid shifted about nervously; she'd seen that look before and knew that her mistress would not just leave it there.

"I think they call him Hunter, my lady. Rumour has it he's captured an injured wolf and is nursing it back to health."

"How odd," Cailean replied.

"Yes ma'am, and I do believe he could be the one who owns that white hawk you mentioned earlier."

"Umm does he now?" Why didn't you tell me this before when I asked?" she queried.

"I shouldn't have said anything my lady...I... I," she replied, almost tripping over her words.

"I don't understand Jiney. What do you mean shouldn't?"

"Please my lady you must speak to your father about these matters," Jiney said nervously. Cailean could see how uncomfortable her maid felt and not wishing to compound matters decided to let the matter drop.

"Then I will speak with my father."

Suddenly they heard the sound of fighting coming from the alley; Cailean couldn't resist the temptation to wander over there to see what was going on. As she got closer to the noise someone grabbed her arm from behind.

"Please my lady, go no further. It is not safe to venture into this part of town."

Jiney's words fell on deaf ears, much to the chagrin of Cailean's personal guard. The young mistress kept on walking towards the corner of the alley way. As the group reached a place where they could get a clear view of the disturbance, Cailean stopped dead in her tracks shocked rigid by what she saw.

***

After leaving the tavern Bael headed for the alley; he felt the need for Vena's special attentions and her non-judgemental company even if it had to be paid for. Crossing the square, he noticed two young women and their four minders heading for the fountain. The alley was poorly lit, but there was enough light for him to spot Vena standing in the brothel's doorway smoking a clay pipe of hicker weed.

Normally his keen sense of danger would have alerted him to the four men lurking in the shadows but his mind was elsewhere; Dogran's earlier rebuttal had affected him more than he cared to admit. Without warning, One-Eye and his cohorts leapt from the darkness daggers drawn. Although he was taken unawares Bael's speed was frightening. One punch floored the weakest of the attackers as the others flanked him from behind. He ducked from a blow that would have opened his throat as One-Eye sliced the air. Bael thundered into the man slamming him hard to the ground. The scrawny one who hit Emma in the tavern, made a lunge for Bael's back, but he was too slow: Bael span around in one flowing movement rammed the blade into the man's thigh. The thug screamed out in agonizing pain.

The noise alerted Vena to Hunters predicament. She dropped her pipe lifted her skirt and unsheathed a dagger strapped to her thigh and never the shrinking violet she burst into action running towards the fight.

Bael floored One-Eye again leaving all four of his attackers writhing on the floor. Momentarily his attention was drawn to four men running towards him swords drawn with two caped women following close behind. It was time enough for One Eye to get to his feet and attack Bael on his blind side.

"Hunter! Behind you."

Bael turned just in time to evade a lethal stab at his back; but that momentary distraction was enough to see the blade slice deeply into his shoulder. Shaking off the pain he smashed his fist into the thug's face with such power it lifted his attacker off the ground dislocating the man's jaw. He looked at Vena whose warning had probably saved his life then to the four swordsmen who'd arrived just as the fight finished. The oldest of the swordsmen approached him.

"You're bleeding, he said.

"Its fine," Bael replied.

"That's not fine Hunter," Vena said, tearing off a piece of her dress. "Here press this on the wound before you bleed to death."

He took the cloth and stemmed the bleeding as best he could. Bael could see these men were no ordinary town's people their swords were military issue, the type he'd seen on men of the Keep. *Why would plain clothed soldiers be guarding two women like this?* he thought.

50

They are obviously not the people their clothes imply and why would they try to hide in plain sight in a part of town where anyone of importance would be in danger?

A small group of the town guard on night duty patrolling the streets had spotted the fight some distance away across the square. The Captain a surly character with a thick brown beard brought his squad to a halt; he looked first to the villains on the floor then to Bael who held a blood-soaked cloth to his shoulder.

"What is going on here?" He asked sternly.

One-Eye tried to stand but fell back onto an elbow.

"This bastard tried to kill us," he said, spitting a mouthful of bloody saliva onto his sleeve.

"One man against four. The odds seemed to be tipped in your favour, wouldn't you agree?" the Captain replied sarcastically. Then he turned to Bael.

"And you Hunter, what have you to say on the matter?" he queried, with an obvious familiarity. "Or should I say…. What did you do this time that would make these fools want to kill you?"

Before Bael could answer Cailean stepped forward sliding the hood from her face. The Captain, shocked, recognized the Lord's daughter immediately: she too knew him well, he'd served in her father's Garrison until his retirement one-year past when he was given the position as Captain of the Town guard as reward for his loyal service.

"Captain Gerrard," she said. "This man's only crime was to defend himself. We saw everything… These men attacked him and tried to kill him."

"M'Lady, but I have had dealings with this man before and I can assure you he will have some part in this, mark my words."

Cailean frowned.

"Captain. Do you call me a liar?"

"No m'Lady, but…."

"Then please-do what I ask of you and let this man be on his way."

"Yes m'Lady," he replied reluctantly.

Bael looked again at the young woman, puzzled. *How does such a woman hold sway with the Captain of the guard?* He thought.

Cailean turned to Bael.

"I think you should take your leave before he changes his mind."

Bael nodded his appreciation; the Captain ordered his men to round up the thugs and escort them to the town jail.

Vena slipped her dagger back into its sheath and took hold of Bael's arm.

"Come with me," she said. "That wound needs tending before you bleed to death."

She pulled him roughly, after seeing the way he looked at Cailean and in all their times together she had never been privy to such a look.

***

Vena's room was as homely as she could make a working girl's room. There were two wooden chairs, a small round table and a large Oak bed covered in sheep skins for clients' extra comfort. It was obvious to all who entered the room that the bed was the main focal point.

Bael sat patiently whilst Vena prepared a poultice of crushed seed of the poppy with the viscous sap of the Amathelia plant known by herbalists for its anaesthetizing qualities. She smeared a copious lump of it onto the wound making Bael wince as it seeped into the open cut.

"That should numb the flesh and kill off any badness that may have entered the wound," Vena said. Sure enough, within seconds he felt the numbness spread easing the pain instantly. She carefully threaded a length of gut twine through a curved needle. "Hopefully you won't feel this. Now sit very still while I close this up, before infection sets in," she said, with an air of confidence that could only come with practice. Hunter stared at the needle with nervous trepidation.

"Surprise, surprise, I'm more than just a pair of open legs" she said sarcastically. "There are times when my girls have needed patchin' up. Not all men are like you Hunter. There are those who like to beat up on women especially after a drink or two. And let's be honest the town healers don't exactly rush to step through my door now do they?"

Bael relaxed a little.

"I feel I don't have a choice. Do I?" he replied.

"Not if you want to hold onto that arm. Now sit still and let me get on with it."

Vena set about stitching him up; she was amazed at his threshold for pain. She knew that the needle would pierce sensitive flesh, yet he didn't make a sound. For a moment, she paused to look at the scars that disfigured the beauty of his upper body; he had never divulged from whence they came and she had not pressed him on it believing that one day he would tell her. But to-date he hadn't. She overlapped the last stitch and tidied up the wound and dressed it with a clean linen bandage.

"There, you are done," she finished. She could see Bael was tired. "Come on get your sorry carcass over here," she said, leading him to the bed. "Make yourself comfortable, I won't be long. I just have to check on my girls."

She wasn't gone long yet in that short time Bael had found sleep. Trying not to wake him she placed a mug of hot herbal wine on the table by the bed then gently slid alongside. He groaned a little as she lifted his head onto her lap; she sipped at the drink then made sure both she and Hunter were comfortable.

She looked again at his scars running her finger along the large crescent shaped one on his right forearm. *How little I know about you Hunter*, she thought. *How does one bare such scars and not know how they came by them?* She took another sip of her drink then began to stroke Bael's hair.

"You are a strange one. You seem to have no trouble making enemies even with those who could be your friend," she whispered to herself. "Yet within the man I have come to know there is so much to offer."

He moved his head slightly as if to awaken, then relaxed back into her lap. She brushed the hair back off his brow and stared at his ruggedly handsome face.

Her girls had only ever seen their mistress sport that look when Hunter was around, a look that carried with it more than just a woman of pleasure doing her job.

Vena drank the last of her night cap and was just about to move Bael's head off her lap when he began to groan restlessly; his eyes flickering under closed eye lids. He began to mumble something incoherently.

"What is it troubles you so?" she whispered. "Why do I never see you smile? What is it that fills you with an anger that drives you to such secrecy?"

***

THE WEAVING.

A huge masked Spirit dressed in a black hooded cape stands by the shores of a gigantic lake. Slowly the cape opens and like a gateway to another realm Bael steps through it to find himself on an island where huge Dire Wolves run free. He follows a winding path until he reaches the massive doors in the jaws of a building shaped like the head of a Wolf. The doors creak open; there are large wooden statues of warriors with a wolf at their sides looming over the long aisle of a huge throne room. Slowly he makes his way through the hall to the figure sitting on an ornately carved throne. The figure wears a glistening helm shaped like a wolf's head. Either side of him are two Dire Wolves; one of them reminds him of the wolf he is nursing back to health but the other is more menacing and bares its teeth at him as he gets closer to the throne. This one is larger and as black as night, with a silver streak of fur running down the back of its neck.

Suddenly there is a burst of blinding light; everything in-front of him begins to fade. Now he finds himself floating high above a black obsidian causeway where a horde of Dark Elven warriors is being led by a strange figure clad in unusual black armour. In-front of him are six grotesque wraith like soul hounds. Bael finds himself drifting uncontrollably towards them. But as he gets close enough to identify them the image flickers and dissolves.

Now he is looking down into an Arena carved into the ground like a huge stone fighting pit. At one end is the King and his entourage high above the crowd on a stone parapet. The baying spectators stand on steep marble tiers cheering as a fighter enters the pit. The image is fleeting. The warrior looks older than most who would survive such a place. He brandishes two swords; one of them has a beautifully balanced long curved blade the other a shorter version of it. The crowd appear to love him. Then, through a gate of spikes eight fighters all with different weapons and armour enter the pit. One of them struggles to restrain two ferocious Grawls tugging on chains attached to studded collars. The older fighter readies himself as the eight surround him. There is a flash of light. Now he looks into a room beneath the Arena, light from a small square portal cut into the solid stone ceiling hardly touches the gloom within. Slowly he drifts towards a giant of a man in a thick leather apron hacking away at something on a huge wooden table with a brutal looking meat cleaver. As he floats closer the true horror reveals itself. The Butcher is chopping the limbs off a human corpse; blood is everywhere. Then he begins to flay the flesh as if preparing it for consumption. There is another flash of light.

Bael now looks down on a battle field. Elves fight Dark Elves-the scene is bloody. In the thick of the fighting, he can see an Elven King in full battle armour. Then again, the scene dissolves.

Bael finds himself cutting his way through Dark Elf after Dark Elf, by his side the Wolf from the lodge, and above, his White hawk. In the distance, he can see a warrior in a Wolf helm leading a pack of Dire wolves into the fray. Suddenly from out of nowhere a huge black shape pounces at him, it is so fast he doesn't have time to react. The abhorrent creature makes the most terrifying sound as it pins him to the ground, its jaws frothing with rage. Bael struggles to free himself but the beast is too heavy: He looks into empty eyes as souls shift in and out of existence trapped by the unholy host as it readies for the kill, its breath fouler than anything he has ever smelt in his life. He feels the air being sucked from his lungs as his very life's essence is being drawn from his body. Another flash of light.

Bael sat up gasping for air as if suffocating; his eyes wide open.

"It's alright. It's alright you were just dreaming," Vena said, wiping the sweat from his wet forehead, totally unaware that this was no dream...

***

Maccon laid his hands on two silver runes inlaid into the marble top of the round Alter. The other warrior priests followed his lead and did the same. They closed their eyes in deep concentration, their minds as one. The twelve feet high Shard of crystal protruding from a hole in the Alters centre hummed into life. A ball of energy materialized above the shard with an almost liquid like quality, shimmering with blues and whites. Maccon opened his eyes and watched as Bael's dream unfolded within it, leaving the Shaman no alternative. He had to speak with Lord Farroth himself...Urgently. For he knew the visions were not only warning of Bael's returning memory, but they also showed a fleeting glimpse of what may come.

***

High Lord Farroth stepped into the Tower's courtyard to receive an unscheduled visit from the Captain of the town guard. The Captain could see why the locals had nick named his Lordship *Fire Beard*; his ginger shoulder length hair and matching full beard looked redder than ever in the bright sunlight. The two men began to chat unaware they were being watched from the balcony above.

Unfortunately for Cailean her father and Captain Gerrard were just out of earshot, but it wasn't difficult to guess what they were talking about; the events of that night in town still fresh in her mind. It was odd, the more these events played out in her memories the stronger her intrigue with Hunter became. Not least the flutter that turned in her stomach each time she pictured his handsomely chiselled face. The conversation below didn't go on for long; her father returned to the Tower, the Captain leaving the grounds the way he came.

Cailean moved from the shade into the bright sunlight at the other end of the balcony where a stone statue of the Great Protector stood sentinel over the room. Jiney joined her carrying a goblet of fresh squeezed orange juice.

"Your drink my Lady," she said, her smile as bright as the morning sun.

"Thank you; this is just what I need."

Jiney handed her the drink.

"You should step into the shade; your skin is too fair for such a strong sun."

"I will be fine, you worry too much," Cailean replied playfully.

She sipped some of her orange then shut her eyes momentarily.

"Don't mornings like this make you glad to be alive?" She said, taking a deep breath.

"Yes, my Lady, they do."

Just then the door to Cailean's quarters slammed shut jolting her from her thoughts. Her father Lord Farroth joined them on the balcony.

"Father," she said hugging him nervously. Jiney bowed and stepped to one side.

"A beautiful morning," he mused, resting his hands on the stone terrace by the statue of the Great Protector.

"Yes, it is father," she replied suspiciously.

Her father kept his back facing towards her, distracted in thought he gazed into the distance.

"I believe there was trouble in town the other day?"

Jiney's face flushed slightly uncertain of how this would play out, for she knew all too well that his Lordship's temper was as fiery as his beard. Cailean's features hardened, it was obvious to her what was coming next; subtlety was never her father's strong suit.

"Yes… A man was attacked by drunken thugs not far from the Town square."

Lord Farroth turned with purpose to face his daughter.

"You were there were you not?"

"Yes father, I was there," she replied defiantly.

"You know my feelings about such visitations into town."

"I was protected by our guards."

"That is not good enough reason to be wandering about the streets in such a manner. There are some amongst the town folk that would see you harmed, just for the coin you may carry in your purse."

Jiney dare not intervene, though she wanted to defend her mistress, silence was the prudent choice no matter how strongly she felt.

"The man who was attacked? Where is he now?"

"I believe they call him Hunter. As for his whereabouts, I have no idea," she replied.

Lord Farroth knew there was more at work here than idle curiosity, he was all too aware of his daughter's insatiable appetite for excitement beyond the confines of the Keep's walls. But this interest in Bael was far and above the most worrying.

"I know this man you speak of. You must stay away from him…. Do you hear me?"

For a moment Cailean was shocked into silence.

"How do you know him?"

"That is no concern of yours."

"And why is that?" she protested.

"Enough! I do not ask you; I am telling you. Stay away from this man," he said angrily, before storming off in a huff.

Alloria-Lady Farroth was readying herself for bed when her husband entered their sleeping chamber. Frustrated, he threw his cape across the back of a chair, poured himself an herbal wine, then sat down on the side of the bed. He took a long drink, clenched a fist digging his nails into his palm to quell the anger that surged within.

"Why does my daughter reap such pleasure in defiance of my words?"

"What troubles you my love?" Alloria asked soothingly.

"She wanders freely amongst the town folk as if one of them. Thoughts of danger cast on the wind."

"We both know how headstrong she can be, but I would not see her spirit broken."

"Nor-I. Yet she laid witness to a brawl between Hunter and some street scum. Worse than this, she is obviously taken with the man…I know her. Our daughter is like an open book in matters of the heart."

"Could this be nothing more sinister than girlish curiosity?"

"If it was nought but curiosity I saw in our daughter's eyes I would not be troubled so. Ten years have we kept her free of such chance meeting."

"I understand your concerns, but I sometimes think your obsession regarding Hunter clouds your better judgement where our daughter is concerned."

Her husband walked over to the balcony; a single line of reflected moonlight danced across the lake like a silver snake worming its way along its rippling surface. He stared at it for a moment as if hypnotised, then turned to face his wife.

"Our alliance with the Elves is fragile at best. Their reasons for leaving him with us all those years ago must not be compromised, a promise we made the Elves when Bael entered our lives, a promise as yet unbroken."

"Then if it will ease your concerns, I will have words with her."

"That would please me, thank you," his tone a mask for a reply riddled in doubt.

***

The song of steel on steel echoed around the grounds masking Maccon's approach as Lord Farroth sparred with his sword master. His friend's sense of urgency brought the practice session to a premature end. The interruption was unexpected, but Lord Farroth knew Maccon would not have done so unless the news was urgent. The Sword Master bowed then took his leave placing both his and his master's practice swords back on the weapon rack. Maccon handed his friend a linen kerchief to wipe the sweat from his brow; then both men sat on a stone bench directly below Cailean's balcony.

Cailean was emptying a vase of dead flowers ready for their replacement when she heard the unmistakeable voice of Maccon. Intrigued, she edged quietly onto the balcony and careful not to be seen leaned over the terrace to be within earshot of what was being discussed.

"You seem troubled?" Lord Farroth said.

"It's Hunter my Lord… I fear he begins to remember."

Lord Farroth shifted around to face his friend.

"How can this be possible?" He asked with growing concern.

"I have laid witness to his dreams. It is no coincidence that these visions, dreams whatever they are began with the arrival of the Wolf. There is more to the beast than the Elves would have us believe."

"What do you mean?"

"I sense a connection, a bond that grows ever stronger between Bael and the Wolf that is far more than just an animal and its master. More than this I cannot say but my instincts tell me that this is just the beginning."

Cailean slipped back into her room flabbergasted at what she had just overheard. There was a knock on the door, then Jiney entered with fresh flowers for the room.

"Jiney, please, put down the flowers and come and sit by me," she said patting the edge of the bed next to where she sat.

"My Lady?"

"I have just heard my father talking to Maccon about that man Hunter. There is something really odd going on and I mean to find out what."

"My Lady is that wise?"

"I would like to know why my father has such concerns about a man whose memory seems to be returning. And why he is so set against me having any contact with the man? There shouldn't be secrets like this amongst family."

Jiney's face turned positively ashen.

"Are you alright?" Cailean asked, aware of her friend's obvious discomfort.

"Ye...Yes my Lady," she replied unconvincingly.

"Are you sure? Do you know more about this Hunter than you would have me believe?"

"No, my Lady," she lied.

"Then I must speak with that wily old priest of ours and see what I can find out."

Maccon was alone when Cailean entered the cavernous Dome of the Inner Circle, where the Shard that revealed Bael's vision lay dormant. He was so invested in the reading of some old scrolls that he hadn't noticed her approach; then his nostrils flared.

"Ah! I would know that scent anywhere," he said looking up.

"So, what brings you to my Temple on this fine day?"

She smiled mischievously and kissed him on the cheek.

"I couldn't help but overhear you and father talking about Hunter the other day."

"I know my child. You are not so practiced in the art of stealth that I could not detect your presence on the balcony," he replied conceitedly.

Cailean's cheeks flushed bright pink.

"What is your interest in this man?"

"I'm just curious, that's all. It is obvious you and father know this Hunter well, yet I have never seen him here in the Keep. Why is that? And why is father so adamant that I should stay clear of this man?" She asked trying to feint indifference.

Gently, Maccon took her hand in his.

"Listen my child I cannot get involved in the ways of the young, but I will tell you this… He is a man from a troubled past with a destiny yet to be determined."

"What do you mean?"

Maccon was no stranger to the pleasures and desires of youth, he too had once fallen victim to their magic. He'd fallen in love with a beautiful young sculptor whose carvings still adorned his dwellings and his heart. But he knew fate could be a cruel master and the day Lamia realized her gift their lives changed forever; and though it went against his better judgement he would not deny another the same opportunity to find that happiness that was so painfully denied him.

"I have said too much already, if you wish to learn more about the man himself then you should speak with the woman called Vena."

"Vena? Who is she?"

"She is an earth maiden, a woman of the night, they have many names. She runs a house for the pleasures of men in the seedier part of town. I believe you may have seen the woman that night in the alley…. But as your father has forbidden your presence in such notorious parts of town, I know of only one place she frequents with any regularity that will afford you at least some modicum of safety."

"And where might that be?"

Maccon paused for a moment of deliberation.

"On the last day of every week she spends an afternoon at the Apothecaries on the edge of town where she is cleansed of the taint of men; not that far from the Keep as luck would have it."

Cailean looked decidedly embarrassed.

"I think I know this place. It's the cottage next to where the stream enters the forest."

"That's the place… But please, your father must not hear I had any part in this."

"Thank you… Do not worry my lips are sealed I promise and again thank you," she said kissing him on the cheek before leaving.

***

Vena loved the smell of potions and herbs that greeted her every time she crossed the threshold of the Apothecary for her weekly cleansing: a ritual she felt not only cleansed her body, but her soul as well, for she loved Alicia the old Alchemist as she would the mother she had always wanted as a child. It would be quite the sight for anyone to see; sitting in an angled chair, her skirt hitched up to her waist with her modesty exposed for all to see. She readied herself, placing her legs over two padded wooden poles sticking out of a very strange looking wooden contraption Alicia had designed herself. The towns carpenter had no idea what he was making when she had shown him her drawings, he could only guess it was some sort of clothes hanging device and that's just what she let him believe. But this clever piece of wooden jiggery pokery allowed Vena to sit comfortably in the birthing position allowing Alicia unhindered access to her wild orchid; the name the old woman had given her exposed genitalia. The old dear placed bowls of different coloured liquids on the floor in front of the jig then positioned herself on a small stool directly between Vena's parted legs.

"I hope your hands are warm?" Vena jibed, smiling.

The old Alchemist placed her hand on Vena's inner thigh, and grinned cheekily, exposing a gap between her front teeth that gave her the comical appearance of an oversized rabbit: Something Vena found totally endearing.

"Is that warm enough for you?" she lisped in her distinctive croaky voice.

"Warm enough… carry on."

She relaxed back and let Alicia set to work on cleansing her.

"I heard about that trouble with Hunter?" Alicia said. "How is he?"

"He's fine. Though I haven't seen him this past week."

"You know I would never question why you do what you do, but it is obvious to eyes that have been around as long as mine, that Hunter means more to you than just a man who would pay for your services. I imagine you have enough money to retire from the path you follow, so why are you not tempted to settle down with such a man?"

Vena was taken a little off guard by the direct and sensitive question. She looked down at the woman crouched down between her legs smearing her with whatever concoctions she had put together and sighed.

"Oh, if life were that simple."

"It is my dear… If only you can believe in yourself and allow yourself to fall to the mercy of change."

"I fear what you suggest will elude me all my life, a fact I came to terms with long ago when I lost my child and found I could have no other. A time I needed the father I never knew and the mother I had all but forgotten."

Sadness filled the old woman's eyes as her thoughts drifted back to that awful day; for she had brought that dead child into the world and had it not been for her skills the mother would have fallen that day also. She remembered too when Vena's fine young fiancé had gone off to war never to return, and how badly Vena had taken it after finding she was pregnant with said child. And how when that tiny living part of her man was so cruelly snatched from her, Vena had turned to a life of pleasing men, where love could never again rip the heart from her beating chest.

Just then the bell inside the door to the cottage rang. Alicia Put down the cloth she was holding and stood up from the stool.

"I will be back shortly; I'll just see who that is?" She said leaving Vena with her legs in the air and her genitals smothered with a gently medicated milky substance.

Within seconds she had returned, escorted by two hooded women who Vena recognised immediately from that night in the alley. Alicia got straight back to work leaving the two young women at the door looking somewhat puzzled and rather shocked.

"Well don't just stand there gawking. Come in I won't bite," Vena said, gesturing for them to stand by her.

"Please forgive us," Cailean replied looking a little embarrassed.

"Don't look so shocked. A woman of my calling has to protect herself from the ills of the flesh that we and men can catch and give in equal measure. And a very wise old woman once told me that warm, moist damp places are the breeding grounds for infestations that would cause us harm," she said, glancing down between her legs.

Both Cailean's and Jiney's cheeks flushed ruddy.

"Come, do not be embarrassed. What can I do for you?" Alicia asked.

"Please forgive my intrusion but I am here to speak with the one they call Vena," Cailean said, unsure that the woman prone on the chair was she.

Vena let the old woman finish drying her clean, then she lowered her skirt and eased herself off the chair.

"And what would you want with this Vena?" she asked, intrigued.

"I am Lord Farroth's daughter."

"I know who you are, but you have not answered my question. What business do you have with Vena?"

"I was told she might be able to tell me something about the one they call Hunter?"

Vena, surprised and more than a bit curious at the question stood silent for a moment before answering.

"I am the one you seek."

"Please sit down, you can use this room to talk. I have things to do in town," Alicia interrupted, before leaving the cottage.

Cailean and Jiney sat at a table in the middle of the room while Vena preferred to stand.

"Can I pour you a drink of herbal wine?"

"No, thank you," the two young women replied, almost in unison.

"Now why would someone like you be interested in a man like him I ask myself?"

"I… I…" Cailean stammered.

In that moment Vena knew the answer to her question, an answer that for some reason played with her very emotions. There was a benevolent envy of such youthful exuberance that she herself had long forgotten, tinged with a more malign jealousy that older women sometimes feel about their younger counterparts. Cailean reached for a small purse in her belt.

"Please do not do what I think you are going to do," Vena said angrily. "I do not want your money."

"Please forgive me I meant no offence," Cailean said nervously.

"Then none is taken… tell me does your father know you are here?"

"Please don't tell him."

"Now why would I do that? Don't worry your visit here will stay within these walls."

There was little Vena could tell her guests other than what most of the town's folk knew, the other things she learned from the confines of her room would never cross her lips. But there was one piece of information she could pass on that was told to one of her girls by a soldier in the Farroth guard.

"There is one more thing I can tell you. This banquet your father is to host for his brother the King. He has asked Hunter to supply venison for the feast, and from what I hear Hunter is heading into the forest one week hence, to fulfil such request."

Cailean thanked Vena for her time and discretion before leaving with Jiney the same way they had arrived; their faces obscured under hooded capes.

4
MUTE

Raen was taller than most youths of his age and at seventeen much broader and stronger than he was as a boy bullied and ridiculed by his peers. Son of the most renowned Smithy in the region; he'd worked for and been trained by Koval in skills past down from father to son for generations.

His schooling as a child of special needs was undertaken by his mother and aunt; but most of all by Maccon, adviser to High Lord Farroth and leader of the Order of the Black Orchid, an elite group of warrior priests. Maccon had a soft spot for the boy and unlike many, viewed the boy's disability not as a curse but as a challenge, and from the day Koval and Tyrna realized their son was a *mute* he had made it his business to help develop the child's other abilities.

The priest had created a special sign language which the lad picked up with remarkable ease. All his family learnt the same, and over time tried to pass on the knowledge to others in the town so that their son could lead as free and normal a life as his disability and the prejudices that surrounded it would allow.

As a boy, Raen had found it really difficult communicating with others, most his age would steer clear more from embarrassment than anything else, but there were a few who were determined to make his life hell. The worst of these was a bully called Toran, son of a drunken father and leader of a small gang of misfits. They lived in Beggars Nest, the poor quarter of town where education wasn't top of the agenda for parents who just wanted them out of the house to bring in what little coin they could, whatever the means. This made for resentment of anyone they considered privileged and as son of a famous Smithy Raen was a prime target.

As an eight-year-old Raen was of average build; he was mild mannered and had an insatiable appetite for learning.

It was a late afternoon; Raen listened to the heavy spring rain beating against the Temple windows as he finished reading the histories of the region. He placed his books of learning in a waxed leather satchel before eating lunch with his tutor. Maccon loved the lad's company; he had a big heart like his father Koval and was such a willing student. It didn't take them long to finish eating; Raen gathered up his belongings and followed the wily priest to the Temple gates.

Within minutes of him hitting the main road into town the heavens opened. Raen was drenched in seconds; with satchel under arm he ran as fast as he could for home. The field on the other side of the bridge connecting the keep to the town was completely waterlogged. As he came to its edge he halted, debating which way to go, the town being the longer route but less of an obstacle course. *I'm already wet,* he thought, *so yes, this way.* He set off towards the woods that would at least offer some shelter but first he had to navigate his way through mud and pools of water which covered his feet. Ahead something moved behind the trees. He slowed down to a jog as he recognised Toran and his gang lurking in the shadows. Raen stopped in his tracks he knew trouble was imminent and though not a fighter nor was he a coward; gripping his satchel tightly he waited. The five bullies surrounded him taunting him with hurtful monkey noises, then Toran snatched the satchel from his grip.

"What is this?" the bully asked throwing it up in the air as if not to catch it.

Raen tried to snatch it back: The satchel fell open exposing his books.

"Books? You fuckin' freak. What do you need books for? Oh-sorry I forgot you can't fuckin' speak," he grunted, laughing like the crazed moron he was.

Raen grabbed for the books.

"Well now what do we 'ave 'ere," Toran jibed opening the satchel and pulling out its contents; within seconds they were soaked. Raen grabbed for them again but it was futile, Toran was two years his senior and much stronger. He brushed the Smith's son aside, then threw the books, satchel and all into the mud. Raen fought back the tears determined not to break in-front of his assailants; he lunged at Toran but was easily over-powered, the bigger boy shoving him head long into a large pool of water.

"Look the little bastards going to cry," the big lad said, turning to the others.

"Pick him up," Toran ordered the two smallest in the gang. Raen hoped that was the end of it, but it wasn't; the gang leader shoved him sprawling into the muddy patch where his satchel and contents lay ruined. Then things took a sinister turn, Toran placed his foot behind Raen's head forcing it into the mud. The lad flailed about unable to breath.

"Eat that you little shit licker," Toran said with cold disdain.

The other members of the gang looked on terrified until the taller of the group and no doubt second in com-mand spoke up nervously.

"That's enough you are killing him," he shouted, his voice shaking. For a moment it looked as though

Toran was about to turn on him, but his anger sated, the thug removed his foot allowing Raen to lift his head coughing and spluttering. Toran waved his hand and the gang disappeared as quickly as they had arrived. His attackers gone the poor lad couldn't hold back the tears any longer; he picked up his satchel and washed off the mud, but the books were ruined, so he just left them where they lay. Still sobbing he ran for home.

Koval was working the forge when his son stepped in from the rain red eyed and covered from head to toe with patches of mud.

"By all that is holy, what happened to you son?" Koval asked. Raen held his head in shame. His father took his satchel and opened it.

"Where are your books?"

That was it; the boy rushed into his father's arms and began to sob uncontrollably.

"There now son it's alright." Koval said, pulling his son into his huge chest. "The silly books are of no importance. Come let's get you cleaned up and into some dry clothes. Your mother has a lovely hot broth waiting for you inside."

Over the meal Koval let the matter drop, he didn't want to stress his son any further; Tyrna was much better at getting information from the boy anyway with a much less demanding approach. After they had finished eating, Koval threw his wife that telling look she knew all too well. Raen with a full belly had calmed down; his mother poured him a goblet of fresh cranberry juice then with that expertise only a mother seems to possess, began to question the events of the afternoon. Raen described his ordeal as best he could, using sign language. Koval was nowhere near as good as his wife with signs but what he did pick up was enough to fuel a father's anger.

"Right son you will come with me," he said, the words almost strangled by temper.

"You are not taking the boy round to that thug's house," Tyrna interrupted.

Koval calmed himself, upsetting his son unnecessarily was never his intention, and by the look on his son's face, that was just what he was doing.

"I will just talk to the little lout's father, nothin' more.... He has to know his son can't get away with that kind of nonsense."

"Just leave it be, I will speak with the boy tomorrow when he is clear of his father's influence," she replied. She knew her words fell on deaf ears, there was no way her husband was going to back down no matter what reasoning she put forth.

"I have to deal with this matter myself, and Raen must face these bullies for his own good."

"Is it really for his good?" She stressed.

"Of course it is, he has to stand up to this bully... They have to realize there is a consequence for such behaviour." He replied. "Raen will be fine."

Koval took his son by the hand and led him outside; he turned around aware Tyrna was shadowing his every step.

"At least the damned rain has eased off," he said.

"Husband... Do not let your temper get the better of you, that is not a lesson our child needs to learn," she replied nervously. Koval gave her a reassuring kiss on the cheek then set off to the rougher part of town.

Toran and his cronies were play fighting outside the front door of his father's house, a small one bedroomed holding in the Nest: a honey comb of rat-infested alley ways where cutthroats, thieves and worse lived out a seedy existence relatively free from the laws that governed most normal people. The smallest of the group was the first to spot the Smithy and his son as they approached. He alerted the others before running off down the muddy street; the others stayed their ground under the arrogant assumption that Toran's father would sort things out.

"What do yer want mister?" Toran shouted.

Koval pulled his son closer and loomed over the young gang leader.

"I take it you are the leader then?" He asked in a tone that made all the youngsters tremble. Toran didn't answer; instead, he just stood there as cocky as you please in dumb insolence. This only went to fuel Koval's anger even further; the big man grabbed the boy by the arm dragging him in front of his son.

"Now, I want you to apologize to my son you little gutter rat or I swear…." Before he could finish, the front door flew open and Toran's father, a big man, more fat than muscle, burst out onto the street.

"What the fuck's going on 'ere?" He bellowed at Koval his breath rank with stale mead. Koval pushed his son behind him and released his grip on Toran's arm.

"This boy of yours and his friends did this to my son, before ruining his books," Koval said, pointing to the swelling under Raen's eye. "I want him to apologize, then that will be the end of it."

"Apologize to that little shit. I hear he can't even speak, so what good are books to him anyways?"

Koval exploded into action, he hit Toran's father with a sweeping uppercut sending him flying back through the door. The man was out cold, blood ran from an impact cut to his chin and two of his rotten teeth lay on the floor next to his face. The boys looked on aghast, mouths open, they all knew Toran's father had a reputation for being tough; not just with his son who sported bruises like a badge of honour but with other hard men in the nest. Koval called Raen over to face the young thugs.

"Now you little brats apologize." The youngest spoke first his voice stuttering with fear.

"I...I'm sorry."

The others were quick to follow.

"And will this ever happen again?"

"No. No," they said, one after the other. Koval stepped into the doorway and turned Toran's father around to face him. The man's eyes were still closed, so the Smithy slapped his face. The eyes opened dazedly; his nose broken, he spat blood and groaned with pain.

"If your son or any of those friends of his so much as look at my boy the wrong way, I will come back here and break your back... You'll be pissing yourself for the rest of your days." His grip tightened around the man's throat. "Nod if you understand me."

He nodded painfully then slumped back down onto the stone floor. Koval took his son's hand and led him away. "Come on son let's leave this sorry place."

Raen looked at his father with a son's pride, although still shaken he was glad and somewhere deep inside he knew that would be the end of it. And it was. From that day, the bullying stopped not only from Toran and his gang but also those who just took childish pleasure from his misery. And in the years that followed, Raen grew bigger and stronger than any of them. And though he felt no need of revenge, he would one day here how Toran's father had been choked to death on his own vomit as his son strangled the life out of him.

But now at seventeen, Raen worked the forge with his father and was loved by all who knew him for his good and gentle nature.

***

Koval, tired after a hard day, put away his tools and hung the new breast plate he'd put the finishing touches to that afternoon. He could smell his wife's cooking through the open kitchen window; it was his favourite, lamb stew with finely ground mint leaves. He knew Tyrna was waiting inside ready to off load the moment he stepped through the door, but she had a point even though he did not agree with her whole heartedly.

Luckily, she was too busy preparing the food by the window to notice him slip past. He freshened up, changed into clean clothes and readied himself mentally for the inevitable.

"Umm! Something smells good woman," he said.

In no mood for empty compliments, she ignored him and stoked the fire under the cauldron of stew. She took a sample on a large wooden spoon and added a few herbs to taste. Then it came.

"If that boy has gone skulking around that Hunters place again, I'll cut his legs off. Huh!" she sighed in frustration.

Koval crept up behind her laying his hands on her buxom waist and squeezed her playfully. For a moment, she responded letting her bottom rest against his thighs, but quickly corrected herself in no mood for any kind of a submission. He squeezed her again with no response; so, he released his grip and poured himself a beer from a keg by the window.

"He's just being a lad yer know," he said defending his son's absence.

A piercing screech drew Tyrna's attention outside. She looked up from the window to catch a glimpse of a white hawk as it plummeted out of sight behind some trees.

"It's not normal I tell yer, a man nursing a Wolf like that; and that bird of his. Who's ever heard of a white hawk? It's an omen it is… an omen."

Koval shifted in his seat, he was first to hear the familiar sound of Raen running up the path. Panting and out of breath the lad stumbled through the back door his face red and sweaty. Koval winked at him and nodded towards the bowl of water he'd placed on a small table by the door of the lads sleeping quarters. He smiled back at his father and sheepishly rushed over to the bowl to freshen himself up. After drying his hands, he joined his father at the table. Tyrna put a platter of freshly baked bread in the middle of the table; her face set in a permanent scowl. She served them both with a generous helping of the stew before joining them, and being a concerned mother, she couldn't contain herself any longer.

"Have you been to that Hunter's place again?" she quizzed.

The look on her son's face confirmed it, no other answer was necessary.

"What have I told you! There's no good in that man. Mark my words," she moaned.

"Let the boy be woman," Koval said in his son's defence.

"I tell you there's something not right about the man. Folks say he's always brawling over one thing or another."

"I don't pay much heed to petty gossip and neither should you. All I can say is, I've never seen Hunter hurt anyone as doesn't have it comin'," Koval replied, giving his son another wink.

Tyrna looked unimpressed. *I can see I'm wasting my breath*, she thought, her face as flushed as a ripe tomato. Relieved the conversation hadn't become a prolonged debate; Koval just broke bread, handed some to his wife and son, then all three quietly tucked into the meal.

5
FATHER'S GRIEF

Kor-yllion paced the room nervously, an emotion not often associated with one so self-assured; his face drawn and troubled. He looked to the balcony where shafts of early morning sunlight entered the room giving life to the rich murals that covered the walls within. Normally such a morning would lift a heavy grief laden heart; but not this day. He knew his life would never be the same again, after that day he left his daughter in the cabin in the woods. It felt like everything that was dear to him was lost, not least the love of a wife. Even other members of his family, blood or otherwise looked upon him with accusing eyes, a burden he was finding ever harder to shoulder. If it weren't for Kor-aviel he was sure he would be absent a friend of any kind, and sometimes he even doubted that. From the first day of his rule over his people he'd known leadership was a lonely companion, yet he never expected to feel the way he did at that very moment, waiting for what he knew was coming.

The Chamber of the High Council was a large room, its walls and ceiling curved like the inside of some enormous egg. The colour throughout was a bleached pastel green only broken by the large murals depicting Elven life from a different time. Two long open balconies filled the room with light and from the largest of these a spiralling walkway gave direct access to the ornate gardens three floors below. At its centre was a large oval table of polished elm supported at either end by two sculpted Stag heads. Twelve ornately carved high-backed chairs surrounded it and in one of these Kor-yllion sat staring at the archway that led to the spiral staircase and his living quarters below. The unmistakable sound of his wife's footsteps sent waves of nervous energy coursing through his stomach as she neared the top of the stairs.

He'd tried as best he could to keep the news of the slaughter on the road from Lessien for as long as he could, but inside he knew it was only time: a whisper from a soldier, a secret shared with a friend or wife. Whichever it was his wife had heard news of that terrible day before he was ready to share such information, and he sensed this day would be one he would not readily forget.

Lessien entered the archway and stormed across the room her face a mask of fury. The King stood to face her. Uncharacteristically she laid blow upon blow across his chest through cries of pure, unfiltered anguish. Kor-yllion offered no resistance to the assault, he just stood there taking whatever punishment she deemed appropriate.

"My daughter is lost to me; your sister is dead and now my granddaughter. Is this the price we must all pay for your ridiculous sense of honour and duty?" She screamed.

The King had no answer he just bowed his head in a shame of his own making. He went to put his arms around her to offer what little comfort he could but she pushed herself clear.

"Your stupid pride. I will never forgive you for this. Never," she cried, as she turned to leave the room. Kor-yllion sat back down and put his elbows on the table, his head in hands.

Kor-aviel passed Lessien at the top of the stairs, he had never seen his Queen so distressed, but its cause was obvious. He tried to speak with her but it was pointless, she barged past him ignoring him completely. He carried on into the Chambers to find Kor-yllion standing on the balcony staring at the forest and falls beyond. The Shaman could see how troubled his friend was but the information he carried had to be relayed without delay.

"My Lord, please forgive my intrusion, but a Falcon has brought urgent news from Maccon. It is in regard to Hunter."

It was as though the Shaman's words were never spoken; the King lost in his own troubles stared to the skies ignoring their import.

"What have I done dear friend? What have I done?"

***

The dusk sky above Hunter's lodge settled in a kaleidoscope of pinks and dusty greys. The Dire Wolf looked beyond the wooden bars of the pen at the youth who had just left the fresh cooked offerings not far from where she lay. There was no threat from her visitor, she knew this and in return she gave him her trust.

Raen had heard about Hunter's latest fight; something about four cutthroats attacking him in an alley not far from the town square. Rumour had it he was spending the night at Vena's place leaving an opportune moment for one of Raen's secret visitations. He'd sneaked some of the chicken leftovers from the previous night's dinner and slipped them through the bars for the beautiful creature beyond. He watched nervously as the Wolf got to her feet and took the offerings into her huge jaws. He had only heard stories of such beasts, so to see one like this was for him a thing of amazement. The chicken breasts were so small the Wolf didn't chew them she swallowed them whole. He stared into her huge golden eyes and swore he could see that she liked him. Well, that is what he wanted to believe and though he didn't know it she did. There was nothing threatening about the beast, yet he knew should the fancy take her she could tear him apart in the blink of an eye. He could see gentleness in her gaze and during these visits had grown to love the animal.

Even with his keen hearing Raen hadn't heard Hunter approach. It was the White Hawk that drew his attention to the back of the lodge as it landed on the roof overlooking the wolf pen. Startled he turned to find Hunter standing by the skinning hut, his shirt bloodied and his face taut with an expression he could not read. Embarrassed at being caught he dropped his gaze, his face as red as a ripe cherry. He looked to the Wolf one last time before backing away; leaving the lodge by a side path he headed for the road back into town.

Bael walked over to the pen, he'd watched the lad feed the Wolf and appreciated his kindness.

The beast lifted her head, the scent of blood from her captors wound filled her nostrils with a hunger that would normally drive her to kill, but all she wanted to do was lick it for him. Now, her strength returned she could feel the bond with this stranger grow ever stronger but with no reason for why. She watched as he knelt before her his face close to the bars.

"It would seem you have a friend," he said smiling at her.

She rested her head back on her paws a growl rumbling in her throat, then closed her eyes in contentment.

In the shadows of the forest at the edge of the lodge a huge Black Dire Wolf watched Hunter's every movement. It bared its razor-sharp teeth and snarled in anger, but it knew this was neither the time nor the place for action. So, it turned and slipped back into the forest from whence it came, the silver streak on its neck catching the sun as it moved.

Bael thought he heard something move in the trees, he looked to the sound's origin, but found only shifting shadows as sunlight filtered through the canopy of leaves. He felt the wetness of fresh blood seep from the closed wound, so without further delay he entered the lodge. Removing his ripped shirt Bael readied a paste of ground herbs and seeds mixed with salted water and applied it under the bandage to the inflamed skin surrounding the cut. Its pain-relieving properties took several seconds to kick in, but when they did he found the movement of his arm far less troublesome. He inserted a clean linen dressing before searching the chest by the bed for a clean shirt. There was a knock at the door. *Who could this be*? He thought, not expecting anyone. He opened the door to find Lord Farroth's personal ward standing on the porch, a face that was no stranger to him.

"I am sorry to trouble you so early in the day but Lord Farroth wishes to speak with you."

"What is it this time?" Bael asked the ward, who had relayed many such messages over the years.

"I am not privy to the details of the request but I think it has something to do with the forthcoming visitation of my Lord's brother the King."

6
TRAINING DAY

Bael hid in the trees watching the lad feed the Wolf, as he had done virtually every day since that night in Vena's place. Not once did he give away his position, he didn't want to scare the lad away again; in-fact the youth's kindness had really touched him. Stealthily he stepped from the shadows and made his way to the Wolf pen; he was almost on top of the lad, when Raen shot to his feet, startled.

"Please…Don't be afraid I mean you no harm."

Bael could see Raen's days on the forge had chiselled muscles not often seen on someone of his age, as the lad's body tensed instinctively.

"Relax my friend. You are the smith's son are you not?"

The lad nodded excitedly.

"An honourable trade… I can see you like the Wolf, and she you."

Raen nodded again, this time smiling.

"Listen, I have a thought. How would you like to stroke her?"

Bael couldn't read the hand movements but the lads beaming smile was all the answer he needed. He unlocked the wolf pen and led the beast into the open; it looked magnificent, its coat the colour of polished amber with eyes that shone like liquid gold. Hunter took her huge head in his hands and gazed into those golden pools.

"You heal well my beauty."

The beast sniffed his face then licked it.

"Here my young friend… Slowly now. Stroke her neck," he gestured to Raen.

Raen cautiously ran his hand along its neck; the beast lifted her head to the touch. Then to the lad's delight she licked the back of his hand; any nervous reservation melted away in that single moment. With his new gained confidence, he nuzzled his head into the Wolf's neck as if it were his pet dog; there was no resistance from the animal, it just stood there proud and powerful. Bael smiled then whistled to the skies: The White Hawk swooped from a nearby tree and landed on his arm; its translucent pink eyes following Raen's every movement. The lad found them unnerving; unlike the Wolf's eyes the birds were penetrating and unforgiving and demanded a different kind of respect.

"Here, slowly raise your hand and place your fingers on the back of his head."

Raen nervously jerked his hand up.

"Slowly, sudden movement will startle him. Now let go of your fear, he will respect that and allow your touch. Trust me you will be fine, but no sharp movements."

Raen took a deep breath and slowly placed his fingers on the back of the bird's head, gently stroking the feathers flat. *That was enough for one day he thought,* slowly removing his trembling hand.

"I'm impressed. Normally my white friend here would have taken a chunk out of your arm or worse," he said grinning. "I think it is fair to say he must like you."

Raen looked pretty pleased with himself.

"You have a natural affinity to animals my friend. It is a rare gift not seen in many," he said pausing for a moment. "I have been hired by Lord Farroth to provide fresh venison for the King's banquet. What would you say to joining me at weeks end to hunt some deer?"

Raen nodded his acceptance.

"Good... But first how about you meet me here after your day at the forge and I shall teach you how to handle my pet?" he said gesturing to the hawk.

The lad couldn't believe his luck; his cheeks flushed with excitement at the prospect of such adventure, so again he nodded his approval.

"Then so be it. I will see you on the morrow." With that Raen stroked the Wolf one last time then left.

The night passed without incident, free of dream or vision, leaving Bael refreshed and ready to face the day ahead. He spent most of it servicing his weapons; re-stringing his two hunting bows, filling a quiver with arrows, sharpening his skinning knives and preparing feed for Wolf and Hawk in anticipation of his young guest. He spent the rest of the afternoon in town where he picked up his half weekly order of bread from Jered's shop. Shortly after, he bumped into Emma who was buying supplies from the market for the Tavern. A chance meeting that somehow lifted his spirits, though if truth be told, he had not said much; and for the first time he sensed an uncharacteristic restraint in her conversation, before they parted company to go about their intended business.

Heading for home he passed through the town square and into the alley where he had fought the four men, the same night he saw the beautiful young woman with her bodyguards. He paused for a moment and looked around; a strange feeling stirred in his stomach: the memory of that night was not filled with images of the fight; it was of her face as it came out of shadow on removal of her hood. He was quickly brought back to reality when he heard Vena shouting him from the door of the brothel; smoking pipe weed. She gave him a verbal dressing down about his absence of the past week, which he took with the grace of indifference before carrying on home.

Whilst he waited for the arrival of the Smith's son, Bael decided to get in some sword practice. A daily ritual he had undertaken for as long as he could remember and never questioned why. It was pure instinct; an art taught him by his father a swordmaster of great renown who had died in a freak hunting accident. Memories it seemed were only known to him and for reasons he had never queried, Maccon and Lord Farroth. He opened the hessian cloth on a table by the fire, revealing two beautifully fashioned swords. One was longer than the other but both had slightly curved blades with intricate engraved carvings along the centre of their lengths; forged from steel that never lost its shine nor its razor-sharp edge no matter what they hit. Qualities in a weapon he took for granted yet qualities others would find extremely unusual and suspicious were they ever to witness what he could do with them.

When the lad finally arrived Bael was engaged in a series of dazzling sword disciplines that were as beautiful in their fluidity as they were lethal in their intent. Raen stopped by the wolf pen and watched in awe at the raw energy needed to perform such a deathly dance.

Hunter spotted the lad as he spun around with the short blade extended behind his back like a scythe; the longer one extended to the front. He finished the move, slipping the long blade into its back scabbard, the other to the open-ended scabbard at his side. His precision was frightening to watch, leaving Raen feeling a little uneasy.

Hunter strode over to the lad, his long black hair soaked with sweat; he could see the uncertainty etched across Raen's face so he removed the short sword from his side and handed it to the lad. Raen took it in his hand and with skilled eyes scrutinized its perfection. The steel was of a quality even his father could not match and the shape was like nothing they had ever forged. His father had told him stories of such weapons but they belonged to the Elves, forged with magic that dated back to a time before the coming of man. Secrets the Elves would share with no one.

"Please… I am sure your father has shown you the way of the blade. I have heard he is no mean swordsman himself. So please… show me what you can do."

Raen stepped back self-consciously swinging the sword in a series of clumsy arcs.

"Forget I am here. Don't over think it. You must focus on the task, nothing more. A battle is won and lost in here," Hunter said, pointing to the side of his head.

"Now try again. I have yet to meet a weapon smith who can't handle a sword."

This time Raen was a little better but the demons of uncertainty still asserted their disruptive influences, again limiting his performance. Whilst the lad fought his imaginary opponent, Hunter slipped quietly into the skinning hut to re-appear holding an iron spit rod.

"That was a little better," he said lifting the rod as he would a sword.

Raen stopped immediately.

"Now. I want you to attack me. Don't hold back."

Raen suddenly became nervous.

"Don't be afraid, no one will get hurt I assure you. Now attack me," Bael said digging the lad in the ribs with the rod.

At first Raen's attacks were restrained, every blow being parried with ease. Hunter gave him a few more digs then stopped.

"Now we have played a little I want you to attack me as if your very life depended on it… Show me what your father has taught you."

This time Raen's muscles hardened, a pre-emptive warning that Hunter read with ease. His blade slashed, parried and thrust with more purposeful vigour; but every blow was cast aside as if he were a child play fighting. Hunter tapped the back of his leg, his neck and his stomach, all blows that had the rod been a sword Raen would either be maimed or dead. Exhausted and somewhat embarrassed the lad let his sword arm drop by his side. Hunter smiled.

"You are better than you than you think you are. Your father has taught you well."

The words do little to lessen Raen's sense of martial incompetence.

"Look. You have nothing to be ashamed of; you fight well for someone your age. I have practiced this way from being so high," Hunter gestured, holding his palm but three feet from the ground.

"I tell you what. Each time you visit me I will teach you the skills of the blade. That is if you are willing to learn?"

Raen stood taller and nodded his agreement.

"Good. But I have one condition. When you can, you must bring me chicken heads from the town's meat vendor."

Though puzzled by the request Raen agreed.

"They won't ask coin for such; they will be only too glad to get rid of them. And one more thing, I would like you to teach me how to speak with my hands. It would please me to understand you more, so if this is how we are to communicate then so be it."

The lad found it hard to believe what had just happened, nobody had shown this much interest in him since Maccon had entered his life, and Hunter was the last person in town he thought would do so.

Bael took his sword back and entered the lodge; a short time later he returned dressed in a chamois leather jerkin and a thick hide arm guard. He let the Wolf out of the pen to roam freely around the grounds. Then he placed a second arm guard on Raen's left arm. Looking to the trees in the distance he whistled the call of the hawk. Raen followed his gaze as the white predator swooped over his head to land firmly on Hunter's arm. Bael kissed the bird on the beak and stroked its neck before placing a soft leather hood over the bird's head. He told Raen to fetch the leather pouch full of chicken heads from the table in the skinning hut. He instructed the lad to fasten the bag to his belt, then braced the bird's legs together with a thin leather strap.

"Hold out your arm?" He said pointing to Raen's protected arm. "Can you whistle?"

Raen stood proud, placed two fingers under his tongue and blew. The sound he made could have cracked glass: though no words had ever passed his lips, his lungs were the size of bellows, and as a child he had taken great pride in making the one sound that he could.

Hunter smiled.

"Well that certainly answered my question… Now, take the end of this strap and wrap it round your hand," he said handing the lad the strap attached to the hawk's legs. Carefully he coaxed the bird onto Raen's protected arm.

"You have to gain his trust, which will take time and patience. What I want you to do now is take one of the chicken heads and carefully feed it to him."

Raen removed the head from the pouch and was about to lift it higher when like lightning the hawk grabbed the head in its beak, then it dropped it into its razor-sharp talons. In a feeding frenzy the hawk tightened its grip, and had the lad not been wearing the leather guard those razor-sharp talons would have pierced clean through his arm. It tore the head to shreds in seconds, ripping flesh and bone with ease. After the third chicken head, the Hawk began to settle; Hunter took advantage of the moment.

"When I remove this," he said taking hold of the hood covering the hawk's eyes, "he may try to take flight. If he does you must swing him around like this, so he lands back on your arm. Otherwise, he could damage his wings and possibly take out your eye." Bael gave the lad a visual demonstration, before slowly removing the hood. The hawk fluttered its wings momentarily, but instinctively Raen fed it another head which settled it immediately.

"You have a way with you. The animals can see it. This is good."

Bael removed the bindings from the bird's legs; making a high and low whistle the Hawk flew to his arm its eyes blinking wildly.

"Now we begin."

***

It was two days to the hunt, Raen as promised arrived after work ready and willing, carrying the required satchel full of chicken heads. His affinity to the Hawk was nothing short of remarkable, the bird like the Wolf seemed to trust him; and except for a few unintentional scars he had come through the training relatively unscathed. On the other hand, the training with the swords was a work in progress; even though the lad had natural skills there was far too much to learn in such limited time. But Bael never expected anything more.

The day's training was coming to an end, Bael and the lad were wet with sweat after a vigorous sparring session. The hawk was high in the trees; the Wolf lay on the ground outside the pen resting. Suddenly it sprang to its feet as Koval entered the grounds. Raen's face already flushed through exhaustion turned rich scarlet when he saw his father approach Hunter.

"You are Koval are you not?" Bael began.

"I am he…."

"So, why am I honoured with such a visit when we have never so much as broken word in the years I have lived amongst you?" Bael asked coolly.

"My son has been rather secretive of late, about his comings and goings… and those scars he bears have caused his mother some concern," he replied in a firm but not unfriendly tone.

"So, you thought you would pay me a visit?"

Koval looked a little uneasy as the Wolf moved to Hunter's side. Bael placed a hand on her head and stroked it reassuringly. Raen edged closer to his father; sword still in hand he scowled at the emasculating interference.

"My son is a simple lad and far too trusting for his own good," the smith said throwing Raen a condescending glance. "I see what his mother does not, he walks with a new-found confidence and though pleasing to see it leaves questions to be answered… And this hunt he tells me about, I would know your purpose for taking him along on such a venture."

Hunter could see what their time together meant to the lad; his face softened.

"I understand a father's concern… Please-wait here a moment there is something you should see," Bael said, entering the skinning hut.

Koval gestured for his son to pass him the sword he was holding. He checked the blade up and down impressed at its lethal beauty. Hunter returned carrying the leather arm guard; he placed it on Raen's arm and stepped back a little.

"Show your father how you got those scars."

Raen looked to the trees and whistled. A white streak swooped from the sky to make a perfect landing on his outstretched arm. The Hawks piercing eyes looked blood red in the fading light; first they flicked to Hunter then to Koval who watched in amazement. It made an ear-piercing screech at the stranger amongst them; Raen stroked its head calming it down. Koval found it hard to believe his eyes, but his heart swelled with a father's pride.

"Your son has a way with animals, a gift rarely seen in one so young... He also wished for me to teach him in skills of the sword."

Koval held up the sword he had taken from his son.

"It is a fine blade… A blade worthy of a Master. If I may ask, how did you come by such a weapon?"

At first Bael's features hardened at the searching question, then he looked to the lad whose obvious discomfort was plain to see.

"It belonged to my father, where he got it from I cannot say, but it was passed down to me with this other," he said pointing to the one in his back scabbard.

"Your son is quite accomplished with the blade. You have taught him well smithy."

Koval began to relax a little, the tension in his shoulders melting away.

"My son is a willing pupil. Eager to learn."

"I have seen these qualities," Hunter replied.

He paused for a moment then stared questioningly at Koval.

"On the matter of the hunt… If this is of concern to you and his mother, then it is best he did not accompany me."

Raen's face was a picture of rejection and disappointment.

"You hunt deer for the feast?"

"I do."

"There are other creatures in the forest, dangerous creatures that my son has no experience of. How would I know he was safe?"

"I have hunted these forests for many years. I know where I can and cannot venture, that is all I can say."

Koval handed the sword back to his son.

"I don't know what I am going to tell your mother, but I can see how much you want this, so yes you can go but on one condition."

Raen's face beamed with joy as he nodded his acceptance for whatever condition his father threw at him.

"You must tell your mother nothing of this, I will think of a reason for your day from the forge. But you must make up the time by working extra hours each day for the coming week. Is that understood?"

Raen smiled, replying the only way he could, his hand gestures exaggerated through excitement.

"Then so be it," he said turning to Hunter. "His mother is not so understanding, but I know the measure of a man Hunter, and you are not the man many in this town think you to be. Please take care of my boy and I thank you for the kindness you have shown him."

With that Koval turned to leave. "I think it is time we went home; your mother will have our meals on the table and we both know how ratty she gets when she is kept waiting."

Raen removed the leather arm guard and handed it back to Hunter; then nuzzled his face into the Wolf's neck before joining his father.

"I will not be able to see you now until the day of the hunt, there is something I must do before then. So, we will meet two days hence. Don't be late," Bael finished.

7
THE OLD CRONE

Bael and the Wolf had been tracking the *child killer* most of the morning, an animal whose usual hunting grounds were much further north where it was said men fought to the death in pits of blood and stone. Bael had never hunted a Grawl before; he had only heard stories of how they were the size of a shadow cat, some it was said, larger even than a fully-grown Dire Wolf. He followed its trail with well-founded caution; Grawls were ferocious killers and one of the few predators that savoured the taste of human flesh above all others.

Twice during the morning, the hunted became the hunter, circling back on itself in a cunning attempt to come up on its pursuers from behind. But Bael being the consummate tracker knew it's every movement; the White Hawk returning every now and then to guide him on the right path, the bird never losing sight of the prey. This game of cat and mouse seemed to thrill the beast more than the kill itself. A game which had brought them to a small holding at the edge of town that belonged to the Old Crone; whom if rumours were true, was blind. He paused for a moment after stepping onto the open path leading from the trees to the white walled cottage in the distance. Kneeling by what looked to be the carcass of a deer was an old woman. He patted the Wolf on the back.

"Wait here. We do not want to frighten her."

As Bael approached, the woman lifted her head and looked right at him as if the rumours of her blindness were unfounded. But as he stared at a face that defied its age, he saw her eyes were clouded over, as ice looked on murky water. Her hand rested on the swollen stomach of the doe; its throat had been ripped out but there was no sign of its killer having feasted off her.

"Please, you are in grave danger, the creature that did this…." Before he could finish he saw the Wolf running towards him; the White Hawk above. Suddenly the Grawl burst from cover, and in that moment Bael realized the deer on the ground was just a ruse, a lure to draw them in while the beast readied itself for the real targets. Them. It was a terrifying visage; eyes a sickly yellow, its head and chest like polished black ebony with hind legs and tail covered in uneven black and white stripes. But the thing that made most men freeze in their tracks was the huge canine teeth; as long as a man's hand from fingertip to wrist, that dripped with poisonous saliva. To die from the bite would be merciful for the death which followed should the beast let you live was slow and agonising.

There was no time to knock an arrow the beast was that quick; it passed the Wolf brushing her aside as though she were a feather. There was only one meat the Grawl wanted to feast on this day and it was human. The beast leapt into the air clearing a good thirty feet, leaving just enough time for Bael to draw his sword from his back. It was over in a second the Grawl's head parting its body as thick muscle and dense bone gave no resistance to the razor-sharp curved blade. The careering body spun end over end landing by the old woman's feet, the head landing further behind spraying Bael in dark crimson.

Somewhat shaken the woman grabbed Bael by the arm; she seemed more concerned about the doe on the ground, than she was about her own safety.

"Please, help me save the poor creature," she said dropping to her knees.

For a moment Bael wondered what she was talking about, as far as he was concerned the deer was dead. But as she laid her hands on the deer's side, he saw the stomach move.

"Please she carries an unborn; if we do not hurry it will surely perish."

Bael pulled out his skinning knife and dropped down beside the dead animal, with deft accuracy he opened her stomach exposing the bluey grey birthing sack and the life chord. He carefully cut the sack and the chord releasing the struggling fawn from the prison of its dead mother's womb. The little creature was weak from its struggle yet Bael could sense its will to live; he picked it up gently, its tiny head falling limp by his hand.

"We must get it to my cottage, please, time is short."

The old woman led them to her home, following the path as if her sight was true, the Wolf following a few paces behind; the White Hawk perched on the cottages thatched roof. Once inside she cleared a thick rough carved oak table of the freshly picked carrots and potatoes; Bael stood by cradling the limp fawn in his arms, still puzzled by the blind woman's ability to move around without ever walking into the numerous obstacles that lay in her path. The Wolf stayed at the open door where Bael had ordered her to stay.

"Your strange travel companion can come in," she said glancing over to the door.

The Wolf slowly moved into the sweet-smelling room without any instruction from Bael to do so.

"Quickly, place the poor creature here," she urged, pointing to the edge of the table next to a small jug of milk and some green herbal potion.

Bael laid the fawn down and watched the old woman clear birthing debris from the animal's mouth before dripping some of the green liquid down its throat. Nothing happened; then it coughed the weakest of coughs before once again lying still, almost lifeless. Bael thought the creature dead, then the Wolf walked over to the table and licked the fawn on the mouth before moving back to Bael's side. The old woman stroked the animal's chest trying to coax some sign of life from it. Then something happened that surprised not just Bael; even the Crone's sightless eyes betrayed her own amazement as a warm pulsating glow emanated from within the fawn's body. Slowly the animal's chest moved up and down as the heart began to beat and air once again filled its lungs. The old woman looked first to the Wolf then back to Hunter.

"Please, there is some straw by the chicken pen," she said, pointing through the open window. "Fetch some so I can make this poor creature more comfortable."

Bael returned with the straw; making a nest shaped bed he laid the fawn down gently and though still weak it raised its head to look at him.

"You are an odd one my boy. You are hired for your skill as a hunter yet you travel with a wolf? And here you are showing compassion for a creature whose life in these forests you may one-day end," she puzzled, pouring him a mug of homemade elderberry wine.

"Here, sit young man and drink this," she said, joining him at the table.

"Thank you," he replied.

"There is no need to thank me, it is I should be thanking you... it appears I owe you my life. And the kindness you have shown here today will not be forgotten."

Bael always found it difficult to deal with praise and was uncertain how to respond; for what he did was just his nature. Again, her eyes became the focus of his attention, their milky glaze definitely suggesting blindness to him.

"Ah? I sense you have questions?" She said, taking hold of his free hand.

Bael pondered for a brief moment feeling an odd tingling sensation as she touched him.

"How do you know I am a hunter?"

"I know many things my dear boy, but for the moment that I know what you are is of little importance."

"Then I would ask about your eyes. They would have me believe you cannot see, yet you move about as if that were not true."

"I am blind in the way *you* see things, but I was blessed with another kind of sight…. I see *light*."

"Light?" Bael replied, puzzled.

"Auras…. Everything has an aura, wood, rock, you me. Your strange companion over there," she said glancing over at the Wolf. "Please- allow me." She stood up and placed her hands on his temples. Gently she let them follow the contours of his face. Then sat back down and smiled.

"You have a handsome face my young friend. Strong yet troubled…. Am I wrong in saying you are not from these parts?"

"What makes you think that?" he asked somewhat surprised by the question.

"So very, very odd. Everything has but a single aura of a colour unique to it or them; a signature that tells me what or who it is. You have *two*. In all my years, I have not seen the like."

"I come from the north, but I have lived here amongst the town's people for the past ten years," Bael said in response to her previous question.

"If that is what you believe then I will pursue the matter no further."

"What do you mean?"

"Forgive me young man, my intention is not to cause concern, but your past it not what you believe it to be."

"I don't understand?"

"There is something very few people know about me; some would call it a gift, others a curse…. I can see into the past, and on rare occasion a glimpse of the future. With you I can see neither. There is a powerful magic at work here, a barrier that prevents you from knowing the truth about your origin. But for what reason I know not."

Bael felt confused. At first, he put her comments down to the wanderings of a lonely old woman, but there was something in her words that troubled him.

"I only know what I have told you," he replied a little defensively.

Behind him the fawn coughed and turned over, leading Bael into another unanswered quandary.

"The light that appeared in the fawn's chest…. What was it and how did you make it happen?"

The old woman turned her head in the direction of the Wolf.

"Like you I am at a loss and would know the answer to that question myself. Your companion, she is a Wolf is she not?"

"She is. But how did you know it was a she?"

"In every living creature, the females' aura is a gentler, softer colour than her male counterpart."

The old woman shuffled around the table and approached the Wolf which was sitting upright by the straw nest as if to guard the sleeping fawn.

"Will she let me touch her?" she asked, placing her hands either side of the Wolf's huge head.

"She will," Bael replied, curious to see what the old woman was up to.

Carefully the blind woman rested her hands just below the beast's ears and looked up as if to listen for something. Then slowly she slid her right hand along the wolf's side until it rested on the healing wound. She winced as if in pain. Without uttering a word, she removed her hands and walked over to a cupboard by the window.

"Forgive me. I forget my manners? Can I offer you some bread and cheese?" she asked, placing a fresh loaf of bread and a chunk of homemade cheese on a wooden platter.

"Thank you. But I am not hungry."

"Is there anything I can give the Wolf then?"

"Water and some cooked chicken if you have any."

"The water I have, the chicken unfortunately I do not."

"Then the water will suffice. Thank you," Bael replied.

The old woman filled a large wooden fruit bowl with water from a pitcher under the window and placed it by the Wolf. As she turned to join Bael again at the table she smiled; the beast lapped up the water quenching her thirst from the offering set before her.

"And now I would have an answer for the question I have yet to ask," she said.

"And that would be?"

"Your name?"

Bael put down his empty wine goblet and stood to leave.

"My name is Bael. Most in the town know me as Hunter. And if I may be so bold, what may I call you?"

"You may call me what you like. Children call me witch; old crone, others Seer. But I am just an old woman who sees the world in a different way. And though I have lived in this town longer than anyone else there are few who call me Lamia, my true birth name."

"Well then Lamia, I thank you for your hospitality but we must go now. I will pass this way each day for a week to make sure there are no more of the beasts we have slain here this day."

"Please. One more thing before you go," she urged. "I believe you have an enthusiastic apprentice, eager to learn the ways of the hunter…. Ranger? Whatever you wish to call yourself."

"You would mean Raen the smithy's son?"

"I do indeed," she replied. "And it is obvious you care for the boy."

"He is a good lad. He has a big heart and above all he listens and is quick to learn," Bael replied.

"As I said, you care for the boy."

"I feel sorry for the lad, that is all. I think he deserves more from *life* than *she* has seen fit to bestow on him," Bael said.

"I take it you refer to the fact that he cannot speak?"

"Yes," he replied, feeling a little uncomfortable with the old woman's line of questioning.

"Ah! Pity…. such an empty vessel. But this I know…. Your heart is full, though you may not see it, for it is not pity that drives you to learn the language of the hands. It is not pity you feel when the boy hugs you dearly as he would a father or a brother," she pondered.

Bael didn't utter a word in response, he just moved uncomfortably in his chair unsure of how to react.

Lamia smiled inwardly at his obvious discomfort.

"Let me tell you a short story, then you can be on your way.... It was a time of terrible conflict. Two brothers, twins, lived in a village high in the mountains far from the wars of men. Their parents were kind gentle folk and would only see the best in people. They believed what you gave in life you received and so it was that the rest of the villagers were as leaves from the same tree, they too were kind and understanding. It was known by all who lived there that one of the twins could not speak, unlike his brother who bore no such affliction his voice loud and clear for all to hear. Yet both brothers were treated the same and loved as one. You see, the people of this village were wise, they knew what the *Gods* denied with one hand *they* made up for with the other.... One day the twins ventured high up the mountains to a secret ridge they'd discovered, where they could sit together and absorb the beauty that surrounded them every day of their lives; without the distractions of adult interference.... Down below was a valley untouched by human kind and both brothers would look to the place and imagine the wonders that lay within. What they could or could not see was the same for both, but when it came to hearing and smelling the things around them it was a completely different story.... High above where they sat were birds that never ventured to the lower reaches, birds that thrived on the cold of the ice capped peaks. They were shy creatures that never came close to the village and were only ever seen as specs in the distance. It was said, their song was the most beautiful of all the birds and only one in the village had ever heard them sing, for the Gods in their wisdom had given the brother who couldn't speak, hearing beyond imagining. And as the twins sat together on that ledge he listened to them play on the wind out of reach of all but him. Now where these birds nested were flowers that no man had ever seen or smelt. They like the birds thrived on the ice and snow; jagged peaks that were shrouded in permanent cloud some called the Veil of the Gods. It was said that the scent from these flowers was so beautiful it intoxicated those very same Gods, a scent that only one person from the village had ever smelt and while he sat on that ledge with his brother he breathed in their beauty. So, who can say which of the brothers had a richer life?"

Bael saw she was finished and stood up to take his leave.

"It is a nice story…. If life were only that simple," he added sceptically.

"You think the story a tale for children? What if I told you one of those twins' lives amongst us to this very day? Would you believe me?"

"That you believe it is enough for me," Bael replied.

"That is very gallant of you…. One-day all will become clear, and what you see as the folk tale of a silly old woman, is in truth not that at all."

She stood up and smiled.

"I have kept you long enough…. Please," she said, leading her visitors to the front door.

"It has been a very interesting morning has it not?"

"It has," he replied, still somewhat bemused.

Before exiting through the door, he looked back to see the young fawn sleeping peacefully on the bed of straw. With that he led the Wolf out of the cottage and along the path. Before leaving the area, he dragged the carcasses of both deer and Grawl into the woods.

As promised, he called each day sweeping the surrounding area for any signs of another Grawl. But he found none. With each visit, the fawn grew stronger. And on his final visit he and the Wolf were greeted in the old woman's garden by the young deer as it walked towards them; shaky and wobbling on its spindly legs.

Bael noticed the old woman standing at the open window; she looked tired.

"Is there anything I can do for you before we leave?" he asked.

"No.... Thank you I am fine. My young lady from the town is due today with my weekly supplies. But I thank you once again for a kindness I will not forget. And should you ever find the need to talk for whatever reason. Do not hesitate to pay me a visit…."

"I will," he replied as he turned to leave.

"And look after your Wolf. She is very special."

The old woman felt a sharp pang of guilt; for as she watched them leave she saw once again both man and beast shared the same double aura, a fact she did not share with Bael when first she realized. She knew in that single touch, when her hands lay on the Wolf's head, that her strange visitors were bound by the same magic that kept Bael from seeing his true past. But she knew also that this secret was not hers to share, it was a secret that Bael must discover for himself. For as she touched the beast, the magic binding its memory faltered; in that solitary moment, she saw a fleeting image of the Elves as they left the injured beast outside Bael's door, and what those Elves had said to one another as they did so.

Shortly after Bael and the Wolf had vanished into the forest, a small custom-made cart pulled by a massive black shire horse appeared along the wheel troughed road that led from the town to the cottage.

As the cart pulled up outside the front gate, Lamia came out to greet her guest, the wobbly young fawn close behind.

"Ah…. Welcome my child. It has been a busy day. Please…. Come in I have a story to tell."

***

Emma enjoyed these weekly visits. She was never greeted with the smell of stale piss and damp clothes that so often accompanied the aged living alone: it was either the sweet scent of freesia, the old woman's favourite flower or as on this day the welcoming smell of home baking, that greeted her.

Emma placed the last basket of fresh fruit next to the small keg of Haraki mead she'd just delivered, courtesy of her father. It was Lamia's one secret pleasure, and from that day she helped deliver his daughter into the world, Dogran had made sure the old woman got a weekly supply of the very same. Nervous of the new guest, the young fawn shied behind the aged pine dresser in the corner. The old woman removed several fresh baked scones from the clay oven and placed them on the wooden platter in the centre of the table while Emma stacked the deliveries in a small pantry at the rear of the kitchen. She filled a couple of small goblets with honey water then sat down to rest her weary old legs. The young deer's curiosity got the better of it; cautiously it edged its way out from behind the dresser for a closer look. Emma closed the pantry door and turned.

"And who might you be?" She asked, almost tripping over the little creature.

Nervously it stepped back; its newfound confidence short lived as Emma bent down to stroke her. With gentle persuasion, the animal dipped its head and allowed the newcomer to stroke her, stretching her neck to the caring touch.

"Please. Come. Sit by me my child," the old woman gestured to the chair by the table next to hers. Emma smiled at the doe, who scurried behind cover again as she stood to join Lamia.

"Where did the deer come from?"

"Please help yourself. I will tell you all," the old woman replied, handing Emma the platter of scones.

Not one to refuse such tasty homemade fare she took one and bit a hearty chunk out of it.

"Thank you. It is delicious…. Can I?"

The old woman nodded yes, before Emma had time to finish the question. The young barmaid broke off a small piece of scone and held it out at arm's length. The doe wobbled over to it, sniffed it, then gently took it in her mouth: Emma patted the back of the deer's head whilst it chewed on the morsel.

Lamia took a sip of the honeyed water, then turned to face her guest.

"I have had a visitor this past week. I think you may know him…. Hunter?"

Emma stopped eating; surprised.

"Hunter…. Yes, I know him," she replied curiously. "But what was he doing here?"

The old woman proceeded to tell her the full story of the past week's events. When she'd finished Emma sat, quiet, shocked but above all relieved that no harm had befallen the old woman.

"You could have lost your life," Emma said. "Thank the gods Hunter was around to protect you."

"I was never in danger my child," she replied with an air of unexpected confidence.

The significance of those few words was lost in the assumption that Bael was there to prevent her demise. But had Emma known the true meaning behind the old woman's comment, her view of her would have changed forever.

Lamia stood up and moved to the open window, letting the cool breeze wash over her face.

"How well do you know this Hunter?" She asked.

"If only that question were easy to answer…. I know he came to our town some ten years past. He is a warden of the forest, and works mainly for Lord Farroth. My father told me the priest, Maccon I think he is called, had some part in Bael's appearance all those years ago."

"Maccon? Now why does that not surprise me?" Lamia mused.

"Do you know this Maccon?" Emma asked.

"It has been a long time…. But yes, I know him."

Emma couldn't help but notice the melancholy in Lamia's voice. It was obvious Maccon was more than a mere past acquaintance, and for a moment sadness furrowed the old woman's brow: for the first time in all her visits, Emma saw the beauty hidden amongst the few lines carved by age and a genteel life style.

"Enough about me. Where were we? Oh, yes. You were telling me about Hunter," Lamia continued.

"Please do not think me rude, but why does my knowing Hunter bother you so?"

"Just an old woman's curiosity, my child. Nothing more…. Please. I do not wish to alarm you, all will become clear, I promise you," she said behind a comforting smile.

Emma relaxed again; though she found the conversation somewhat strange, she had only ever received kindness in her dealings with the old woman.

"He calls at the tavern on occasion, more now than he has ever done. Though my father would prefer otherwise."

"Ah. Your father, how is he?"

"He is well and sends his regards."

"Please, give him my love when you see him."

"I will be sure to tell him."

Lamia pondered for a moment.

"Why does your father not look upon Hunter with favour?" Lamia asked, picking up on Emma's previous comment.

"Oh…. He just thinks Hunter is trouble. My father has had occasion to ban him from drinking at the tavern."

"And why is that my dear?"

"My father believes he turns up just to annoy him…. It's just. Well…. Hunter has gotten into his fair share of fights, and though in all the cases I know of he is justified, my father believes they were fights that could have easily been avoided. But I believe there is more to Hunter. I can see it in his eyes."

The old woman returned to her seat and took Emma's hand in hers.

"I feel there is more to your father's concerns about Hunter than you wish to share," she said caringly.

Lamia watched Emma's aura change colour slightly, telling her the young woman was blushing.

"Please. Ignore the ramblings of an old woman. What views you and your father share regarding Hunter should be yours and yours alone, so please forgive such intrusion."

"You have asked nothing that would offend me. It's just I have had little occasion to speak of such matters. So please, go on," Emma insisted.

Lamia sat up straight and tapped the back of Emma's outstretched hand.

"What I am about to tell you, I would have you keep to yourself, for I do not fully understand its meaning myself. Promise me this will be so?"

"I will never speak a word of it to anyone."

"Well then, I believe my meeting with Hunter did not happen by chance. I am convinced he entered our lives for a reason. A reason I don't yet think even he understands. I can only tell you what I feel, and I feel there is a mystery woven around this man and his wolf, and once uncovered it will alter the lives of all who know him."

Emma was completely transfixed as more of the Old woman's thoughts revealed themselves. She could only sit there and listen.

"You are one of a very few who know, that though blind in the true meaning of such a word, I can yet see as others cannot."

Emma nodded.

"Well.... These auras' I have mentioned in many of our welcomed conversations; I see them around everything. Everything, living or not has this unique signature, and from the first day I realized what I was seeing I have only ever known these signatures to have but one colour, or that was my belief. That is until I met Hunter and his wolf for the first time."

The old woman paused, and for a moment she just sat there, quietly gathering her thoughts.

"I do not wish to get embroiled in the games of men, so I would ask you once again never to speak to anyone especially Hunter, of what I am about to tell you."

"I promise. But do you think it *wise* to share such information with me? Would it not be more prudent to keep this to yourself, then there would be no need for concern," Emma suggested, more than a little bewildered by what she was hearing.

"Wise? Only time will tell, but I believe you should hear what I have to say, for the very same reason your face reddened when I asked about your father's concerns regarding Hunter.... It is obvious to an old woman that you have feelings for this young man, strong feelings. Am I wrong?"

Again, Emma blushed, but this time she gave voice to her embarrassment.

"Yes, yes, I do care for him," she mused.

"Does Bael know just how much you like him?"

"That is one question I cannot answer. He is such a private person. If he has such feelings, he keeps them well hidden. Just when I think I am getting to know him something happens that makes me question whether I know him at all."

"I am sure the Bael you know is but a very small part of who the man really is; and that is my concern. I fear that Bael himself has no idea of who he truly is. The two auras I mentioned…. They suggest two different entities, but even more puzzling; the colour of one of those auras is shared with his wolf."

"What does it all mean?" Emma asked, now totally bemused.

"I wish I had an answer for you, but I have not. All I know is; whatever Bael believes his past to be is but a lie. There is powerful magic at work which I believe holds the secret to Bael's true identity. And when a secret is this deeply hidden….One can only wonder."

"You are making me nervous. If he isn't who we think he is, then who is he?"

"I am sorry. I feel I may have shared such misgivings, before discovering the facts…. I only wish for you to be armed with such information that will prevent you being hurt by events that are already beginning to unfold."

"Then what must I do?"

"Nothing. Hunter is still the man you care for, he knows no different, and as such you should deal with him as you have always done."

Emma had no reply. She just sat there staring at the passing clouds through the open window, lost in thought. She finished her drink, then before leaving she turned and gave Lamia a warm hug and a kiss on the cheek. At the door, the old woman stopped her.

"You will be fine. Just be your usual beautiful self and treat Bael no differently."

As she waved the young woman off, she thought back to the earlier conversation. There was one fact she did not feel it necessary to share as she had no idea what it meant herself. She felt, the sharing of this information would only go to unnerve her guest unnecessarily. On their first meeting Lamia had noticed a small shadow separating the two auras that surrounded Bael, but what was even stranger, when last they met, the shadow had grown and seemed to have form. It was a mystery whose answer she believed lay with an old friend.

***

Like his fellow knights Cirius de Santo came from and represented with pride one of the kingdoms twelve regions. Being the youngest member of the Black Orchids landed him with many of the Temple's less savoury duties; unlike most other knightly orders who would see such tasks undertaken by squires or the like. Maccon their leader was a firm believer in character building, and as such believed there was no task to highly or lowly considered to be beyond their undertaking. But other older members of the order didn't wholly share their leader's enthusiasm for such beliefs and would frequently assert their seniority by petitioning their youngest member with these menial chores. By his very nature he was an easy target for this kind of authoritative manipulation, but he took it in good humour: really, it could be said that amongst the Twelve he seemed to be the only member who had one, and no matter what task was thrown his way, you would very rarely see him without a smile on his face. But, though most of the Order *were* a humourless bunch, the one unifying thought they all shared when Cirius came to mind was respect; respect for his skills in combat, proved beyond questioning during the invasion of the Northern Territories where his sword and shield were put to devastating use.

Maccon had a particular fondness for the young man, although when one would say young, Cirius had actually seen thirty-eight name days. But to all the others he was deemed young, and though a few of his companions were not much older than him it suited their purpose to look upon him so; especially when Maccon dished out the daily chores.

This day he was in charge of the messenger hawks. His bird and favourite, wasn't a hawk at all. It was a falcon. A Kaila Falcon from the deserts of Fereise he named after his sword *Razor,* for its ability to cut through the air with such effortless speed that made him by far the fastest of all the messenger birds. Part of his duty was to clean the Eyrie of bird shit and any leftover food that might contaminate their living environment. He did this with a verve that betrayed his bubbly personality. He tended the birds with a loving care they all sensed and respected, in fact on many an occasion when either Maccon or one of the others came to inspect the Eyrie, they would often catch him conversing with the birds as if they were human. But Maccon never brought it up and would not allow any of the others to make ridicule of it either; for he saw how much the hawks loved Cirius, and just maybe, it was these little conversations that were the reason why.

Twelve birds service the Temple and Keep, one for each Knight. And at first each Knight trained and saw to the needs of his particular hawk. But as time went on it became clear to all that Cirius had a natural affinity to the birds; so much so, that he became known as the Knight of Hawks. A title he wore with a not to unexpected pride. These hawks were messengers of choice for only the most important of missions: the lesser left to scores of pigeons, which were kept and cared for by a group of the town's orphans. Four boys and four girls, snatched from a life of misery by Lady Farroth herself.

High on the roof of the Temple, Cirius tucked into one of several apples he had picked from the orchard earlier. Almost a month had passed since Maccon had given orders for his bird to deliver a message to the Elves at Grayspire, the Elven Fortress. His gut told him Razor was coming home and his gut was very rarely wrong. He cast the last apple core over the wall and made his way to the open wooden bridge connecting the Temples two highest towers. Daylight was fading; the wind had picked up carrying with it the threat of heavy rain. It wasn't long before large droplets began to fall, bouncing off the stone roof in a rhythmic pitter patter that Cirius found both soothing and a warning. And he was right; within seconds thunder ripped across the heavens, followed almost instantly by a streak of lightning which lit the whole sky above the keep like some huge godly lantern. Cirius ran for shelter; it was no place to be wearing chain mail and if he had waited much longer he would have been soaked to the skin. Just before entering the east tower he held out his arm. He knew Razor was close, and not one to let him down the bird gave its familiar screech and landed on his out stretched hand.

"It's good to have you back old friend," he said. "Come. Let's get you home…. I have got something special waiting for you, your favourite."

Razor ripped small pieces of flesh from one of the two shrews Cirius had saved him; courtesy of Lia, one of the orphan girls who had captured them in the Keep's garden. The Knight let his bird have its fill, before placing it on a freshly cleaned perch to remove a small leather pouch attached to its leg.

Maccon was engrossed in conversation with an elderly woman when Cirius entered his quarters, message in hand. The leader of the Order seemed uncharacteristically nervous with his female guest; not a look Cirius was accustomed to.

"Please. Forgive this intrusion my lord, I believe this is the message you have been waiting for."

"Let me deal with this, then we can continue our conversation," Maccon said excusing himself from the woman's company.

"Sur. As you requested."

"Thank you," Maccon replied, with a look that ended the conversation. The young Knight took pause for a moment, half expecting an introduction that never came.

"Thank you," Maccon repeated.

This time Cirius bowed graciously, smiled at the woman, and then he quietly slipped away.

The old priest returned to his guest sitting at the table with a smile on her face.

"A nice young man," she gestured as the Knight left the room.

Maccon made no reply and sat back down next to her. He took pause for a moment to look at her. The sunlight that entered through the open window lit up a face he once loved. There was hardly a wrinkle, unlike his, which was littered with what he preferred to call his lines of wisdom. In fact, if it wasn't for her greying hair and the texture to the skin which comes with time, you would never have guessed that she was a lot older than Maccon. It seemed like a life time ago, but he could still see the beauty that seduced him all those years ago before the *change*, when her eyes clouded over and her gift was realized.

"You are still beautiful," his whisper tinged with an air of melancholy.

"Your words are flattering, but untrue," she replied with a wry smile.

"Not so."

"Well, who am I to question the wisdom of a Knight of the Order.... But I am not here for flattery, no matter how well it is received."

Maccon shifted uncomfortably in his chair and was just about to place the message in his pocket.

"You should read that," she said. "It comes from the Elves, I think."

Maccon should have been surprised. But in reality he wasn't. He knew all too well what secret lurked behind those clouded eyes. He walked over to the open window and carefully removed the letter from the leather pouch. As he held the message up to the sunlight he momentarily let his guard down, allowing the words to enter his thoughts and by so doing, hers as well. His face became stern; he was more annoyed at himself than his guest for he knew it was foolish to open such a thing whilst in her company.

"Please forgive me Maccon? Old habits."

Maccon rolled the note back up and placed it in the pocket of his gown.

"If you will excuse me? I have to take this message to Lord Farroth."

"I am sure he can wait just a little longer," she replied.

His fingers played with the note, then he stopped.

"If you were a man, I would see you here as a member of the Order."

"Then thank the gods for the little mercy they bestowed on me when they made me a woman," she replied playfully.

"The years haven't changed you I see? But I am sure you did not come to the Temple to exchange pleasantries as nice as they are."

Silence followed. And for a moment he swore she was looking right through him, so intense was her clouded gaze.

"Why did you never visit me after you joined the Order?" she asked, in a poignant but civil tone.

As the final word left her lips, she saw his aura fade slightly and though she could not see his eyes she knew they were filled with sadness.

"I…. I," he stammered. "I think that is a conversation for another day."

"Yes. Maybe you are right…. Well then, to other matters. This week past I had a visitor, well two really. I believe they call him Hunter. A strange young man with an even stranger travel companion."

The silence that followed her comments spoke volumes.

"Well, he saved my life, or thought he had and it was from the honour in that thought that I allowed him into my home. The creature he so readily despatched had no place in these parts, a Grawl I believe, a fearsome beast."

"A Grawl. Why would such a creature be hunting this far east, so far from home?"

"Why indeed? The very same question that troubled this strange young man….. I believe you know him?" She said, more from intrigue than need for an answer.

Maccon's aura brightened.

"Yes. I know him…. But why would he be the reason for this welcome though unexpected visit after all these years?" He asked, knowing to deny any knowledge of the man would be futile.

"You are one of the few who know and understand my gift, and why such chance meeting would leave me with such unsettled thoughts."

Maccon gave an acknowledging nod, but remained silent.

"During my meetings with Bael I saw things that trouble me greatly. Amongst these visions I saw you…. A fleeting glimpse of a moment past. Yet a moment I believe has some bearing on why the young man is absent memory of his past. A past I am certain you and the Elves I saw know more about than you would have people believe."

Maccon was stunned. He'd hoped this day would never come, a naivety he had courted all these years. Instinctively he emptied his mind of any thoughts regarding Bael and none too quick as he felt Lamia's thoughts probing his. But as powerful as she was her mind was still no match for his.

"You are still as wily as a snow fox I see. What is it about this man's past you seem so eager to protect?"

"These are questions I cannot give answer to, no matter how much I wish I could…. It has been quite the burden all these years harbouring such a secret. But…."

"Your words are safe with me, if nothing else you know this to be true, she interrupted.

"Of course, I know this, yet it is more than word or duty that keeps me from parting with such information. More than this I cannot say on the subject. But let me allay your fears about the man himself…. Know he is a man whose intentions are honourable. Of this I am sure," he said reassuringly, aware of the doubts that occupied Lamia's thoughts.

"I saw a glimpse of things that I fear intent will not be his to control."

"Then please, tell me what worries you so?"

"I know that Emma has opened her heart to this man and fool that he is, he does not realize by how much. Sadly, I fear his heart will never be hers, not in the way she would like anyway. He cares for her, yes. But in my vision, I saw someone else his heart desires, yet he is unaware of that person's existence, because such memories have been hidden from him, and I sense you had a hand in this. We both know there is no force more powerful or unpredictable than love of the heart, and I believe his love for this person will eventually pull down the wall that so cleverly hides his past."

Maccon shifted uncomfortably in his seat. But he let her continue without interruption.

"Something which troubles me even more is this connection he has with his strange travel companion."

"What do you mean?" Maccon asked.

"The wolf he travels with. You know of this?"

"Yes."

"Then I am sure you know of its origins?"

Maccon sat forward in his chair uncertain of how to respond.

"Again, your silence is deafening…. There is something which may interest you even more; this creature is somehow bound to Hunter."

"Bound? In what way?" he asked with concern.

"I am not sure of the manner in which they find themselves connected; I have had only fleeting glimpses of events that leave me absent understanding. But what I do know is that man and beast share the same unusual auras."

"Could this not be mere coincidence?"

"I would come to the same conclusion were it not for the nature of these auras," she replied.

"In what way?"

"They both share two…. I have never seen the like. Ever. Everything has but a single light or so I believed 'till now, and I cannot offer explanation. Part of my understanding of the light that surrounds them is that it is a reflection of their souls, and if I am correct then it would mean that both have two souls. But how can this be?" She asked, hoping Maccon could make her a little wiser.

Sadly, he couldn't. There was very little he knew of Bael's life before the Elves brokered that odd arrangement all those years ago, yet even then he believed Koryllion was holding back on information of who the man really was.

"There was something stranger still. The auras around Bael were beginning to separate. At first, I thought it but a shadow. But on my last meeting with Hunter I noticed the shadow had grown, and more than that it had appeared to take form."

At this point, Maccon was completely invested in the conversation. What it all meant? He wasn't sure, but he believed it was of great importance.

"Do you have any clue to what the shadow might be?"

"I am not sure. I feel it may have something to do with his returning memories, and the Wolf. I will not say the shadow is a living thing, but it has form…. A wisp like human form. I can't pretend to understand what it is or means but I feel it is all connected to the Wolf. She has shown me a glimpse of a power far beyond my imaginings. A power I believe she does not yet know she possesses. A power she cannot fully realize without Bael at her side."

"Why do you tell me all this when you know I can give nothing in return?" He asked guiltily.

"Because I believe the secrets you and this Hunter share are beginning to unravel, and such secrets so deeply hidden must bring with them consequences that will affect all who know this man and worse: there is another, someone already involved with this man I would not see hurt. Someone close to my heart I fear could be in grave danger.

"What is this danger you speak of? And who is it gives for such concern?" he asked caringly.

"The wolf bares a wound on her side that should have killed her. Yet she lives. This is a miracle in itself. But when my hand touched said wound, I saw a fleeting glimpse of what made it. Maccon….it is a creature not of this world. A '*thing*' that filled me with a feeling of such dread the like I have never felt before."

"What is it you saw," Maccon asked, concerned.

"I do not know. The image was but a flicker in time. But know this, a terrible thing is coming, and I only hope we are ready when it does."

Maccon looked pale. She knew most of what she said had come as no surprise to the white fox, yet he looked deeply troubled. But she continued.

"As for the person I would not see harmed, I cannot say. It might be time will change that, but for now I will say no more on the matter."

"As you wish."

"Though you know Bael better than most, I think there remains a lot hidden from even you," Lamia suggested.

Maccon pushed back in the chair and stood up.

"I wish I could share more with you, but for now I cannot. Know that I really appreciate you taking me into your confidence like this. Especially as we have not spoken in such a long time. Hopefully, one day I can offer you the same courtesy. Anyway, I would love to continue with this conversation, but I have to go. Lord Farroth gave strict instructions that this message be taken to him the moment of its arrival…. I will have Cirius take you home."

He paused for a moment and took her hand in his.

"It is sad that it takes such concerns to bring us back together like this. It has been too long and such regrets should not be allowed to continue. So, if it please you,

I would like to continue our meetings on a more regular basis," he said, his voice reflecting a sadness truly felt.

"That would be nice," she replied, her eyes filling with tears for all the past years she had shared with no one. Regrets that held a troubling secret.

"It has been lovely to see you. But before I go, tell me, why has it taken you thirty years to come to my Temple? Did you hate me that much?"

"I never hated you," she replied, her head dropping slightly. "The answer you seek lies within the grounds of my cottage. There is something I should have told you a long time ago, something that is too important for such passing conversation. A conversation long overdue."

Maccon was totally bemused by Lamia's heartfelt comments.

"Then I will come to see you as soon as I can. But for now, I have to go, and as I said before, Cirius will escort you home."

8
THE HUNT - BLACK WOLF - THE BEAR

Cailean was awakened from a night of troubled sleep by the chatter of finch, crow and blackbird that inhabited the thick creeping vines that grew up the side of the keep. She stretched and yawned before sliding out of bed to see what all the fuss was about. Normally she found their morning chorus comforting and somewhat melodic, but this particular morning it was different, it was loud almost manic in its intensity.

Still a little fuzzy she stepped out onto the terrace, the fresh air nipping at her skin giving her goose bumps. It took a moment before she noticed the ghostly white of Hunter's Hawk perched defiantly on the head of the Great Protectors statue at the end of the balcony. The sight of it caught her off guard for a moment, its penetrating red eyes causing her to gasp a lung full of cold air that almost set her to coughing: eyes that followed her every move. She quickly gathered her senses, *why would this creature be here on my balcony when it had the freedom to roam wherever it so wished?* She thought. Little wonder the birds around her were so unsettled. She took a step back, then without warning the hawk flew off heading in the direction of the forest in the distance.

Cailean's breathing had been short and laboured, so she filled her lungs with the warming air as the sun rose above the mountains on the horizon. She walked to the edge of the balcony to follow the bird's flight. Movement where her father's land touched the edge of the Kingswood caught her eye. Across the fields of grazing cattle where lambs sprang playfully through the low-lying mist, she spotted a group about to enter the woods. Straining her eyes, she could just about make out the figures of two men; following behind them was the largest Wolf she had ever seen. With the Hawk heading directly towards them and the Wolf following, she knew it was Hunter leading them. *But who was that with him?* She thought. From what people said about him, of the few people he could call friend none of them were men. Intrigued she returned to her room, dressed herself quickly, then stepped out into the torch lit corridors of the Keep.

There was no one to be seen at this early hour, not even the kitchen staff who were usually first up in preparation of the Lord and Ladies morning meals. It didn't take her long to reach Jiney's room two floors below, where without knocking she entered. Her friend lay fast asleep, seemingly oblivious to the commotion that had so rudely awakened Cailean earlier.

In her excitement Cailean caught the leg of a chair with her foot raking it noisily across the hard-stone floor. Jiney shot up with a start; for a moment, the young maid's eyes refused to focus, she wasn't sure if the blurry figure that approached the bed was not part of a dream. She shook her head and was about to scream out, when her sight cleared.

"My lady…What? What are you doing here?" She asked, her voice quivering nervously.

"Sssh," Cailean whispered pressing a finger to her lips. "I will explain all as we travel."

"Travel my lady?"

"Yes, we are going for a ride. So, get dressed."

"As you wish my lady," Jiney said still confused.

She dressed herself quickly if somewhat clumsily.

"Where are we going at this time in the morning?"

"You will see soon enough, but hurry, I would be away from this place before my father wakes."

After sneaking past the guards at the rear of the keep and taking their horses from the stables, the pair sped across the fields to the trail where Hunter and his group entered the forest a little earlier. They paused for a moment while Cailean explained her strange behaviour; Jiney was all too familiar with the look that filled her friend's eyes and knew that any attempt at persuasion was pointless. Cailean nudged her horse into a canter, the mist swirling about its feet; Jiney followed her lead.

Above, the clouds were gathering letting intermittent bursts of sunlight break through the trees like spears of light, a threatening sky that appeared to go unnoticed by Cailean, but not Jiney. She pulled her mount alongside her friend.

"My lady I think we should go no further. I fear a storm is brewing," she said anxiously.

"Then we should hurry. It is just a little further; there is a valley ahead where I played as a child. Deer roam there in abundance, we will be safe, my father's game keepers have kept this part of the forest free from danger for many years."

"If you are sure my lady," Jiney said, not fully convinced.

"I promise, if we don't see Hunter there, we shall return to the Keep."

The trail climbed the side of a hill that overlooked the valley she mentioned, where a fast-flowing river cut through its centre like a crystal serpent. The two women tethered their horses to a nearby tree and walked the rest of the way to the brow of the hill. Cailean led them from the trodden path to a group of bushes whose delicate white flowers were beginning to open, coerced by the large droplets of rain which cascaded from the black clouds above. Cautiously the pair made their way down the hillside to a small rise overlooking the valley below. As they broke through the cover of the dense undergrowth Cailean's breath was taken away by what she saw.

In bright shafts of sunlight that spread like an ethereal fan between the trees, a huge Wolf stood facing Hunter in the middle of the shallow rapids of the river. Above them the White Hawk circled around, gliding gracefully on the warm air currents; it was a scene of tranquil beauty that hadn't gone unappreciated by Jiney either. For a moment, they just stared in silence at the spectacle before re-entering the cover of the bushes behind. When they were again settled, Cailean peeked through the open branches; Hunter and his group had gone.

***

Bael led the group out of the rapids, across a clearing to a small rocky shelf, giving them a clear view of the valley below. Not far from a narrow section of the river stood a magnificent Stag. It grazed peacefully unaware of the intruders. Raen passed Hunter his bow and removed an arrow from his quiver. The shot would be difficult, as rain began to fall heavily making everything slick and slippery to control. The very skies themselves became threatening; swirling clouds that cast everything below in menacing grey shadow. The bow string slipped into the crease of his two wet fingers ready to release the arrow; suddenly the stag's ears pricked up and without warning it dodged into the safety of nearby trees. Bael lowered his bow looking to the river beyond. A bolt of lightning lit up the clearing, something stirred in the shadows on the other side of fast flowing rapids, it was a fleeting glimpse but something moved, Bael was sure of it.

Within seconds of the lightning the heavens erupted. A young bear cub broke cover, frightened it splashed through the shallow waters and on to the centre of the clearing. Raen looked to Hunter and was about to head for the clearing.

"Stay where you are. Where there is a cub the mother will not be far behind. You would not like to face her, believe me she is a ferocious hunter," Bael said knowingly.

The Hawk circled high above the trees from whence the cub came, telling Hunter he was right. The Wolf pulled up by his side; she sniffed the air and growled nervously. Raen moved to the edge of the rock for a better view, movement to his left caught his attention; he tapped Hunter's shoulder and pointed to some bushes not a hundred paces from where the cub stood shaking. Bael couldn't believe his eyes.

***

Both women were soaked as they entered the clearing and made their way cautiously towards the bear cub, neither had ever seen such a cute little creature. Their womanly instincts to protect drove them carelessly across the open ground without a thought for why the youngster was alone. For a moment, the cub watched them nervously then boom! Another clash of thunder sent the frightened beast running scared and confused towards them. Cailean held out her hand and coaxed the animal to come to her. Shivering and frightened it was strangely willing. She picked it up in her arms and stroked it gently, it's fur dense and wiry to the touch.

"There, there you poor thing, you are safe now," she said, as Jiney joined her in stroking the creature. Then common sense finally kicked in, and the true danger they found themselves in hit them like a thunderbolt. Jiney looked piercingly into Cailean's eyes.

"Where is its mother?"

Before Cailean could answer, a blood chilling roar echoed menacingly around the clearing. The two women froze with fear, for both knew its origin. Then everything happened so fast it seemed that time itself had slowed down. Out of the shadows burst the mother, a juggernaut of muscle, fang and claw she thundered across the rapids to protect her offspring like any mother would. Jiney turned ashen and collapsed unconscious; Cailean remained standing but her legs seemed rooted to the spot, and though her brain told her to run, she could not. Then, as if to appear out of nowhere Hunter and the boy appeared.

Bael ran like the wind, his bow knocked and ready he knew he would not be able to reach the women before the charging mother. He could see one of them had fainted, so there was no use in telling them to run. He stopped some twenty paces from them and levelled his bow, he had to hit the beast in the head, the eye if he could, it was the only shot that would take down such a creature. Raen pulled up by his side, sword drawn, though what good that would do was anyone's guess. Carefully Hunter gathered himself and took aim, the mother was incredibly quick for such a large beast and in mere seconds she would be on top of the two women. He let the arrow slip then just as he loosed it he was bowled to the ground making the shot fly wildly into the trees.

The Wolf hit him with her full weight and in a blink put herself between the women and the charging mother. Though herself big for a wolf she was dwarfed by the bear she now faced. Unfazed she stood her ground. Instinctively Cailean dropped the cub which surprisingly moved towards the Wolf. She could see Jiney was regaining consciousness, but she could only stand and watch in amazement at what was unfolding before her.

The charging mother ground to a halt not far from the Wolf and her cub; she reared upright in defiance giving out a ferocious roar of challenge. Then something quite miraculous happened. The mother dropped on all fours; it was as if she knew her cub no longer faced danger. In the meantime, Hunter had gathered his senses and once again readied his bow: still uncertain of what was happening he lined up the shot for the bears head. Without warning a huge black shape knocked both him and Raen to the ground. Another Dire Wolf, bigger even than the one that already faced the bear joined her, its fangs bared ready for combat. Bael lifted himself from the mud, with Raen close behind, and looked on in astonishment as the huge black wolf with the silver streak readied for a fight that would surely see its death: but a magic was abroad that none in the clearing had any knowledge of, not even the one that wielded it.

Something in her stirred, filling her with a warm comforting energy. She first looked with surprise to the Black Wolf by her side, which seemed ready to kill for her. Then she turned her attention to the bear that cautiously approached on all fours, she could feel the mother's fears as if they were her own. A mother's instinct to protect her child, an action she should not have to die for. Again, she turned to the Wolf by her side, its fears were of a different kind; it feared death, her death. Their minds linked filling both the bear and the Black silver-streaked intruder with thoughts of calm and peacefulness. As if born to it she just let the energy flow between them, uncertain herself of what was happening and unable to control it; yet there was something familiar about it, something locked away in a memory.

The mother stopped and let her cub run to her; the huge beast nudged the youngster with her snout then snorted loudly into the air. The bear cub turned back to look at the strange creatures it had left behind before mother and cub set off for the river.

Bael lowered his bow and waved Raen to follow him, he wasn't yet sure who these two women were but he was about to find out and no mistake.

Raen was too busy watching the Wolves to notice movement in the shadows across the river, and Bael having recognised the two women was also too preoccupied with giving them a piece of his mind to notice the same; but as he reached Cailean instinct took over. He paused for a moment and listened. Other than the sound of the beating rain, the forest around them was smothered in an unnatural silence.

"Something is wrong," he said, his voice thick with anxiety. "Go! Go. Now!" he shouted, pointing to the rock ledge he left only moments before. Still shaken Cailean was only too glad to oblige; she quickly grabbed her friend's hand and headed for safety. Hunter armed his bow and looked beyond the mother and her cub to the tree line across the rapids. Raen was already moving towards him with sword drawn, his obsession with the wolves broken by their disquieting growls towards the very same shadows which seemed to have Bael transfixed.

Before the mother and cub had reached the centre of the clearing, something huge exploded from the trees and charged across the rapids, its speed frightening for a creature so monstrously large. The rogue bear was half a size bigger even than the one with her cub and Hunter knew it was neither father nor mate to those it sped towards. Bael had seen this kind of creature before when hunting the rain forests of the southern swamp lands. This bear was a cannibalistic killer, its face battle scarred leaving one of its eye sockets empty and deformed.

It hit the mother with such force it sent her spinning through the air. Then it reeled, around cutting deep troughs into the sodden earth; it's true target…. the cub. Hunter was the only one moving, Raen froze on the spot, even the two wolves seemed stunned by the shear ferocity of the attacker.

He glanced behind to see the two women reach relative safety, then in one flowing movement he raised the bow. The mother was on her feet but she was too late. The scarred monster tossed her cub across the clearing as if it were a rag doll. The gentle creature hit a tree with a sickening crunch; it's lifeless body falling to the ground…. Dead. Even though she was herself badly injured the mother charged, launching herself at her attacker in sheer desperation. The rogue bear brushed her aside with ease, his razor-sharp claws tearing open her throat. She hit the ground bloody and still.

Again, Bael knew the only arrow that had even the remotest chance of bringing down such a beast, had to hit it square in the eye. His aim was steady; breathing with the shot he loosed the shaft. Thud! It hit the bear in the neck, in a blink he loosed another, this hitting closer to its mark digging deeply into flesh and bone just below the empty socket. The bear went berserk, shaking its head and upper body with such ferocity it snapped the shaft of both arrows. In its rage, the bear spun around to catch Hunter knocking a third arrow. In an instant, it threw its whole-body weight forward and bound towards its attacker. The last arrow hit it in the neck, but it still kept coming. Dropping the bow, he pushed the still stunned Raen behind him sending the lad sprawling through a deep puddle of water. Before Raen had stopped sliding through the mud, Hunter had drawn both swords and was running at the bear. The monster reared up on its hind legs, its massive claws splayed like deadly fans. Hunter was fast, dodging a blow that would have torn him in half. He spun around, his long blade cutting deeply into the bear's hind leg. Blood ran freely from the gaping wound forcing the beast to drop on all fours. Hunter tried to flank the bear, but the ground was like a bog. His right foot slipped kicking up a sod of grass and mud. He went down on one knee; the beast reared upright and roared ferociously, then out of nowhere his Wolf leaped for its throat. The bear swung around hitting her in mid-air. She whimpered in pain before hitting the ground close to where Hunter knelt. Suddenly the Black Wolf sprang onto the monsters back sinking his teeth into its neck. The bear roared in pain and shook with such force it sent the Wolf arcing through the air, its mouth full of flesh and fur. Crunch! It hit a tree and slid limply to the ground. Before the bear could drop on all fours, the White Hawk swooped out of the rain filled sky its razor talons ripping out the animals one good eye.

This was the opening Hunter needed. He shoved the short sword deep into the monster's side cutting through muscle and bone on its way to the liver. It turned to face him and was about to rear up, when like lightning Bael rammed the long blade home, penetrating under the bear's lower jaw up through its neck and on into its brain. The monster wobbled for a moment then fell, its life blood washing away in a river of red as it was carried by the rain into the surrounding puddles.

Bael's first concern was with the Wolf. Thankfully though shaken she wasn't badly hurt and was already on her feet. The mother and her cub were less fortunate, Bael could see there was nothing to be done for them;

nature though beautiful, had her cruel side, a side he had experienced more times than he cared to remember.

Raen, his pride dented by his stunted performance was also on his feet and though his face was covered in mud it was obvious to Bael that the lad felt awful. But he offered no words of consolation. He believed lessons had to be learned the hard way and this was one such lesson. Bael looked to the tree where the Black Wolf fell. It had gone. He was glad and knew that was a mystery to be solved another day. For now, he was thankful that all were safe, and his thoughts focused on the two women watching in nervous disbelief from the rock shelf overlooking the clearing.

***

Cailean was still shaking from the ordeal as Hunter and his followers approached, bloodied and covered from head to foot in mud. Jiney was still ashen white and felt as though she would vomit if she tried to speak.

"You have our thanks," Cailean said shakily.

For a moment Bael stood quiet.

"Your thanks. Well, isn't that nice. Your madness could have cost everyone their lives. Does your father know you are out wandering about the woods this early in the morning?" Bael asked coldly.

Both women were too traumatised to offer up any kind of reply, but Cailean was more than a little surprised he recognized at all. Especially as they had only met for the briefest of moments the night he fought off those four villains trying to take his life.

"You are Lord Farroth's daughter are you not?"

"I am," she replied abruptly.

"I don't know what possessed you both to come here, but whatever the reason, I am sure Lord Farroth would like to hear it."

"How dare you talk to me in this way," Cailean interrupted, finding her voice again.

"Oh, I dare," he replied. "And if you allow another word to pass those pretty little lips of yours, I will leave you here to face whatever else is lurking out there in the shadows."

Cailean kept silent, the prospect of being left to fend for herself more frightening than the urge to retaliate.

"Good. Now that is settled, me and my friends here will take you home and rest assured, one word from either of you and I will let you walk alone."

Though angered by his remarks, Cailean did not wish to test his resolve and did as he asked. Jiney couldn't have said a word anyway, but she had noticed for the first time how good looking the young man following Hunter was, and though she hadn't heard him utter a word she had noticed his gaze upon her on a number of occasions as they made their way to the keep.

Finally, on reaching the open road in sight of the Town, Hunter stopped.

"This is as far as we go."

"But I thought? I imagined you would want my father to hear what happened this morning?" Cailean said sarcastically.

"I don't pretend to understand or want to know what madness led you into those woods. I have no desire to punish you further; I think or hope you have learned a hard lesson this day. So, whatever your father hears about all this, will only come from you," he said, with an indifference that annoyed Cailean.

"Then I thank you for your courtesy. I am sure this is a day I will never forget," she muttered, with an air of sarcasm that failed to mask the gratitude she felt inside.

"Yes, thank you, thank you both," Jiney said looking toward Raen who nodded his acknowledgement; his shyness glowing red through the spots of mud on his face.

The Wolf was already on the move, heading along the road to town. With nothing further to say, Hunter and Raen followed.

Cailean and her friend led their horses back to the keep, both hoping their absence had gone unnoticed. But high in the Tower Lord Farroth was watching them approach the keep, had they seen his face they would know there would be consequences.

9

SONS AND DAUGHTERS

Cailean threw off her soaking wet cape and flopped onto her bed; the ordeal in the forest had taken more out of her than she cared to admit. Her encounter with Hunter had not gone at all as she would have liked, and though in truth she hadn't really known what to expect, it certainly didn't involve being almost mauled by a bear.

Jiney snatched up the wet cloak and looked to her mistress, who sighed out loud; both women unaware they were being watched from the balcony.

"My Lady you should get out of those wet clothes before you catch your death."

"I will. I just need a moment…. What happened today?"

"I'm not sure m'Lady. But what I do know is, we are lucky to be alive. If it weren't for Hunter and those wolves, well I fear that bear…."

"What do you mean? Lucky to be alive," Lord Farroth interrupted. His voice cold and unforgiving.

Jiney looked terrified as he stepped from the shadows, his temples throbbing with anger.

"Forgive me my lord, I had no idea you were standing outside," she replied nervously.

"Otherwise, you would have chosen your words more carefully no doubt?"

"Yes sur. I mean no sur."

Cailean sat bolt upright, and though taken aback herself, she was in no mood for any of her father's overbearing nonsense, and was not about to see her friend squirm so.

"Leave us. I will deal with this," she ordered Jiney.

Her friend didn't need any further encouragement; she curtsied and scurried away like a scolded cat, carrying the two wet capes.

"Deal with what? I don't like your tone young lady."

"Nor I yours," she replied with a growing disdain.

"Do not speak to me as if I were a lowly servant, child…. You will show me some respect."

"As will you. And I am no child."

"Quiet!" He bellowed sweeping a vase full of flowers off the table, smashing it against the wall. "Or I swear by the gods I will have you locked in this room until I deem otherwise."

Cailean slid across the bed, away from her father. She couldn't remember the last time she had seen him so animated and it frightened her. For though she had always believed he would never lay a hand to her, at this very moment she wasn't sure.

"Can I at least change from my wet clothes?" She asked quietly.

"No. We will get to the bottom of this if it takes all day…. Now tell me, what happened that would see you in such a state?"

Cailean dropped her gaze and stared at the dried mud on her feet, her face still a picture of silent defiance. Her father knew her all too well and was having none of it. This went way beyond ignoring his fatherly guidance.

"I'll not stand for your dumb insolence. Speak!" he bellowed, hitting the table with his fist so hard it broke the skin on his knuckles.

Frightened she looked up. Shaken she began to talk.

"I only wanted to show Jiney where I played as a child," she lied, her voice quivering.

Lord Farroth walked to the open balcony and stared to the forest in the distance. He was about to speak when the door behind him creaked open.

Alloria stepped into the room to see her daughter wet and forlorn on the bed and her husband red faced and angry by the window. She'd bumped into Jiney on the way and had coaxed what little information she could from her about the events of the morning. And though there wasn't time for a full story, there was enough to know that Cailean was in deep trouble. Ever the peacemaker, this was one of those occasions that demanded a mother's diplomacy.

"What is going on? Can you not see our daughter is soaked to the skin?" She said, placing her hand on Cailean's wet shoulder.

That was all it needed. Almost childlike, Cailean leant into her and began sobbing uncontrollably. Lady Farroth pulled her daughter's head against her bosom.

"There now. There is no need for tears. Go. Go and change from those wet clothes," she urged, staring down her husband defiantly. Lord Farroth showed no sign of softening, which surprised her.

"This isn't the end of it. Do as your mother says, then we will finish this conversation."

Cailean left the room and entered the small chamber at the back which housed most of her clothes. She could hear her mother trying to calm her father whilst she was out of the room, but from the sound of it she was failing. Cailean removed her wet garments, underwear and all, then briskly washed away the dirt, the cold water stinging her wind dried skin. She patted herself dry then removed a soft silk gown from a pole sticking out from the wall. Quickly dressing herself, she moved to the slightly open door and listened momentarily, wishing she didn't have to go back and join her parents. But she accepted the thought was redundant and with a sigh she pushed open the door and stepped out to face her fate.

"I am sick and tired of wasting my breath. I told her never to see this Hunter again…. So, what does she do? She follows him into the woods," he said, addressing his wife angrily.

"Are you sure she followed him? She may be telling the truth."

"There is no way this was a meeting of chance. I know my daughter well enough, as I thought, did you. I cannot believe you to be so naive as to think this was mere coincidence. No. She knew he would be in those woods, but who would tell her?"

Alloria stood silent; she had no answer to this. She was herself all too aware that such coincidences didn't exist, especially when it came to their daughter.

"And not only this. I heard her handmaiden mention how lucky they were to survive a bear attack…. That had it not been for Hunter's intervention they both might have been killed."

Alloria stared at Cailean, shocked by her husband's latest comment. In her short conversation with Jiney earlier, she had cut the explanation short at the mention of Hunter's name, thinking that was the only reason for her husband's angry outburst, not realising there was far worse hidden in what was unsaid.

"A bear. Is this true?" She asked Cailean, frowning.

Cailean sat up and nodded, *yes*. Before her husband could intervene Alloria took her daughter's hand in hers.

"Please? Tell us what happened today…. Everything."

Cailean explained how they had ridden into the forest and come across the bear cub. Then followed in great detail with what occurred afterwards, but not once admitting the adventure was in anyway planned. She could see as she rounded off the story her mother looked troubled.

"I am afraid your father is right. You should never have been in those woods alone."

"I am sorry mother.... Only for the concern it has caused you. I am a woman not a child, I should be able to go when and where I please.... And the consequences of such actions should be mine to bare and mine alone."

"If only life were that simple. Your actions today could have so easily seen another ending to your story. And had it not been for Hunter.... Well?"

Lord Farroth had stood silent, in the hope his wife would be more successful at getting the full story, but he knew what he had heard was only a part truth and he had heard enough.

"You think me a fool? Sorry you say? How empty this word sounds passing *your* lips? I will get to the bottom of this, mark my words. If you will not listen to me then I shall speak with Hunter and see an end to this nonsense. As for yourself, if you mean to act like a child then as such you will be treated as one. You will be confined to your quarters until you learn how to behave as an adult."

"You can't do this," Cailean shouted furiously.

"I can and I will.... Now enough."

With that he stormed out of the room and placed two guards outside the door. Alloria watched her daughter defiantly move to the door only to find her path blocked as the two guards crossed spears.

"You will let me pass."

"I am sorry my lady. Your father gave strict instruction that you cannot leave the room," the taller of the two men said, with unquestioned resolve.

She slammed the door shut to join her mother on the side of the bed.

"He can't do this. I will not be made prisoner in my own home."

"You cannot carry on behaving like this in front of your father. I do not know what is wrong with you two, but some common ground has to be found…. I have never seen your father this incensed."

"What is it mother? Why does he treat me so? He seems more concerned about my meeting with Hunter than he does about the fact that I could have been torn apart by a savage bear."

"That is where you are wrong. If he did not care he would let you do as you pleased, the fact that he is so angered shows how strongly he treasures your safety…. Though sometimes he has great difficulty in articulating such."

"I know you mean well mother, but even you are aware of my father's darker side. If he is not careful his temper will see him undone, one day he will lose it with the wrong person. I fear had you not arrived when you did, he would have hit me."

"Nonsense…. Your father would never raise a hand to you."

"Are you sure of that mother?"

An uncertainty washed over her face, for in truth she was not. When Cailean was a child her arms bore many a bruise, something she had never shared with her daughter; but fortunately, as her child grew to adulthood the bruises got fewer. Time and patience had been great teachers and slowly she had learned how to ride the storm and quench the fiery rage she had seen burn so brightly whenever her husband was stressed or angered.

"Listen. I will have words with him. But for now, please try to stay out of trouble."

She kissed her daughter on the forehead, then left.

***

When Alloria entered their quarters, she had expected her husband to be waiting, but the room was empty. Thwack, thwack, the sound of metal on wood told her exactly where he was. The table downstairs had been set for the evening meal, so she knew it wouldn't be long before one of the kitchen maids would be calling them for dinner.

She took this opportunity to change from her formal gown into a soft white linen dress that afforded her a lot more comfort. As expected the maid knocked on the door and told her the meal was ready. Glazed pheasant and plum sauce were the order of the day, a favourite of both her and her daughter, though she doubted she would have the company of Cailean on this particular evening.

The sound of steel on wood still echoed around the courtyard, so Lady Farroth stepped out onto the balcony. Lord Farroth was venting his anger on a practice dummy, the keen blade of his sword dulled from its continuous contact with the hard wood. Red faced and wet with sweat she thought it best to let him finish, hopefully leaving him more amenable.

Nervously, the squire handed Lord Farroth a cloth to dry the sweat from his brow; he was never sure when his master was in this frame of mind, whether or not he would be victim to his Lordship's acid tongue and venomous temper. This day he was lucky.

"My Lord… Dinner is ready to be served."

"Yes, yes. I will be along shortly."

The servant was so relieved at the measured response, he hesitated for a moment.

"Well then? Get on with it. You can't stand there all-day gawking like an idiot. Go."

"Yes, my Lord. Sorry my Lord," he replied scurrying back into the keep like a wounded rat. Lord Farroth sheathed his sword, wiped his forehead then glanced up at the balcony. Alloria waved at him uncertainly. He acknowledged with a grunt and a nod signalling that both should make their way to the dining hall.

The pair sat facing one another at either end of the long food filled table with the unloving formality so often seen amongst those of high standing. Something which quietly angered Alloria, yet she would never voice such. For though, as now, this husband of hers could be a pompous oaf, there were still enough times in their relationship she saw the young warrior she fell in love with all those years ago. Before eating, she ordered one of the serving girls to take Cailean a platter full of food; thankfully without any interference from her husband, which led her to believe his wood smashing in the courtyard had worked its exhaustive magic. She broke bread and dipped it in the piping hot carrot, turnip, lentil broth and watched her husband down two goblets of wine without taking a breath. His appetite dulled by the day's events, he picked half-heartedly at the feast laid before him. Alloria knew no matter which way she tried to open the conversation she would be treading on hot cinders. But try she must.

"Are you looking forward to the fair, my love?"

For a moment all seemed fine, then her husband took a deep breath and slammed down the goblet, spilling what little wine remained across the table.

"Fair! How can you think about the fair, when our daughter behaves as if all common sense has abandoned her for this reckless insanity she seems so eager to embrace?"

"I know she can be infuriating at times, but that fire she has in her breast is what makes her strong. And I know, you as I, would not have that fire dampened, it is what makes her your daughter. She is a spirited girl and unfortunately as is so often the case, rebellion is the shadow of that very spirit. A rebellion that comes of immaturity and something she will grow out of with the passing of time."

She could see the tightness in her husband's shoulders slowly melt away. He looked to the stairs that led to Cailean's room.

"There is truth in what you say, yet your words give me little comfort. This goes way beyond anything she has done before. I am sick to my stomach of her insubordinate behaviour; she tries to undermine my authority at every turn. It has to stop."

"You frighten me sometimes. You talk about her as if she were a soldier in your garrison and not a daughter cherished by a loving father. Is it any wonder she seeks the love of a man when that of her father seems so lacking?"

The look on Lord Farroth's face softened, her words hurting him as intended; so often the weapon of her gender when all else failed. Words she knew would cut deeper than any blade, words that carried a truth he could not defend or deny and though she felt shame she continued.

"I cannot pretend to understand what it is about this Hunter and our daughter that has you so rankled, I can only assume there is a lot you haven't told me, and would know the reason why?"

Her husband waved at the serving wench to fetch another drink. She filled his goblet and looked to Lady Farroth to see if she wanted any more. Her mistress shook her head declining the offer, then Lord Farroth quickly dismissed all the servants leaving just the two of them in the hall.

"If I do not understand your reasoning over this matter, then how can you expect Cailean to understand, unless you tell her why?"

"I have good reason. That should be enough, for both of you… But it would seem my words lack weight as master of this house, for I appear to be failing in my mission as both father and protector of this family when my views are met with such open hostility."

"You are twisting my words to suit purpose. I am not looking for an argument, just a few simple truths without the mind games you so frequently employ when the opposite is your agenda. It is not just our daughter's indiscretions that has you so tightly strung, there is more," Alloria suggested.

Lord Farroth finished his wine and resting his elbow on the table ran his fingers through his beard thoughtfully.

"There is much I cannot tell you. I swore an oath to the Elves all those years ago when Bael was brought amongst us, and though you seem to believe otherwise I have shouldered this burden so that the people dear to me would remain safe. But you are right; it is not the problem of our daughter alone that sees me this way. There are things about Bael I too do not pretend to understand, I don't know whether you have noticed, but from the day he joined us he hasn't aged a day."

Alloria looked stunned. Her husband always dealt with Bael himself, keeping her at a safe distance, so in truth she hadn't really taken much notice of him, accepting these were the matters of men.

"How can this be?" she asked.

"I don't know. There was much both Maccon and I felt the Elders were not telling us. They were uncertain times; settlements close to Elven lands that had prospered for years, were being attacked and burned to the ground. My brother believed it was the Elves, though none of those attacked had lived to bear witness to such. But he felt our mysterious neighbours resented our presence so close to their sacred boundaries. Maccon and I had readied all our men at arms ready to join my brother in what seemed like the inevitable conflict between our two races. But to our great surprise and relief, Kor-yllion requested a meeting with my brother. He agreed without reservation. So, with a hundred of his finest guard, Maccon and I escorted my brother to an Elven outpost nestling in the peaks of the Taelyn Mountains. During that meeting the Elder King denied any part in the attacks on our kind. But I could see my brother had his doubts to the authenticity of his words. I on the other hand believed him, but I knew my thoughts on the matter would have no influence on my brother's stubborn mind. Kor-yllion swore he would find out who the perpetrators of these atrocities were and would bring them to task. And as time has proved, he was true to his word, though to this day we are no closer to knowing who they were. What we do know is the raids stopped. On that day, a treaty was forged that has kept us all safe from a conflict I fear we would have lost. Elven kind populated these lands long before we were capable of leaving the trees and caves we inhabited as mindless savages. Maccon is the most powerful mage I have ever seen in my lifetime, but even he admits his knowledge of the arcane arts pales into insignificance when compared to the magic of the Elves. So, you can imagine our relief when Bael was brought into the meeting escorted by Kor-aviel the king's head shaman, who requested but one thing from us."

"That Bael lives amongst us. But why?" She interrupted.

"In truth, I do not know. It seemed such a simple request considering the enormity of what was agreed upon that day, so my brother and I accepted without question their condition. Bael carried only the blades and bow he carries today; now, thinking back he looked lost, and I could see that Maccon pitied the young warrior, so too did Kor-aviel, who made it his business to pull our leader of the Order to one side. He told Maccon as much as he dare, which was that Bael's memories had been wiped clean and fresh ones put in their place. Memories which must never be allowed to resurface. That is why Maccon has kept such a close eye on Hunter all these years."

"But why would the Elves be so intent of getting rid of Bael. What is it about his past that would lead them to take such drastic measure as to remove any evidence of it?"

"Maccon believes it has something to do with Koryllion himself, for it was he that looked upon Bael with accusing disdain that day, when there was only pity in the eyes of Kor-aviel and his mages."

"Did it not worry you that there was much you were being kept in the dark about?"

"Of course, it did, I am not a fool. But at the time we just wanted peace and anyway what problems could one man bring down upon us, thoughts that until now have proved fruitful."

"What do you mean until now?" she asked.

Again, he played with his beard.

"Maccon knows it was the Elves that brought the Dire Wolf to Bael."

"Are you sure of this?"

"Yes…. Not only that, since the beast has come into his life there are signs his memory is returning, and Maccon says the longer they are together the bond between man and beast grows ever stronger. To add to this my brother is on his way here, intent on supplying our daughter with a suitor of his choosing, which we both know will go down like a Tic falling through the ass crack of boar. And if that weren't worry enough, Kor-yllion has requested our presence once again at the Outpost we last frequented all those years ago."

"Is it your belief this has something to do with Bael and his Wolf?"

"It is…. And now we may get a better understanding of what this with Hunter is really about. But Maccon thinks there is something far graver involved, but we shall see. So now you can understand why I have troubling concerns when it comes to our daughter and this Hunter."

"I am sorry I doubted you my love…But we can't leave Cailean locked in her room forever."

"She will stay as long as I see fit and that will be the end of it."

It was pointless pushing the point any further, her husband's mind was made up and nothing was going to change it. She stood up and made her way over to him.

"I am going to bed," she said kissing him on the forehead.

"I will join you shortly."

As his wife left the hall, he drew the note Maccon had given him from a pouch on his belt. It read.

My Lord Kor-yllion requests a meeting with yourself Lord Farroth and the one you call Maccon in matters regarding our agreement surrounding Bael, matters which give us great concern. There is also another matter to discuss that is of the gravest importance; it is not something I can put in this message. But know this; I cannot overstate the importance and urgency of this meeting. I await your reply. Kor-aviel of the Council of Elders.

***

Emma finished clearing the tables and scattered fresh saw dust on the floor, whilst her father closed up for the night, shutting the door behind Koval and Tyrna who were last to leave. Raga the old war hound wandered around the tables sniffing out any meaty remains left lying about. It snapped up a partially eaten leg of lamb as Emma was about to pick up the same; she smiled as the old hound carried the tasty morsel over to the fire and began chomping away at it. She closed the last of the shutters as the rain outside began to fall heavily, then she put out the candles and joined her father in the living quarters. He was sprawled out on his chair exhausted from a very busy day behind the bar. As she approached, he sat himself upright.

"I've been meaning to ask, how was the old dear yesterday? You have been rather quiet since you met her…. There is nothing wrong with her is there?"

"No, she is fine…. But she did tell me that Hunter slew some strange beast the other day, saving her life."

"What kind of beast?"

"I'm not sure, but she said it was ferocious and not from these parts."

"An old woman's mind can play tricks on her. It was probably a mountain lion, wandered from its hunting grounds."

"I don't think so; I believe she would have told me that," Emma said, changing the subject. "It's nice of Lord Farroth to put on a fair for us all before his brother the King arrives."

"Keeping us sweet 'ats all it is. Sweet and preoccupied. But whatever his reasons you can bet your life he has more to gain from it than we do and that's for sure," Dogran replied.

"Ever the pessimist, father? It will be a welcome distraction and a chance to catch up with people we haven't seen in a while."

"I suppose you are right. There is no point delving into the whys and wherefores of the likes of the Farroths and that's no mistake…. I believe entertainers are coming from all around and even wrestlers from the capital…Should be fun."

"Yes father. *Fun.* No fighting, you know what you and Koval are like when you get together, reminiscing about your days together in the militia."

"Now would I embarrass my daughter like that?" he said grinning mischievously.

"Yes, you would."

"Never."

"Well, we shall see."

"That we will my little one. That we will."

***

Koval was aware of a change in his son, the days following the hunt. The lad's mother hadn't noticed, and he didn't want to alert her to it before he understood himself what was going on. He watched Raen busy himself pushing the bellows to fire up the forge. The lad placed a length of steel in the flame that would eventually become a Bastard sword. As Koval watched through the window he too was putting the finishing touches to a sword he had been working on for the past two days. He lifted it to his cheek and glanced along its edge; the light capturing its beauty casting shadows in the two furrows cut down its centre, running virtually the full length of the blade. Between the furrows he had carefully etched the swords name. All that was needed was to leather bind the hilt and it was finished. Raen in the meantime was hammering the piece of red-hot metal on the huge anvil by the barrel of water.

Koval watched him for a while longer then turned to cross the room where his wife was busy grinding herbs from the garden. He placed the sword on a small bench in the corner and removed wet strips of leather from a bowl of water to his right. Carefully he began to wrap the strips of deer hide around the hilt.

"You work that lad too hard," Tyrna said.

"It will do him no harm. He will be stronger for it and he enjoys what he does, so why interfere with that?"

"I'm not against hard work. But between the forge and his time with Hunter, our boy has little time for himself."

"I think if he wanted it any other way he would let us know."

"I hope so," she said intrigued by her husband's attention to detail as he made the finishing touches to the sword he had so carefully kept from Raen's sight.

"I can't remember the last time I saw you take such loving care over a blade?" she quizzed.

"Well, I hope our son feels the same.... I have made it for him."

"Now that's a surprise, considering the fact that you made sure he was either off on some foolhardy errand or just too busy on the forge, to notice you were making such a sword," she said smugly.

One side of Koval's mouth dropped slightly making his grin look cheesy as she often enjoyed telling him, but grin he did and she loved him for it.

"Nothing gets past you, does it wench?" He jibed.

"Not a lot-my love. Not a lot."

On a more serious note, she stopped what she was doing and sipped the cold remains of a hot mug of elderberry wine she had left standing too long.

"That is a lovely thing you have done..."

"But?" he interrupted.

"But, do you really think he is ready for such a weapon?"

"I believe he is…. I have seen how much he has come on since Hunter took him under his wing. In fact, I would be hard pressed to match him in matters of the blade so accomplished has he become, and in such a short time. He is a natural I swear."

"I would rather see our son make such weapons as weald them. He has too bigger heart to be a fighter of any kind. And I worry he is being led along such a path that could see him harmed…. I still don't like it that Hunter teaches him these things."

"The lad will only do what *he* wants to do. I have seen him grow into a man these past weeks we can both be proud of, and like it or not Hunter has played no small part in this."

"Argh! Men. It is like the weapons are your toys and combat the game you play, but to us women this deadly game can rob us of a husband, lover, brother or son. If only our world was ruled by women, by the gods what a different place it would be."

"You worry too much desire of my loins," he said trying to lighten the mood.

"You can be such a fool… All I know is, most young men of his age will be looking to take a girl to the fair tomorrow, whereas our son seems to be more pre-occupied with thoughts of jousting and combat tourneys. Don't you ever worry that he will never meet a girl; settle down and one day bless us with a grand-child?"

"There is plenty of time for that, you are wishing the lad's life away…. I'm sure when the time is right the grandchildren you so wantonly desire will be ours to love. I have seen some of the town's young ladies looking his way, especially that pretty young thing that follows Farroth's daughter around like a shadow. In fact, it was only the other day I saw her eyeing our son in the market place, where I saw her buy a monk fish, only to give it to a beggar by the fountain in a vain attempt to mask her true intention. And if I am not mistaken our son noticed the same, that's if his grin from ear to ear was anything to go by. Listen, I have an eye for such matters."

"And who told you that?"

"Well, I chose you didn't-I?" he laughed.

He finished binding the leather strips with gut twine, then hefted the finished sword.

"There. Done."

His wife smiled sarcastically, before Koval joined his son outside.

Raen quenched the hot blade in the barrel of water and laid it down on the work bench ready for the following morning. His father walked towards him swinging a blade that looked very much like the one Hunter let him use during his training.

"Is everything alright son? You seem somewhat preoccupied after your hunt the other day."

Raen nodded he was fine. But Koval knew his son too well to believe that was the truth, yet he pursued it no further.

"I'm sure if something *is* troubling you, you will tell me when you are ready."

Raen gave him a tired smile.

"I have something for you, son," he said, handing Raen the sword he had worked on for two days.

The lad's face lit up; all signs of tiredness faded immediately. He took the blade and felt its balance. It was perfect. His eyes followed the slight curve of the blade before spinning it through the air in a series of dazzling arcs. When he was done getting a feel for the sword, Raen spotted the word etched between the parallel furrows running down its centre. It read. Fortune.

"Yes, my son, fortune. And if ever you need to use the blade in combat, may the only fortune it sees fit to bestow on you be *good*."

Raen placed the sword on the work bench by his side then threw his arms around his father's neck, hugging him lovingly; each squeeze telling his father how much he loved his gift also.

"Now son you should freshen up, your mother awaits our presence at the table, and you know how cranky she gets when we keep her waiting."

Raen picked up his sword and made his way back into the house. Just before he entered the door Koval grabbed his shoulder.

"Before we go inside, I have a little secret to share. Your father and that old war horse Dogran are going to put on a show tomorrow at the fair. I haven't told your mother so that's between us," he said winking like an over grown child. "Also, if my sources are correct, a pretty young lady, Jiney I think they call her, will be there too."

Raen's face lit up like a red lantern.

"I just thought you would like to know. Now son lets fill our bellies."

10
SHARED SECRETS

The cottage was just as he remembered it. There was an air of tranquillity that surrounded the place, which the passing of the years had preserved. Maccon tethered his horse to the fence and looked around. It was like a painting in his memory had come to life: rabbits ran free and unafraid around a pond. Butterflies displayed their beautiful colours whilst basking in the sun. Bees collected honey from the sweetest of flowers as birds of every size and colour filled the air with their summer song. And though Maccon guessed magic was in some part responsible, wasps and other garden pests were never an issue in the grounds where all this wild life lived in harmony. There was a great feeling of life here and Maccon suddenly realized how much he had missed the place.

The old gate squealed on rusty hinges as he approached the cottage. Before he could put a foot on the porch, the door opened and out sprang a young deer. It stopped dead in its tracks, uncertain of the new visitor it backed away shakily. Maccon dropped to one knee, held out his hand and clicked his fingers.

"Here. Come now. Don't be afraid."

Lamia stepped from the door giving the fawn a reassuring glance.

"Go on," she said. "He won't hurt you."

As if the creature understood every word it edged its way cautiously towards Maccon. The Priest tickled her throat; she seemed to like it turning her head so his fingers would find another place to tickle.

"Your new friend here is a delight," he smiled.

Lamia sat on the bench under the window, the sun catching her beauty in its light. Maccon could see, even in what he believed was her sixtieth year she still retained an elegance you would expect in someone fifteen years younger. Nature had been kind to her; porcelain skin with hardly a wrinkle line to be seen, all her curves in the right place with no sign of sagging breasts or rounded shoulders that so often came with age.

For a moment, he just stared at her his heart filled with sadness. She was tall for a woman, at most an inch shorter than Maccon and he was six feet tall. He could see she had made an effort as if she were expecting his visit. She wore a simple oatmeal coloured dress of soft cotton that showed the gentle curves of her body to the full. Her greying black hair was tied back in a bun, a style in the past he'd always complimented her on. He too had made an effort, wearing long turquoise robes with a white sash around his waist. On the back was the emblem of the Black Orchids, colourful raiment's that told the uninitiated that he was leader of the Order. And though his robes reflected more his priesthood than the chain mail he usually wore, he still carried a sword at his side.

Before sitting next to her he glanced again at the abundance of colour that surrounded the property; flowers, shrubs and trees of every kind bloomed in full spectacle.

"May I?" He asked gesturing at the bench.

"Please. You do not have to ask."

"How lovely you look. It is nice to see you with your hair up like that."

If he hadn't known better, he could have sworn he saw the faintest hint of a blush warm her cheeks.

"Ever the charmer, Maccon. It is nice to see time has not changed that."

Gently he took her hand in his and stroked the back of it.

"It is such a fine morning. Would you walk with me a while?" he asked softly.

She didn't answer but stood up as he did; she linked his arm feeling the hard muscle as he squeezed her hand against his side. They passed through the gate where his horse was tethered and took the path which led to the woods, the very path where Hunter had killed the Grawl. As they passed the spot, there was no evidence the beast had met such a violent end, nature had worked her magic erasing any tell-tale evidence that might have suggested otherwise. Following close behind the fawn jumped about, chasing bright blue dragonflies as they hovered and darted away at will. A veil of fine white cloud gathered above making the air heavy and muggy.

Not long after entering the woods they reached a clearing, where several paths overgrown through lack of use, spread away like open fingers amongst the trees. Lamia halted for a moment, then she led them along the path furthest to their right. Maccon was still amazed at how she could navigate so accurately without true sight. The path wound through the forest like a grass serpent, until they reached a clearing; Maccon realized where they were. He took Lamia by the hand and walked her to the spot where they first made love: the grassy knoll overlooked a beautiful crystal rock pool, which was fed by two cascading waterfalls. He had all but forgotten this wonderful place, but as he ran his fingers through the ice-cold water of the pool, memories came flooding back. Once again, he felt the burning passion in the pit of his stomach, a flame he had thought long extinguished. He looked at Lamia and could see the sadness in her eyes. He took her hand again and kissed her gently.

"I am so...so sorry it has taken this long for us to return to this place, I had forgotten how beautiful it is." A single tear ran down her cheek as his lips touched hers. He caught it with the tip of his finger and kissed it. The fawn nuzzled against her side as if to comfort her. She stroked it lovingly, then the young deer ran over to the water's edge and stared at its own reflection, seeing itself for the first time. Cautiously it dipped its nose into the pool causing ripples to break the glassy surface, the ice-cold water making it jump back in shock. After a few more nose dips the fawn began to drink fearlessly, no longer frightened by the little creature staring back at her from the water's surface. Lamia wiped the remainder of the tear off her cheek and sat back taking a deep breath of the clean moist air.

"So, you do remember this place?" She asked searchingly.

"Yes....I remember. How could I forget the first place we lay together? It still holds the same beauty it held all those years ago. Is it not a cruel irony of nature that sees us wrinkle and wither with age whilst all around us; the trees, the fields, the rivers, the mountains all stay the same? Waiting patiently as another generation replaces the one before."

"Such thoughts are for the foolish," she said affectionately. "I have learned to love what I have in the moment. Thoughts of the things that maybe, seem such tiresome folly."

"Yet you possess the power to see things that have not yet come to pass."

"Not because I wish it, as well you know. It is a gift I was blessed or cursed with depending on how you view such a thing. But do I wish it? Mostly not."

They both sat quietly for a while neither speaking a word. Maccon watched a delicate Empress Butterfly land on Lamia's arm. Again, he was mesmerised by the precise way she extended a finger, which the insect stepped onto willingly.

"Are you going to the upcoming fair?" he asked.

"It is not for the likes of me. Many in the town still think me a witch."

"And many do not.... And those that do must lead such boring lives that they can only find solace in the trouble of others."

This made her smile.

"Time is such a fickle master is it not? It must be thirty or more years past since we last lay on this hill together. Yet as I look at you now it could have been yesterday," he said thoughtfully.

Something in Maccon's comment took her back to that day her life changed forever; the last day they slept together. They had just finished making love, she noticed something different in his body language this time, intangible but definitely different. Her powers of perception were nowhere near fully developed but she knew something was wrong and though she pressed him many times about her feelings, it wasn't till days later that he gave her the devastating news. Words that would see their relationship broken beyond repair, her heart broken the same. A heart she would never give to another.

She sat up and pulled her knees into her chest rocking backwards and forwards nervously.

"Why did you never seek me out when you returned from the wars?" She asked.

Maccon dropped his gaze.

"I was young.... Foolish, and afraid. Many times, I hoped you would be the one to come to me, selfish as that may seem I did not have the courage to break my vows. I was then only second to Osias, the leader of the Order who was grooming me at the time to replace him in his retirement. And though it was never written that a leader of the order should take no wife, it has always been the way.

"If your love for me was true, should you not have challenged such pointless tradition?" Lamia protested.

"Wisdom is the slave of time.... The years have taught me truths I was too stupid to see back then. I deeply regret some of the decisions I have made and would see them undone."

"When you told me you were leaving to fight for the King, I felt empty. And for a while I hated you for it.... But hate is such a poisonous emotion and in time that hate turned to indifference."

"I knew the campaigns in the North would see me gone from here for many years, though none of us serving could have foreseen the ten years it took from our lives. It tore me apart leaving you that way, but I could not see you waiting all those years only to find that the man who returned was but a shadow of the one that left."

Lamia snatched her hand away.

"Should that choice not have been mine to make?" She said angrily. "Could you not see how terrible it was to have such decisions denied me, no matter how well intentioned?"

Maccon shuffled about uncomfortably.

"Back then, sadly no. A young man's ambition and loyalty to his King saw my judgement clouded, misguided whatever you would call it, decisions I cannot defend as wisdom has taught me some hard truths."

"We both know what the real truth is, don't we Maccon? She urged. "Was my fate not sealed the day my gift manifested itself? Powers that were bestowed on me by whom or what I still have no idea. But you were unwilling to see past your selfish ambition and the ignorance that still festers in the laws that rule the land to this very day. Nothing could have steered *me* from the path our relationship was traveling, I loved you that much. But *you* allowed this fear and hypocrisy to destroy everything we had together. A young woman in love, and…" She couldn't finish, the lump she felt in her throat strangling the last words.

Maccon put his arm around her shoulder and hugged her dearly.

"I deeply regret causing you so much pain," he whispered.

Her eyes filled with tears, not because of anything that was said; these tears were for another truth she should have shared with Maccon long ago but couldn't. She wiped her eyes again and corrected herself. Maccon let her sit up straight and took her by the hand again.

"In truth, I didn't know what to do. Even though the law condemning women for practicing magic is outdated and hypocritical, I could not risk the consequences of anyone finding out about you. It states even to this day that women shall not practice magic of any sort, Dark or Light. That such was solely the practice of men. When your gift finally blossomed, I was terrified. Lord Farroth is a fair man but rigid in his interpretation of the law, I was afraid had he discovered your secret his judgement would have been swift and unrelenting. That much I knew of the man."

"But how could you then and now serve such a man, and not question the kind of morals that would see women disadvantaged in this way?"

"Because underneath I know he is a good man who makes questionable decisions he is burdened to execute. I knew in his ignorance and many others like him that you would be branded a witch, and had it been discovered that I courted such knowledge, then gods know what both our fates would have been. But my thoughts on the matter then and the ones I have now are but a world apart."

Lamia had nothing to come back with, she understood but was still disappointed with what she heard. During his explanation, she had probed his mind and saw that everything he said was true and heartfelt. Yet it made no difference, she felt had he shown more courage all those years ago, their lives could have been so different.

For a while they both sat there, not a word passed between them. Then Maccon stood up and walked to the rock pool. He removed his sandals and dangled his feet in the water. The deer ran up to him and nudged him with its nose. He smiled at her and stroked her neck; she jumped back playfully and ran to Lamia who was getting to her feet. She brushed her dress down trying to flatten the creases and joined Maccon by the pool.

"When we met the other day, I felt guilty that our conversation had been so one sided. I have made mistakes in my past I do not wish to repeat.... You deserve better than that. A lot better. There is something I want to share with you that I should have then, concerning Bael."

Lamia leant forward and stared into the bubbling water where the falls broke the glass like surface and listened.

"Just over ten summers ago, the Elders you saw in your vision brought Bael to our town. In truth, I still no not the reason why. It was Kor-yllion and Kor-aviel his head shaman. At that time, our relationship with Elven kind was fragile at best. The land of men had grown ever closer to their sacred boundaries, and at one point most believed a war with the Elves was unavoidable. Luckily this was not to be. Something must have happened, something that Bael, Hunter which ever name you want to give him, was party to, a secret only known to the Elves. A secret none the less so powerful it drove Kor-yllion to set up a meeting with Lord Farroth, myself and the King. At this meeting, we discovered Kor-aviel and his council of mages had performed an ancient rite, locking Hunter's memories away forever.... Or so we thought."

Lamia sat back down on a large rock next to his and sighed, some of the unanswered questions from their last meeting finally had some clarity.

"What could Hunter be party to that would advocate such devastating consequences?" She asked herself out loud.

"They had their reasons but we were never privy to them. King Agramar couldn't afford another war both politically and financially so soon after the Northern campaigns, so a treaty was forged. Hunter was to live amongst us and reassurances were made by Agramar that we as a people would never settle anywhere beyond our side of the Neck that narrow stretch of land that separates our Races. With my help Kor-aviel gave Hunter a new set of memories which would allow him to integrate with us more easily. As you know Bael has accepted his place in our town without much difficulty.... Now those very same Elders that brought *him* to us all those years ago, have burdened Hunter with the Dire Wolf that follows him like a shadow. Not only this, we received a message the other day asking Lord Farroth and myself to meet them at one of their outposts on matters of grave importance."

Lamia frowned as she listened intently to his words.

"You must be careful Maccon. I fear there is more to these Elders than they would have you believe. I sense something terrible is coming and I believe they know what it is.... And I feel Hunter and his wolf are part of it."

A breeze whipped across the clearing carrying the threat of rain. Lamia shivered a little then again sadness filled her eyes.

"We should head back to the cottage; I think rain is coming."

"I think you are right. Come take my arm," he said guiding her back along the path.

It didn't take them long to get home, the rain just beginning to fall as they stepped onto the porch. Lamia let go of Maccon's arm and opened the front door letting the fawn run in, but instead of following she closed it and turned around.

"Last time we met you asked me why it had taken me all these years to finally come to your Temple," she said nervously. "The answer you seek is here at the cottage."

She took his hand and led him behind the house, past the pond at the back of the garden to a small circle of bushes with a single opening. As they got closer, he could see through a curtain of fine rain a small mound with a headstone. Maccon looked puzzled.

"A grave?"

Tears ran down both of Lamia's reddened cheeks.

"Your daughter's," she whispered, hardly able to speak the words.

It was like the very air was stilled, sucked into a vacuum that only those words could fill. Maccon was stunned. It felt like a burning blade had pierced his heart. Suddenly, as the reality of what she said settled, he dropped to his knees, his head bowed in anguish.

"Why did you not tell me?"

She couldn't answer.

"What happened?"

Lamia paused momentarily, gathering herself.

"She died of a fever, two days before her tenth name day. There was nothing I or anyone could do."

"But why? Why did you not try to get word to me? I may have been able to do something."

"You could have done nothing."

"Then why did you not tell me you were with child at the beginning?"

"You had gone to war. I was hurt beyond telling by what you had said to me before you left. I felt like an outcast for something I had no control over, then to discover I carried your child. It was too much for a young woman to bear. I hoped you would do the right thing by me, but as time passed and I hadn't heard a word from you, only resentment filled my heart. Before she was born, I cried till I had no more tears left to cry. I thought of you always as I carried her to birth, a birth that only one person in the town knew about. So, our secret could never jeopardise your position in the Order should you live through the Campaign that could so easily have taken your life. Remember I heard nothing from you for ten years, and because of your status I thought she would never be part of your life. So, I stopped worrying."

Maccon calmed down, her words and tears filling him with a mixture of guilt and sadness he found hard to rationalize.

"What was her name?"

"See for yourself," she said pointing to the headstone.

Maccon stood up and moved closer to read the engraving in the fading light. It simply read.

RENYA

A cherished soul

Taken

Before her time

"Everything you have told me I understand and regret beyond what any words could ever convey. But you should have told me about this, it breaks my heart," he said, more sad than angry.

"You lost that right the day you left me the way you did. But now? Well that is a different matter. Time has healed the wound you dealt me and now I understand more your reasons for why you did what you did. I still don't agree with them but I can see that it too left a hole in your life as it did mine."

"I am sorry Lamia I have to go. I cannot speak about this any longer. I regret deeply what I put you through, but this you should have told me about. I am sorry, I must go."

Lamia was left standing alone by the graveside her tears lost in the rain. She gathered her thoughts and headed back to the comfort of her cottage. Though soaked to the skin she stepped onto the front porch her thoughts filled with more serious matters. There was one piece of information she hadn't shared with Maccon; it just didn't feel like the right time. The child that lay in the grave had a twin, a daughter she had not seen or spoken to for many years. A daughter who still lived in the town, but sadly a daughter she felt Maccon would have difficulty accepting. A daughter who had brought shame to the family.

11

THE WEAVING - GATES OF LIFE AND DEATH

Most people in town knew, prying into Bael's private life especially if that involved rumour and town gossip, was to risk a look that could freeze any normal person on the spot. But Vena wasn't one of those normal people. Stories on the streets, embellished as some undoubtedly were, were filled with tales of heroism or madness, depending on which story you were privy to at the time. In just one day, Bael had gone from being an annoying recluse the sadder people in town took great pleasure in ridiculing, to being a reluctant town hero everyone wanted to talk about. The killing of the rogue bear and the saving of the Farroth girl and her handmaiden was the stuff of legend; or so the song, a minstrel known simply as Red; due to his weathered cheeks, would have you believe. The rendition of this little ditty in Dogran's tavern the night before had left Bael squirming with embarrassment, especially as Emma had pestered him constantly about said events, whenever she had a spare moment between serving a full tavern of regulars. He was for now anyway, the town's centre of attention and he didn't like it, one bit. But at least someone reaped the benefits from it all, the Tavern was bursting at the rafters prompting Dogran to prance about the place sporting a grin that stretched from one ear to the other. That was yesterday. Today....

Vena's monthly blood cycle had been heavier than normal, and the stomach cramps that accompanied such an occurrence were almost unbearable. This was usually a time in her schedule that she would take a well-earned respite from the rigours of her demanding profession. A time for rest. A time to reflect and keep tabs on her wealth. But there was one client she would forgo such a ritual.

Hunter arrived as expected, his hair tied back in a ponytail, she couldn't help thinking how handsome he looked; but tired, as if he carried the weight of the world on his shoulders. He was greeted by the welcoming glow of several lit candles which filled the room with scented jasmine. Vena was sometimes conscious that her scent of womanhood could be strong when her show of blood was this heavy, no matter how clean she kept herself. A condition that wouldn't normally have bothered her, but with Hunter arriving she found herself feeling quite self-conscious about it. It also helped that the old apothecary who cleansed her body of men so regularly, had developed a wool filled pad that she could place on her womanhood, stemming the flow of blood; and in so doing protecting her clothing from such unsanitary stains as would inevitably occur on such an occasion as this.

She led Hunter to the bed and removed his leather jerkin. Leaning into him she greeted him with a kiss that hid within it a passion she felt for no other man, but his response was one of indifference as if his mind was elsewhere.

She lay back on the bed and took his hand guiding him next to her. She was wearing a simple night dress of some worth, made of blue silk, for though many in the town found her profession deplorable, she had accrued considerable wealth from such unsavoury indiscretions.

Vena could see that Hunter was preoccupied in thought, he was staring at the wall as if she wasn't there. What she didn't know was that his thoughts were filled with memories of Cailean and the warning her father Lord Farroth had given him. It had upset him more than he cared to admit, on top of which he was finding it harder and harder to shake her image from his thoughts. He wasn't sure why, when she annoyed him so much, but fill his mind she did and it unsettled him somewhat. Add to this the constant questioning by Emma the night before, with the whole Tavern whispering about him; was it any wonder he sought a little peace and quiet. Well, that is what he had hoped.

Instead of resting Hunter's head on her lap, she lay down and pulled it gently into the softness of her breasts.

"You seem troubled Hunter, what is it?" she asked, a little disappointedly, as she had been looking forward to this night for the past few days.

Hunter hesitated momentarily before answering.

"There is nothing wrong, I am just tired. I have been hunting deer for the King's table, and most of today I have exercised the Wolf by taking her into the mountains."

"But they are leagues away," she replied. "Is it any wonder you are burnt out. Anyway, how is the Wolf doing?"

Bael shifted in the bed a little, trying to find a more comfortable position.

"She is coming along fine. She grows stronger by the day."

"So, it's a She-Wolf then?"

"It is, and she is becoming a handful. Her energy shows no bounds now her strength returns. If she had her way, we would be out hunting all day every day."

"Well, you can relax now," she said stroking his hair. She waited a short while not wishing to sound over eager. Then she risked it. "I heard about the bear; the whole town are talking about it."

Bael didn't answer, but she felt his body tense up.

"And what was that foolhardy Farroth girl doing in the forest anyway?" She queried, jealously.

Now Bael was annoyed. He sat up and gave her the stare.

"I do not wish to speak about it. If you need to know any more, go speak with the local gossip, we seem to have a town full of them…If you wish to continue along this path, I will leave. I came here to get away from all that nonsense, not have it rubbed in my face. So, if…"

"Alright. Alright I am sorry. I will speak no more about it," she replied, a little upset with herself for being so tactless. "Please. Lie down and relax, I promise that's the end of it."

She pulled him back to her, and thankfully he didn't try to resist. She kept quiet, running her fingers through his hair in short soothing strokes.

It wasn't long before the welcoming heat and comfort of the bed worked its magic, luring him into the warm embrace of a deep and troubled sleep.

**

THE WEAVING.

The subterranean network of tunnels and pens beneath the arena reek with the smell of death. Two figures sit alone on a square stone bench in the centre of the Cornerius Quintas – the Chamber of Hope: the last room and entrance to the tunnel which leads to the Gate of Life through which the fighters enter the Arena, and should they endure, leave by. Shafts of light flicker through gaps on the wooden door, shimmering on sand and rock salt as it sifts through cracks in the wooden floor above: The added rock salt the brainchild of a sick mind, to cause the wounded excruciating pain should they fall upon it.

The fight above would soon be over; the older fighter knew this from the response of the screaming crowd. If he was lucky one of the fighters would re-enter the Gate of Life; the fallen by the Gate of Death which led to a room adjacent to the one, he and his younger companion are sitting in. A room none of the fighters cared to look in as they awaited their fate, for what lay within was a horror beyond imagining. It seems like the older man's thoughts are his own, yet Hunter has no idea what the younger man is thinking, something or someone is blocking the connection.

Determined to get a closer look at the strange young warrior, Bael floats like a phantom towards the two men who seem to be totally oblivious of his presence. As he gets within earshot he stops, the only face visible to him is the older man's, the younger one has his back to him. But there is something unsettlingly familiar about him. The crowd above cry out in perverted delight. The fight is over. For one at least, maybe both? The older man looks towards the tunnel waiting for the victor to appear, leaving just enough time for the sand men to scatter fresh salt and rake the sand ready for the fight of the day. Theirs. Bael senses this will be no ordinary fight; he can't understand why but somehow, he just knows.

The winner of the fight above appears from the tunnel. He limps into the room, blood pouring from a spear wound to his thigh. But he will live. The older warrior looks towards the younger, his eyes tired and strangely knowing.

"By the gods, Galas, it is hard to believe that after this fight we are free men."

Bael waits for a reply from the young man, but there is none, only silence... Galas? Galas? Should I know that name? A question his dream can't answer.

"If I should fall this day, I would make you a gift of these," the older man says pointing to his swords. The very same blades Bael now carries. Again, there is no reply, but this time the young warrior places his hand on top of his father's and shakes it reassuringly. The older man's-tired eyes fill with tears of pride and a finality which he knows will be determined in the moments to follow. Then a voice calls to them both from the tunnel of Life. "Joren you old lion, this is your time. May the gods look down on you this day and favour you with a victory." The guard is a chubby man with a jolly face, it is obvious he likes the two fighters, but there is concern and doubt in his tone. "Galas, protect your father."

There is a blinding light.

Now Bael looks upon the arena from above as the visions of his earlier dreams unfold. Just like his previous dream the eight fighters enter the pit arena, but not from the Gate of Life as would be expected. Instead, they come through the Gate of Death; but this time the older warrior facing them is not alone. By his side is his son whose body is a sculpture of muscle and sinew, which glistens with an oil of his father's making; an oil he knew would make his son more difficult to hold, should their opponents get close enough. As Bael watches, a White Hawk lands on the young warriors protected arm, it's eyes as red as fire. On seeing the bird, the fighter with the two Grawls struggles to pull them back so crazed are they. But Bael can see doubt burn its way into the Beast Master's eyes. Suddenly there is a blinding white light.

This time Bael sees a babe wrapped in linen, left in the forest to die. As nightfall swallows what is left of the daylight, he sees the eyes of a beast in the shadows. Slowly the eyes move behind one tree then another red and menacing, until a huge Black Dire Wolf steps into the open, close to where the child lie's; not the one with the silver streak standing by its King, no, this one is different and much more powerful looking. Bael can only look on in horror, his muscles frozen, locked by some unknown force. The beast seems to be protecting the babe. Bael is uncertain of its intent, until it takes the child in its massive jaws and carries it as if it were a cub. The image fades, and now he finds himself looking down upon a log cabin high on a ridge. The snows have begun to fall, its stark white blanket broken only by the Black Wolf as it appears from the forest. Still holding the babe, it moves cautiously to the wooden porch and lays the bundle outside the door, which it begins to scratch with ever increasing urgency. Then it quickly disappears back into the forest, where it waits, watching from the shadows as the door opens and the young man within picks up the child. Bewildered the man looks around for any sign of who might have left such a gift, but the only prints he sees that have broken the settling snow are those of a Wolf. He looks to the forest but doesn't see the Wolf staring at him from the darkness. Then he glances down to the bundle in his hands.

"What are you doing here?" He says stroking the child's forehead. "Who could leave you like this so far from anywhere?" The young man looks around again before taking the babe inside. Again, there is a blinding light.

This time Hunter awoke to find himself still in Vena's arms, shaking as if his body lay naked in the snow. He sat up sharply, head butting her squarely in the face, instantly causing a swelling under her left eye and a bruise on her cheek. She pushed him away, concern turning to anger and for the first time she was actually frightened of him.

"By the gods, Hunter, what is it? What is going on with you? Look at me. Look what you've done to my face," she cried, shakily.

It took a moment for Bael to gather himself, realizing what he'd done he cupped her swollen cheek with his hand and caressed it gently. She relaxed to the affection of his touch.

"Forgive me. I would never wish to cause you…."

"I know you would never harm me intentionally, yet here I sit bearing a face my paying clients might find somewhat disconcerting," her sarcasm easing the tension. "Something is troubling you deeply, troubling you enough to leave your body soaked in sweat and trembling like a frightened child. So please, do not, like every other time I have asked you about these dreams, answer me with the silence that so conveniently befalls you. Not this time Hunter, something is going on with you and I would know what it is."

Bael slipped off the bed and stood as if about to leave. Vena stared at him disappointingly, and then to her surprise he stopped, turned around and joined her back on the bed. Sitting by her side he turned to face her. She saw that gentleness in those vivid blue eyes that sadly seemed to appear with ever increasing rarity. He began to speak, and for the first time he shared with her every mysterious detail of his recurring dream. By the end of it Vena's left eye was all but swollen shut, the pain never once abating. She stroked his hair; he dropped his head to stare at the floor by his feet.

"It is strange you would have such a dream reveal itself in such detail, and on so many occasions. Does it hold any kind of meaning for you at all?" she asked.

"I am not sure. Yet there is something familiar about the fighter with the hawk, though his face is masked by his helmet."

"You must find it strange that the bird you see in your dream describes perfectly the very hawk you possess."

"Yes, I agree, it is puzzling, but aren't dreams the place for strange things?"

"I suppose they are; I remember someone told me once that dreams were the mischievous children of sleep," she pondered, her features saddening with a deep sense of melancholy. "Yet I feel there is more to these visions than you might realize."

Vena slipped out of bed to sit next to Bael. She placed her hand on his and squeezed. She had never seen a man more tormented by his past than Hunter and was one of the few people who knew him, that was aware just how much of that torment he kept hidden. "There is somebody I believe might be able to help you make some sense of it all. She is an old woman I hear possesses the gift of Sight, a gift that allows her to see what we cannot. She lives in a cottage where two streams meet on the edge of Deep Pine Woods."

"You know this woman?"

"I did, but that was a long time ago," she replied, sadly.

Hunter was more than a little surprised by Vena's reaction to his question, he had never seen her look so vulnerable before, which touched him.

"I think we have already met. She is blind. Is she not?"

"Most believe that to be true and yes she is blind, but not in the way one thinks of blindness. No, the fact is she sees the world in a far different way to the rest of us. That is all I know.... You should call on her again and tell her about these dreams, hopefully she will shed some light on what is going on."

"I will think on it," Bael said, as he slipped his hand from under hers and stood to leave. She grabbed hold of it again, her face looking almost pitiful as she pulled him back.

"Why don't you stay?"

"No, I must go, I feel I have caused you enough damage for one night," he replied, not wishing to risk another episode like the one that left her looking like she had done a round in the fight pits. He ran his finger over her swollen cheek.

"I will survive. Stay," she urged.

"Another time."

Bael kissed her on the forehead and walked to the door. As he was about to step out of the room Vena called to him.

"How was the blind woman, was she in good health?"

"She looked fine," he replied. "As to her wellbeing, I can only tell you what I saw. She seems to possess a strength that women of lesser years would be only too happy to possess."

"I am glad," Vena replied, quietly.

Bael nodded good buy and left, not quite sure of the question. Then Vena lay back down and cried, something she hadn't done since the death of her husband.

12

RAIDERS

Vaeyu was a hardened veteran. Leading his gang of thieves' cutthroats and worse was punishment for simply speaking his mind. Not so long past he was known by another name, Kal-Adynn; *the killer in the shadows*, the first in an elite brotherhood of assassins whose sole purpose was to serve the brutal King of the White Isles: Hingar. A King who was known for his cruelty and his craving for blood, and if whispers could be believed, blood he would bathe in.

Cor-Leonese raiders were infamous seaman, smugglers, pirates and slavers, their Galleys small and fast and Vaeyu's ship the Savage Eel the fastest of them all. This was the farthest they had ever ventured from the sea, the targets of choice were always towns and villages along the coast, but it had become almost impossible to fill their manifest of human cargo with each passing year. Patrols along roads were becoming more frequent, especially the high roads and major trade routes between the regions. This forced the Cor-Leonese Raiders to seek alternative routes which were not ideal for the movement of prison wagons and the huge horses that pulled them.

Vaeyu and his crew had been on the road for several weeks, this was to be the last wagon load before sailing for the islands; there was room for three more, then his cargo would be at capacity. He was almost tempted to leave the last places unfilled, the last of the summer raids had been particularly uncomfortable, with temperatures higher than they had been in years, causing the raiders delicate skins to come out in an irritating heat rash, fuelling discontent amongst the crew. But Vaeyu had never returned with a less than a full cargo and though this had been his most trying raid to date, it would not be the exception.

The end of the hottest day of the raid was coming to a close; as the sun vanished on the horizon and the temperature became more bearable Vaeyu removed his hood, exposing his sweat soaked head to the cool breath of a gentle breeze. Like the rest of his kind Vaeyu's skin was as white as goat's milk, which looked thin and translucent with thin blue veins visible beneath. A skin that was void of any bodily hair. A skin that welcomed night over day. He slipped his hand across his tattoo covered head; for him an intricate mark of honour that commanded respect and fear, a fear for his speciality: *Death*.

His scouts returned with news of a settlement not more than a day's ride from where they were camped. They reported of easy pickings from several farms in the region and a town overlooked by a Large Keep at the edge of a lake.

Vaeyu joined some of his crew who had lit a fire and were already eating the half raw meat of a freshly cooked boar. Through the wooden bars of the wagon, children's faces glowed orange from the fire, their eyes hungry and wanting. Over his years as a raider his cargo was almost always children; a duty for the realm that had slowly eaten away at him leaving him empty. But he had been raised from birth to serve the realm no matter what, and he had to believe that these unfortunates would mostly find a new and better life: but on that terrible day when he had confronted his King, the very day he was exiled from the brotherhood he was awakened to a very different truth. So much so, that he began to question his very role in keeping such a savage leader on the throne; feelings which tore at the very fibre of his humanity.

He looked to the wagon again; there were five boys and six girls; if they were lucky they would get half eaten bones his crew would throw their way after first gorging themselves: otherwise they would have to feed on some grey tasteless sludge that would leave enough meat on *their* bones to fetch a good price at auction. He lent over the fire and tore off chunks of the darker meat and threw it into the wagon. The strongest ate first the weakest whatever remained; there was no question of etiquette when faced with starvation. One girl sat alone, dark of hair her clothes torn and tattered, no older than her tenth name day she stared at the others as they ate leaving her with nothing. One of his crew, a hunchback, stood up and with a half-eaten bone from the boar's leg, walked to the cage. Vaeyu was surprised, in their tasteless profession there was little room for emotion but he never believed in cruelty for cruelties sake so he watched with interest. In a language, she couldn't understand, the hunchback whispered.

"Here. Eat."

She turned to receive the morsel that her captor dangled through the bars, but as she reached out to take it he pulled it away laughing and slobbering. He placed his free hand on the girl's leg and squeezed.

"Not so quick my pretty. What will you give old Fengr for such a fine piece of meat?"

The girl pulled away terrified, for though she understood not a word, she was sure of what they implied.

A master of deception, Vaeyu's face didn't reveal the anger that welled inside. He tore off another piece of meat and approached the cage. Coolly he handed the food to the frightened child, who snatched it nervously as hunger overrode any fear she felt.

"You are too generous with the food," the hunchback said drunkenly, picking meat from between his rotting teeth.

"I am what I need to be. No more no less… if this is not to your liking, then leave. I will not hold you back."

A silence befell the camp, most had worked with Vaeyu before; they knew how this could end and they didn't want any part of it. The hunchback reached for a dagger strapped to his arm, but in a blink Vaeyu had it out of his hand and in one flowing movement slashed off every finger from the hand that had touched the young girl's leg. The hunchback screamed in agony as blood and fingers arced through the air. Then with a single powerful downward blow Vaeyu knocked the misfit to the ground.

"You leave. Now! If ever my eyes rest upon you again you will die," his threat cold and emotionless.

He called the healer, who was resting against the massive roots of a giant Emperor tree with that look of expectancy one would often see in a man waiting for the inevitable.

"Bind his wounds and see him from the camp, I weary of his twisted soul," he said with some reluctance. For had they not been on the road the hunchback would have surely died; Vaeyu new that death would not bode well with his raiders, but it paid to let them see he still possessed his skills.

Two days had passed since they kidnapped their last child: it was a small village south west of the Taelyn Mountains. They had been discovered escaping with the young daughter of a local farmer who had been mercilessly slaughtered with his wife by three of Vaeyu's reavers, whilst he oversaw the shackling of the girl unaware of his men's pointless savagery.

Vaeyu lost four of his men to those hardy mountain people, who had put up a fight they could never win armed only with knives, scythes or whatever else they could use as a weapon. This kind of pointless killing was like a cancer; slowly eating away at Vaeyu. For him there was no glory in such victories, he found the killing of innocents abhorrent and sadly these incidents were becoming commonplace as the mainlanders ramped up security. He knew the days of easy pickings were over; after years of such raids it was only time before the populace would get wise to their movements and that time had arrived.

Weary boned he retired to his blanket by the fire and before long was asleep, with one eye open; a skill perfected during his time as an assassin. He was awakened the following morning by a heavy summer downpour. The hunchback was gone as ordered, left to whatever fate the gods had planned for such a vile and twisted creature.

Already saddled and ready to ride, his first scout, a tall imposing figure of a man approached bringing Vaeyu his mount. The leader jumped to the saddle and pulled the bit tight against the animal's hardened mouth, reigning it in as it fought to run. He spun the beast around to face his scout.

"Come. I have had enough of this land…Is this town you speak of heavily guarded?" he asked.

"Yes. It must be a town of some importance for it has its own fortress. But there is an abundance of farms and small holdings surrounding the town that would see us in and gone before anyone would realize.

"Good. Then we ride."

13

THE WEAVING-THE FIGHT-
THE RUNE STONE

Even through the dizziness of his dream like state, Bael knew death was the accepted punishment for a careless lapse in concentration; the failure to heed the obvious, kill or be killed. There was an unnatural beauty in the splashing's of red that soaked into the arena sand: a canvas of death whose only colour was that of blood. In this prison of his mind's own making Bael carried no weapons, he drifted from one existence to another. A helpless spectator, whose only option was to watch and listen as scenes unfolded that bore no resemblance to any part of his conscious existence; yet inexplicably yielding moments of familiarity that were both unnerving yet at the same time fulfilling. Times forgotten. Times lived.

Bael looks down, as he floats freely above the fighting pit, viewing it as if he were in several places at once. A hush befalls the arena, the crowd waiting for what they hope will be a bloody spectacle. The eight fighters surround Galas, the young warrior with the hawk and his father Joren. In the pulpit, the King gives the signal for the sport to begin, delighting the crowd into a mindless chant, "Kill. Kill. Kill."

Bael feels himself being drawn ever closer to the fight; it is futile to resist. Whatever power is at work, he can't stop himself from drifting towards the young warrior with the hawk, until finally he finds himself looking through the man's eyes: almost like his spirit possesses the man.

Galas looks at the hawk on his arm, then just off to his right the huge dark-skinned fighter brandishing a brutal looking double-edged battle axe, rushes him. The bird instinctively takes flight; it is so quick the axe man doesn't have time to react. The hawk tears into his exposed shoulder, giving Galas time enough to dodge the axe as it passes only inches from his face. Before the lumbering fighter can bring his weapon back up, Galas opens his stomach in a spray of entrails and blood. The fighter drops to his knees spilling all that bloody gore into the sand around him. This prompts the two fighters facing the older warrior to attack. The first to reach him is a tall young man, an Altaerian fighter at least six feet five, whip lean, his weapon of choice a spear and a small round buckler with short blades along its edge. He lunges at Joran, but his spear is easily parried. The old warrior head butts him breaking the man's nose as the second fighter, a smaller but more robust man attacks him with a spiked mace in one hand and a short-curved sword in the other. The spearman reals back in pain hardly able to see.

Meanwhile Galas makes short work of dispatching another fighter armed with a whip and large spiked hook, leaving his head rolling across the arena floor.

The old warrior takes a rib shattering blow to his side, but like lightning he severs his attacker's sword hand clean off, spraying blood all over his face. The burly fighter tries to recover but he is too late, Joren rams his short sword up into the fighter's groin, the blade exiting his belly button. He drops to the sand, dead.

Galas can see the beast master struggling to hold back the two young Grawls, waiting for the right moment to unleash the beasts. Through Galas' eyes Bael can see this fighter is more battle savvy than the rest and keeps him in constant view. Next to him is a young fighter who can't be more than sixteen name days old; he is handsome with olive skin, a shaven head, and a single braid of beaded hair hanging to one side. Bael has seen his type before; from the Summer Isles to the south, in the Sea of Hope. Natural fighters, they are a clannish people, the colour of the beads in their hair representing their clan and their prowess as a warrior. Bael can see this fighter is a fledgling. He nervously wields an exotic curved long blade with a jagged upper edge and judging by his reluctance to attack, this is probably his first time in the pits. The young fighter rushes Galas. His jagged edged sword is easily parried, leaving him wide open to a thundering blow from the hilt of Galas' sword. Instead of finishing the job, Galas leaves the young man prone and unconscious on the ground.

Out of the corner of his eye he spots his hawk attack the back of a muscular fighter; Phaelesian, a desert dweller of bronze complexion. He brandishes a kind of spear, but heavier, with a spiked metal ball at one end. Bael can see the older warrior has Galas' back and with the help of his hawk their attacker will be dispatched of quite readily. He isn't wrong, the man's face arcs through the air, passing by Galas' right shoulder, having been separated cleanly from the fighter's head.

This distraction is just what the beast master is waiting for, he unleashes his frenzied pets, poison saliva foaming from their gaping jaws. Galas is quick but the hawk is quicker: it hits the lead Grawl with the speed of an arrow, ripping out one of its eyes. The creature screeches in agonizing pain, shaking its head, blood spraying from a ruined socket. Disoriented, the beast careers into its partner forcing the animal out of Galas' path; this is all the time he needs to turn and decapitate the injured creature, sending its head spinning across the sand. But the other Grawl is incredibly agile, and before the young warrior can finish the job, the beast passes him to attack his father. The old warrior is slow to react, the Grawl rips half of his left calf muscle away, coating the open wound with its deadly venom. Joren drops on one knee and vomits into the air; the hawk hits the beast on the back of its neck, but too late. The Grawl clamps its jaws around the warrior's throat, shaking its head savagely. For a moment, the warrior's body convulses, then it stops as his head lolls grotesquely to one side. Galas screams out." No, oo!" and leaps at the creature. But its agility is frightening, it spins on the spot dodging his blade with ease. Galas rolls across the sand, blooded fangs missing his face by inches. He gets to his feet but the beast is on him, knocking the air from his lungs it pins him to the ground. Galas drops his sword and grabs the Grawl by the throat, struggling to prevent the creature from biting his face off. But it is too strong. Its razor-sharp claws dig deeply into his shoulders forcing him to loosen his grip. Poison saliva falls from its mouth onto his forearm, it burns like acid. Galas wrestles to hold its gnashing teeth inches from his neck, just when all seems lost the hawk dives onto its face ripping frantically to save its master. Galas' hand searches the sand for his sword, his fingers touch the cold hilt, he grips hold of it and rams it repeatedly into the Grawl's head. The animal's blood covers him as it drops dead on top of him. Though badly wounded from its claws, he manages to push himself from under it. As he stands, a hand grabs hold of his ankle, he looks down to see the Altaerian coughing blood in his last moments. Galas topples headlong into the sand; behind he hears the Beast Master scream in rage at the death of his monstrous pets. Pulling two daggers from his belt, dripping with the same poison that inhabited the Grawls mouths, he leaps at Galas. The young warrior cuts off the hand gripping him and turns just in time to see a jagged edged blade punch through his attacker's chest. The Beast Master drops to his knees, a look of horror, frozen, as the blade slowly withdraws. Towering above him is the young fighter Galas spared earlier in the fight. The crowd go wild. Slowly Galas squares up to the young fighter. It is a moment of uncertainty; neither man moves until the young warrior drops his sword. Without uttering a word Galas takes hold of his hand raising it into the air. Both men turn a full circle to acknowledge the crowd, then Galas lets go of his opponent's hand and walks to within earshot of the Royal Parapet. The bloated Emperor stands, puts up his hand to hush the crowd. Then through the silence that follows he bellows.

"You have earned your freedom this day, and by right of combat I must grant you one request...What would you wish of me?"

Galas looks over at his father's corpse with a lump in his throat.

"I would have my father buried with the honours that befit a champion."

For a moment, the Emperor ponders the request.

"Then he shall have it," he replies with obvious reluctance. "But what are we to do with you?" he shouts, pointing to the young fighter with the jagged edged sword. The crowd are quick to react shouting, "Live, live, live."

There is a blinding light. Bael once again finds himself outside the stone dwelling, where the black Dire Wolf left the babe. The snows have melted, the sun is right above for what appears to be a summer's day, yet

Bael feels no heat, nor the gentle breeze that dances through the leaves of the Red Maple tree at the front of the cottage. Again, he experiences an odd sense of familiarity, he feels he has been to this place before. But when? Why?

Off to his right he hears the sound of a child's laughter. A short distance along a narrow path, a boy of about ten appears from behind a large rocky prominence, chased by a feisty young Elk hound. Following not far behind is the man who took the babe in after the wolf left it by the door. Bael watches intently as they get closer to him, neither aware of his ghostly presence. The boy grabs the dog around the neck and wrestles it to the ground. It pulls itself free, putting its full weight on the lad's shoulders, pinning him down it licks his face playfully. Bael begins to float closer to within six paces from the group. As the boy's protector gets closer, he whistles. The hound jumps off the lad and in two bounds leaps into the man's arms hitting him in the chest, almost knocking him off his feet.

"Alright boy, calm down," he says, dropping the animal on the path. "Galas the fun is over, time to practice," he indicates, sliding the curved sword from his back scabbard. The boy stands and stumbles forward, his foot catching on a large stone half buried in the ground. As he straightens up a disc shaped rune stone swings out from his open shirt. Bael stares in amazement.

There is a blinding light.

Now Bael finds himself in a place of tranquil beauty. He sees the face of an Elven woman. She is mesmerizingly beautiful, her cheekbones bathed in the restless light of a full moon, her forehead drenched by the same silver glow; her eyes turquoise wells of yearning. Tiny lines etch her mouth, her smile welcoming, her arms outstretched beckoning him to follow, as she drifts back like a ghost lost in time towards a building shaped like a wolf's head. Then it registers; she can see him.

This time Bael wakes from his troubled sleep to find himself lying in the pen outside, his head resting against the side of the Wolf. It was still dark, so he stood up and entered the house. He stripped from his soiled clothes and jumped onto his bed; still weary and tired it wasn't long before he fell back into a dreamless sleep; the disc shaped black medallion around his neck clear to see.

14
ALONG THE EMPEROR ROAD

It was well known amongst the ranks that Fraene Caulder came from a long line of military brats. He had two older brothers who served and died in the northern wars and a younger one whose life ended during a training exercise, his throat closing from the sting of a cotton fly ending three years of martial training without ever seeing real combat. But it was his father who had left him with an indelible reminder of what it took to be a true man, qualities he never forgot, but ones he would never embrace.

Jon Caulder was a General in the King's finest for many years, hated by officer and soldier alike; fortunately, he was no longer around to enforce his rigid beliefs on either his men or his family. It turned out that this fine upstanding example of moral integrity, died of some syphilitic variant after distributing his seed into as many harlots as would have him. And there were many; for he had been a handsome man and in uniform quite the dashing young officer. A quality Fraene was glad he had *not* inherited, for in truth he was his father's nemesis; conducting himself with honour and living his life to a code of his own making.

What the General did to his mother was unforgivable and his hatred for the old man had never wavered. He watched her die a slow agonizing death, wasting away from the same debilitating disease that feasted so unforgivingly on his father's brain; a degenerative gift, for the rare occasion he took to her bed when not rutting in the gutter with the trash.

There was this one time he remembers, whilst serving as a simple archer under the General's command: The old man gave him every shitty task he could think of and then some, but Fraene was not going to allow the evil bastard the pleasure of breaking him.

They were hunting down a small army of bandits led by a savage named Gorasalai, which in common tongue translated to Bringer of Death. He and his cutthroats were pillaging every town and village in their path with no allegiance to anyone but themselves. There was a moment on the plains of Dead Man's Reach that his hatred for his father had never burned so brightly. All but a few of the bandits had been killed or captured; ahead the General bellowed his final orders.

"Leave none alive, take all their weapons and anything else of worth. This scum deserves no better. Leave them to the carrion, a feast for the rats and crows. Then let us get out of here, I tire of this shit hole."

There are a few like Fraene who let the chaos wash over them, there was no honour in robbing the dead no matter who they were; again, it was a stark reminder of the brutality he had suffered as a child at the hands of such a sadistic task master. He could never understand how someone as gentle and fair minded as his mother could love such a man, but she did and that was possibly the one reason the old tyrant still drew breath.

Now less than thirty feet away the General afforded him a rare opportunity to settle all debts; Fraene nocked an arrow he picked from a bandit's quiver and lifted his bow, it would be so easy to end this now, he thought; a chance shot from a fleeing bandit. No-one would be any the wiser. Instead, he let the arrow fall to the ground; something told him fate had other plans for the wicked old man. But had he known that fate held the same surprise for his mother, the arrow would have surely found its mark. That was then…. Now….

Fraene Caulder sensed the heightened spirits of the men as he wandered through the centre of the camp. Whether it was because they were only three days from Farroth Keep or the infamous whore house he and his men had heard so much about, it didn't matter: he was glad to see the morale of the King's own guard lifted so. It had been a long march from the capital, longer than any of them had expected, and the heavy rain hadn't helped, making their armour almost unbearable to wear. Added to this, food was in short supply and as all fighting men knew, an army marched on its belly: the thought reminded him of a statement his father once made when introducing him to the one person in the world his father could call friend; Brelt a military cook, who sadly still worked for the King.

"*A hungry army is an unhappy army my son, and no matter what loyalties a King's purse can buy, a soldier with an empty belly will never realize his full potential.*"

He remembered the coldness in his father's voice as if he were speaking to a complete stranger and not a son he should love.

On his way to the Royal tent, he passed by one that was only second in size to the King's. Through an open flap he spotted Prince Selaas Graegor, the chosen suitor for the daughter of the King's brother. He was a pallid, insipid young man who walked with rather an effeminate gate. He was heir to the reigning Queen of the Western Isles; a subtropical archipelago, renowned for its rich mineral deposits and the inhumane mines that supplied her treasury with a wealth almost unmatched anywhere across the Kingdoms. Not only this, she was also blessed with one of the most notorious armies that money could buy. A mercenary army trained from birth to do one thing; kill-with such efficiency the very utterance of their name put fear into the hearts of any who were unfortunate enough to face them in battle. Fraene knew his King well enough to see, the driving force behind this most unlikely of unions was the huge dowry that such an alliance would bring to his own coffers. The army of elite warriors was a welcomed bonus should all go as planned. But Fraene had heard rumours about this Cailean, a feisty, head strong woman they said. And by all accounts what he had seen of this Selaas Graegor, it was going to be no easy task pairing such contrasting opposites together. Thankfully that was not to be a problem he would have to deal with.

As he trudged through the mud most of the men he passed gave him a friendly nod of recognition and respect. He had shot up the ranks quicker than any before him, now he was Commander in chief of the King's elite guard and nothing like his father. There would always be some amongst the ranks, who didn't like his methods, but they were few and he paid them no heed.

King Agramar Farroth loved his food, his ever-expanding waistline testament to his culinary over indulgence. He tried to surround himself with as many home luxuries as was logistically possible, filling his tent with fineries more befitting the rooms of a castle. The smell of fresh roast pig and scented Jasmine oil kept the smell of piss and shit from the mud outside at bay. The soldiers were told to relieve themselves as far from the camp as possible. But with the pouring rain there were a few who just stood behind their tents and did what they must.

Brelt the old cook was busy slicing the pork when the door flaps of the tent flew open. There was no mistaking the person silhouetted against the shaft of bright sunlight that broke through the grey rain cloud outside.

For a moment, the King thought it was the young General himself stepping into the tent, Fraene being so much like his father in stature. Brelt grumbled under his breath but continued to cut; he'd never had a fondness for the Commander, thinking him soft hearted and nothing like his old friend.

Agramar felt the tension in the room every time these two were together, but he chose to ignore it; he liked to be around the General's son there was something calming about him: and the cook? Well, he was the best damned cook he had ever employed, and in a fight, you would want him by your side.

"Ah! My young commander. Please…. Join me," Agramar said handing Fraene a goblet of fine wine.

"My Lord."

"So, what brings you to my tent on this wet, miserable day?" The King asked, to a background of mumbled obscenities.

"Sire we…."

"Forgive me," the King interrupted. Scowling, he turned to face the cook. "Leave us I wish to speak with the Commander alone."

Brelt stopped slicing the meat and left it by the side of the large platter.

"Would you like the food served now Sire?" He asked in a voice as rough as gravel.

"No, I am sure we can look after ourselves, so please," he indicated, pointing to the tent entrance.

The cook and his two young serving squires gave a quick bow and left the tent, the cook moaning every step of the way.

"He really likes you, doesn't he?"

"It seems that way my Lord."

"I believe a whore faking pleasure would moan less than that miserable old bastard," the King said with a wry smile. "I swear if that man had nothing to grumble about he would think the world was coming to an end.... What is it with you two anyway? I have never understood how he could hate the son of his best friend so."

Fraene couldn't give him an answer for he too had no idea why.

"Maybe I just don't smell right. Who knows," he replied with cold indifference.

"I have never met a man who can stretch a few rangy rabbits and a bucket of potatoes as far as he can, and make them into some semblance of a meal. And that meat cleaver of his, well let's just say it split many a man's skull when the battle blood is up and you are in the thick of it. So-I suppose I have learned to ignore his ranting's, otherwise I fear his head would have decorated a pike long before now.... But I ramble, please help yourself to the food and tell me what bothers you."

Fraene filled a metal plate with two thick slices of spiced pork.

"Can I get you something my Lord?"

"I am fine for the moment," he replied sipping some more wine. "So, pray continue."

Fraene swigged down a chunk of half eaten pork that had burned the roof of his mouth and coughed to clear his throat.

"We are a week's march at most from your brother's keep. I think it would be prudent to send out scouts my Lord; check the road ahead...Just a precaution."

"You worry too much my friend. Can we not sit here, fill our bellies, drink our wine and think of the wives we have left at home, lying alone absent a husband's touch?"

"That may work for you my Lord. Unfortunately, I am not married." He smiled.

"A fine figure of a man like you should be," the King replied, consciously trying not to stare at the young man's face. In truth, the King had always envied Fraene his lean whip like physique. At six feet two inches the young Commander carried his armour with a grace very few could match. His jet-black shoulder length hair only partly covered a large disfiguring plum coloured birth mark which stretched from his shoulder blade to cover most of the left side of his face. He tried to cover it by growing a beard but for reasons unknown, hair would not grow on that side of his face. The King believed that was the reason why Fraene's father had given his son such a hard time. On numerous occasions, he had overheard his General talking to the cook after drink had loosened his tongue, saying the birthmark was a curse for his own infidelity; as if he was the one baring the disfigurement. And as tough a man as he was himself, the King was touched by the young man's plight.

"Come on spit it out. I can see you will not rest 'till you do so."

"Sorry my Lord, I do not wish to cause unnecessary concern…. It's…Just. The other day sire, when we passed that caravan of merchants along the road."

"Yes, I remember, I saw you talking to one of them, one of those olive skinned Phaelesians if I am not mistaken?"

"That is correct sire…Well- he told me he had heard stories of raiders attacking farmsteads across the region."

"But that was two days' past, why the concern now?"

"This very day sire, before entering your tent, I was in conversation with a messenger from one of the outlying villages. He was passing through camp on his way to your brother's keep. He told me a rider came to his village less than a week past, the man was mortally wounded. The healers did their best to keep him alive but he was too weak from the ride and died a day later. Before he journeyed to the afterlife, he ranted about the massacre of everyone in his village. He kept repeating the same words before he drew his last breath. Daemons, black demons. They take no-one alive."

"Daemons. What does he mean?"

"I have no idea sire, but this messenger said he had heard stories of such massacres stretching from as far away as the Eastern Coast to the Apolesian Tundra; but like his fellow villagers he thought they were exaggerated rumour. Until now."

"It could just be the ramblings of a broken mind," the King said uncertainly.

"It could be just that. But if it is true, whatever these daemons are, they are headed this way."

"I believe daemons are for the superstitious, I think it more likely raiders, and they are still far from here. But if it helps you sleep at night, send out a dozen riders to cover our flanks and another dozen to scout ahead and behind."

"Yes sire," he said, a little easier.

Fraene finished his wine and bit into a large slice of fresh pineapple. The King picked at a small bunch of grapes having left a plate full of half eaten pork; his appetite dulled somewhat by the conversation.

"Now, onto other matters. How is that milk sop Selaas? Has he stopped puking his guts up yet?"

"I believe he has sire. I'm not sure the food agrees with his delicate stomach."

"Now isn't that just a terrible inconvenience…. He is his father's son alright, but his mother. Now there's a woman. Since the death of her husband she has proved to be quite the resourceful leader. No beauty I fear, but quite the resourceful woman, and not one to suffer fools lightly. It's hard to believe she spawned such a weakling, but he is her only son and unfortunately Cailean is the only daughter in a family cursed with sons."

Fraene smiled in agreement. No comment was necessary, for as much as the King looked upon him with favour his personal opinion on such matters would be deemed inappropriate.

"What do you think about this union I propose between my niece and this...? Bah! It is such a pity. But one must do what has to be done."

"It is not my place to say sire."

"Of course, it is. By the Gods man speak, give me an honest opinion."

Fraene walked over to the tent entrance and looked to the skies as the heavens opened and the rain began to fall.

"I hear your niece has grown into a beauty? And by all accounts, headstrong and fearless."

"It would seem, you feel my future nephew unworthy of such a prize?"

"No sire I...."

"I jest. Please, we both know the man's a fool," the King said reluctantly. "So, pray continue."

"From what I have seen of this Prince Graegor, convincing your niece to marry him will be no easy task. What if she refuses to take his hand?"

The King frowned at the unexpectedly frank question.

"There is no question here of choice my good friend," his reply prickly to say the least. Agramar could see his tone had made his commander uncomfortable, so he tried to relax the tension in the room by filling both goblets with more wine.

"Here, drink this," he said handing Fraene the drink. "I have asked myself the very same questions more times than I can count. I love my niece, but sadly gold reserves are all but depleted, my Council of Auditors advise me against further tax increases and this fool's mother sits on the richest throne in all the kingdoms. So, you see my dilemma. I have no heir as yet myself, the rest of my kin have been cursed to bare sons only, except my brother. And he knows my needs are dire, for a bankrupt King is no King at all. And this must not happen. It will not happen. So, you see, as much as I pursue this venture of ours with heavy heart, it cannot fail."

Fraene finished his drink. Surprised by the King's candid and revealing comments, he struggled to reply. In the ten years, he has been Agramar's first protector, he knew there would be no changing the man's mind. His leader was a brilliant military tactician, on the surface he could appear amiable and understanding, while in reality he was driven, highly intelligent and ruled with a rod of iron. Never a man to be underestimated.

"Though I can't pretend to understand the financing of a kingdom, I had no idea things were that bad?

"It wouldn't have been this critical had it not been for the particularly harsh winter we suffered these past two years. Our biggest trade with surrounding regions has always been our Olives from the south, our wheat and corn from the east and our timber from the forests to the west. The income from such products is crucial to balancing the treasury books. But as we all know, money coming in from supplying such goods has all but dried up. A strange black blight has attacked our forests and severe winter storms have decimated crops. So much so that we have had to buy in grain from foreign lands even from pirates as unsavoury as that might be. Otherwise, we would have a starving population to contend with, and anyone with any sense knows what that can bring?"

Fraene finished his wine and stood ready to leave.

"Well sire if it pleases you, I must get along and organize the scouting parties.... I am sure all will go well when we reach your brother's keep," he said hiding his reservations about the latter.

As he turned to leave, Omaar the burly quartermaster entered the tent. He was a heavily built man, nearly as broad as he was tall. In the low light of the interior he was quite a frightening visage. The men called him *old smiley:* during a raid against Solician mercenaries, a dull blade caught him in the mouth cutting upward in an arc that after stitching left him with a grotesque extended smile. In fact, his body was covered in scars from wounds that would have killed most people, and as ugly as he was the men looked at him as a lucky charm having cheated death as many times as he had.

The man lumbered over to the King.

"Sire we have a problem…. Supplies are running low. I believe there is a village not far from here; it should take less than a day to return by horse and cart. I can buy fresh meat and grain from the farmers, who I hear have had a better than normal yield this year," he said, almost spitting the words from his disfigured mouth.

"That is a good idea. Take a dozen men with you and the cook, you may need him to butcher some livestock, and he can advise on the best produce.... Speak with Brabien my treasury Maester in the next tent. He will supply you with the coin you need."

"Thank you sire I will."

"Good. Now I am tired. Both of you have duties to perform so if you don't mind I would like some time alone."

Both Omaar and Fraene excused themselves and left the tent. The mud outside was ankle deep and the rain relentless. Before heading off to organize the scouting parties Fraene addressed the quartermaster who he respected more than any other man in the army.

"Be careful out there. I have heard rumours that slavers are afoot."

"Don't worry my young friend, a few scurvy ridden fuckers don't frighten me none, and that's for sure."

"I know. But just take care all the same, there are strange things going on in these parts, things that should worry any sane man."

"So, being a mad bastard helps then, aye?" he smiled, grotesquely.

Fraene slapped the man on his huge shoulder, then both parted company.

The Captain gathered up the men he wanted for the expedition, the last being Gelac, a young man who over the past year had caught his eye. He saw in the young man, qualities he too possessed at that age; driven but fair minded, showing early signs of the skills required for good leadership. Fraene had made it his personal mission to take Gelac under his wing, and make sure these qualities weren't snuffed out by the less mindful of the other commanders.

Walking over to the campfire close to Fraene's tent, both men sat on a large log dragged there as a make shift seat. Gelac watched his Captain, there was weight in his gaze, penetrating eyes that had a mature depth behind them. The young warrior had a deep respect for Fraene and would literally follow him into the jaws of death should he so order. "You look troubled sur."

"It is nothing my friend. It's just; sometimes I have to question why we do what we do. Nothing more sinister than that," he pondered.

The young soldier could see his Captain was troubled, more than he was prepared to admit. In the relatively short time he had been under his command, he had never met a man who lived his life with an honour and integrity that was almost impossible to find in times such as these.

"There is a story that sometimes comes to mind on nights like this," the Captain reflected, staring at the young man he admired and cared for, like so many young soldiers whose names were forgotten in memorium. "I knew a woman once; she was the most intelligent person I had ever met. She married a man who saw such intelligence to be a threat. And so, whenever they were in the company of their peers, he took great delight in belittling her; making her feel foolish, and feeble. And try as he did to smother such wisdom with ridicule and infidelity, he could not break her spirit. In his many absences, she found strength in passing on her knowledge to the four sons she loved above all else. Sadly, three of those children no longer walk amongst the living, but the one who survived lives by a code that was born of love and respect for the woman he called mother…. She once told me, *War is a terrible thing. It feeds on itself, for the sake of greed and power. Young men, just like yourself serve believing they fight for honour; a naivety the instigators of such wars like to propagate. Wars are the food on which old men feed, men who would see the young pay with their lives, all in the name of arrogance.* Words that haunt me every time I lay witness to another pointless death. How ironic then that such a wonderful woman should marry a warmonger and spawn four sons to follow in his footsteps. I have seen soldiers, little more than boys watch as their friends are disembowelled or worse, turn into mindless killers they would normally abhor. Blood, piss and shit are the perfume of the battle field. A smell that will never abandon you, no matter how hard you may try to shake it."

"Then why do you fight in these wars and put yourself through such torment, when you so clearly hate them?" Gelac asked.

Fraene stared at the ground by his feet.

"I do it to save as many of those *boys* as I can, and I believe our King, for all his flaws, is, at his core an honourable leader, given the unsettling times we live in."

The Captain stood up, patted Gelac reassuringly on the shoulder and said.

"Tomorrow, stay close to Omaar. Be observant as I know you can be, and don't be afraid to speak your mind. I feel we are about to embark along a path that will pit us against an enemy we have yet to face."

With that Fraene left for the welcome confines of his tent.

***

The wheels of the supply wagon creaked and groaned as Omaar led his group along the stony farm track. The only other sound to break the eerie silence was that of the horses snorting nervously, their hooves clip clopping on the travel worn rocks embedded in the path. The quartermaster spurred his mount forward passing the cook, who was already pulling on the reins trying to control the two spooked horses pulling the wagon. Omaar grabbed the bit of the stronger of the two horses and pulled back hard.

"Whoa! Whoa there."

All came to a halt. It was a small holding, having only three fields a farmhouse and a barn. Omaar and his men looked around them finding it hard to accept what they were seeing.

One of the fields where there should have been a fresh harvest of corn ready for picking, there was only charred stalks protruding through lingering wisps of smoke like the landscape from some nightmarish netherworld. The next field was littered with the dead carcasses of cattle in various stages of mutilation. Some looked as if they were partly eaten; others killed more for the sport, their bodies like grotesque porcupines peppered with black arrows. Not a word passed between the men as Omaar waved them forward towards the farmhouse. First to draw his sword, he leaned forward slightly, ready for what they might encounter.

The last field before they reached the house was also littered with slaughtered livestock. Sheep, goats and several geese lay strewn around a pond, its water like a gaping wound, red with blood. The group reached the barn first. Brelt pulled the wagon to a stop and jumped down from the seat, meat cleaver in hand. Omaar and the rest dismounted ready for the worst.

"Spread out, you three follow me. You two stay with the horses," he said pointing to the youngest of his group. "The rest go with cook, look 'round the farmhouse."

Omaar could sense the strange unease in his men, all had seen battle many times and atrocities which go with that, but this kind of pointless slaughter was pure savagery. As he led his men to the open barn door, he couldn't help thinking how odd it was that amongst all this wanton carnage there was the sweet smell of cooked corn, which on any other occasion would see his mouth water.

Swords drawn they entered the darkness. Suddenly, screeching for all they were worth, two small piglets scurried past the four men, zig zagging frantically into the yard. Omaar was the only one not rattled; the other three looked at each other shocked by the sudden break of silence.

"Well at least something has survived," he said in a commanding voice, trying to calm the nerves.

After a few minutes, it was obvious the barn was empty, so Omaar led his men into the yard. Brelt and his group came out of the farm house holding the two piglets by their back feet. He walked over to Omaar who was standing by the wagon.

"The house is empty."

"The barn too," Omaar replied. "Who ever lived here must have escaped to the village, there are no horses in the barn and none are amongst the dead. Just to be sure, go and check the fields, make sure we missed nothing," he ordered pointing to the men behind the cook.

"Whilst they are doing that I will prepare these little beauties," Brelt said, handing one of them to the youngest member of group guarding the horses. Then with the skill of a butcher he drew his knife and slit the beasts throat letting it bleed out onto the stony ground. Without hesitation, he took the other off the guard and did the same.

"There. Got you, you little bastards," he said hanging the limp bleeding bodies on the side of the wagon. Stepping around the back he pulled out a hessian sack.

"There are vegetables in the house, might as well find a use for them. I'm sure the owners wouldn't mind."

Omaar threw the cook a disapproving glance but said nothing. If by chance the farmer was at the village and still alive, he would pay whatever coin was owed; he was a hard man but never a thief.

"As soon as you are done we must move on to the village, gods only know what we will find there," he said to Brelt and the two men he was leading into the farmhouse.

***

Not a word passed between the men as they approached the outskirts of Stony Hollow. The same unnatural quiet that greeted Omaar and his group at the farmstead earlier couldn't have prepared them for what they were about to discover. Hardened veterans, all of them, yet none had witnessed the like. Ever.

15

THE FAIR-THE FIGHT-THE TREE-THE PLAN

The kiss of a warm summer breeze greeted the first of the crowds; early bird's eager to claim prime position at their favourite venue. Tents and stalls of every shape and size littered the shore of the lake, stretching from the bridge by the Keep, to the forest almost a league away. People arrived from far and wide, some by invite, others eager to see for themselves the spectacle that Lord Farroth had become so famous for staging. Even before the sun peaked over the horizon, exhibiters and merchants alike had begun to stock their shelves. Carpenters, weavers, jewellers and toymakers; clothiers, shoemakers, herbalists, sculptors of stone and wood, all busy as a nest full of bees in preparation for a day of spectacle and frivolity.

Unfortunately, such occasions offered easy pickings for every thief and scoundrel brave enough to risk capture, and Beggars Nest was full of them. As usual Maccon was tasked with organising security. Extra town's guard patrolled the streets, making sure empty households weren't burgled, whilst some of the Keep's guard dressed in plain clothes mingled amongst the crowds. Meanwhile Maccon busied himself with preparations for the day's events, making sure everything was ready. He gave Garrus, an efficient but rather surly member of the Order the responsibility of overseeing the smooth running of the barge that was to take Lord Farroth and family to the fair via the lake. The various other duties he allocated to the rest of the Black Orchids.

Cirius knocked on the door and entered the room. Maccon tightened his sword belt and threw a long white cloak off his shoulder exposing his sword arm. He looked quite splendid in his finest chain mail, yet Cirius felt something was wrong.

"And what can I do for you my young Cirius?" Maccon asked.

"Sur, the barge is ready to take Lord and Lady Farroth to the fair whenever they wish to go."

"Good, I am just about to meet up with his Lordship. I will let him know," Maccon replied.

"Is everything alright Sur? You look troubled."

"I am fine. I have a few things on my mind, that's all."

"Is there anything I can do to help?" Cirius probed. He cared for his leader like a son would a father, and he knew very well that it was more than a *few things* that would see Maccon so subdued on such an auspicious day.

"Don't worry about me, enjoy the day for what it is. You have worked hard, you deserve to have a little fun in your life, whatever form that takes," he said with a warm smile.

"Thank you, Sur, I will.... One other thing if I may be so bold?"

"Go on spit it out."

"Miss Cailean, Sur? She has been confined to her room now two days' past. It would seem a little harsh if she were to miss today's events. Will Lord...?"

Maccon cut him short.

"That is no concern of yours, his Lordship has his reasons and who are we to question them?"

"I know how much you care for her; it must bother you...?"

"Whether it does or it doesn't, such concerns are mine and mine alone to ponder. Now go before I change my mind and have you cleaning out the stables," the old Priest said, noticing for the first time the look in Cirius' eyes at the mention of Cailean.

Cailean watched from her balcony as Cirius passed by the courtyard on his way to the jetty where the barge was moored. She turned her attention to the gates of the Temple in the distance; Maccon appeared to be staring at the youngest member of the Order as he disappeared into the dock area. Then his gaze fell upon her. She waved at him, but he didn't wave back. *He mustn't have seen me*, she thought, turning her attention now to the hustle and bustle of the fair goers milling around the shore of the lake.

The two days confined to her room had done little if anything to sate the anger she felt towards her father. Her mother had visited her several times during this period to little avail; she was in no mood for her parent's sanctimonious meanderings, which her mood so graphically confirmed. Jiney though was luckier. Her visits were welcomed by her friend, she was a good listener and the past few days had given her plenty to listen to: she was all too aware that when Cailean was angry; by the gods could she talk.

On the morning of the fair Jiney joined Cailean on the balcony. The pair of them stared across the lake as visitors arrived by cart, horse, donkey or foot to join the increasing numbers of townsfolk who were already seated or standing around their favourite areas. They could see quite a crowd was already gathered around an open compound closest to the Keep, where a local farmer was showing off his livestock, something he did every spring at the town's own farmers market. But a fair like this afforded him the rare opportunity to show off to a much larger and diverse audience: which on this occasion consisted mainly of women.

Word had got around about his prize possession, a black longhorn bull from Orania. A rare beast indeed, it was rumoured to be the largest bull in the land. So, large in fact he had trouble mating it with his local cows and it didn't take a vivid imagination to understand why. It was for this very reason that such a large female audience had gathered. There had been rumblings weeks before the fair about the bull with balls the size of coconuts, and the beast hadn't disappointed. Women young and old pointed, giggled, some flushing with exited embarrassment at what their eyes couldn't believe. A lot of the men folk left them to it, having seen the bull before at livestock shows, though for some men it was simply the feeling of inadequacy in the company of such a well-endowed specimen. It was all in good humour and this set the tone for the day.

Jiney watched Cailean as she scanned the crowds, there was only one person her mistress was looking for, as was she. But from what they could make out neither Hunter nor Raen had arrived yet. Cailean couldn't hide her disappointment.

"Jiney. You should go to the fair and enjoy yourself."

"I can't leave you here alone on such a day milady."

"I will be fine. I doubt my father would let me go anyway. Even before I was confined to this room. So please I insist, you must..."

Before she could finish, there was a knock on the door and her mother entered.

"Well, you two do look a pair of miseries," she said, trying to make light of the situation.

The comment was greeted with a mixed response; Jiney smiled courteously, Cailean stood stony faced and unimpressed.

"I am not in the mood mother."

"I know my love, but I come the barer of good tidings.... Your father has set up a stand by the jousting and archery, and I have persuaded him to let you join us this afternoon."

Cailean managed a half smile while Jiney beamed with agreement.

"Thank-you mother." Cailean said gratefully.

"Yes. But first promise me you will do nothing to antagonize your father? Leave all this unsavoriness behind you. I have been given strict instruction that you are to stay under the protection of Maccon and the Order at all times.... Promise me you understand?"

"I promise," she replied reluctantly.

"Good. Now get dressed into something cool and comfortable. It is going to be hot out there today."

**

Hunter would normally never partake of such festivities preferring to leave such celebration to those of a more sociable nature; but today would be an exception. During one of his nightly visitations Vena had expressed her desire to attend the Fair, something she herself had never done before. More surprising, she wanted Hunter to be her escort. Though caught off guard he felt it was the least he could do for the one person in the town who had been there for him unconditionally, whether paid for or not.

She met him at his lodge, a place she had only visited once before when he was too drunk to find his own way home. He was already waiting when she arrived, his Wolf by his side. Nervously she approached him, her eyes never leaving the Wolf. Though she knew of the beast, the knowledge hadn't prepared her for just how big it was.

"She won't harm you. Come stroke her."

Vena trusted in Hunter and did as he bade, surprised at how tame the animal appeared to be.

"It is magnificent," she said stroking the Wolf more confidently.

"Yes, she is."

Vena stopped stroking the beast and faced Bael.

"Do you think it wise to bring her to the fair?"

"She comes or I do not," he said coolly.

"I was only saying. Town's folk know about her, but strangers will find it odd, frightening, to see a Wolf this size, especially those with children."

Bael smiled.

"I will make sure she eats none of them, so please, do not concern yourself and let us go to this fair of yours."

***

The morning went without a hitch, the atmosphere amongst the crowd boisterous and full of merriment. Bards sang their songs and recited their poems as they mingled amongst the visitors. The smell of food permeated all around from spit roast boar, duck and pheasant cooked to perfection over open fires.

Dogran's tent was filling quickly; people spilling out onto the grass, drinking their favourite tipple, kept as cool as the weather would allow. The Tavern was closed for the day, both, he, Emma and a few friends made sure there was plenty in the tent to cater for most people's needs.

Koval wandered about for an hour or so trying with his wife to keep Raen occupied before the afternoon's main events. It was difficult, as Tyrna only seemed to be interested in the merchant stalls, where exotic spices, fruits, trinkets and many other items from faraway lands tempted the willing. Koval still hadn't told his wife about the fight he had entered with Dogran, so if wandering mindlessly around a few stalls kept her sweet, then so be it. Although, his son's face told a different story.

"Father, do we have to keep following ma from stall to stall. It is so boring," Raen grumbled. Or so his father deciphered, having a less than adequate understanding of his sign language.

"Just a little longer son, then we can make our way over to the fighters' compound," Koval said shaking his son's shoulder with his huge hand.

Raen reluctantly nodded his agreement. He left his mother and father at a hand-crafted Jewellery stall where Tyrna embarrassed Koval into buying her a filigree silver bracelet. He looked everywhere for any sign of Hunter, but mostly to see if the young woman from the woods was amongst the town's folk. Up until midday neither could be seen, to the lad's growing disappointment.

The melee tournaments weren't far off starting, the preliminaries in the archery had been decided and the finalists were about to compete. Now she sported the fine bracelet on her wrist Koval was finally able to drag Tyrna away from the stalls. He secured a place by the fence for the three of them to get a clear view of the finals.

"Whilst we are waiting, I'll just nip over to Dogran's tent. Say hello to the old goat."

"We will come with you," she replied looking at him suspiciously.

"No, you stay here; it wasn't easy securing this place. I will be back shortly."

"Make sure you are. I don't trust you two when you get together."

"I will," he replied shiftily. "You look after your mother son."

Raen wasn't impressed.

Dogran served Jered the baker a mug of his favourite ale, surprised that his old friend had somehow managed to lose his domineering wife.

"She's let you off the leash then?"

"Very witty, Dogran.... You should try living with the woman."

Dogran laughed out loud, a laugh so contagious it had all around him laughing as well, though they hadn't got a clue what they were laughing *at*.

"I couldn't resist old friend," he replied. "Anyway, where is the good lady?"

"You should have been a Jester. As for my wife." He smiled mischievously. "I left her talking with that Myra, you know the fishmonger's wife. I swear those two were forged from the same anvil."

Dogran looked to his friend and shook his head affectionately.

"Now, now, is that any way to speak about the love of your life? Anyway old friend enjoy your drink you deserve a break."

Meanwhile Emma was busy collecting empty mugs; she kept glancing to the entrance hoping to see Bael walk in. Instead, she saw Koval waving frantically at her father. Dogran checked to see if Emma was watching, then waved back. This was the signal for him to change into his leathers ready for the fist fighting competition that both he and Koval had entered many times before, when the opportunity presented itself. The prize on this occasion was a sizable purse, funded straight from the Farroth coffers. The last time they met, Dogran and Koval made the finals, much to the chagrin of Tyrna, and Emma was none too amused either. It was a brutal fight, but both men loved the battle more than the purse, unfortunately the battle saw Koval suffer a broken nose and Dogran a fractured little finger.

Emma knew what was going down the moment she spotted Koval waving, plus, in his other hand he carried a round bag, and it obviously held her father's fighting gear. She dropped a couple of mugs into the water trough, then quickly caught her father's attention.

"I know what you're up to father.... Please. Correct me if I am wrong, but did you not promise me there would be no fighting at this tourney?" She queried, deriving great pleasure from seeing him squirm.

"You can't deny your father one of his few pleasures in life. Now, can you my sweet?"

"My sweet, is it? How can knocking the seven bells out of each other be a pleasure?"

"Well maybe that was the wrong word.... Let us say indulgence then."

"If I am not mistaken, the last time you two faced one another, that old bull over there had his nose rearranged and you ended up with a broken hand."

"Finger."

"Finger? Hand? does it really matter?" Can't you both reminisce about your days in the militia in a less brutal way?"

"It's just our way my love."

She was wasting her breath, but she enjoyed the friendly banter with her gentle giant and could not begrudge him his eccentricity no matter how difficult to understand.

"You go father…We have everything in hand."

"Thank you my sweet," he replied kissing her on the forehead.

"I will be over to watch you both later…But please. Please be careful. Neither of you are the sprightly chickens you once were."

"You worry too much but I love you for it."

Jered couldn't help overhearing the conversation, he truly cared for the inn keep and his daughter and would see no harm come to either of them.

"Listen to your daughter, you old fool. At your age, bones break and cuts don't heal so quickly. And she's right; you are no longer a spring chicken."

Like some lumbering child, he slapped his friend on the shoulder and made his way over to Koval clucking like a demented chicken.

It was just past midday. Lord Farroth's barge approached the long wooden jetty close to the rear of the main jousting area. It was a boat of purpose; nothing fancy, it did its job efficiently with the help of ten strapping oarsmen. The Royal party sat on a raised platform at the rear of the vessel, surrounded by Maccon and six of the Order. The rest of the warrior priests sat in between the rowers.

Lord Farroth loved the privileges his position offered him and his family, the barge just one of the few examples he felt set him apart from his people. A social division he endlessly reminded his family of, especially Cailean. *There are the likes of us and there are the likes of them and neither the two shall mix*, he would say. *Treat them fairly but firmly and they will respect you for it.* It's fair to say he did both but not in equal measure. Many felt his punishment for certain indiscretions to be more than a little severe. But as the boat eased its way alongside the jetty he was confident the day's events would more than satisfy his people.

Unobserved, Raen climbed a tree by the water's edge to get a clear view as the Farroth entourage stepped ashore. He was extra vigilante, recognizing faces of some of the town guard commissioned to police the event as they mingled with the crowd not far from where he hid. High in the tree he lay along a thick branch to avoid detection. Jiney was offered a helping hand by Cirius. As she stepped onto the jetty her ankle gave way causing her to stumble forward. Instinctively Raen dropped his arm to catch her, an involuntary action that almost unseated him from the branch he lay on. He slipped to the side ending up holding on for dear life underneath it. Luckily no one below saw or heard him; he righted himself just in time to see Cirius supporting Jiney on his outstretched arm. Raen felt a pang of jealousy as he watched her smile at the warrior priest, her face pink with embarrassment. It was a moment of chivalry he wished was his, especially as he was not the recipient of such an engaging smile.

Maccon led the group along the board walk to the Royal stand, surrounded on both sides by townsfolk waving and cheering. Before being seated Cailean and Jiney looked amongst the spectators, but still neither could see who they were looking for.

Raen climbed stealthily down the tree and made his way around the far end of the jousting area on his way to watch his father fight. As he passed in clear view of the stand, Jiney spotted him, her stomach turning with excitement. For a moment, it looked as if he was going to wave at her, but he didn't; she too wanted to wave, but she knew it would be deemed improper. Cailean noticed the secret altercation between her friend and the young smithy and placed her hand on Jiney's giving it a reassuring squeeze.

Lord Farroth stood up and addressed the crowd opening the main contests of the day. Before the jousting tournament, half a dozen horse archers with short bows demonstrated their prowess by riding at full gallop towards straw filled dummies whose heads were the target. It was the first of a few warm up acts where various weapon masters showed off their marshal skills. Usually at this point Lord Farroth would wander off on his own to watch the fist fighting, his own personal favourite. But on this occasion Alloria had persuaded him to stay by her side. She always deemed the fist fights barbaric and too lowly for someone of her husband's standing to patronize. Normally he ignored her request on the matter, but he had caused enough upset in his family for one week, so he grudgingly reneged.

Emma removed her apron and asked her friends to cover for her. She made her way to the fight pen, passing by the archery contest to the cheer of the crowd as the winner, a young farm hand put his last arrow through the eye of the target. She arrived at the compound just before the last fight of the knock out stages was about to begin. She spotted Raen and his mother by the fence in an area reserved for family and friends. She weaved her way through the growing crowd until she reached Tyrna.

"Am I too late? Have father and Koval fought yet? She asked Tyrna, who didn't look at all impressed.

"Your father is through to the finals and that fool of a husband of mine is about to fight to see who will face him."

Emma could see the concern on Tyrna's face, when she saw who Koval was about to fight she understood why. They called him the Bear. Not a pretty sight, he bore his scars like a badge; half an ear bitten off by a desperate opponent who drew his final breath during an exhibition fight in the Capital. A nose, flat and shapeless, hardly bone or gristle left in it and scars from stitched old wounds, all a visual testament to a punished face. Yet a face unbeaten. This was a very hard man indeed; whose fights lacked any kind of finesse other than brutal strength and a savage will to win no matter what the cost. A fact witnessed by the crowd when he left his first opponent with a jaw so badly smashed he would be sucking liquids through a length of hollowed out bamboo for weeks to come. And a second with a broken arm as the northerner grabbed him in a bone breaking clinch whist pummelling his face into a bloody mess with his other fist. Even Emma's father looked concerned about his friend's safety, but Dogran Knew all too well there was no turning back; the fight would have to reach its inevitable conclusion, whatever that may be. Emma waved at the three of them but stayed with Tyrna, both aware this was the time for men where women played no part other than stand in the side-lines to watch and support as best they could. Emma offered Tyrna a slice of homemade pie from the tent which was accepted gratefully. Then a commotion across the compound drew both their attentions. When Emma saw who it was, her face hardened.

Hunter and Vena arrived via the lake to a plethora of whispers and disdainful looks as the crowd parted, making a clear path to the fence surrounding the fight pen. Vena realized the people were more upset about the Wolf being there than they were about a woman of her calling walking amongst them: though along the way she chose to ignore a few unfriendly comments from women whose husbands dropped their gaze guiltily as she passed.

"Well, we *have* caused a stir and that's for sure," she said to Hunter, who chose not to answer. "If only half of these women knew I had entertained their husbands one time or another, what would they say then, I wonder?"

Bael could see the look on many of the men's faces supported her comment and that she derived some kind of selfish pleasure from it. She held her head high in defiance as they passed through the parting crowd making sure she was one side of Hunter, the Wolf the other. Bael wasn't interested in any of the idle chit chat, he was here for two things only. The fights and to support a man he had great respect for, Dogran. On reaching the fence he leant his elbows on the top horizontal rail and stared across the compound. Raen was waving at him excitedly, his mother far too engrossed in what her husband was doing to take any notice and the burly in-keep just stared at them with indifferent curiosity: But Emma was a different story. First it was disbelief, it wasn't so much about the appearance of the Wolf as the fact that he could bring such a woman to an event like this without even considering whether she herself would like to go or not.

Even at this distance Bael could see her features redden and had the stare that followed been a dagger it would surely have pierced his heart. He nodded at her but she turned away as if not to see him. Vena sidled next to him her hip resting against his.

"It would seem someone is more than a little upset at our presence here today," she said looking in the direction of the barmaid. "My, my, who would have thought such a quiet, unassuming man like yourself would have so many admirers?"

Hunter ignored her comment; his attention was fixed on the corner where the Northern brute was having his hands wrapped in wool padded leather straps, the brainchild of the local tanner. He watched the fighter's second, bind his master's fists, which Bael knew was more for the protection of the fighter's knuckles than his opponents face. He could see Koval's hands were already bound and the big man was moving into the centre of the compound ready to face off with the Northerner. Bael turned his attention back to the brute; his second finished the binding and looked about him unable to hide his sheepishness. This gave Hunter room for concern, he respected Koval, not just as a man but as a good father to his son Raen, who was about to join him after running across the compound to the rumbles of a disapproving crowd.

"Should you not be back there with your mother, my friend? I think she could do with some sibling support," Hunter said, pleased to see his prodigy. Raen either didn't hear Hunter or chose to ignore the words; instead he dropped to his knees in-front of the Wolf and nuzzled into its massive neck. The beast responded by licking him across the face.

Vena was surprised at how fearless the lad was with the animal and how both seemed to love the company of the other. Bael turned and smiled at the lad, but this was not enough. Raen stood up as if to hug his friend and mentor, but Hunter turned back to watch the fight. Vena could see the lad's disappointment and moved close to the Wolf, bravely stroking its head.

"You must be Raen?"

He nodded-yes then bowed slightly. It really touched Vena to see this handsome young man treat her with such unexpected courtesy.

"It's nice to meet you Raen; I have heard many good things about you. Even if this oaf of a man won't admit it," she said prodding Bael in the back with her finger.

Raen's face lit up. He wasn't used to the compliments of women especially one he found so attractive, in a worldly sense of the word. His face reddened slightly, and pleasantly embarrassed he turned away to watch the fight. Vena touched by the lad's innocence turned to join them, and though this was not her venue of choice she was just glad to be there.

The two fighters faced one another in the centre of the compound. Koval was starting the fight with a swelling under his left eye whilst his opponent only had a few superficial bruises on his chiselled cheekbones. The referee looked at them both.

"You know the rules. No rounds. You fight 'till one of yer drops."

The Northerner couldn't keep still; wild eyed he banged his fists together and growled within inches of Koval's face. The Smithy ignored the taunt and pushed his opponent back. The referee backed away quickly as a flurry of punches from both fighters started the fight. Blow for blow there wasn't much in it, though the swelling under Koval's eye was beginning to bleed a little, Dogran didn't give it too much thought as his friend had suffered far worse and won. Tyrna on the other hand had to turn away as her husband absorbed blow after blow to his kidneys. Emma joined her father, concerned about his friend.

"I don't like this," she said to him. "Koval is taking too many punches. This brute of a man is dangerous."

"Koval will be fine… Keep Tyrna company she needs comforting. Leave this to me, I promise if I think my friend is in any danger I will stop the fight myself."

Emma wasn't stupid, she could see the uncertainty in her father's eyes, but she trusted him and did as he asked.

Fights like this were usually over pretty quickly if not from a knock out, one or both would succumb to exhaustion. Koval moved around the compound blocking several blows to his face, then leaving his head exposed he drew his opponent into throwing a punch that he was able to dodge with ease. This left the brute open to a thundering uppercut to the jaw that rocked him where he stood.

Bael had seen fighters like this Northerner before; in the Nest. Thugs, capable of taking extreme punishment as if their bodies felt no pain, backed up with fighting skills as raw as they were barbarous. He watched the fight with an intensity shared by very few. He could see there was more skill to Koval's way of fighting, blow after blow glancing almost harmlessly off elbow and forearm. But when the thundering uppercut smashed into the Northerner's jaw, Hunter saw the fighter open the straps covering his knuckles as he backed away from Koval, desperately trying to shake off the dizziness. For a moment, it looked as though Koval would once again face his old friend in the final. Then his opponent hit him in the face with a combination of vicious punches that could have killed a lesser man, leaving the Smithy on his knees rubbing his eyes. Koval was quick to get his guard up, but something was wrong. Dogran could see his friend was in grave trouble and was about to stop the fight when Tyrna rushed across the sand covered ground, unfortunately not quick enough to stop a savage right hook that burst the swelling under Koval's eye in a spray of blood. The big man staggered backwards and fell to the ground. By this time Dogran had rushed to join Tyrna who had placed herself between her man and the brute.

"What kind of man lets his woman fight his battles," the beast from the north bellowed, turning to the crowd arms outstretched. Koval lay deathly still, then his eyes opened as he desperately tried to shake his head clear. He tried to stand up but his legs were shaky and without strength. Tyrna bent down and placed her hand under her husband's head.

He forced himself onto one elbow.

"Leave me be woman."

"Men!" She muttered, tears streaming down her cheeks.

Dogran was quick to intervene. He grabbed his friend under the waist and armpit and lifted him to his feet.

"I'll take it from here," he said, leading his friend over to where Emma waited with a healer.

During the obligatory rest period between fights, Bael chose to investigate the Northerner's tent. He left Vena and Raen to make their way over to where the lad's father was having the wound under his eye stitched. The Wolf followed him through the growing crowd to the water's edge. Bael could see she wanted to relieve herself and told her to *go,* pointing to the forest. The beast didn't need telling twice, she was away to the woods.

Standing on a small grassy knoll, he could see clearly the Northerner's tent below, the fighter and his aid still within. He waited patiently, until both figures re-appeared and left to return to the fight. Making sure no one saw him, Bael made for said tent and entered unseen. He gagged. The air that greeted him was thick with the stench of sweat and foul bodily odours blown or excreted from every orifice the previous two occupants possessed. These Northerners were known for their consumption of Arleisian red chillies, raw and uncooked the hotter the better leaving them with this never-ending need to evacuate their bowels of built-up gasses. Bael Quickly looked around the place not wishing to stay a moment longer than was necessary. As he suspected, he found a mulch of freshly ground chillies in a make shift mortar and pestle. Careful not to get any on his skin he picked the red mess up and headed back to the fighter's compound, not caring this time whether he was seen or not.

As he approached the area where Dogran and his friends were readying themselves for the upcoming fight he was careful not to let the Northerners see what he carried. Emma spotted him first, her face a picture of mild disdain. At first it looked like she was going to ignore him, but it seemed she thought better of it leaving her father's side to meet him. She could see he was holding something in his hands.

"Tell your father to watch the man's hands. He has smeared his knuckles with this," he said staring at the red mess.

At first, she wasn't sure what to say, the thoughtful concern for her father's wellbeing somewhat disarming. She tried to sound indifferent but couldn't.

"What is it?"

"Here. Be careful it is hot. If it touches your skin it will cause a rash," he said, carefully handing her the crushed chillies. "They are the very hottest of peppers, crushed for the juices the Northerner has rubbed on his bare knuckles. I have seen men in the Nest win fights this way."

"How would you know such a thing?" She queried, surprised by his knowledge of such barbaric practices.

"That matters not. Just show your father."

By this time Raen had spotted his friend and joined them both. It was obvious even to his inexperienced mind there was a tension between Hunter and Emma.

"Is your father alright?" Bael asked, showing genuine concern as the lad arrived.

Raen nodded yes, then looked to the red mess in Emma's hands.

"That is why your father's eyes burn with tears of fire," Bael continued.

Raen frowned angrily.

"I will show this to father, the fight is about to begin," Emma said. "Thank you for bringing this to his attention. I will speak with you...."

"Go, he must see this," Bael interrupted before she could finish.

There was a moment she wanted to slap him then kiss him but did neither, both she and Raen turning to join their fathers, leaving Hunter to re-join Vena, who watched the altercation with a woman's curiosity.

Emma showed her father the red chillies; she explained how Bael had brought them to her. The big man glanced up and watched Bael as he made his way across the compound.

"Huh!" He grunted. He dipped his finger in the mess and licked the small amount of juice off the end of it. His tongue felt as though someone had placed a fiery torch on it. He spat it out onto the ground.

"I thought as much."

"What do you mean?" she asked surprised.

"I have seen this tactic used in fights during the Northern Campaigns."

"What is it with you men," she said frustrated. "Hunter gave me a similar answer.... Anyway, should we not have the fight stopped?"

"No!"

Koval stared at him and nodded in agreement. Tyrna was furious with what she was hearing. She went to take the chillies.

"Do not interfere woman," Koval said, grabbing her hand before she could touch the fiery concoction.

"Are you two fools? People should know what has taken place here today."

"And they will. But first we must show this Northerner what it is to cross one of our own. If we bring this to light now the fight will be stopped," Dogran replied.

"And?" Emma challenged, astounded by the comment.

"And! This is not up for debate. I will hear no more on the matter."

Both women sighed with impotent frustration in the knowledge that justice could be done if Dogran were to win. Though looking to his opponent both women were not secure in the fact that this would be a forgone conclusion. Tyrna grabbed Dogran's arm.

"If this is the way it must be, then forgive my unlady like request Dogran. Make bloody that bastards face. Teach the Northern thug a lesson he will take with him the rest of his fighting days."

Dogran placed his giant hand on hers and smiled, then without saying a word he walked to the centre of the compound to face his opponent. A tumultuous cheer filled the air. Shouts of kill the bastard, amongst other punctuated obscenities floated amongst the heightened anxiety as the fight was about to begin.

The fighters parted, the Beast from the North swaggering about the crowd as if he had already won. He had faced many before like Dogran and always came out the victor. The Inn Keep paid no heed to the man's bragging, he was intent on one thing-making it a short fight. It was time. Both men returned to the centre and began to circle one another. The Northerner threw the first punch which glanced harmlessly off Dogran's blocking forearm. Dogran moved quickly head butting his opponent square in the face, shattering his nose. Three thundering punches followed smashing a rib and badly bruising the Northerner's kidney. Winded the hulk of a man stepped back as Dogran released his grip. Within seconds the brute had recovered his senses and charged like a crazed bull. Dogran took a barrage of body blows that would have felled most men his size. But he was unfazed and driven to avenge the honour of his friend.

Blow for blow there was naught between them, both men showing facial swelling and bruising. Up until this point Dogran had avoided most punches to the eyes but a sudden flurry of blows changed that and then he felt it. Burning. The Northerner could see his knuckles were at last reaping their reward, the fight would not long continue. With this in mind he went for the killer blow. Dogran read the move, body movement told him the first blow would find contact with his upper stomach forcing his face into the path of the vicious uppercut that would follow. He was right. The Northerner let fly with a pounding blow to his midsection, but instead of hitting soft tissue it smashed quite literally into Dogran's outstretched elbow; a move he had learnt from his fist fights in the camps up north. There was a sickening crack as fingers shattered and dislocated leaving the brutes hand limp and useless. He pulled back in pain, but not quick enough to avoid Dogran's final revenge. The crowd who had been nervously quiet throughout, were now screaming with anticipative vigour for the visitor's almost certain demise. And it came. *Bang!* A murderous uppercut sent the brute arcing through the air, teeth and blood peppering nearby spectators as the man's lower jaw seemed to come loose and wobble freely like the unhinged chin of a wooden marionette. To the delight of the crowd the Northerner hit the ground with a sickening thud. The noise was deafening and though she had made her disapproval of the fight perfectly clear, at that moment Emma's heart swelled with a daughter's pride.

Lord Farroth was suddenly awakened from his sleep by the roar of the crowd surrounding the fighters' compound.

"What did I miss?" He asked groggily.

"The whole of the jousting my dear husband," Alloria replied, with an air of disgust.

"I am sorry my love. Preparations for this day have proved to be more tiring than I had imagined."

He turned to see Maccon on his feet.

"Did I miss anything?"

"No, not really my Lord. The odd broken rib here and there, nothing really of note."

"Then what is all the noise about?"

"If I am not mistaken my Lord it looks like the Inn Keep has won the fist fighting," he said, as he watched Dogran being paraded on the shoulders of Koval and his son Raen.

"If I remember rightly, he fought at the Battle of Nordengaard, handy man to have around in a scrap?" Lord Farroth added.

"That he was my Lord. Singlehandedly bludgeoned ten men with that mace of his before reinforcements arrived to secure Malanon's throne room."

"Ah yes. I remember. One tough old bastard."

"Language. You're not with the men now." Alloria said sharply, still annoyed by his lack of interest in the joust.

"Sorry my dear."

"Bring him over to us. I would like to congratulate this, Dogran is it?"

"It is my Lord."

Maccon quietly instructed Cirius to fetch Dogran and his group to join them on the Royal stand. Without hesitation, the Knight leapt over the wooden barrier in front of the Royal hosts and made his way through the growing crowd.

Emma recognized the Knight from his frequent visitations to the town markets. She didn't know his name but it was obvious people liked the man for his good humour and friendly disposition. Koval and his son lowered Dogran to the ground as the young knight approached.

"Lord Farroth would like you all to join him on the Royal stand. And if I may, congratulations on your victory. I hear your opponent has never been beaten. "

"He has now," Koval interrupted.

"Husband!" Tyrna said nudging Koval's arm.

"That he has. And truth be told I didn't like the cut of the man. A mindless brute at best," Cirius said. "But please follow me I am sure his Lordship would love to hear your story."

Raen couldn't believe his luck as he arrived at the stand and from the look on Jiney's face neither could she. Lord Farroth spoke with Dogran and his group for a while getting a blow-by-blow account that would see bards singing of the fight for years to come. Eventually they were seated just behind the Royal group, Raen making sure he was sat directly behind Jiney, a manoeuvre that hadn't gone unnoticed by his father. He looked to his son and winked. Cailean welcomed the group as they sat down ready to watch the main event of the day. Jiney smiled at everyone and almost in a whisper shyly said, "hello," to Raen, who bowed his head in a military type nod and a newfound confidence he had gained from his time with Hunter. Jiney blushed and turned around. Cailean ever the romantic laid her hand on her friends and squeezed it reassuringly.

"Father?"

"Yes, what is it?" He asked sharply, irritated by the interruption of his conversation with Dogran. And not least because he realized he had missed such a grand fight.

"There is a vendor selling honeyed water by the lake. Would you mind if I sent Jiney to fetch me some? I have such a thirst from all this heat."

"I will send one of the guards," he replied.

Jiney's face dropped.

Cailean quick to react turned around and faced Raen.

"The Smithy's son can go with her…. Can't you?"

Surprised, but willing, Raen nodded his agreement.

For a moment, there was a pause and from the disinterested look on her father's face she knew he was going to decline the suggestion. Thankfully, Alloria unlike her husband was not blind to the passion of youth, so she intervened before another word could pass his lips.

"I think that is a good idea. Here," she said, handing Jiney some coin from a purse on her belt. "I too would like a drink so please take this and treat you and this young man to a drink as well."

Jiney accepted the money willingly and thanked her mistress more for the timely intervention than the drink itself. Lord Farroth was too eager to hear the final details of the fight than argue his point any further. Cailean lip mimed *thank you* to her mother then sat back looking around the crowd for any sign of Bael. Raen in the meantime took Jiney by the hand and led her off the stand.

After worming their way through the crowd, the pair found themselves at the tail end of a long queue, all in need of hydration after the suffocating heat of the day. Neither of them had tried to communicate, Raen believing she wouldn't understand his hand gestures and Jiney finding herself emotionally choked by a sudden bout of shyness.

The queue was moving much too slowly for Raen's liking, the final event couldn't be far off starting and he didn't want to miss a second of it. As fortune would have it, the vendor Imogen and her daughter Amile were close friends to his family, so he took Jiney by the hand and led her away from the line, to the side where they could see him.

"What are you doing?"

He smiled then waved at Amile who had always held a dear spot in her heart for the Smithy's son and was one of the few children that understood his hand language. The eleven-year-old waved back and handed her mother another mug of water.

"Ma, Raen is over there. He wants something."

"Go and see what he wants then, but don't be long we are busy here."

Without another word, the young girl ran over to Raen and Jiney, who were standing beneath the sheltering branches of the large oak tree by the lake, still holding hands. The youngster looked to Raen her eyes betraying the childish adoration she felt for the young man.

"What do you want Raen? Ma says I can't be long," she said ignoring Jiney.

Raen explained the order to her; Jiney surprised to see the young girl understood every hand gesture put before her. Amile ran back with coin in hand and returned with three small leather mugs filled with honey water. She handed them over and gave Jiney back the coin.

"Ma says the drinks are on her."

"Please thank your mother for us, she is very kind," Jiney replied.

Amile managed a half smile but positively beamed when Raen leant over and kissed her on the forehead. The youngster ran back to her mother, while Raen and Jiney passed by the queue to rumblings of discontent from some of the locals for the obvious display of favouritism.

Raen led them back a different way avoiding the crowds. Not far from the stands he halted. A weeping cherry tree surrounded by a gathering of wild flowers, filled the air with the sweetest of scents. Holding hands had given Raen an all too needed boost in confidence. He carefully placed the mugs down and picked a small bouquet of freesia handing them to Jiney. She blushed slightly and raised the bunch to her nose sniffing their scented perfection.

"Thank-you. They are lovely," she said, heartfelt.

Raen bowed playfully and picked up the honey water; he seemed to stand a little taller.

Back at the stand he handed out the drinks then seated himself behind Jiney again. Maccon was on his feet and introducing the last event of the day, Sylas a Master Swordsman from the Amalphii Coast. His reputation wasn't wasted on the crowd, most had heard of his skills through travel, merchants, bards or gossip in taverns and market places. Unlike most other Sword Masters of great renown, he was tall, six feet six inches without a helm. His armour was light, an amalgamation of leather and mail exquisitely tailored to fit his lean sinewy physique. The man stepped out in front of the crowd with self-assured arrogance, followed by a small entourage of warriors all carrying weapons of various kinds. The group made their way across the make shift arena until they reached the Farroth stand. Sylas was the first to bow the rest following his lead. Lord Farroth nodded his acceptance of the courtesy and settled back to enjoy the performance.

The display started with a series of dazzling routines where he demonstrated his martial artistry against different opponents brandishing mace, sword, axe it didn't matter which; the whole thing was meticulously choreographed. Even so his skill was breath-taking he could turn the blade in the blink of an eye avoiding injury by a hair breadth. The crowd was jubilant, cheering with every strike of steel. After some twenty minutes of routines his trained opponents bowed and left the arena, not a drop of blood spilled. Sylas looked around the crowd searching out would be opponents, then turning to the stand he addressed Lord Farroth directly.

"My Lord, I would take six of your finest who deem themselves handy with a sword to join me," his voice clear, showing no sign of exhaustion.

Lord Farroth leant forward.

"I am sure many in my Order would like the challenge, unfortunately it is forbidden to partake of such matters. Though I am sure there are many amongst us who will not disappoint."

"So be it," Sylas said turning to face the crowd. "Please I require six Knights with skills in the sword to join me."

It wasn't long before six Knights of varying size and racial background joined him in the arena, he had a quick word with them explaining the rules of combat. The six men then formed a close circle around him swords in hand; one by one they attacked him random and unpredictably. Sylas made short work of all six disarming four and leaving two prone on the ground with only their pride injured. Everyone cheered at the spectacle having never seen the like. When all was done, the guest fighters were excused leaving one last demonstration. Sylas once again addressed the crowd asking for a volunteer to face him one on one assuring whoever faced him would not be hurt.

There was a silence as people looked at one another, then without warning Raen stood up and before his parents could intervene Sylas shouted out.

"Ah! We have a challenger. Good. Please come join me young man."

There was a gasp of surprise from all around even Hunter looked shocked, but he could see what was really at play, the lad obviously thought he could impress the pretty young lady in the stands.

Sylas called over one of his exhibition fighters whose bodily proportions were similar to Raen's. The man removed his leather cuirass and bracers and gave them to the young volunteer. Then Sylas offered him a selection of fine swords. The lad chose a longsword which felt perfectly balanced in his hand.

"Now I want you to attack me as if you meant to kill me," Sylas ordered.

Raen looked a little nervous now his bravado was beginning to wane. The warrior who supplied his armour handed him a small hide buckler for added protection then the fight began. Raen not sure how much force to put into his blows made a series of skilled lunges then found himself defending strike after strike forcing him backwards. A spinning blow hit the buckler with such force it sent Raen tumbling to the ground face down and arse up. It was quite the most embarrassing position he had ever been in.

Sylas stepped back whilst the lad got to his feet. The crowd were silent, most loved Raen and would not see him humiliated so. He readied himself and made a move Hunter had taught him, so arrogant was his opponent he was caught with his guard down. Raen's execution of the move was far from perfect and lacked restraint, his blade nicking the back of Sylas' sword hand. What followed was ugly, unnecessary and only went to fuel the crowd's dislike of the visitor further. In a series of dazzling moves Sylas managed to completely disarm Raen of both shield and sword leaving him once again prone on the ground, his opponent's foot on his chest and the point of his blade at his throat. Jiney was on her feet as was Maccon who was just about to end the proceedings, when out of nowhere Bael leapt over the fence and faced off the Sword Master.

Sylas removed his foot from Raen's chest to face his knew adversary. Hunter picked up the long sword from the ground. Sylas removed a second sword from his back scabbard; there was something in Hunter's eyes that told him he was no stranger to violence.

"A little unfair don't you think? Let's see how you fare against someone with a little more knowledge of the blade," Hunter said threateningly. Raen stood up and moved away as steel clashed with steel. The speed of the attacks from both men was frightening. No quarter was given by either fighter; you could hear a pin drop. It was obvious the fight was getting out of hand; Raen feeling responsible made a move towards the fighters to show Bael there was no harm done. But something in Hunter snapped, and in his rage, he hit Raen with the hilt of his sword, knocking the lad onto his back; then he unleashed a series of strikes that drove the Master Swordsman backwards. Bael seized the moment disarming Sylas of one of his blades opening his body to a flying kick to the chest that flawed the swordsman. In a blink, Hunter was upon him blade to his face; his Wolf pounced into the arena, lips snarled exposing huge canines. Guards around the compound raised their cross bows all aimed at the beast. Lord Farroth was now on his feet, red with anger.

"Enough! If that wolf moves, kill it," he bellowed.

Maccon quick to react stepped in waving down the nervous archers. Although still a little out of sorts Koval was quick to join his son with Jiney close behind, her station momentarily put aside. Cailean was so shocked by Hunter's behaviour she didn't dare move from her father's side, so furious was he. Bael stood down and moved to calm his Wolf.

Lord Farroth found it hard to speak, the words trapped as his throat tightened. His feelings towards Sylas were no different to the rest of the crowd, he hadn't liked the humiliation of the lad, but what happened with Bael and the Wolf was far more concerning.

"Pay that fool his promised purse then have him and his men escorted from the town with instruction never to return. Then I want to speak with Hunter in my chambers. We are finished here. And get him to cage that wolf or so help me I will have it put down," he ordered Maccon.

At day's end the sky was the colour of blood, bruised by wisps of purple blue clouds. Bael left the Wolf to wander freely through the woods and make its way back to the lodge, whilst he followed Maccon to the Keep where he faced the Farroth wrath with arrogant indifference.

Maccon was left more troubled than not, with what motivations unleashed in Bael such a ferocious outburst and though a Master of the sword himself he had never seen the like. In all the years of dealing with the man he had never seen or got an inkling Bael possessed such skills. It was becoming abundantly clear now the Elves had kept much from them the day he was delivered into their midst.

Bael finished his night in the lap of Vena who caressed his brow through another sweat inducing nightmare.

***

Cailean returned to her room. She was more disappointed than shocked by the afternoon's fiasco. Hunter filled her mind with every passing thought, the bonds of family preventing her from communicating her true feelings for him, to near breaking point. She felt a prisoner of the Farroth name and with the urges that befell a young woman of her age no matter how irresponsible; the seeds of rebellion were sewn.

***

Raen returned to the forge with his parents, baring a smile of contentment whose origin saw him through an hour of his mother's ramblings on how she had been right about Hunter all along. Koval stepped into another room, choosing to sooth his swollen face with a piece of freshly cut beef. He was pleased that his son was alright, and being his father, saw the events of the afternoon in a totally different light to his wife. His views on Hunter would stay his own, for he knew this was not the moment to share them.

***

Jiney returned to her own quarters after making sure her mistress was settled. She had her nightly duties to perform before retiring for the night but she too had the faintest of smiles as she did them, comforted in the knowledge that she had asked Raen to meet her under the great Oak by the Lake the next day.

***

Dogran sat by the fire, Raga at his feet licking his outstretched hand. Emma joined them, handing her father a mug of warmed herbal wine which would help him sleep. The events of the afternoon concerning Hunter weren't lost to Dogran but his thoughts were with his friend Koval. He was glad the Smithy had only suffered an injured pride; a story he knew all too well could have had a different ending. Emma chose not to talk about things any further, she was proud of her father no matter how misguided she thought his antics. And her thoughts on Hunter would wait for another day, though those very thoughts would keep her awake all that night.

***

Eight Cor-Leonese raiders tasked with the capture of the last slave met under the very Oak tree Jiney and Raen had met earlier. Vaeyu had explicitly ordered them to stay clear of the town, an order Simaeyu the leader of the six chose to ignore. They had split up into pairs, hooded to keep their delicate skins covered from the sun, their separation making them less conspicuous from the searching eyes of the town guard. Earlier that day they had visited a farmstead several miles from the town leaving behind a dead father, a raped daughter and mother all put to the blade in a pointless, merciless act of violence that left them still needing a final prisoner.

Whilst seeking the shade of the branches of the Old Oak tree, Simaeyu and his companions overheard the conversation between a young man and a beautiful young woman, who arranged for a meeting under said tree the very next morning.

Simaeyu looked to his cohorts and he had a plan.

16
THE BEGINNING TO THE END OF ALL THINGS

The Palace of Dax-Barh stood like a Black Monolith, its twisted Obsidian spires looming menacingly above the surrounding landscape. The grounds facing the Royal suite were huge, filled with giant trees their branches sculptured into strange filigree like buildings with roofs open to the wonderment of the skies. There was a beauty here one would not expect to find garnishing a land housing a race possessed of such dark intent.

The King of the Dark Elves was rarely victim to nerves but looking down at the abomination both he and his Shamen had brought through the portal, sent tendrils of uncertainty coursing through his stomach. Down there in the grounds was a power far beyond anything he or Kor-yllion of the High Elders could ever hope to singularly possess, but for now it would do his bidding. The creature had come to them a gift from the void with a singular purpose, the annihilation of all, other than those he served; or that is what Dax-Barh and his elders liked to believe. But as he stared at the warrior, the King couldn't help thinking this *thing* had an agenda all its own that only time would reveal.

Dax-Barh was so lost in the moment he didn't see his wife and youngest children join him on the balcony. This was soon remedied when his son Kalek grabbed him around the leg. Equivalent to a human child of ten years he was the apple of his father's eye. The King patted his son on the top of the head then put a finger to his lips.

"Sshh! He whispered, turning his head to face his wife and daughter.

Anumii was a tall dark beauty her skin like his, the colour of flawless ebony, smooth, with no sign of age lines that could betray her three thousand years. Ceisa, the daughter holding her hand, like her brother, had a fairer skin that would darken with time. But being half her brother's age would see many years before such change would take place. As soon as the youngster saw her brother grab their father's leg she let go of her mother's hand and rushed over to grab the other leg. Anumii looked to her family, either side of her husband the lights of both their lives and he, tall with long black hair framing a chiselled face that commanded attention. Her heart swelled with pride, but she could see the nervous uncertainty that the King's deep violet eyes failed to hide from her. She knelt down and coaxed the children back to her side.

"You seem anxious my love?" she said, holding back her son, who was struggling to return to his father. Her grip tightened as the youngster tried to pull away whining in frustration. Dax-Barh stared disapprovingly at the child.

"Do not be a trouble to your mother," he urged, his voice deep, resonating with authority.

Kalek ceased his tantrums immediately. Anumii quickly led the children back into the main living quarters where she left them to play, then re-joined her husband on the balcony. Still sensing his unease, she followed his gaze to the grounds below.

"I would prefer our children did not see this," he said without turning around.

This was the first time she had seen the Devourer of Souls close up; it was a sight that left her with a growing sense of foreboding. She knew all too well the reasons the King had conjured such a thing, for his hatred of his once good friend Kor-yllion showed no bounds, yet she feared this was a move that could see all their undoing.

For thousands of years both Dark and High Elves had lived in relative harmony until the *purge.* She remembered; it was a time of change. Young from both races were beginning to rebel against the old doctrines. Children of mixed blood were being born out of wedlock. Births hidden in shame, from old beliefs passed down through generations; beliefs rigidly adhered to by Kor-yllion who deemed these half-bloods of light and dark skin a subversion of his idealistic views. In his eyes, they were not purebloods.

Dax-Barh and his kind were never as practiced in the old ways as their brethren. They saw racial integration as a way forward; too long had the racial inequalities been ignored. Yet this frail harmonious balance between the two races had been held together by the long-lasting friendship of both leaders; until Dax-Barh's eldest son Miica and his halfbreed daughter were exiled with all the other half-bloods. That day a friendship ended.

A thousand years of bitter conflict followed which saw Dax-Barh and his kind outcast to an area which became known as the Shadow Lands. Miica and his daughter were never heard from again. A loss that to this day had never been sated. Even though Anumii understood all this, she was frightened that what lurked in the grounds below would unleash horrors of such magnitude that none would be safe. Her husband had tried to allay such fears, telling her the very scrolls scribed by the ancients themselves would keep the creature bound to their will, a fact she was willing to believe 'till now. Her first impression when laying eyes on the Devourer was the lethal, aesthetic beauty of his black armour, the likes of which even the legendary forges of the High Elves would be hard pressed to match.

The King took hold of his wife's hand as they shared a moment to watch the figure on the grassy mound by the waterfall; his arm outstretched holding the hilt of an extraordinary black bladed sword which was stuck in the ground in-front of him: His head bowed, obscured by a black helm that looked as if it was attached to the armour. The armour itself was a thing of Dark, shadowy beauty, crafted to perfection to fit his seven feet frame like a second skin. It was made from small strips of sharpened plates overlapping one another in such a way as not to restrict movement. But had the King and Queen been able to look closer they would have seen neither rivet nor ring held these razor-sharp shards in place; instead they were bound by some invisible force whose origins stemmed from demonic shadows. But all this said, the thing that troubled the Queen the most was the creatures that circled the strange warrior in a constant state of agitation. Six grotesque *Hounds* each the size of a small pony that reeked of death and decay, minions of the afterlife, dark, menacing and ferociously protective of their master. Anumii linked her husband's arm pressing it tightly against her side.

"I hope for all our sakes you know what you are doing? These things terrify me," she said.

Dax-Barh's only reply was a look of growing uncertainty. The warrior below didn't move, his head still bowed he appeared to be in some kind of meditative state, but the alpha, the largest of the six hounds turned its massive head towards the balcony. The sight of its piercing red eyes sent shivers down Anumii's spine.

She watched in amazement as the tortured faces of trapped souls phased in and out of existence in some futile attempt to escape their unholy host.

The children returned to the balcony running straight to their father's side, both of them terrified by the leader of the King's Elite Warriors who followed close behind.

Sereg was a massive specimen and unlike most of his kind who were revered for their agility; he was a powerhouse of raw unbridled strength which helped him brandish his monstrous two-handed mace. He never smiled or wasted a word that he deemed pointless or unnecessary. He stood a brutal killer whose methods sometimes shocked even the King who was himself no stranger to the brutality of the art of warfare. But his loyalty to the throne was unquestionable.

"My liege. The council is assembled. I can also report the scouting parties have returned," he told the King, his voice quiet but deep and full of menace. Dax-Barh kissed his wife and children, then followed Sereg down the twisting stairway to the Council Chamber adjacent to the huge throne room two levels down. He never liked these meetings. He hated the smell of smouldering opiates that hung in the air; a fog of ochre smoke emanating from several metal dishes suspended from the ceiling by tarnished discoloured chains.

Sereg took his seat next to Craban the head Shaman. Next to him Etzuc Master of Audits whose sole duty was to manage the Royal coffers, overseeing everything from the King's personal expenses to the funding of the armies. A person of considerable influence, with an inherent dislike of the eight summoning mages who faced him across the massive black Obsidian table. Next to him sat Maril the Shadow Maester, a skeletally thin Elf whose skin was as black as night. His was a position of intrigue and secret, whose spies kept the council informed about any potential threat against the realm, either internal or external. Not a group to be underestimated or trifled with, these were masters of covert surveillance and deception.

The council stood as the King entered the chamber. He seated himself at the head of the table, his Obsidian chair twice the size of the others. Before addressing the group, he paused for a moment and looked to the eight Summoners. He couldn't help thinking how it was possible for them to function properly when the smoke that filled the chamber also wafted around their living quarters dulling their eyes after years of saturation. They believed the smouldering pollen opened their minds allowing them to channel their magic more freely, with one drawback; they always appeared to be in a semi-trance like state, their mud coloured eyes never quite focusing on those they faced.

Dax-Barh addressed the Shadow Maester for any news from beyond the Neck.

"My Lord, as you suspected the wolf still lives," Maril said, his voice deeper than one would imagine for someone so thin. "She lives in the realm of men. Nursed back to health by a hunter of sorts; a loner who it seems is not well liked amongst his kind."

The King stroked his short black beard in puzzling contemplation.

"Why would he leave the beast with such a man?"

"Whatever the reason, we all know such a union will have a hidden purpose, you can be sure of that. This King of our enemy is no fool. We must not underestimate the importance of such an undertaking, no matter how strange it might first appear," Craban replied. "There has to be a reason why Kor-yllion chose this man above any of his own kind. He knows as do we, that without this creature the prophesy that would see the end of his kind will not come to pass."

Sereg stood up, his size and presence intimidating to all but the King.

"My Lord we must act swiftly and without mercy. This wolf would already be wandering the afterlife had I been in charge when those fools killed all but the one thing they were meant to kill. You were too lenient my Lord. I would have decorated the battlements with their heads." In truth, he still held resentment for the fact that the Devourer and his pets had led that particular raid.

Craban had never liked Sereg's way of dealing with conflict; though effective, he found it brutal and savage and lacking anything that resembled finesse.

"The wolf was protected by strong magic. I doubt even you would have been able to detect it?" he said.

Sereg snarled at the shaman.

"What would you know of such things? Hiding away in that temple of yours." Sereg had little time for the Shamen, if he had his way he would see the lot of them impaled on spikes, screaming for a mercy that would never come. But he was all too aware they were a necessary evil the King relied upon, so he kept his baser thoughts hidden away for another time.

Maril shifted in his seat, himself agitated by the brute's arrogance.

"Always ready to blame someone else for your own incompetence I see. What a surprise," he said, making no attempt to mask his sarcasm.

Sereg loathed only one Dark Elf more than the Shamen, so whenever he and Maril shared the same room together there was always going to be trouble. The huge warrior jumped to his feet. No longer able to contain his contempt for the Shadow Maester his temper exploded.

"You worm. Slither back under the stone from whence you came. I face my foes like a warrior, not as a coward fighting in the shadows."

"What does it matter where we fight, so long as the results are the same," Maril said, calmly.

"You have no honour worm."

"You speak of honour. Is it honour, when you butcher mothers and their children without showing a shred of remorse? I think not," Maril said, taking the high ground as if he wouldn't do the same.

The muscles in Sereg's neck bunched like sculpted ebony, his knuckles turning white as he clenched his fists.

"You scum! The day will come when I will feed you that clever tongue of yours, and…."

"My, my. How blessed we are that such meaningless words spill from your mouth like mindless vomit," Maril interrupted.

The King's patience finally exhausted, intervened.

"Enough! We are not here to fight amongst ourselves, harness this anger for when we face our enemies."

Sereg grunted as Dax-Barh threw him a look the warrior knew all too well would be foolish to ignore. Reluctantly he seated himself. Maril apologised for his part in the pointless banter and turned his thoughts to the matters at hand.

"Another matter was brought to my attention Sire; I have news that this King of men they call Agramar, is escorting the son of a powerful ally to wed the daughter of his brother in the south. A powerful union which could cause us considerable problems when we are finally able to turn our attentions to reclaiming the lands that were rightly ours to command."

"Where do you get such information?" the King asked, puzzled somewhat by the comment.

"I have my sources my Lord, more than that, I prefer such knowledge stay with me at this point in time.

A conversation for another time perhaps my Lord. Suffice to say the less amongst us who know my methods, the less chance that such important information is prevented from reaching your ears Sire."

"Yes. Yes, as you wish, for now," Dax-Barh replied. "But why should a matter like this be raised now when our most pressing concerns are with our long-lost brethren to the east."

"My Lord. What nonsense is this our learned Shadow Maester would have us consider? When all our focus should be on killing the Wolf and all who aid her. Then with the help of whatever that thing is out there, we should take back the lands we were so unjustly driven from all those centuries ago," Sereg gestured, nodding disapprovingly in the direction of the Palace grounds, where the Devourer still knelt, surrounded by his demonic pets.

Before the Warlord could go any further, his head Shaman Craban intervened, demonstrating his usual well practiced diplomacy.

"Sire what Sereg says is true, our priority has to be the prevention of the Prophesy, which we all agree, revolves around this Wolf and her protector. But what our Shadow Maester here says, also has merit."

The King sat forward.

"I agree my friend. As you have told me yourself, this Agramar has some deep-seated alliance with Koryllion that still puzzles me to this day."

"Yes Sire, and if my sources are correct, a meeting has been arranged between Agramar's brother and the Council of High Elders," Maril quickly followed. "The true nature of this meeting is as yet unknown to me, other than to say it has something to do with the mystery surrounding the Wolf and this Hunter who protects her."

"If what you say is true, it would be sheer folly to attempt to fight a full-blown battle on two fronts, this would see our end long before the prophesy was fulfilled. No. We have the opportunity to cut the head from the serpent without engaging in full scale war," Dax-Barh pondered.

"What do you propose Sire?" Craban asked.

Sereg interrupted with his usual vicious rhetoric.

"I can take a hundred of my best warriors and finish this King Agramar on the open road,"

"I would have to agree, Sereg." Dax-Barh replied.

"Would it not be more prudent to adopt a subtler approach?" Craban added.

"And what would you have us do? Sit around a table and talk them to death. No. Our attack must be swift and merciless," Sereg interrupted.

The Shadow Maester sneered at Sereg with the contempt of a superior intellect.

"That shouldn't pose a problem then, should it? The bloodier the better."

"That is enough," the King intervened. "I understand your concerns Shadow Maester, but time for subtlety is long past." He stood up, knowing that if he left Sereg and Maril in the room absent his company, that blood may very well be spilled. Although, if truth be told, he wasn't certain who's blood that would be. For though his Warlord was a force to be reckoned with, there was something about Maril that unnerved him; he possessed a strength of a different kind, subtle and dangerous. "Sereg I would have you join me on my balcony."

"As you wish my Lord," Sereg grunted.

In truth, the War Lord was only too glad to be rid of the council, in his mind they were the planners, he the executioner, the spearhead of whatever battle strategy they deemed appropriate and for all his loathing of them he respected their tactical prowess. Though they would never know it.

Before leaving the room Dax-Barh addressed the remaining council.

"The Wolf and this Hunter must be our priority, but as you suggest this Agramar situation cannot be overlooked…. Maril. Let the rest of the council know every piece of information your acolytes have accrued, on this King's whereabouts."

"Yes Sire."

"Good. Then I want you all to come up with a plan and have it for me on the morrow. Sereg and myself will make sure our warriors are ready to move at a moment's notice."

Raj-aat, the leader of the eight summoners, had remained silent throughout the meeting, but he could hold back no longer.

"Sire one more thing?"

"Yes, what is it?"

"What of the creatures we summoned from the void."

"My plans for them have already been set in motion, that is all you need to know for now."

The King took a moment to reflect on the few meetings he'd had with the Devourer of Souls and realized that not once during their meetings did the Dark Knight remove his helm. For had he laid witness to who or what resided in that black helm, his views on all matters regarding this daemon would take on a very different meaning.

17
TERRIBLE THINGS

Jiney could choose any day of the week to be free of her duties, so it came as no surprise to Cailean why her friend had chosen this particular day. Intent on making it special she gave Jiney a beautiful white linen dress to honour the occasion. The hem line was set halfway between knee and ankle and considered quite the fashion statement amongst young women of substance. Unfortunately, not a view shared by older women of the court who felt the length provocative and unbecoming for a lady. But in Cailean's eyes this was more of a reason to wear it.

"Turn around. Let me look at you."

Jiney gladly obliged, spinning around the room like a child at her first dance.

"Thank you, my lady. It is so beautiful."

"As are you."

"But are you sure about this? I mean it is…"

"Of course, I am," Cailean interrupted. "The dress is yours, my gift to you…Now stay still a moment I have one more thing left to do." She searched around the room until she found what she was looking for.

"Ah! There you are," she said, walking over to a small wooden box by the window. She removed two lengths of scarlet silk ribbon and gestured for Jiney to seat herself in a chair by the balcony. As she sat down

Jiney smoothed the creases out of the dress while her friend fiddled with her hair.

"There done. Here, take a look."

Jiney took the highly-polished steel mirror from her mistress and turned her head in its reflection. The hair was styled into two pigtails giving her face an almost childlike innocence. Wearing her hair this way had never occurred to her before, but she was pleasantly surprised at the transformation.

"How can I ever repay you for this?" She asked.

"By just enjoying yourself…Now speak no more about it."

Jiney went to kiss her mistress's hand, but Cailean pulled her close and hugged her dearly.

"Now go. Don't keep this handsome young smithy's boy waiting."

Jiney gave one final squeeze and left excitedly.

Cailean headed out onto the balcony where she watched her friend make her way across the bridge to the lakeside beyond. It was odd, she thought, how feelings could be so mixed and confusing; on the one hand a feeling of delight, whilst on the other envy. There was no question, given the choice she would have preferred that the meeting was between her and Hunter. But for now, she accepted this was impossible. She had overheard her father's comments to Hunter following the fiasco with the guest sword master. He made it abundantly clear that Hunter was to stay well away from her. Though how Hunter would react to her father's dressing down was any one's guess. He didn't act like a man who would be influenced by such an outburst, no matter how persuasive her father tried to be.

***

The night of the fair Raen took great delight in telling his mother of his planned liaise with Jiney. Still annoyed at Koval for his part in the fight, this news came as a welcome diversion.

"It is a mother's joy to hear such news my love. She looks to be a good girl, pretty but more importantly kind," she said, warmly.

Raen gave her a hug and a kiss on the cheek before retiring to his room. As he got into bed he could hear his mother milling about the kitchen, but after such a tiring day it wasn't long before his snores competed with his father's.

Raen rose earlier than usual the following morning. He wanted to make sure the forge was prepared before leaving to meet Jiney. His own work was almost finished. There was a ceremonial breast plate for the leader of the Royal guard which needed polishing in readiness for the King's visit. It took him less than an hour to complete. He hung the piece of armour where his father couldn't miss it and laid out his tools in preparation for the day ahead. Before leaving he had one more thing to do. He sneaked back to his room trying not to disturb his mother and father who were fortunately still sleeping soundly. He quickly changed from his work clothes into his dark grey linen trousers and soft chamois leather jerkin that tied up the front with a thin leather lace. Finally, he slipped on a pair of fine leather ankle boots then he was ready. He quickly tied his hair back in a ponytail, a style he favoured from his time around Hunter, and then entered the kitchen. In the centre of the table by the window was a large bundle wrapped in a white linen cloth. By it was a note from his mother. It read: *Have a lovely time son. I have put a few morsels together for you so you can both have a bite to eat by the lake.* Raen looked towards his parent's room and smiled. He picked up the bundle; made sure he hadn't forgotten anything and left.

***

Jiney spotted Raen standing under the huge canopy of the old oak tree staring across the glass still lake to the mountains beyond. As she approached, he appeared to be completely unaware of her presence. With each passing step, her stomach churned over with nervous excitement. Some hand gestures were obvious, but Raen's knowledge of the hand language was way beyond her understanding, which only added to her nerves. She made her way alongside the lake keeping out of sight so she could playfully surprise him. Just as she was about to put her hands over his eyes Raen turned around sporting a grin from ear to ear. She laughed with embarrassment.

"How did you know I was behind you?"

Raen tapped his ears and pointed to her feet and the brown fallen leaves beneath them. There was warmth in his smile that was rare in young men of his age and it touched her. Most of the teenage boys she met growing up were self-absorbed pigs as she liked to call them: Interested in just one thing and that was a flower only the right one would pluck. A decision she made the first day she bled.

She moved closer to him hoping he would take her hand. He didn't. Instead he pointed to the bundle he carried and raised a hand to his mouth as if to eat something.

"You have brought something to eat?" she asked.

He nodded yes, then turned and gestured for them to walk along the banks of the lake in the direction of the forest where Hunter's Wolf would often hunt for vermin.

"That would be nice," she said, the kindness in his eyes the perfect antidote for her jittery stomach.

They walked a short distance until they reached a thin strip of sandy beach that stretched a good half league along the water's edge. Raen looked for a dry spot of grass on a raised embankment overlooking the widest section of sand. He opened the bundle he carried and laid out the white linen cloth for Jiney to sit on. While she got herself comfortable, he began to un-wrap the waxed paper that covered each small parcel of food, passing them to her for inspection. She checked each one appreciatively and passed them back to him with a welcome look of approval.

For a while they just sat staring at the lake, its stillness broken by a dance of circular ripples as fish fed on insects that scurried across its surface. Then Raen did something completely unexpected. He whipped off his shirt and boots and ran to the edge of the beach diving headlong into the lake. It took Jiney by surprise. *But why not,* she thought, as she felt the heat of the sun bear down on her.

He surfaced after what seemed like an impossible amount of time underwater to find Jiney on her feet looking more than a little apprehensive. Sweeping back his hair he waved for her to join him. There was a moment of uncertainty. She wasn't going to undress down to her undergarments, that was for sure, but there was something inviting about the thought of cool water touching her skin. Not least because for the first time she became aware of Raen's chiselled physique as he stood waste deep in the water. Her first reaction was to wave *no*. But Raen wasn't going to give up that easily. He waded into the shallows until the water was just below his knees and splashed playfully waving for her to join him. This time she smiled, hitched up her dress and quite lady like stepped into the cool water. Like a child, he jumped backwards splashing her with his feet, soaking her to the skin.

"Raen!" she screamed…Look at me I'm wet through." Not wishing to let her new dress get ruined, Jiney turned and walked back to the picnic area, where, to his welcome surprise she undressed down to her undergarments.

Whoops! He thought uncertainly, looking at the scowl on her face. *Maybe I went a little too far.* Then quite unexpectedly she ran back into the water and splashed him back. Raen jumped backwards, but not quick enough to avoid a mouthful of fresh water. He resurfaced, feeling a little guilty in the realization, that maybe she just didn't want to swim. Or maybe it was that she just couldn't; a thought which bore fruit when she suddenly lost her footing in a deep trough, leaving her neck deep in the water flailing like a beached fish. Raen quickly grabbed her arm and pulled her to safety, carrying her back to the grass. At first, she didn't know whether to laugh or cry until she saw how mortified Raen looked.

"Well, you got what you wanted," she said with a somewhat sarcastic smile.

He mimed; *I am sorry,* and found himself staring at her breasts, her nipples hardened by the chill of a slight breeze. He quickly averted his eyes and blushed. Surprisingly she didn't make any attempt to hide herself; in fact, she was flattered by his attentions and without being conceited was proud of her womanly proportions.

The sun was directly above, and now the breeze had dropped Jiney could feel her clothes begin to warm up nicely. Standing there in her undergarments, her dress splayed out on the grass drying in the sun, he once again found his eyes wandering involuntarily, this time towards her legs which were bare from the knee down. Her skin was the gentle cream colour of goat's milk, smooth with a light scattering of freckles. As he stared at her, he couldn't quite believe how someone so beautiful would even contemplate being his girl. Yet here she was and by the gods he was glad.

This time when she caught his gaze, she shyly crossed her arms in front of her. Raen blushed again, looked to the ground where his leather shirt lay and proceeded to open it out on the grass. He gestured for her to sit on it, which she did, pulling her knees into her chest. Raen then removed the linen cloth from under the food and placed it over her shoulders.

"Thank you," she whispered, touching the back of his hand affectionately.

He'd had very little experience dealing with the opposite sex, in-fact almost none at all, but the thrill he got from that simple touch sent his heart racing. Clumsily, he began to open the food parcels, his nervy fingers fumbling over the wrappings. This touched Jiney, she found his gentleness towards her refreshing, unlike most of the young men who had courted her attention.

When all was laid out in front of them, they began to eat, and for a short while after just sat there basking in the heat of the sun.

It wasn't long before Raen's chest began to turn red, so he stood up and started searching around the ground until he found a small piece of fallen branch. Jiney watched him with growing curiosity as he walked over to the wet beach not far from where she sat and began writing in the sand.

Sorry about dress.

"It is fine…All in all I have to say it was fun. Well, until I nearly drowned that is." Smiling, she felt the hem of her dress. "There," she said. "It's almost dry." With that she stood up and put the dress back on, leaving the lace at the front slightly open to expose her adequate cleavage. Raen's shirt was also dry, so he did the same, then cleared away the waxed paper wrappings and placed them back in the linen cloth. Some distance away over the embankment they could hear the market vendors dismantling their stalls. But that was the only sound. Raen was the first to notice the disquieting silence that hung over the lake. Then somewhere in the distance a dog barked. Not long after a wolf howled, a call Raen recognized immediately.

***

Lamia followed the young fawn into the garden where it mithered a duck and it's young around the pond. Day by day the gentle creature grew stronger and was a source of new found joy for an old woman who asked for little out of life. The mother duck wasn't standing for any of its playful nonsense even though her ducklings seemed to be enjoying the chase; she pecked the fawn painfully on the nose sending her scurrying back to the old woman.

The trees around the cottage were unnaturally still. Lamia was all too aware of the silence and it left her with an acute sense of foreboding. It was the stillness she felt before the threat of a storm, yet the sky above was as clear as a flawless sapphire. It was as if nature herself held her breath in anticipation of some impending disaster. She tried to shake the feeling, focusing on the beauty that surrounded her, but the oppressive humidity of days like this made her tired and less able to keep her emotions in check.

She felt the fawn by her leg nursing its injured pride. She bent down to stroke the creature then gave it a name.

"Come along Kela! I have something for you," she said, leading the young deer over to a vegetable garden, shaded by the westerly facing wall of the cottage. Kela sprung back to life in anticipation of what would hopefully come next. Not one to disappoint, Lamia picked a fresh cauliflower and a handful of carrots and then made her way back to the shade of the porch where she broke off the tip of a small carrot and fed it to the fawn's already waiting mouth. It didn't take long for the deer to finish the offering, so Lamia broke off a small chunk of cauliflower and placed it on the porch floor before sitting down on the bench under the window. The animal was quick to take up the fresh morsel and chomped away heartily.

"What a strange day this is," she said stroking the creatures back. Then it started.

The strength in her legs began to drain away, leaving her weak and unsteady. Next came the throbbing pain behind her eyes and temples. This was confirmation that her sense of unease earlier wasn't a coincidence, and though she wished it was, she knew all too well that these symptoms were the prelude to one of her visions.

***

Emma was so preoccupied with thoughts of the previous day, that any sense of time was lost to her. Now here she was, right outside Lamia's cottage not quite sure how she got there. She jumped down off the small cart, tethered the horse to the fence and pushed open the gate. She saw the old woman cradling her head in her hands as if distressed, whilst the fawn munched on something by her leg.

Lamia looked up as the gate creaked open, she recognised Emma immediately from her aura.

"To what do I owe this welcome visit?" She said, trying to look less troubled. "I'm sure you have better things to attend to than indulge in an old woman's daily meanderings."

Emma smiled.

"I have a short while before the Tavern opens and thought you might like to hear about the goings on at the fair.

"That would be nice...But first, let me get you a drink. This heat is unbearable."

"I would love one but please let me get it."

"Thankyou my child. There is jug of honey water in the bucket," Lamia said, glancing over at the well just right of the pond. "I keep it down there on days like this to keep it nice and cool."

"What a clever idea," Emma replied.

"Well, if you say so...Who am I to refuse a compliment when one is freely offered? I'll get the mugs and some milk for Kela here."

"Kela? What a lovely name. I've never heard it before?" Emma said.

Lamia stood up ready to enter the cottage still holding the cauliflower and carrots in her hands.

"It's elvish I believe. It means little gift."

"That's beautiful," Emma replied, coaxing the fawn to follow her to the well.

By the time she had retrieved the jug and returned to the porch, Lamia had placed a bowl of milk on the floor and was sitting on the bench holding the two clay mugs. The fawn ran straight for the bowl as Emma carefully filled each mug and sat down beside the old woman. They both took a sip and as Lamia had said, the water was still surprisingly cool.

"Ahh! That's better."

"Much better," Lamia replied.

Emma sat forward. It was unusual to find her old friend looking so drawn and pallid of complexion. Cheeks that were usually rosy seemed pale even in the stifling heat, which was getting hotter with each passing moment.

"Are you feeling alright?"

Lamia took a couple of heavy gulps of honey water and rested her back against the cottage wall.

"I'm fine my dear...It's this damned heat, I find it so oppressive. But I'll survive," she replied, tapping the back of Emma's hand caringly. "Now, enough about me...Please, tell me about the fair."

Emma described the previous day's events in great detail, covering the fight, the winners of the various contests and was about to finish with the story of Hunter and the visiting Sword Master, when without warning Lamia's eyes blinked shut. Within seconds they opened again, this time only the whites were visible. For a moment Emma was taken aback, but concern quickly pulled her together.

"Lamia. What is it?"

There was no answer. Lamia just stared into the distance. The image was fleeting. First one, then another, neither making any sense. But sometimes this happened. There was no reason for it, whatever source these images spawned from, they prevented any kind of censorship. Clarity wasn't a given. Messages like these were often questionable; sometimes they were warnings of things to come. Sometimes they portrayed events that were taking place that very moment, whilst others were the results of things that had passed. It was a paradox; the only time she saw things as she did before losing her sight, was during these visionary episodes. Again, it flashed, this time it lingered long enough to show her four men almost invisible in the tree shadows of the forest. There was an impending sense of doom and it frightened her. Then she saw a wolf but couldn't make out if it was Hunter's or another one entirely. A sharp pain coursed through her temples as another image materialized, this one much clearer. A huge black hound burst into a clearing in the forest by the lake, barking frantically at the four figures skulking in the shadows. She couldn't see the face of its owner but she knew by his size who it was. Her blood ran cold as two of the men in the shadows raised their cross bows.

Lamia screamed. "Nooo!" And fell backwards exhausted.

Emma watched unable to do anything, uncertain of what might happen should she try to bring the old woman out of her trance. But as Lamia cried out she reacted instantly, grabbing her friend's arm as she collapsed to the ground. She shook Lamia nervously until her eyes rolled back revealing her clouded pupils.

"What is it? What did you see?" Emma asked anxiously.

Lamia couldn't answer.

***

Maccon gathered the twelve in the Temple. The shard hummed into life, activated not by the warrior priests but by an outside source. This had never happened before and all twelve looked to one another with puzzling concern. Each member of the Order followed Maccon's lead and placed their hands on the runes inlayed into the altar top surrounding the shard. Osor a thick red bearded member, pressed his knuckles down hard.

"What is happening? It appears we have no control over what takes place in our very own Temple?" He said, directing his question to his leader. At this point all eyes were on Maccon looking for the same answer. For a moment like the rest he just stood there watching images flicker in and out of existence totally void of their influence.

"I am as much in the dark as the rest of you."

"It would seem we are dealing with a power greater than the sum of all our minds combined, would it not?"

Interrupted Arbar, a tall inspiring figure of a man and by far the oldest in the group. Before Maccon could give reply Cirius spoke up unhappy about the tone of questioning.

"Surely this is not a time for such debate, should we not be more concerned about what message the shard presents us," he said, angrily as the flickering images became clearer.

A respectful silence befell the room as all thirteen averted their eyes to the mystery unravelling before them.

"Thank you Cirius. As usual you are correct. For now, let us all focus as *one*, for the answers we all desire may well be hidden amongst these images put before us."

Now resigned to the task, the thirteen calmed themselves and focused their energies towards the ball of light expanding and contracting at the tip of the shard. What they saw was quite incredible. *Bael walked as if towards the group watching him. He bent down in front of what or who's ever eyes they were looking through and stretched out his arm.* In that moment, it became clear to the collective consciousness where part of the Temple's invading power originated. Only part, for all recognised there was another force at work; menacing and dreadful in its nature.

***

Bael bent down and stroked the Wolfs huge head; he knew full well she sensed danger long before he did.

"What is it my beauty? What troubles you?"

The Wolf licked his hand and set off through the trees in the direction of the lake beyond. Bael slipped his bow off his shoulder and followed cautiously. This venture into the woods was part of a daily ritual he and the Wolf shared to help keep the beast's senses honed so her natural instincts would grow with her strength. The hawk was elsewhere this day, honing his own abilities and would no doubt be waiting back at the lodge for Hunter's return having satisfied his appetite on his many kills. Bael picked up the pace. The Wolf was away out of sight and he knew she had caught the scent of something in the clearing less than a hundred paces ahead through the trees. As he got to within spitting distance of the tree line the Wolf appeared from behind a cluster of bramble bushes. He could see the agitation in her eyes. She was waiting for him, but *why* he thought. What lay beyond these trees that would see her this unsettled? He patted her head.

"Shsh!" He whispered. "Stay by my side."

Bending low and using shadows as cover Hunter and the Wolf made for the clearing. As they approached the last row of trees before breaking cover a dog barked angrily not far ahead. But within moments it yelped as if injured. Bael threw caution to the wind and burst into the open, the Wolf by his side. Across the clearing, he saw a big man running towards four men nestling amongst the trees. At first, he wasn't sure who the man was, not until he saw the large black war hound lying dead still at the feet of the raiders, then he knew. His blood ran cold as he watched the big man fall, unable to reach him in time before a third cross bow bolt hit him in the chest. The Wolf gave out a blood curdling howl and sprang towards the attackers.

***

Dogran was on his way back to the town when he and Raga his old war hound entered the clearing not that far from the lake. It was like any other summer's day for them both, hot, humid, but today Dogran had chosen to exercise the dog a lot earlier than usual having closed the Tavern for the day to rest after his fight the day before.

The sun was right above and the grass they trod was scorched brown from its relentless heat. Half way across the hound stopped dead in its tracks its instinct to protect its master alerting Dogran to impending danger.

"What is it? What can you smell, my old friend?" He said stroking the dog's neck. Before he could stand up straight the hound made for the trees just ahead of him barking ferociously at the shadows beyond. A figure stepped from cover with cross bow raised. Before Dogran could move, a bolt hit the animal just above the right leg not far from its neck. It yelped from the pain. Most other dogs would have been downed by such a shot but Raga kept on going until another bowman stepped out, his bolt hitting the dog square between the eyes. The animal dropped like a stone. Dead. Dogran was already on the move towards his dog's killers, his rage overwhelming any sense of caution. As he got closer there seemed to be four attackers three with cross bows and one wielding a sword. The two who had fired theirs were busy reloading, the other though fired his. Dogran tried to dodge out of the way but the bolt hit him high in the chest. It slowed him for a moment but he kept on going. He hadn't seen Bael and his Wolf enter the clearing behind him until he heard the animal howl. Thud! Another bolt hit him, this time in the leg and before he hit the ground another thumped into him. Then all turned black.

The gentle giant never saw the Wolf rip out the throats of two of the raiders while Bael deftly disembowelled a third and severed the head of the fourth.

***

Raen plucked up courage and took Jiney by the hand. He kissed her on the cheek and wrote another message in the sand asking how she ended up in Lord Farroth's employ. Jiney stared at him for a moment saddened by a memory, shared only with the members of the Farroth household and that was some time ago now. But here she was, ready to share details of her past with a man she hardly knew, but for some reason she wanted to.

"My family were farmers. My father like his and his father before him were cattle men. They bred some of the finest bulls the shire had ever seen, selling to other breeders across the land. It turned enough profit to give us a more than comfortable life. They were proud people but kind."

She paused and stared at the ground.

"It was my sixth name day. Mother had cooked a turkey and baked a special almond cake, my favourite. Me and my older sister Cora set the table ready for father's return from the cattle auction. When all was finished, we heard father's horse pull up outside, snorting heavily having been ridden hard," Jiney said, swallowing back a lump in her throat.

Raen squeezed her hand reassuringly.

"Father burst through the door screaming for us all to get to the hideaway under the floor boards of the kitchen. We were terrified. By the time we reached the trapdoor, several more horses pulled up outside. Father only had enough time to drop me into the cubby hole before the first of the strangers following him entered the house. He quickly dropped the door shut pulling the table over it; two men entered the kitchen. I could see everything through gaps in the floor boards. Six men took both my sister and my mother, raping my mother in front of my father. When they were done with them, they slit both my parent's throats."

Jiney faltered, a tear running down her cheek. Raen pulled her head into his chest. And shook his finger to say, no more. But she wanted to finish.

"I am alright. Thank you," she said, sitting back up. "They took my sister and left. I was trapped in the hideaway for two days covered in my parent's blood, before friends of my father came looking for him after his absence from the cattle market. They knew it was so unlike father to miss collecting his money from the sale, a thing he did without exception the morning following an auction. They found all our farm hands butchered in the same way. It was terrible. I was taken to Lord Farroth who took pity on me and let me live amongst his servants. In time, a young girl of his household befriended me and that is how I came to be mistress Cailean's personal hand maiden. A position I have enjoyed ever since."

Raen kissed her forehead and again wrote in the sand. Jiney pondered the question for a moment.

"No. I have never seen or heard from my sister since. I don't even know if she is still alive."

Raen sat back down, he looked sad. He took her hand again but this time she leant into him and kissed him passionately on the lips. In that very moment, he realized he loved her and as she lay back he followed her, their lips never parting. All around them faded like a soundless dream, it was quite beautiful. His world began to swirl with an overwhelming passion he had never felt before; something stirred in his loins.

Jiney was still a virgin, but she knew this was the day she would surrender her virginity for the man she loved. Their hands searched each other with ever increasing eagerness as they caressed intimately. He was incredibly gentle with her, which helped to overcome her fear of the pain she had heard sometimes accompanied loves first penetration. Her legs slowly parted to accommodate his entry into the sanctity of her body. Instinctively she began to guide him in, for a moment his body tensed at her touch, but he surrendered and began to enter her.

A sudden feeling of nausea filled his throat with bile as he fought to remain conscious. The blow to the back of the head almost rendered him senseless. What the pair hadn't noticed in their moment of passion was the approach of four men, armed and full of deadly intent. Two of the men dragged Raen off Cailean so violently she screamed out in searing pain. They kept him on his knees whilst a third man grabbed his hair and pulled back his head. He tried to break free but his assailants were too strong.

"You'll not miss this, my friend," the slaver said coldly, nicking Raen under the eye with a dagger. "That pretty thing over there is going to find out what it's like to be fucked by a real man. Then another and another 'till we've 'ad our fill. And if you so much as close an eye, I'll cut the fucker out."

The biggest and leader of the group mounted her first. As he ripped open her dress Jiney fought for all she was worth. But he hit her bloodying her face before ruining her. As soon as he was spent another of the men jumped between her legs, but Jiney still had enough about her to spot the knife in her attacker's belt. Just as he was about to enter her she grabbed the dagger and rammed it into his groin, piercing his scrotum, pinning it to his inner thigh. The slaver screamed out in agony. He quickly pulled the knife out, slid back and turned Jiney onto her stomach. Raen looked on in horror, helpless to stop the savage from cutting her throat so deeply she was almost decapitated. She would never know the blade that ended her life so cruelly, was the very same blade that ended her mother's all those years ago. Raen fought to free himself, his face twisted with inconsolable anguish. But it was pointless; another blow to the head sent him spinning, his body going limp. And in that moment, something changed in him forever.

18

THE EMPEROR ROAD
(part two)

Agramar's head was pounding from a hangover following a night of over indulgence and lack of sleep. The guards outside his tent were given strict instructions that he not be disturbed, but by the sound of the commotion outside it became obvious to the King that his request was about to be ignored.

"Listen you fuckin' imbecile. We have to see the King," Omaar bellowed, after the two soldiers guarding the tent refused to let him pass.

The guards nervously locked spears and repeated the King's orders only to find it angered the quartermaster even more. The noise alerted the rest of the camp to the party's return; slowly men began to pour out of their tents and in no time at all a large group had gathered in the centre of camp. The quartermaster moved towards the taller of the two soldiers, a young man no more than nineteen but strongly built and battle hardened. It took a lot to make him nervous, but nervous he was, his legs feeling weak as Omaar shoved his face inches from his own.

"If you don't get out of my way I'll shove that spear so far up yer arse yer eyes'll spin," he spat.

Both guards looked to one another in the knowledge that Omaar was more than capable of executing such a threat.

The gathering crowd parted as Fraene cut a path through them, his dishevelled hair covering half his face.

"What's going on?"

Omaar recognising the voice turned. Fraene arrived half-dressed trying with some difficulty to fasten his sword belt; the leather made slippery by the rain. The young officer could see from the look on the men's faces that something was terribly wrong.

"You can all go back to your tents now. There is nothing more to see here," he ordered. Reluctantly the crowd began to disperse mumbling with one another as they did so. Finally, when all but a few stragglers had disappeared Fraene turned back to face Omaar and his group outside the tent entrance.

"What is it Omaar?"

"I must speak with the King. Now," he replied, agitated.

Fraene finished buckling his belt and stepped up to the tent's entrance.

"It's alright. Let them pass. I will take full responsibility," he told the guards.

Relieved, both men lifted their spears and stepped back, thankful for the commander's timely intervention.

Fraene led the party through the tent flap to find the King nursing his head in his hands trying to shake off a pounding headache.

"Sire, forgive the intrusion. It would seem Omaar here has pressing information I believe you would wish to hear without delay," Fraene urged, looking back at the surly quarter master.

"Yes, yes, I am not an idiot," the King replied impatiently. "One of you pass me that water," he ordered, pointing to a clay pitcher on the table by his bed. Fraene didn't wait for one of the others to take the initiative, he quickly grabbed the jug and filled a goblet with the water.

During his years of service to his leader, Fraene had laid witness to many such alcohol related mood swings and was all too aware of how quickly things could turn sour. In moments like these, the King's judgement on matters could be swift and unpredictable. But fortunately, the Captain was one of the few people in his leader's employ who could weather such volatile situations; but not without personal risk. And though he didn't know it, a risk Agramar had not been so self-absorbed as not to notice. And during their time together, was one of the many qualities he had come to respect and make him look to his Captain as he would a son.

The King raised his head from his hands, took the drink and gulped it down, half of it running down his chin to soak his chest. Partially hydrated, Agramar stood up shakily. Fraene went to help him steady himself but was angrily shaken off.

"I will be fine.... So, what information do you have that would encourage such blatant disregard of my orders?" The King asked Omaar.

"My Lord. We did as you commanded. We got the food."

"Yes. Yes, and?" Agramar interrupted, still agitated by the intrusion.

Omaar, angered by the King's attitude had to consciously censor his response or find himself in chains or worse.

Fraene could see the old warhorse was struggling to get his words out, his disfigured mouth spitting saliva with every word. It was frustration the young Captain knew could lead Omaar into saying something he would definitely regret.

"What happened?" Fraene asked, directing his question at Brelt the cook. Normally this line of questioning from the Captain would have induced a bout of mumbling obscenities, but on this occasion the surly cook responded with an unexpected willingness to speak. Though he still managed to scowl as he readied his reply. Edging his way to the front of the group Brelt directed his answer to the King. In his deep gravelly voice, he explained how they had first arrived at the farmstead where they found all the dead livestock and burnt out crops. Then he paused for a moment before describing what they found when they entered the village.

"As we said, we got some of the supplies we needed from the farm, but we still needed grain and barrels of fresh water, which we hoped we would get from the nearby village. But when we got to the village." He paused and sucked in air through tightened lips as his thoughts drifted back to that very moment.

Before he could continue, Omaar intervened, having calmed himself enough to take over the conversation; as leader of the group he felt he should.

"Some way off we could see the smoke in the distance. We all knew after finding the farm the way we did, that something was wrong. We hid the horses and wagon amongst the trees not far from the only road into the village. As we closed in on the place we were hit with a smell we all knew too well. Burning flesh. It looked like some of the cottages had been put to the torch, burning all those left inside. But what we found next, well," Omaar looked at the others.

"Get to the point, I haven't got all day," the King interrupted, still in an agitated state.

Omaar continued.

"As we moved further into the village, we realized that this was no ordinary raid. We passed two dwellings that were burnt to the ground, but the thing that struck me first was the silence. Not a sound from the wind, birds, nothin'. Wasn't natural I tell ya. I know evil when I see it and what we saw in that village was pure evil and that's no mistake. Everyone here knows I have seen my fair share of brutality over the years, but this was somethin' else." The king's demeanour visibly changed; now he hung onto every word the quartermaster spat out.

"The few cottages that remained were untouched by fire. Not a body lay on the ground. Then we saw why…." Omaar paused momentarily to wipe the excess saliva from his lips. "Bodies of men, women and children had been butchered; heads, legs, arms, all cut off and nailed to doors. They formed some kinda symbol or somethin', never seen anythin' like it."

"What do you mean? Symbols," Fraene interrupted.

"That's what they looked like. Body parts were bent and twisted into some kinda pattern, they weren't just nailed up there, is what I mean. It was some sick fuckin' warnin', was what it was," Omaar said, forgetting himself momentarily. "Sorry mi-Lord."

The King just gestured for him to carry on.

"I gave the order to torch the rest of the cottages, body parts an' all. Nothin' else we could do," he looked to the King.

"Yes, yes, I understand, please continue."

"We scoured the area for any sign of the attackers. At first, we found nothin'. Then cook here finds this pile of animal shit. It weren't from any beast I've ever seen, an' that's for sure. Then we all hear the lad here a hollerin'," Omaar said, turning to look at the youngest of the group, the thin wiry lad called Gelac, who was standing by the cook, holding a cloth bundle. "We made our way over to the deep ravine he was standin' over. Lyin' at the bottom were the dead bodies of women and children the menfolk must 'ave hid there for protection. Babies, mothers, all stuck with the same black arrows that killed all the animals back on the farm. These arrows sire," he said, gesturing to Gelac, to open the bundle on the table by the King.

Before Gelac reached the table Fraene intervened.

"Here, I will take those lad," he said, taking the bundle and rolling it open on the table. Arrows still covered in gore splayed out. The King stepped forward and picked one up to get a closer look.

"These haven't come off any bird I have ever seen," he said, scrutinizing the black and red fletch. Fraene picked up another arrow, turning it around in his hand. He saw the head of the arrow was strange as well. It was neither iron, steel or bronze or any kind of metal used by any army he knew. It was expertly crafted from black obsidian, with an edge sharper than any metal.

The King turned inquisitively to his captain.

"What do you make of it?"

"I can't say for sure sire but," Fraene hesitated.

"Go on spit it out man."

"Sire, they look to be Elven in origin." A silence filled the room. The King looked thunder struck.

"How can this be?" he asked. "We have done nothing to break our treaty with those sharp eared bastards."

"I have no answer sire. It doesn't make any sense…." Before the Captain could finish, the sound of steel on steel and men screaming filled the tent. Fraene was quick to react. He drew his sword and ran to the back of the tent.

"To arms, protect the King," he ordered as he cut a large slit into the rear wall. The commotion outside got closer and louder. Fraene grabbed the King by the arm and yanked him towards the exit he had cut in the canvas. Agramar was through the hole first. Fraene turned to order the rest to follow; Omaar stood facing the tent entrance his massive mace at the ready. Brelt the cook was already drawing his meat cleaver from its protective leather pouch strapped around his waist.

"Quick follow me, protect the …." Before he could finish the command, the head of one of the sentries standing outside the tent entrance, rolled across the floor. Omaar turned to face Fraene.

"Go, we will hold them off for as long as we can," he spat, then an arm brandishing a huge war axe punched through the open tent flap. Fraene's instinct was to rush forward and help his friends, but discipline took over: before following the King, he was delayed enough to see Brelt's meat cleaver come down, sending the severed arm spinning through the air, axe still in hand. But as the Captain turned to follow Agramar, he saw the huge figure of Sereg enter the tent, his massive two-handed mace obliterating young Gelac's head beyond recognition.

19

AFTERMATH

Bael had been on the trail of the foreign raiders for little over a day. They had zig zagged their way off the most direct route back to Vaeyu, in a vain attempt to lose their pursuers. But the white hawk above never lost sight of them.

Tracking them on the ground on the other hand was being hampered by a summer storm that had blown in from the sea, destroying all but a few of nature's telltale signs used by a tracker such as Bael. Luckily, whenever he wandered off the proper path, the hawk would return, directing him ever closer to his goal; the Wolf at times wandering off to try and pick up the scent herself.

It was obvious they were heading South East. It made sense, this was the closest coastline to his town; it was littered with small sandy coves that could easily shelter the raiders vessel.

The rain was heavy, but thankfully the winds were warm allowing Bael to ride hard without too much discomfort. He had to makeup whatever ground he could; the coast was at most a day away. He looked to the skies as the hawk screeched above, steering him one last time off the misleading path set by the raiders.

After several hours of hard riding, Bael reined in his horse; white froth gathering around all the leather that touched the animal's body. He had hoped to catch up to the slavers before the onset of dark, but Daylight was fading. They had reached the mouth of a narrow gorge and he couldn't let his need for urgency cloud his judgement; it told him, this was the ideal place for an ambush. The Wolf circled him for a moment and slowly set off down the gorge, sniffing the air as she did so. Bael heeled his mount forward cautiously, his bow in hand, ready.

***

Dogran awoke to the wet tongue of a young deer licking his sweat drenched face. He had been unconscious for two days, unaware that if it weren't for the healing skills of Lamia he would surely be dead.

"Well. You have finally decided to join us," Lamia said, removing a bloodstained dressing from one of his wounds. Dogran was too weak to even lift his head, but he did manage a half smile and an acknowledging flick of his right hand.

"Those arrows that Hunter removed from your body were coated with a poison that stopped your blood from thickening. It would be fair to say you owe that young man your life. Had he not acted as quickly as he did, your blood would have spilled from your body until you were dead. The herbs he used stemmed the flow of the poison long enough for him to get you back here to me. The young man never fails to surprise me."

Dogran felt his hand being squeezed affectionately. He painfully turned his head to see the light of his life; tears streaming from her tired eyes. The deer sprang backwards shocked by the unexpected movement, emptying its bladder as it did so. Lamia carefully removed the animal from beside the big man, waving her hand from side to side as he tried without success, to sit up.

"Now, now. We will have none of that," she said. "Are you so eager to open your wounds? Please, do not try to move until I deem it is the right time to do so.... Dogran, show me you understand."

He moved his hand up and down before his eyes closed and he fell into a welcome sleep. Lamia took this opportunity to remove the remaining dressings and apply the strong-smelling poultice both she and Emma had concocted during their two-day vigil.

"I am so grateful to you and Hunter for saving my father's life, I have never felt so helpless. I wouldn't know what I would do if I lost him, I have never thought about a life without him in it, and just how quickly that can change without warning."

"I understand my child, but you can rest assured, your father will pull through this and will in time regain all his strength."

Lamia finished dressing the remaining wounds and looked over at Emma and could see how the young woman's aura had lost its clarity. She understood the fear that filled the tavern girls heart, she had fallen victim to that very same fear all those years ago, when Maccon left for the war.

"Listen, we have done all we can for now. You should go home and try to get some sleep yourself. You will be better prepared to help your father, if you are fully rested. So please. I can deal with things here." Before Emma could respond there was a knock at the door. "Maccon," Lamia whispered to herself. She opened the door and sure enough it was Maccon who greeted her.

"Lamia."

"Maccon. Please, come in."

The priest stepped into the cottage, Cirius close behind, he'd insisted on escorting his leader; sharing a fondness for the burly inn-keep and his daughter. The young Knight made his way over to Dogran, who was lying asleep on a makeshift bed by the fireplace. For Emma's sake, he tried to mask his surprise at how drawn the big man looked and how grey his skin had become.

"How is your father?"

"He is improving and thank the gods he will recover fully. He awoke just moments ago but fell back to sleep just before you arrived."

"Sleep is the best thing for him at this time. It is the bodies way of healing itself," Cirius said reassuringly. "Your father is a strong man; the strongest I have ever met in-fact. I am sure he will soon be himself again." He could see from her dishevelled hair, how much the two days at her father's side had taken out of her. "You look tired."

"I was just about to leave as you arrived, Lamia says there is little else to be done here."

"Then please. Let me escort you home."

"I would not wish to put you out, I will be fine, thank-you."

"Nonsense, I'll not hear of it. It would please me. I insist," he said, offering her his hand.

Before leaving, Emma kissed her father's fevered forehead and took Cirius' outstretched hand to stand up. She gave both Lamia and Maccon a heartfelt hug, then left with her handsome escort.

As they made their way across town people stopped them in the streets showing their support for their favourite Inn keep.

Eventually Emma and her escort found themselves standing outside the open door to the Tavern. Cirius had a quick glance indoors and saw the Inn was full to the rafters, with regulars and friends alike. It was a heartwarming sight, but he could see it was just too overwhelming for Emma to deal with at that moment. They all meant well, but it was obvious she just wanted some peace and quiet and a chance to sleep. Cirius took her hand in his and turned to face her.

"Will you be alright? If you wish, I can come in with you, and tell everyone you need your sleep. If it helps, I can answer any questions they have about your father. Please, let me help you."

His kindness was the final straw, she just fell into his chest and sobbed uncontrollably. Cirius held her close and stroked the back of her head.

It wasn't long before her shoulders stopped shaking, and through sheer strength of character was able to compose herself.

"Thank you, I will be alright now. You have done more than enough for me already. I am really grateful, so please, I am sure Maccon must be wondering where you are."

"Then may I visit your father when possible, until he regains his strength?"

"That would be nice, it is so kind of you."

"I have a deep respect for your father and would wish for nothing else."

For a moment, she found herself gazing into his dark blue eyes where she saw a kindness that unexpectedly moved her. Then as he met her gaze, she turned away shyly.

"If I may be so bold? I would also like to call here to make sure all is well with yourself." The awkward silence that followed made Cirius a little uncomfortable. Then.

"I would like that."

The Knight's face lit up.

"Then I shall see you on the morrow."

"That would be nice and thank you for escorting me home." With that, he took her hand and kissed it.

"I best be going, otherwise my leader will be conjuring up all manner of unsavoury chores for me to do on my return to the Temple."

She let go of his hand, stepped into the open doorway, but before entering she turned around.

Cirius made his way across the town square; on reaching the fountain he turned his head. To his delight, Emma was still standing in the doorway looking his way. He waved goodbye and was pleased to see the wave returned before the young barmaid disappeared into the Tavern.

***

Maccon walked over to where the big man lay, his concern plain to see.

"Will he recover fully?"

"Yes, after plenty of rest. His will to live astounds me. The wounds he suffered should have killed him. Had it not been for Hunter's quick wittedness they surely would have."

Maccon couldn't hide his anxiety from her, Hunter was missing and this didn't bode well with either himself or Lord Farroth. A matter further complicated by the death of that poor young girl Jiney; leaving Cailean in an inconsolable state of mourning, and the Farroth household up in arms that such a dreadful atrocity could take place so close to home without it being detected by the Temple.

"We found the bodies of the men that did this to Dogran, all dead at the hands of Bael and his Wolf." Maccon looked sad. "It would appear that these raiders have abducted young Raen." He paused for a moment. "Did you hear how we found that poor girl?"

"Only what Emma told me, that her body was found by the lake."

"The killing was brutal beyond imagining. She was raped before her throat was cut. We found cut rope by a tree not far from her body, I fear this is where they had

Raen tethered. I am almost certain this is the reason for Hunter's absence."

"I felt a darkness, and saw what happened to Dogran in a vision," Lamia replied. "But I had no idea that at that same moment the young girl's life was being so violently ended. There is powerful dark magic at work here, Maccon. I can feel it, as I am sure can you. What or whoever is capable of wielding such power is beyond my understanding. But it all began when Hunter's Wolf entered our lives."

Maccon took her by the hand.

"I believe you are right. Under normal circumstances, events such as these killings, so close to the Temple, would be made known to us through the Shard. But like yourself, we felt we were only being allowed to see what someone or something wanted us to see. A troubling mystery I believe the Elves we seek possess the answers to. Lord Farroth and I ride to meet our old allies; let us hope they can shed some light on all the issues involving Hunter and his Wolf."

"But what of the King's arrival? Shouldn't you be here for that?" Lamia asked.

Maccon's aura changed, the uncertainty she saw in its colour reflected in his voice.

"The King should have arrived three days' past. We have waited for as long as we can, but I know this. The meeting with the Elves has had to take precedent over all other matters. I have sent Dorodir one of our best tracker's, and a search party to hopefully find and escort the King back to the Keep. I just hope nothing ill has befallen them." Maccon let go of Lamia's hand and walked over to the door. She followed him, a growing sense of the unknown filling her with nervous unease.

Behind them, Dogran groaned, his eyes wide open.

"Maccon," he croaked, his throat dry and sore.

"Rest my old friend. I fear we will need that strength you possess in times to come." Dogran managed a half smile before closing his eyes once more.

Lamia stopped Maccon from leaving. She edged closer to him and kissed him gently on the lips. It took the Mage by surprise. But it was a welcome surprise.

"Please be careful Maccon. I believe these Elves you so readily seek will draw us into a conflict beyond anything we have ever faced before. Don't trust all they tell you. Whatever it is they are withholding from you is a secret I fear they will not wholly share. I would hate to lose you again." Her final comment caught him off guard, but he wasn't going to let this opportunity to re-kindle a relationship he thought lost to him, pass. He drew her towards him and hugged her dearly.

"I promise I will heed your words, and this time I will return to face whatever fate has in store for us." With that, he returned her kiss and left, repeating the promise as he did so.

***

Koval returned home after visiting his old friend, who lay unconscious all the time he was there. He entered his main living quarters to find Tyrna sitting at the table; in-front of her a bowl of broth he had made for her earlier, completely untouched. In-fact she hadn't eaten a morsel for over a day. Concerned for her wellbeing he urged her to eat, but his request was ignored.

She sat like that for nearly two hours, not a word passing her lips. Then without warning or explanation she stood up, placed a shawl over her shoulders and made to leave.

"Where are you going?" Koval asked, as she opened the door.

"I need to walk. Clear my head. I just can't bear to sit here doing nothing when our son is…." She couldn't finish the sentence, the grief-stricken words caught in her throat.

"I will walk with you then," he offered.

"No. I wish to be alone."

Koval was shocked, he couldn't remember the last time she had shunned his company like that, if ever. But he knew better than to fight it.

"If you must, then I shall not interfere."

"I must." With that she left.

Tyrna had never been inclined or found it necessary to visit Hunter's home before; yet here she was, uncertain of what to expect or find. She made her way around the side of the lodge; her every step watched by piercing red eyes high above in the trees. She made her way past the skinning hut and empty wolf pen to find Hunter saddling his horse, the Wolf by his side. Normally the sight of the Wolf would have been enough to dissuade her from going anywhere near the place, but she was driven by a mother's love.

Bael ignored her and continued to tighten the straps underneath the saddle. It was known to most in the town how she felt about him, not least by Bael himself. Yet he understood why she was there, and though his feelings towards her were those of indifference she was still the mother of his friend. His features softened as she crossed the garden to face him.

"I know my feelings towards you have always been plain to see. I am not a woman who hides behind whispers like so many in this town. Yet here I am and would ask you to put your thoughts on my past behaviour to one side," she said, with an impassioned servility Bael had never seen in her before.

"And so here we stand," he replied. "Only now do you wish to talk."

I… I am sorry. I only thought….." She couldn't finish the sentence before tears filled her eyes. "I…I have made a mistake coming here, I must go." As she turned to leave Bael grabbed her by the arm.

"Please forgive me. I know why you are here," he said, with a softness in his voice she had not expected. She turned back to face him and found herself drawn to those incredibly light blue eyes that radiated with a willingness to help. She let her shoulders drop and slowly but surely, she began to relax.

"My son loves you like the brother he never had, Hunter. I believe these raiders we have all heard about, the ones who killed that poor girl, have kidnapped him. And whatever feelings I have about you Hunter, I truly believe you are my son's best chance of survival. Please. I beg you. Hunt these bastards down, show them the same mercy they showed that poor girl."

Bael didn't reply immediately. He jumped into the saddle, armed with bow and swords. "The path I take now is uncertain. But I promise you I will do everything in my power to return your son to you. And take some comfort in the fact that he is both strong and sharp witted," he urged, before heeling his horse forward.

Through clenched teeth Tyrna muttered to herself, "Kill every last one of the bastards, and bring my son home safe."

Hunter never heard the words as he, his Wolf and the Hawk disappeared into the distance.

***

Alloria paced up and down nervously. She was deeply concerned. Her daughter hadn't eaten a thing for nearly two days. The death of her friend Jiney had been so devastating, that it left Cailean crying inconsolably for almost all of the first day following the terrible news.

"I am worried about our daughter. We both know how stubborn she can be. She won't eat, and it has taken me all of my time to even get her to drink…. I have never seen her like this," Alloria finished, as she watched her husband roll up a map he had been looking at. It was obvious his thoughts were elsewhere; this angered her.

"What is up with you? Are those maps more important than your own daughter's wellbeing?"

Lord Farroth stepped back from the open balcony where he was watching his stable hand ready his horse for the journey to see the Elders.

"Make her eat. Force it down her if you must but I tire of her moods. I have more pressing concerns than the death of a servant girl."

Alloria was furious.

"How can you be so cold? How can the death of such a young girl who has worked in this house for so long, mean so little to you? Not to mention the affect it has had on Cailean."

"Of course, it concerns me."

"I begin to wonder," she replied angrily.

"Rest assured, I have already sent fifty of my best men to hunt down those bastards and bring back their heads. As for our daughter, she will get over it. Just find her another maid, that will be a start."

"That's your answer? Find another maid."

"Bah! Cailean loves no one but herself, do you not think I have enough to worry about. My brother is three days late. Hunter has gone missing with that confounded wolf of his. And I have to meet those bastard Elders. So enough about all this, deal with it as you must, and that is my last word on the matter."

Alloria couldn't contain her contempt for her husband any longer. She threw a goblet of water she was holding, smashing it against the wall by the door. She was so angry; words deserted her.

"Careful woman. It's been a long time since you felt the back of my hand, but do not push me," Lord Farroth threatened. His face the colour of beetroot. Alloria couldn't take any more, she stormed across the room and slammed the door behind her as she left.

***

Cailean lay on the bed. Her face pallid and drawn looking. There was a knock at the bedroom door and shortly after, her mother entered. Cailean watched her cross the room to her bedside, carrying a clay bowl.

"I have brought you some soup," she said. "Your favourite."

Cailean didn't respond and continued staring at the ceiling.

"I know how much Jiney meant to you, but it won't help anyone if you make yourself ill," her mother continued. "So please, just try sipping a little, I am sure your friend would wish it."

Alloria placed the bowl close to Cailean's nose in a hope that the smell would encourage her to eat. Sadly, it didn't get the response she had hoped for; so, she placed it on a small table by the bed.

"Please my love, talk to me, I can't help you if you won't let me."

Cailean moved her head slightly, avoiding her mother's gaze.

"Ever since I spilled from your womb without a piece of dangling flesh between my legs, I felt my father's disappointment."

Alloria was stunned that such vulgarity could come from her daughter's mouth.

"How dare you speak to me in this manner. I have done nothing to deserve such disrespect," she pressed, more shocked than angry, for she knew, though the language was strong its message was true. With that Cailean burst into floods of tears.

Alloria softened as a mother does, it was true her husband had always wanted a son, but sadly that would never be. Maybe it was natures cruel way of punishing her husband's lack of understanding, who knows, she thought, whenever her mind visited such matters. Whatever the reason, her womb was barren and would never again bear child; and was why she never lost sight of just how precious Cailean was to both her and her husband. Though sadly he just didn't see it, and though she still loved him, it was the thorn in their relationship which dug ever deeper.

Alloria took Cailean's head in her lap and gently stroked her hair.

"I am so sorry about your friend. I too miss her. She was like a ray of sunshine about the place. And I know you think you will never get over this terrible thing, but you will…. Time is a great healer. And though this will live with you the rest of your life, you will learn to deal with it. This I know…." For a moment she sat quietly, then took a deep breath. "There is something I have never told you…. You had a brother."

Cailean turned onto her back and stared at her mother in surprise, her tears reduced to snivelling.

"What do you mean?"

"I had intended to tell you all about it when I deemed you were ready, but as time passed by and I saw the bitterness between you and your father grow the way it did, I held back."

"What happened?" she asked, watching as the memory glazed her mother's eyes.

"We named him after your father, Anwald Il. Sadly, he only lived amongst us for one week before joining his ancestors. He was born too early and was not strong enough to hold on to his fragile life.... I felt then as you must now, that I would never get over such loss, but I did, and somehow learnt to celebrate his life no matter how short. And each year on his name day, though I feel a sadness I have learned to control, I cherish that he was a part of my life, no matter how fleeting."

Cailean stopped sobbing and sat up on the bed.

"I feel so helpless, I want to do something to help find her killers, but what can I do? I have no skills to speak of. I live off my father's name. I am expected to marry some stranger, I have yet to meet."

Alloria stared at her in amazement.

"How do you know about this?"

"I'm not a fool, mother. Rumours abound throughout the town. The King brings a suitor for me to marry, some Prince from the Isles they say. As if that wasn't bad enough, now my friend is murdered, and here I lie as useless as ever."

"You must not talk this way. You are a beautiful young woman, highly intelligent, if a little misguided at times, but loved by all who know you. For now, there is little either of us can do, other than pray the men we so readily depend upon will see justice done. And though I should not mention it, I believe Hunter is endeavouring to do just that."

"What do you mean?"

"I have said more than I should have. But. Well let's just say, Hunter and his Wolf are missing. We both know how he cared for that smithy's boy, I believe this to be the reason for his absence. Let us hope the gods favour his quest for justice, and that his justice is swift and merciless."

Cailean seemed to perk up a little. Alloria handed her the cold soup, and this time her daughter took it willingly. She stood up and kissed Cailean on the forehead, ready to leave.

"Thank-you mother, I do love you. I really wouldn't know what to do without you."

"I love you too. Now try to get some sleep and I will see you in the morning. I have an idea."

And on that note, she left.

20

THE STRANGER

Vena was no stranger to tragedy, but the news of the young girl's murder and the abduction of the smithy's son had left her with a growing sense of foreboding. Nothing like this had ever happened to her town before. Murders tended to be between rival gangs and were mostly committed in the confines of Beggars Nest. The kidnapping however was a first. She had, like the rest of the town heard about such raids, that for whatever reason, until now, they had been lucky enough to avoid.

Bael had visited Vena before leaving town to find Raen. She was his only confidant, and other than Tyrna, was the only person he'd told of his plan to hunt down Raen's kidnappers. His only request of her was that she check on his lodge from time to time, until his return. This she did willingly.

The death of Jiney saddened her; what few times their paths crossed, Vena had found her to be nothing less than kind and respectful. And far too young to find her life cut short in such a brutal manner. The news of Dogran had also bothered her; she had a soft spot for the burly inn-keep, who unlike his daughter, had treated her with nothing but kindness. And for her part she held him in high esteem for being one of the few men of importance in the town that hadn't at one time or another patronised her establishment.

Three days had passed since Hunter set off to find Raen. As promised she had just finished checking his lodge; realizing that time was getting on, she decided to make her way back into town.

The sun had all but disappeared behind the mountains to the East, leaving just enough light for her to navigate the streets and alleyways without too much difficulty. Instead of going back to the brothel, she headed for Dogran's Tavern.

Most of the regulars were already present when Vena entered. It was obvious the main topics of conversation were the terrible events surrounding the murder and kidnapping. But as she passed people on her way to the bar, a hush befell the place, and not unexpectedly the whispers began.

"What's *she* doing here," the baker's wife asked. Not really directing her question to anyone in particular. A few other women in the room seconded the question. But all were met with silence; as most men in the establishment didn't want to get involved, for obvious reasons, and in fairness none had any grievance with the woman anyway.

Emma looked uncomfortable as her unexpected guest approached the bar. But there were more important things to think about, than her patrons' petty misgivings regarding the woman who now sat facing her across the counter.

Vena placed her small leather purse in-front of her; ignoring the pathetic meanderings from behind, she leaned forward.

"Would you be so kind as to pour me a mug of your finest cider?" she asked.

Emma didn't answer, she just walked to the end of the bar, filled a goblet full of local cider and returned, her hand outstretched to receive payment. Vena took the drink, ignored the snub and handed Emma the coin.

"How is your father?" She asked, as Emma placed the change on the counter in-front of her.

"He is fine."

Vena took a sip of her drink; annoyed by the measured response she said.

"What have I done to warrant such contempt?"

Emma's cheeks flushed with embarrassment at Vena's directness, and though normally she would not shy away from an answer, she found herself uncharacteristically tongue-tied.

It had never been Vena's intention to make Emma feel uncomfortable, with all the emotions the woman was having to juggle regarding her father's health.

"Look. I haven't come here to make you feel awkward. I am here out of a courtesy to Dogran, one of the few honourable men left in this town…. Please when you see him tell him I was asking after him, that's all."

Vena gulped down the last of her drink, placed the empty mug on the counter and made to leave.

Emma's face softened.

"Please forgive my rudeness. Stay a moment and let me pour you another drink, courtesy of the Inn."

Vena sat back down and acknowledged the gesture with a smile.

"No apology necessary, and that drink would be welcome."

The two women chatted for a while, Emma explaining how the old woman had saved her father's life, and how Hunter had played no small part in it. The mention of Lamia seemed to trigger a look of melancholy Emma had never expected to see from Vena. But she never thought to question why and carried on.

As time passed, she found herself warming to this woman of the night. A feeling shared by Vena. Just as the conversation was coming to its conclusion, a tall darkly handsome stranger entered the room. Vena being an excellent judge of character could see this was no simple wanderer. He had a presence about him that certain men possess, a presence that makes one stop, look and wonder.

The stranger made his way over to the bar and ordered a drink, surprisingly nothing stronger than honeyed water. Vena could see Emma found the man handsome, and not being shy herself, turned to face him.

"So, what brings you to this small town of ours?" She asked.

The man drank half of the honey water in one gulp and answered.

"Nothing of any note, just passing through. Why do you ask?"

"Just curious nothin' more. We don't get many of your kind visitin' these parts."

"My kind?" He smiled.

Vena could see the stranger found her line of questioning a little prickly, so she adopted a more tactful approach.

"I meant no offence. It's just, we don't get many from the Summer Isles traveling this far East," she said looking at his single beaded braid of hair.

"Then no offence is taken," he replied. "Do you have a room for the night? I have been on the road for quite some time and would welcome a bed and a well-needed bath."

"We have a room, just let me know when you are ready to retire and I will get one of my maids to pour you that hot bath."

"Then I thank you for your courtesy and would welcome another drink, an ale this time I think." Emma poured his drink and returned to finish her conversation with Vena. They talked for a little while longer before Vena decided to leave. She stood up, picked her purse off the counter.

"One last thing," Emma asked. "Is it true Hunter has left town with his Wolf and that white hawk of his?"

Before Vena could answer, the stranger interrupted.

"I am sorry. I couldn't help overhearing your comment about the man with a white hawk…. This hawk, does it have the reddest of eyes?"

His question left both women somewhat surprised and naturally defensive. Vena no longer in any rush to leave ordered another drink. She was aware that Emma, like herself was more than a little intrigued by the stranger's question. And neither woman was willing to just leave it there.

"Why do you ask?" Vena quizzed.

"Please, forgive my bluntness. I am just curious nothing more. Only I knew a man once, a long time ago, who had such a bird. That's all."

Emma stared at Vena, a look that shared the same question. Could this stranger hold answers to the mystery surrounding Hunter that had eluded them both for as long as they had known him.

"You say you knew such a man? How? And how long are you talking about?"

The Stranger pondered Emma's question carefully before answering. Vena's innate ability at reading peoples body language left her in no doubt that whatever secrets this man held, they gave him pain on recollection.

The strain wrinkles on the stranger's forehead softened, his eyes became rounded once more and taking a deep breath, he finished his ale in one large gulp. Emma instinctively refilled his mug and waved no coin was necessary. She gave her two friends working behind the counter a friendly nod and asked Vena and the stranger to join her at an empty table by the door. When all were seated Vena took the initiative.

"This man you speak of, how old would he be now?"

"I think he would be in his sixtieth year. It has been almost thirty years that I last saw him. I remember the day as if it were only yesterday. It was the day this man earned his freedom. It was his thirtieth name day, I recall."

Both women looked disappointed with his answer.

"Then the man we know cannot be the same," Vena replied. "For the man we know, can only be half that age.

"At most," Emma seconded.

Though in truth neither woman was sure about Hunter's age, but both were certain he definitely hadn't seen his sixtieth name day. This time it was the stranger's turn to look disappointed.

"What name did this man go by?" Vena asked.

"He was known to us all as Galas. He was a great fighter."

"Fighter! What do you mean? Emma interrupted.

"It will help I think, if I tell you a little about myself.... I was captured as a child and trained as a slave to fight in the pits up North, for the entertainment of the King. I was in my fifteenth year when I fought for the first time in the Grand Arena. I was put with seven seasoned fighters from lands far and wide, our opponents, a father and his son. The men I was to fight beside were Brutal killers, champions of whichever country they represented. I presume I was set amongst them to present the crowd with an early death, so that the fight would not look to be weighted unfairly against the crowd's favourites. This Galas and his father.

Galas had built up a ferocious reputation with this white hawk of his, a creature that accompanied him from the day both he and his father were first introduced to the games.

Both fighters should they win, would gain their freedom, but King Malanon had other ideas. This monster had eaten the hearts of many of his fallen champions, and was hoping to feast on the two he hoped would fall that day."

"What? Eat their hearts, why? What would drive a man to such barbarism?" Vena asked, in disgust.

"The man was mad, he believed, to eat the hearts of fallen champions was a way to draw their spirits into his body. The greater the champion the more powerful he would become. But as fate would have it things were not going to go his way. That was the day Galas lost a father and spared my life. I don't know why he let me live, but whatever his reason was, I have always been grateful and hoped that one day I could meet the man and thank him for my life. Sadly, from what you tell me, I am no closer to fulfilling that wish. Yet I still find it strange that such a man as you both describe should be accompanied by such a rare and unusual creature as a white hawk. The like in truth, I have never seen since."

How strange indeed, Vena thought, *the man the stranger described could have been Hunter himself, but how?*

Emma was more pragmatic; she felt the likelihood that Hunter and his hawk were one and the same as this stranger described was beyond ridiculous.

"There is no possibility that the man you speak of is the same man we know as Hunter."

"His name is Hunter?" the stranger asked.

"His real name is Bael. Most in the town call him Hunter, a name favoured by those who just haven't taken the time to get to know the man."

"Where can I find this Hunter?"

"He has gone, nobody knows where or when he will return," Emma replied.

Vena didn't offer any further information, letting the moment pass.

Both women went on to tell him about the terrible events that had left the town in such a solemn state. The stranger looked genuinely sympathetic on completion of the story, but it was easy to see the man was tired.

"I am sorry that such a terrible thing like this should befall what I perceive to be a nice town. Events such as these take their toll on people, I have seen it far too often. You will all find the strength you need to get over a tragedy like this, by looking to each other. Now I am afraid I must take my leave. If you would be so kind, the bath you promised would see a welcome end to a tiresome day," he said, smiling wearily at Emma.

"Of course. I must get back to my duties." She excused herself from Vena's company and showed the stranger to his room. She showed him where everything was, but before leaving him to relax, she had one more question.

"Do you intend to stay for long?"

"I am not sure yet."

"Well so long as you can pay, the room is yours," she replied, before leaving.

The stranger removed his clothes and slid into the hot bath left for him in the small annex room next to his. He let himself soak away the weariness of his long journey and found his thoughts drifting back to that day in the arena.

He lay in the water until the skin on his fingers began to wrinkle; that was time enough to wash away the stench of travel. He stepped out of the bath, wrapped a towel around his waist and entered his room. Before sprawling out on the welcoming cot bed he walked over to a small oak table close to the only window in the room. He opened it and let the cool night breeze in to tease his still damp skin, then he slowly undid the string tie to the bundle he was carrying. Inside were a number of extra clothes he had picked up on his long journey; he removed them and placed them flat over the backs of the two chairs by the table. There was one item that remained. Carefully, he picked it up, the flickering candle light running along its shiny edge. He moved over to his bed and rested the jagged edged sword close to where he lay: the very sword that punched through the chest of the fighter standing over Galas all those years ago.

21
AMBUSH

Raen opened his eyes. His head still ached from the blow that laid him unconscious two days earlier, his hair matted with the dried blood that covered half his face. His captor's arrogance had led them to believe their evasive manoeuvres would fool any who might try to follow. They were wrong.

Raen's hands and feet were tightly bound as he lay staring up at the moonlit sky. Something circled above the campfire his captors had lit to ward off the many predators they knew roamed the land. Luckily it was only Raen who spotted his friend, with those bright red eyes. This and the sound of a wolf in the distance filled the lad with renewed hope, his adrenalin filled muscles straining at his bonds with fresh vigour, fuelled by chance.

Goren, the vicious leader of the group posted two men at opposite ends of the clearing to keep watch, while the rest sat by the fire eating their fill of under cooked dog they killed on the trail. When their bellies were full, Goren ordered two of them to change places with the two on guard duty.

Raen hadn't been fed once during the whole journey, his only consolation being water, provided with reluctance and a frequent boot in the stomach. He'd tried to keep his attempt to free himself from the ever-roaming eyes of his captors and had thus far succeeded.

Goren stood up. Out of the corner of his eye he caught the slightest of movements. His prisoner was wriggling about trying to loosen the leather straps binding his wrists; traitored by the orange glow of the fire. The ugly brute of a man walked over to Raen who now lay still.

"What the fuck are yer up to, you stupid bastard," he bellowed, his voice thick with anger. "Tried to escape did ya? If you weren't worth more alive, I'd 'ave cut yer fuckin' throat when we fucked that whore of yours."

Raen, filled with uncontrollable anger sat up and fought with every ounce of his being to break free, but the bindings held true, stripping his wrists raw.

"Yer dumb fuck," Goren grunted, booting Raen squarely in the face rendering him instantly unconscious. Returning to the fire he ordered the youngest in the group, a thin wiry thug with face scars to match his violent nature, to sit by the prisoner.

"If he tries to move take a finger or two. That should stop the fucker," Goren ordered.

Master of twin daggers, the young thug knew better than to damage the cargo any more than had already been done. Vaeyu wouldn't tolerate damaged merchandise, and he feared his leader far more than the monster staring down at him. Fortunately, it looked as though the captive would give no further trouble that night, so the young thug rested against a nearby tree and fell asleep.

***

Bael edged his way to the tree line, just out of reach of the fires revealing glow. He patted the Wolf on the neck and gestured for her to stay hidden in the shadows. Slowly he circled his way around the camp taking account of all the raiders. He had one chance, outnumbered as he was by such hardened killers. He kept out of sight of the prison wagon which was situated the opposite side of the camp, some thirty paces or so from where Raen lay. He couldn't risk one of the captives giving away his position no matter how un-intentioned it might be. The Hawk circled above, waiting for the moment it knew wasn't far away.

Hunter could see Raen wasn't moving; the first to die had to be the thin raider by the tree. The arrow thudded through his face pinning his head to the tree trunk. The guard closest to the dead reaver was first to his feet.

"We are under attack," he screamed, before an arrow whizzed across the clearing to end his screaming. The rest of the group were on their feet. In the confusion Bael stepped from the shadows to cut Raen's bonds, but as his blade cut the rope a crossbow bolt thudded into a tree behind him. Raen didn't move.

Goren armed with his battle axe made for Hunter. One of the other raiders readied his crossbow, before he could fire the bolt, the Wolf pounced over two men brandishing swords, knocking both of them to the ground. In one savage moment, the bowman watched on helplessly as his throat was torn out, drowning on his own blood. The two on the ground were quick to their feet. They stood back to back uncertain from which direction the Wolf would make its next attack. What they didn't expect was an attack from above. The Hawk took out the eyes of the smaller of the two leaving him on his knees writhing in agony. The Wolf pounced again savaging the other fighter until he was dead.

Meanwhile Goren and the three remaining raiders circled Bael, weapons drawn. Bael made short work of the first two to attack him, leaving one a headless corpse the other wrestling his guts as they slipped through his fingers. Goren ordered his last man forward, Hunter took his leg off, leaving him to bleed out. But before he could despatch the leader of the raiders in a similar manner, he saw his Wolf topple head over heels as a crossbow bolt punched into her. He knew she was beyond his help, he had to finish what he started. His blades flashed like lightning, one piercing his attacker's groin, the other opening his throat. Goren fell to the ground in a spray of deep red. Dead. But it was all for naught. A group of riders appeared through the trees the other side of the fire.

Bael looked to both Raen and the Wolf, neither moved. His Hawk plummeted from the darkness, attacking the rider at the rear. But it wasn't enough. Another rider close by hit the bird with his mace, sending it plummeting into the shadows, broken. Hunter's bow was where he left it, too far to consider, but before he could make his move a blade dug into his throat.

***

Vaeyu's dagger cut into Bael's neck, just deep enough to draw a line of blood, but not deep enough to sever the artery that throbbed with anticipation. In that moment, Hunter expected his life to end. Surprisingly it didn't.

The rest of Vaeyu's men stood around him waiting for that final cut, but instead of the blade finishing his captive's life, it supported a chain with a black rune medallion at its end. Vaeyu ordered two of his men to force Bael to his knees. Then he too knelt down to face his prisoner. Again, he lifted the medallion on his dagger's blade.

"Where did you come by this?"

At first Bael refused to answer. Vaeyu looked more closely to make sure there was no mistake.

"I will ask you one more time, where did you get this?"

Hunter could see in his captors eyes some sense of recognition but couldn't understand why. But he also knew further silence would see his death.

"It was my father's." Then all went black.

Vaeyu placed the dagger back in its scabbard, after rendering Bael unconscious with its hilt. None of his men could understand why their leader didn't finish the job, but they all knew enough not to question his motives. Vaeyu had Raen put in the wagon with the rest of the captives and left the camp as he found it, leaving the dead as appetisers for the wild. But there was something about the captive he'd allowed to live, that troubled him, but for now that mystery would have to wait.

22

CAPE OF STORMS

The Cape of Storms. A graveyard for ships unlucky enough to get trapped in the Tempests that gave it, its name. There was no other route for Vaeyu's ship to travel without adding weeks to their voyage. And that just wasn't an option.

Luck had seen the ship's outward journey, free from all but the mildest of storms. But on its return, luck was not so kind.

The nose of the Savage Eel cut through the water like a knife, dipping into a swell that exploded over the bow. The sound of the waves pounding the hull was like thunder to those below fighting to plug holes that would see the ship to a watery grave. The timbers creaked and groaned; the sound of resistance to a force that could tear the vessel apart. To weather the Tempest, the ship had veered off course in an attempt to traverse its outer edge.

Two crewmen lost their lives, dashed from the rigging by the unforgiving water. The remaining crew still working the deck were lashed to the main mast by lengths of rope that allowed them to perform their duties.

The quartermaster, a thick set man with the tattoo of a green eye staring from the back of his shaven head, fought next to the pilot to keep the vessel heading into the waves. He knew all too well what a cruel mistress the sea could be; a lesson hard learned over years at her mercy. His skills as a seaman had prevented the ship from being broadsided by waves that would have sheered the masts and broke the vessels spine.

As the ship rose out of a fifty-foot trough to crest a huge swell, the horizon came into view. Thankfully the rain and thunder had stopped, but forked lightening stubbornly lit up a sky that turned day into night. His knowledge of the waters they were traveling, told him the worst was over. It wasn't long before the swells got smaller; the quartermaster felt the time was right and ordered the main sail dropped to catch the wind and steer them back on course.

Within a day of leaving the storm behind, the ship found itself stranded in becalmed waters sailors call the doldrums. For two days' nerves were shredded, tempers frayed and tolerance levels were almost non-existent, as a baking sun dried everything in its path. On the third day the wind howled through the rigging; the flapping canvas a sound the sailors called the song of the sea. And then the clean-up began.

Before entering the captain's quarters to speak with Vaeyu, the coxswain looked to the area on deck that housed the prisoners. Luckily it was still intact, but the rough seas had taken its toll on the young cargo within, leaving the deck around them soiled with more than their usual quota of vomit and other bodily excretions.

Raen was beginning to feel his strength returning. He noticed during his moments of lucidity, that the captain of the ship didn't appear to share the same penchant for needless suffering as the rest of the crew. Well, most that is. There were others amongst them that given the choice would have preferred an easier life, but fate in all its mischievous glory, had dealt them a hand where choice just wasn't an option.

Both he and the other captives were chained together on the ships forward deck. Their only protection from the elements being a canvas canopy supported at the front by two wooden struts and tethered at the rear to the roof of the cabin holding the ships food supplies. Surprisingly all the puke, excrement and other bodily fluids that surrounded such a group like this, were flushed away at the end of each day to prevent any kind of disease spreading around the ship. Vaeyu had seen first-hand how quickly a disease such as dysentery could decimate a crew and he wasn't about to let that happen on this ship.

Unfortunately for Raen, both he and a girl who was maybe in her sixteenth or seventeenth year, fell fowl of this responsibility. It was getting close to that time in the day; Raen and the girl were released from their chains. Two empty buckets attached by a coil of rope to wooden cleats, were waiting for them at the side of the ship closest to their canvas shelter. They threw the heavy buckets over the side and let them down into the crystal blue water below. Each bucket had a lead weight attached to one side of the rim, so it would tip over on impact. When full, they hauled them up the side of the ship's hull; trying not to spill too much in case they incurred the wrath of the more sadistic crew members.

After the first four bucket loads were used, Raen and the girl threw the empty buckets over the side again. Normally four buckets would have been enough, but the sea had been incredibly rough during the storm, inducing a particularly bad bout of sea sickness amongst the group. What made matters worse, the sun was intense, drying the mess into solid clumps.

The buckets hit the water. This time though, the girl's strength had abandoned her. She couldn't even pull hers free of the waves. Raen by contrast, had no problem with his. Pulling it over the side he threw its contents across the deck, brushing what remained of the human waste into troughs, then on through holes in the side of the hull to the sea below. He hadn't taken much notice of the girl behind him until he heard a member of the crew screaming at her. Raen dropped his brush; the girl began to cry as the raider, a surly looking low life with half his nose missing screeched obscenities at her.

"Listen you little cunt. I don't want to be smellin' yer shit all night, 'cause yer too fuckin' lazy to pull up that bucket," the thug bellowed. "Now pull it up or I'll throw yer over the side with it."

Fear helped the girl pull the bucket of water almost halfway up the side of the ship. The raider leant over the rail to check on her progress.

"Well, come on pull. We 'aven't got all fuckin' day."

No matter how hard she tried she had nothing left to give, the bucket fell back into the water, leaving her with painful rope burns to her hands. Raen just couldn't stand there and watch such brutality, he moved quickly to the girl's side, removed her bloodied hands from around the rope and began to pull up the bucket for her.

"Well. Well. Well. The fucker's in love," the pirate jibed, as Raen hauled up the full bucket.

"If that's how it is, then maybe you can clean up *all* the shit from now on."

The commotion had drawn Vaeyu out of his cabin. He stormed across the deck to where the girl knelt sobbing, her hands bloodied and his crewman kicking Raen along from behind as he spread the last of the water along the floor.

"What are you doing?"

"This lazy bitch dropped the barrel back into the water, then this dumb fuck thought he would 'elp 'er."

Vaeyu looked at the girl first, then at Raen. He helped the girl to her feet and tried to open her clenched hands. At first, she resisted, keeping them tightly shut for fear of what he might do next.

"It's alright, I will not hurt you," he whispered, in the common tongue she understood.

This time she allowed him to open them, but not without great discomfort. He turned to face his crewman again.

"These wounds won't heal before we reach shore. And because of you I will lose coin on her at the auctions."

"I. I am sorry captain. I...."

Before he could finish his apology, Vaeyu's dagger appeared from nowhere, opening up a gash from his nave to his chest. Before the man's guts could spill out and soil the deck, Vaeyu kicked him in the chest catapulting both man and his offal overboard to feed whatever lurked below. The rest of the crew turned away and went about their duties, some mumbling to themselves whilst others had the sense to keep quiet.

It wasn't the loss of money that saw him execute his crew member, that excuse was solely for the benefit of the rest of his men. In truth, he was sick of the mindless violence that seemed to be getting worse and more frequent with each passing trip. And though his King did not yet no it, this was to be his last.

Vaeyu called on the ship's healer, a bearded man with dark skin, a foreigner, captured during a past raid and used for his skills. He dressed the girl's wounds and left her unchained as instructed. The poor girl had suffered enough. To his surprise Raen also found himself untethered. Instead, the healer asked him to follow.

Vaeyu poured a mug of fresh water and handed it to Raen, who was preoccupied with the cabin's interior. It was the first time he had been allowed to enter the place, the space was fascinating. Stuffed animals from different lands adorned ornate shelves. Lanterns filled the room with a welcoming warm glow that cast enough light to allow the captain to read the many maps and charts that littered the massive desk by the stained-glass window. The picture in the glass was of a giant eel attacking a boat at sea. Raen accepted the water willingly and downed it in one. He placed the empty mug on the floor by his feet, all too aware he was being scrutinised by his strange captor.

"There is something about you boy, what is it? Why would a man face such overwhelming odds and risk his life to get you back? And why did this man you know travel with a dire wolf?" Vaeyu asked, in his native tongue.

Raen couldn't understand a word the man said, until the mention of the wolf. A word that for one reason or another, was the same in his language as it was in his captor's.

Vaeyu noticed the lad's eyes widen at the mention of the wolf. He realized he had to speak in the common tongue to make himself understood.

"I will do best to speak in common tongue so you understand, yes?" He said, nodding at the prisoner. Raen nodded back that he understood.

"Good, then we get somewhere. Before we left mainland a man with wolf tried to save you, yes?"

Raen didn't acknowledge the question, instead he faced his captor with a look of hate fuelled defiance. Vaeyu could see recognition written all over Raen's face and was in no mood for childish games.

"Look, I would have you answer me or suffer consequence for your stupidity. Choice is yours." Raen reluctantly nodded he understood.

"You can speak, not worry," Vaeyu said, expecting a verbal reply.

Raen pointed to his lips and shook his head.

"So, you cannot speak, now I see this will be difficult. First, I wish you to know, I had nothing to do with the death of that young woman. Maybe some comfort can be had knowing your friend saw an end to those men."

For a moment Raen fought to contain the anger that if released would surely see his death. Even through the hatred he felt for his captor, he could see the man spoke the truth. Softening, he pointed to a stick of charcoal on the desk and a scroll of empty parchment.

"Yes. Yes, please," the captain said, gesturing for Raen to pull his chair to the desk and pick up the charcoal. He did what the captain requested and opened the parchment ready to write.

"I will try to ask questions that require simple answers, otherwise we will run out of paper," he said struggling with the language. "Only speak the truth. I will know lie. You don't want to lie."

Raen looked tentatively at the man, he could sense there was something special about him, and that any attempt at deceit would be futile, and such action would be dealt with vigorously.

"This man I speak of, the one with wolf. What is his name?"

Hunter, Raen wrote down.

"And the wolf, how did man come by such beast?"

Raen paused to think how best to answer. Then he wrote, *the Elves.*

Vaeyu sat down at his desk and pondered over his next question.

"The stone around Hunter's neck, how did he come by?"

The question puzzled Raen, he had seen the stone pendant many times and thought it nothing more than a fancy trinket. But it was obvious in this man's eyes it held far greater significance. The lad shook his head.

"Are you sure you don't know?"

Again, Raen shook his head.

Vaeyu could see he was telling the truth and couldn't hide his disappointment.

"A pity. I have only ever seen a stone like this once before. The person wearing it saved my life." he whispered, putting voice to his thoughts. "So, that is enough for today."

He shouted the guard outside the door and ordered the man to escort Raen back to the other captives, but like the girl, was not to be chained.

Raen joined the group, who were waiting with hunger induced anticipation for the food that was about to be handed out. Their one meal of the day. Now they were on the ship it was distributed more evenly amongst the group, by a young steward. A scrawny lad, who looked as though a decent square meal would have done him no harm either. When the other crewmen weren't looking, he seemed to be a kindly sought, rough at the edges but soft inside. But if any of the others stood over him with a watchful eye, he pretended he was made of sterner stuff.

Sadly, on this occasion the man approaching was the ships cook, a fat ugly brute with a bad limp. Instead of sharing it out, he threw the pan of salted fish and bowl of bread on the floor in the centre of the prisoners. Not a care for who got what.

Raen noticed each time this man served the food, the smallest amongst them, a girl no more than twelve, edged her way close to him.

The girl had suffered on the road at the hands of a cruel hunchback. And had seen the kindness in the leader of the raiders when he fed her some meat and cut off the fingers of the hand the hunchback laid on her leg. She saw a strength in Raen she didn't see in any of the others except maybe the girl with the bandaged hands.

On these occasions one of the captives, a tough looking lad with the chiselled cheekbones of a hard life, made sure he got more than his fair share of the offerings. And on two such occasions Raen found himself sharing his portion with this young girl by his side. The lad was possibly a year younger than Raen but was the sought you would see wandering the streets of Beggars Nest. Not wishing to draw unnecessary attention on himself Raen had let it pass, but not this time.

As usual, the bully was first to tuck in, leaving just enough for the rest to forage through. The young girl kept her head down and was ready for tears. Raen sat down beside her and gave her half his bread and all his fish. She grabbed the food hungrily, but before she let it touch her lips she looked up.

"Thank you," she whispered. He smiled at her reassuringly, then stood up and walked over to where the bully sat stuffing himself. Raen pointed to the fish, and waved *no, no*. The lad's immediate response was to smart mouth his way out of the problem; until he saw Raen's chiselled biceps and thought better of it. Raen took what was left, handing some to the girl with the bandaged hands, who was now sitting next to the youngest in support of Raen's kindness. He sat down beside them both and handed half of what remained to the young girl; a kindness that wasn't lost to Vaeyu, who watched from the pilot's platform.

All three ate together, and for the first time during their gruelling ordeal, found comfort in each other's company. Something they did for the rest of the journey; the bully never bothering them again.

23

NEGLECTED ALLIES

A week of hard riding, staying no longer than one night in any one place, saw Lord Farroth and his party within spitting distance of their final destination.

Traitors Pass was a ten-league long road that snaked its way through high white rock cliffs, to its destination, a bowl type valley with only one way in and one way out.

Lord Farroth's father, King Mailo Farroth it was said, though never fully corroborated, led a small army of mounted fighters into the Pass to search out an Elven Fortress that was rumoured to have been built there. A fortress they were never to see.

The Elders had carved massive plateaus into the cliffs; their only access, stone steps hewn out of solid rock that would accommodate two men abreast. These lookouts could each hold as many as one hundred archers at any one time, which for the unfortunates below they did.

Less than half way into the Pass, King Mailo lost half his men and horses to a rain of arrows that left the rest with nowhere to hide. Before the King could issue the order to retreat, some fifty of his men broke ranks and headed back the way they came. Mailo was so angered by this display of such unforgivable cowardice, he had the men nailed to stakes high above the canyon mouth: where it is said, their remains lie to this day.

Mailo never returned, and never met the military genius who orchestrated his humiliating defeat: *Koryllion*.

Shortly after his run in with the Elders, Mailo took a vacation with his family, visiting his cousin Alderan, Prince of the Shimmering Isles, a small group of islands nestling like jewels in the Sea of Hope. He and his eldest son Agramar were out swimming one morning in the palace's own private cove. Mailo never lived out that day, he was bitten on the face by a deadly sea snake and died almost instantly in his wife's arms, on a small deserted beach far from his own Kingdom.

It took his son Agramar, years to broker a truce with his Elven brethren, and now as fate would have it, here they were about to enter the very Pass that was party to his father's humiliation all those years before.

Maccon ordered two outriders to scout ahead, whilst he and Lord Farroth led the rest of the escort into the pass. Just over a league in, the outriders returned with ten Elven Lancers riding close behind. The Captain of the Lancer's welcomed his guests and bade them follow.

The few times Maccon had come into contact with the Elves, they had never failed to impress him. Their uniforms were always pristine and their weapons polished; they had remarkable symmetry in the way they moved, whether it be marching or a military manoeuvre, their uniformity was breath-taking.

More than three quarters of the way into the pass they approached a rock face, which appeared to be the end of the road, but it was an illusion created by distance. On reaching the rock face, the road veered sharply right to reveal a huge bowl-shaped valley surrounded on all sides by the snow-capped peaks of the Taelyn Mountains.

The sight as they rounded the corner was a marvel of both nature and Elven ingenuity. The valley was probably two leagues across. At its centre, a crystal blue lake whose waters were fed from half a dozen waterfalls cascading from high in the mountains. Surrounding the lake was a pine forest, honeycombed with well-trodden trails, all culminating on the lake's stony shores. At the rear of the lake high above the pine trees was the fortress. A masterpiece of engineering it was hewn out of solid rock, demonstrating their race's uniquely delicate architecture. And though both Maccon and his leader had seen it once before when they signed the peace treaty, the sight still took their breath away. It was a mystery to those who were privileged enough to lay eyes on the place, at how this far from anywhere such a structure could be built. A secret the Elders had never shared with anyone.

The procession of riders followed the road up and around the curved rock face. A half league from the fortress entrance the escorting lancers drew to a halt. The road came to a dead end; a deep gorge some thirty feet wide cut right through it. On the other side of the gorge two large stone-built towers groaned into action. The chain mechanisms held within, slowly lowered the huge wooden draw bridge to allow the approaching party to continue on their journey. Four sentinel warriors waved them across.

It wasn't long before Lord Farroth and his party entered the massive gates of the fortress. They were greeted by the Shaman Kor-aviel and half a dozen archers. Lord Farroth ordered his group to dismount. Kor-aviel waved over a number of stable hands who were stood in waiting at the other end of the courtyard. They took charge of the tired horses, leading them off for a welcome feed, and grooming. Once that was done the Shaman approached his guests.

"Welcome. I am sure you are weary after your long journey. I will have your men escorted to their quarters where they will find refreshments and a hot bath should they require it."

"Thank you that would be most welcome," Lord Farroth replied.

"And if you would both be so kind as to follow me, I will show you to your chambers where the same will be waiting."

They followed the Shaman along winding corridors, lit by torches placed in alcoves cut into the walls. Eventually they arrived at their adjacent rooms some two floors up from the courtyard outside.

After a night of well-earned rest, Maccon and Lord Farroth were ready to meet their host. Most of the men accompanying them had overindulged on elven wine and were more than happy to just wander the halls and corridors and bathe in the structure's magnificence.

Maccon fastened his sword belt and was just about to call on Lord Farroth, when someone knocked on his door. A beautiful, tall, slender Elven maiden entered holding a wooden platter carrying a portion of freshly baked bread and a small clay pot of Royal honey. It was a customary ritual that was afforded guests to welcome them into the Royal household; and was considered to be a great honour and an acknowledgement of a visitor's importance. Maccon accepted the gift, as did Lord Farroth who was standing in the open doorway confronted with a similar offering from a second maiden who could have been the twin of her companion, so alike were they. Maccon broke bread, dipped it in the honey, and smiled at his leader. But no smile was reciprocated. Lord Farroth did what he considered courteous, placing the remainder of the offering back on the platter.

Both maidens beckoned their guests to follow them to the Great Hall, where Kor-yllion would be waiting with his high council.

The Hall was magnificent. At one end, a throne adorned the top of a platform, hewn from the very same white stone that made up the rest of the fortress. Above that were three massive stained-glass windows, the middle one being the largest, depicting a scene that saw Kor-yllion slaying a mighty warlord in some distant conflict. Stone statues of Elven leaders looked down from dizzying heights upon a grand oval table where Kor-yllion and his council were already seated.

On entering the hall, the two handmaidens excused themselves, leaving their guests in the capable hands of four lancers. They escorted their guests the rest of the way.

Kor-yllion sat at the head of the table, next to him was Kor-aviel his head Shaman. The rest of the council was made up of ten apostates, a High Minister and the commander in chief of the Elven army Anaras: Taller than the King, he had shoulder length white hair with a small pointed beard and eyes the colour of emerald. He was a member the King held in high regard, and after Kor-aviel was his closest confidant.

The council stood up as their guests approached the table, but Kor-yllion remained seated as his office demanded.

Lord Farroth was placed next to the King as a common courtesy, whilst Maccon was placed across from his equivalent, Kor-aviel, and it was quite obvious both Mage and Shaman held each other in high esteem. In contrast, it was obvious to all who knew the King well, that he viewed Lord Farroth as a necessary evil who had the ear of his brother King Agramar. A man the King had no fondness for, but a man he respected as a military tactician whose skills would undoubtedly be useful, should or more likely when the occasion present itself.

Kor-aviel was the first to speak.

"Lord Farroth. Maccon," he said, looking to each as he addressed them. "My Lord and this council would like to welcome you to Grayspire."

Kor-yllion nodded his support of his Shaman's greeting but found it difficult hiding his anxiety for what was to follow. He again nodded at Kor-aviel, this time as instruction to share what he and his council had discussed during the early hours whilst their guests slept.

Kor-aviel stood up, his gaze firmly fixed on Lord Farroth.

"I have some grave news regarding your brother, the King."

Both Maccon and Lord Farroth sat forward simultaneously, shocked by the comment.

"What do you mean?" Lord Farroth, asked.

"King Agramar I am told, was attacked on the Emperor road."

"Attacked. And you tell me this now. Why was this information not given to me the moment I arrived here?"

Kor-yllion stood up, vexed by his guest's tone and wearing a look more akin to condescension than one of anger.

"We tell you this now, because we were only privy to such information while you slept in the night."

Lord Farroth softened slightly. His anger making way for concern.

"Forgive me. Please continue."

"We believe he was attacked by those we have brought you here to discuss," Kor-yllion explained.

Maccon like his counterpart, the Shaman, deemed this conversation one for their leaders to meat out. So, both kept quiet vigil, waiting for their moment, should the opportunity present itself.

"Is my brother alive?"

"I can only tell you when last seen, he was. With only three other men besides. I fear the man they escorted, a Prince I believe, has parted this life with all the others in your brother's party," Kor-yllion continued.

"How did you come by this information? And how reliable is your source?" Lord Farroth asked, suspiciously.

"I am not at liberty to disclose the identity of my source, but you can be sure of this- what I have told you here should not be mistaken for idle gossip or be ignored as mere conjecture. My source is true. You must believe that."

"Did you help him?"

"Unfortunately, we could not. The messenger of this news is but one."

"Where is my brother now?"

A look of concern etched the King's features as they did his Shaman's, Kor-aviel.

"They have found safety in the hands of a search party, led by some of your order," the King said, glancing over at Maccon. Then he took a deep breath to reveal the real reason behind his obvious anxiety.

"Accompanying them was Hunter and the Wolf."

Maccon couldn't maintain his silence any longer.

"When did all this take place?"

"Some two days' past," Kor-aviel intervened.

"How fairs King Agramar now? Will he survive?"

"That is a question I cannot answer. This is something only time will reveal when you return home to your Keep," the Shaman replied, taking to his feet. "I am sure Maccon, like the rest of us here, has noticed how certain information is being withheld from us. How or why, we are not certain. There is a dark power at work here, it would be foolish to ignore."

"At the Temple, we have witnessed the very same. And I too have no answer for the power's origin," Maccon replied.

"This is the very reason for your visit here this day. You must have noticed, that ever since the Wolf was left in your care strange and unsettling things have begun to manifest themselves."

Maccon nodded his agreement, and Lord Farroth sat forward resting one arm on the table.

Then Kor-yllion took over.

"We believe, those who attacked King Agramar were Dark Elf followers of one Dax-barh. A ruthless and brutal leader I know all too well."

"Why would they attack us, when their grievance is obviously with yourselves," Lord Farroth interrupted.

"They must believe we would turn to you as allies in the conflict we will all inevitably face," the Shaman replied.

"To what conflict do you refer?" Maccon followed.

"Why would we be drawn into a war that has nothing to do with us?" Lord Farroth interrupted.

"The attack on your King should be answer enough to that question. Though you seem not to wish it, I believe we must face this enemy as one," Kor-yllion added.

A look of anger came over Lord Farroth's face.

"You knew this day would come, when you left that confounded wolf amongst us. Your actions were calculated, with no regard for the horrors that have befallen my people"

Kor-yllion moved about uncomfortably.

"It was never our belief or intention to draw you into any of this. We thought the Wolf would be safe amongst you, but unforeseen, we were wrong."

"What has the Wolf got to do with all this?" Lord Farroth asked.

The Elven leader glanced around the table.

"Everything."

The King paused for a moment to reflect and choose his next words carefully. Before continuing he ordered the distribution of welcome refreshments. Then carried on.

"This Dax-barh I speak of. He is a great warrior I have battled in the past. The way he fights is to attack and retreat. I believe you would call it a war of attrition. He knows he cannot win a war against us with a full-on assault, especially if it is on two fronts. So, in his madness I fear he has unleashed an abomination, that should it be allowed to take hold will see an end to all we know."

Lord Farroth couldn't hide his concern and displeasure at what he was hearing. Maccon just looked concerned.

"And what part does your Wolf have to play in all this?" Lord Farroth asked, hoping at last to get some clarity to the secrets surrounding the animal.

"She is part of a prophesy passed down for generations. A prophesy written by the Ancients. A race that held such powers that you would call them Gods. They told of someone or something entering our lives at a time of great peril. The ancient scripts predict, he will be neither one nor the other yet stronger than both, and when the time came, he would unleash a power beyond imagining. The power of the Ancients themselves. For this will be the only thing that can defeat what is coming. And as incredible as it might sound, we believe the key is the Wolf," Kor-aviel added.

"You put your faith in a fairy tale. A bed time story for children," Lord Farroth replied, his tone riddled with contempt. "We have such tales. We call them folk lore. Stories passed down through the ages. Stories that with every passing generation get more outrageous in the telling."

"This has never been a story for children. There are things about my kind you will never understand," Koraviel interrupted. "Know this. Our Dark brethren have summoned something through a portal. A doorway to a realm that resides somewhere between this life and the next. A place that is home to a great evil. We know this, for it was the Ancients who cast it there. An evil those Ancients faced at the Battle of Sith-llyan. The greatest battle our world has ever seen."

Still not convinced of the story's credibility, Lord Farroth pressed further.

"Again, I would ask. What has the Wolf to do with all this? And where does it come from?"

"It matters not from whence she came. There is naught to be gained from your knowledge of such information. As for your other question, we have already offered an explanation, whether you believe it or not. Well, that is something you will have to discuss amongst yourselves," the King said, agitated by his guest's arrogance.

Lord Farroth's face turned almost as red as his beard.

"You mean to say you have dragged us all this way, on the assumption that some prophesy written gods know when, is more than a tale for fools and old maids."

It was extremely rare to see an Elder lose his or her composure, letting their belief in logic prevail. But Commander Anaras had sat through the meeting, paying resolute attention to every word that was uttered. He felt the tone of Lord Farroth's questioning was more than enough to warrant a response.

"Choose your next words very carefully."

The King waved him down but smiled appreciatively. Experience told him, this was neither the time nor the place to alienate a would-be ally, no matter how ignorant they may be.

"You doubt my words. So be it. But I think when you return home, you will see things differently…. I hope you find your brother alive and well. For now, I think there is little point in our trying to explain things any further. So, I will bid you good day. I hope next time we meet, you will be more agreeable, and understand what we have told you here this day is a truth we must all embrace," the King finished.

All those around the table rose to their feet as the King made to leave. Anaras led the council out of the hall, except for Kor-aviel. Lord Farroth excused himself and left for his chambers in no mood for any kind of pleasantries. Maccon held back, aware that the Shaman wanted to speak with him.

Kor-aviel brushed the creases out of his robe and ushered Maccon out onto the balcony overlooking the courtyard. The song of steel on steel ricocheted off all surrounding walls, some twenty or so Elven knights were honing their skills with sword and lance. For a moment Maccon stood, mesmerised by their graceful discipline. Then.

"Before you leave in the morning, I would like you to ride with me to the lake. There is something I think you should see," Kor-aviel said.

"Of course. I would be honoured."

"Good. Then I shall detain you no longer. The kitchens have been given instruction to supply you and your men with whatever your stomachs desire," he smiled. "You should find our tastes not far removed from your own."

Maccon thanked his host before wandering back to his chambers.

The following morning saw Maccon up bright and early. The air was crisp, the sky azure blue with a dusting of clouds that looked like feathers. It was a fine morning for a ride.

A stablehand guided their guest through the maze of corridors that led to the stables where Kor-aviel was waiting, seated on a magnificent white stallion.

"A beautiful morning is it not?"

"It is. But please. Time is short, Lord Farroth will be awake shortly, he means for an early departure," Maccon replied, heeling his horse forward.

Kor-aviel edged his horse alongside his guest's, ordering the guards to open the gates.

It wasn't long before both riders found themselves exiting the woods, high on the eastern edge of the lake. The view was breath-taking. The lake was still, like glass. Its colour a reflection of the sky above. The waterfalls feeding it were like cascading jewels, every drop capturing the sun light as it peaked above the snow-capped mountain tops. Both riders stopped for a moment and bathed in its magnificence. Then.

"Yes. I can see how intoxicating this place can be. But I am sure you did not bring me here to revel in its beauty," Maccon said.

"You are right my friend. Please," he said, dismounting his horse.

Maccon did the same and followed his guide to the edge of a high rock promontory overlooking a stony beach, just west of where they were standing. A figure wearing a hooded robe, a bit like a monk's habit, stepped back from the lakes edge unaware he was being observed.

Kor-aviel pondered, as the figure below dropped his hood to reveal his long black hair, the silver streak visible to his onlookers.

"This is our source of information."

Maccon could see the figure was that of a young Elder, but it was still unclear why his friend had bought him to this place. It was obvious, by the very nature of their approach that it was never the intention of his host to allow any contact with the person they now gazed upon. *So, what was the point.*

"Please. Watch," Kor-aviel urged, sensing Maccon's scepticism.

Maccon did just that, still unsure of what to expect. The robed figure entered the cover of trees not far from the stony shore line. At first nothing appeared to be happening, then slowly the sound of someone in pain echoed through the trees. Shortly after, a huge black Dire Wolf appeared from the same place the Elder entered just moments before, a silver streak running down the back of its neck, clear to see. Maccon was speechless. He watched with dumbfounded silence as the beast sped off into the distance, to exit the valley.

Kor-aviel completely understood his friend's disbelief at what both had just witnessed, but time was short.

"I know you must have many questions, but we have little time to share all the answers. I believe you deserve more of an explanation than my leader is prepared to give you. So, I will tell you what I can without dishonouring my position as my Lord's chief adviser."

"Thank-you," were the only words that Maccon could muster at that moment.

"What you've seen here, no man has ever witnessed before. The figure you saw enter the woods is a Prince amongst his kind. He comes from an Isle where all are like him. His father the King of Wolves comes from a family lineage dating back to a time before even my kind roamed these lands. It is believed they are the direct descendants of the Ancients themselves."

"But they are Wolves. How can this be?" Maccon asked, regaining his composure.

"It is believed, they fought by the side of those Ancients, to help in the final exile of an evil so great, it would have seen the end to all we love. You as a people would never have come to exist were it not for the bravery of those I mention. After the battle of Sith-llyan the Dark Ones were cast into the abyss, where they fester for eternity. But before they departed this world, they placed a curse on the those who helped in their defeat. A spell so powerful even the Ancients themselves could not reverse it."

Maccon led his horse to a nearby rock and seated himself down. He was fascinated at what he was hearing and didn't doubt for one minute, the story's authenticity. Kor-aviel took his lead and sat down beside him.

"Why Wolves? What is the significance of such an animal?" Maccon asked.

"No one knows for sure what their motive was. We believe that they viewed the wolves as vermin, as we think of rats. But more than that I cannot say. The Isle which is home to these wolves retains a magic dating all the way back to those Ancients Gods. And so long as they stay on this Island these Elves can wield a power far in excess of any we possess. But should they leave its boundaries their power diminishes, and with it their former selves. For it is only as a wolf that they can wander the lands beyond."

"Yet I saw the Prince before he became a wolf. How is that possible?"

"Some like the Prince and his father have the power to change back to their original form, but only for a short time. That is what you saw. But this transformation comes at a cost. The pain they endure as they go through that change is excruciating. The cries we heard before the Prince left the woods are testament to my words. Once, the world we all now inhabit, was full of magic. The land itself was the source. Trees, rocks, everything we all take for granted possessed it. But when the race of men entered this world the magic was slowly forgotten. And after thousands of years, there are only a few places left, where men reside, that any semblance of this magic exists. You Maccon, and your Temple are one of those rare examples."

Maccon had nothing of import to add to the conversation and was quite happy to sit quietly and listen.

"The reason that my kind are so protective of their lands, is because, it is in those lands the magic of the Ancients still resides. And none more so than at the Isle of the Lost. The Isle of Wolves if you wish."

"But what has all this got to do with Hunter and his Wolf?"

"Everything. Is it not obvious, from all I have told you that, the wolf in Bael's possession, is not merely *a wolf*?"

"Then what or who is it?" Maccon asked, hoping at last for an answer long overdue.

"I have shared far more than was my original intention, Maccon. I beg you to respect my silence on the issue. For now, I cannot give you an answer to that. But there is one more piece of information I will share with you. There is a darkness growing inside Bael. His love for the Wolf is the only thing keeping it at bay. I don't know why, but when that thing came out of the void the darkness in him began to grow."

Maccon stood up, his eyes full of troubled recognition, filling his thoughts with a conversation he had with Lamia, days before setting off for Grayspire.

"I know someone who told me something similar."

"I know of the woman you speak. When the land around her chose to give her its gift, you abandoned her. Now I believe you have seen the error of your ways. This gift is very rare indeed in the land of men. Don't let the ignorance of those around you influence what I know deep down you believe unjust. This woman will play no small part in what is to come. There is something she withholds from you that will test your resolve. In time, she will share with you a secret that has been her burden for far too long."

Maccon shifted about uncomfortably. His mind full of pointless speculation.

"I have already seen the grave of a daughter I did not know existed. Is this not the secret you refer to?"

"I feel sorry that such news should be relayed to you in such an untimely fashion. To find that one has a daughter, only to discover she is no longer there to love. It is a tragedy no one should have to bear. Yet this is not the secret I have mentioned. There is another, but only time and understanding will allow her to share it with you. In this, you must respect her wishes. Allow her this courtesy. Wounds of the heart, cut the deepest and by their very nature, take the longest to heal."

Maccon's face softened, reflecting his understanding.

"I would not dream to press her on matters relating to the past, she has earned that right. I hope I will face whatever it is you mention, with the dignity she deserves."

"I am sure you will, old friend." Kor-aviel smiled. Then his features took on a sterner appearance. "It would appear that the land surrounding Lamia has gifted her with an insight into what is happening to Bael. Know this. Bael has a power growing in him he is not aware of, and until now, neither were we. She has seen it, when she touched the Wolf. I believe like us, you felt Bael's memories were beginning to return because of the Wolf?"

Maccon nodded his agreement.

"Then like us you would be wrong. I cannot say for sure, but I believe it has something to do with the shadow that Lamia witnessed when Bael last visited her. Maccon, we must make sure Hunter and his Wolf survive whatever is coming. Because I believe without both of them the prophesy will never be realized, and all will be lost."

Maccon stood up and stretched. Unfortunately, he had to get back before his absence was noticed.

"It would appear I have a lot to think about. I thank you for this time we have spent together, sadly I fear we must return. Lord Farroth and I have a long journey ahead of us."

Both mounted their horses, but before leaving Maccon had one last question.

"The wolf I saw today, tell me, does the one you left with Hunter come from the same Island?"

"She does."

24
THE RETURN

It was early morning when they arrived back in Stonehaven. Most of the townsfolk were still in their beds, except for the odd drunk or homeless vagrant unlucky enough to have slept rough through a night of heavy rain. The group cantered down the main street towards the bridge and the lake beyond, the morning mist hugging the ground like a gossamer blanket.

It had taken Lord Farroth and his men little less than a week to find themselves riding towards the Keep's gates. The journey home only marred by one minor incident: a small but desperate gang of robbers made a futile attempt at parting Lord Farroth and his group from what little money they were carrying. Maccon and his men made short work of their attackers, after pleading with them to back away and leave, a warning they ignored that resulted in at least a dozen corpses playing host to an even greater number of eye feasting carrion.

As they approached the lake fed moat at the front of the Keep, the drawbridge creaked into action. Maccon noticed the extra sentries placed strategically along the ramparts, maybe twenty or thirty archers alone, faced the town. He presumed the same number manned all the remaining battlements and were testament to the sense of growing anxiety he felt on entering the gates.

Alloria was awakened by the Sergeant of the garrison, a short stocky man with a thick greying beard and a bald head that was as smooth as the shell of hardboiled egg.

"My Lady," he nodded, as she opened her bedroom door to see what all the knocking was about. "Forgive me my Lady. Your husband approaches the gates. I thought you should know."

Alloria thanked him, grateful for his timely message, leaving her just long enough to freshen up, slip into a gown and make her way to the Great Hall. The final corridor led her past Cailean's room. Quietly she opened the door and peered in. Her daughter thankfully, had at last found comfort in a sleep that night after night was so cruelly denied her. Though it was nearly four weeks past, the murder of her friend still laid heavily on her, and Alloria wasn't about to interrupt her daughter's well-deserved rest. She closed the door and followed her escort, to meet her husband. When she entered the Hall, Lord Farroth and Maccon were already making their way over to the door that led to the guards' room and the Temple beyond.

"Thank the Gods you are both safe."

"My Lady," Maccon smiled respectfully.

Before she could return the courtesy, her husband intervened without any apparent consideration for *her* wellbeing.

"The King. Where is he?"

"He heals well. They look to his needs in the Temple," she replied tersely.

His Lordship's unpredictable mood swings towards his family hadn't gone unnoticed by Maccon. The Mage cared deeply for Alloria, he found her kind and big hearted to all around her, always trying to see the good in people, which made these awkward moments all the more uncomfortable to witness. And if truth be told his Lordship's intolerant behaviour was beginning to annoy him.

"My Lady. How is Cailean?" he asked.

"She still mourns for her friend, so I left her to rest. Since you left to visit the Elders she has been unable to sleep through one full night."

"I don't have time for this. I must see my brother," Lord Farroth, barked, making his way to the door that led to the Temple grounds.

This coldness in his Lord's behaviour worried Maccon. He was all too aware, of how, like a knife, indifference could sever the bonds of what was once a loving relationship; and how that very knife was already making its mark.

"He is tired, our meeting with the Elves didn't go as we had hoped. And then this with his brother," Maccon said, looking to Lord Farroth as he exited the Hall.

"He has changed Maccon. I know you can see it and I don't know what to do about it. I have never seen him this unsettled."

"Try to give him time."

"Time! It would seem things are only going to get worse, if what the King told us is true."

Maccon felt uncomfortable, he wanted to stay and talk with Alloria, but for now duty demanded he join his friend.

"My Lady, I am sure all will be fine," he lied. "But for now, I must go to the King." Before leaving he took her by the hand and kissed it gently. She managed a half smile and left; returning to her quarters. Maccon exited the Hall and through a sudden downpour, made his way over to the Temple.

***

Dogran spent a full week at Lamia's cottage, before he was anywhere near well enough to move back to the Tavern. The Old woman with the help of his daughter had tended his every need during that time; both working tirelessly to nurse him back to health and see him strong enough to sit up and feed himself.

The two weeks that followed saw him in his own bed, with welcome visits from his closest friends, and the young Knight of the Order.

Koval had visited him as often as he could, though not as often as he would have liked. Four weeks on from their son's abduction had only seen Tyrna grow more morose and unpredictably volatile; driving Koval to be constantly by her side, knowing full well his absence would allow her depression to fester and take hold.

The Tavern was almost full every night in support of their favourite Innkeep. Nearing the end of the second week, Koval with the help of Cirius, tried at Dogran's request, to get him to his feet. One man under each shoulder helped the big man walk shakily into the main Tavern to surprise his unsuspecting guests. When he finally appeared behind the bar propped up by his helpers, the room burst into cheers of welcome. Jered the Baker, stood up, lifted his tankard and smiled warmly.

"Well, you stubborn old bull. You had us all fooled there for a moment. We thought you for the afterlife, yet here you stand looking somewhat healthier than I do," he said, his eyes glazed with emotion as his friend faced him, pale and hardly able to take his own weight.

Then a voice from the back of the room lightened the moment.

"We all look healthier than you Jered. You old fool."

The place exploded into laughter, Dogran joining in briefly, for as long as the pain would allow. He supported his own weight by leaning forward and bracing his arms on the bar top. With some reluctance both Koval and Cirius let him do it, both ready should his legs give way. Emma watched nervously as her father thanked everyone for their kindness, but she could see, what little colour filled his cheeks was slowly beginning to drain away. She began to move towards him, but thankfully Koval had noticed the same, and quickly took charge of his friend. Cirius followed the Smithy's lead, taking Dogran by the opposite arm he helped take the weight off the big man's shaking legs and turned him around. Both men led their friend back to the comfort of his chair by the fireplace, where he welcomed his well-earned sleep.

By the end of the third week Dogran was up and walking about, Lamia and his daughter constantly warning him not to overdo things; words that never seemed to reach his ears.

It was early morning, two days had passed since Lamia's last visit, and Emma was still sleeping. Dogran could feel his strength returning with the passing of each day. He dressed himself and moved into the main room. Seating himself by the fireplace he looked to the empty spot where Raga would lie and rest its massive head on his outstretched feet. He'd tried not to think about that terrible day during his time recovering, but now a sadness washed over him as he remembered the moment his hound fell.

A noise across the room jolted him from his thoughts.

"What are you doing father?" She asked, frustrated, but happy to see him up and about by his own hand.

"The dizzy spells have all but passed now, my love. I need to get back to some kind of normality before I go insane."

Emma could see, pressing the matter any further was futile. He did look better, but Lamia told her it would still take several more days for his body to be free of the poison that infected it. She made them both a tasty breakfast of ham and eggs with a hot mug of herbal tea. Whilst they ate, both were quiet, happy in sharing such a moment that for the past three weeks was so cruelly denied them.

Dogran was first to finish. He placed his plate on the floor by his feet and just stared at the love of his life. She had tended his every need and weathered his odd bout of frustrated anger, without one word of complaint. And as self-assured and proud as he was, he knew a life without her was no life at all.

Emma finished the last of her meal and turned to catch her father staring at her. She smiled lovingly, it warmed her heart to see him, almost back to his usual boisterous, larger than life self. Without uttering a word, she picked up the empty dishes and placed them by the washing trough in the kitchen area. On her return, she found the room empty.

"Where have you gone now?" She mumbled to herself.

A clatter of pottery broke the silence. Hurriedly, she made her way into the Tavern, that later in the day she knew would be full of well-wishers. Dogran was behind the bar preparing things as if it was like any normal day. Even though it lifted her spirits to see him like this, she placed her hands on her hips.

"And what may I ask, do you think you are doing? You are still not well enough to be prancing about as if all is right with the world."

Dogran understood her words came from a good place, but he knew his own body better than anyone.

"I will be fine, my flower. I couldn't spend one more day moping around like an invalid. No. I am ready to get back to living."

"I can see I am wasting my breath….So, please promise me, the first sign of pain or discomfort, you will let me take over."

"I promise," his lie, well intentioned.

Something in his posture told her he was the happiest he had been in weeks, making her swallow back a lump in her throat.

For the following half hour, they both went about their business, preparing the place for the mid-day regulars. And for a brief moment it was as though nothing terrible had happened. It felt good for them both to suspend the tragic reality of those past three weeks, and work together, as they always had since the death of both a mother and wife.

Dogran finished washing down the counter and then sat down at a table by the window.

"Emma! Come and sit with me."

"I will father. Just give me a moment," she replied, making her way over to the bar. She filled a couple of mugs with Monks ale and joined him at the table.

"Here father," she said passing him his drink. "To the Gods for your safe return."

They tapped their mugs together in a toast, then Emma sat down and stared out of the window, finding comfort in watching people going about their daily business.

"I see that young Knight, Cirius is it?"

"It is father, as well you know," she said, smiling sarcastically.

His face took on that boyish, mischievous look, that anyone who knew him, loved.

"I see or should I say, believe, his visits of late have become more frequent."

"And? What are you trying to imply father?"

Dogran gulped down a mouthful of ale, still sporting that mischievous, boyish grin. It felt nice to be able to put to one side the horrors that the town had, had to endure, no matter how brief such moments presented themselves. In reality, they all knew the town would never be the same again, but for now it felt good to pretend all was as it used to be.

"You could do a lot worse my love. He is a Knight, a man of honour, and if I am not mistaken, has the looks most young ladies would… You know what I mean."

"No father. I don't know what you mean," she replied, trying hard to keep this suspension of reality going.

"Such naïvety. Any fool can see the man can't keep his eyes off you. And for once, I am glad to embrace the idea that such a man has made his intentions so blatantly obvious. Though why you would wish to ignore such welcome attention, I cannot begin to understand."

Emma's cheeks blushed, warm and pink.

"He is nice, and I do welcome his visits. And I know he is kindly and has a big heart. Who would not welcome such pleasant company? But he is a friend, nothing more," she said, half believing her comment to be true. But something stirred inside her when he entered her thoughts, that would suggest otherwise.

Dogran was no fool, he could see also, that her body language spoke a different truth.

"And what of Hunter?" he asked. This time his face reflecting a more serious matter. Emma couldn't hide her disappointment and hurt at the question.

"I haven't seen him once, since your injury," she said, unable to mask the sadness in her reply.

"I must go and see him. I believe in no small part; I owe him my life."

"It is true. Without his knowledge of healing, the poison that entered your body would have seen your end. An end I could not bear, father," she said as the reality of that day came flooding back.

Dogran reached across the table and squeezed her hand gently.

"You do not have to concern yourself with such matters. When I am ready, I will go and see the man.... Now before I forget, what of this stranger you mentioned? The one who thought he knew Hunter."

"It is odd, father. He left here two weeks ago, some of his belongings are still in his room, which he paid a full month in advance. He said he had business in the village of Waycrest. He hasn't returned. Yet he told me he would be back by the week's end, and as I said, that was two weeks ago."

"Maybe whatever business took him there, has taken longer than he expected."

"Maybe. But something doesn't sit right, I'm not sure why, but I fear something has happened to him. He seemed to be a man who, if he said a week, then a week it would be."

"Well, only time will tell," Dogran replied.

But Emma couldn't shake a growing feeling of unease.

25

THE RESCUE-THE PACK

When Dorodir and his men came upon the slavers final encampment they found Bael tied tightly to a tree surrounded by the dead bodies of the fallen reavers. Other than a large plum sized lump to his head, he'd only suffered a few minor cuts and bruises and was lucky enough to find this the full measure of his injuries; considering what the alternative could have been. The Wolf was in a lot worse condition, as too the Hawk which lay trembling and broken by a bramble bush. It was evident to Dorodir, from the ashes of the campfire, that the raiders were long gone, but for the moment he had to focus on the injured.

Arbar, Maccon's second, loomed over Bael who was on his knees looking at the blood on his hands after running them over the wound to his head. As he looked up he recognized the crescent moon hilt of the sword Moonwraith and knew right away who was stood over him offering him a helping hand.

"Let me take a look at that," the Priest knight said, pushing back Bael's hair to look at the damage. "You will live my friend."

Bael wasn't concerned about himself, through the haze of his pounding headache he began to recollect what befell the Wolf and Hawk. Turning quickly, he saw Dorodir tending the Wolf, who was lying still, not far from where the Hawk was encompassed in a nest of soft firs.

Bael shook his head, struggling to focus.

"The Wolf? How is she? He asked.

"She is fine. We removed the bolt from her side and did what we could for the wound. And by some miracle, beyond our endeavours, she already begins to heal. As for the Hawk, well, Cirius is the expert, but unfortunately, he is not amongst us. He is back at the Temple, but your Hawk is strong and is at least alive. Dorodir, like yourself has a way with creatures of the wild, and has made the bird as comfortable as he can for now, and I am sure on our return to the Keep all will be put right, and he will fly again of that you can be certain."

Bael's relief was clear to see.

"Thankyou."

"You are welcome my friend," Arbar replied, as a group of his men placed the last of the bodies on a pyre, ready to burn. Nodding towards the fallen, he smiled. "It would seem this scum have come to regret crossing your path this day. But what of the Smithy's lad?"

Bael looked angry with himself.

"He's gone. Taken by the rest of those bastards."

"You are lucky to be alive. It is strange is it not? That they let you live, especially considering the carnage you left in your wake."

"I am as confused as you are. All I remember is the blade at my throat, and the leader of those men over there, staring down at me before laying me unconscious with the butt of his dagger. A rare weapon indeed…. He appeared like a ghost hiding in the shadows, it was like the very air around me had spewed him forth. In arrogance, I underestimated my enemy. You can be sure that will not happen again."

Leaving Arbar to go about his business, Bael quickly made his way over to the Wolf, who was now on her feet.

"Thank the gods you are alright," he whispered, stroking the back of her head.

Dorodir patted Bael on the shoulder.

"The animal has a love for you I think."

At first Bael didn't answer, his attention drawn to the now burning pile of bodies.

"Why don't you leave them to the crows?

Dorodir paused for a moment as the sweet, sickly smell of freshly cooked meat assaulted the air around the camp.

"They deserve no better, I know. Yet my Order does not allow me the privilege of choice in such matters. We have to honour the dead, whether they be one of ours or those we are in conflict with. In our Gods eyes, all life is precious, even scum like these. And for which ever God their souls are headed, we have to send them on their journey in the manner given. Even though we might be the ones to send them on such a journey. Complicated I know."

Bael didn't look convinced. He still believed fire was too good for this scum who took his friend and killed his girl. Then his thoughts settled on another matter.

"My horse?"

"I'm afraid he is dead. Mindless slaughter," Dorodir reflected, knowing how important *his* own horse was to *him*.

Arbar approached Dorodir with a look of recognition on his face. He still felt somewhat uneasy around the Wolf, keeping Bael between him and the beast.

"It would seem we have picked up the slavers trail," he said pointing to a pile of horse droppings. "They can't be more than a few hours ahead of us, and the wagon will be slowed by the rough terrain."

"Then we should delay no further," Dorodir replied.

"You should stay here. I will leave a dozen men to protect you and your injured companions," the leader said to Bael.

"I am fine. If you can spare a horse I would rather I joined you."

"As you wish. But who will tend to the Wolf while you are gone?" Arbar interrupted.

"I will make sure she understands what is expected of her. I believe she is too weak to follow us anyway. She will just wander the surrounding woodlands as her nature dictates, and wait for our return."

Bael could see they didn't share his belief that the Wolf would do as he said, but still they gave him the benefit of the doubt. In an attempt to quell their concerns, he walked over to where the Wolf lay licking her wound. He removed a handful of crushed herbs from his belt pouch and carefully dusted it with them. Then he took her huge head in his hands and placed his forehead against hers with the hope she would understand.

"I want you to stay here. Do not try to follow me."

The Wolf licked his face, then wearily rested her head on her front paws as if in surrender to his request. Bael gave her a final pat on the back and made his way over to the Hawk; he placed a couple of fine leather strips around the wings, bracing them to its body to help prevent any further damage.

Dorodir approached him leading a horse. Arbar and the rest of the men were already mounted.

"We must make haste, you should find this an easy ride," he said, handing over the reins.

Bael leapt into the saddle, his swords and bow on his back and heeled his mount forward to join the rest, who were already on the move.

Dorodir it was believed, could even rival Hunter as the consummate tracker. He was able to pick up any deviation in the trail; Bael quietly acknowledging his decisions without interfering.

As they thundered towards the coast, Bael felt they had made up precious time, hopefully time enough to prevent the raiders reaching their ship. But as the group drew to an abrupt halt after cresting a hill leading down to the sea below; what they saw put pay to any chance of that happening.

At the bottom of the track leading down to the bay, the slave wagon was reduced to a skeleton of burning embers. On the beach, right by the water line were the slaughtered remains of the raiders horses. Bael assumed that such barbarism was probably executed to save time and make sure nothing was left that might prove useful to their pursuers. Then he stared towards the horizon. The Savage-eel was almost out of sight.

Arbar could see the painful, jaw clenching frustration sculpt its way across Hunter's face.

"There is nothing to be done here. We should return to the Keep, without delay," he said, spinning his horse around on the spot. Dorodir nodded his agreement, ordering his men to follow. Bael didn't utter a word, all the way back to camp.

The Wolf was finding it difficult keeping up with the horses during the first day of the groups homeward journey. Though her wound healed miraculously quick, the muscles were still weak from the trauma impacted on them. By the second day the rendered flesh had almost completely closed and scarred over, leaving Bael pleased, but once again, puzzled as to what could trigger such a quick recovery. The herbs he had applied he believed were in some part responsible, but after his meeting with Lamia at her cottage, he knew there was a far greater power at work here: though welcome, it was a phenomenon fraught with unanswered questions.

With daylight fading, Arbar decided they should make camp for the night before continuing on the final day's ride back to the Keep. A few of the men collected what dry wood they could find and lit a fire near the tree line where the trail they travelled crossed the Emperor Road. Dorodir set up four separate sentry points, each manned by two lookouts. Bael checked on the Hawk making sure it was as comfortable as circumstances would allow, then he and the Wolf set up their place to sleep, not far from the roaring fire.

Somewhere in the night two owls called out to one another, the full moon above, an eerie backdrop to their haunting song. Bael lay back, resting his head on his saddle bags he stared at the flickering stars above. The Wolf shifted her head as the tall figure of Dorodir approached. Tired after the hard day's ride, he sat down on a large bolder next to Bael.

"How fairs the beast," he asked, nodding towards the Wolf.

Bael lifted himself onto his elbows.

"She is fine. Her wound already begins to heal," he replied wearily.

"Quite the miracle I would say? I have never seen a wound like that heal so quickly. Some of the men believe magic is at work?"

Bael at first, didn't respond to the comment. But he respected the Knight's bluntness, aware there was no malice intended.

"Maybe they are right. Who can tell? For in truth it is as much a mystery to me as it is to you."

As the last word parted his lips, the Wolf sprang to her feet; her lips snarling back exposing huge canines, she growled threateningly towards the dark tree line. Bael was first to react, drawing his sword he was closely followed by Dorodir, Arbar and then the rest of the men; all on their feet ready to meet whatever threat the shadows spewed their way.

Four figures melted out of the blackness. From what the light of both fire and moon would allow, it could be seen one of the intruders was being supported by two of the others, whilst the fourth, a powerfully built individual, seemed to be nursing a bloodied arm.

"Halt! State your intention," Arbar bellowed, taking no chances.

"It's the King. Agramar," came the gravely reply. "He's badly wounded."

Dorodir ordered four of his men to assist the injured men.

The man holding his arm dropped to the ground. Bael was closest and was quickly by the man's side. Even in the low light he could see the man's face was badly scarred, giving him a grotesquely extended smile. Carefully, he opened the bloodied rags exposing what lay beneath. The hand was missing, severed off a few inches above the wrist. He could see the stump had been crudely cauterized and had the arm not been tourniquet as it was, the soldier would have surely bled to death. It took three of them to lift the warrior off the ground and place him by the fire.

Dorodir recognized the King immediately and looked to the two men holding him up.

"Please, we will take care of the King now."

"He has taken an arrow to the stomach," one of the men said. His face half covered by what at first looked to be blood, but on closer scrutiny was revealed to be a plum coloured birth mark. The other man, a surly looking character carrying a bloodied meat clever at his side, repositioned himself under the King's armpit.

"We have him, where can we lay the King? He is exhausted."

"Please, set the King down here," Arbar instructed, pointing to a bunch of bedding he'd placed not far from where Oromar lay. Agramar fell back, the shaft of the arrow still embedded in his stomach. And whether it was luck or intention, the fact that the arrow was left in situ had helped stem the bleeding. Unfortunately, the poison it carried was already doing its job; black vein like tendrils stained the skin around the point of entry, spreading outwards like the veins of a leaf. Dorodir called over one of his men; Garon, a lean looking man in his mid-fifties, shoulder length hair the colour of dark amber, his face a map of freckles. Known for his limited knowledge of medicine, having served with numerous field surgeons during the Campaigns, he knelt down to get a closer look at the wound. With some reluctance he said.

"I don't think anything can be done. The poison in the wound has already begun to spread."

"We must do something. We cannot let him die without trying something," Fraene urged.

"I fear we might not have an option Sur," Garon replied, shaking his head.

Bael moved over to where he left his saddle bag, took out a small pouch of crushed herbs and a corked water bladder. Whilst everyone else was focused on the King, he readied a poultice, placing the herbs and water in a small clay bowl he always carried with him in case he had to deal with the unforeseen. Holding the bowl of paste, he pushed his way through the crowd gathered around Agramar. He placed his hand on Garon's shoulder.

"Let me take a look."

Garon stepped back to give Hunter access to the King, the Wolf, now by his side. Bael placed the bowl on the ground and ran his finger over the rendered flesh. He could feel the heat of infection get warmer the closer it got to the imbedded arrow. Luckily the King was still unconscious.

"I must remove the arrow. Its head could be barbed, so I will have to cut it out."

Fraene walked to the fire and placed his dagger in the embers. When the blade glowed red, he removed it and returned to the King. Bael took the hot knife from him, nodding his appreciation of the Knight's trust. As he placed the blade on the hissing skin, Dorodir intervened.

"Are you sure you know what you are doing?"

Bael didn't waste time answering, he just let the blade cut, creating two extensions either side of the arrow's entry wound. Blood began to flow freely now, Bael then placed a clean rag on it drying the area as best he could, but before he could smother the gash with his poultice, the Wolf edged him to one side.

"What is it doing? Brelt bellowed, excitedly.

"Wait! Let her do this," Bael reassured.

The group looked on in astonishment as the beast licked the bloodied wound, its saliva thick and shiny. She turned her head as if beckoning Hunter to act. Without thinking Bael placed his concoction over the open wound and placed a thick piece of clean cloth over it.

"Now we must wait. We must leave the wound open so the poison and underlying infection can be drawn out. Someone must hold the dressing, putting enough pressure on it to stem the flow of blood. Fraene was first to volunteer, followed by Brelt and several others from the surrounding group. Bael showed the Knight what to do, explaining the dressing must be changed every few hours.

"If he survives the night he will live," Hunter said, more than a little hopeful that this would be the outcome.

***

For over two weeks following the kidnapping of his son, Koval had tried to balance his work at the forge with the thankless task of looking after his wife. As the days passed, Tyrna just seemed to go from bad to worse. For the first time in his life Koval had run out of ideas. He'd tried to focus on his work in a vain attempt to stem the grief he was suffering, and to some degree it worked, but his wife's incessant rantings put pay to that endeavour.

On a couple of occasions, he'd paid Hunter a visit to find out what really happened out there on the trail. Tyrna had accompanied him on the first visit. During that particular meeting, he learned about his wife's previous liaison with Hunter; when she had asked him to find their son's kidnappers and kill them, a fact she had never shared until now. When Hunter explained what had happened after he eventually caught up with the raiders, Tyrna went hysterical. On that occasion Koval realized any further pursuit of the facts would have to be done alone, and on the second visit, he did just that.

He listened without interruption to Hunter's detailed description of the events that took place during those dreadful days. While he listened, he couldn't help but notice how the Wolf never once took its eyes off the man. And how Hunter would go over to the beast and check on its wound. Koval had never seen a man more caring and loving towards an animal, especially an animal of the wild, and as the time passed, he began to understand why his son was drawn to such a man. By the end of the meeting Koval could see Hunter was struggling with something within himself.

"You did all you could, you have nothing to reproach yourself for. And I must thank you for that. But I can see, something troubles you?"

For a moment Bael made no attempt to answer, he just stared over at the Wolf, his eyes lost in thought.

"I should have saved your son. Instead, I let a creature of the shadows place a blade at my throat, only to spare my life. Though I know not why. I was helpless to stop him taking your son to face whatever fate this creature has planned for him. I was so close to achieving my goal, which would have seen Raen back where he belongs. But instead, I underestimated an adversary who was worthy of my full attention. A mistake I shall not make when next our paths cross. And make no mistake they will, and when that day comes, that meeting will have a very different outcome."

"The blame is not yours to shoulder. You did all that you could. No one could have asked more of you. The fact that you did what you did, was a miracle in itself. So once again I thank you, as would my wife if she weren't so overcome with grief. I offer an apology for her behaviour when we last called upon you."

"There is no need for an apology. She is a mother who just wants her son back."

"That is so," Koval replied respectfully. "Anyway, I believe I have taken up enough of your time. I will take your leave now; my wife will be wondering where I have got to."

Both men locked arms.

Koval returned home to find his wife fast asleep; only having eaten half the meal he had left out for her. Yet it gave him some comfort to see she had at least eaten something. Over the next few days, things seemed to get a little easier. Tyrna began to eat more and showed signs of improvement; going about her usual daily chores. This change in spirit allowed Koval to get on with the back log of work that had accumulated during his many absences from the forge.

It was five weeks to the day since Raen was abducted. The sun was up to begin a bright new morning. Koval readied himself for a full day at the forge, leaving Tyrna in bed asleep. He pumped the bellows to fire up the furnace, sweat and coal dust running down his arms. He turned to look up as a tall figure of a man approached. Even though the man wore no armour, Koval could tell he was a Knight. As the man got closer the Smithy couldn't help but notice the large plum coloured birth mark that almost covered half the man's face.

"And what can I do for you sur?" Koval asked.

The Knight removed the cap off a leather tube he carried and opened up a parchment of paper on the workbench.

"I would commission you to make this for me," Fraene said, pointing to the diagram filling the page.

Koval scrutinized it carefully.

"Umm! I see."

"My friend lost his arm protecting the King. I once fought a man brandishing one of these, he too had lost part of his arm. This part goes over the remaining stump," he pointed out. "A metal collar of sorts, to cup over the end of the wound, filled with either sheep skin or goat skin to pad and protect the stump from impact damage. The two short thick blades protruding from the end of it can act as a weapon, but can also be used to trap and break a sword blade. See how the two blades are set further apart at their tips than at their place of attachment to the arm," he said, running his finger over the diagram. "Can you make it?"

"I can. Very ingenious. I too saw such weapons used in the Northern campaigns. And very effective they were to, when used by a trained fighter. I will do this for you, gladly. But I fear it won't be ready 'till weeks' end, unfortunately I have a back log of work I have to get through first."

"That will be fine. My friend will first have to heal before any kind of training can be contemplated. Then on our return to the Capital we will find the trainer he will need."

26

RECONING

Dax-Barh found it almost impossible to contain the anger boiling up inside him, as what remained of the raiding party entered the Palace grounds. Even at such a distance he could see Sereg slumped over the back of his armoured lizard. It was obvious both were wounded, the lizard favouring its right-side as it limped towards the Palace; blood pouring profusely from a gash to its right foreleg. It was a sad sight indeed to witness, yet it did nothing to extinguish the raging fire that burned inside the King.

The Council were seated and waiting as Dax-Barh stepped back into the room. The atmosphere was thick with anxiety, for all around that table knew how dangerously unpredictable the King could be in his present mood.

Maril, amongst the group was the hardest to read. It was difficult to say whether he was smirking or not, but Dax-Barh cast his Shadow Maester a warning glance, wiping away whatever expression that was, with immediate effect.

Craban the Head Summoner hated such meetings, the tension in the room so tangible you could almost taste it. Experience had taught him discretion and silent observation were the best course of action; but in the moment, he felt he should start the proceedings.

"Sire. As we are already aware, Sereg and what is left of his party enter the grounds as we speak. What would you have us do?"

The King sat silent, lost in thought. He couldn't believe his situation and wouldn't rest until he got to the bottom of how such a well-planned raid could go so incredibly wrong.

"It is obvious Sereg does not fare well. Get our best healers, see to his wounds, then bring him back here, I will know the cause of this unforgivable failure."

"Yes Sire," Craban replied, leaving the room in some haste.

Dax-Barh, unable to keep still, he left the meeting, walked out onto the balcony to stare in disbelief as Sereg's ten remaining assassins nursed wounds of varying severity in the courtyard below. Agitated even more by what he saw, he stepped back into the Council chamber, where the remaining members sat pensively. He looked to Maril again, this time his expression absent any kind of emotion.

"Maril!"

"Yes, my Lord."

"Come with me. The rest of you are dismissed," Dax-Barh ordered.

There followed a few acknowledging nods, while the rest mumbled their disapproval for being cast aside so readily. Dax-Barh ignored the irritation and was first through the door, Maril right behind.

It wasn't difficult to guess where they were headed, Dax-Barh wasn't known for his patience, yet it surprised Maril how nonchalantly the rest of the Council were dismissed: a thought he kept to himself, feeling honoured to be the one chosen to accompany his leader, whatever the outcome.

Sereg lay prostrate and bloody on top of a low-lying cot bed. A healer loomed over him, his robe red with viscera, trying to close a deep wound to the warrior's upper chest. Dax-Barh brushed the apostate aside, seeing him lose his balance and in an undignified fashion, send him sprawling face down on the sawdust covered floor. No apology given, and none demanded.

"Leave! I wish to speak with Sereg alone," he ordered, addressing the two healers only. "You can stay."

Craban acknowledged the King's request, seating himself at a table not far from the bed, his nostrils flared from the rank smell of sweat, blood and stale piss: Sereg had slipped into unconsciousness, allowing his bladder to involuntarily relieve itself of whatever bodily waist it contained.

Maril stayed uncharacteristically quiet. For even though he had no love for Sereg, it pleased him not to witness such a sight.

Dax-Barh was in no mood for sitting around, he stepped over to the side of the bed, his feet surrounded by swabs of soggy linen, all stained with the warrior's life blood.

"Craban!"

"Yes, sire?"

"Can you do something here? So that I might question him."

Craban nodded his understanding and made his way over to a shelf full of bottles, herbs and a variety of odd-looking plants. From an ornate wooden box, he removed a strange looking flower, its deep red petals speckled with dots of the deep ochre pollen that fell like dust from its centre. Even across the room the King and Maril could smell its pungent aroma. Both of them watched in silence as Craban administered the fowl smelling dust, tapping it around Sereg's huge nostrils. It did the trick; the warrior sneezed back to consciousness. It took him a moment to become aware of his surroundings, before calling upon what little strength he had left, to find himself sitting upright. As the haze cleared, he looked around at the other three figures occupying the room, all staring down at him, expectant, unforgiving. Dax-Barh came alongside the bed, his eyes cold, humourless, demanding reason for such abject failure.

It was the first time Maril had ever seen the slightest hint of fear manifest itself on Sereg's brow. Though he shared not a single, agreeable thought with the brute, it again gave him no pleasure to see such a proud creature broken like a wounded animal waiting on death. Failure of this magnitude was only ever met with a finality that was sure to come. Maril also knew the recipient of this justice would not put up any kind of resistance, no matter how swift and brutal; that was the measure of the Royal subject facing his leader.

"What happened out there? Twice now have you failed to bring me back a victory," Dax-Barh said.

Sereg tried to reply, but his throat was so dry and sore it set him to coughing uncontrollably. Craban was quick to react, he filled a ladle full of water from a barrel by the door and got Sereg to sip it slowly. Most of the water dribbled down his chin and on to his chest, but it had the desired effect. Still with some difficulty the warrior began his explanation of the events that led to his present demise.

Several times during Sereg's explanation of events, Maril noticed the King's hand caress the hilt of his sword, only to remove it. As the story reached its conclusion he watched as his leader once again touched the hilt, this time gripping it with intent.

Sereg explained how his party had come across Agramar's encampment. And in as much detail as memory and the pain that racked his body would allow, he described the onslaught that should have seen an end to the King of men.

He, like Maril, had noticed the King's obsession with his sword hilt, waiting each time it happened for an end to his story. But it didn't come. Something stayed his leader's hand, and though he had surrendered to his inevitable fate, he was glad to see its execution unexpectedly postponed.

Dax-Barh's hand finally slipped off the hilt of his sword; it was at Sereg's mention of the Wolf pack.

All three in the room looked to one another. Sereg coughed again. This time it was Maril that gave him the water to sip.

"Wolves! What do you mean?" the King asked.

Sereg once again dug into his body's reserves, and sat up straighter, aware of the change in Dax-Barh's demeanour that would see his life returned. Then he continued.

"We sent all in Agramar's command on their journey to the afterlife. I saw this King dragged off into the forest, with three by his side that survived. I seek not to make excuses for my failure, but these we fought were hardened fighters, the toughest we have ever faced from the race of men. Yet victory was surely ours, as only four remained, one amongst them the target we were sent to kill. We followed them into the forest and caught sight of these men as they reached the centre of a clearing, surrounded on all sides by trees. I thought this is where they would meet their end. I was wrong. As we entered the clearing the heavens began to weep as if the very Gods themselves were displeased. It was obvious to us all that these men we hunted down, knew that escape was now impossible. They turned to face us one last time, weapons drawn, ready. It was then that the Dire Wolves appeared from the tree line to both our flanks. There must have been at least fifteen of the beasts, the biggest Wolves I have ever seen. They tore us to pieces, leaving only those you have seen return with me. One of the men protecting Agramar gave me this," he said pointing to his wound. "I took his hand before another amongst them injured my mount. They fought like they were possessed, to protect their leader."

"You say that as if you admire these men?" Maril interrupted.

Sereg didn't respond, ignoring the question, he continued.

"When this King was led to the safety of the forest beyond the clearing, the wolves disappeared as quickly as they had appeared. The last of them to leave, and the biggest of them, bore a white streak on its head and neck. I was in no doubt this was the leader."

Maril turned to face Dax-Barh and Craban, both of whom shared the same look of troubled concern.

"This is bad. We all know from whence these wolves came. They have never interfered in our affairs before; that they should do so now is to say the least, worrying," he said.

Dax-Barh agreed with his Shadow Maester. Intervention of this nature could not have been foreseen by any of them, even with the powers that Craban and his followers possessed. In this knowledge, the King found mercy in his heart.

Back in the Royal chambers Anumii joined her husband on the veranda that overlooked the grounds where the Devourer and his pets once stood. She could see the furrows that worry carved into his troubled brow and it moved her. She loved her husband dearly; this was her time to support him. She knew better than anyone what it had taken out of him to chisel out an existence for their kind, when so much of what they believed in betrayed them. To co-exist for thousands of years with their Elder brethren that deemed them somewhat inferior, was no easy task; one that became even harder when all that they fought to achieve was taken from them so unforgivingly. But where many in his position would have broken, her husband instead found strength; one that would see her and her kind find purpose in a world that at the time felt so unjust. This King she loved so dearly, had paid the price for his unwavering beliefs, but the full extent of that cost was only his to own.

As the two of them stood alone in the darkness, Dax-Barh's hand searched for his wife's waist. Slowly he wrapped his arm around her slenderness and pulled her into his comforting chest. He kissed the side of her head gently, his thoughts, elsewhere. He could sense her unease as they stared at the blackened ground which had hosted their unholy guests. His arm tightened around her, pulling her tightly against his body, as if to reassure her all was well. For only he knew where the Devourer and his pets had gone.

A day before Sereg and his party returned, Dax-Barh had set in motion a plan only shared with Maril and Craban. Whatever powers these daemons from the void possessed Dax-Barh believed this was the moment they would be truly tested.

***

The Devourer rallied his pets around him. He looked across the lake to the jewel that nestled at its centre. The Isle of the Lost, the very Isle that spawned those who saved the life of the King of men. A place he knew all too well. A place that in time would see his return, but for now there was another matter that for him took president.

A decision his masters in the void would disagree with had they been privy to it, as they waited impatiently for a report on his progress that as yet was not forthcoming, a fact that was to have far reaching ramifications.

27
HUNTER-CRAB GIRL-WEAVING

After returning home, Bael decided to spend his first two days sleeping, eating and tending his injured companions. The Wolf faired the better of the two, she had almost completely recovered, the only evidence that there was ever a wound at all was a crusty scab and a bald patch where the fur was removed. The Hawk's recovery on the other hand was going to be more long-term, and as promised the Knight called Cirius visited each day to help the bird along its path of healing.

Bael was fascinated by the Knight's skills, setting the broken wing was simply masterful and something he was eager to learn. Each time Cirius paid him a visit he made it his business to watch the young knight perform his healing magic. He was also quietly impressed by how quickly Cirius was able to earn the bird's trust, normally it would have ripped a chunk out of the Knight's hand or worse. Even young Raen hadn't been able to calm the Hawk in such a short period of time, taking home a few scars to prove it.

On the third day Cirius arrived early. Before heading to the skinning hut where the Hawk was recovering, he knocked on the lodge's back door. Bael invited him in; they broke bread and shared some freshly prepared goats' cheese. Unlike Hunter, Cirius was the master communicator, some might go as far as to say gossip. There was hardly ever a quiet moment when the two were together, Bael being the recipient of most that was said. Yet strangely, he found the young man's enthusiasm for life a welcome distraction from his own increasing sense of failure at not saving Raen.

"You are early today my friend," Hunter began.

"Maccon has found it necessary to burden me with extra duties. I swear he just makes them up to keep me occupied…. But more importantly I wish to relay a message from the King himself."

Bael picked up the empty plates and placed them into the washing trough by the window.

"And why does our King want to speak to me?" Bael asked, curiously.

"It would appear he wishes to thank you in person for your part in saving his life."

"It isn't necessary, I would do the same for any man I deemed worthy."

"Well, it would seem he feels it is necessary," Cirius smiled. "So, when I am finished here, I have been asked to escort you to the Temple, where his Majesty grows stronger with each passing day."

Bael hated occasions like this; if he could have got away with ignoring the invite he would have. But it was the King. A man he believed to be honourable, and really, he wasn't so arrogant as to believe he had a choice in the matter anyway.

Cirius could see how uncomfortable it made Hunter feel and couldn't hide his amusement as he made for the door.

"Well! A Royal invite no less. How much fun can one man take in a day? I ask."

Hunter just stood there pan faced.

As the young Knight made his way over to the skinning hut Bael was sure he could still hear the man chuckling; which in itself drew a smile out of himself. Being around Cirius was almost like taking a tonic. He had this Gods given talent at being able to lift Hunter's spirit, lightening the burden he had carried with him since the disappearance of his friend. Bael remembered something someone once said to him, who or why alluded him, but the memory was clear. *"If there is one thing in life you can bet coin on with any certainty, it is that, at some point you will suffer the pain of loss-grief-sadness; it has many faces. But happiness is another kind of animal altogether. Happiness has to be sought out, like a beast on the run, it is illusive."* But from what he could see, the Priest Knight never seemed dulled by such negative feelings; his lust for life was obvious to all around him and it was contageous.

Whilst Cirius attended to the Hawk, Bael walked his Wolf over to the lake, letting her roam as she wished. He sat for a short while tossing pebbles into the lakes still water, its surface the mirror of all above and around it. He lay back as the greyness of an impending storm smothered whatever sun light remained; a creeping darkness he knew was almost ready to unleash her fury on the land below.

He was quick to return home. He found Cirius waiting patiently on the wooden bench by the back door.

"I think we should be going," Bael urged.

"I think you are right. Let's hope we make it to the Keep before the heavens open."

It was midday when the pair arrived at the Temple. Thankfully the storm held off. But on entering the courtyard there came a tremendous *boom* as nature unleashed her anger. The thunder ripped across the sky. The lightning that followed lit up the darkness and within seconds both men were soaked to the skin. It was pointless running, so both strolled across the yard as if they carried not a care in the world.

Hunter on introduction, took his Kings appreciation with his usual bemused indifference. One thing he couldn't deny was his admiration for this leader who wouldn't accept any kind of physical assistance, even though he still suffered considerable discomfort. Bael was quick to recognize a man with a battle-hardened pedigree; not a man to be trifled with. As he wandered about the room, he recognized the King's guard he met on the road home. He, like those riding with him that day had learned of the events leading up to their King's crushing defeat at the hands of the Dark Elves. But the story Bael just couldn't shake or ignore was that of the Wolf pack; especially the part that contained the description of the Black Alpha Wolf, the very same that had intervened when he faced off against the bear with Raen all those weeks ago. But he kept his thoughts to himself, he felt this was a mystery to solve at a later date.

When all the pleasantries were over, Bael approached the Knight with the unusual strawberry birth mark on his face. He locked arms with the man; both glad to be meeting in more goodly surroundings.

"How fairs your friend? The one 'as lost his hand."

"He's around here somewhere. Never was one for get togethers like this," Fraene replied.

"I know how he feels."

"I'm sure he would like to see you again and thank you for saving his arm the way you did. We can go find him if you like?"

"No need. I must be leaving now," Bael said. "Just tell him I hope all goes well with his recovery."

"That I will."

Again, they locked arms, then Hunter sneaked away quietly, he'd suffered enough frivolity for one afternoon.

Outside the skies were still overcast, but the rain had eased off a little, the eye of the storm having moved to the mountain range on the horizon. Hunter filled his lungs with the moist fresh air that followed such inclement weather before making his way across the Temple courtyard towards the main Keep building that led to the causeway beyond.

Something caught his eye as he was about to pass the wooden two storey building that housed the carrier pigeons and the orphan children who tended them. In the low light, Hunter could see it was a young girl sitting on the cold wet cobbles, propped up against the front wall by the rickety oak door; she was sobbing. He changed direction and slowly made his way over to the girl. He assessed from her size she would have seen her tenth name day, or there about; he was never good at guessing the age of a female, and like most men found such observation fraught with miscalculation.

There was a lantern over the door which cast its flickering orange glow over an area that just fell short of where the girl sat, but it cast just enough light for Hunter to see there was something really odd looking about the girl's silhouette. It was her arm. The left one was shorter than her right, and instead of a hand the girl had what could only be described as a crab's claw. But on closer study it could be seen she had but one finger and an opposing thumb. A disfigurement Bael had never seen before.

Her head was still bowed as he came alongside her: she didn't look up at him even though she was aware of his presence. Not wishing to loom over the girl, Bael sat down beside her on the wet cobbles. The rain now turned to a drizzle, neither of them showing any concerns about being soaked to the skin.

"Why are you crying?"

At first, she didn't reply. So, he took her small hand in his and squeezed it affectionately.

She raised her head to look into his eyes. It was rare to have someone touch what most judged to be the result of a curse or punishment the Gods had seen fit to suffer upon her. It was a cruel world to live in for someone like her, and even at such a tender age she had learned the hard way how to survive its prejudices. She felt kindly to the man who now sat beside her and seemed not to be swayed by such ill-conceived ignorance. In that moment, she saw something in Hunter very few were privy to: an unexpected tenderness, a safeness all children unknowingly desire that sadly some never find.

Bael noticed in the flickering light, a large bruised swelling under the girls left eye, which was almost closed. He didn't make an issue of it at first, instead he asked the girl her name.

"Lia." She replied.

"Lia. What a beautiful name. Well Lia, you mustn't be afraid, I would never hurt you. Tell me, what happened to your eye?"

For a moment, Lia seemed hesitant to share such knowledge. It was obvious she was frightened.

"Look, if you don't want to say. That is alright. I understand," Bael said caringly.

"It was the new boy. Kory. He said I was a crab," she sobbed. "So, I kicked him. Then he hit me."

"Where is this Kory now?"

"Please mister, don't do anything."

"Don't worry I will not hurt him. Is he in there?"

She nodded-*yes*. Bael stood up, kept hold of her hand and led her into the pigeon house.

Downstairs was split into two rooms, both containing rough cut wooden cot beds. In the room closest to the door, were four beds, three were occupied by girls the fourth was obviously Lia's. Bael guessed the boys were in the next room. He looked about him as he led Lia to where the boys lay. There was enough light from two half burned candles to see the room was sparsely furnished. Three small chairs and a goat skin rug were situated in front of an oven type fireplace that would see the children warm enough through the harsh winters. As they entered the back room Bael found four cot beds each occupied, this time by a boy; chairs, rug and fireplace all the same as in the girls' room. He whispered for Lia to point out the offender. Even in the low light Bael could see the boy was a head bigger than the others. They were all asleep, the short chubby boy occupying the bed in the corner snored as if he were constantly about to choke. But none of the other lads budged, a hard-full day would probably see them sleep through to the morning. Bael looked down at Lia, his finger up to his lips.

"Ssh! You wait here," he whispered. "Let's try not to wake the other boys."

Lia nodded nervously, frightened at what was about to happen. It was all so unexpected, but there was nothing she could do about it now anyway, so she stooped down as if to hide.

Bael loomed over the bully. Carefully he put his hand over the boy's mouth and pressed down with enough pressure to wake the lad. Kory looked terrified. Bael put his other hand up to his mouth and placed his finger on his lip, kneeling down beside the bed he put his mouth close to the boy's ear.

"Do you Know who I am? - Nod if you understand."

The boy shook his head from side to side frantically.

"My name is Hunter. Have you heard of me?"

The lout nodded *yes*, this time.

"Good. Then you know I have a Dire Wolf?"

Again, the boy nodded yes, his eyes bulging with fear.

"Now listen very carefully. If you so much as look at Lia the wrong way, or any of the others here for that matter. I will take you in the night and feed you to my Wolf," Bael whispered, cold and unforgiving.

The boy nodded again and pissed his bed. Then like a phantom Bael was gone, Lia with him, leaving Korey to spend a night lay in his own waist, too terrified to move.

Bael put Lia to bed, he could see one of the girls had awakened and was peeking out at them, the rough woollen blanket she lay under, wrapped tightly around her head. Bael knelt down.

"I don't think he will be bothering you again. Just to make sure, I will call to see you now and again, if that is alright with you?"

Lia smiled.

"That would be nice," she whispered.

Just as Bael was about to stand, her little hand grabbed his sleeve. She sat up and kissed his cheek with the unconditional love you only get from a child. Bael smiled back and stroked her forehead. This strange poor child had found a place in his heart. He just didn't know it yet.

Outside, as he left the building, a figure moved stealthily in the shadows. Whoever it was stayed hidden and watched the whole altercation between Bael and Lia before they entered the house; and then waited patiently until Hunter reappeared.

***

Toran remained in the shadows until Hunter left the grounds, then made his way over to the pigeon house. He'd sheltered as best he could from the rain, but his clothes were stuck to him, his long blonde hair flattened against his head making him look every bit as tough as he was. Without knocking he entered the building, the other girls appeared to be asleep, but he knew his sister Lia would still be awake. He was right. She sat up immediately, even in the low light there was no mistaking the identity of her night caller.

"What are you doing here?" She whispered, as he leant over to kiss her forehead. The silvery light from the full moon outside shone through the only window in the room, to highlight the swelling under her eye.

"Who did this to you?" Toran asked angrily, running his finger gently over the swelling.

Frightened by what he might do she made a fruitless attempt at playing down the incident.

"I am alright, he didn't mean it."

"Who? Was it one of the scum in the next room? Tell me, which one was it?" His voice no longer a whisper, and loud enough to wake the rest of the girls. Carla the oldest of them was first to sit up, she like the rest, frightened by his sudden appearance. Then she recognised who it was.

"What are you doing here? If anyone from the Keep see's you 'ere we'll all be fo'it."

"That's not your concern, Carla. I just want to know who did this to Lia?"

"It was the new boy, Kory, 'e did it. Called Lia crab girl, 'e did," Tilly, the youngest of the bunch, chirped up.

"Did 'e now. Where is this new boy? Show me Tilly."

The young girl was only too pleased to oblige, they all were, they all liked Lia, for the kindness she always showed them.

Not wanting to miss out, the girls were up and out of bed, following Toran into the lads' room next door.

All the boys were sat up in bed, wondering what all the commotion was about. All that is, except Kory, who lay shaking under his wet bedding.

Tilly ran straight to the culprit's bed, pointing accusingly to the crumpled mound of blanket in the middle. Toran dragged it back, exposing the boy beneath crying in fear, he raised his hand to slap the lad, but Lia stepped between them.

"Please Toran, don't. He's learn'd 'is lesson. Haven't you?" She said, turning to the boy.

"Yes. I am sorry. The man as was 'ere before, said 'e would feed me to 'is wolf, if I did anythin' like that again," he cried.

Toran stayed his hand and knelt down in front of Lia.

"That man I saw leavin' a while back, does he go by the name Hunter?"

"Yes."

"What was he doin' 'ere?"

"He saw me crying outside. He was kind. Told me he would make sure I was alright, and said this would never happen again," she said, pointing to her bruise. "He is nice, he told me he would bring his wolf to see me."

Toran looked surprised. He turned back to the new boy, and not wishing to compound the lads suffering any further, he stood up, put his arm around his sister and said.

"You'll never do this again, or say such cruel things, not just to my sister, but to anyone 'ere, do you understand?"

"Yes," the boy replied, shaking his head in relief.

"Then we shall say no more about it."

Toran led the girls back into their own room. He spoke for a while with them all, before returning to Beggars Nest.

The days that followed not only saw the new boy abstain from his bullying ways, they saw him actually go out of his way to help Lia with her chores, and through it, the most unexpected of friendships was forged.

***

When he could, as promised, Bael visited Lia. She had become somewhat of a celebrity amongst the other girls, the boys giving her a wide birth, especially on the odd occasion he arrived with his Wolf. On those occasions, Kory looked terrified. But in time that would change. Bael would see to that. But for now it suited his purpose that the lad should learn a hard lesson.

During his visits, Lia took him into her confidence. He discovered she had a brother. His name she said was Toran. He learned how Toran had saved her life the day she was born. How her mother had died at her birth, and how her father in his anger had left her tiny body by the fire at the mercy of his savage dog. She would have been torn to pieces had Toran not intervened, killing both his father and the dog. It was a carnage she thankfully had no memory of, but even at such a young age she knew what a toll it had taken on her brother. There was no way he could bring up a child, especially living in Beggars Nest as they did, so he left her swaddled on the Temple steps. Maccon had taken pity on her and asked Lady Farroth to help.

She had a nurse maid tend to the child's needs, uncertain whether she would live beyond the first week. But the Gods were just. She lived and grew stronger by the day. Unfortunately, her disability was never accepted by Lord Farroth, he didn't share his wife's maternal instincts, sadly he just saw the disfigurement; not the child that had the roundest eyes the colour of blue ice, and a face that was blessed with a childish beauty which masked a vulnerability that yearned to be loved. And like Lady Farroth, Maccon and all those in the Order who cared for Lia, Bael saw beyond the disfigurement. He saw the inner beauty she radiated like light in a dark room. He saw the child.

***

Vena hadn't seen Hunter in over a month since the disappearance of the smithy's boy. It felt ironic, that the one man who had kept her from performing her usual duties with any other, was the one person keeping away; and it hurt. Whether it was a wise move or not, it was her choice to let her girls fulfil the needs of the many, while she surrendered her body to only one man; Hunter.

Neira, a small buxom wench and the girl Vena let run the place whenever she was absent, sat on the bed next to the inexperienced young patron; spent and red faced. Sadly, for the young soldier the pleasure was fleeting; for her it was easy money, but she felt for the lad.

A few of his friends had secretly organised the whole thing; he being a virgin, they thought it would be fitting to pop his cherry at their expense. Unfortunately, his experience with the opposite sex was almost non-existent, and after two or three pounding thrusts, he'd exploded his life's milk into Neira with such a copious delivery, it Left her with a warm stream running down her inner thigh. Feeling his embarrassment, she decided to sit with him for a while. She put her hand on his and tapped it a couple of times.

"Listen my sweet. It happens. Bein' your first time an' all. There is no shame in that. Let me tell you, you'd be surprised just how often it does happen, to men a lot more experienced than yourself. But by the Gods your sack must have been ready to burst," she grinned, pulling her wet hand from between her legs.

This comment brought a smile to the soldier's face. They talked for a while longer, a conversation which in some part, touched on Hunter's whereabouts. She stood up to escort him to the door, leaving just enough time for her to convey what she had learned to Vena.

"Listen! You must call again. Ask for me. I will teach you how to please us ladies, so, as when the woman of your heart comes along. Well. Let's just say she won't be disappointed."

The young soldier left the room with a bit more spring in his step than when he entered.

Neira cleaned herself quickly, ready to accommodate her next client, the town's fishmonger. Not one of her favourite turns; he always reeked from his catch of the day, even though, if what he told her was true, that he bathed himself in anticipation of their weekly liaison. Anyhow, she thought, it was good money and he was a kindly man to boot. She changed her underwear and left the room, heading for Vena's quarters before the *fish man* as she liked to call him, arrived.

She'd made it her business, whenever the opportunity presented itself, to coax what information she could from her clients, regarding Hunter. She truly cared for Vena, who had shown her nothing but kindness, and it didn't take a genius to see that Hunter meant more to her than just a client. Not only that; Vena had taken her from a life on the streets that offered no protection from the often-brutal nature of men. When Vena found her, she was beaten bloody by a thug in the Warrens. Vena took her in, giving her a roof over her head, and as safe a place as she would ever hope to find, being the nature of her profession.

Of late, she couldn't help but notice Vena's erratic mood swings and she knew why; so, whenever possible she would coerce what information she could from her clients, in search of Hunter's comings and goings.

Vena was like the older sister she never had. Though in truth, Vena wasn't much older than Neira, yet anyone meeting them both for the first time could be forgiven for believing the complete opposite. The hardships of street life had taken a heavy toll, the marks of which were all too clear to see. Her skin ravaged by filth and what scarring disease it contained, then there were the other kinds of scarring, the healed bruises and dried jagged wounds one gets from a good beating. But here, in Vena's brothel she had gained a family; strange, but the closest thing she had ever known to represent such.

She was put to the streets from the age of eight. Orphaned to poverty as so many children were, living in the Warrens, she turned to sex as a way to feel loved and wanted. As empty as those feelings truly were, it was only through Vena and the other girls help, that she began to realize how terribly misguided such beliefs were. It was only now, the sorrow and emptiness that followed her like a cursed shadow, was at last the fading memory of a life no child should ever have to endure. Vena was her saviour, a woman she would never betray, a woman she knew possessed a bigger heart than she would ever admit.

Neira made her way up the wooden stairs to the second gallery which housed Vena's private quarters.

It was a strange looking building. Hexagonal in shape and made entirely of timber, it rose up two floors. Inside, the stairs led to two tiers of gallery landings which stretched around the whole building; each wall housing three adjacent rooms. The landings themselves looked down to the ground floor below, to the centre of the structure where the guests could peruse the fleshy merchandise, before retiring to live out whatever fantasies their desires could concoct. It was a place where very few secrets remained sacred.

Neira was only ten paces from Vena's room; unexpectedly the door opened. A young man exited, and if rumours were true, and more often than not they were, the man who stepped out onto the gallery was father of two, whose cheating wife was sleeping with the Sargent of the Garrison. She was shocked, not so much by the appearance of the man, but more because Vena used those quarters for the sole entertainment of just one client. Hunter.

The man was sweating profusely and smelt of sex as he passed by Neira, head bowed. She paid him no heed and carried on to the room.

"Well?" Vena ventured, in anticipation of the well-intentioned criticism she felt was sure to follow.

Neira just smiled as she entered the room. The covers on the bed were dishevelled, exposing the soiled horse hair mattress beneath. She could see Vena had what the girls like to call the *glow*; a dead giveaway that all carnal urges had been satisfied.

"Well? What can I do for you?"

"No judgement." Neira's reply tinged with a hint of sarcasm.

Vena, with an air of indignation straightened her skirt and pulled the bedcovers over the mattress.

"Don't even go there. Do you know how long it's been since I last had a man between my legs?"

Neira walked over to the only window in the room, that overlooked the shaded street below. She was surprised to see amongst the people going about their business, Hunter, who passed the building without giving it a second glance. She chose to keep her observation quiet for the moment. Instead, she began to relay what information she had.

"I have news about Hunter."

Vena at first, tried to appear unconcerned. She finished making the bed and walked to a table that had a clay bottle and several hardened leather mugs on it. It wasn't long though, before wanton curiosity got the better of her.

"Sit with me," she said, pulling out one of two wooden chairs.

Neira did as Vena asked, accepting the offer of a mug of fresh wine.

"What have you heard?"

"A young soldier from the Keep, says Maccon, you know, that priest whatever he is, says this Maccon is troubled by Hunter's behaviour of late."

"What do you mean?"

"It seems he's been keepin' away from folk more than usual. Other than seein' some poor orphan girl at the Temple, he's kept away from town."

Vena was surprised by the comment. *Orphan* she thought. *Why would he take an interest in such a girl?*

"Orphan girl?" she puzzled. "Why would he visit such a child?"

"I don't know. That's all what was told me by this soldier. Anyways, it seems he's been frequentin' that dump in the Nest. The Severed Hand. You Know. That place as welcomes every cutthroat, thief and boar shagger in the Warrens."

"Yes. I know it. But why? Strange," she pondered. "Carry on Neira, what else have you heard?"

"Whatever is goin' on with Hunter, is definitely concernin' Maccon and Lord Farroth and that's for sure. It looks like the only other person he's been visitin' is that old crone in the woods."

"She's an elderly woman, not some old witch to be ridiculed so."

"I meant nothin' by it," Neira said. Surprised that her words gave such offence to Vena.

"Anyway. Please go on."

"These are just rumours mind-yer. It seems one of the soldier's friends overhears Maccon talkin' to that young knight of 'is. You know. The ones been hangin' around Dogran's place these past weeks… Cirius I think they call 'im."

"Yes. I know him, he's been sniffing around Emma I am told. Good lookin' young man."

"That he is. Wouldn't mind a slice of that pie meself. It would appear the young Knight 'as taken an interest in Hunter's whereabouts. So Maccon tells 'im how Hunter is becomin' more distant, and that somethin' dark was growin' in him."

"What do you mean? Dark?"

"I Don't know. That's all the lad told me. But whatever it is, Maccon said the Old Woman in the forest 'as seen it too."

Vena was convinced, the worrying events that had transpired all stemmed from the disappearance of the Smithy's son, and was somehow connected to the dreams Hunter was having. She knew how much he cared for the lad, but something more-deep rooted was at work, but what that was she could only guess.

"I have never seen Hunter like this. When have you ever known him to stay away this long?"

"It is strange, and that's for sure," Neira said, trying to sound supportive. "Well if it be any consolation, he passed here just before we started talkin'. Looked like 'e was headin' over to Dogran's place. Maybe he'll call 'ere on his way home."

Vena made no attempt to reply. She looked sad. Lost almost, as if she knew things were about to change. Things she had no control over.

***

Bael entered the Tavern. Dogran was behind the counter, some of his regulars were busy chatting with him. Contrary to many of the other times he approached the bar, the group stopped talking and one by one raised their mugs in welcome. Bael gave an acknowledging nod and continued on to the bar. Dogran poured him his favourite ale, placed it on the counter in front of him and put up his hand.

"No payment necessary my friend. Not seen you around for a while?"

Bael took a long sip of his drink, savouring every welcome drop.

"I've been busy," came his short reply.

"Well, it's good to have you back."

Bael walked over to the empty table by the stairs. He sat down and sighed heavily, as if his shoulders were laden with the weight of the world.

Emma had watched his every step, disappointed that he hadn't once glanced her way. She couldn't understand why she felt so awkward sitting alongside Cirius as she did; but as confused as her feelings were, she was glad to see Hunter return.

Cirius turned to see what had taken Emma's attention. When he saw Hunter sitting alone at a table the other side of the room, he raised his tankard as to say *hello*.

Emma was surprised when Hunter returned the courtesy as if she wasn't there; and though she enjoyed the company of the man next to her, she felt hurt. Hurt because there was no sign of jealousy: That his feelings about her were so indifferent that her flirting with another man seemed to have no effect whatsoever.

Cirius waved Hunter over to join them. Bael raised his hand, declining the kind invitation. The Knight pressed the matter no further. He guessed from Emma's frown, that the pair shared some kind of history together. Though, it would appear it meant more to her than it did to Hunter; but he chose to ignore the matter and continued his conversation.

Hunter finished his drink, returned the empty mug to the counter and was about to turn and leave.

"You leaving so soon," Dogran asked.

"I have things to do," was all Hunter could muster.

"How fairs that Wolf of yours? And the Hawk?"

"She has healed well…. The Hawk will fly soon."

"I am glad. Don't be a stranger," the big man urged.

Hunter smiled tiredly and left without uttering another word.

***

Hunter stepped through the door of the brothel. He felt tired, drained. He passed some of the girls chatting with one another, taking advantage of what little time they had between tricks. Neira was amongst them and seemed happy to see him.

"She's been missin' yer," she said as he made his way up the stairs.

The door to Vena's room was ajar as he approached. He knocked once and entered, before permission was granted. Vena was sat on the edge of the bed in just her underwear, not expecting a visit by anyone other than her girls.

"So! You've finally decided to grace me with your company," she whispered.

He ignored the comment, removed his jacket and flopped on the bed next to her. She wasn't really sure how she felt; guilt at sleeping with another just earlier that day, something she had never done before. Anger at the man who just saw her as a place to lay his head whenever he was troubled, and now absent promise of sex as pleasurable compensation for her troubles. And finally, and somewhat disconcertingly, found herself at the mercy of a man who could disarm whatever grievance she might harbour against him, in an instant.

Unsettled, Vena slipped off the bed and closed the door. For some obscure reason, she felt slightly nervous, not a feeling she was used to dealing with. But she needn't have worried. Hunter was fast asleep when she joined him on the bed. He was dead to the world and in this state, he could sleep through almost anything. She pulled his boots off, followed by his deer skin britches; he groaned a few times but his eyes stayed firmly shut. She turned him onto his side to face her and joined him in bed, pulling the cover over them both. She put her arm over him, slipped further down in the bed and put her face to his.

"What's a woman to think? Hunter," she whispered. "It's been a month, and what do I get for my troubles. You snoring like a stuck pig. Bah!" Vena let herself drift off, *at least I might get a good night's sleep*, she thought. But she was headed for disappointment.

Not long past midnight she was awakened to find Hunter lying face up groaning as he so often did when lost in a troubled sleep. His face was slick with sweat, his eyes moving about under closed eye lids. She sat herself up, swept back his wet black hair and stroked his troubled brow. She sat there, reserved to the fact that any attempt at sleep was futile. There was but one thing to do and that was sit it out until Hunter woke up.

***

THE WEAVING.

Bael drifts through the forest, as a bird on the wing, trapped in the chaos of unpredictable air currents. There is no sense of direction. He lets himself surrender to whatever force is guiding him. His progress becomes slow and laboured. The wild life below ignores him as if he was just a ghost passing through.

Eventually he exits the canopy of trees to find himself floating above bright grassy flat lands whose variants of green compliment the dusty peach-coloured clouds drifting gracefully in a sea of azure blue. Ahead he spots a huge castle, which seems to grow out of the horizon like an Elven monolith. As he drifts closer, he can't help but be impressed by its graceful majesty. Slowly, he flies above the battlements, between spiral topped towers and on to beautifully landscaped gardens that stretch all the way to the foot of a mountain whose waterfalls act as a backdrop of breath-taking beauty.

Without any kind of warning he begins to slow down, to hang in the air like a hawk before a kill. Below, water from one of the falls in the distance feeds a stony stream whose waters culminate in an almost lake sized pond. So clear he can see the stones below being caressed by long flowing pond weeds trapped in an ever-swirling undercurrent. The area is home to an abundance of birds of every colour, size and variety imaginable. Then he sees them. Two figures lying together not far from the water's edge, under the cover of a weeping cherry tree.

Again, there is no warning. Bael finds himself drifting uncontrollably closer. He tries to consciously resist, but to no avail. He stops right above them, literally just feet away, but still neither of them aware they are being observed. He is close enough now to realize the couple are completely naked. He can see that the one on top is in fact an Elder and not a man as he previously thought. He is tall, slender but muscular, not an ounce of fat on a chiselled physique that is perfectly proportioned to his height. Beneath him lies the most beautiful woman Bael has ever seen. In her nakedness, he can see she has lightly tanned skin unlike the Elder atop her whose skin is the colour of moonlight on frozen snow. On closer scrutiny, Bael can see that unlike her ears, which are human, his are pointed confirming his Elven origin.

Even in this voyeuristic state, Bael feels a deep sense of intrusive guilt. It is obvious he is watching two lovers bound in the dance of procreation, and it feels wrong. As that singular thought enters his mind, he thankfully starts to drift up higher and onwards, back to the castle. This time he moves just beyond a balcony high up on the tallest of three central towers. A single figure stands alone like a sentinel, his face drawn thin and unforgiving. He is staring at the couple. His radiant violet eyes filled with the burden of the heart, it is obvious he cares for one or both he looks upon. Bael can feel his sadness. He is tall, proud, on his head the Crown of a King.

There is a flash of light.

Bael now finds himself traveling above an island in the middle of a huge lake, surrounded on all sides by glacier faced mountains. Slowly he begins to descend, passing by a crescent moon shaped harbour, past a strange building shaped like a wolf's head and on, over open areas where Dire Wolves roam freely.

There is a flash of light.

Now he stands in an egg-shaped room, unnoticed by a group of Elders sitting around a massive oval shaped bed. Lying on top in the throes of childbirth lies the beautiful woman he saw by the pond. There is blood on the sheets, an Elder woman wearing a fine filigree Crown Bael felt must be the Queen, is holding a newborn child in her arms, the babe covered in a mother's blood; she is sad. The father he saw by the pond is kneeling, holding onto the hand of his suffering partner. Bael can feel his gut wrenching, overwhelming grief as if it were his own. It felt terrible, all-consuming and in that very moment it felt like part of him was being ripped away.

He tries to leave but can't. Instead he drifts towards the Queen and the babe. He can see the child is pink of skin with ears the shape of its mother, not pointed like the father's. Bael finds the whole scene incredibly moving and finds himself staring through tear filled eyes.

There is a flash of light.

Bael is back at the house in the mountains where in an earlier dream he saw the huge black Dire Wolf leave the baby outside the door and later where the boy and his father played with a dog. He is drawn closer, in the doorway stands a young man. This time there is no mistaking the man's identity. It is Bael himself.

***

Hunter woke to find his head resting on Vena's lap. The only evidence of his dream like journey, the sweat soaked bedding he was lay upon.

Vena had stayed awake all night; glad he was once again a guest of her bed. She wasn't sure why, but she had this undeniable feeling that these special nights in her life were about to end. The last few times they shared her bed she felt the distance growing in him. At first she chose to ignore it, passing it off as her own insecurities; but finally the realization that such thoughts were not the product of an overzealous imagination became all too clear. He was going to leave and she didn't know whether he would ever return, and as angry and frustrated as he could make her, she was determined to cherish every moment they shared together. Unfortunately, she knew with Hunter she rarely got what she so wantonly desired. In all her years in the profession, she had never come across a man whose moods and habits were so difficult to predict. Yet still, she cared for him like no other.

"What did you dream about this time?"

"It matters not," he replied. He just couldn't be bothered trying to decipher the why's and wherefores of his latest vision; his waking mind was set to one purpose: To find and return with Raen no matter how long it took.

"You have changed, Hunter. Something tells me you will be leaving us soon," feeling, as the words left her lips, like she had been punched in the pit of her stomach.

His silence confirmed her worries.

It had been a long time since she felt such an acute sense of impending loss; not since the death of the father of her child had she experienced such feelings. Being a woman of means, always able to keep her emotions in check, was what made her present state of mind so hard to rationalize. Yet hidden away deep in the realms of her inner thoughts was the realization that the man by her side would never be hers; not in the traditional sense. He paid for her company; a fact they could never get past. She was never supposed to fall in love. That wasn't the path she chose to follow. But love, like the flame of a fire is unpredictable in its nature. It can sneak up on you, intoxicating in its allure, burning down the barriers of the unsuspecting, to disarm them as it had with Vena.

Hunter moved as to leave the bed, only to find himself naked on top of Vena, as she yanked him back onto her. He placed his arms either side of her, lifted himself up slightly, enough to be able to kiss her on the breast, her stomach but instead of continuing down he pushed himself back up to kiss her on the lips. She couldn't deny her disappointment in such a move that sent a clear message to a woman of her experience.

"You are off-then?"

"I must. There are things I have to do." He sat on the edge of the bed and pulled up his britches.

"Don't be a stranger…. You know how much you miss me."

"I won't," he lied.

Vena felt awkward, her dilemma was; she wanted him to stay without appearing desperate. Not a quality she admired. So she said the first thing that came into her head.

"Are you off to see that girl at the Temple?"

"How do you know about that?"

"I have my sources."

"Why am I not surprised," he said, brushing his hair back and tying it into a pony tail. "But in answer to your question. No. I am riding to Woodcrest, there is someone I must seek out."

"Who?" she asked.

"I'm not sure."

"How can you not be sure?"

"Emma, Dogran's daughter…"

"I know who Emma is," she interrupted. "So please, carry on."

"Emma told me about a stranger staying at the Tavern who thinks he knows me from the past. The person she described to me sounded like one of the fighters from my dreams. The young one whose life I saved."

"Yes, I remember, the one with the jagged edged sword," she replied, choosing to withhold the fact that she too had met the man.

"That's right."

"How strange," she continued, verbalizing her thoughts out loud. "Be careful Hunter. Who knows what this man's intentions might be? It is a troubling coincidence, is it not? That he should appear at the very same time an attempt has been made on Agramar's life."

"If there is a connection, I mean to find it. But first I want to know if he holds answers about my past that I now believe to be questionable," he said, as he sprang to his feet. He couldn't ignore how shapely her body was, as she followed him naked from the bed. Seductively, she placed her arms around his neck and drew him into her. She kissed him with a passion her lips hadn't surrendered for a long time. His lips returned in kind, his hands searching for the round softness of her buttocks. His fingers pressed into the soft flesh as he pulled her pelvis against his arousal; only to let his hands fall away teasingly.

"Not fair! Hunter. You can't do that to a girl, then get up and leave."

Hunter smiled.

"As much as the body is willing, I have to go." He kissed her forehead, picked up his cape, threw it over his shoulder and made for the door. "I promise I will see you as soon as I can," he said, as he stepped out of the room.

Vena held the door ajar to watch him make his way down the stairway.

"Make sure you do," she shouted, as he disappeared from view.

"I will."

She closed the door, not realizing the next time she would see Hunter, it would be for a very different reason.

28

OLD CRONE

Bael fed the Hawk the last of the chicken heads he carried in the leather pouch hanging from his belt. The bird's blood red eyes blinked at him knowingly as it turned to take flight. Its razor-sharp talons tightened, digging into the hardened leather bracer protecting his arm; a signal it was ready.

"Fly my beauty," he urged, relieved and glad his friend could once again take to the skies like he was born to do. The bird flapped its wings as proof that Cirius' magic had actually worked, and as the confidence in its healed wing grew the Hawk took to the air; flying above and beyond the trees bordering the property.

Cirius was quietly pleased with himself as the bird disappeared from view. He could see how much it meant to Hunter and how the Hawk didn't so much serve a master, rather it was a union of mutual respect in which both served each other. It was rare to see, indeed; he considered himself a kindred spirit for he too shared such a bond with his own falcon.

"Well, my friend, it would seem I am done here."

Bael locked arms with the Knight, the Wolf by his side raising her head approvingly.

"Thankyou. I hope one day I can return the kindness," Bael replied.

"You owe me naught. It is in my nature to help such creatures, as it is in yours. This much I have learned about you. To see your Hawk return to full health and fly free is reward enough for me."

"I will not forget what you did for him. You are welcome to visit any time you wish; my door will always be open to you."

"Thank you," Cirius replied. "Sadly, I must take my leave. The King readies himself for the long journey back to the capital today. Unfortunately, duty calls as they say."

But before leaving, there was another question he wanted to ask, that had been simmering from the time he saw how Emma looked at Bael back at the Tavern. Now was as good a time as any to get some clarity on the matter.

"Hunter! Please do not think me presumptuous and if you wish not to answer, I understand and take no offence, but do you and Emma share a history of some kind?"

Such a question would normally be met with a threating silence, but on this occasion Bael wasn't about to subject the man to such a discourteous response.

"I have a fondness for her, who in his right mind wouldn't. I can see you are taken with her."

Cirius' cheeks warmed to pink, which to anyone in his company was confirmation that Hunter's words struck true. Bael patted the young knight on the shoulder.

"There is no shame in it my friend, it obvious to anyone seeing you together."

Cirius seemed a little uncomfortable.

"That obvious? Yet I am filled with uncertainty."

"Why? She is a beautiful woman, within and without. It would be a fool that didn't find such a woman desirable, so again I say, where is the shame in that?"

"My Order forbids me such intimacies when absent the prospect of marriage, and unlike most relationships, it is the woman who must choose the man…. Yet when I am in her company, I feel such vows tested."

"I can't pretend to know or understand, why an Order like yours would court such rigid practices. Only you can answer that. You are a man, she is a woman, what more is there to say. Why deny yourself what is only natural."

Cirius found Hunter's frankness, surprising. It was obvious he did have feelings for Emma, but wished not to act on them, for whatever reason. He could only assume that Hunter's well documented visits to the town's brothel was all the commitment the man was prepared to embrace. It was a contradiction he could not understand.

"You speak so kindly of Emma, have you never thought to ask her how she feels about you?" he asked.

Bael couldn't summon an answer. Inwardly, out of all the women he knew, he deemed her the finest, yet; he'd never stopped to wonder why he only pursued the company of women requiring little or no commitment, other than what coin he held in his purse. It was easier, less demanding. He'd abandoned any semblance of meaningful companionship, in a lost past. A past, now fighting back to regain its rightful place in his memories. A past that conjured up an odd feeling he couldn't understand or recognise, but a feeling that somewhere in another place, another time, he belonged to someone. A feeling his conscious mind had kept hidden all these years.

Cirius could see his question made Hunter fidget uncomfortably.

"Please forgive my rambling. I should not presume to ask questions of such a personal nature, though void of malice I fear my enthusiasm got the better of me."

"No offence is taken my friend."

"I'm glad… So, now I am afraid I must leave you. Oh! And before I forget. Let me say how kind it is of you to visit our little Lia the way you have."

"She is a lovely child. It is nothing."

"You are wrong. It is everything. I have watched her grow these past few weeks, in a confidence she lacked so desperately. The girl loves you Hunter, like a child would a kind and loving father. A love so pure, is not to be taken lightly, I think."

Hunter once again seemed lost for words; set to thinking, he mustered a half smile. Cirius locked arms with him and left the house.

The rest of the morning, the words haunted Bael. There was an undeniable truth in what Cirius said to him regarding Lia, a truth that carried with it, uncertainty… responsibility.

A full month had passed since the disappearance of Raen. King Agramar and his ensemble were headed back to the Capital with two hundred militia men as protection. The town's people had settled into some semblance of normality and Bael was ready to take up Lamia's invitation.

Autumn was advancing on summer. Trees other than evergreens tried with varying success to hang onto their seasonal foliage, but most were littered with leaves of orange, brown and yellow. Nature's sign, that change was on the way. The winds were colder, and for a land to be so rich and green there had to be a cost; that cost was heavy rain.

As Bael arrived at Lamia's cottage, the heavens opened. He and the Wolf were lucky enough to reach the front door before it began to pour down so heavily it bounced off the stone pathway.

"Come in, come in, you'll be catching your death out there," Lamia said, waving from the open doorway.

As they entered the main room the young deer, though grown in size and strength, darted under a chair by the table. Being a natural source of food for the Wolf, survival instincts and a growing sense of preservation took over.

"There, there… There is nothing to fear," Lamia said, coaxing the animal out of hiding.

Bael handed her a parcel containing a loaf of her favourite rye bread and a clay bottle of her favourite mead, all courtesy of Dogran, who Bael had seen earlier that morning.

"Can I put these somewhere for you?"

"Down here will do fine," she replied, pointing to the table by the window.

Bael obliged, then sat down at the larger table in the centre of the room where Lamia was already seated.

"I haven't had the pleasure of your company since the abduction of Koval's son. So, what brings you to my home *this* day?"

"In truth, I am not sure," he replied. "Yet here I am. I wanted to see you were alright."

"I am, but I sense that is not the only purpose for your visit. Am I, right?"

"There is something. It concerns Raen's whereabouts… your gift allows you to see what others do not."

"So, you think me a witch, do you? A purveyor of dark, malevolent sorcery I presume."

"I mean not to offend."

"And why should I believe your words bear truth in their delivery?" Lamia said, unable to keep up the pretence that she was offended by his question. "I play with you young man… please, pour us both a drink, then come and sit by my side." She smiled, handing Bael the bottle of mead he'd given her. Bael did what the old woman asked of him, then she extended her arm, in a toast. Hunter tapped mugs, not sure why.

"For better days to come," Lamia said. Her clouded eyes giving nothing away.

Bael took a long drink, almost emptying his mug in one take; putting it down on the table he leant forward as if to whisper, but she put her hand up to stop him.

"I know what you seek, I knew it from the moment you crossed the threshold. I want to help you, but I fear what bits of information I impart, will offer little in the way of comforting expectation."

"Please? Whatever you can tell me will help."

"I can only tell you what I saw that day. With what you know, well, maybe you can piece it together to reveal something of import. It is obvious you have heard about the powers I possess, so I will not waste your time explaining them. The day Raen was taken, I saw a fleeting image of those that took him, the very same that also attacked Dogran and killed that poor girl. A terrible day indeed."

Bael sat quiet, not wishing to interrupt he filled both their mugs with what remained of the mead and sat back tentatively.

"I think you already know these slavers were not from these parts, their skin is too delicate for our hot summers. That is why it surprises me that they should undertake such a venture when this has been one of the hottest summers I can remember. I believe these people originate from a group of islands, far to the west in the Sea of Tears."

"I have heard of these islands you speak."

"I am afraid, such knowledge is of limited value. It is said there are a thousand islands nestling in this area; groups of which, go by different names and as varied a number of leaders. No! To find these terrible people you must get more information, how I cannot say, but I know you are a resourceful man. Yet I still must warrant caution."

"I will not make the mistake of underestimating my adversary a second time," Hunter said. "I faced the leader of these men on the road, only to have his knife at my throat, and watch, helpless to prevent Raen from being taken away. A fact that haunts me every day."

Lamia could feel Hunter's pain, but something she witnessed worried her deeply.

"Please? Give me your hand."

Bael reached out and rested his right hand on hers, gently she closed her fingers around it and closed her eyes in concentration. Slowly her thoughts meld with his and one by one his memories are probed by an invisible assailant, painless and friendly in its intent. Lamia's psychic voyeurism allows her access to scenes that play out in a random almost chaotic order. *First, she lays witness to Hunter saving Dogran's life. Bael's mind is strong and wilful; it takes all of her powers of concentration to navigate them with any sense of understanding. She feels a pain behind her eyes as she presses further, this time she watches as Bael helps save the King's life. She feels warmth on her lip as blood drips from her nose, but she maintains her focus, there is a forest, slavers sit and drink around a fire, as Hunter enters the camp she sees Raen tied to a tree, blood encrusted across his face. Hunter puts all of the captors to the sword, until a blow to the back of his head renders him semi-conscious. As he looks into the face of his aggressor, she not only shares the man's identity but fights to stay the image as the slaver's mind resists her probing, as if, even in this mindful state he is aware of her presence.* This shocks her back to reality. Bael is instantly aware of her distress and holds her hand concernedly.

"Are you alright? Your nose is bleeding."

"I am fine," she replied, wiping the blood away with a kerchief removed from a pocket in her skirt.

"This happens sometimes, it is an unfortunate symptom of my condition; powers like mine come at a price."

"What did you see?"

Lamia described everything she witnessed, unfortunately there was nothing new that Hunter was not already privy to. Then she added.

"I saw the leader of the men you seek. His head bore tattoos of a runic nature. They have meaning of great significance. You must be careful Hunter. This man is very dangerous, I sensed a power beyond the mortal"

"What do you mean?"

"My powers allow me to penetrate thoughts within the realms of another's mind, some call *Weaving:* as I did when I saw this man through your own mind's eye. But it was as if he was aware of my presence and somehow kept me at bay. This I have never experienced before, and as such, I find it extremely troubling."

"I know this is no ordinary killer, such a man would never have been able to steal up on me the way he did, as if from the very air itself. But he is a man, and he can bleed like a man. The next time we meet I will be prepared."

"There is something else. Your thoughts revealed a tavern in the Nest. And a young fighter brandishing a jagged sword."

"It is incredible that you have seen so much in such a short time."

"Sadly, not enough," she replied. "But why must you venture into the Warrens? They are so dangerous for those of us who don't prey on others, yet I believe, you are no stranger to the place."

"I have heard rumours of a hunchback, boasting he knows the identity of those who took Raen and killed his woman. If what I hear is true, then by week's end I hope to have such information in my possession. I am told this hunchback frequents that drink hole in the Nest called the Severed Hand."

"An apt name for a place whose landlord plays host to every cutthroat, thief and rapist in the Warrens. This is no place for the likes of you Hunter."

"I have had occasion to visit the place, so I am aware of the nature of those who reside there. You can be sure they offer me no threat… I can take care of myself."

Lamia still looked troubled. She stood up to clear away the empty mugs and bottle.

"I do not doubt that, but please heed my words. Be careful. There are those you will meet who would wish you harm in this establishment and they are very dangerous."

"I will do as you ask," Bael said, warmly.

Lamia washed the empty mugs, rinsed out the clay bottle and poured goats milk into a bowl on the floor for the young deer, and water for the Wolf. Both animals were asleep, the deer resting its head against the Wolf's, the sight touched the old woman, it was almost a shame to disturb them, but she tapped them both gently on the head. The Wolf was first to respond, she walked over to the bowl and began lapping up the water. The deer followed shortly after, but rather than drink the milk she joined the Wolf and drank with her, without interference.

Lamia joined Hunter back at the table. This time she scrutinized the aura surrounding him more closely; she frowned, but again said nothing. This time she faced him from across the table.

"What of the young fighter with the jagged sword?" she asked.

"I was told this man visited Dogran's Tavern some weeks back. He told a friend of mine, Dogran's daughter, Emma, he thought he knew me. The person described to me reminded me of a fighter I saw in my dreams."

Lamia leant forward towards Bael, her mind once again linked to his. On description of the man, she is taken to the fighting pits. *The warrior brandishing the jagged edged sword moves against another fighter who stands over Galas, prone on the ground. As the fighter standing over Galas is about to execute the final blow, the jagged sword punches through his back, out through his chest.* Lamia fell back in her chair exhausted. She is troubled.

"I must find this man," Hunter urged.

"What will you do, if you are indeed fortunate in your endeavour?"

"I'm not sure. I only know he may offer clarity to questions that have troubled me since my dreams began."

"Then I hope you find what you seek. But for now I would beg forgiveness. My weary bones press me for rest, an unfortunate by-product of an aging body."

"There is nothing to forgive.... I thank you for your time, and if you are agreeable? I would like to visit you again before I leave to find Raen," he said, as he walked towards the door.

"Please do, that would be nice."

The Wolf was already waiting. The fawn jumped backwards frightened by the sudden movement. Bael bent down to tickle the animal under the chin, its immediate response, to lift its head to the touch. Then to Lamia's surprise, Hunter turned and kissed her affectionately on the cheek. Before he could step outside, she took hold of his hand.

"There are those around you who are not what they seem. Look out for them, I believe amongst them you will find an unexpected ally."

Hunter smiled, then left: Puzzled by her last comment.

Lamia stayed at the open door, the deer at her feet. What she hadn't shared with Bael earlier was what she saw when he first entered the cottage. A condition that was still present as she watched him disappear down the path, the Wolf, ever close to his side.

There was no mistaking, the two Aura's he shared with the Wolf had dulled, yet hers remained radiant as before. But what troubled Lamia most, was the darkness separating Hunter's. It had grown. At times it flickered wisp like, then lashed out as a black flame, to dissolve in the air like soot in water. It was the final phenomenon that gave her most concern, the darkness took the form of what could only be described as the shape of a person, which too, on appearance would flicker and dissolve into the air.

29
JACK'AND - SEVERED HAND – TORAN

The Severed Hand was a true den of iniquity. It earned its less than savoury name from the fact that the innkeep and owner displayed his severed left hand on the wall behind the bar; the story of his loss changing frequently on the telling.

The place greeted all who entered with a smell of piss, unwashed clothes, unclean women and men whose bodily habits were questionable in the least: ripe was to understate the obvious. Most who entered the place, probably hadn't seen water in weeks, and the whores that serviced the place weren't much better either.

Fights broke out nightly, some resulted in maiming or worse-death. The removal and disposal of these bodies wasn't a problem for Jack'and as they called him, being his name was Jack and the fact that his hand was parted from his arm. No. Jack had quite the novel way of disposing of such unfortunates: out back of the Tavern he housed several large sows and a couple of hogs, whose insatiable appetites found such human fare a welcome tender delicacy. Some even rumoured, that a number of these poor unfortunate bastards ended up in the tavern's pies, said to be, pork, beef and the like. Most didn't care, as they tasted so good, but on occasion if one scrutinized the meat they would find it pale of colour, stringy in texture.

In truth Jack lost his hand in a fight with a rival gang leader. He and his men killing every last one of an enemy trying to infringe on his territorial boundaries. Following this altercation Jack shocked all who followed him, when, after all the blood was spilled, he, without rhyme or reason knelt down, picked up his severed hand and stuffed it in a pouch on his belt.

Jack was no ordinary villain. He'd gained a reputation for being just, for those as deserved such justice, but any he deemed unworthy of such judgement were dealt with swiftly, ruthlessly, absent any sense of remorse. Jack, unlike most of those who followed him and there were many; was highly intelligent, savvy and who through years of clever investment in both people and property, had accrued the means to run an underworld empire that oversaw most of the unlawful goings on in the Warrens. If rumours were to be believed, Jack's simple beginnings came from the barrels of contraband liquor he stole from the ships wrecked on the coastal reefs. Led to their watery graves by fires placed strategically along the beach; all manoeuvred by design when Jacks men infiltrated the shipping companies, offering false information to the ships Captains for their return with their cargo of liquor and whatever else was of worth. Now Jack ran his seedy empire from the Tavern, its construction funded by those early takings.

Like Dogran, Jack kept himself well informed about the regulars who patronised his establishment. He was a big man, a good half head larger than most who frequented the place and cut quite an intimidating visage. Behind the counter holding pride of place next to his hand, shrivelled purple like rotten fruit, was Blood Bane: a huge blood encrusted club, its head peppered with six-inch nails. A brutal weapon that saw a bloody end to many a fight, its nails ripping through flesh and bone with equal ease to render the skull a pulp like broken mess. He feared no man and wore his wounds with pride, many on display for all to see.

He'd watched his regulars come and go throughout the day, Hunter, sitting alone by the window wasn't one of them. Jack knew or made it his business to know about everyone who passed through his doors, Hunter no exception. He considered Hunter to be an odd one, the Wolf and white Hawk set him apart from anyone else he'd investigated. He was all too aware of the man's penchant for a fight. On one of the few occasions Hunter wet his tongue at his Tavern, he witnessed such; the man laying waste to the Venger brothers, a couple of drunken low life debt collectors, with a willingness to remove fingers and other more personal extremities, using the two daggers they both carried. Fortunately, on this occasion neither of the brothers were to be seen, otherwise Jack felt his pigs would be feasting on an excess of fleshy delights.

Jack lent over the counter, a woman possibly in her late twenties lent across to face him. She was hard looking but not unattractive like the rest of the whores.

"Keep an eye on that-'ne," he whispered, glancing over to the table by the furthest of the three windows facing the dirt road outside. "He's fucker as keeps that mangy wolf as a pet, not shy of a scrap o' two either. Not sure why 'ed show is face 'ere again after showin' those idiot Venger twins what it's like to chew on sawdust."

"Leave it to me, I'll sway 'im with some o' me female charms," she said, tapping her more than ample breasts.

Hunter took a long swig of ale, keeping his face in the shadow. On the next table not far from his, four tough looking thugs laughed heartily at something the hunchback said, unfortunately too quiet for Hunter to make any sense of. He noticed the man was missing all the fingers of his left hand as he waved it about, being drunk, loud and obnoxious. The men around him seemed to be intrigued by the verbal horseshit that spewed from the man's mouth, no matter how bizarre and outrageous the levity of his words. Hunter listened in disbelief as they all exchanged childhood escapades with a pride befitting the mindless morons they obviously were. One of the thugs, a thin wiry individual who continually spat mouthfuls of phlegm onto the floor, missing intentionally the spittoon by his feet, burst into laughter. Hunter couldn't hear what the man considered so funny, though he felt it was nothing to miss. Another at the table the others called Cutter, chipped in, this time loud enough for anyone close by to hear.

"So 'eres one for yer. Me and Tiny 'ere," he said, elbowing the grossly overweight thug next to him. "We was ten I fink, we raid this farmer's orchard, sweetest apples you ever tasted. By the time we be finished, Tiny 'ere's eaten that many of the fuckers 'e starts complainin' of the belly ache. Next thing I see is 'im runnin' over to the nearest tree, drops 'is britches an' starts to shit out this white fuckin' froth. Fermented apple juice, whatever it was, 'e shits the stuff all over the fuckin' tree. Tiny looks less than impressed by his friends oversharing, but the rest crack up laughing, bearing an array of rotten teeth in varying stages of decay. Another at the table whose name Hunter didn't catch, banged his mug down in demand of attention.

"I got one better 'an that. There's this kid I knew, right? No mother an' a father tighter'n a cat's arse 'ole. One mornin' I goes to call on 'im, see if 'e wants to climb a tree an' piss on them walkin' below. When I get to where he's livin' I finds the little fucker lay on the ground suckin' on a bitch hound's teat. Thing was, 'is mad fuck of a father killed the bitch's pups 'cause 'e didn't want 'em runnin' about the place. Trouble is the bitch is broodin' and still makin' milk, so this kid 'alf starved thinks, why not."

For some reason the rest of the group didn't find his story funny; Hunter assumed the reason being, one it was an awful story and secondly because they had suffered the same kind of degrading poverty in their own childhood. For a moment the conversation dried up.

"Well, I thought it was funny."

"You would yer sick fuck," Cutter said. Then he turned to the hunchback. "Your turn."

The hunchback dribbled ale from his twisted lips; to Hunter it seemed the man did not share his colleagues' childish sense of camaraderie. But Cutter wasn't about to give up.

"Come on, tell again 'ow you lost them fingers, Tiny 'ere 'asn't 'eard it yet."

"No point to that now is there? I've told it more times 'an I care to remember," he replied.

Hunter had seen this many times before; that moment amongst drunks when just one wrong word or look can change everything, laughter one moment, the next, a broken bottle in the face.

The hunchback was quick to rethink his last comment: if looks could kill, he was already wandering the afterlife.

"Alright, one last time. Yes?"

"Yes," Cutter replied, as if triumphant.

The hunchback drank the last of his ale, placed the mug back in front of him and proceeded to tell his story.

"As I have told yer before, we was on the road and made up camp for the night. Vaeyu, our leader got us to cook up a pig we killed from one o' farms we raided."

"This Vaeyu, tough fucker is 'e?" Cutter asked.

"The most dangerous man I ever known," the hunchback replied.

Bael's ears pricked up at the mention of this Vaeyu's name, a single piece of information that in itself he felt warranted his visit to such an unsavoury place.

"Before Vaeyu was a Captain 'e was a King's assassin. A King it's said, drinks the blood of his victims and is rumoured to even bathe in the shit."

"Sounds a real sick bastard," Tiny interrupted, hanging on every word, exaggerated or not.

"Yeh! Well, that's what 'e is. Anyways, we got this bunch o' kids to take back with us. I see's youngest of 'em, little girl lookin' hungry eyed as we start a cuttin' that there pig. I look to meat in me hand, and decides to give 'er some," he lied. "Now I knows Vaeyu don't take to any of us bein' kindly and the like, but I feel I should do the right thing. So, I goes over to the wagon, gives her a chunk o' this meat. Next thing I know, Vaeyu grabs me 'and pulls out his knife, then one be one he cuts off me fingers."

"Go on, this is best bit," Cutter said expectantly.

"So, he picks 'em up off the ground, walks over to the fire an' drops them into some hot ashes. I can here 'em crackle, spit an' the like, cookin' good an' proper. Then the fucker picks 'em out of the ashes an' eats 'em right in front o' me. Was lucky to come away with me life."

Hunter couldn't believe how these morons hung onto every lying word, wishing them to be true and better in the telling. He knew the man that put a blade to his throat was not the man this low life was describing, but this was the break he was hoping for. The hunchback was who he was rumoured to be and could be the only chance anyone would have of finding out where Raen had been taken. Finishing his drink, he readied to leave, when a young whore walked up to him pressing her pelvis against his shoulder.

"You goin' to buy a girl a drink? Could give yer some o' this for a bit extra," she said, lifting her skirt, exposing her thigh, which looked cleaner than the rest of the place would suggest. Bael ignored her advances and eased her away from his side.

"Don't like girls then? Boys, is it? No! Sheep then? More's the pity. Pretty lookin' fella like you, could 'ave 'is pick o' the bunch," she said, sarcastically. She dropped the hem of her skirt and wasn't about to let Hunter leave without suffering some degree of indignity: she deftly removed the tiny cork stopper off a small phial she kept hidden in her cleavage.

"If yer not 'ere for girls, boys, drinks then what are yer 'ere for?"

"Not your concern… Whatever it is yer sellin' I'm not buyin."

She looked over at Cutter who gave her the nod. Flirting, she sat down onto Hunter's lap and in an unseen movement dropped the contents of the Phial into what remained of his drink. Hunter unceremoniously shoved the whore off him, to a mouthful of obscenities. Almost losing her footing she went to slap him across the face, but something stayed her hand.

She stepped back uncertainly, many a time she'd seen the darkness in some men's gaze, but something in Hunter's eyes sent a chill down her spine neutralizing any further attempt at sarcasm. Not wishing to waste any more time on him, she turned and made her way back to the counter where Jack was waiting for an update.

Nothing happened in the Tavern without Jack's say-so, Ayla and Cutter's little scam being no exception, but he chose to overlook it, instead choosing to bed her when she wasn't occupied with a client; and her being the best of the crop was payment enough.

Hunter had had enough for one day and didn't want to spend another moment longer than he had to in the shithole. He swigged down the remainder of his mead and got up to leave. Crossing the room, he noticed the whore and the Innkeep whispering to one another, watching his every step.

The street outside was ankle deep in mud following the day's heavy rain. Hunter kept to the shadows and waited; then it began. First, he threw up a mouthful of bile, but not enough to stop the sedative doing its work; he started to go dizzy giving the outward appearance of gross overindulgence. He tried to shake off the feeling, which only made things worse. He dropped to his knees but was conscious enough to recognize the hunchback and his colleagues heading towards him. Their voices echoed around his head like a bad dream and stopped just before Cutter's foot hit him across the side of the head sending him sprawling through the mud.

What he missed in the Tavern, was the whore spike his drink with a colourless, odourless sedative, her and Cutter used to subdue and rob those they felt carried something of value, although in this case it was something far more sinister. If the night was to go Cutter's way, Hunter would be pig food by the end of it, after they questioned him, that is.

Hunter tried to stand but fell back into the mud. All those surrounding him stuck the boot in kicking him over and over, knocking the wind out of him. Finally, Cutter's foot hit him squarely in the face splitting his lips.

"Saw yer in there, listenin' to us talkin'. Who the fuck is yer?" Cutter bellowed, menacingly.

Hunter tried to lift his weight on outstretched arms, but again collapsed. Then something totally unexpected happened: it all stopped.

"Leave 'im be," came the unfamiliar voice. "You all know who I am? Now get!"

The hunchback went for his dagger, but Cutter stayed his hand, preventing the blade from leaving its sheath.

"Yer know this fucker then?" Cutter asked the man leading six other men, all carrying a variety of weapons favoured by cutthroats and those of a similar persuasion.

"That is no concern of yours. Now go, before me lads 'ere get restless and gut the fuckin' lot o' yer."

Cutter could see the odds were completely stacked against them, so reluctantly he rallied his group and led them away. Before he disappeared around the corner close by, he turned.

"You've not 'ered the last of this and that's for sure," he threatened, as both he and his group faded into the darkness.

Hunter lifted his mud caked face out of the dirt, to look at the man who just saved his life. He was under no illusion, had there been no intervention, his present condition would have left him wanting. It was hard to make out anything through the mud over his eyes. He scraped away as much as he could with his fingers, shaking off the excess. All he could see was that the leader of the gang was tall, blonde and well built, not heavily, rather sinewy like a fighter.

"Who are you?" he mustered.

"You've showed a kindness to me sister, Lia. For that you have my gratitude. Best be getting back home before they return to finish the job."

Before Hunter could get to his feet and thank his saviours, two of them took him under the arms and lifted him to his feet.

He had no recollection of how he got back to his lodge and find himself prostrate by the door, the Wolf licking his bloodied face. He ran his fingers through his hair, feeling the irregular contours of several egg-shaped lumps. Then it registered. Lia said she had a brother. Toran! *That's it,* he thought, *his name is Toran.*

30

TROUBLING MESSAGE

The night was pretty uneventful. Jack closed down a couple of fights, Blood Bane stayed on the wall; it only took him and two of his henchmen to incapacitate all concerned and see them cast out into the muddy street finding themselves lucky they weren't guests of the pig pen. He was about to close the doors for the night, when a foot appeared, wedging it open. Jack yanked it back ready to meet the intruder with his bludgeoning fist.

"What the fuck do *you* want at this god forsaken hour," he asked, recognising Scab, one of Cutter's gang. The thug was a low life petty thief, wiry and thin, his scurvy ridden face a mask of perpetual sores. The man was well known for not being a scrapper, a coward in fact, if appearance and what Jack had heard bore truth.

"Are you hurt?" Jack asked, aware the man's face was covered in spattering's of blood.

"It's not mine," he replied, fighting for breath.

"Well, I suppose you better get in 'ere."

Ayla and a few of the girls were still finishing what cleaning they could. Duties Jack expected of them; extending beyond the bed sheets to see them emptying spittoons and cleaning up the vomit. Gifts of the inconsiderate, not tasks to be relished but ones that were responsible for regular complaint. She was lucky, if washing down tables and clearing away empty mugs could be described as such, but she knew on the face of it she didn't do too badly, Jack giving her the more menial of the tasks to undertake.

She dried the last of the clay tankards and hung it on one of the small hooks running along a wooden rail that stretched the length of the bar. She saw Jack open the door to whoever it was paying them a visit at such an unsociable hour, but the moment the man entered the room she knew something was wrong.

The late visitor was one of Cutter's, she didn't like the man, feeling he was a degenerate creep who never stopped ogling her breasts whenever she was unfortunate enough to be in his company. But she knew he would never come to the tavern at this hour without Cutter, he was like the man's shadow, always slinking behind like a frightened rat.

"What are yer doin' 'ere? Where's Cutter?" she asked, concerned as she realized the man was covered in blood.

"That's why I's 'ere," he replied, breathing in short nervous gasps. "Cutter's dead."

"What do yer mean, dead?" she choked, her voice almost betraying the secret fondness she held for her partner in crime.

Before he could reply, Jack butted in, grabbed Scab by the arm and almost threw him on the nearest chair.

"Sit! What the fuck da yer mean, he's dead?"

"They are all dead. Cutter, Tiny, Yold, an' Ben. Fucker cut 'em to pieces with 'is two swords. It was fuckin' slaughter, I tell yer, I was lucky to escape with me life."

Luck had nothin' to do with it yer fuckin' coward, Jack thought, but didn't share. He remembered it was these four that were sat talking with the hunchback two nights before. He had also heard how they attacked that Hunter fella on leaving the Tavern that night, and how

Toran and his gang had split it up, an incident he hadn't wasted a thought on until now. Ayla went quiet. Jack could see the news had hit her hard, but he was't about to let such emotion interfere with his current line of questioning.

"This man you saw, what did he look like? Was he so high, hair black, tied back in a ponytail?"

"That's 'im. Fighter if ever I saw one. Cut 'em down quicker than a blink. Never seen anythin' like it."

"Was that hunchback 'as been hangin' around Cutter these past weeks there as well?"

"Yeh! He was. But the fucker didn't kill 'im as far as I know. He just cuts 'im under the knee an' drags him off into an alley. That's last I seen of 'em."

"Strange how 'e left that one alive. Gave no hint to why?" Jack asked, not really expecting any answer of worth. But he had to try at least.

"No. As I say, fucker just dragged him off."

Jack told Ayla to wait for him back in his room. What he was about to say was for Scab's ears only, he felt her unnecessary suffering a pointless exercise that would only add further complications in its execution. She was only too glad to oblige, her lips quivering as she ascended the flight of wooden stairs at the back of the room. Jack walked over to the washing trough behind the bar, soaked a rag with water, then returned to Scab.

"Here clean yer self-up we 'ave work to do."

Scab wiped what blood he could off his face, the blood on his clothes had dried, so there was no point in trying to remove it.

Jack left him alone for the moment and returned after a few minutes escorted by half a dozen of his strongest men. He knew what was coming, a coward he might be, but he wasn't an idiot like many in Cutter's gang. He knew Jack had to get rid of any evidence that might attract the attention of the town guard, and bodies cut to pieces like this was just such a thing. The guards' presence and their subsequent investigations into the warrens would only go to interfere with Jack's hold on the movement of contraband within the place, a position he wouldn't surrender lightly. No. He knew what fate awaited Cutter and the rest, and the only ones to get any kind of satisfaction out of all of this were the pigs and sows in the yard out back.

"Right, show us where these bodies are," Jack ordered, grabbing him under the arm and dragging him off his seat.

31
CAILEAN - THE ORPHANS

The days felt long, the nights even longer. Many seeing Cailean deprived of sleep. Her mother had asked Maccon to council her, which he did, thankfully with some degree of success. The Temple was the only place she had made any effort to visit since that terrible day. On occasion, she was allowed entry into the Chamber of the Shard, a privilege afforded to very few women. One time, inadvertently, she walked into the Chamber while the members of the Order were meditating around the Shard. For just a fleeting moment she witnessed what no woman before her had; the appearance of an image shimmering in a ball of blue light above the black stone. She wasn't around long enough to see what the image contained, Maccon breaking the circle and escorting her from the proceedings offering no explanation for what she had just witnessed. She knew by his demeanour, that was a question not worth broaching.

There were days she would watch the Knights during their weapon training, it was a discipline they executed with some vigour at least three hours of every day, honing skills to peak efficiency. In fact, this had become the main reason for her frequent visits; her mother Alloria had asked Maccon to school her in the way of the sword, feeling such diversion would help to take her mind off everything and see her to purpose.

Maccon allocated the task to Garrus; being only a year Cirius' senior it made him the second youngest in the Order, his speciality being the long sword.

It turned out to be a rewarding idea. Pleasing Alloria immensely whenever Maccon relayed the welcome news of her daughter's speedy progress. Cailean's willingness to learn made for easy teaching, making such meetings fun for both pupil and teacher.

Cailean was a week into her early morning sessions. It was getting colder by the day, morning dew making the stony ground slick with moisture. Garrus was a stickler for punctuality, but he discovered he had no need for concern. Cailean, in contradiction to most men's perception of women was of like mind and never late for their meetings. Garrus was always first to arrive, waiting for her with blunted steel practice swords in hand. For him, there was none of this nonsense of using wooden swords favoured by most who taught the way of the blade. He believed it was better to feel the weight and balance of a real blade from the outset, believing it carried advantage over the use of wood.

Another thing that made these times more enjoyable was the professionalism with which her teacher conducted himself. It was refreshing to find herself in the company of a man, absent the baser values so many men of her age exhibited when in the company of such a beautiful woman; values shared by many of those in her father's Court, young and those of advancing years who should know better. Thankfully, Garrus like his counterparts performed his duties impeccably. She found him to be a man of simple tastes, his looks bordering on the plain, neither handsome nor ugly he stood a good six feet tall, thin yet sinewy, his face made more distinguished by the neat goatee style beard decorating his long chin.

This particular morning the sky was overcast, she felt the chill in the air, a warning that the snows of winter were almost upon them. On a few of her previous visits, she made a point of calling in on her Uncle, to see his recovery set to completion. Though she loved him dearly, and even as her King; she felt his idea of seeing her to wedded bliss in the arms of a Prince she had never met, naive in its execution, and did not bode well in her understanding of such. Yet she would not have wished to see it concluded in such a mindless, violent fashion, leaving her Uncle wounded and her betrothed dead. But she forgave her Uncle his self-fulfilling indiscretion and though the consequence of these actions was terrible, they had saved her from a day of mourning that by its very nature should have been the complete opposite.

The King was only a few days from leaving, Maccon and most of the Order set to task in preparation thereof.

Cailean arrived earlier than usual. She wanted time with her Uncle alone, absent the company of her father who was visiting later that morning. On her way over to the King's chamber, a few of his men nodded to her in recognition of her status. The one with the strawberry birth mark she knew as Fraene and another whose name eluded her, stood sentry outside the door.

"My lady," Fraene welcomed.

The other man quite frightened her; his extended grin and saliva slobbering lips twisted into some semblance of a smile; his words spat more than spoken.

"My lady," Omaar seconded. His handless stump, dressed, with blood still seeping through.

Fraene was quick to assist. He opened the door and led her to the King, who was waiting by an open window staring to the gardens beyond. As she approached he turned to greet her, still picking food from between his teeth, oral debris left behind from his early breakfast.

"Come! Let me look at you," he said, coaxing her over to the light from the window.

"Uncle."

"My how you have blossomed from the child I last saw, what was it? Ten name days past?"

"It was Uncle."

"If only time was as kind to the aged," he sighed.

"You are too hard on yourself; I have seen younger men look and act older than you."

He squeezed her hand gently and looked outside at the clearing sky.

"What say we wander the Temple grounds and spend a little time together before my brother arrives to bother me with his well-intentioned but mithering presence."

"That would be nice Uncle."

The grey clouds made way for the sun, whose warmth out of the shade still required the appropriate attire to be worn. The King donned a beautiful deep purple velveteen cloak with his house Sigil emblazoned on the back: a golden sword set against a disc of flickering flames. Cailean was dressed in her fine leathers in preparation for training with Garrus later, but her Uncle felt she would be cold and lent her his hunting cloak made from heavy woven dark green wool.

They walked side by side, both taking in lungsful of the sharp fresh air. The King talked about his journey home, his brother organizing a protective ensemble of two hundred militia men. The rest of the conversation covered mainly matters of the family, neither wishing to revisit earlier conversations involving all the terrible events that led them both to that very moment.

For a short time, they explored the wonders of the extensive gardens to the rear of the Temple, giving life to plants and trees from lands stretching far and wide, whose temperate climate was shared with theirs. As time grew short and Cailean had to leave for her sword lessons, they found themselves not far from the building that housed the carrier pigeons. Turning the corner at the front of the Temple, the glare from a low-lying sun made a clear view of the building nigh on impossible, but through the haze they could just make out the figure of a man, surrounded by children and a wolf.

Bael watched the two figures appear from the light, their silhouettes shimmering as if spewed out by the sun. On realizing who it was that approached he stood up, the children turning to see what drew his attention. The Wolf rolled a growl in her throat, before a familiar touch stayed her protective anxiety.

"My Lord," Bael said, without showing a hint of the formality a meeting like this demanded. He looked to Cailean and just gave her a quick nod of recognition.

"It is good to see you again, my friend. How fares the Wolf and that hawk of yours?"

"They recover well, thank you Sire."

Cailean counted the number of children to be eight, four boys and four girls. One girl in particular took her attention, the hand of her left arm having but a finger and opposing thumb. By her side was the largest boy in the group, who placed himself in-front of the girl as if to protect her. She had never given these orphan children a second thought before now, all she knew was, that Maccon and her mother for reasons of their own, found it in their hearts to save these children from an awful life on the streets. How odd, she thought, that a man she deemed to be a self-opinionated hermit of sorts, would find himself in the company of such children. Unexpectedly, she was also aware of how much these children were taken with their guests, especially the Wolf, a creature very few had the privilege of touching. This was a side of Hunter she had never been privy to and could see by the King's demeanour that he held the man in high regard.

Strangely, on this occasion she found herself void of any urge to impart her usual blend of sarcastic wit; the temptation dulled by circumstance. The young girl with the disfigured hand stepped out of her protector's shadow and took Hunter by the hand.

Cailean addressed the children with an almost girlish sense of curiosity.

"What are you all doing out here?"

Lia was the first to speak, quietly proud that it was her hand Bael was holding.

"Bael tells us stories and lets us stroke the Wolf."

Cailean was surprised that the children addressed Bael by his true name; she like many in the town only called him by the name they had created for him, his real name forgotten in time and convenience.

The King nelt down in front of the youngest and smiled warmly.

"What kind of stories does Bael tell you?"

The little girl blushed; her voice tiny with nerves.

"He tells us about when 'e goes hunting, and about the animals in the woods."

"Ah! That sounds exiting, he will have to tell them to me, sometime," the King said. He winked at Hunter, who just stood there expressionless. "I tell you what, children. You must get him to tell you the story of how he saved my life, now there is a story worth telling. Bael is a true hero."

"Please? Tell us that story," they all repeated.

"Another time maybe," Bael replied, embarrassed by the title and universal adulation exhibited by all except Cailean.

Bael saw a vulnerability, shadowed eyes that betrayed Cailean's many sleepless nights; eyes that had lost their brightness, victims of the same anguish she shared with him. This was the first time since that terrible day, that they both found themselves in each other's company. Taken up with his own thoughts he hadn't made any attempt to pass on his condolences, knowing how much Jiney meant to Cailean; now such opportunity was afforded him free of her father's influence, he said with disarming sincerity.

"I am sorry for your loss. Your friend was a kindly girl, I know you loved dearly."

Cailean's lip quivered, she had no answer for his unexpected show of compassion, that saw her unfettered emotions strangle her response in a tightened throat. There was a warmth in his words she found comforting and she too realized that both shared a loss, neither should have to bear alone.

The King being an astute observer of human behaviour was aware, even though first impressions might suggest otherwise, that Bael and his niece were trying hard to mask their true feelings for one another. Bael he perceived, feigned indifference, yet his words bore sentiment of the heart, whilst Cailean hid behind an anger born of that very indifference. He was all too aware of the unification that shared grief could instil in people, having shared such loss with his wife, the queen, when they lost their two babes, passed prematurely in a river of blood.

An uncomfortable silence ensued, so Agramar took the initiative. A great believer in dealing with a problem head on, and never one to shy away from a direct approach, rested his hand on Bael's shoulder.

"I believe it is time for me to leave."

"As must I, my Lord," Bael replied.

The King turned to leave without addressing Cailean, who made to follow, while Hunter said his farewells to his young followers. The children dispersed, and Agramar, not getting the response he believed he might, stopped to face both Cailean and Hunter before they too moved on.

"It is obvious to me, that you both share a common grief, that neither of you has made time to discuss. Whether you wish to believe it or not, in this grief you also share a bond. Make time, share thoughts and see the burden lessened, you might be surprised by the result of so doing. Believe me when I tell you, I know this to be true."

The King's words ambushed the pair of them in their unexpected yet observant delivery, and there was no denying on both counts they carried weight. Caught off guard in this way saw them both uncertain of a response, but it was Cailean who found voice.

"Even if I wished it, my father has given strict instruction that I not see or speak with Hunter."

"Though I love him, my brother can be an oaf at times. You are no longer a child that seeks a parent's guidance, you must become the woman you were meant to be and strive to make your own decisions. When I was your age, none could steer me from the path I chose to take. If it is a mistake you make, learn from it, grow stronger, but I know what I suggest is not a mistake… Really, I should not speak of this, but what my stubborn brother does not know will not give him cause for concern."

Cailean couldn't believe her ears, but it was undeniable, there was truth in her Uncle's words. Even Bael couldn't ignore that the King's comments had touched a nerve, although his outward demeanour suggested otherwise.

Agramar smiled.

"This time I must take my leave."

"I have to go also. Garrus will be waiting," Cailean said.

Bael just nodded his understanding at her. Then he faced the King.

"My Lord."

Then without uttering another word, both he and his Wolf left for the Keep.

The following morning Cailean decided to pay the pigeon house an unscheduled visit, before moving on to her training session.

The older boy, who the day before stepped in-front of Lia as if to protect her, answered the door.

"Is your friend Lia, awake?" Cailean asked, in a gentle tone, not wishing to alarm the boy.

"Yes, mam," he nodded. "I will get 'er for yer."

It wasn't long before Korey returned, Lia by his side rubbing her tired eyes. Cailean smiled at them both and knelt down so she could look at them face to face.

"Good morning Lia."

"Good morning mam."

"Would you mind if I spoke with Lia alone?" Cailean asked Korey.

The boy nodded his approval and stepped back into the house. Cailean took Lia by the hand and led her outside. They talked for a while. She asked how it came about that Hunter visited the place. The answer surprised her in its simplicity, it would appear Hunter just liked the child. It was obvious to Cailean during the conversation, just how much he meant to Lia. Before leaving, she had one more thing to discuss with the child.

"Now! What I am about to ask you might come as a surprise. So, you don't have to answer right away, but how would you like to come and live in the Keep?"

Lia wasn't sure how to respond, her young mind struggling to process what she was hearing. That a woman she hardly knew, should offer such a life changing opportunity, was difficult to comprehend, yet at the same time exiting for a young intelligent mind.

"You would be my personal handmaiden, help me choose what clothes to wear, little things like that. We would speak every day and you would no longer have to tend those mangy pigeons. I hope too, that in time we would become friends. What do you say to that?"

Eventually plucking up the courage, she replied.

"That would be nice,"

"Then I will make sure it is done. I will come to see you again in the morning. First I must speak with mother."

32

A PROMICE REVISITED

The King's departure from the Keep, was as low key as circumstances would allow; most in the town still sleeping, the sun not yet risen.

Lord Farroth, Alloria, Cailean, those of the Order and others of the Keep who wished to witness his departure, watched as Agramar and his two hundred strong entourage headed out of the main gate. There was no pomp and ceremony involved. Only the sound of hoof upon stone and the rickety chorus the axels made, as the supply wagon's wheels sang out the strain of riding the well-worn troughs of the old road. It was an eerie spectacle to behold.

As the last of the horse guard disappeared from view, the Farroth family made their way back into the Keep. Most of the Order set about duties allocated to them the day previous; while Maccon prepared himself for later when, through a growing sense of concern, he was to activate the Shard.

At the break of dawn, Cailean made her way to the kitchen's, helped herself to fresh baked bread and a cut of ham the maids were preparing for the family's early breakfast. Eating as she walked, she made her way through the Keep to the pigeon house beyond.

Lia the day before, had told all the other children of Cailean's unexpected offer. The older ones in the group offered nothing but support for the idea, telling her to accept the position. It was a different matter when it came to the two youngest amongst them; they just burst into tears begging her to stay. But, it was Korey who finally helped her to come to terms with a decision she inwardly knew, would be foolish to avoid.

He, like her was an old head on young shoulders. He would miss her, that went without saying, but for her to pass up such an incredible opportunity like this would be a sacrifice too far. Selflessly, he told her to accept the offer and that they could see one another anyway.

Lia hadn't had a chance to tell her brother about it all, but she believed he would come to the same conclusion.

She, like the rest of the children had risen early that morning to witness the departure of the King and his armed escort. It wasn't often that such opportunity presented itself, that would see Lia and the other children of low standing in the presence of such exalted company, and they weren't about to miss it. Lia, like the older members of her group knew they were in the presence of a great leader, whilst the youngest, bemused by it all, were content just to follow and enjoy what little spectacle was afforded them.

Lia saw to the care of the birds earlier than usual in the hope and expectation that Cailean would visit her on her way to the Temple: looking out of the window, she wasn't disappointed.

Cailean had spoken with her mother about taking Lia as her own personal handmaiden, which without involving her father with the details, saw her mother to agreement. All that was required now, was that the girl herself was agreeable.

Standing outside the pigeon house door, she was about to knock, when suddenly the door flew open; Lia stood before her, nervous trepidation written right across her little face. Her fears were quickly allayed when Cailean's lips curled into a welcoming smile, conformation that all would be as she had hoped.

Cailean explained to Lia that she would only have one more day to wait and once her room was ready, she was to move into the main Keep. For the other children it was like drinking lemon and honey, bitter sweet. All wished the best for her departing, but there was still a sense of sadness that she would no longer be amongst them. It was fortunate indeed, that her piers were of like mind; whether it was a reflection of the kindness shown to them by Lady Alloria and those of the Order, they all, youngest to oldest, offered nothing but support.

33

AN INTRUDER

As nightfall saw an end to the last of the sunlight, Maccon rallied the rest of the Order to join him around the Shard. The little heat that radiated from the numerous candles adorning the walls gave a little comfort to those residing within as chilly drafts watched the temperature plummet. One by one the members of the Order placed their hands onto the runes inlaid into the alter. Slowly the Shard throbbed into action and almost immediately an image began to materialize.

Maccon and the other priests closed their eyes as they all drifted into a meditative state, minds bound by a power that made images available to them; all unaware they shared the room with an intruder.

Cailean, following her training with Garrus, overheard Osar and Arbar the oldest of the Order, talking about Maccon's worries concerning Hunter's troubling behaviour. Furthermore, she heard mention of the gathering he had arranged for later that evening when they would see the Shard set to purpose.

She watched from the shadows of a pillar just inside the chamber not far from the huge wooden doors.

Following Maccon's example, they all began to chant words spoken in the old tongue; a language she didn't understand. Whatever it was they said, the Shard hummed into life, a ball of bluish light pulsated and grew ever larger as she watched what no woman before her ever had.

She felt her heart racing, anxious but exited as images flickered into existence. What she witnessed shocked her to the very core, and as scene upon scene revealed their dark secrets, she saw a side of Hunter that was terrifying to behold.

34

KOVAL - TYRNA - THE VISITOR

Koval and his wife Tyrna, chose to visit Dogran's Tavern together for the first time since Raen's abduction.

Jered with his surly wife, joined others in the Town to make special welcome for them both, especially for Tyrna, whose suffering was heart felt by everyone there.

Emma served each of them with a drink, courtesy of her father, who she could see was happy to entertain the notion that this gathering represented some kind of return to normality. Whether it did or it didn't, it was an idea worth courting, just to see people she loved smile again. Friendly banter a welcome distraction from the reality that simmered beneath the fragile illusion.

Tyrna stayed quiet most of the time, responding to direct questions with brief one-word answers. And though on the surface it might appear otherwise, she was glad to be amongst friends.

Koval felt his spirits lifted, as this for him was the first sign that his wife's foot had stepped firmly on the path to recovery.

Jered's wife, though a constant bane for her husband, could be quite the acid tongued comedian, a quality they all seemed to enjoy and one that saw Tyrna more relaxed and open minded. It lightened an otherwise tense atmosphere and slowly but surely Tyrna became more engaged in the conversation, delighting Koval. For his part, he kept relatively quiet throughout, glad to just sit back and watch as those around him took on the mantle of his wife's supporters.

While Tyrna was occupied, lending opportunity for his absence, Koval quietly slipped away to have a welcome chat with his old friend Dogran who was busy wiping spilt ale off the top of the bar.

"It's good to see Tyrna acting more like her old self," Dogran said.

"It is old friend. I thought this day might never come. She has hardly uttered a word in weeks, to see her like this amongst friends, swells my heart."

Dogran patted his friend warmly on the shoulder and poured them both a drink.

"Here's to new beginnings," he cheered, tapping his tankard with Koval's.

So busy were the pair watching their friends, that neither noticed the appearance of the young Knight of the Order. Emma on the other hand was quick off the mark, ushering Cirius off to a table away from prying eyes and inquisitive ears.

Dogran glanced up and smiled. Koval turned around to see what had taken his friend's attention.

"Emma seems quite smitten with this young man?"

"She is. He is a kindly sought, but I fear it will all come to naught," Dogran replied, with quiet concern.

"What makes you think that? From what I can see they both enjoy one another's company. Surely that is a good sign?"

"Have you forgotten the vows they take, being part of such an old and revered Order," Dogran replied. "And I fear this infatuation she has for Hunter, is far from over."

Koval pondered the question for a moment, realizing his friend had a point.

"Surely for one as young as he, such vows can be, let's say, bent a little. Am I wrong to believe we live in such times that should see outdated ideals like these revisited? Laws set a thousand years ago should hold at most, limited sway in the running of our lives. Surely I can't be the only one who believes this to be true?" Koval rationalized. "As for Hunter, I'm sure it will pass given the proper distraction."

"You might be right old friend, and it helps none to worry about it. It's just, Emma has had to bear more than her fair share of uncertainty in her life, and that's for sure."

Koval chatted a little while longer, then returned to his wife and friends. He could see she was once again quiet and withdrawn and felt this was as good a time as any to leave. He put his hand on her knee and in a low voice asked was she ready to go. She nodded, she was, so Koval took the initiative and excused them both from the group. Kisses and hugs ensued, then both left the Tavern for home.

***

Hunter sat astride his horse outside the front of the Forge. He'd waited for some time and was about to give up and leave, when Koval and his wife appeared at the top of the road. He dismounted, tethered the horse to the wooden rail in front of the porch and waited.

Koval was first to spot Hunter, Tyrna's mind elsewhere.

"What is Hunter doing here?" he asked, thinking out loud and drawing his wife's attention to the fact.

"Do you think he has news of our son?"

Koval didn't answer and quickened his pace, leaving his wife trailing behind him.

Hunter stepped off the porch as Koval approached the door, he could see the apprehension written across the Smithy's face and understood.

"Greetings."

"Greetings my friend," Koval replied, locking arms with his unexpected visitor. "I have to ask, what happened to your face?"

"I will tell you everything," Bael replied, turning to face Tyrna as she arrived shortly after.

"What brings you to my house? Is there news of our son?" She asked excitedly.

"Of sorts."

"Then please come in, let us not speak out here," Koval said, opening the door.

Once inside, Tyrna, picking up on Bael's last comment, again pressed for more information.

"Please! Tell us, what have you heard? Do you know where our son has been taken."

Koval saw Hunter was uncertain how to respond, it was obvious from his expression that he didn't want to fill them both with false hope. He glanced at his wife.

"Let us press no further 'till we offer our guest some refreshment."

Tyrna showed no sign or intention of responding to his comment, so Koval quickly poured a mug of honeyed wine and offered it to Bael. He accepted it more out of a courtesy than wanting and stayed on his feet when Koval suggested they all sit. He sipped the wine, just enough to wet his tongue and taste its sweetness.

"Please Hunter, tell us what you have heard?" Tyrna pleaded.

"Before you answer my wife's questions, tell us first what happened to you?"

Bael fixed his gaze on the Smithy, placed his drink down on the table in front of him, then caringly glanced at Tyrna.

"This is why I am here," he said, pointing to his swollen face. "I heard rumours of a hunchback in the Warrens bragging about the taking of slaves and the name of the man who led the raid."

"Where did you come upon such rumour?" Koval urged.

"That matters not. On hearing this, I visited the Severed Hand in Beggars Nest where I was told the hunchback and his friends would be drinking. At first, I wasn't sure if such rumour was true, but when I entered the place my doubts were laid to rest."

"Do you know where our son is?" Tyrna interrupted.

"Not yet. But I hope by the end of this day I will have more to tell you."

"Why? What do you plan to do?" Koval asked.

"The reason my face ended up like this, is because I was careless enough to allow myself to be drugged."

"Drugged? What do you mean?" Tyrna asked.

"I fear my drink was laced with a substance that saw my wits dulled to the point of unconsciousness. I could hardly stand. The hunchback and his group ambushed me in an alleyway just by the Tavern. If it hadn't been for the timely intervention of another, who knows what the outcome would have been? But that is a conversation for another time. What little I was able to pick up whilst in the Tavern, leads me to believe, this hunchback possesses information that should set us on the path to finding your son. I thought you ought to know this in case something should happen to me…. My intention is to revisit the Warrens this very night. This time though, I will be prepared. I will see to it that this hunchback imparts whatever it is he knows about the slavers leader, and where they have taken Raen."

"Then I must go with you. There is no need for you to face this alone," Koval offered.

Tyrna looked worried. She had lost a son; she didn't now want to lose a husband too.

"Is it not enough that our son has been taken from us? I do not wish to find myself a widow as well."

"I would do this alone. Your family has suffered enough. No, you should stay."

Tyrna's eyes were awash with tears. Reluctantly, Koval surrendered to her request, he didn't want to see what improvement she had made undone in his eagerness for revenge.

"Then you must be careful. These men you speak of are no better than savages," Koval sighed.

"I will. This time I know what I must do... So, I shall bother you no longer and as soon as I know anything further, I will return."

Koval locked arms with him again, then to Hunter's surprise, Tyrna lent forward and kissed him dearly on the cheek.

"Thank you," she whispered.

35

TROUBLING REVELATION

The light above the Shard grew larger, shimmering with an ever-increasing clarity to grow large enough that all in the Chamber could see clearly the secrets it began to reveal.

Cailean knelt quietly, trying desperately not to cough from a throat dry from nerves as the scene above the Shard took form. Within the pulsating ball of energy, she saw Hunter step from the shadows, his Wolf by his side. In the low light of the muddy alley two figures appeared from the entrance of the Severed Hand. Those watching didn't recognize the men, but it was obvious Hunter did. As instructed the Wolf stayed hidden behind the corner of a shanty type dwelling. Bael stepped out into the middle of the street.

"You! Cutter shouted, not drunk enough to be absent recognition. The thug pulled out his two daggers: Tiny, next to him removing a small hatchet from inside his long coat; both following Bael into the side alley.

"This time I'll finish the fuckin' job," Cutter threatened, rushing Bael like the demented killer he was.

Even in the low light Cailean could see the brutality with which Hunter dispatched of the two: leaving Cutter absent his head and Tiny screaming in the thick mud holding his entrails as they spilled from a gash that stretched from his chest to his pubic bone.

Again, he joined his Wolf in the shadows and waited. It wasn't long before the hunchback and the other men from the previous night stepped into the open. This time Bael and the Wolf held back and stealthily followed the three men; waiting for them to enter a place that would make easier what he had planned.

Maccon and the Order, still unaware of Cailean's presence, watched with growing concern. Maccon was shocked by the viciousness with which Bael handled himself, such bloody revenge came from a place of darkness; a darkness he was made aware of when last he spoke with Lamia.

Cailean couldn't fully comprehend what she was seeing. If these men had something to do with Jiney's death, then they deserved no less. Yet when faced with such visceral savagery, it left her unsettled, even though secretly she too wished them dead.

The three thugs made their way across a small muddy square where the street from the Tavern intersected with several arterial alleyways. Bael looked around quickly to see if there were any passers bye; seeing only two drunks propped up against a wall he decided this was the place to launch his welcome. He whispered something into the Wolf's ear, then removed his hand from her mane to unleash her fury. In a heartbeat, she burst across the clearing, ripped the throat from one of the men, then tore into the other's crotch, bringing him down before biting away most of his face. The man's arms and legs jerked involuntarily as his life's blood soaked into the mud until, like his cohort, he too was dead.

The Wolf readied to finish the job and attack the last man standing, but Bael was quick to raise his hand and stay the beast. He drew his two swords and moved with purpose towards the shaking hunchback; it was obvious the man was in shock and looked to the Wolf with terror eyes. Before uttering a word, Bael sliced his victim, just below the knee causing him to drop to ground as the blade severed the tendons. Then speaking loud enough that all those watching in the Temple could hear, he began his planned interrogation.

"I want answers. Lie and I shall know it… Believe me when I say, do not lie. Nod, you understand my meaning," he said, each word riddled with unrelenting menace.

The hunchback groaned in agony but was still lucid enough to nod his understanding of the weighted proposition laid before him.

"Good. Then I would have you tell me the name of the one you followed and called leader?"

The hunchback looked up defiantly; anger from the pain overriding any rational understanding of his predicament, he displayed only moments before.

"You bastard. Why are you doing this?" The hunchback croaked. "You're mad."

"Wrong answer," Bael replied, ramming the blade of his short sword through the man's foot, turning it slowly.

The hunchback screamed out in agony, teetering precariously on the edge of consciousness. Bael removed the blade and hit him in the mouth with the sword's hilt, sending the man sprawling face down in the mud. For a moment the hunchback didn't move. Not sure whether he was unconscious, Bael bent down and dragged the man unceremoniously back onto his knees; shook him a little until his head came up and then lifted the man's chin with the blade of his long sword.

"I will ask you again?"

"Vaeyu! It's Vaeyu, yer mad fuck," the hunchback croaked, spitting words and mud simultaneously.

"That's better. Now how difficult was that? - These children you kidnapped, one amongst them was the mute son of the town's smithy. Taken after being forced to watch his lover, raped and brutally murdered."

"I know nothing about this," words falling too easily from his cracked, plump lips.

Bael hit the man in the face again, this time spraying blood and rotten teeth through the air.

"You lie."

"No more, please, I tell the truth." His words drowning in overwhelming desperation.

"Then speak. Convince me your words are not false and all will be over."

"I speak the truth when I tell you I did not see this mute you speak of. I was cast aside by Vaeyu long before he and the rest raided your town."

Bael could see the venom in the words as the hunchback spoke of his leader and felt his truth in the telling.

"This Vaeyu was your leader, yes?"

The hunchback held up his fingerless hand.

"The bastard did this to me."

"The man you speak of has a shaven head that bears strange tattoo's? Am I right?"

"That's - 'im. A very dangerous man to have as an enemy. He kills without feeling, but he would not kill this woman you speak of. For him death holds meaning. Such pointless execution would carry no merit."

"Then who would do such a thing, if this Vaeyu you speak of is such a paragon of virtue?"

The hunchback fell back onto his heels exhausted: the man whose name Bael so wantonly desired had been no friend to him when this Vaeyu casually removed his fingers, so this was not a time for false loyalty.

"I believe the man you seek is the one they call Kengar. A vicious cunt if ever there was one. I was told he killed his own wife and child because he thought she slept with another and the child she cradled was his. When he found out he was wrong, he mourned their passing not in the slightest."

"That your leader would choose such a man to accompany him on his quest, says a lot about the man himself. Why would this Vaeyu allow such an animal to lead his raids, when clearly the man is absent any remorse for acts of such pointless savagery?"

"We can't always choose our companions."

"Now answer me true, where will I find this Vaeyu and his followers?" Bael asked in a simmering, belligerent tone.

"Do you think me to be a complete fool? I tell you this, then what is there to stay your hand from seein' an end to my life?"

"Your life was forfeit, the very day you embraced a profession that saw you reave, steal and pillage… Yet, tell me what I need to know and see an end to all this."

"And my life?"

"Answer me true and see it spared."

"Our ship sailed from the Port of Thenen on the largest of the White Isles."

"What will happen to these children when this Vaeyu delivers them to said Port?" Bael asked, cutting a deep gash across the hunchback's cheek.

The thug became light headed and struggled to steady himself as he rocked weakly from side to side.

"They'll be taken to market and auctioned off to those with enough coin and inclination, good or bad, to buy them."

"What do you mean, good or bad?"

"There are those amongst my kind who seek such cargo to satisfy their baser desires, even the King, whose buyer is very careful in his choosing. For his desires are of a more extreme nature," the hunchback said, his lips curling into a malformed sneer.

Bael, unable to hide his growing anger grabbed the degenerate by the throat.

"How is this so?"

"It is said that our beloved King believes, that if he drinks the blood of certain children he will be rewarded with an endless life. This mute you speak of, he is a strong lad?"

Bael moved behind the hunchback as if ready to leave. An overwhelming need for revenge smothered any thoughts of mercy; in one swift blow, he cleaved the man's head in two, on through to finish between his shoulder blades.

***

Maccon removed his hands from the rune inlay, the image above the Shard disappeared immediately. The rest amongst the Order looked to one another in astonishment, to the man, troubled at the sheer brutality of what they just bore witness to. But they weren't alone.

Cailean felt the bile rush to the back of her throat, its acidity causing her to cough out loud as she tried to swallow it back down.

Cirius was the first to spot her, the shadow she inhabited obscuring her identity. Maccon was next; his face set in a frown he drew his sword. Most of the others were quick to follow his lead, drawing their weapons also.

Falon was closest and as the intruder stepped from the shadows and into the light, he sheathed his sword.

"My Lady. What are you doing here?" He bowed.

"I am sorry. I meant no harm."

Maccon recognized the voice immediately. He ordered the rest to leave him alone with Cailean. The men one by one sheathed their weapons and left as requested. Cirius was last to leave and smiled at the unexpected guest in an attempt to let her know, that the law which said women were not allowed to see the Shard reveal its secrets, was not one he shared with most of his Order. Sadly, the gesture went unnoticed as Maccon took her quite forcibly by the arm and led her outside to the courtyard.

"You know it is forbidden for women to enter the Temple when we are in meditation around the Shard. Why would you do such a thing?"

"I am sorry Maccon. I meant no disrespect, only I heard talk of your concern for Hunter's behaviour, and that you planned to observe him this very night."

"Then why didn't you just come to me and discuss openly what it is that sees you so invested in Hunter's wellbeing? I thought you knew me well enough to be able to do that, rather than have you skulking about the shadows like a common thief."

"I know. I am sorry Maccon," she said, not wishing to upset a man she loved dearly, any more than was necessary.

Maccon couldn't stay annoyed at her for long, she had from being a child, developed this disarming ability that saw his cross words fade through guilt for having voiced them. Such was his love for her and the fact that such manipulation of his affections held no malice; for he always knew she loved him like an uncle and aged confidant.

"Will you tell my father about this?" she asked.

"No. but I want you to promise this will never happen again."

"I promise."

"And?"

"And?" She said, pre-empting the condition.

"And promise me you will speak to know one about what you saw this night."

"I will say nothing of this Maccon, I give you my word… but please, may I ask *you* a question?"

"You can but understand there are some things I am not at liberty to share."

"I know those men deserved to be punished, but what I saw Hunter do, was brutal… frightening. Why would he commit such violence?"

"I'm not sure, but I mean to find out. What I do know is, a darkness has manifested itself around Bael, a darkness he fights without realizing it."

"I don't understand?"

"I have already shared more than I should have, my Lady. I would be grateful if you would kindly take your leave, for there is little else I can tell you at this time. Trust me when I say, I will find out what is going on and when I do we shall have the conversation you presently desire. But for now, I must go and speak with someone I believe might have some insight into what is happening."

"Who is this person you speak of?" She asked, her curiosity once again getting the better of her.

"That is not your concern… Please, Cailean. You must leave now, and again I beseech you, speak to no one about any of this."

"I promise, my lips are sealed," she replied, before exiting the Temple, both troubled by what she had just witnessed, yet strangely satisfied to see justice done; as bloody as it was.

36

LESSIEN – AN UNEXPECTED THREAT

Lessien the Queen paced up and down the empty Throne room in the knowledge that her husband Kor-yllion was in troubling talks with his High Council: a group of Elders whose family lineage dated back thousands of years and represented what some would say, were the best of their kind. Such meetings that saw all the Elders present like this were rare indeed, and more often than not spelt trouble for someone.

The years since the exile of her daughter had done little to quell the anger she felt for her husband; yet she couldn't ignore an undeniable truth. She still loved her King, and though at times she struggled with that reality, the anger she felt still hadn't dowsed the embers of an enduring love that simmered unpredictably with varying degrees of intensity.

Knowing her daughter lived safely on the Isle of Wolves was at least some consolation and comfort, and the fact that the Wolf still lived, even though it was amongst the race of men, gave her hope. Hope, that one day all would be re-united, a project that both her and her secret ally Kor-aviel worked on relentlessly. She could see, though her husband pretended otherwise, he too wished for a conclusion absent the prejudices of old outdated doctrines that sadly accompanied his office.

But she was all too aware of what a difficult undertaking that was to see to fruition; as outdated and questionable these beliefs might be, her husband was stalwart in their execution.

The death of Melia the King's sister was not so readily cast aside. She had loved her like a blood sister and felt she had never really gotten to the bottom of what happened on the road to the human settlement, where all in Melia's party were slaughtered. What little she was able to pry from Kor-aviel on the matter was more than a little suspect. In truth, she always believed his response muted; a persuasion of loyalty to her husband, and an honourable sense of duty. The only information she was sure held any true credibility, was that the Wolf survived the attack and lived amongst the humans with one they called Hunter. And though she understood the reason behind this unusual partnership, such knowledge did little to lessen her sense of loss.

Now, fed up of waiting for her husband's return the Queen decided to take a ride out into the forest beyond the Palace. She spoke of her decision with Aedor the stable master, who with reluctance, ordered a young stable hand to ready the beautiful white mare Moonsilver for immediate departure.

When the horse was saddled and ready Aedor took hold of the reins close to the bit and held her steady whilst the Queen mounted her.

"Is this prudent, my Lady?" He asked, in the knowledge that the King never liked her to ride alone.

"I will be fine, there is nothing in the forest that would present a danger to me. And please, worry not. I will make sure my husband knows it was I that demanded to ride alone.

"But my…?"

"My mind is made up." She interrupted. "There is no need for concern, though warmly received. I assure you all will be fine, you know my knowledge of these woods is second only to your own," she said, remembering how as a child Aedor took her riding, allowing the forest to reveal its secrets the more they ventured into it.

Moonsilver was one of the Royal Whites whose pedigree dated back a thousand years; like her stable mates she stood a good sixteen hands high and was capable of speeds very few horses could match.

Once they were beyond the Palace grounds Lessien heeled her into a gallop, racing along a well-worn bridle path that ran the length of the river she was following; heading for a massive water fall in the distance.

It was times like this she felt liberated from the Royal burdens she endured being wed to such a steely, uncompromising leader. There was no feeling like it; the speed, the wind in her hair, it felt so…. Freeing.

Some two leagues from the Palace, Lessien slowed to a canter; Moonsilver shied at something just beyond the tree line, jerking its head so far back it almost unseated her. The horse then began to winey, skittering from side to side, causing Lessien to tug on the reins, the bit cutting into its soft mouth in a desperate attempt to settle the animal. Eventually the horse settled and Lessien lent forward to whisper in her ear.

"What is it my beauty? What troubles you?" She asked, patting the animal on the neck. Then without warning Moonsilver reared up to defend itself as three huge black shadows burst from the cover of the tree line. Lessien ended up spinning head over heel down the steep river embankment to land just short of the water's edge. She fought to clear her head, dizzy from spinning and as she rose to her knees she heard the cries of a dying animal.

The first Soul Hound to reach Moonsilver took her under the inside of her left rear leg downing the animal in a beat. Another ripped out her throat leaving the third hound to target whatever part of the dying animal it liked.

A black mist curled its way from the shadow of the same tree line and began to swirl around the fallen beast turning everything in its path black and burnt looking as if all were attacked by the blight. The Devourer of Souls and his three remaining pets materialized in the centre of the mist. Before Moonsilver could draw her last breath, the Devourer laid his hand on her head and like a scourge of tiny flesh-eating insects, virulent specs of darkness devoured all flesh and bone to leave a shadow in the shape of the horse, burned into the ground like some indelible silhouette. The Devourer then turned his attention to the area where he saw the Elder Queen fall.

Lessien became aware of the smell of decay as a black shadow crept over the edge of the embankment above her. The cries of her horse had ceased by the time she was on her feet and ready for the climb back up to the top to find out what happened. That was her initial thought, which was quickly replaced by one that said, *run.* As she turned to do so, she heard the howl of a wolf, then she ran and slipped her way towards a spot up river where the embankment sloped down to the same level as the water's edge.

The Devourer drifted around as a huge black Dire Wolf pounced at one of the hounds; it bowled the beast over. Then at least a dozen more wolves appeared, most targeting the remaining hounds, but three of them made for him. In a blink, his sword was unsheathed and cut two of his attackers clean in two. The third he grabbed by the throat, half its face disappearing as the darkness feasted on it. The beast dropped to the ground, dead. The first wolf, with the silver streak on its neck tried desperately to get the hound it knocked down, by the throat. But the beast was too strong and brushed him off as if he were a pup. Two more of the pack were savaged by the hounds and another losing its head as the Devourer unleashed his fury.

The Wolf Prince knew now they couldn't win the fight, but hopefully they had given the Queen a window of escape. Taking a bite to his side that blackened and burned the Prince howled for those that remained of his pack, to follow him in retreat.

Eventually, Lessien reached the level embankment out of breath, muddied and wet in the hope she was able to evade whatever attacked her horse. A moment, allowed her to believe she had. Then to her horror a black mist engulfed her feet turning every blade of grass, every bush and leaf into a charred looking mess; with it came an unnatural cold that chilled her to the core, carrying with it a sense of deep foreboding. She looked to the top of the slope to find a huge figure dressed in the strangest Shadow Armour staring down at her, either side of him the biggest, blackest hounds she had ever seen.

***

The walls of the Royal stables were unable to contain the sound of whinnying distress as all the White's kicked and reared up on hind legs as they felt the life of their soul mate ebb away. Each horse was bound to the other like twins in the womb, no one really understood why, but bound they were and when Moonsilver died, they felt her pain.

Aedor and the three stable hands tending that morning had never witnessed anything like it. It felt like chaos, that met every attempt to calm the beasts with heightened aggression.

Quick to realize that something was terribly wrong and that it more than likely involved Moonsilver and the

Queen, Aedor ordered his three helpers to do what little he believed they could, until he returned with the sole rider of each mount. But first the King.

***

Kor-aviel sat quietly whilst the King addressed the High Council; every seat around the huge table occupied.

"I do not have to remind you, that all sitting at this table swore an oath many years ago. Without exception, we all agreed never to get involved or interfere in the troubles that the race of men so frequently embrace. Yet as much as it grieves me to admit this, I fear such abstinence is no longer an option. Kor-aviel and his seekers have happened upon very troubling news that I will leave for him to explain."

Kor-aviel stood up as the King seated himself. All at the table knew him well enough to believe his concern carried merit and demanded nothing less than their full, undivided attention.

"My Lord," he acknowledged. "All of us here are aware that our dark-skinned brethren have set in motion, events that I believe are the reason that the Sith-llyan Prophesy will soon become an inevitability. We know it was Dax-barh who made to end the life of King Agramar, and had it not been for our friends from the Isle of the Lost, he would have been successful in this endeavour. And as hard as it is to accept, this King of men will play no small part in the war that will surely follow. A bitter drink to swallow, I know. But one we must, if we are to have any chance of surviving what we all know is coming. So, how can we in their hour of need, look the other way as if their allegiance mattered not. We would do this at our peril."

Themiel, the oldest and many deemed the wisest of the Council stood up in defiance. It was common knowledge how much he hated the race of men, especially those of Agramar's lineage; who during the Battle of the Seven Sisters, slayed his two sons, never to be replaced. Such talk of compromise with those he still deemed an enemy, saw the High Elder drawn tighter than a bow string in his objection.

"This is not a decision to be taken lightly. Are our memories so short that we forget men's greed and thirst for power corrupts all they touch? We have fought our own wars for thousands of years, why then should we seek to ally ourselves with such an unpredictable and unworthy King as this Agramar. I believe, whatever it is you and your Shaman fear for these men," he said glaring at Kor-aviel, "Should be theirs to deal with, absent any kind of intervention on our part."

"As much as I understand your logic Themiel, circumstances beyond our control are already beginning to affect our lives, and though you wish otherwise, you know my words are true."

Ferond, a portly member of Council took to the floor. Known for his more tempered approach to solving a problem than his friend Themiel: Kor-aviel welcomed his timely intervention.

"It would be prudent, would it not? To let Kor-aviel tell us all what he has seen that gives him such concern. So, we can ponder such information and give criticism or approval as we see fit."

Anaras the leader of the King's army, seconded the comment, in his powerful disquieting way.

Themiel couldn't argue with his jolly friend's logic either. He'd said his piece and respected those around him to be fair and balanced in their judgment of the facts as they are presented. He saw no reason to give further voice to his grievance and sat back down.

Kor-aviel sighed quietly to himself. Grateful to his friendly colleague for defusing what could have escalated into a long and heated debate, aware that arguing about racial differences was almost as pointless as debating those of differing religious persuasions.

"You are all aware, as Shamen we possess the ability to dream weave?"

"Yes. We know what you mean to do," Themiel said, frowning as were most of the other members, for a practice none of them fully understood or liked.

"The Seekers and I have seen a great danger approach, not Agramar himself, but his brother who we took council with not so long ago, when we met at Grayspire. This threat does not come from Dax-barh and our dark brethren; it comes from an old adversary of Agramar's, Malanon, as brutal a leader as we have ever seen."

"Men killing men. Why should we care? This surely is not our fight?" Themiel again interrupted.

Throwing his co-member a hard look of condescension, Kor-aviel replied.

"Did I say we would fight? No! What I am saying is, we warn our allies of an evil that spreads from the North like a plague, setting villages and towns to the torch and worse."

"What does this Malanon gain by destroying lands and settlements that once were his to rule? This fool is destroying farms that once supplied food and livestock for his Kingdom, mills that supplied his grain, forges that once produced his armour and weapons. Surely this is a madness that we should have no part of. So, I ask again, what is his purpose?"

"Revenge. The purest of reasons for those that seek it, the opposite side of a coin whose face is forgiveness." Kor-aviel replied. "As we all here know,

King Agramar fought and brought to task this evil despot of a leader, driving him and what remained of his followers, North of the Frozen Needles."

"What does this Malanon hope to achieve with these raids? Surely if he means to retake what was his, a full out assault would be the better option?" Ferond asked.

This time the King stood up to address the group, most of whom, still didn't look convinced.

"This savage who calls himself King, is as wily as he is brutal. He knows to face Agramar on the battlefield would be suicide. The lands north of Farroth keep are the Kingdoms main source of crops and when food is short, all will suffer. This will force Agramar to march his armies North. And we saw how the lack of raw materials, prevented Agramar from achieving what he set out to do during those Northern wars. He secured the North, yes. But was unable to end the reign of this madman who escaped beyond the Needles to regroup and create the greatest fighting arena the world has ever seen. The men who are making their way to Farroth Keep are fighters of this arena, experts in butchery, and masters of the weapons they wield. I believe his final assault will be Farroth Keep, there he will be part way to getting the revenge he so deeply desires. Lord Farroth himself, his family and all those he holds dear. My scouts have counted three hundred strong, all hardened killers. And we all know what will happen if that Keep falls and the Wolf dies."

"So, what would you have us do?" Ferond asked.

"It is too late to send any of our army to assist. It is too great a distance even, to send what few fighters we have guarding Grayspire. What I suggested before, would seem to be the only practical course of action left to us. And this I believe we should do without delay."

"Couldn't we send a bird?" Themiel suggested.

"There just isn't enough time."

"What about the Order of the Black Orchids? Surely they can see what threat approaches?"

"They have been committed to keeping an eye on Hunter after the death of that poor girl and the kidnapping of the Smithy's boy. And there is a dark power at work, I fear it comes from that abomination Dax-barh has summoned from the void."

The council sat quietly for a moment, they all knew this dream weaving Kor-aviel proposed, didn't come without its own dangers. When free of the body the spirit of the seeker could be trapped in the mind of the sleeping host, trapped and lost forever in the realm of dreams. But from what they had just heard, the execution outweighed the risk.

"We must do what has to be done," the King intervened, impatient and in no mood for any further debate. But he saw no resistance to his comment.

"Then we must delay no further," Kor-aviel agreed.

Before he could sit down and finish his honeyed wine, the chamber door flew open and Aedor the stable master rushed in, panting heavily.

"My Lord, forgive the intrusion. It's the Royal Whites… They go wild, I cannot calm them."

"What do you mean?" Anaras asked.

"We all know the bond the Whites possess; I fear something has happened to Moonsilver, and this is the cause of their distress. The Queen took Moonsilver out this morning, she told me she wanted to ride alone."

"What?" Kor-yllion raged. "Why did you let her ride without an escort, when my instructions were clear?"

"I am sorry my Lord, she insisted. She knows the forest better than anyone here, and there is nothing I can think of that would cause her harm. But now I am worried. Neither Queen nor horse have returned."

Kor-yllion ordered Anaras to summon his guard and get them to the stables without delay. He then excused himself from the Council meeting and made haste, with Kor-aviel and Aedor close behind.

Each rider calmed his horse and it wasn't long before Kor-yllion, Anaras, Kor-aviel and the King's guard were all mounted and in hot pursuit.

Kor-aviel used his powers of perception to pick up the Queen's trail. They followed the river until they reached the area where the embankment gradually sloped upwards. What they found horrified them. There was a large patch of ground that was blackened as if burnt, at its centre, a shadow of what looked like ash. It was obvious from its shape that it was all that remained of the Queen.

37

PORT OF THENEN – SLAVERS WAREHOUSE

The helmsman eased the Savage Eel into her moorings to the thrall of men, women and children adding sound to the hustle and bustle of a busy harbour. Ships of every shape and size littered the Port flying sails of varying shape and colour giving a hint to their origins.

The first thing Raen noticed as he was dragged on deck was the huge array of smells: fish, prawns, meats from different lands added their own distinctive aroma's, some cooked, most freshly caught in the nets of local fishermen ready to be sold by enthusiastic venders. Raen had never seen anything like it.

As he and the other captives were led ashore, they faced merchants selling their wares, plundered from lands far and wide. Whores stood by tents others by small hovel style shanty huts and some, more up market used their feminine guile to lure willing sailors back to the harbour brothel.

Exiting as it was for the young cargo to find their feet at last, firmly on land, there was also a nagging fear of what unknown hardships they would face next. All of them friend or not, found themselves huddled together offering what little comfort it could afford them.

Raen made sure his two new friends were by his side, especially the young one for whom he had taken on the mantle of guardian; and protected them both as much as his captivity would allow.

Throughout the voyage, he'd watched Vaeyu more than anyone else amongst his captors. He could see the man was different from the rest, not by position as Captain or leader but something else.

During their time on the Savage Eel Raen got to know the oldest of his female companions as Tala, and the younger girl he later discovered went by the name of Mara. Both were daughters of farming families, Tala's home being Stoneholt, a farming community not more than twenty leagues from Farroth Keep, while Mara came from further afield in the village of Oakridge a good day's ride North east of Raen's home of Stonehaven. He showed them *his* name by writing it on the deck of the ship using his finger and the grey gruel they were often served up during the journey.

Raen had only ever looked at Tala as a girl with a dirty face and dishevelled clothing, who helped him with the ship's chores and care of Mara. But since they had all been washed and cleaned up ready for the Auction, he found himself seeing her in a completely different light.

Not far from the warehouse to which they were headed, was a large pool fed by the cooled hot water of natural geysers that exploded into the air from radiant green sulphur wells scattered for miles behind the Harbour. Clothes and all, they were told to jump into the water which only immersed the smallest of the children up to their wastes. When their captors deemed they were clean enough, the children were ordered to sit by the pool and dry out in the hot midday sun. This was the moment Raen became aware of just how pretty Tala really was absent the mud mask she had hidden behind, though not by choice during their arduous sea crossing.

Not only that, he hadn't fully acknowledged her age being the same as his, and now as they sat in the heat, steam coming from their drying clothes, he found his gaze following the contours of a womanly body as her damp dress revealed the well-proportioned curves of a fully developed young woman. Lost to his thoughts he didn't notice Mara scowling at him, for even at her tender age she was aware of what his lingering gaze suggested. Tala blushed. Realizing what had just transpired, Raen turned away the moment she became aware of his attentions, and though a little unnerved by it, she found herself more than a little pleased also. But she couldn't help but smile when Mara in her cute girlish way, showed her disapproval by scowling like a wronged child. Raen flushed, turned his face to the sun as if to suggest its heat was the reason for his red cheeks. After about an hour the group were ordered to stand and follow the slavers.

Vaeyu and half a dozen handpicked crew members escorted their young cargo towards the massive warehouse, where they would be incarcerated until required for auction the following day. All in all, there were thirty-eight children, most in reasonably good condition, Raen being the oldest of them. There should have been forty, but the hazardous journey through the Bay of Storms saw two of the youngest girls swept overboard, lost to a wave that almost capsized the ship.

Vaeyu was the consummate perfectionist when it came to whatever work he was commissioned to see to conclusion. He'd built up a reputation that over time made him the highest paid slaver in the Isles and coming short of his manifest like this would normally have filled him with self-derision. But the last few raids had seen his disillusionment with this ship grow to such an extreme, that he now deemed this trip to be his last, a decision he knew was going to be a problem.

Vaeyu had noticed Raen watching his every move during the crossing. There was something about the lad he couldn't help but admire. He could see how the smithy's son helped two of the girls with their chores and respected how he looked out for their wellbeing. It stirred in him a feeling suppressed for so long he felt it might never surface again; *compassion;* and for the first time, he found himself thinking about what fate had in store for these three unlikely companions.

"Captain," the quartermaster repeated, snapping Vaeyu from his thoughts.

"Yes. What is it?"

"That fucker, Ketch, sez he wants more coin for storin' the cargo. Says he was told we would only be bringin' half the number of kids and unless he gets double the agreed amount, he ain't lettin' us past the doors."

"Move!" Pushing his man to one side Vaeyu snarled.

Ketch could be an awkward bastard at the best of times, he was big, fat and had a face that to describe as ugly was to do the word an injustice. His skin was permanently slick with sweat, his nose pitted and redder than his ruddy pockmarked cheeks; and his breath; this added to the smell of piss that hung around him like a cloud, made him one foul excuse for a human being.

Usually, Vaeyu avoided dealing with the man directly, he refused to subject himself to the man's unsavoury company, he'd send one of his crew instead. But on this occasion he was in no mood for the misfit's belligerence. On his way to confront this warehouse owner, Vaeyu passed Raen and the two girls who were at the front of the line waiting to be led to where they were to spend the night. They watched as he stormed over to the big man blocking the warehouse door; and he didn't look happy.

"It's been a rough journey. You have been paid your dues, so I would suggest you move from that door and let us pass," Vaeyu demanded, his nostril's flaring as the pungent scent of the man assaulted them.

"More coin or you find another place to take these little shits," Ketch replied. His false bravery born and reinforced by his consumption of a locally brewed beverage they called ratsblood.

"If you have a grievance, take it up with the King. But know this, if you do not move and let us pass, I will gut you like a fish and leave you for the rats."

Ketch felt the sudden urge to evacuate his bowels, his fake courage deserting him in an instant of realization that he faced a killer who was more than capable of carrying out such a threat.

Without giving voice to any smart mouthed reply, the unkempt lump of a human being moved his pungent bulk from in front of the double doors, his head bowed in a coward's uncertainty.

Vaeyu waved the line of children to follow him through the doorway down a long wooden balcony that acted as a viewing gallery, so those privileged buyers of courtly favour could weigh up the human merchandise prior to the auction.

There was no hiding the smell of the warehouse's previous occupants. It smelt of stale piss, sweat and whatever else was excreted from their persons during their brief stay. Fresh saw dust had been laid down at least two knuckles deep, a pointless attempt to mask what dried human waste soiled the wooden flooring below. Most of the children looked frightened as they descended the wooden stairs at the edge of the viewing gallery, on their way to the area they were to spend their last night together.

Raen squeezed the young girl's hand with a reassurance he could not truly promise, but he did it anyway hoping her young mind would believe his well-intentioned deceit. And it did. She looked into the dark brown eyes of her Hero and smiled, rubbing the back of his hand lovingly across her cheek. Raen smiled back and kissed her caringly on the top of the head, a mask he wore with ever increasing difficulty as the fear of what fate had instore for them all, fought to reveal an ugly truth. Whatever might become of him and his two newfound companions was in the hands of the Gods and the strangers of this strange land who treated them more like animals than human beings; and there was nothing he could do about it.

Vaeyu and his men rounded the children up in a corner of the warehouse that resembled more a huge hay barn than a place that was once used to store crates of contraband, containing anything from small livestock ready for shipment, to rock salt and olive oil, the natural produce of this main Island. He noticed Raen and the two girls huddled together at the back of the group, and though he shouldn't, he found himself saddened by the prospect of what he knew was to befall them during the auction on the morrow.

The older girl saw Vaeyu staring at them and nudged Raen in the side nervously, unsure why they were of particular interest to this leader of their captors. He found himself staring back at a man he had come to respect; in that strange twisted way a prisoner can come to care for his or her kidnapper. For just the briefest of moments Raen was sure he saw sadness in Vaeyu's eyes, before the Leader of the slavers turned away.

There were only three exits from the area, one being the stairs the group had just come down, the other two being a door at either end of that floor; the one nearest the children leading further into the warehouse the other to the docks out front. Part of the deal with Ketch was, that he supplies the men to guard the children until the following morning, which he did, placing two thugs at each of the exits armed with sword and dagger, to the man a brute.

It was early evening, the sun outside had all but surrendered to a night that was a lot cooler than the heat of the day promised. All the children had eaten what portions they were able to lay their hands on; bread, cheese and water that Vaeyu and a few of his men made available. It wasn't long before some of the youngest were asleep huddled on the bed of saw dust that afforded them little or no comfort. Raen couldn't sleep; his mind reeling about what tomorrow had in store for him and his two friends. Tala was also far from sleep. She stroked Mara's brow and moved carefully over her to sit in the space by the side of Raen. It didn't take a genius to realize they both shared the same misgivings. She leant into Raen pushing her body close to his for both warmth and a comfort they might never share again.

"I am frightened about tomorrow," she whispered.

As am I, Raen thought, making hand gestures he hoped would convey the same.

"What if they split us up? What will we do? I fear more for Mara than myself… I feel like I could be sick."

Raen had no answers for the very same questions that had haunted him for days, more frequent in the asking the closer the moment of the Auction became. The only response he could give her was the gentle squeezing of her hand, and a smile that had given her so much comfort in the times she felt at her lowest. A smile she would miss terribly. And she knew at that very moment, she loved him, not like a brother or a friend but her life's first true love. Raen sensed a change in her demeanour as she pressed herself closer to him, tears running down her cheeks. He placed his finger on her chin and caught the first tear to collect there. He gently lifted her face as if to tell her there was no need for her to cry, then put the wet finger to his lips and tasted the salt of her distress. She fell into his chest sobbing uncontrollably like she had done the first few days of her capture. Raen put his arm around her as if to protect her, he kissed the top of her head, then she looked up and their lips met. Her lips moist with tears, danced with his as if awakened to desire for the very first time, made more desperate by the thought that this might be the last time such opportunity would present itself. He pulled her onto his leg and felt the warmth of her womanhood press against his thigh, stirring in him a feeling he thought would never be his again to experience. His arms held her tight.

"I only feel safe when I am by your side. In the morning, all that will change and it terrifies me," her voice cracking with fear.

Suddenly, there was a cry of help from one of the other children not far from where Mara was sleeping. One of the older boys jumped to his feet pointing to another younger boy who was rolling about in agony on the floor.

"What's up with 'im?" He screamed, frightened by the blood infused froth pumping from the boy's mouth. It wasn't long before several of the other children started screaming too.

Raen was quick on his feet and rushed to see what all the fuss was about. Before he could reach the area where the child lay struggling, he felt a heavy hand grab his shoulder and pull him out of the way.

"It's one o' those fuckin' yella backs," the heavily built guard said, knocking a yellow dotted black spider the size of a chicken egg off the lad's face. The other guard who pulled Raen out of the way flattened the insect, spraying its green slime either side of his boot.

"It's too late for this poor retch."

"That's another one gone… Vaeyu is going to be pissed, and that's for sure," the heavy-set guard added.

Unceremoniously the smaller guard grabbed the boy by the feet, dragging his body away to the double doors close to the group.

"Bastard can't blame us for that."

Unsettled by it all, some of the children were crying, whilst some of the older ones moved away from that corner of the room.

Two of the remaining guards told the children to be quiet and herded the ones that had wandered off back to the corner they had moved from; both guards aware it was almost time for a few chosen buyers to peruse the merchandise.

Raen couldn't sleep, he sat awake all night his back propped up against the wooden wall. Mara lay with her head on his lap, and from sheer exhaustion, she like most of the other young children found at least some respite in sleep.

Tala couldn't sleep either and sat beside Raen with his arm over her shoulder affording what little comfort he could on a night that pre-empted a day of so many unknowns.

"What are they doing?" she asked Raen, as a group of half a dozen people walked out onto the wooden balcony overlooking the area the children occupied.

Raen had no answers, even if he had, she wouldn't understand the reply his hands would give her. But he watched these men dressed in their finery move from one end of the balcony to the other, escorted by Vaeyu himself and a couple of his men. One of the observers in particular drew his attention. A tall thin man dressed in robes of red and green silk with the sigil of the Royal family emblazoned in gold on his shoulder; no doubt a person of office, being shown more favour than the rest. Raen dropped his gaze; the man seemed to be staring his way pointing directly at him, saying something to Vaeyu as he did.

Whatever it was the stranger said, Raen knew no good would come of it. Instinctively, he pulled Tala that bit closer to him, more fearful than ever of what the morning would bring. But even at that distance he could see; whatever the tall thin man said to Vaeyu, it left this leader of cutthroats and rapists unsettled.

38

THE CORPSE

The last time Bael visited the Tavern, he asked Dogran permission to look around the missing stranger's room.

Emma shadowed his every move, leaving her father to service the regulars while she accompanied Hunter, more from intrigue than the desire to chat about issues closer to her heart that she was almost certain he would avoid anyway.

Even though her relationship with Cirius looked like it was developing into something more than just platonic, the flame her heart burned for Hunter was far from extinguished. But this only saw her frustrated, as it was obvious once again he was his usual annoyingly indifferent self, and though she should know better than to expect anything more from this man of many silences, she did and it unnerved her.

"What do you hope to find?" She asked, as Hunter removed the jagged edged sword from its cloth wrappings. "And anyway, what is it about this stranger that has you searching through his belongings as if you know the man?"

No answer followed, Hunter seemed to be more than a little intrigued by the sword he was holding, but it was more than that, he looked puzzled.

He lifted the blade into the light of the window the way only an artist of such a weapon does.

"How can it be? And why would he leave such a weapon behind?" He thought out loud, oblivious of the questions pondered by Emma, as if her words were never spoken.

"Is it true then? Do you know this man?"

"I'm not sure," he replied, the words spilling from his mouth uncensored through lack of concentration.

"Then why is it you appear to recognize that sword you hold?"

"I'm sorry Emma, I don't wish to be secretive. This is as much a mystery to me as it is to you. There are questions concerning my past that have troubled me for some time now, and with all that has happened lately, I mean to have answers. It was never my intent to live in the shadow of lies spoken by those who don't really know me, and as you are aware there are plenty in this town who fit that description. You not amongst them."

Emma softened. His apology disarmed her totally. And for the first time in all the years she had shared such moments with Hunter, she was beginning to see the man beneath the veil. He was different, she couldn't put her finger on how or why, he just was.

She made her way across the room to sit on the edge of the bed and gestured for him to join her. Hunter obliged, placing the sword back in its wrapping and back on the table. She couldn't be sure if the butterflies she felt sitting so close to Hunter were the product of an anxious mind or the hormonal beckoning of a young body. Whichever it was, it caused her cheeks to flush an endearing pink. Hunter glared at the floor in-front of him lost in a place she hoped he would at last share with her, and for the first time, she laid her hand on his and it felt nice; for both of them.

"What is it about this stranger that sees you so troubled? Is it the story he told me regarding the man he thought you might be, a man who fought with him in those arenas up north?" She asked, seeing her words resonate with Hunter.

"In truth, it is that very reason. I know you are aware of how many in this town sought to judge me without ever trying to know the measure of the man I am. So, as you know, rightly or wrongly, I have kept my own council…"

"That is not altogether true, if rumours hold any sway," she said, almost accusingly.

Hunter turned his head with a half-smile of confirmation that said her words were true, so he continued.

"Vena, ah! Yes Vena. You two have had cause for conversation I believe. How I would like to have been a fly on the wall that day. Anyway. Since the Wolf was placed in my care things have begun to unravel that throw doubt on details of my past I have always believed to be true. And as time moves on I am discovering that some people I have placed my trust in all these years, know things about me, I do not."

"What do you mean? Who are these people?" She pressed further.

Bael lent forward, rested his chin on his hand and rubbed his forefinger between his lips, uncertain of his reveal, but he was tired of secrets and lies, so his explanation began.

He'd just finished telling her about his dreams and his connections to the Farroth household, and about how Raen and Lamia had come to play a part in all that had happened, when a knock on the door silenced him.

Lysia, a close young friend of Emma's who was helping her father man the Tavern in her absence, sheepishly stepped into the room not quite sure what she would find. Given the chance to occupy a room with a man she liked as much as she knew Emma still liked Hunter, such opportunity would be seen to advantage. Thankfully Emma wasn't so loose with her emotions;

Lysia finding nothing more than Hunter and her friend sharing the edge of the bed together, talking,

Bael stood up, Emma following straight after.

"Father?" She asked, in anticipation of the question.

"Yes, he sent me up here to see if you had fallen asleep, were his exact words."

"Tell him I am on my way. We are almost finished here."

Lysia looked first to her friend, her gaze slowly drifting across to Hunter who was a little uncomfortable; she grinned as if she knew something they didn't and left. Hunter picked up the stranger's sword and one of the man's well-worn shirts that luckily still held his scent for the Wolf to pick up.

"Would your father mind if I borrow these?"

"I am sure it will be fine... I hope you find what you are looking for, and please come back when you are done. I would have you tell me good or ill what has happened to our missing resident," she concluded, feeling the sudden urge to move closer and kiss him. But she didn't and quickly said her goodbye before joining her father back in the main Tavern.

Bael exited the Tavern by the rear door not wishing to cause any more reason for gossip than both his and Emma's prolonged absence might already have. Now he had what he came for he was ready to depart on his search for a stranger he had never met and answers this stranger may or may not possess.

***

Bael rode hard to be within half a day's ride from the village of Woodcrest. He'd wanted to have the company of his Hawk, but the bird was off somewhere, probably hunting and rather than waste time waiting he decided to go it alone with the Wolf.

Before departing, he got the Wolf to sniff the stranger's clothing in the hope that her keen sense of smell would help them pick up the scent; and up until now the animal showed no signs of doing so.

This part of the road they travelled cut its way through five square miles of Pine Tree Woods. In front of Bael the road turned sharply right, on either side a naturally formed ditch continued along its length for a further two miles. Most of the ditch was hidden from those traveling the route, its edges overgrown with bush, shrub and weed. The area was less travelled than the stretch leading out of Stonehaven to the crossroad he'd left about half a day back. As he came out of the bend, he pulled his horse to a halt, the Wolf showing signs she had picked up the stranger's scent.

Circling around sniffing the ground, the Wolf left the trail and entered the ditch disappearing from Bael's line of sight.

Not more than a hundred paces from where he pulled his horse around, the Wolf burst from the undergrowth, she howled once, to disappear the way she came.

"Ha!" Bael shouted digging his heels in, spurring his horse into a flat-out gallop. He headed for the skeletal remains of a pine tree split in half by a lightning strike, broken and covered in moss; the place he lost sight of his Wolf. He leaped down from the saddle, leaving his horse to graze on the long grass.

The Wolf had left a tell-tale path for him to follow, the freshly trodden grass guiding him some twenty paces beyond the broken tree to a row of wild hawthorn bushes, hiding the ditch behind. There was enough of a gap between two of the bushes to allow him access to what lay beyond; and instinct told him it wasn't going to be good.

Once through, his instincts proved, as ever, reliable. The Wolf stood at the edge of the ditch staring down at the remains below. Bael patted her neck and told the beast to stay where she was, then he slid to the bottom of the ditch which at that point was about six feet deep. He landed close to the feet of the stranger's corpse, it looked odd, almost like he had fallen asleep, his knees pulled up into his chest, like the foetal position assumed in the comfort of bed. But this was no bed and there was no comfort to be found here. Reluctantly Bael rolled the stranger onto his back the rigor-mortis keeping the legs bent up in a bizarre almost comical pose. It wasn't a pretty sight, half the man's face was missing, eaten away by the wild. It was obvious to him that the injuries were suffered post mortem and were not the cause of death. On closer inspection, Bael's eyes followed the gore until they reached the wound that so brutally did end the stranger's life. A maggot ridden gash across the man's throat, stretched from ear to ear in the method of an execution. It was clean, precise, the signature kill of a trained assassin.

Bael scowered the murder scene hoping it would reveal some evidence of who the killer might be, but it didn't: no footprints, torn items of clothing, nothing. To a skilled tracker like Bael it was like chasing a ghost. What he did deduce from the body was that the murder had been committed elsewhere. Blood from a neck wound like that would have sprayed everywhere, and though there was blood around the area it just wasn't enough to suggest otherwise. Finally, he methodically riffled through the man's clothing, yielding absolutely nothing. If he'd been carrying coin, it had been stolen. The whole thing looked for all intent and purpose to be that of a robbery.

"There was no time to bury you, and just in case you were found the killer wanted it to look like a robbery gone wrong," Bael said, talking directly at the corpse. "But why were you really killed?"

Before leaving for Wayrest, Bael took one last look at what remained of the stranger's face in the hope it might trigger something in his memories. Sadly, there just wasn't enough of it left to afford any kind of recognition, no matter how hard he tried.

Then amongst the viscera he spotted the single braid of platted hair, confirming his fears. He did what he could to cover the remains, using fallen branches, leaves and whatever else he could find inhabiting the forest floor.

Making his way back up the side of the ditch, he led the Wolf over to where he left his horse, this time taking more notice of the path he'd taken there. As he thought, dried blood lay hidden amongst the overgrown grass, on reaching the broken tree he discovered the place of murder. Behind the tree was the remains of a campfire. Blood was everywhere, soaked dry into the hard ground. Again, the killer had left nothing incriminating.

Bael whistled his horse over. He jumped into the saddle, then all three left for Waycrest.

39

SLAVE MARKET

It was just getting light outside the warehouse. The harbour slowly coming back to life after a colder night than the day promised. Some of the children were already awake, hearing the noise of a new day. Many, like Raen and Tala got no sleep at all worrying about what the day had install for them. A few of the youngest were a little more fortunate, they were still asleep but that all changed when Vaeyu and six of his most trusted men arrived to check all was well with the cargo.

The smallest of the children cowered against the wooden wall as their captors chained their shackles, forming groups of three and four. But when it came to Raen and his two companions Vaeyu intervened, relieving his men of their duty as the auctioneer's men, a dozen strong entered the area. These men were sent to escort the children to the designated place of sale.

Whilst the escorts busied themselves organizing the children into two straight lines, Vaeyu seized the opportunity to pull Raen and the girls to one side, just out of earshot of the last child in the line. Mara was terrified, her little mind thinking the worst. But their captor did something none of them expected: he removed the locks off their shackles so the iron pins could be removed.

"Do you trust me?" He asked in common tongue, directing the question more towards Raen and Tala.

Raen nodded *yes,* Tala doing the same. Mara on the other hand left all responses to the older more experienced members of her group.

"Listen to me carefully and do exactly as I say, no more-no less… When you leave this building, you will follow the guards through the market place towards a fenced open-air compound where you are to be sold. Before you reach this place, you will pass a stall that sells fruit. To the side of this stall will be a woman dressed in blue, wearing a red head scarf. When you see her and not before, slip your chains and run. Not directly to her… this is important. Instead, run past her until you reach a small wooden holding with a hanging basket of red flowers on the wall by the door. Enter the building and wait for the woman in the red scarf to join you and do whatever she says…. do you understand?"

Raen and Tala acknowledged they understood, Mara, again going along with their decision.

"Good, then I must…"

"But what about the guards?" Tala interrupted.

"The guard at the back is overweight, and I made sure he was plied with plenty of free ale. He has slept little, so escaping him should not be difficult."

"What if the vendors behind the stalls close to the house should give up our position?" Tala whispered, still not convinced.

"They won't. They know me well and know what I have planned… just make sure you do everything I have told you."

Raen squeezed both girl's hands, as confirmation that all would be fine, but Tala still felt it all sounded too easy.

It wasn't long before they were being led out of the building; through the front door to the harbour beyond. It was cooler than the previous day, many of the locals welcoming the cloud filled sky that promised rain.

It was just as Vaeyu described, the line of children wormed their way past vendors selling everything from livestock, fish and more exotic food stuff, to cutlery, jewellery, armour and weapons. One stall even sold brightly coloured parakeets that swore in different languages as the children passed by.

Raen never took his eyes off the guard nearest the end of the line. Still suffering a hangover, the man found it hard to walk a straight line, trying without success, to appear sober. This gave him some comfort in the knowledge Vaeyu was at least true to his word. But one thing he had learned being around Hunter, was never leave anything to chance.

Until now, an opportune moment hadn't presented itself, but as they approached a stall selling swords, maces and other weapons of combat, Raen had a plan.

Coming alongside the stall Raen pushed the last boy from the adjacent line, into a small wooden bucket containing daggers of varying weight and length. The boy fell to the ground knocking the knives everywhere. Tala and Mara hadn't got a clue what was happening, but in the confusion Raen managed to pick up a small dagger that was poking out from under the fabric covering the front of the stall.

The vendor was mad with rage, screaming obscenities in a foreign tongue, whilst the boy struggled to his feet bewildered at why the stall owner directed his abuse at him.

The drunken guard came over to see what all the commotion was about. The boy getting up from the ground shouted that Raen had pushed him. The guard grabbed Raen by the scruff of his shirt.

"Do that again and I'll cut yer fuckin' hand off," he threatened, slapping Raen across the side of the head.

By now the line had drawn to a halt, the other guards aware something was going on. The drunk waved all was fine and shouted.

"Get movin' yer little bastards or I swear I'll put a whip to yer."

Tala looked at Raen in disbelief, still unsure of what his motive for causing such a ruckus was.

"Why did you do that?" she pressed.

Raen rolled back his sleeve to produce the hilt of the dagger he was hiding there.

"How did you…?"

"Ssh!" Raen replied, putting a finger to his lips.

Unfortunately, drunk or not the fat guard nearest them watched them like a hawk. Vaeyu's words came flooding back. *Do as I say, no more-no less.* Raen realized he had already broken that promise and it unnerved him.

The line of children followed the path around a long curve, and as it straightened, Raen spotted the fruit stall. At first it looked as though part of Vaeyu's plan had gone wrong, then the woman with the red scarf stepped from behind another stall and waited.

Raen nudged his companions and slipped the pin out of his shackles. Tala followed his lead but Mara wasn't strong enough to release hers. Raen quickly took hold of her hands and banged the pin clear, but not quick enough to evade the attention of the drunk guard.

"Hey!" He bellowed, pushing some of the children out of his way as he made a run for Raen.

Raen told the girls to run. They didn't need telling twice. At full stretch, they ran past the woman in blue making a direct line for the house with the hanging basket.

It all happened so fast for the guards down the line to realize what was going on, and when they did, it was all over.

The fat guard was quicker than he should have been, but anger and adrenaline seemed to more than compensate for his drunken incompetence. He grabbed Raen by the neck, drawing his short sword ready to strike.

Hunter had told Raen, *when using a knife, the quickest way to kill a man is to pierce his heart, if that wasn't possible in a situation like this, aim for the groin, hopefully you will hit the main artery and the man will bleed out. If not, you will at least bring him down to afford your escape.*

Raen did just that, his dagger punching through the guard's groin, slicing away the tip of his manhood, missing the artery but sending the lump of a man screaming in agony as he fell to his knees. By the time the other guards were aware of what was happening, Raen was already on the move. Being a fast runner saw him pass the woman in blue and on to the house with the hanging basket, before the slavers could barge their way through the line of children and continue their pursuit.

The woman wearing the red head scarf turned slowly, ignoring the chaos that erupted behind her. Four of the guards split away from the rest, the one nursing his groin pointing in the direction the three escapees had run. In their eagerness, they passed the woman in blue, to be misdirected by some of the vendors close to the house where Raen and his friends hid.

Vaeyu's friend entered the wooden house. The place smelt of damp, there was little in the way of furniture; it was somewhere to stay for the night after a hard day's trading, rather than one you could call home. There was just the one room, in it, a table, two chairs and a makeshift cot bed, its wooden frame riddled with wood worm; an infestation that was slowly devouring the place. In the corner was a bucket of saw dust used to replenish the dust that covered the floor, infused with rat droppings and whatever dirt found its way in from the harbour outside.

Huddled together in the corner farthest away from the single muddied window obscuring most of the light fighting to enter and illuminate the gloom within, was Raen and his two companions.

It touched her to see the young man crouched in front of the girls offering what little protection he could, from what or whoever entered the room. Luckily for them it was her. In the dim light, she removed her red scarf, shook her head allowing her shoulder length brown hair to drop and swirl across her face.

Even in low visibility Raen could see the young woman was neither pretty nor plain but somewhere in between. Feeling no threat from her he stood up straight, the two girls waiting a little longer before doing the same. The woman seemed at first to ignore them, the three watched in silence as she slid the table across the floor to expose a trap door hidden beneath the scattering of saw dust. She bent down, grabbed the metal latch and lifted it open.

"You must all hide in here," she said, resting the heavy door against her thigh. "Those men will come back to look for you, if they catch you here all will be lost... So quickly, get in. and whatever you do don't make a sound, no matter what happens up here. Until I open this door you must stay put."

None of the three made to question the woman. Raen entered first, stepping down a small ladder and into a space that allowed enough headroom for them to stand. Tala followed next, then Mara put her foot on the first rung; Raen moved to assist the little girl but before he could reach her, her foot slipped. She cried out, biting her tongue as her chin caught on one of the rungs; Raen's arms shot out and caught her. She began to cry.

"Please you must be quiet," the woman whispered, as she heard the sound of the guards returning.

Raen pulled Mara into his chest to console her. Tala used her sleeve to wipe away the tiny bit of blood that seeped from the youngster's lips. Then the door above them closed, stirring up saw dust as it dropped. The gaps between the floor boards surrendered a little light but not enough to illuminate the darkness they found themselves in. But if this was the cost of safety, it was a price worth paying.

The woman in blue lifted the bucket in the corner, spreading the saw dust to obscure the trap door's edges. When that was done, she slid the table back over it making it nigh impossible to see. For a moment she took stock of the situation; the trap door and table a poignant reminder of the moment in her childhood the world she cherished fell apart.

The memories as painful as they were, came flooding back, she saw her mother raped as she and her father were made to watch, then to see both parents brutally murdered like animals to the slaughter knowing her little sister Jiney lay hidden beneath the trapdoor, listening and watching. Images she would carry the rest of her life.

The sound of the slavers outside the house snapped her back to the reality of the moment. Now all she could do was wait.

Doors close by slammed shut as the slavers checked the surrounding properties, the young woman's stomach felt hollow, her heart racing as the sounds got steadily closer.

"Pull yourself together," she whispered, scolding herself for allowing the nerves to take hold. "They see me like this and we are done." Outside, she heard a couple of the guards swearing, followed by a shuffling then a series of muffled thudding noises. Unnerved by it she wiped the thick dirt off the inside of the window only to spread the filth even further, obscuring completely what lay beyond. Instinct guided her right hand through a slit in her dress that resembled a pocket; her fingers found purchase around the hilt of a concealed dagger. Only as a last resort would she use it; for whoever walked through that front door her first line of defence would be diplomacy. Should that fail, the blade would see its purpose fulfilled.

Not seconds after hearing the last thud! The door flew open. Vaeyu entered, covered in blood. The woman in blue was standing by the table, hand on dagger, her eyes bulging with uncertainty.

"Come. We must leave," he said, sliding the table across the floor.

He opened the trap door to find three anxious faces staring up at him.

"We must go. Now! All the harbour will be looking for us… Quickly," he urged, pulling each one of them out and into the room. Vaeyu led them out through the front door; outside, four of the auction guards lay dead from stab wounds. He moved past them as if nothing had happened. Making his way around the back of his dwelling he guided the group through the myriad of sulphur pools and the red-hot geysers that intermittently filled the air around them with steam clouds. It wasn't long before their clothes were damp, the pools giving off a stench of rotten eggs, the sulphuric fumes stinging their red rimmed eyes as if they were crying.

Eventually they arrived at a road where Vaeyu's quartermaster was waiting with a horse drawn wagon. Vaeyu linked arms with the man, gesturing for Raen and the girls to get onto the open back, the woman in blue taking her place up front.

"Thank you, my friend," Vaeyu said, in his native tongue.

"We will meet again soon, I hope?" The quartermaster asked.

"Someday, if the gods are just... Take care my friend."

Raen could see how much Vaeyu respected the man holding the horses and as he stepped up to join his female companion his friend looked sad.

Just out of sight of the harbour the heavens opened, the rain was torrential, the open back wagon offering no protection. Raen and the girls huddled together bracing themselves against the jolts of an unforgiving road and the seemingly welcome downpour that helped wash away the stench of the sulphur pools.

Tala nudged Raen urging him to follow her gaze: it was obvious the woman in blue had affection for their captor, she was lent into him with her head resting on his shoulder. Vaeyu was a lot older, so maybe he was her father, a thought which Raen felt carried more weight than the alternative; an older man and his young lover, or wife even. No this was something else, and though he didn't know it, in time he would discover what that was. And through an incredible twist of fate, he would also discover the true identity of the young woman who had just helped save his life.

40

WAYCREST – WITCH

It was nightfall when Bael and the Wolf arrived at Waycrest. To reach the village they crossed a small white stone bridge spanning the river that gave the place its name. He let the Wolf wander off, feeling her appearance would alarm the locals, hindering what would more than likely be a difficult and delicate investigation at best.

Once across, he passed through open farmland that stretched for as far as the eye could see. The village itself was the hub that several surrounding farms worked around. It consisted of a dozen or so dwellings of varying size, all of them topped with a thatched roof. Amongst these buildings was the village Inn, of moderate size, its white washed walls gave the place a real country feel. For generations, other than the odd summer fete, this was the villagers' main source of entertainment and centre of neighbourliness and would be Bael's first port of call.

He glanced up at the swinging wooden sign suspended above one of the two doors leading into the establishment; it read – The Dancing Rooster. It gave him a good feel for the place; the detailed painting on the board saw a rooster dancing, its face and stance quite comical in their presentation. Close to the other door to his right, was a large wooden porch filled with a group of boisterous locals, farmers and farm hands, if the snippets of conversation he was able to pick up were anything to go by.

Like so many times before when entering these insular close communities, he could be welcomed in the least with suspicion, that would often escalate into varying degrees of outright unfriendliness. Fortunately, on this occasion it was the former, most of those on the porch just looking his way with nothing more sinister than a peeked curiosity, some even managed a smile.

Bael stooped down to avoid banging his head; a small sign nailed to the thick wooden lintel above the door had the words Duck or Grouse carved into it. The place was old. *The first occupants must have been dwarves*, he thought, as he ducked under relieved he was able to stand up straight on the other side. Once inside he found himself in the larger of two rooms. He could see those around him were drinkers only, whilst the smaller room at the back was reserved for customers who wished to sample the Inn's culinary delights.

The first of the rooms was nearly full. Again, he was met with harmless curiosity, most of those around him were farmers, farm hands and their families, a pleasant crowd by any standard. Conversations halted sporadically as a few of the revellers followed his movement towards the bar; but by the time he reached it, the place was again a cauldron of lively conversation.

Two buxom serving wenches waited on the tables. The landlord, a rather plump individual, slightly less than average height with a clean-shaven head, entertained four of his regulars. Seeing the newcomer approach, he excused himself from the conversation and walked to the end of the counter where Bael had found space.

"And what can I get for you my fine young friend?" he asked, in a refreshingly boisterous tone.

"Can I bother you for a mug of your local ale? Thankyou."

"No bother at all. Would you like me to bring it to you?" The landlord nodded in the direction of an empty table close to the door at the back room.

"No. I will be fine here." Bael replied.

One of the barmaids, possibly in her late thirties, and not unattractive for a woman of her stature, passed behind Bael on her way to re-fill the four empty tankards she was carrying.

"My, aren't you the handsome one. Not like this bunch of leather faced reprobates."

One of the men standing at the bar, heavy set, his cheeks the weathered red of a farmer, lifted his mug and turned from his conversation with the landlord.

"And you would know Sally. Look what a catch you got," he jibed, staring at her husband, sitting with a friend at a table close by.

"That's right Tom, but at least I can keep a wife," the man replied with playful sarcasm.

The place burst into raucous laughter, even some in the back room joined in the harmless banter.

Bael welcomed the pleasant atmosphere, especially after the grisly discovery he had made on the road in. For a while and during his consumption of several ales, he quietly soaked up the normality that had, for one reason or another deserted Stonehaven.

Weary from the journey and not wishing to dampen the atmosphere, Bael decided to leave the questioning until morning, before setting off for home at the end of the day.

He paid for one night's board and stabling of his horse, then retired to his room one floor up, where he dropped fully dressed onto the bed and fell into a well-earned sleep.

The morning sky was overcast, but the early light was enough to wake Bael from his dreamless slumber. He freshened himself up and joined four other guests of the Inn, who were getting tucked in to a hearty breakfast in the back room overlooking the valley beyond. He sat at a table on his own, close to the large bay window that offered panoramic views of the stunning scenery it overlooked. Breakfast was ham, fresh baked bread, goats cheese and a refreshing mug of apple juice to swill it all down. But as relaxing and tranquil as the place was, it couldn't erase the image of the stranger's body by the road, the day before.

After finishing his meal, he walked over to the window and looked across the valley beyond. The river he'd crossed on his way to the village, snaked its way along the basin, most of its waters hidden by early morning mist that lay across the landscape like a gossamer grey blanket.

His hunger satisfied; he was now ready to look around in the hope he might discover the reason for why the stranger chose to visit such a place. He thanked the landlord for his kind hospitality, the portly man looking as refreshed and full of life as he had the night before.

The room was his for the remainder of the day, so he left the stranger's sword and clothing where it lay, deciding he would show the landlord later before his departure.

He ducked under and through the door, filling his lungs with the fresh country air as he stepped into the open.

After a couple of hours or so of searching around, the village had surrendered not a thing. There were no fighting pits that a man owning a jagged sword like the stranger possessed, might frequent. It would appear on the face of it that there was nothing to suggest that anything other than farming took place in the area. There was no guild of thieves, no brothel, no cock or dog fighting rings; nor anything else that might suggest activities of ill repute.

Before venturing back to the Inn Bael visited the stables. His horse was busy nibbling fresh hay from a deep stone trough; the beast looked up, snorted a couple of times, then carried on eating ignoring its master as if he wasn't there.

Bael left him be, the animal had earned the privilege. He entered the Inn, which was busy again but not as full as the night before.

Retrieving the stranger's sword from his room he headed back downstairs to speak with the landlord. Not wishing to cause undue alarm, he asked the landlord to join him at the end of the counter where they could speak in private. He unwrapped the sword and placed it down on the counter. The landlord was somewhat bewildered.

"What is this?"

"It belonged to a man I believe may have visited your village. Please take a good look at it and tell me if you knew the man?" Bael urged, handing the landlord the blade.

Though, still at a loss, it hadn't escaped the landlord's notice that Bael's reference to the stranger was spoken in the past tense.

"You say it belonged to this stranger, yet it is in your possession. Why?"

Bael gave as short but detailed account as time would allow. He told the story of how the stranger had appeared in Stonehaven and what had transpired since then.

The landlord looked flabbergasted, especially on hearing about the grizzly remains Bael discovered along the road. On hearing the story to completion, his attitude to Bael became more amenable. He picked up the sword, held it above his head so all around him could see.

"Please. If you can spare me a moment of your time," he said, drawing the attention of everyone in the room. "Does any amongst you recognize this sword, and know the man it belonged to?"

What followed was a mixture of head shaking and chorus of *no's*. The landlord turned back to face Bael.

"It would seem this stranger of yours is as much of a mystery to us, as he is to you. I am sorry. I wish I could tell you more my friend, but it appears your journey was for nought."

It became blatantly obvious that to invest any more of his time in the village would be pointless. He thanked the landlord for his generosity, had one more drink, then gathered his belongings and returned to the stables. He saddled his horse, tied the wrapped sword to the pommel and was ready to leave, when his Wolf appeared at the exit.

"What are you doing here?" he asked, tying the horse's reins to the wooden rail. "What is it?"

The Wolf brushed against his leg, then headed out into the road beyond; Bael followed her.

Those members of the village who were outside going about their daily business couldn't believe their eyes. Mothers grabbed their children pushing them indoors, a farmhand carrying a scythe made ready should he need to use it and a young girl screamed running into her father's arms for safety. It wasn't until Bael stepped beside the Wolf that the growing crowd's anxiety, though still uncertain, was reduced to one of bewilderment. They watched, many with open mouth, as Bael and the Wolf headed for the last cottage that looked out on acres of yellow corn fields.

Still not sure of why the Wolf was leading him this way, Bael could only think his four-legged companion had uncovered something he had missed; a thought that proved to be well founded.

Sitting alone on a log bench in front of a canvas of succulent yellow corn stalks stretching as far as the eye can see, was an old woman. His first thoughts were that she was well past her seventieth name day. Her skin was sun soaked brown, wrinkled, leaving features thin as if undernourished, giving her quite a hard-unforgiving countenance. There was a strange expectancy in the way she followed his every step, as if she had been waiting for them both.

As he got closer the hardness of her features softened, she patted the top of the bench with gnarled arthritic fingers.

"Please my boy, sit with me," she rasped, her voice deep and assertive for a woman of her years. "I have been expecting you."

Normally Bael would have been surprised by the comment, but after all the strange things he had witnessed these past months, he was sure *this* and more stranger times were to come. He sat beside the old woman, the Wolf dropping to the ground by his side, a gentle growl rolling around her throat. Bael stroked the back of her neck as further reassurance that all was well.

"Your Wolf is special, is she not?" the old woman croaked, looking upon the animal with caring eyes.

"She is," Bael replied.

"I had her bring you to me... You see, I know why you are here... Does that surprise you?"

"It should, but in truth it does not."

"Then you are learning," she smiled. "So, ask the question you came all this way to ask."

Bael was starved of words, there was no sword or item of clothing to show her, they were back at the stables and it was quite obvious by her comment she already knew the question anyway.

"I came here seeking answers about a stranger who visited my town, a stranger that believed he knew me from my past. A past I can't explain, but one I believe I have seen in my dreams."

"And now this stranger lies face down in a ditch covered with leaf and twig as food for the worms," the woman whispered, knowingly.

"How…?" Bael again stuck for words.

"I see many things. Like my sister I have the sight… And I have seen the one who mercilessly took your stranger's life."

This time Bael was surprised.

"Tell me, who is it?" He asked, with heightened urgency.

"Before I do, I must tell you something. Time is short, but you should know I have been waiting a very long time for this moment. Your fate is bound to mine and another like me, someone you have already had the privilege to meet… My sister; like me a Witch. A calling she still refuses to embrace, yet a witch she is… You know her as Lamia."

Bael was dumbstruck. This was not a meeting or eventuality that anyone could have predicted, certainly none that he himself could have envisaged anyway.

"Please, give me your hands," she asked.

Bael responded without a second thought, allowing the old woman to turn them palm up.

"Death follows you like a shadow, though your heart is pure your past is bathed in blood. From the day you were born you were destined for greatness, but this birth right will put those close to you in grave peril. You are right to question your memories, for these are lies, figments of someone else's imagination. You are protected by a great power born of darkness. A darkness that now grows within you. Its origin is hidden from me, but my sister has seen this shadow on your life and though she does not realize it, through her I have seen the same…. Though our gifts are similar, she can see what I cannot. Her blindness allows access to the realms of light and dark, colours, auras, in truth I know not what to call them, but she can see what no other can. And during her hours of slumber I have probed her mind to see what she has seen, and so you are here, not by chance for the gods themselves have seen fit to awaken in you the power you are meant to wield. And I believe the Wolf by your side plays no small part in this awakening."

Even though her words seemed outrageous, Bael couldn't ignore the fact that some of what she said gave answer to questions that had troubled him from the day the Wolf became an integral part of his life. His bond with the animal was undeniable, incredible by any stretch of the imagination. He always felt his dreams were more than the inventions of a sleeping mind. But from what he had just heard the mystery surrounding his past was now even more confusing. A mystery, he was more than ever determined to unravel. But for the moment, all he could do was listen.

"There are things about your past I have no answers for, someone or something has hidden your memories so deep, that even with the powers I possess they are beyond my reach. What I can tell you with certainty, your dreams reveal a truth and a lie. The truth is, you have been granted a look into events and people, pieces of a puzzle of a life lived. As for the lie, the man you called father, the man who raised you as his own, the man who helped gain you freedom in that terrible arena, was not your true father. *His* identity is unknown to me. What I can tell you is," she hesitated. "I know your mother."

It wasn't lost on Bael that his mother was mentioned in the here and now. It was a mystery he never thought to question, believing she had died during his infancy, his thoughts always focused on the man he thought saw him to manhood. Now here he sat beginning to believe everything about his past was indeed a fabrication of someone's making. That his mother could really be alive was more than he could handle.

"You speak of my mother as if she still lives?" Bael pried.

"She does."

"You must tell me who she is. What is her name? Where, where can I find her?"

"Unfortunately, I cannot tell you these things. I am sworn to secrecy. The things I tell you now, I do so at great risk to myself. In truth, I should not be sharing any of this, but when I said our destinies are bound, that was only part of the reason I talk with you here this day. You see, we are also bound in blood in a way you cannot imagine. I am sure all you are hearing, leaves even more questions to be answered, but these I cannot, not at this time."

"I understand your concerns regarding my past, what I don't understand is how you can keep my mother's identity hidden from me?"

The old woman can see the pain in Bael's eyes, but she doesn't let it weaken her resolve.

"Because the woman I speak of does not know you are her child. She believes she only loved one man in her life. It is a falsehood she like yourself has lived, it is those who created this falsehood you must surely seek out, the Elders: for it is only they who hold the answers to the lie that is your life."

"But why would these Elders do such a terrible thing, to rob me of my true identity, not only me but my mother, and what of my father? My real father, who was *he*?"

A sadness came over the old woman, filling her eyes with tears of frustration, knowing how wanting it must be to believe a parent dead all your life, to then discover they lived. Your heart would want to burst from your chest, but she couldn't share such information before the mother herself realized the same and with the knowledge of what was to come, the time for such disclosure was sadly not now.

"My heart weighs heavy, that I cannot give answer to the many questions I know must be pressing you for conclusion. The pieces of the puzzle that Maccon, my sister and myself possess, when put together, still do not reveal the truth about who you really are. The moment your memories were revealed to you through your dreams, I felt it my duty to help you as much as I am able to understand part of what is happening to you. This I have done, the rest will come in time, you have to trust me in this. Soon I must leave you…. So, onto the matter at hand, this stranger you mentioned."

"If what you told me is true, then this man was the person I believed him to be, the young warrior in the arena whose life I saved?"

"He was. He spent years trying to find you. Sadly he almost did, before his life was so cruelly cut short. During his travels he met me, again not by chance. But the gods can be fickle, for I cannot see any reasoning behind his death. From your dreams, I knew who he was the moment I laid eyes on him. He told me something your dreams have yet to reveal, knowledge I believe was in part the reason for his murder. When he told me this story, I sent him back to warn you. For that he died."

"Please, do not talk in riddles. What information did he possess that would see his life ended in this way?" Bael pressed, sad but angered that such an act could be committed on his behalf.

"Your final fight in that terrible arena was to be your last. As you saw in your dream, the father who fostered you all those years, died trying to gain you a freedom promised should you survive triumphant. You did. But your King had other plans, he schemed to have you murdered, believing the blood running through your veins was more powerful than any he had taken before. He wanted you dead, so he could consume it believing your strength would then be his. You heard about this plot, from the young warrior whose life you saved that day. He'd overheard a conversation between Malanon and the assassin chosen weeks before; a killer who was to see the deed to its gruesome end. The killer the stranger was trying to warn you about: a man I believed dead, until I saw him kill this young man we speak of. A killer I know very well. My brother."

"Your brother? Why would he wish to see me dead? What have I done to him that would warrant such a deed?"

"Forgive me, my mind wanders. I mean to explain. After hearing about the plot to end your life, you took the swords of your father, promised should he fall. With them you fought your way out of the palace grounds where you were to be dined and entertained before your execution. Amongst those you killed was Malanon's only son, a son he loved above all else. His grief has never waned. And for years my brother has hunted you down, amongst many other victims beyond counting, in his misguided loyalty to a tyrant leader. That the Elders gave you a new identity helped your cause considerably, an inadvertent act that till now has kept you alive."

Bael turned to lock eyes with the old woman, there was so much for his mind to contemplate. Some things had become clearer, but much was still unanswered. It felt like they had been speaking for hours seeing his emotions drawn thin through anger and disbelief that all he was hearing was true.

"All this said, why did the Elders bring me to Stonehaven? And why was I chosen to take care of the Wolf?"

"This, as I said is mystery only they can unravel. All I can tell you is what I know to be true."

For a moment, Bael reflected on the story so far, one issue his thoughts kept returning to was the mention of his old friend.

"You said that Lamia is your sister, yet not once during my conversations with her did she ever mention a sister, or a brother. Don't you find that odd?"

"Because she believes me and my brother dead. And I wish it to stay that way, for the moment at least."

"But why?"

"That is no concern of yours, you must respect my wishes in this matter, believe me when I tell you, I do not exaggerate its importance. But one day we will revisit that conversation."

"If all that you tell me is true, why is my living a lie of such importance that people must die in its protection?"

"I do not have an answer for that. But whatever it is, it means more to the race of Elders than it does to that of man. Now listen to me carefully. What I am about to tell you I have told no one and this knowledge must stay between us."

Bael nodded his understanding.

"If I told you my age you would not believe me, Lamia and my brother the same. We are what Elder kind view as an abomination, for the blood that runs through our veins is both Elven and human."

"You are a halfblood?" Bael suggested.

"An astute observation young man," she replied sarcastically. "Our father was an Elven shaman; I believe still lives. Our mother was human, she died many years ago of a broken heart. The gift me and my siblings possess come from our father's bloodline. Out of the three of us, my brother's gift was the weakest. As we grew older, he became consumed with jealousy, that my sister and I developed the power to see moments of the past, present and in my case the future. He was only blessed with the ability to read the minds of others, but he possessed something we did not, incredible agility. As a child, he could climb a tree like a monkey, he could wrestle a boy twice his size, to the ground such was his speed. The mindfulness he let slip into memory, concentrating more on this ability that would aid him in the profession that made him its slave. And now he is a lethal killer. Soon I must leave you. But there is something else you should know; the real reason I believe you were meant to meet with me… When my brother caught up with the unfortunate stranger, he read his mind before killing him. I told the young warrior about my sister's part in all this. Now my brother is aware of not just my sister's involvement, but mine also. I fear he is already on his way to find you in Stonehaven. But now I worry he will find my sister first and see her life ended. You must hurry back, go to her if it isn't too late. Protect her from this monster, for all our sakes, see an end to his miserable life. Please, save her…. Now, I am afraid we must part company. Make haste Bael, time is our enemy. But rest assured we will meet again.

41

DREAM WEAVERS

There was no time to waste following his meeting with the High Council, Kor-aviel with the King's blessing rounded up five of his fellow Seekers.

Whilst he waited for their arrival, he used the time to prepare the beds for the Weaving. The Spirit Chamber was by far the oldest part of the Palace; an ancient cave whose only access was the two-huge metal ribbed panel doors, built into stone walls, constructed as protection for this ancient site. Permanently moist stalagmites grew out of the floor like white stone soldiers, faced by their opposites, hanging from the ceiling in slick, wet defiance. Six low lying cot beds arranged in the shape of an open fan, took up the cave centre. Each bed had an Elven runic symbol carved into its aged wooden headboard.

Collectively, they read *Free Spirit,* but individually each rune was the unique signature of the Seeker it belonged to; the same symbol tattooed on the back of each of their shoulders. For thousands of years each sign was bound by magic to members of that one family and could only be changed should Kor-aviel and his fellow shamen deem otherwise. An event that had only occurred once in his lifetime, when the remaining members of that family were killed fighting the War of the

Seven Sisters, ending a family lineage dating back to the Ancients themselves.

But a feature that made this cave truly unique was the collection of long, clear, six sided crystals that formed a natural circle around the beds. Some amongst the Elders believed the crystals were the work of the Ancients themselves so perfect in symmetry was the circle. But in truth no one knew for sure what their origins were, what they did know was, this crystalline perfection held a power that helped in the Weaving.

No matter how many times Kor-aviel frequented the chamber, he was always amazed at the place's ability to maintain a constant temperature no matter what weather change occurred outside.

The beds were ready for the ritual, in which each Seeker released his spirit to weave his way into the dreams of the chosen.

Eleroth was the first to enter the cave. He was tall even for an Elder, a long-pointed beard, like his long hair, as white as snow, giving him a mature distinguished look. Being the eldest of the Seekers, and most powerful after Kor-aviel, he liked to be early, to help settle his mind in preparation for the task ahead.

The next two to arrive were Aelron and Anwed, the youngest of the group, his beard short almost goatee like and as black as coal. His face always looked stern, making him less approachable than his fellow members. In contrast, Aelron who was around the same age, looked and acted younger. He was clean shaven with long flowing blonde hair that stretched down to the small of his back; this paired with his quick wittedness and razor-sharp intellect, made him very popular with many of the young females of his kind.

The final two, were always last to arrive, to the constant chagrin of Kor-aviel, who was a stickler for punctuality. And no matter how many times he addressed the issue with them they always had an excuse. Azaele was the shortest of the group and quite portly for an Elder. But his dedication to the task could never be questioned, allowing the head Shaman to stay his tongue on some of the occasions his time keeping came into question.

Loras was a completely different proposition. He was around the same age as Kor-aviel and came from one of the richest families in the land. His skin was the colour of sand stone, his hair looked almost golden, possessing a constant sheen no matter how many times he washed it. He was almost as tall as Eleroth, his golden beard, cropped, framing a strong square jaw line. His lack of punctuality stemmed from his annoying self-belief that his station was a cut above everyone else in the group. Kor-aviel had given up trying to change him a long time ago, leaving that duty to Eleroth, whose sharp intellect and unique style of sarcasm allowed him to pull his colleague down a peg or two without appearing overly offensive.

Now all the Seekers were present, each removed his outer clothing and without uttering a word lay down on his own bed. Kor-aviel stood at the base of his bed and one by one spoke each of the runic names representing each member.

The circle of clear crystals began to resonate with a very low humming sound, this was the que for the head Shaman to take his position on his bed at the centre of the group. The thrum of the crystals became slower, quieter and sang to an almost hypnotic beat.

During the ritual, the Seekers didn't actually fall asleep, this was a misconception of the uninitiated. Instead, their eyes stayed open and rolled back to expose their whites, signalling a deep meditative state.

Kor-aviel lay back to join his colleagues. Being head Seeker, he led in the weaving, his breathing reduced to a bare minimum, his body temperature dropping to that within the cave. The rest of the Seekers followed his lead until they all maintained the same level of meditation; breathing so shallow it left their chest movement almost undetectable to the untrained eye.

Having done this many times, it didn't take long for all of them to reach the state of contemplative repose needed for the separation. All six of them lay as still as a corpse, eyes wide white and strangely unnerving. Within moments their combined consciousness linked, releasing Invisible spirits from the confines of their bodies. Many amongst the Elders believed it was the Seeker's very soul that departed his body during this process, a thought that Kor-aviel believed was up for interpretation.

The Weaving could only be performed on the mind of someone the Seeker had already met in the real world. This day only three minds were the target, and as a precautionary measure two Seekers would search out each individual; one entering the dream whilst the other stayed outside should there be a problem. In that case he would enter the dream to assist in the extraction of his colleague's spirit.

Each of the Seeker's spirits turned to look at one another as they rose up into the cave roof. Kor-aviel gazed down at his soulless body, then in a blink they were all gone.

***

The vanguard was made up of more than a hundred of the Northern Arena's best fighters, granted their freedom for their service to the King: warriors whose armour and weaponry were as exotic and varied as the lands that birthed them. Behind them, over one hundred-cavalry flanked by a further one hundred, foot soldiers, all dressed in full ring mail bearing the Emperors own sigil; a silver crossed broadsword and mace.

In the background were the undulating hills known as the Spine. Facing the Northern insurgents was the forest of Blackwood, named after the black barked pine, a rare tree only found in this area, a half-day's march from Stonehaven.

There was no sound. Not wind, not the chinking of armour, nor the sound of man and horse. Nothing.

Maccon found himself floating above the Northern fighters, an undetected spectator moving around at will. The dream seemed real, he didn't question his ability to fly, he just accepted he could.

He found himself moving towards the forest, influenced by a hidden force. On reaching the tree line he began to descend. To his side he heard the flapping of wings. Turning, he was confronted by a black hawk. The bird circled around him, guiding him below the canopy of trees. To his astonishment, the hawk vanished as his feet touched the ground and in its place stood Kor-aviel.

"Am I dreaming this?" Maccon asked the shaman.

"Yes and no. You were dreaming, but what I have shown you is a vision of the danger that is almost upon you."

"How do I know you are not just a figment of my imagination?"

"I take you back, to the morning you and Lord Farroth were to leave Grayspire. We both went for a ride. Do you remember what you saw?"

"I do."

"I showed you, what no other man has seen," Kor-aviel continued.

"The Wolf Prince."

"Yes."

"How are you able to do this?" Maccon asked apologetically, looking around himself.

"This matters not. You must believe all I have shown you as time is short. You must convince your Lord of the danger you have seen here. And prepare as best you can for what is surely coming."

Maccon walked to the edge of the tree line and stepped out into the open field beyond, the Northern invaders were no more than a hundred paces from where he stood. To the man they were motionless, statues of time, frozen by a magic he didn't understand. Cavalrymen, half on, half off their horse's. Foot soldiers bending down to pick up their weapons and others just walking about; all of them caught and frozen in that moment, like detailed figurines carved for some elaborate battle plan.

One after the other they began to dissolve into rivulets of blood, until there wasn't one Northerner left standing. The red arterial streams flowed towards the forest, coming together as one, then separating, reaching out like long bloody fingers to soak the ground around the two figures standing alone. Maccon turned. Kor-aviel was gone. He turned back, the river of blood was gone and as he awoke he knew what he must do.

***

It was a risk he had to take, entering the mind of the Witch could be troublesome at the best of times, but Eleroth knew he faced more than just the powerful will of such a woman; the fear of recognition. They had a history, one that at all costs must stay hidden. This for him was a complete unknown, but because of her connection to Hunter it was a risk he had to take. He was specifically chosen for the task, after Kor-aviel himself, his powers of Weaving were by far the strongest; and as the head Shaman couldn't be in two places at once, it was agreed that he should be the one to enter the dreams of Lamia.

Lamia, like Maccon, found herself floating above the Northern fighters, camped just beyond Blackwood Forest. She swooped and glided amongst the frozen Northerners as a bird on the wing; by her side a Kaila Falcon, its feathers the colour of bronze; the bird spirit of Eleroth's choosing. She followed his lead as the two of them flew towards Stonehaven. They passed over her cottage near Farroth Woods and on to Hunter's place. Here everything changed. The skies around them swirled with darkening storm clouds, and as they approached the streets of the town Lamia saw Hunter and his Wolf, side by side looking down the main street to the Keep beyond; like the Northerners before, frozen mid movement. Then out of nowhere came Hunter's white Hawk.

Eleroth tried his best to ward off the white demon as it attacked from above. This was as he feared. Lamia's sleeping mind was trying to protect itself, and in so doing, was somehow changing the images his Weaving spirit guide had so meticulously created. His spirit Hawk ducked and dived trying desperately to protect itself, and all seemed lost; until out of the swirling darkness his friend appeared.

Aelron could see his friend was in trouble. His spirit-self looked down at Lamia as she slept, lost in her dream. His mind link with Eleroth showed him everything that was happening, and there was nothing left for him to do, he had to Weave his way into Lamia's dream.

The Golden Eagle hit the White Hawk so hard, it sent him spinning uncontrollably towards the ground, but just as it was about to hit and be broken, it disappeared. Aelron, flew next to his friend, the White Dove by his side; this though she couldn't see it herself, was

Lamia's dream spirit. The three of them landed by the fountain in the town square.

Vendors selling their wares, people going about their daily business were again, frozen, like toys of a God child, placed in a town that was made for his amusement.

It was Eleroth who materialised first, followed by Lamia and then Aelron who like the others, was totally bemused by what was happening to them.

"Lamia, please, you must not be alarmed. We are here as friends…. We wish you no harm," Eleroth said, warmly.

"What is happening to me?" she asked, believing her Elder companions posed no threat. "Why are we here?"

"We have entered your dream, so we can show you the danger that is almost upon you and your townfolk. We are aware of the bond you have with Hunter and his Wolf. This is why we chose you. You are in grave danger from another, Hunter is on his way as you sleep. You must awaken, for there is nothing we can do to help you, only warn you of what is to come. You have to survive or all will be lost. You must tell Hunter of what you see here, death comes from the North and it must be stopped."

As the last word fell from his lips the heavens above exploded in thunder, and the rain began to fall. The three spirits started to walk towards the Keep in the distance. Then it happened. The rain turned into torrents of blood. The cobbles under their feet ran slick with it. Black rot ran down the walls of the buildings, the frozen figures occupying the streets were covered in it, as if they were being devoured by some virulent wasting disease. The blood ran like a *river of red* around them, filling the mote around the Keep with the colour of death, its battlements dripping gore like some macabre tapestry.

Lamia could see her Elder companions were as shocked as she, and even in her dream state she felt what was happening now was none of their doing.

"Lamia you must wake up, now. There is a dark power at work here, I can't begin to understand why or how this should be. But it is connected to you and this town, and from what I have seen here, it has something to do with Hunter and the Wolf," Eleroth said. "My spirit grows weak. It is time for my friend and I to leave."

Aelron bowed and concernedly, he disappeared. Eleroth looked deep into Lamia's green eyes, his anguish that he could help no further, reflected therein.

"You must survive. Tell Hunter what you have seen, then seek out the one you call Maccon. He and your Lord have shared part of your dream, but not this," he said, looking around the curtain of blood rain. "This is a warning of the true horrors which threaten us all, a threat written by the Scribes of the Ancients themselves. And in this, you, Hunter and his Wolf have no small part to play. But if any of you should fall this day, all may be lost."

Lamia woke up, her brow wet with sweat, her heart racing, her eyes once again colourless. Outside, the early morning mist was beginning to evaporate, and she heard a sound of footsteps on the porch at the front, she knew who it was, but there was someone else.

***

Agramar awoke from his dream, sweating and bad tempered. He was shown the same images as Maccon, on this occasion, his spirit guide being an oversized black raven. There was no mistaking the identity of the spirit that replaced the bird, it was

Loras; a member of the Elder High Council he met during the signing of the peace treaty many years before. Then as now, he found Loras aloof, condescending and thoroughly obnoxious. But one thing he couldn't question was his integrity.

He ordered one of the two soldiers on guard outside his tent, to wake up and fetch Fraene Caulder to him. The guard reacted immediately.

It wasn't long before he and his commander returned to the King's tent. The guard stayed at the entrance whilst Fraene entered.

"Sire. You wish to speak with me?" he asked, trying his best to shake off the tiredness of a disturbed sleep.

"I do. Please, sit," the King instructed, pointing to a wooden stool not far from where he sat. Fraene obliged, uncertain of what to expect, but certain it would be troublesome being dragged from his bed this early in the morning.

Agramar described in great detail the vision he was shown, and how he was able to authenticate its reliability. Fraene too, remembered this Loras both he and the King met from his dream, and he, like Agramar hadn't liked the Elder; but he believed the story bore a truth, as bizarre as the whole incident might appear.

Agramar, still only half dressed poured himself a goblet of wine offering Fraene the same. But, often after eating some of the meals prepared for him during these times out on the road, he suffered bouts of severe stomach acid, that would often burn the back of his throat. The venison stew from earlier that night caused just such digestive discomfort; prompting his refusal of the King's offering.

"I am fine. Thank you, sire…. What you tell me is troubling. It is a pity we didn't end the reign of this Northern despot when we had the chance. I have always felt we had not heard the last of this degenerate, and here we are."

"I know. I think time, and years of relatively peaceful rule have softened my resolve to revisit the North and finish what the weather and lack of resources stole from us during those Northern Campaigns. And as the years passed, I thought the threat from this Malanon diminished. It would seem I was wrong in this assumption."

Fraene could see the thought troubled his leader deeply, but there was one thing he knew about the King; the man would not make the same mistake twice, and whatever he had planned at this moment it was only the beginning.

"What would you have me do my Lord?"

"Take half the men, those you know to have the fastest horses and return to my brother. Do what you can to help prevent the siege of his Keep. I know, the day we left he sent half his garrison back to their fort a good two days ride from the town. Even if he gets word to them, I fear it will be too late. From what this Loras told me, these Northern raiders are at most only a day's march from the Keep and are already on the move as we speak."

"Are you sure that is wise my Lord? I will not feel easy, leaving you with only half our men to protect you. Would it not be safer, if I took only a handful of them, and left the rest to bolster your protection?"

"No. You must do as I ask…. I am grateful for your concerns, but I am sure I will be quite safe. I would join you myself, but I must get back to the Capital and prepare for what is to follow. So please, chose your men and make haste, and ride as fast as you can. Help my brother."

Fraene didn't try to resist, it would be futile. He excused himself, then set about fulfilling his King's command.

Two of the men he was leaving behind were Omaar and Brelt. The cook didn't resist his Commander's order to protect the King, but Omaar was a different proposition, though still healing from his injuries he wanted to fight.

"I would rather come with you," he spat. "I owe those people my life."

"I know old friend and were the King back in the Capital where he is safe, there is no other I would have by my side. But I will rest easier, knowing you are here protecting our King as you have done so loyally all these years."

Omaar grunted a few times in reluctant acceptance that what Fraene was saying was right. Fraene patted him on the shoulder, leading him back to his tent.

"We will meet again my friend, you will have healed and once again we shall fight side by side," he finished, trying desperately to mask his uncertainty.

Omaar gripped hold of Fraene's arm and locked elbows.

"Be careful, these Northern fucker's can be tricky bastards. Just make sure you and the lads come home?"

"I will do my best," Fraene smiled, before leaving to prepare for his journey to Farroth Keep.

42

TO KILL A SISTER

Maccon couldn't shake the feeling of unease as he opened the rickety old gate to Lamia's cottage. The front door was ajar. Normally, at this time in the morning Kela would be outside playing, with Lamia looking on from her bench under the window, a ritual she had told him she enjoyed from the day the young deer was well enough to do so.

Instead, his only welcome was an eerie silence. Instinct drove his hand to his sword hilt. Cautiously, blade at the ready he approached the door: being left-handed, he moved to the right, placed the tip of his sword against it and slowly pushed it open. His grip tightened on the hilt ready for what might come next; nothing did, the room was empty. Without letting his guard down, he entered the cottage, looking first behind the door, before carefully scanning the rest of the room.

There was no sign that an early morning meal was being prepared; the table was completely clear. The only evidence of any kind of any activity at all, was the pool of milk on the stone floor, spilled from the deer's upturned bowl.

"Where are you?" He whispered to himself, as he looked around the room for any clues that might give answer to his question. Then it hit him. The smell. Subtle, out of place. As his nose became accustomed to it, it got stronger. It was the smell of death: *Loves kiss,* a misleading name given to a rare lethal poison extracted from the skin of the equally rare tree frogs of the Southern Swamplands.

Maccon felt the adrenalin surge through his stomach, aware, that such an exotic poison was only used by assassins of deadly renown to coat the blades of their daggers. The sword in his hand got lighter, reducing greatly any sense of fatigue he might experience in a prolonged engagement. This like the other members of the Order, was part of his gift as a Mage, the other: he slid his hand along the edge of his blade leaving behind a freezing coating of frost, zinging with a sharpness that could penetrate any armour.

It was odd, there was no sign of violence; everything was where it should be. Other than the open door there was no visible evidence to suggest that an intruder had ever been in the place. But the pungent smell that assaulted his nostrils told another story he knew could have dire consequences if ignored. Making his way into the sleeping quarters, he found the same.

"Where are you?" He repeated, in the knowledge that Lamia would never leave the door open when the cottage was unattended. There was only one place on the property he felt she could hide; the tree lined enclosure containing his daughter's grave.

Throwing caution to the wind, he quickly turned and ran outside. The heavens opened; thunder ripped across the skies as if the Gods themselves were warning him of the impending doom. Through the heavy rain he ran to the back of the cottage and on past the vegetable and herb garden. Then he felt it.

***

Lamia woke from her dream, sweating nervously, the warning from the Elder Seeker playing over and over as she dressed herself quickly. Whoever it was coming for her fortunately had not arrived. She threw a cloak over her shoulders and readied to leave.

The fawn was still sleeping when she picked it up; there was no time to prepare any kind of food for either of them. As quickly as her blindness would allow, she rushed through the front door leaving it ajar behind her. The early morning dew that coated the grass had made the wooden porch slippery; in her haste Lamia lost her footing driving one leg across the other. She tumbled quite heavily, catching her forearm on a sharp corner of the bench under the window. The jagged edge of wood tore through her sleeve, then her flesh, gouging a nasty gash just in front of the elbow. But she still held onto the fawn she knew would run off in all the confusion should she let her go.

As painful as her injury was the bench broke her fall, luckily no bones were broken, but the wound began to bleed. She clenched the inside of her lower lip with her teeth and grimaced as the initial shock made way for the pain. Resolute, she pushed herself up using her injured arm, steadied herself, then carefully made her way across the remainder of the porch and out onto the garden path along the side of the cottage.

She felt the change in the weather as she headed through the vegetable patch and on to the circle surrounding her daughter's grave. There was no mistaking the smell of imminent rain. *But better wet than dead,* she thought as she knelt behind a small group of bushes that afforded her a clear view of the garden and the cottage beyond. The fawn was shaking, it had obviously picked up on Lamia's sense of danger.

"There. There now," she whispered caringly. The animal visibly calmed, as her bloodied hand stroked the back of its neck. Now all she could do was wait. Wait and prepare.

***

Aelard Dane had long ago forsaken his birth name for the one given to him by his adopted Northern counterparts, led by the vicious tyrant known to his enemies as Malanon the Merciless. He wore his new name with pride, not for the name itself, but what it suggested; Shadow Hunter, more a title, earned through years of honing talents that had seen him rise in the ranks of killers whose sole purpose was to serve a psychotic leader.

Years of searching had finally born fruit, and now it was time to collect; but first, he had to deal with his sister.

Experience taught him to keep away from the hustle and bustle of the main town, instead he stayed where no one would question his presence; Beggars Nest. He found a Tavern with a one handed Innkeep right in the heart of the cess pool of dark alleys and shanty dwellings. He paid for a bed for the night, to his surprise it was cleaner than he would have imagined. He was offered a woman for the night, but declined, instead he chose to wile away the hours listening to all the local gossip in the bar room down stairs. Being no stranger to such rabid dens of iniquity, it came as no surprise to hear thieves bragging about their nightly raids, or the fence trying to sell such ill gains to anyone ready to part with coin.

Resting back in his chair, he sipped a mouthful of ale, placed his money pouch on the table by his tankard and watched and listened with interest to the pox faced scrawny looking low life on the next table. His ears pricked up at the mention of Hunter. The not unattractive wench caught up in the man's drunken babbling became uncomfortable, nervous even at the mention of Hunter's name. She glanced over to the bar where the one- handed Innkeep was busy plotting something with a small band of cutthroats.

"Better keep yer voice down *Scab*. If Jack 'eres yer talkin' about Hunter, he'll gut yer for sure," she urged.

"I don't get it. I should be goin' with 'em. Cutter was *my* friend. I 'ave a right to kill the fucker that ended his life."

Anyone passing Aelard would never guess he was listening in to the next table's conversation. His eyes looked as though they were closed, but through the tinniest slit between his eyelids he could see all. Not only this, one special ability he had developed over years of training was to isolate peripheral sounds so he could focus his hearing on the target of his choosing. This, with his internal amplification of sound allowed him to listen into conversations even a room away; a very powerful weapon to have in an arsenal of many. From what he could make out, there was some kind of plot afoot to kill this Hunter, and this pox ridden lack wit was more than a little disgruntled at being left out of it.

He could see the girl standing next to this Scab was getting more concerned by the moment, worried about what mindless utterances he was going to blurt out next. It was obvious she wanted to part company with the man but was too nervous to leave him alone. This presented what could prove to be a fruitful opportunity. Aelard noticed the madam of the place had finished her conversation with the Innkeep and his cronies.

Ayla turned; after the talks of Hunter's demise had drawn to an end, she saw the hooded figure at the table by Scab's waving her over. Using her forearms, she hitched up her breasts and pranced over to the stranger; flaunting all of her feminine assets that most men in the place had sampled at one time or another.

"So, what can I do for you my lovely?"

"The girl? He gestured, nodding at the girl talking to Scab. "How much for the night?"

"'till mornin'?"

"Yes."

"She don't come cheap. One o' me best girls. Can teach yer a thing o' two and no mistake, not that a man like you would need it mind yer. All the same you'll find there ain't much she won't do to please such as yer self."

"How much?" He repeated, ignoring the over inflated rhetoric surrounding the whore's seductive charms.

"Ten in silver should cover it. No markin' her mind. You won't be disappointed I can guarantee it."

"Ten it is," he agreed, removing the coin from the money pouch by his drink on the table in-front of him.

Ayla took the money, blew on it and deftly dropped it into the leather purse attached to her belt.

"Sally! Come 'ere girl. Say 'ello to the gentleman."

Sally was thankful for the timely intervention. Even though she disliked Scab, she wouldn't wish him dead from running off his mouth. In her own way she had tried to shut him up, but enough was enough and now she was glad to be rid of him. She cut the conversation short and joined Ayla at the next table.

Aelard could see, as the girl arrived by his side that she was younger than first appearances would suggest; at a guess, maybe seventeen at most, he reckoned. Not unattractive, a bit weighty for his taste maybe, but it mattered not.

"Hello," she said, betraying her inexperience.

Aelard smiled but didn't offer a reply.

"Man's paid for the night. See he isn't disappointed," Ayla winked, failing to mask the underlying threat in her voice should the girl fall short of her demands.

Sally took hold of the stranger's hand, gently coaxing him to follow her. Aelard picked up his money pouch and allowed the girl to guide him over to the stairs, still holding hands.

"Remember. No markin'- 'er. Right?" Ayla shouted, letting all around her know she was still queen of the establishment.

Again, Aelard didn't grace her with an answer, his face a blank canvas lacking any kind of tell-tale expression. Climbing the stairs behind his young host, he was acutely aware that the one handed Innkeep hadn't taken his eyes off him once after stepping through the Tavern door. He knew the man was not one to be trifled with. But being the master deceiver, he'd expected no less from a man whose reputation was feared by all who resided in the Warrens. And there was nothing he had done that would lead this Innkeep into suspecting anything more, than he just wanted the pleasure of this young woman he was following. So, he let the thoughts drop and surrendered himself to a night of welcome pleasure.

Sally led him along the wooden veranda to her room at the end. On entering, it was obvious the space was used for one thing only, the pleasure of others.

It was clean, but the scented sheets couldn't mask the smell of past endeavours, no matter how much she tried. He recognized the oil she used was the bi-product of jasmine. Though, mixed with a cocktail of sweat and men's bodily secretions; to his practiced nostrils it somehow smelt off. But this was a miner sufferance he had to ignore. He followed the young whore to the waiting bed. She pushed him back so he was sat on the edge, then removed her dress to reveal her milk white nakedness. Trying to appear experienced beyond her years she pushed him onto his back and began to undress him. He surrendered willingly, allowing her to believe she was in control. Once he was naked, she straddled him. "Which way do yer want me?" she asked, lacking the finesse that only came from years of practice.

What he wanted, her body couldn't supply; it was just a means to an end, and in its pursuit, he could enjoy the journey. So once again silence followed. But this time he gently took her by the arms and guided her down beside him. Just as she was about to speak, he put his finger to her lips and to her surprise she felt herself uncharacteristically compliant with his request. He explored her, caressed her, allowing her to enjoy him like a wife might a husband or a girl her boyfriend.

After two hours of pleasure, she lay back exhausted, her cheeks glowing with the redness of satisfaction. In her short time as a whore she had never been treated so gently or expertly by a man and it was a whole new feeling she liked. She lay in his arms and allowed his fingers to comb through her damp black hair.

"That was a surprise," she said.

"You have learnt your trade well."

"It is obvious you are no stranger to women of my kind?"

"You sell yourself short. Believe me when I say, you are a dish to be savoured."

"Well. Now we are done with the flattery, what are you really here for?" she asked.

Not expecting such directness from one he deemed inexperienced and non-too bright, he realized there was more to the girl than he gave her credit for.

"Well now, aren't you the bright one," he smiled, leaning over onto his elbow to get a clear look at her face. From the hips down she was covered by the sheet, the rest of her nakedness was in full view. He licked his finger and ran it teasingly around her belly button.

"I admire your bluntness, so I won't insult you with a lie…. That man you were speaking with downstairs, Scab I believe you called him? He mentioned a man who goes by the name of Hunter?"

"Why are you so interested in *him*?"

"A man's curiosity, nothing more. I knew a man by that name and haven't seen him in years," he lied. He turned around, lent over the bed and rummaged through his clothing until he found his money pouch. He grabbed it and turned back to face her.

"Here," he said dropping two more silver into her hand. "Will this help loosen your tongue?"

She looked down at the offering, leaving her hand open. He dropped another two coins into it.

"You drive a hard bargain," he flattered, her half smile confirming the amount was to her liking.

"Listen! I shouldn't be tellin' yer this, but this Hunter your talkin' about killed a few of Jack's friends."

"Who's this Jack?"

"The man who'll skin me alive if 'e finds out I been tellin' yer any of this. The man that runs this place, a merciless cunt if ever there was one," she said unable to hide her hatred for the man. "Anyway, heard tell this Hunter cut them to pieces and now Jack's ready to return the favour."

"Is he now?" Aelard pondered.

Sally was no fool, she could see mischief in the stranger's eyes, and it bothered her.

"You can't go askin' questions about this Hunter. What I tell yer has to stay within these walls. Do yer understand? If Jack gets a sniff of what we are talkin about, he'll feed both of us to the pigs."

"I promise, I won't breathe a word of this to anyone else," he said dropping another two silver onto the pillow by her head.

Something in his tone made her believe him.

"What do you want with 'im anyway?"

"I have a long-standing debt I must see collected. If your friend's downstairs get to him first, I will forfeit the purse that has been years in the coming. Do you know when all this is going to take place?"

"Day after tomorrow. I heard Jack's got somethin' else to attend to first," she said, staring into dark brown eyes; empty like those the dead stare back at you with. But it was too late, the blade slid effortlessly across her neck, the cut so clean that for a moment only the thinnest line of red was visible. Then the tip of the blade severed the jugular; the wound yawned open causing the blood to spray violently upwards. Aelard quickly drew up the sheet to avoid being soaked in red. Emotionlessly, he dressed himself, opened the window and in a blink, was gone.

***

It was early morning, the ground leading up to his sister's cottage was wet with dew. He leaped over the gate, his feet making no noise whatsoever, as if he were treading the very air itself. He moved cautiously towards the open door that was almost beckoning him to enter. One thing experience had taught him, it was foolish to trust in the convenience of luck. From the moment he stepped onto the property, any action from then could only occur by his design.

Once inside it was immediately obvious the place was empty. A spilled bowl of milk was the only visible evidence that his sister had left in a hurry. *She knew I was coming,* he thought as he made to leave.

His heightened sense of hearing picked up the sound of an approaching rider. With gazelle like agility he stepped outside and sprang up onto the thatched roof. Hiding around the side, shadowed by the low-lying sun, he watched as the figure of a man approached the gate. The man drew his sword and carefully made his way to the open door.

Aelard heard the visitor rummaging around inside, but it wasn't long before he saw him exit the door. It began to rain heavily, in a blink he was off the roof and with a dagger in each hand, vanished.

***

Maccon looked down. The dagger was imbedded up to the hilt in his stomach, but his reflexes weren't dulled by the poison whose effects were delayed. His sword came up quick enough to parry the second dagger that would have opened his throat; but when he spun around to deliver the killing blow, his assailant was gone, vanished.

The blood, helped on by the rain ran down his crotch and onto his inner thigh. It wasn't long before he began to lose muscle function, which he knew would quickly turn into full paralysis, suffocation, then death. His legs went first. He dropped to his knees; then as fast as his attacker had vanished, he re-materialized as if from thin air. Maccon bent his head in wait for the killer blow, but it didn't come. He looked up to find the assassin frozen, motionless, his dagger held ready to strike, but stayed by some invisible force. Through the curtain of rain, he could just about make out the figure of Lamia, her hands on her temples, the pain of her exertion etched across her face.

Somehow, she was able to control the killer, Maccon was almost sure of it. The man's face contorted with the pain of trying to free his mind of her grip. But as powerful as she was, Maccon could see she was weakening. He tried to get to his feet; his muscles just would not respond. Now, he could feel the poison's effects stiffen the joints of his arms, and he was all too aware that by the time it reached his neck all would be over. But he was completely impotent to do anything about it.

In his agony, he saw Lamia collapse, the young fawn by her side licking her face like it would a wounded mother. His arms locked up, his breathing became laboured, death wasn't far away, and the assassin showed signs of movement.

***

Hunter's horse ran like the wind, the white froth of exertion gathering around every piece of leather touching its hide. The gate of the cottage in sight, he pulled heavily on the reins and jumped from the saddle before his horse had even come to a stop. He pulled his bow from over his shoulder, leapt over the fence, the Wolf close behind and was about to make for the open door when thunder ripped across the sky. Lightning followed within seconds, lighting up the greyness around the property. Like highlighted statues, Bael saw two figures frozen in the rain; one was kneeling the other standing over him, dagger in hand. Beyond them, almost indistinguishable, was the old woman. Before he could issue a command, the Wolf was already on the move. She passed the two frozen figures to reach Lamia as she collapsed to the ground. Hunter knocked an arrow whilst he was running. As he got closer to the two men, he recognized Maccon. Suddenly the figure standing over him showed signs of movement. There was no time to aim, Bael had to trust in his instincts.

"Hey," he bellowed, the distraction allowing him precious moments to get off the shot. He let the first arrow fly. It hit the assassin just above the right breast bone punching its way out through his back. The impact knocked the killer backwards away from Maccon, but Hunter was shocked that the mage didn't try to move.

Without giving it a second thought he loosed another arrow, but just as it was about to pierce the assassin's face, he vanished.

Bael dropped his bow, drew both swords and rushed towards Maccon; the man was struggling for air, but still he waved Hunter on to aid Lamia instead. He could see the old woman getting back on her feet, so he ignored the mage's request. He took hold of Maccon and laid him down on the muddy, waterlogged ground. The wound was still bleeding through the hole the dagger had made passing through the ringmail shirt. Bael lifted it up to expose the rendered flesh beneath. Bluish branches of poisoned veins spread out around the wound, time was short, both men knew it.

"This is going to hurt. A lot," Bael threatened, removing his own dagger from his belt. He cut deeply; Maccon screamed out in pain. The first cut lengthened the already existing wound, the second passed through its centre to form a bloody cross. The blood ran freely covering his stomach, diluted in the rain. Bael cut away a piece of his own shirt and placed it over the affected area stemming as much blood as he could. In all the excitement, he didn't notice Lamia come up beside him; shaky, but still full of her faculties.

"Quickly! Get him inside," she urged.

Bael picked him off the ground; Maccon had passed out from the pain, but his breathing was less laboured. Once inside the cottage, he laid the mage onto Lamia's bed; she was already grabbing a large jar from a shelf by the door. She tried to remove the cork but was still too weak. Bael took the jar from her, pulled out the cork and gagged as the smell from it assaulted his nostrils.

"Spread it over the wound and the skin around it," she instructed.

He dug his fingers into the mushroom-coloured poultice and scooped out a good handful; but before he could administer it the Wolf brushed past him and began licking the infected area, lapping up the blood like it was water. The saliva seemed to stem the bleeding.

Lamia watched with growing curiosity, remembering what happened when she first brought the fawn into the cottage. With this in mind, even though weak, too weak to conjure anywhere near the same healing energy she did back then, she placed her hands on the wound. Slowly, she felt the warmth begin to increase under them. She concentrated as much as her strength would allow, then once again, it happened. A ball of light appeared beneath her hands, its glow leaking from the gaps between her fingers. First, the angry purple bruising around the cuts began to fade, then the bluish veins started to clear and the cuts themselves were sealed by an invisible bonding agent. It was miraculous.

Maccon opened his eyes, his breathing almost back to normal, but still he was too weak to lift his head.

"You will stay here for the night," Lamia ordered, caringly.

Maccon managed the faintest of smiles, then fell back to sleep.

"Will he be alright?" Bael asked.

Lamia stroked the Wolf, then leant in and kissed Hunter on the cheek.

"He will thanks to you and your companion here…. I am truly grateful," she said, her eyes filled with tears. "I hope one day I will be able to repay the debt I owe you."

"It is payment enough to see you both still amongst the living," he replied, affectionately.

Then Maccon coughed, choked for air, his chest heaved once; and quietly he died.

43

AN INJUSTICE-SERVED

Toran and his gang sat around the barrel tables outside the dockside Inn, drinking mugs of the local ale, watching Jack'and's crew bringing ashore their cargo of contraband hides and crates of exotic weapons off one of his clippers. The Lobster Pot was now the drinking hole of choice for Toran and his thugs. After hearing what chain of events saving Hunter's life had triggered, they thought it wise to give the Severed Hand a wide birth.

Toran liked hanging around the docks, there was a buzz of activity about the place, a constant movement of people and goods that seemed never to abate, day or night. It was just nice to relax, sit back, feet on barrel with drink in hand and just people watch. But more importantly, observe what curios those people were smuggling into the Warrens. It was his way of keeping tabs on Jack and his Empire's nefarious activities. He had learned through a hard life in the Nest that knowledge was power and that it paid to stay ahead of the competition in a place where one man was a King among thieves.

He slid his foot off the barrel, sipped the last of his drink and ordered Jed one of his cohorts to get him another. The rest of them dragged two of the tables over to his, while Toran in an attempt to avoid unnecessary attention, quietly placed the nights takings on them.

Earlier that evening they had broken into a High Lord's house on the outskirts of town after hearing that the family were away visiting relatives in Newport, leaving only four servants behind to look after the place. Masked, and armed to the teeth, they terrified the servants, who offered no resistance at all, then tied them up and pilfered the place at their leisure. All in all, a good night's work.

Amongst the items on the tables were jewellery, household silver, some kind of ceremonial dagger, which Toran had earmarked for himself and a pair of women's cream silk pantalets.

"Whoa! What the fuck are these, you little pervert," Garret, Toran's second laughed, digging the youngest of the group in the ribs.

"So?" Will replied indignantly, grabbing the frilly item and stuffing it into his pocket, not the least embarrassed.

"What the fuck Will, yer not turnin' into a girl now are yer?" The chubbiest of the gang gibed.

"Fuck you! Nobby."

"Alright, that's enough," Toran intervened, relieving the tension slightly. But he couldn't resist the temptation. "So, you'll be changin' yer shit stained unders for those little beauties, aye?"

Just for a moment it looked as though Will was going to blow a blood vessel, but of the group he was the consummate fool; his face changed and instead he stood up, removed the panties from his pocket and paraded around the barrels, shamelessly flaunting his inner female. Some of the other patrons sitting at barrels close by looked on in amusement whilst others mumbled obscenities under their breath.

Toran and his group had come to terms long ago with Will's obvious penchant for partners of the same sex. The lad had never tried it on with any of them, and kept it all low key, offering no offence to his burly friends. And by the time they had realized his sexual preference he had already become a valuable member of the gang.

Jed returned with Toran's drink wondering what all the laughter was about, until he saw Will prancing around holding a pair of women's underpants in front of his nether regions. He could see his young friend was drunk and left him to it; he handed Toran the drink and sat back down next to him.

"We're goin' to have trouble fencin' this lot, now Jack's on the war path," he said, glancing at the takings on the tables. But as the last word fell from his lips Jack appeared from around the corner with at least a dozen of his hardened henchmen.

Toran sprang to his feet, the rest of his group following his lead. They all knew why Jack was there; they just misjudged the inevitability of it would come so soon. The door of the Inn slammed shut behind them, it was a setup.

Axel, the most insular and moody of Toran's gang backed away from the rest his eyes giving away his betrayal. Men at the surrounding tables did the same, not wishing to get embroiled in what was to follow.

Toran's realization came too late; the nails of Jack's club Blood Bane ripped part of Will's head away as he brought it down with a tremendous, violent blow. The lad died instantly. Toran fended off an axe to the face and buried his dagger into his attacker's heart. Quickly he turned as another of Jack's men rushed him swinging a short sword, he dodged the blow and slit the man's throat, then he felt a pressure in his side. He winced as the pain registered; the sword had gone clean through. He could feel the blade being slowly withdrawn every inch of its exit causing excruciating pain. He just had enough strength to turn, parry a killing blow to his head and ram his dagger into the thug's eye. The scene was carnage. Toran fought to stay conscious, only to see his friends dying brutal deaths, one after the other. He knew if he tried to keep up the fight he would die. There was nothing to be done for his friends, so in the confusion he slipped away. Unfortunately, not without being spotted.

He reached a back alley only to find his assailant closing in on him. In his attempt to escape, he hadn't had time to think about the pain, but that was changing. He could feel the blood running down the front and back of his left leg and with that reality came the pain; he winced and slipped into the shadows behind the corner of a deserted broken-down shanty dwelling. He drew the stolen dagger from his belt; Jack's henchman appeared from around the corner. Mustering every ounce of his remaining strength Toran rammed it home. The man dropped to his knees gurgling as his lungs filled with his own blood. Toran quickly pulled the blade from his attacker's chest leaving him to die a slow agonizing death. There was only one place he could think of going in his present state; a thought that surprised even him. But he could think of no one else and time was running out as quickly as the blood ran from his wound.

***

Meanwhile, Jack ordered his crew to remove the bodies from in-front of the Inn. *The pigs'll be well fed this night, and the rest of the week looking at this lot*, he thought without remorse. Axel approached him with a confidence born of being accepted into the fold. Jack could see the full purse he'd used to bribe the man was still attached to his belt; he looked up and smiled.

"What can I say? Yer held up your end of the bargain. So, I decided to give yer a bonus for yer troubles," he said, giving the nod to his man standing behind Axel. The blade opened his throat, his eyes bulging with shock he fell forward. Jack grabbed him with his huge hand, holding him in front of his face.

"Did yer really think I'd let a slimy little low life like you join my crew, yer dumb fuck," he snarled, before letting him drop to the ground, dead.

Jack got his men to remove the body and put it with the rest on the back of a small horse drawn cart that now approached. He made his own way back to the Severed Hand with only one thing on his mind. Hunter. But that would have to wait till the next day. For now he wished for nothing more than a stiff drink and to have Ayla his madam whore, de-stress him in her own inimitable way.

44

THE DELIVERY – KILLER'S GOOD FORTUNE

Kaleb and his son Sam, with the help of a couple of farm hands placed the Keep's order on the back of the wagon.

"Check we have everything, son. I'll just say bye to yer ma, an' we'll be off."

"Will do," Sam said, smiling. He made sure the six large barrels were tight and secure, then took an apple from one of them and sat on the edge of the wagon to wait for his father.

One of the helpers, a strong freckly faced lad tapped the toe of Sam's boot.

"Give that Cailean a kiss from me when yer see 'er," he winked.

"I'll see what I can do Tom."

"Bit too skinny for my likin', prefer 'em to have some meat on their bones. Somethin' yer can really get hold of," the other lad added.

"You'd be s' lucky Byrnie boy. With a face like that you'd be lucky to get a kiss-off Sam's prize sow," Tom joked, running to the other side of the wagon, Byrne hot on his tail.

Sam jumped down off the back, threw his apple core into the field of cauliflowers close by and climbed onto the seat up front. He placed two fingers under his tongue and gave one mighty whistle. His two friends stopped wrestling one another and looked up as Kaleb stepped out of the farmhouse door, his wife close behind.

"Look at those two, they're at it again," he said, as she kissed him on the lips.

"Leave 'em be. They've been workin' hard all mornin', the lads are just havin' a bit of fun. Anyway, it's nice to see it isn't all about work 'round here. Bit of fun now an' then, hurts no one."

Kaleb returned the kiss, ignored her comments and headed back to the wagon.

"You two. No work to do I see," he shouted sarcastically. "Tom, go an' clean out the stables, and don't finish 'till you can eat off the floor. Byrne, you've really touched lucky, you can clean out the pig sty and give them some fresh feed."

Both lads got up off the ground, mumbled something to each other, not loud enough for Kaleb to hear and with shoulders dropped, left to do said chores.

"Everything ready son?"

"It is father. Two barrels of apples, two of potatoes and two of cabbages and carrots."

"All secure?"

"They are."

"Good. Then let us be off then," Kaleb said, climbing onto the bench seat next to his son. He let Sam take the reins of the two shire horses pulling the wagon; at the speed they were traveling it would take about half a day to reach Stonehaven. He was eager to make his delivery, spend as little time as was necessary and get back to the farm ready to welcome in the newcomer: a calf from pregnant Betsy one of his prize heifers.

***

Two hundred Northerners were less than a mile from Stonehaven. Braxus, a brutal champion of the arena led the fighters given their freedom and promise of a sizable purse on the success of this mission. His men were tasked with the infiltration of Farroth Keep under the cover of night; take out the guards manning the front gates and make sure the draw bridge was down. First, they would head through the forest by the lake, move stealthily along its edge and somehow gain access to the Keep without being spotted. Though at this point nobody was sure how they would achieve this.

Yold, a veteran Captain of the Northern campaigns and battle-hardened fighter who led many successful attacks against Malanon's enemies was ready to move. Night was closing in, the hundred and fifty men he was in charge of were hungry for blood; there was just one problem: Braxus and his fighters. He and his soldiers were no stranger to brutality, but what he witnessed from the pit fighters went far beyond anything he had been party to before. By right of combat, his men would take an ear from the fallen. Some fanatical members of his group would make grotesque necklaces of them and wear them around their necks. But other than what wounds their victims suffered in battle, mutilation was kept to a minimum.

These restraints held no meaning for the others in his party. On entering some of the villages on their journey to Stonehaven, he and his men watched with morbid curiosity as Braxus and his followers casually dismembered the fallen; placing men's genitals in the mouths of severed heads, turning them to look upon whatever bodyparts they could remove and nail to doors like nightmarish sculptures. The women and children did not escape this savagery either. Women found in their dwellings were systematically raped then dealt with in the same manner, whilst those found huddled together in dug outs with their children were slaughtered with arrows as a quick and convenient way of ending the assault.

Yold was himself a master swordsman, he fought with his shield and longsword better than any fighter he had faced to date, but this Braxus was something else. He had watched this savage dispose of his enemies with an almost inhuman brutal efficiency; in his right hand a short sword, in his left a spiked hammer. This pit fighter had already earned his freedom and was elevated to a leader of Malanon's free fighters by the King himself, with a sizable chunk of land and dowry to go with it. This was the only reason Yold had any sway over the man at all; though, the large pay-out promised after success of this mission did help considerably in the matter.

The order of attack hadn't exactly been agreed upon by both Captains. Braxus wanted the glory, Yold just wanted a successful result and allowed the pit fighters the privilege of laying siege to the Keep; by far the most dangerous of the planned assaults. He would lead his men through the town, taking out as many of the inhabitants as they could to prevent any capable of brandishing a weapon from supporting the attack on the Keep. He believed this task far easier as most of his targets would be sleeping.

The time was almost nigh, the skies were already darkening as the full moon cast its silvery glow across the forest ahead of them; this wasn't a night for horses, they would be left in the hands of a dozen of the youngest soldiers. Yold readied to give the order to begin the assault, unclear on how Braxus intended to gain access to the Keep without raising the alarm. Then as if the Gods themselves had sent the solution, the wagon appeared down the road.

***

Kaleb slept for most of the journey, the work on the farm had been particularly gruelling that day, taking its toll on his weary bones. Sam nudged him awake.

"Father! Father, wake up."

Kaleb snorted a few times and awoke with a start; blinking his eyes to clear the sleep in them.

"What is it son?"

"Look! Ahead of us."

Kaleb stared in disbelief. He saw at least two hundred armed fighters camped just beyond Farroth Woods. He felt sick as the reality of his predicament became frighteningly clear and the realization that it was too late to do anything about it.

"Son. Run!" he shouted, as a dozen or so riders headed their way.

"But father? I can't leave you here."

"There isn't time, please? Run," Kaleb pleaded, before he saw an arrow punch through his son's neck. "No, oo." Everything around him seemed to slow, he grabbed for Sam as he started to fall, then another arrow hit his son in the chest. There was nothing left to do but fight for his life. In desperation he jumped down from the wagon unsheathed the short sword he carried on journeys like this and readied to face his death. It came quick as the closest rider passed him, cutting off his head with one clean swing of his broad sword.

The Northerner, with bloody sword in hand jumped from his horse, handed the reins to one of the other riders and climbed onto the wagon. Then, leaving the two bodies where they fell the raiders returned to their group.

***

It didn't take a genius to work out what the plan was, never the less Yold took charge, leaving nothing to chance. He chose to speak with Braxus alone first, letting him deal with his own men. But Braxus was no fool.

"Opportunity favours us this day, does it not?" he said, before Yold could speak.

"It does. It appears we have the means for you to enter the Keep unseen."

"I will put a man in each barrel and have two upfront with the horses," Braxus interrupted, not wishing to be outshone in front of his men.

So as not to steal the man's thunder Yold measured his response.

"That would seem the best course of action. Then so be it."

Braxus ordered two of his men to return to the place where the owner of the wagon and his son were killed. They were to remove the victims' clothes and bring them back.

It didn't take long; the two fighters arrived back with every piece of clothing, leaving the farmer and his son in just their underwear. Braxus chose two men he trusted of similar size to the victims, and got them to put on the bloodied garments. Under cover of darkness and the dim torch light at the Keeps entrance, he believed the stains would not be visible. Then he ordered the six barrels emptied. When that was done, he got six of his smallest fighters to climb into them before placing the fruit and vegetables over the top of each man, effectively obscuring them from view. Now they were ready.

Yold in the meantime was busy preparing his own men for the assault. He could see the Pit fighters were finished and in position. He readied to give the order to advance, only to find Braxus and his group already on the move. He kept his contempt for the pit fighters hidden from his own soldiers; this was neither the time nor the place to show even the slightest sign of weakness in his leadership. Inwardly, as he watched those fifty savages head off, he hoped most would see an unfortunate end, leaving him and his men to make the deciding assault.

There was no need to speak, he had already briefed his men earlier that evening. He picked up his shield and began to bang it with his sword, a battle ritual that raised moral and got the adrenalin pumping; his men did the same. And now they were on the move, filtering through the forest like an army of ants.

45
A DESTINY UNFORSEEN

The Temple possesses a natural force that helps the twelve Knights of its order become mind collective when summoning the power of the Shard. None can explain its origin. Maccon believed it was an intangible, invisible creation of their combined minds, held in some kind of stasis until called upon by a magic permeating from the Holy grounds themselves. All the members were inexplicably bound to this force and when the balance was altered each Knight could feel it. And by definition, each one at that very moment knew something was terribly wrong.

Cirius crossed quickly past the alter and entered the circular dome covered annex housing the Shard. All his fellow Knights were stood at their places around the black crystal, all except their leader, Maccon. Cirius rushed over to join them, he felt sick, as if he had suffered a great loss. He could see by the look on everyone else's face, they too felt the same. Being the youngest, the experience was something new, strange, filled with uncertainty, its intensity unpredictable and different for each member. On reaching his place by the Shard he stopped, and before placing his hands on the runes infront of him he looked to Arbar, his eyes wanting.

"Where is Maccon? Why is he not here with us?" He asked, almost afraid to receive the answer.

Arbar being the oldest, had only ever felt this level of change in the balance once before; when Osias passed away leaving the Order leaderless. The question was the same for all of them, and there was only one way they were going to find an answer.

"I'm not sure, but I mean to find out. This is the reason I summoned this meeting. All of us are aware are we not? That something profoundly troubling has occurred, and Maccon's absence cannot be rationalized as just mere coincidence."

One by one they all placed their hands on the Alter's runic inlays. It only took a short time before their minds linked and the Shard hummed into life. The knights focused on the images as they materialized. What they saw left them speechless, numb, with the spiralling sense of loss that follows the death of a loved one. And in a faraway land an unsuspecting mute son of a Smithy felt a deep sense of loss without ever understanding its origin.

***

Cailean thought it would be nice to show Lia around the Keep's inner grounds, allowing Korey, the girl's new-found boyfriend and self-appointed protector to join them. The wind made the weather changeable, the darkening grey clouds blowing across the sky as quickly as the white ones left it. She felt the first spot of rain on her outstretched hand and decided to call it a day. There was just one more place she wanted to take them. In truth it was more for Korey than Lia as reward for the way he kept at her side the whole time, taking Lia's hand when she would allow it.

They passed through the kitchens; Cailean took a couple of freshly baked tarts, handing one to each of her young followers. By the time they entered the weapon training area where her father practiced daily, all that remained of the freshly baked fare was the fragments of jam and pastry waiting to be wiped from their lips. Luckily, Lord Farroth was preoccupied. He was in the stables taking delivery of his black stallion, a horse he had just purchased to stud his prize mares.

The three of them stepped out into the training yard, the rain now a fine drizzle. Korey wiped his lips clean on his shirt sleeve, his face a picture of excitement, Lia not so much, but she went along with it for his sake. He looked around at the racks of different weapons. Swords, maces, spears, flails, just about every weapon you could think of were on display. He ran over to the swords, his favourite, like many boys of his age he imagined himself as a Knight, sword and shield in hand.

"Can I?" He asked pointing to a short sword that was just about small enough for him to handle.

"Not that one," she said. "When you are a bit older maybe. Before then you will need a lot of practice." She was touched by his restrained disappointment. Lia shook her head in a beyond her year's kind of way, as if to say *boys*.

"These are the practice swords we all use when learning the ways of the blade. Here try this one." His smile returned. Like any lad with an ounce of adventure in him he began whacking the practice dummy with it, swinging at the wood and straw for all he was worth.

"I tell you what. You take the sword, and in your spare time, practice with it."

His face lit up. Even Lia was happy; though she could never quite fathom out why it was that boys were so obsessed with toys of violence, even at such a tender age.

"Can I keep it, can I?" He replied excitedly.

"The sword is yours to keep. But you must promise me, you will never hurt anyone with it. Promise?"

"I promise miss."

"Good. Now we must get you back before my father returns. I fear he would not take kindly to me giving away one of his practice swords." As she turned to exit through the stone archway leading to the pigeon house and the Temple grounds beyond, she heard her father's voice.

"Quickly," she urged, grabbing Korey by the hand. "This way. We mustn't let father see you." She led them to a wooden door further along the wall, which opened up to a field of grape vines the Keep used to make local wine. It was a longer way around, but at least the boy would get back to the house undetected.

Cailean let Lia accompany Korey, allowing her to quickly return to the archway to see if she could pick up on what her father was saying. She hid behind a large palm tree on the Temple side of the arch. She recognized Arbar immediately, his whole demeanour an uncharacteristic one of sorrow and anguish. She could hear clearly what was being discussed and when it became obvious the conversation was about Maccon, she couldn't contain herself: she stepped out into the open her face ashen.

"What do you mean, Maccon is dead?" She stammered in disbelief. "He can't be. You must be mistaken." It was obvious from her father's reaction that Arbar was not mistaken, and for the first time she saw true grief in her father's eyes.

"I am soo sorry Lady Cailean. I know you loved him dearly, as did we all. Truly, I don't want to believe it myself, but the Shard never lies, it revealed all…."

Lord Farroth waved him to finish, believing it only right that he should tell his daughter what happened to their dear friend.

"It would appear that Maccon was trying to protect some woman, who lived in a cottage by the woods. An assassin's blade saw an end to his life…." Before he could utter another word Cailean's lip began to quiver, then she burst into floods of tears. Her body shook and to his surprise she fell against his chest. For a brief moment he just stood there, uncertain what to do next, then slowly his arms encircled her and drew her tight against him and for the first time in their turbulent relationship his eyes filled with tears.

***

Cirius couldn't get to the cottage quick enough; Maccon had become the surrogate father he always wanted. Unlike his blood father who retired from the Order years before and was in no uncertain terms, a bastard.

With his horse at full stretch, Dorodir, Osor, Falon, Hengar and Lonin found it difficult keeping up with him.

They were all chosen, after Arbar had assumed command and though every member of the Order had volunteered he felt that some should stay back and man the Temple. Chosen or not Cirius would have gone anyway, so there was never any doubt in Arbar's mind that he would be part of the group.

Bael heard the thunder of hooves as several riders pulled to a halt by the cottage gate. He could see Lamia was too grief stricken to notice the arrival of their unexpected visitors. He left her crying inconsolably by the ashen face of Maccon whose body he had carried into the cottage, placing it onto the table in the hope that by some miracle they could save him. But the secondary poison which the killer had piggy backed onto the back of the primary one had done its job well. The leader of the Order never stood a chance, his heart just stopped.

It was still raining heavily when the riders came to a halt, their horses ridden so hard that water vapour steamed off their hides like water on smouldering embers. Cirius was first to jump down from the saddle, leaving his boots ankle deep in mud. He was half way down the path before his comrades did the same.

Bael stepped out onto the porch, swords drawn, just in case the killer had returned. He was relieved to find such cautionary tactics unnecessary. He instantly recognized the young Knight and his friends as they approached the cottage. Their mood was sombre. No one spoke. Cirius was first through the open door, the rest followed, only Bael and Dorodir chose to stay behind.

"I am sorry about your friend, he was a good man," Bael said, respectfully.

"Maccon was the best of us. I cannot believe he is no longer with us," Dorodir replied thoughtfully.

"I did all I could. Sadly, it wasn't enough to save his life."

"No one could have asked for more and I thank you for that. But before I go in there, tell me what killed him? For, what we saw through the Shard led us to believe he would live."

"As did I. But the killer's blade carried poison. We treated the wound and thought we had the better of it, and as you saw he looked to recover. What we didn't know was, there was a second poison carried on the back of the one we treated him for. It would seem the steps we took to save him were what actually killed him. A rare poison indeed. Then just as he looked to improve, his heart stopped."

Dorodir was at first surprised by Bael's apparent knowledge of such things, until his thoughts took him back to that time on the Emperor Road when he witnessed the man play no small part in saving the King's life. Though on that occasion the Wolf had been by his side and like him the beast showed extraordinary powers of healing. Sadly, on this occasion the animal arrived too late. Had it been there, he thought, maybe Maccon would be alive to tell the tale…. He became aware of Bael staring at him as if reading his mind.

"It was the old woman who discovered the second poison, she said it had a distinctive smell which wasn't evident until the first poison was treated, by then it was too late," Bael added. Then, as if to predict the next question he continued. "I wounded the killer, I would have seen him to the afterlife, but he vanished before my blade could find its mark."

"This we saw also. I have never seen anything like it. I would have said it was a trick of the mind, but that we all saw the same would suggest otherwise. I can only think it was a force of darkness. If this is so, I fear we have not seen the last of this assassin."

"All men can die and if our paths cross again I will finish what I started this day."

"I hope you do," Dorodir replied, patting Bael on his shoulder. "I will not forget what you tried to do for my friend, if ever you need my help with anything you only have to ask. Now I must join my friends inside."

The image was almost saintly. Maccon lay outstretched, a lit candle either side of his head with the rest of the order looking down at the body, the flickering light moving shadows across their faces like fragments of emotion whose whole was a deep sense of mourning. Dorodir joined them all in prayer. Bael walked over to the cot bed where Lamia lay sobbing, he removed one of her capes from a hook on the wall and placed it over her shaking body. As his hand brushed over her shoulder she placed her hand on it and squeezed it caringly, acknowledging his kindness. Through the sobs he could hear her mumbling something. He leant over to try and make some sense of it.

"She will never meet her father.... She will never know his love.... He never knew, he never knew," She cried, in a broken whisper.

Bael didn't understand her, but whoever it was she was talking about, the thoughts distressed her beyond reasoning. And through circumstance, the father she mentioned could only be Maccon, he thought, but what did she mean, *she will never meet him*?

It wasn't long before the Knights of the Order had finished their short vigil. The sound of a horse drawn wagon drew closer, breaking the silence in the room. Dorodir organised the removal of Maccon's body. They all lifted him carefully off the table, not a word passing between them. Riayas was waiting for them outside by the gate holding steady the open wagon as his friends placed the body on it. Cirius headed back into the cottage to make sure Lamia was going to be alright, remembering how much Maccon liked the woman.

Dorodir was the last to leave, he stepped outside onto the porch to find Cirius returning.

"I think we have done all we can here," he said to the young Knight.

"I will follow shortly. I just want to make sure she stays safe." Cirius replied.

"So be it. I will see you back at the Temple," he said, understanding his friend's motivation.

On entering the room, Cirius found Bael sword on lap sitting in a chair watching over the old woman, who by now had cried herself to sleep.

"Will she be alright?" He asked, concerned.

"I mean to stay and make sure she is," Bael replied.

"I will go to the tavern and see if Emma can join you here. I know she is very fond of the old woman."

Bael was grateful for the thought. As much as he wanted to stay the night, there were things he had to do back at the lodge and having Emma there would at least temporarily relieve him of such responsibility.

"That is kind of you my friend. I believe Emma will offer welcome comfort."

"Then I will see it done."

With that Cirius excused himself and left. Bael poured himself a mug of homemade wine, then returned to his seat by the bed and waited.

In less than an hour he heard the sound of the Tavern's shire horses clip-clopping their way towards the cottage gate, the wagon's wheels groaning with every stony bump. Quietly, he got to his feet and made his way over to the door. Before he had a chance to open it the hulking figure of Dogran entered, Emma close behind.

"How is she," the burly innkeep asked, concerned.

"She sleeps."

"It is a blessing," Emma added, her face pale from the shock of it all. "Cirius told us everything. In all the years I have known her, she never once led me to believe that she and Maccon were once so close."

"She must have had her reasons. The more I think about it, maybe he was the father of the little one buried out back?" Dogran pondered, compassionately. Emma looked puzzled.

But this was neither the time nor the place for pointless questions, so she let her father continue.

"What better reason not to share such information. Were I in her position I would do just the same, and if our suspicions are true, how sad that after all these years it has come to this," he finished.

Lamia didn't move. She kept her eyes shut as if still asleep and listened to her friends' heartfelt words that once again moved her to tears. Each time Maccon entered her thoughts it felt like her heart was being ripped from her chest. But this thought was haunted by the memory of her daughter, not the one lying in the grave outside, but the one still living in town. The one who deserved to know about her father, a father she would only see in death. With the grief came regret. As wise as she was, whatever excuses she made for such selfish decisions; the error in denying a father a daughter and daughter a father was through circumstance, moot. For now, she had to put such thoughts to one side, even for *her* disciplined mind it was just too much. Instead, she tried to focus on those around her. And in truth, if asked, she couldn't have wished for better company than the three-people sharing the room with her, and in this thought she was beyond grateful. And though Hunter didn't know it, she loved him for the man she knew he was, a man others in the town had been too ignorant or reluctant to recognize. But what neither he nor she realized, the bond that was growing between them had far deeper roots than anyone could imagine.

The cloak covering her began to slide off. Not wanting to appear awake Lamia let it fall to the floor.

Emma saw the cloak flop off the bed; as quietly as she could she took hold of it and gently laid it back over the old woman trying her best not to disturb her. Lamia didn't move, so Emma assumed she was still sleeping. She then turned to face Hunter who was sliding his sword into the scabbard on his back. She was sensitive enough to realize he wanted to leave, and it touched her to see how protective he was towards her old friend.

"We can take it from here," she whispered. "There is no need for the three of us to stay."

"Are you sure? I was ready to stay the night anyway, in case the killer decided to return."

"I'm sure you have things to do. We will make sure she is well looked after, you can be sure of that,"

Dogran added, his feelings in keeping with his daughter's. "Anyway, from what I gather, you wounded this retch. I doubt he will be eager to return."

Bael wasn't at all convinced, so he did something he had never done before.

"Here, take this," he suggested, handing Dogran the larger of the two swords he carried.

Dogran accepted the offer gratefully, never a man to leave anything to chance he nodded his thanks and looked to the blade with the expert eyes of a veteran. Just by holding it he knew how special it was, forged to a perfection even Koval couldn't match and as far as Dogran was concerned, he was the best weapon smith around. He swung it around a few times finding its balance surprisingly perfect for his huge hands.

"Careful father," Emma said in a loud whisper. "There isn't enough room in here for that."

Dogran stopped immediately.

Hunter gave the innkeep a wide birth while he swung the sword about, and made his way over to the bed. Ready to leave, he stood over the old woman for a moment and just stared at her thoughtfully. Emma placed her hand in the middle of his shoulder blades and rubbed his back affectionately.

"You don't need to worry; I promise you she will be fine." She said, aware of a sorrow in him she had never seen before, a vulnerability even. Seeing him like this put a lump in her throat. Without thinking she took hold of his hand, to her surprise he didn't resist. She squeezed it caringly and led him to the open door where her father stood holding it ajar. As they passed through onto the wooden porch outside Dogran gave him a friendly pat on the shoulder and nodded good bye.

Luckily, when Maccon's body was removed, the rain had temporarily subsided. Now the edge of the porch was once again a curtain of water, tiny jewels caught in the light of the lanterns hanging over the door.

"Why don't you stay? At least until the rain stops," Emma suggested.

"I must be getting back, a little water never hurt anyone. I will call in the morning to see how the old woman is doing."

"That would be nice. Lamia, I am sure will be glad to see you," she said, hiding the fact that she too would be glad of his company. "I didn't know Maccon that well but I believe he was a good man who will be sorely missed."

Hunter didn't respond, he just stood there preoccupied, his thoughts lost in the sound of the rain. Instinctively she squeezed his hand tighter.

"I don't pretend to know what you must be feeling right now, what with everything you have been through these past months and now this. I just want you to know, you are not alone. My father and I are here for you, as you have been for us." She turned him round and hugged him so tightly it took her breath away. And though their bodies had never tasted the delights of the other, he was and would always be her first true love.

As if they had a life of their own Bael felt his arms wrap around her and for the briefest of moments he allowed himself the comfort of her embrace. As he held her tight against him she raised her head and wanted to kiss him, a comforting kiss, nothing more, but something stayed the urge. She lowered her chin and cherished the moment. Slowly, he released his grip and eased her backward; he gave her as much of a smile as he could muster, then gently placed her hand in his cupping it affectionately. And for the very first time in all the years they had known each other, she saw in those deep blue windows of the soul, her love returned; a friend's love, but that was enough. Then without uttering another word he disappeared into the rain.

***

Bael made his way along the forest perimeter. Not far from home he heard movement through the trees. Quickly, he drew his sword ready for whatever the shadows were to spew his way. Visibility was hindered by the incessant downpour. It came again, closer this time, crackling, crunching, like twigs crushed underfoot; the sound once again swallowed by unforgiving winds. Muscle, sinew and tendon twitched in nervous anticipation. Crack! His sword came up, then out of the shadows his Wolf came running towards him. Above, he heard the familiar screech of the White Hawk.

Like a sixth sense, he knew something was wrong. The Wolf and Hawk had come to rally support, he trusted their judgement and through the bond they shared an inner voice urged him to return to the cottage. Something terrible was on the move, and whatever this voice was, it warned, should he not heed its message all those he'd left behind there would surely perish. Before he could turn to retrace his tracks the Wolf brushed against him, forcibly pushing him in the direction of the lodge, which was only minutes from where they stood. The Hawk was on the low branch of a nearby tree, its head facing the same direction the Wolf was trying to push him. Bael took pause, then decided to follow his insistent companions who were already on the move.

It was really dark when they entered the rear of the property via the forest path. Even so, Bael could just about make out the figure of a man slumped against the wall by the back door. He drew his sword, but inwardly he knew, had the figure been a threat, both Hawk and

Wolf would already have attacked. Yet experience dictated he should still keep his weapon drawn. Passing by the skinning hut he removed a torch from the iron grate inside its open doorway. The man by the door didn't move a muscle whilst he did this, in fact Bael thought he may well be dead until on closer inspection he discovered otherwise.

He knelt down, lifting the stranger's face into the flickering light. "You?" he whispered, in surprise. "Lia's brother, you saved my life in the Warrens.... But what are you doing here?" Lowering the light, he saw the lad's shirt was soaked in red, his hand still covering the wound. It was obvious he had passed out through loss of blood, but he was still breathing.

Bael lit another torch on the wall by the door and dropped the one he was holding so he could help the injured lad to his feet. As he placed his arm under Toran's arm pit the lad lifted his head; he winced with pain and tried to take his own weight, but his legs gave way. Bael held strong, throwing Toran's arm over his shoulder he led him inside and onto his bed by the far wall. He lifted up the bloodied shirt to inspect the wound; it was deep but not fatal. All this time Bael couldn't shake his growing concern for those he'd left earlier. There was no time to stitch the wound that would have to wait, and who better to do it than Lamia, should she still be alright. He sat Toran up, went over to the table and prepared one of his concoctions filling a small clay bowl with the green milk, then returned to the bedside.

"Here, sip this it will help. I don't have time to explain but we will have to leave. This should help you stay conscious."

Toran was too weak to question anything. He was just grateful to be alive. He sipped the drink until the bowl was empty, fortunately it didn't taste as bad as it looked. The drink contained herbs that helped his body produce adrenalin, Bael called it battle blood and it worked. The colour began to return to Toran's cheeks and though it was only temporary he felt some of his strength return also.

"Thankyou."

Bael nodded acknowledgement of the courtesy but couldn't hide his anxiety to get moving.

"Do you think you can ride?" he asked."

"I think so."

"Good, we can share my horse…. For the moment keep this pressed against your wound, there is something on the cloth that will prevent infection taking hold. All being well, the person we are going to see will do are far better job of stitching you up than I ever could."

Toran took hold of the impregnated cloth and placed it directly over the open cut. At first it stung like crazy making his eyes water in pain, then the flesh began to slowly numb. With difficulty he swung his legs off the bed and shakily stood up.

"I am ready."

"So be it, then we should leave."

46

AND SO, IT BEGINS

The barrel wagon pulled up outside the portcullis, as fortune would have it the gate was still up. One of the two guards manning it stepped forward, the tip of his lance still pointing to the skies.

"It's a little late for makin' deliveries."

"Almost shed a wheel back at the crossroads," one of the Northern drivers, lied.

"Took us a while ter fix it," the one next to him added. The second guard moved towards the wagon.

"Where is Kaleb and 'is son?"

The question caught both Northerners by surprise, but the taller of the two closest to the guards thought quickly.

"One of 'is cows ready to calf. Yer know what 'im an' 'is boy are like… didn't want nothin' leavin' ter chance. Aye?"

"Yeh! Sounds like Kaleb. Goodly sought an' no mistake," the first guard replied. "Come along then, kitchen's 'ill be glad of this lot." The two guards stepped aside allowing the wagon clear passage through the gates. Not far in they came to a halt. A guard was running towards them from the direction of the main tower. The Northerners' slid their hands onto their weapons. But instead of confronting *them* the guard passed the wagon to address the two manning the gate. The raiders relaxed and waited.

"You have to drop the 'cullis and raise the drawbridge. Lord Farroth's orders," the messenger shouted, out of breath.

"Why? What's goin' on?" One of the gatemen asked.

"Not sure. All I know is, 'e wants the gates closed, an' he looks non-too happy 'bout somethin'…. So, you better be gettin' on with it," the messenger said, impatiently.

"Right. We get it. Just askin' that's all. You best be gettin' back, tell 'is Lordship it's done." And when the messenger was out of earshot. "Go on run, yer ignorant fuck. Next time yer speak ter me like that I'll put my boot up yer ass."

The Northerners' waited until the messenger was beyond the cottages and out of sight, then, just as they were both about to shed their cloaks, one of the gate guards pointed his spear towards them.

"Wait! Why would you be carryin' an axe?"

Before he could sound the alarm, a dagger punched through his throat leaving him gurgling on his own blood. The Northerner who threw it was already down off the wagon, his axe ready to strike, but the second guard fell backwards with the other raider's axe sticking out of his chest. They dragged the bodies into the shadows, removed the guards armour and dressed themselves in it.

Arms began to appear; pushing away the vegetables that covered them, each fighter one by one emerged from the barrels to melt into the night.

It wasn't long before all the remaining guards manning the walls close by were dealt with in the same brutal but efficient manner. Two of the Northerners' took charge of the wheel house for the portcullis and drawbridge. Now, all they had to do was wait and that wasn't going to be for long as one of the raiders on the wall gave Braxus and the rest of his men the signal. He waved the wall torch from side to side, then in the distance along the side of the lake small groups of shadow amalgamated as one and slowly that *one* expanding mass of living darkness made its way towards the Keep.

47

CRIMSON RIVER

Fraene led his fifty riders either side of a wagon and its cargo of six large barrels obviously headed in the same direction he was. There was nothing about it to suggest that it carried anything other than the farm produce that bobbled about its open back. The soldiers thundered past without giving it a second glance.

It wasn't long before they reached the edge of town. Fraene led his riders along the outskirts, past Farroth woods and along the lakeside so as not to alarm the town folk unnecessarily. Slowing to a canter they crossed the bridge to the Keep. The guards recognised the King's colours and let them pass unhindered.

The outer walls of the fortress housed a huge area with the main Keep at its centre; their destination. Before reaching it, they passed cottages; homes of staff and workers tasked with the upkeep of the main buildings. It was like passing through a small village, carpenter workshops, gardeners potting sheds there was even a small farm which carried its own limited number of livestock. And finally, the Temple, nestling in its own huge grounds at the rear of the Main Keep, stretching out into the lake beyond. They eventually pulled up alongside the large stables attached to the right wall of the main tower. Fraene jumped from his saddle and ordered the head stable hand to look after the horses. The old man recognized Fraene from his earlier visit and responded immediately. He and several of his young hands tended each mount as its rider stepped to the ground. The Captain asked six of his men to follow him into the tower, leaving the rest to man the front entrance as extra support for the two guards already stationed there.

Lord and Lady Farroth had been made aware of the approaching riders and were already waiting for them in the main hall. As he walked towards them Fraene could see something was terribly wrong. Both the Lord and his wife look troubled, sad even and as he got closer he could see they had both been crying, their reddened eyes a betrayal of a grief suffered. Half a dozen Knights of the Order were present, Cirius and Arbar amongst them, their leader Maccon conspicuous in his absence; all looked concerned about their visitors return.

Lord Farroth stepped forward.

"Why are you here? Surely it is your duty to protect my brother?"

"It is my Lord. But the King insisted we come here to warn you of the grave danger that is almost upon you," Fraene replied, respectfully. "Our orders are to help you fortify the Keep."

"Please, forgive us, my apologies for this cold reception," Ever the level headed, Alloria interrupted. "Would you come and join us?" She gestured to a seat at the head of the long hosting table that the rest of her group were all waiting by. Fraene welcomed the invite; asked his men to join the others outside and then stood rather than sat where suggested, the Knights of the Order doing the same, leaving those that remained to find a seat. Before sitting himself, Lord Farroth ordered one of his guards to head to the gates and have the portcullis dropped and the drawbridge raised as a precautionary measure, until he got to the bottom of his visitors warning.

Time was short, Fraene kept his curiosity under wraps as to the whereabouts of Maccon feeling it best to explain all that happened back on the road with the King. During his explanation Cailean wandered in, she was pale, drawn as if suffering an illness. The Captain paused for a moment and followed the young woman's every step as she sat by her mother. He could see the grief she shouldered and was beginning to think it might have something to do with Maccon. But still he continued.

It wasn't long before the guard returned from delivering his message, he approached the table.

"Sur. The gates are being closed as we speak. The last to enter was a cartload of vegetables ordered by the kitchens," he said, apologising for his untimely interruption.

"Good. Good, then that will be all," Lord Farroth replied, dismissing his guard irritably. "Please Captain, carry on."

In what remained of the explanation, Fraene noticed Cailean didn't look up once and though he had only recently got to know her, it troubled him greatly to see her this way.

Lord Farroth wasn't so much concerned as he was impatient. What with the death of his lifelong friend and now this; a warning born of his brother's night terrors. It was just too much.

"Maccon has just been murdered and now I have to listen to the rantings of my brother's dreams. How can I take such a warning seriously?"

Fraene was shocked. Not by Lord Farroth's reaction to his news, but by what he had just heard regarding the leader of the Order.

"Maccon is dead? What happened?"

"An assassin took his life, poison on his blade," Arbar replied.

"Could this assassin not be party to what I have just told you?"

"I think not." Arbar reflected. "This was no Northern raider, he is something else entirely."

"My thoughts are with you all and with you my lady," he said addressing Cailean directly.

She looked up, then quickly turned away as her eyes began to fill with tears. Fraene, frustrated that his warning wasn't being taken seriously enough addressed Lord Farroth again.

"My Lord, you must listen to me. It is imperative we place your archers on the battlements. Like your Temple's Shard, the Elders have the ability to see what we cannot. This warning I bring you is true."

"Sur? I believe we should act immediately; something is wrong I can feel it. An unknown force is leaving us partially blind to what might be coming. Just before it gave up the death of our friend, we saw but for a fleeting moment, a large group of warriors. The image was so scant we took no notice of it believing it to be a glimpse of the King's return to the Capital. Then, after witnessing the death of Maccon the image was soon forgotten. Now it all makes sense. We must get word to the town folk before it is too late, bring as many as we can inside the Keep walls," Arbar finished.

Without any prompting Cirius took the initiative, telling everyone he would summon the rest of the Order to do just that.

This time Cailean spoke up, fed up of her father's indecision and seemingly constant need to be disagreeable.

"Father we have to move. If what the Captain tells us is true, we have very little time."

"She's right. This is no time for debate," Alloria seconded.

As stubborn as he could be, Lord Farroth couldn't deny the sincerity of the man giving him the news on top of which his wife was more than a little distressed by it. Without further ado, he snapped an order to two of the guards by the door to the hall, ordering them to rally every available archer to the Keep's battlements. Arbar and Cirius left immediately, heading outside towards the Temple. Fraene walked over to Alloria and Cailean, while Lord Farroth was busy organizing his men.

"My Lady, I think it best that you and your daughter retire to your room at the top of the tower, just in case these Northerners breach the walls."

"Do you really think they will?" Alloria asked, nervously.

"Hopefully, no. But it would be foolish to believe it was impossible."

"I can use a sword, I will help," Cailean offered, the urgency of the situation dispelling any sense of grief she had for the death of her dear old friend.

"That would not be wise. These men we face are savages capable of terrible brutality. I urge you both to do as I ask. I will have six of my men stand guard for you and if the worst should happen, I will make sure I am there with them."

"Thankyou Captain, I will not forget your kindness. Come, we must make haste," she urged, taking Cailean by the hand.

At first, she was going to resist, but quickly rethought the action when she saw how distressed her mother was becoming. Reluctantly she succumbed to her mother's calling and followed her up the spiral stairway to the top room of the tower; the six guards promised, right behind. On reaching their destination two guards followed them inside leaving the remaining four to guard outside the door.

Both women felt uncomfortable with their male protectors sharing the same room, offering no privacy other than the small balcony. Alloria stepped outside, taking in a deep lungful of the cool night air. Before joining her, Cailean armed herself with one of the swords her father kept in the weapon rack by the large stone fire place, then headed outside to join her mother on the balcony. They both looked down to the lake, the half-moon breaking through the thickening rain clouds; intervals brief but long enough to highlight a large dark shadow moving towards the Keep.

"They are coming," Cailean said, nervously. "I cannot just sit here waiting. For once in my life allow me to do something to help those who would help us…. Mother, I have to go."

"You mustn't. I need you here with me, you may be able to handle a blade but these are not practice swords you will be facing and the men that weald them are hardened killers. No! Cailean you must stay. Please, I can't lose you, not now, and I fear should you leave this room I will never see you again alive."

Cailean ignored her mother's plea and made for the door. The two guards crossed their spears barring her passage.

"Let me pass," she shouted, her frustration turning to anger.

"We can't my Lady. Until our Captain joins us we are ordered to protect you at all cost, and that means keeping you here. I am sorry," the youngest of the guards apologized.

"You can't keep me prisoner in my own house, I will see you punished for this," she returned angrily.

"I understand, my lady. But I fear my Captain's wrath more than I fear yours."

In sheer frustration she backed away from the door; her mother walked over to her holding out a glass of wine.

"It's a brave thing you offered to do, but I know it is for the best," she said, relieved at the guard's timely intervention. Cailean took the glass, stepped out onto the balcony her mother by her side, and waited. Neither of them noticing the disappearance of the moving shadow by the lake.

***

The Northern fighters liked to attack in specialized groups of eight to ten men, each splinter cell having a sub-leader. After passing through Farroth woods undetected Yold gave each group leader his orders; it was getting late and as planned he hoped most in the town would be to their beds. One by one all the groups separated.

Kobien led his men in the direction of the lake. He was a *hard, unforgiving son of a one-legged whore,* a title only uttered by his men in whispers, for if heard a brutal death would swiftly follow. The first dwelling they came across was a lodge of sorts, not far from the forest edge. Stealthily they entered the grounds. There was a large wooden pen that must have housed a large animal or many small animals, but it was empty. Moving on they passed an open skinning hut; two hunting bows were still hanging from wooden pegs. The biggest of them, a giant of a man the rest called Lofty, booted the door in with one thunderous kick. The place was empty. There was no time for pointless plunder not that there was much to plunder anyway.

Kobien led his group onward towards the next property on route to the lake. It was a cottage. Two lanterns were still lit, casting unwanted light onto the wooden porch at the front. One of the raiders began opening the small iron gate at the end of the pathway, its rusty hinges resisting with a chorus of creaks and groans. Kobien grabbed his arm, stopping the man in his tracks. He gestured they all climb over the small hedges surrounding the gardens. Keeping to the shadows they made their way to the porch. Lofty stepped forward and booted open the door. But this time waiting sword in hand was a big man equal in size to the brute who destroyed the door; to his right a smaller man armed with a dagger in each hand, struggling to stay on his feet protecting a doorway to the back room.

Dogran gave out a mighty war cry and charged the huge intruder. The savage was quick, bringing down his mace with such power it should have shattered the parrying sword, but the blade held true. Another raider entered the room blindsiding Dogran and burying his sword into the inkeep's side. Before he could retaliate the attacker fell dead, a dagger in his face. Toran dropped to one knee dizzy from the exertion of the throw.

Emma and Lamia watched from the relative safety of the sleeping quarters as Bael's plan unfolded. Dogran was forced backwards towards them as the brute he faced kicked him in the chest. Emma jumped to her feet, she could see her father was winded; she launched herself at the raider landing on his back, her only weapon her teeth. She bit deeply into the man's neck as he tried desperately to shake her off. Dogran ignored the pain; fuelled by the danger facing his daughter he rammed the sword home, the blade rising up through the stomach and into the man's heart. He fell to the ground with an almighty thud, Emma still locked around his neck. As he hit the floor face first, Emma released her grip and spat out the piece of his neck she still gripped tightly between her teeth. Dogran put his arm around her leading her into the back room with Lamia where she gagged from the taste of rubbed metal that came from swallowing the raider's blood. He then turned around and lifted Toran to his feet, helping him into the back room with the women. Without uttering a word, he left the three of them to join in the fighting he could hear coming from the porch. His wound was painful but he had suffered far worse during the Northern campaigns and thought nothing more of it. He had to help Hunter at all costs.

***

Jack ordered his men to spread out. Never one to underestimate the target he approached Hunter's lodge with experienced caution. Four of his gang carried light crossbows made for quick loading and accurate at close quarters, lethal in situations such as these. Each man a tested marksman notching more than a hundred kills between them in the past year alone. But their victims were men and women who more often than not came to a violent end from a bolt in the back; a Dire wolf was a completely different proposition and it found each marksman nervously stoking the trigger with fingers slick with sweat.

Jack made it his duty to collate as much information as he could before making a raid like this: the stories of Hunter and his Wolf he believed to be exaggerated ramblings of drunken fools who loved to embellish an otherwise boring story. That was until he witnessed the aftermath of the Justice Hunter meted out on Cutter and his crew. He could feel the tension amongst his men; his primary target was a man to be reckoned with, of that there was no doubt. But it was the Wolf that filled them with anxiety as their formation took the shape of a crescent across the grounds.

"If that wolf so much as sticks its nose out, kill the fucker," Jack ordered the four marksmen.

They acknowledged the command, nervously looking side to side for any sign of movement. Jack, brave as he was, was no fool. He let his other eight men armed with sword, dagger and axe move ahead of him towards the open back door. *Something isn't right,* Jack thought, *if that wolf and hawk of his were here they would have attacked by now.*

The place was in total darkness. The animal pen was empty and other than the wind, not a sound could be heard. The closer they got to the door the more it became obvious the place was deserted. *Others must have been here*, Jack thought as he stepped in muddy footprints left by the Northerners; at least half a dozen men he reckoned from the evidence.

As a cautionary move, he pointed to the door with the head of his club Blood Bane. The two men closest eased it wider and then rushed in. As suspected the place was empty. One of the intruders, an ugly brute missing all his front teeth stepped back into the open doorway and waved the all clear. Before following his men inside, Jack gave those with the crossbows their orders.

"You two, over there," he said pointing to an open area by the skinning hut. "You over here by the door. Stay sharp. No tellin' when they'll be back."

After a quick search of the place Jack decided it wasn't worth hanging around, it was clear Hunter hadn't been there all day. But he didn't just want to head back to the Tavern, his men were expecting the bonus promised on termination of target and Jack knew all too well it wasn't fear alone that bought their loyalty. He pondered the situation for a moment uncertain of what to do next, then Scyler stepped forward.

"Looks like someone wants the fucker as bad as you do," he said, looking around at the muddy footprints.

"It's strange, an' that's for sure," Jack puzzled.

"Anyway, I think I know where he'll be," Scyler lisped, through the gaping hole where his teeth should have been.

"Where?"

"Up to 'is stones in that cunt as runs town brothel, Vena I think they call 'er. Yeh, Vena."

"I think yer right," the man next to him, chirped up. "I've 'eard she gives herself to no other. Loves the fucker, me cousin tells me."

"Cousin?" Jack looked surprised. "Are you sure about this?"

"Sure, as I be standin' 'ere. Tells me everythin' does Sally. Worked this Vena's place couple of years now. Bedded her a few times me self. Let's her mouth run way with itself, like. But she's never lied to me."

"Then we should pay this Vena a visit," Jack came back.

The gang moved quickly through the myriad of alleyways that made up the Warrens. Eventually, they arrived at one of the three roads that lead to the high ground and the town beyond. It was the central of the three that zig-zagged its way up the steep incline to an alleyway not far from the brothel. The streets were quiet. Most in the town would be to their beds. But as a procurer of such fleshy delights Jack was all too aware that women of the night followed no such time limitations.

Standing in the shadows just across the street he watched for any sign of patrons either entering or leaving the place, as the doors would be locked and would only be opened by appointment. The man whose cousin worked there moved to Jack's side.

"I will get Sally to come with us, I wouldn't like to see any harm come to 'er."

"You do that. The rest of yer listen up. When we get in there, Vena is mine. Take what you will and any girl wants to come an' work for me leave unharmed. The rest, do as you will," Jack finished, as a middle-aged man stepped out of the brothel door. Before his female host was able to close it, Jack rushed across the street, caving the man's head in before he knew what was happening. Scyler was quick to grab the whore from behind gagging her mouth shut with his hand. Within seconds the rest of the gang poured through the door and spread through the place like a plague of rats. Jack dragged the dead man's body inside, then all mayhem broke loose.

***

Bael kept himself well hidden on top of the thatched roof as the Northern invaders entered the property. He waited until he saw the Wolf come out from the side of the cottage, then he jumped.

His sword sliced the top of one man's head clean off just above the nose, his boot knocking another to the ground his blade cutting into the man's crotch, severing his main artery. The Wolf took out three more in quick bloody succession, leaving their bodies convulsing as their life blood swirled away in red rivulets to fill muddy footprints by the edge of the porch. Another soldier flanked Bael, raised his hatchet, but before he could bring it down he raised his head to the screech above. He lost both eyes, one to the hawks curling talons the other to its razor-sharp beak. The man dropped to the ground screaming in agony; silenced mercilessly by Bael's dagger to the throat.

Dogran made short work of those who got past the door, until there was only Kobien standing. Slowly he backed his way off the porch, only to find Hunter waiting, the rest of his soldiers' dead or dying where they lay.

Dogran didn't wait for Hunter to make his move, he barged at the Northerner, parrying a killing blow without thinking and thundered a punch into the man's face breaking his nose and leaving several teeth imbedded in his knuckles. The raider hit the ground with his back, spitting blood and teeth in his fight to breath. Dogran raised his sword to end the retches life.

"Wait! We need to know what they are doing here," Hunter shouted.

Dogran reluctantly dropped his sword arm, picking the man off the ground with his other and dragged him onto the veranda.

***

Emma couldn't wait any longer, she had to see what was going on outside with her father and Hunter. Lamia, who was already tending to Toran's wound waved her to carry on.

"Go on, I will be alright. This young man needs my help," she said, aware that the only sound coming from the porch was that of Dogran and Bael talking. Emma acknowledged her old friend's well-intentioned command, stepping over a body in the doorway to the mayhem outside. It was like a slaughter house. Bodies lay everywhere. The carnage left her speechless, her father covered in blood was holding the only survivor by the scruff of the neck. She watched as he threw the man to the ground, Hunter's intervention staying his intent and the only reason the man still drew breath. Even though she knew her father was capable of such action it shocked her to see it first-hand. It felt quite surreal. She moved to her father's side and took hold of his arm hugging it tightly as if he might fade away. Maybe it was shock, she didn't know what it was that held her there as Hunter stepped over the injured raider and drove his sword, mercilessly twisting it into the man's shoulder.

The words that were spoken didn't register, they floated about her head as indistinguishable sounds, dreamlike, echoing as if she was stood in an empty hall. Her legs went weak, the air passing through her nostrils smelt strangely off; suddenly she felt faint. When Hunter placed his blade to the soldier's crotch it was too much.

Dogran felt her legs give way slightly and could see her fight back the bile as her face turned ashen. Without another thought he led her back into the cottage where Lamia was tending to the young man's wound.

"What happened?" Lamia asked, tying up the last stitch of Toran's wound.

"She's a little shaken up. Not something a woman should have to see out there." He sat Emma down next to the fire and wiped her wet forehead

"I feel sick."

"It's alright my sweet. You just sit here and rest," Dogran whispered, running his finger down her wet cheek. "I must return to Hunter."

"Do what must be done," Lamia intervened. "There is nothing for you to do in here. I will look after Emma," she added, placing a damp cloth on her forehead.

"Are you sure?"

"I am fine, father. Go! I think Hunter might need you more than we do."

Dogran squeezed his daughter's hand and dragged the body blocking the doorway outside with the others.

***

Bael was too busy trying to extract what information he could from the man lying prone between his legs to notice Emma join them on the porch. He placed his foot on the soldier's chest and pressed down heavily, pinning him to the floor.

"Why did you attack this place? What would you have to gain killing a defenceless old woman?" He pressed, unforgivingly.

Kobien lifted the back of his head up and spat blood and phlegm over Hunter's leg. In response Bael rammed his sword into the man's shoulder and twisted it mercilessly, wiping away the oddly distorted grin that curled his lips.

"Fuck you. Fuck all o' yer," Kobien returned.

Hunter showed no sign of emotion he just slid the blade effortlessly through the man's side. The Northerner screamed out in agony.

"I will ask you again. Why are you here?"

Kobien repeated his last response, this time spitting blood over Hunter's boot.

"I will ask you one last time, then you will lose whatever hangs down 'ere," he gestured, prodding the intruder's crotch with his blade. This move caused a shuffling behind him, throwing a quick sideward glance he saw Dogran step into the cottage with Emma, her face the color of chalk.

Calling Hunter's bluff Kobien remained defiant, that was until his britches were sliced open exposing his genitals.

"Alright. Alright. Enough. It is too late anyway."

Unseen, Dogran returned. Incensed by the Northerner's arrogance he stamped down hard on his extended foot to the sickening crack of surrendering bone as it broke at an odd angle. Koban writhed around in agony.

"Lie and I break the other one, you fuck" Dogran threatened,

"No more. No more," Kobien begged, raising his hands in pursuit of a mercy not promised. "Malanon wants the Farroths dead, all of 'em. Braxus and the mad bastards followin' 'im should already be at the Keep."

"Braxus? Who is he?" Bael asked coldly.

A thin line of blood ran between Kobien's lips, curling into a menstrual like grin.

"You will soon find out."

The blade of Bael's sword sliced into his captive's scrotum, the man turned quickly ashen.

"That doesn't explain why you would attack an old woman in her home," he said menacingly.

"Our orders were to pass through the town as you all slept and kill any we felt might offer resistance."

"Does that include old women and children?" Dogran stepped in.

"I do not kill women and children," he lied. "But Braxus follows no such code. He is a savage I have been forced to work beside," he replied in a tone that sounded almost regretful. Then his features hardened.

"How many are there of you?" Dogran continued.

"Too many. Will likely be all over should yer make it to the Keep."

"How many?" Bael repeated, kicking the broken foot.

"Three hundred. Three hundred," he screamed, the pain overriding any thoughts of defiance.

Hunter stepped off Kobien driving his sword through his heart without even a second thought.

The Wolf had taken to pacing up and down the edge of the property not far from the gate, licking blood off its fur. The Hawk stood sentinel on the apex of the thatched roof its eyes flickering constantly for any sign of movement. Bael followed Dogran's lead, dragging all the fallen onto the grass allowing the rain to wash away some of the gore. Then both men stepped back inside the cottage.

Toran was sitting on the floor whilst Lamia administered a healing ointment to the wound. Emma was back on her feet shaking, a large kitchen knife in her hand trying to look strong. It moved Hunter to see how fragile she looked. He walked over to her, gently removed the knife from her grip and pulled her into his chest, hugging her dearly.

"Remind me never to get on your wrong side," he whispered, staring at her blood covered mouth and chin. The remark gave her cause to smile nervously, but this quickly turned to sobbing, now more from relief than shock. Bael stroked the back of her head running his fingers through her sweat drenched hair. And as she pressed against his chest she wished that all around them would fade away and allow her to stay in his embrace for as long as she could.

In any other situation this move would have seen Dogran animated, but as he watched them both embrace like that it warmed his heart. This was the gentle side of Hunter; Emma had so often tried to convince him about and at last he understood the truth of her words.

Lamia finished dressing Toran's wound. He put his shirt back on turning his attention to the curious little creature sniffing his leg. He bent down to stroke the young fawn but it ran straight to the old woman, nestling shyly in the hem of her skirt. Weak from the wound he sat on the floor by the fire not sure what to say.

Bael released Emma from his arms to have Dogran take his place. He could see the fear in Lamia's eyes as if she knew something else was about to happen.

"We have to leave this place. The town is in grave danger," Lamia said. A sadness washed over her as she turned to face Hunter. "There is someone in the town needs your help. You know who she is. Her life depends on it. There is no time to waste."

Emma knew immediately who she meant and by the look on Hunter's face he was in no doubt who that person was, *but why?* She thought. Why would Lamia show such concern for the mistress of the town brothel.

Dogran returned the sword to its rightful owner. Bael placed it back in its scabbard with the other and addressed the big man directly.

"Lamia is right. I must leave. There are several small boats not far from here by Millers Landing. You should make your way there and take safe haven in the middle of the lake."

"What about you?" Dogran asked.

"I must help those in the town. Get as many to the Keep as can fight."

"Come with us. If you do as you say, you might die," Emma beckoned fearfully.

"If the Keep falls, we all die. No. I must do what I can."

Dogran stayed surprisingly quiet during his daughter's interruption. She thought he would want to go with Hunter, though she would have done all in her power to prevent that from happening. Instead, he seemed to go along with Hunter's suggestion. All she could think was, that hers and Lamia's wellbeing meant more to him at that moment and in part she was right. Only Lamia knew his true intent and understood it completely.

***

Groups of Northern fighters swept through the Town like a wave of death. Most of their victims as expected were asleep when they met their bloody end.

Some of those still awake were lucky enough to escape to the streets, most only to find another group of soldiers waiting for them. The few that made it to the town square gathered together for the comfort in numbers, most in a state of shock, many of them women and children whose husband, boyfriend, and father sacrificed themselves to give them time to escape.

Screams from those on the run gave many residing in the part of town closest to the Keep, enough warning to see whole households out in the street and on the move. Unfortunately, the forge was not one of them.

Koval was working late. He'd seen Tyrna to bed; she had been tired all day, most of which she just moped around in a lethargic state of negativity. It was a blessing that these off days as he liked to call them had become less frequent. They were at their worst whenever she dwelled on thoughts to whereabouts of their son doubting he was still alive. Koval had watched her on days such as this, wander over to Raen's bed and though nothing needed doing to it, she would remove the bedding and reset it on the off chance that he would make a miraculous return. He found days like this extremely taxing and had come to the conclusion that the best course of action was to give her a wide birth and allow her mood to burn itself out.

The embers from the forge still glowed red hot, bathing the area in a dim orange light. Moving past the furnace Koval caught a large pair of metal tongues with his hip sending them clanging to the stone floor. As he bent down to pick them up he heard a shuffling noise coming from the darkness not far from the back door of his house. He knew Tyrna was fast asleep and that nothing good came from an unscheduled visit that late at night. Arming himself with a heavy hammer he knelt down behind the still warm kiln.

The back door was open, he was sure he hadn't left it that way. A shadow moved, then he saw the man and another and another. His heart sank. He couldn't tell whether any of the intruders were already in the house but the thought spurred him into blind action, attacking without any thought for how many he might encounter.

***

The noise outside caused Tyrna to stir from an already troubled sleep, but it was too late. The blade slid across her throat cutting the thinnest of lines. For a second her eyes opened; a young man no older than Raen was stood over her, there was hope in her smile.

"Raen, you are home," she whispered, until the wound yawned open to see hopes illusion fade away in a river of red.

***

Koval caved the head in of one, hitting another of the soldiers so hard in the chest his ribs broke puncturing his lungs leaving the man drowning in his own blood. Then he froze in horror as a young Northerner stepped out of the house with blood all over his ringmail. Koval knew the love of his life was gone. He exploded in overwhelming grief.

"No, ooo! gods no," he screamed, before obliterating the man's face. He mindlessly made for the door. But before he could reach it he heard someone come up behind him. He spun around in time to parry a sword attack that would have struck where neck meets shoulder, only to feel the bludgeoning pain as a mace shattered his arm. All was lost, there were just too many. In desperation, he charged head first at the raider closest to him cannoning him to the ground. Such a move would bring certain death, *but at least,* he thought, he could take one more with him. As they fell together the soldier caught his head on the point of the anvil killing him instantly. Then a shadow stood over him. *Now* he thought *I meet my maker.*

***

Vena drew her dagger. Chaos was abroad. The only sound she could hear outside her room was her girls screaming, men jeering, laughing and killing. Before she could slip the catches on the door it flew open.

Jack burst in brandishing Blood Bane. She made a futile attempt to bury her knife in the intruder's chest but was met with a thundering punch to the stomach. She collapsed to the floor gasping for air and retching to the point of vomiting. Jack stood by her feet and kicked her legs apart.

"Hunter! Where is 'e?" he asked threateningly.

Still gulping for air, she couldn't answer. He kicked her again, this time between her legs. She raised her hand for him to stop. There was no pity in him, but he knew there was no point in knocking the wind out of her completely, so he let her breath.

"Now then, speak. Tell me where this fucker is and it'll all be over. From what I hear you know 'im better'n anyone."

"I don't know where he is," she replied.

He bent down and lifted her to her feet, this time making to strike her across the face.

"My answer is the same, no matter how many times you hit me."

Jack was a great reader of people and could see she was telling the truth.

"Well, no doubt…" Before he could finish the place was filled with the sound of death. Steel on steel, men and women screaming in terror.

He hit Vena so hard she fell to the floor unconscious. There was no time to finish what he had instore for the mistress of the brothel; he stepped out onto the gallery and looked down at the carnage below. Bodies were strewn everywhere. Women bent over furniture some missing limbs; his own men and some they were fighting locked together in death like patrons of the afterlife seeking the pleasure of soulless whores. The screams kept coming; closer and closer. Most of his men dead, Jack moved to the top of the staircase. The Northerners were systematically trying every door, killing those within and by the sound of the screams, raping whenever they could. Two of the raiders spotted him as he descended to the next level, his one overwhelming thought, *better to die fighting.* Blood Bane crushed the face of the first attacker, he swung again to finish the second but his club arced harmlessly past the man's head. The raider lunged at him cutting Jack just below his rib cage, but not deep enough to see his guts spill out. The innkeep booted the soldier in the chest sending him sprawling head over heels down the stairs. He jumped down after him, a mistake realized as his ankle gave way and three other Northern raiders spilled from nearby rooms. He tried to right himself using his club to assist, but now there were six men moving around him ready for the kill. The numbers were too great even for him, but death was never a stranger to a man like him. Resigned to a certain end he spat blood into the face of the nearest raider, a powerfully built man swinging an axe its blade already christened with the blood of his followers. Jack swung Blood Bane, but he missed and, in that instant, resigned himself for a quick and bloody death.

One by one the Northern invaders fell to the ground, dead from a variety of blade wounds a sword master brandishing two swords can inflict. When Jack lifted his head he found Hunter standing over him covered in blood.

The Wolf was elsewhere in the building killing those who remained that Hunter's blades hadn't seen to the afterlife.

Bael wasn't sure whether to finish the job and kill the Innkeep where he knelt, but a singular realization stayed his hand. Instead he grabbed hold of Jack and hauled him back up. The irony of the situation wasn't lost to the gang leader, the man he came here to kill just saved his life and even to a man like him it meant something.

"The debt is paid…. A life for a life." Jack ventured.

"I care not about such matters; we have more pressing concerns to consider. And a common enemy who would see an end to all of us."

"I cannot deny that," Jack replied, looking at the carnage surrounding them.

Bael was about to reply when Vena came storming down the stairs behind them and before Jack realized what was happening, she made to stab him in the back. To her surprise Hunter's hand lashed out to grab hold of the offending arm.

"What are you doing?" she screamed through cut swollen lips. Incensed by the untimely interference.

"We need him," Hunter replied, holding her fast.

"Why? He's a killer. Look at my face, can't you see what the bastard did to me? And my girls, what of them?"

"One day he will pay for what he did here. But, for now we need a killer. A killer who leads other killers."

Jack was completely unperturbed by her outburst. He had twelve men dead and probably most of the whores he had hoped to employ.

"Twice you have saved my life," he exclaimed. "Yer could have finished me yourself, yet yer didn't. It is obvious you have somethin' else in mind?"

Bael removed the dagger from Vena's grip and let her go. Instinctively, she launched herself at Jack, scratching deep bloody furrows down his right cheek, her long fingernails raking through layers of skin. The man didn't so much as flinch. Bael pulled Vena to one side and held her close.

"There will be time for revenge another day," he whispered in her ear. "For now, we need the fighters he can provide."

The Wolf re-joined Bael and the others, her jaws caked in gore.

Vena slowly began to relax; the next thought to enter her mind, her girls or what was left of them. She broke free of Hunter's embrace. He was in no doubt what her next move was going to be and knelt down.

"Go with her, keep her safe," he whispered in the Wolf's ear as Vena went from room to room in the hope of finding survivors.

In the meantime, Bael returned to face Jack who was busy wiping blood off his face.

"How many men can you muster?"

"Why should I muster any?" he pondered.

"Because we both know, if these Northerners take the Keep there'll be no nobles to rob, no spoils to be had. And how long do you think it will be before they kill us all. And they will, make no mistake…. Where will your empire be then? And should you survive you would be a leader of what?"

Jack couldn't argue with Hunter's logic and had already made up his mind anyway. The delayed response was a little bit of theatre, to empower him a little in the naive belief that he was getting some of his control back.

"I should be able to rally fifty, maybe sixty, the rest are out of town," he said, unwilling to elaborate.

"That will have to do. Head for the Keep as soon as you can and pray all is not lost by then. I will round up as many from town as I can then head there myself."

Jack nodded assertively and left, making his way as quickly as he could to the Warrens below.

There was no time to waste, Hunter joined Vena in her search for survivors; and by its end they found only four of her fifteen girls alive, the rest slaughtered like animals. Thankful for small mercies, Vena looked to her friend Neira who was lucky enough to survive: She had taken her attacker in the mouth and bit off his manhood, bashing his skull in with a poker from the fireplace.

All four women hugged one another, each sobbing uncontrollably in support of the other. Bael felt sympathy for all of them but they had to move, and quickly.

"Please, we have to go, others can't be far behind…. Go to the lake, you will find boats at Millers Landing near Farroth Woods. Dogran the innkeep should be there with his daughter and the old woman from the cottage nearby."

Vena broke away from the other three women at the mention of the old woman; Hunter could see it gave her concern.

"This old woman? Is her name Lamia?"

"It is. She means something to you?" He replied, surprised.

"Is she hurt?"

"Not physically. No. But she grieves for another, a man called Maccon. He died at the hand of an assassin. Hopefully she, and the others are rowing to the centre of the lake."

Stepping over the bodies, Hunter and his Wolf led the four women out onto the street past a number of dead town's people, women and children amongst them, to arrive at the town square. There was quite a gathering of those lucky enough to have escaped the blades of the invaders, most in a state of shock and disbelief. The Wolf stayed back as Hunter ordered not wishing to stress the crowd any more than was necessary. Before making his way to the fountain in the centre he once again told Vena and her girls to go to the lake. The girls were only too willing, begging their mistress to join them, but she had other plans. She kissed her girls good bye and marched back to Hunter who was already making his way through the crowd. Before he could reach the fountain she grabbed his arm.

"What are you doing? You should be on your way to the lake." He stressed, exacerbated by her refusal to heed his advice.

"I am going with you and that's, that. I'm as good as any man with a dagger as well you know. So, there is no point in trying to persuade me otherwise."

He didn't even try; time was of the essence and other than put her over his shoulder and carry her to the lake himself there was no chance she was going to leave his side.

There was quite a gathering in the town square, most were women and children, a third of them men but only half of *those* fit to fight. Bael jumped onto the stone surround of the fountain to address the crowd.

"Listen!" he shouted. The silence was contagious as one by one the people stopped what they were doing. "We have little time. Women, children and the elderly should make their way to Millers Landing. You will find boats there."

"What about the rest of us?" Logan, apprentice to the town's barrel maker asked.

"Those of you strong enough to fight will come with me to the Keep."

"But only a handful of us are armed?" Another young man in the crowd shouted.

"The forge is on the way; you will get weapons there. Other than that, you must take what you can from the fallen." Hunter added. "There is no time for debate we must move quickly."

"I will lead the women and children," Toman the fishmonger interrupted. The eldest and most respected of everyone around the fountain.

"Good," Bael said, thankful for the man's assistance. "There aren't enough boats for all of you, so give priority to the weakest and most vulnerable. The rest of you should make for the woods."

Hunter, jumped down off the wall and rallied the rest of the men to follow him down the main street towards the forge and then onto the Keep. Vena pulled up alongside him her dagger already drawn, her hand shaking; he could see she looked frightened.

"Whatever you do, stay by my side. I promise you we will survive this," his optimism well intentioned.

The Wolf was again by Bael's side and for the first time Vena found its presence oddly reassuring.

On their way to the forge Hunter and his Wolf made short work of a few Northern stragglers intent on filling their pockets with whatever valuables they could carry. The encounters were dealt with so quickly none of the others in his group had to do a thing, not even Vena.

Bael halted and put up his hand for everyone else to do the same. He looked to the forge which was to their right, less than fifty paces from where they stood.

"Why are we stopping?" Vena asked.

"Listen."

The sound of steel on steel rang out to the backing chorus of men in the thick of a fight. The sound came from the forge. Hunter faced his group.

"All of you wait here. If I do not return, make your way to the Keep, it is your only hope."

"I am coming with you," Vena intervened.

"So am I," Logan added. As did another half dozen of the strongest members of the group.

"Alright but follow my lead."

With that, Bael and his Wolf led his followers into the shadows and on to the forge.

***

Dogran made sure Emma, Lamia and Toran were safely on the row boat before shoving it away from the mooring with his foot.

"What are you doing?" Emma cried out in disbelief.

"I have to make sure Koval and Tyrna are safe."

"No father. I can't go through this again. I nearly lost you once, please, not again."

"I have to do this my sweet. I promise I will come back to get you," he said, as the boat drifted slowly away.

Toran took up the ores, he knew what he had to do pain or no pain. As he began to row, he felt the stitches on his wound stretch and the flow of fresh blood begin to seep through tiny gaps along its length. But Lamia's work held true.

Emma wasn't about to give up that easily, she leant forward almost capsizing the boat.

"Don't do this," she said in a desperate attempt to change her father's mind. As she sat back down to steady the boat, she felt Lamia take her hand.

"Let him go child. The gods haven't finished with him yet," Lamia said with an undeniable confidence.

Emma softened. With eyes full of tears she resigned herself to the fact that her father was never going to surrender to her wishes, and that Lamia's gift of foresight was the reasoning behind her confidence.

Dogran watched as the boat disappeared into the darkness of the lake, he would have wished Emma by his side where he could keep an eye on her, but what was coming next was far too dangerous.

48

THE FORGE – A FRIEND'S GRIEF

Koval's hand slipped in the thick bloody mess as he tried to push himself up off the body beneath him. If he was about to die he would prefer to meet his end on his feet as any fighting man would. But the final blow never came. Instead, the fighter standing over him suddenly fell to one side with the top of his head caved in like the mouth of a volcano, but instead of lava spewing forth it was brain matter in a wash of blood. As the man's body hit the ground, Koval turned his head up to see his saviour. Dogran was standing like a giant, brandishing a heavy steel maul he'd acquired from one of the forge's weapon racks set far enough away from the fighting as to prevent his detection. He offered his hand to help Koval to his feet. In his wake were the remainder of the attackers all of them smashed to death though a variety of lethal bludgeoning's.

"You are injured," he said, looking to his friends limp broken arm. But before he could ask where Tyrna was Koval turned around and without saying a word ran for the open door, the pain from his dangling arm completely ignored. Dogran followed, and like his friend he feared the worst and knew should such fears be realized, he would have to be there for his friend. Once inside, Koval made straight for the stairs leaping up them two at a time, his heart beating out of his chest. The bedroom door was ajar. The fact that Tyrna wasn't awake to greet him sent chills down his spine. He moved to the open door as though part of a dream where his every step was being hindered by some invisible force, slowing every footfall as if to delay the horror he might have to face. Finally, he reached his destination. Almost too afraid to discover what lay within, he fell forward almost tripping over himself. The door gave way to his weight and the only thing he could remember as he fell to his knees the tears streaming down his weathered cheeks, was red. The colour was everywhere. He couldn't shake the image. He dropped onto all fours his stomach surrendering its contents all over the floor as he retched and threw up: it wasn't the blood, he'd seen plenty of that in his life time. No, for a man like him to see the love of his life slaughtered like some lowly animal and unable to do anything about it, was a sense of helplessness beyond description. His arms and legs felt weak as if they might collapse under his weight. He lowered his face to the ground and cried and cried.

Dogran stood behind his friend in the open doorway; he looked to the bed beyond and then to the broken man by his feet. Tyrna lay as if sleeping, her head almost severed from her shoulders, her face a mask of red. But beneath all that she seemed to be smiling, as if in that final moment she had found piece. Dogran passed by his friend and slid the bed covers over her body. As terrible as all this was, he knew there was no time to waste, he had to get his friend on his feet and out of there. He fought back the sadness and knelt down, resting his hand on Koval's shoulder.

"I am so sorry my friend. Such a loss is beyond imagining. But there is nothing more to be done here, we have to go," Dogran whispered with heartfelt sympathy, swallowing back the lump in his throat. Koval mumbled something but Dogran couldn't make out what he was saying. At first Koval resisted any attempt at getting him to his feet, then something changed. He took the weight on his good arm and pushed himself up onto his knees. He wiped away the blood and vomit from his face and with the help of his friend, stood up. His features became cold, resolute with a stare that had no focus. Dogran was all too aware what that look meant, he had seen it too many times on the battle field. His friend was in total shock. The type of shock that numbs the mind of all reason.

"Go my friend. You have a daughter to protect," Koval mumbled, loud enough to be heard this time.

"If you stay you will surely die," Dogran replied.

"Then what better place to do so. No! My place is here with my wife."

Dogran accepted there was no way Koval was leaving that room unless he carried him over his shoulder, an option that was merely the thought of a desperate man.

There was one thing left for him to do before leaving his friend to face whatever would come through that door after he leaves. Dogran walked over to a chest of draws under a window that looked out over the forge. He removed one of Tyrna's dresses and ripped a large strip off it. While he was doing that Koval made his way over to the bed and slid down the cover, just enough to expose his wife's face. Dogran watched as he wiped the blood off Tyrna's face, in such a way that he half expected her to open her eyes to the caring touch. Though it would never happen the image was moving, and for a moment he let his friend indulge himself in the tender care of his dead wife. He made his way over to the bed and placed his hand on Koval's back.

"If nothing else, let me tend that arm of yours," he said dangling the piece of cloth in-front of him.

Koval finished what he was doing and stood up to face his friend. The arm was shattered and the hand was already turning blue. Dogran could see it wouldn't be long before the flesh became blackened, facilitating the removal of the arm should he by some miracle survive what will surely follow.

"Here, this is going to hurt," Dogran warned. The bone was shattered and beyond setting. "All I can do is brace it against your body, at least it will hold it steady."

Koval nodded his consent to go ahead. He didn't cry out once as the dying arm was strapped tightly to his midriff. This was the one benefit that shock such as Koval was suffering carried with it; Dogran had seen its effects when men had limbs amputated after battle. Somehow it was able to dull the most extreme of the pain induced until as in most cases unconsciousness ensued. All that done, Dogran reluctantly picked out Koval's favourite weapon of choice a longsword and handed it to him.

"I have to go. May the gods protect you my friend? If you change your mind head to the Keep."

No reply followed. Instead Koval wrapped his good arm around Dogran and the two men hugged, neither wanting to let go.

"Think what you are doing here," Dogran choked, "and if this life is just, we will meet again old friend."

A tear ran the length of Koval's cheek as his friend disappeared through the door. He returned to the bed and closed his wife's eyes. Now all he could do was wait.

49

A CALLING

The Devourer of Souls found himself inexplicably drawn to the cottage. Bodies lay about the grounds and by the look of them their deaths were quite recent. Darkness swirled all around him blocking out any other magic that might be abroad that night. It interfered with the natural balance and was the sole reason the Temple's Shard had such difficulty seeing what had to be seen.

Something inside a lost memory called to him from the depths of an existence long forgotten. There was a powerful energy surrounding this place where magic of the light flourished. It was unusual to come upon such a place in the realms of man and in part it was this that drew him to the place.

The darkness seeped out from every blade that made up his armour as if what resided inside was reduced to a smouldering fire. It spread out along the ground reaching out like Godless fingers to touch those who had fallen. The unholy tendrils wisped around and entered every orifice of the bodies it came in touch with, in search of answers only the dead can reveal and slowly but surely each corpse gave up its own story.

The dark revealed everything that these fallen had witnessed that day. He saw the plan to overrun the town and take the Keep. He saw the death of Kaleb and his son and then all that followed. Finally, he saw what and who sent these unfortunates to the afterlife and as quickly as the darkness left his being, it dissolved into thin air without a trace. The Wolf had been here, the images leaving him in no doubt. But there was something about the man with her. He felt the bond they shared and it troubled him. And though he couldn't see the aura the man and beast shared; like Lamia he could see the dark entity growing from within the man like some invisible shadow. It had form and was almost half the man's size and it was growing.

There was opportunity here to bring to conclusion unfinished business. Though such an endeavour didn't carry the same sense of urgency for him as it did the Dark Elf leader who had tasked him with it. He didn't wish to have his presence here compromised in any way, and the power it took to conceal himself like that was incredibly draining. The energy emitted by the Temple Shard was ever present and in constant need of blocking. He was able to do this but he was weakening. If he made a move to find the Wolf in his current state, he would surely give himself away; something at this moment in time his masters in the abyss would look upon as a betrayal of his original orders. Not only this, Dax-barh's explicit command was to reconnoitre the Isle of the Lost, observe and at all cost remain undetected. He had already broken that order when he visited an untimely death on the Elven Queen. Fortunately, there was nothing to link him to this atrocity his anonymity still intact. Yet his actions would have terrible repercussions making the bond between man and Elder ever stronger.

He had no love for those that created him. Bastions of pain, horrors and the unimaginable corruption that he had to suffer to become the abomination he was. But even as far away as he was in this land of the living, he could still feel his connection to those demi-gods and the power they possessed, and what that power could do when it was finally unleashed. The task they'd burdened him with was far from complete. On top of this the Wolf was still alive. But most troubling of all was the Tome of the Ancients; the only relic that could free them from their deathly prison was for the moment unassailable. In his search he had discovered it was the Wolf King who held the key to achieving his goal. But to underestimate the greatest hero the Elder race had ever birthed was to do so at his peril. Though he suffered the arrogance that those of great power possess, he was no fool. When he stood on the shores of that great lake surrounding the Isle, he felt a power way beyond his expectations. At that moment, he knew that whilst on the Isle this descendant of the Ancients would be almost invincible and that only those Dark Lords would have any chance to defeat him. But they were still in Vul-Sarh and without access to the Isle and the Tome within, they were going to stay there. A situation he had to remedy and quickly.

The Wolf King was by far the most powerful purveyor of magic in both the lands of Elder and Man, of that there was no doubt. But when the Devourer observed the comings and goings of the Isles inhabitants he noticed how, when they took on the form of a wolf their magic seemed to weaken. Not only this, it seemed that once they had crossed the lake they had no choice but to become such a beast. This had to be their weakness and he had to find a way to exploit it. Somehow, he had to lure the King from the Isle where his power would gradually diminish, or so he thought.

When the darkness had dissipated the six hounds moved in on the bodies ready to feast on their souls only to find disappointment in the fact that the souls of those lying there were long gone. In part from anger but mostly intrigue, they began to feast on the flesh, a delicacy new to them after a life in the void and they found they had a real taste for it.

Their Master let them eat their fill. Then a different kind of dark mist began to spread around him; tiny particles, spore like with a virulent appetite to devour whatever stood in their path dissolved what remained to leave behind a shadow of what once lay there. This was not the time to get involved in the concerns of man. Something was coming. Something terrible. He could feel it. It was the Dark Ones; he was sure of it.

Before leaving through the portal his spies had told him his masters were up to something so secret that only a chosen few of their denizens had access to it. Sultry necromancers all of them and they all hated the Devourer for the power he had become. Envy could be such a motivator and susceptible to manipulation by those who were cunning enough to know how, a quality the Dark Ones possessed in abundance. So, it wasn't difficult to keep their project a secret from their other creation and his six hounds.

The Devourer wanted to stay and finish what he started but there was no ignoring the sense of foreboding he was feeling. Even though he was far from his creators he could feel their malevolence through a change in the balance of the force that bound him to the place. Somehow, they were reaching out to him. There was no time to waste, he had to return to Dax-barh and the Circle of ancient stones that brought him here. For there was one fact that Dax-barh's shamen had no concept of when they opened that portal: once open it could only be closed by the Dark Ones themselves allowing them access to this world unhindered.

50

THE LAKE-A POWER REALIZED

Tiny swells lapped against the sides of the boat as is it bobbed up and down to the rhythm of the winds that created them. Emma found its sound strangely comforting. She looked at her odd companions. Now they were a good half league away from the beach area they'd set off from, Toran pulled in the oars and laid them along the sides of the boat. Emma could see he had nothing left to give; blood loss and exhaustion had finally taken its toll. But what concerned her most was the condition of Lamia. Since entering the boat she hadn't said a word or even lifted her head to see where they were going. She was just sitting there, head bowed as if asleep. Even in his weakened state it was obvious to Emma that Toran shared the same concern.

"Is the old woman alright?" he asked weakly.

Emma paused for a moment, then she leaned forward and touched the back of Lamia's hand.

"Forgive me, I don't know your name?" she said glancing over to her male companion.

"Toran."

"I'm not sure Toran. I think she is just exhausted," Emma replied, gently shaking Lamia's hand. But the old woman didn't move. "Lamia? Lamia?" There was still no response, which only heightened Emma's feeling of anxiety. Taking the initiative she let go of Lamia's hand and gently lifted her head. The old woman offered no resistance. Emma bent down to take a closer look; Lamia's eyes were wide open but only the whites of them were visible. In the moonlight it was quite an unsettling sight and had she not known her old friend the visage would have scared her rigid. As it was she had seen Lamia in this state before. She was in one of her trances and as before Emma was unsure whether she should try to awaken her. But before she had time to act on a decision Toran intervened. He sat upright and pointed to the shoreline near Millers Landing.

"We have visitors," he gestured, pointing to the silhouettes of people arriving in mass at the beach.

Emma followed his gaze and watched as some of the people entered the remaining boats while others made for Farroth Woods. The fact that there were children amongst them confirmed Emma's belief that they were surely town's people, though from this distance she couldn't say who had survived.

There was comfort in the thought that they would now have friends joining them; a fact she would have liked to have shared with her old friend. But in hindsight she decided to leave her alone in the hope that when their friends arrived she would naturally be drawn out of her trance.

"The old woman doesn't look so good," Toran mused.

"Her name is Lamia," Emma replied, prickled by the young man's tone.

"Lamia doesn't look so good," Toran corrected himself, not wishing to sound disrespectful.

Emma's face softened. She had served men like Toran many times. Tough on the outside but inwardly and in the right environment could show they did possess a heart, in-fact Hunter it could be argued may very well have been tarred off the same brush. But before she could reply Lamia lifted her head, her eyes still staring white.

"Someone is coming," she croaked.

"It's people from the town," Emma replied.

Lamia stared pensively in the direction of the approaching boat.

"No! It is not."

***

Gayn was a young man, no more than eighteen if appearances were anything to go by. He'd been forced to join the Northern Army by an unforgiving father who thought him a waster of no ambition. His father, a retired veteran officer felt that being his only son he should follow in his footsteps even if that was a constant embarrassment to him.

He was well educated there was no denying that, but he was a conscientious objector who hated war and the violence it courted. He and a bunch of his friends had tried to create political unrest amongst their peers only to find themselves slapped into the Malanon's dungeons for soliciting negative propaganda against their Governing Council. This could have seen him executed like his friends all of whom lost their lives in the fighting pits where death came from the very violence they abhorred. Only by his father's status in the eyes of the King and his agreeing to fight in the Crowns army did he manage to avoid such a terrible fate; and now here he was rowing across a lake about to commit a violence he had no stomach for with bloodthirsty bastards his father would have loved.

Terek his leader had spotted the three in the boat when a big man pushed it away from the jetty. His decision was to take a boat used by poachers, hidden amongst the bushes by the stony shore a good half league away around the shoreline by the woods. Two of the seven soldiers had to stay behind, as fully armoured the combined weight would be just too much for the boat handle. Unfortunately, Gayn was not one of them.

The darkness swallowed them up as the two remaining soldiers pushed the boat away from shore. Under the dim light of the crescent moon Terek reckoned they wouldn't be seen until it was too late to do anything about it. Two of the strongest in the group rowed for all they were worth whilst Terek knelt at the bow guiding them to the target. What set Gayn apart from the rest was that he wanted to be anywhere but there. Killing two women and a man about his age presented him with anything but glory. As they got closer, just before they entered the moonlight that their targets boat bobbed in and out of, he could see one of the women was old like his grandmother the other young enough to be a sister. The thought of killing them so pointlessly made him feel sick to the stomach. He wanted to protest against the mindlessness of it all but knew to do so would see him join in their fate. So, like the time he was given his previous orders to attack the town, he said nothing.

Terek drew his sword the moment the front of the boat broke out of the darkness. His men followed his lead ready to pull up alongside the three who were now alerted to their presence. All except Gayn. Unseen by the others he left his sword sheathed. He was unwilling to slaughter two women and from the looks of it an injured man as well.

***

Emma was the first to spot the approaching boat. It came out of the darkness unexpectedly from behind. Toran reached for his daggers. Emma looked terrified, but Lamia very slowly raised her head, her eyes unblinking like a wraith's. Emma placed herself in-front of her old friend and picked up an oar almost toppling into the water as she lost her balance. Toran quickly dropped a dagger and grabbed her arm to steady her but before he could pick it up again the other boat banged into theirs. Emma swung the oar, missed and fell backwards. Toran lunged at Terek who was the first to step onto their boat. The northerner parried the blow knocking Toran overboard. Then it all happened at once. The air around the two boats seemed to muffle all external sounds. One by one Terek and his men felt the pounding, a throbbing sound pulsating with an ever-increasing regularity.

Lamia looked at the auras of their attackers. All showed the reddish hue of hostility, all but one, a young man at the back. His showed no sign of intended aggression, instead it was the colour of Jade of peace and regret. All but him held their head in their hands as the pressure grew stronger and stronger. It was as if the very air itself had taken on a life of its own. The same invisible force threw Gayn into the water. The rest of his comrades were frozen where they stood unable to move a muscle. Blood started to seep from their eyes, ears and mouths. They screamed in agony as their brains turned to mush and where they stood they died.

Terek writhed in pain, like the others blood poured from every orifice but unlike them his eyes began to bulge until they blew out onto his cheeks in concert with the total destruction of his head as it exploded leaving torn flaps of flesh where his neck once was.

Emma fell back onto her seat in shock, she had never witnessed anything like it. Lamia dropped back down and collapsed into Emma's lap completely exhausted by the ordeal.

Toran pulled himself aboard. Dagger still in hand he was ready to kill the last of his attackers who was hanging onto the side of his boat trying desperately not to sink under the burden of his chain mail.

"No! Do not hurt him. He is not like the others," Lamia intervened.

The young man fell backwards as Toran's blade cut across his forearm luckily only to slide helplessly off the ring mail covering it. Gayn looked up nervously as Toran loomed over him.

"Please I wish you no harm," he said surprisingly.

"He speaks the truth," Lamia said staring at Toran. Then, to both Emma's and Toran's disbelief she gestured to the front of their boat. "Join us young man, for if the town's people catch you in that boat they might forget to ask questions and see you to an early grave."

Instead of ending the young soldier's life Toran offered an outstretched hand and hauled him back onto the boat. The Northerner gazed at his fallen comrades his face drained of colour. He was visibly shaking beneath his soaking garments. Carefully stepping back onto his own boat Toran with the help of his captive, tipped Terek's headless corpse over the side, the water turning black as the blood spread in the moonlight.

Gayn was as shocked as anyone at the suggestion, but he was savvy enough to realize the truth it held. He gave up his sword to Emma not fully trusting the wounded young man who had just tried to kill him. Like those two, he was still in shock from what he had just seen and was grateful to have not suffered the same fate. As much a mystery to him as it was to them, he could see that. Now all he could do was wait as boats containing others from the town approached.

51

THE KEEP-AN AWAKENING

On his way back to the Temple Cirius called at the pigeon house to collect the orphans. His first thought was to ignore his duty and rush into the town to make sure Emma and her father were safe, but he couldn't ignore his oath to the Temple and his dear friend who once resided over it. It pained him greatly to succumb to protocol like this; for his heart pulled him in one direction his duty another. A conflict that could see only one outcome at a time such as this. His stomach turned with the thought that hope upon hope she and her father were already safely in the Keep, though how safe that was now was anybody's guess. A question he would soon discover had no favourable answer.

In the meantime, he entered the darkness of the orphans sleeping quarters to find them all huddled together on Lia's old bed. Korey, her boy-friend was stood in-front of the rest with a make shift dagger in his hand made from sharpened bone. In the light of the single candle Cirius could see how much the lad was shaking, but brave he was and Cirius respected him for it.

It was Lia who recognized him first. She leapt off the bed and virtually threw herself against his chest in sheer relief that it was he and not one of those attacking the Keep stepping through the door. He stroked the back of her head and then ordered them all to follow him back to the Temple.

Arbar was already addressing the rest of the Order when Cirius and his young entourage arrived. Lia could see that they like Cirius were all suited up in mail armour and ready to battle. She had watched them many times in martial practice, never once thinking the time might come that they would need to utilize such skills. But it had, and she hoped that all that training would now prove its worth.

The battle in the Keep was now well underway and loud enough that they all could hear its deathly chorus. Being the wisest of the orphans Lia was aware of one horrible realization; some of the people they had come to love and respect by nights end would no longer be with them, and it terrified her.

Emat, the smallest of the Knights walked over to the children whilst Cirius conferred with Arbar and the others. He was a kindly man with an oddly funny face the children found welcoming and safe. Whenever circumstances allowed he would act like a court jester juggling fruit and the like, the smile on every child's face his well-deserved reward.

"Now listen children, there is nothing to be afraid of. I will take you to a safe place, you can be sure of that. So, I need you all follow me," he said in a tone that masked the true gravity of the situation.

"Where are we going? Can't we stay here with you?" Lia asked nervously.

"You will be safer up here," he replied, leading them all to the steps of the bell tower. "Don't worry, Osor and Garrus will be down below to protect you."

"Where will you be?" Korey asked.

"I will be with my brothers in the Keep," he replied, kneeling down to face Lia who he knew would follow his request to the letter. "Listen very carefully. You must not move from this place until we return to collect you. If anything should go wrong Osor knows what to do. Do you understand?"

"Yes," they all returned.

"Good. Then I must leave you. Remember, stay here and all should be fine." With that he turned and made his way back down the age worn steps of the spiral stairway.

Osor and Garrus looked none too pleased about their assignment to the children, they thought their presence better served with their companions in the Keep, but an order was an order. Emat joined Arbar and the rest and before heading over to the Keep they performed a little ritual passed down to them by their ancestral counterparts. Each withdrew his sword, then all of them formed a circle and raised their blades until each tip touched.

"Protector. Let your light be ours. Protect us as we protect you, for there is no glory in death," Arbar chanted, the rest echoing his words. A liquid blue light snaked down from the Shard to the tip of their swords. It shimmered down the blades to imbue their armour with an invisible shield of protection and their blades with a keenness that could penetrate mail, leather and plate without resistance. When the swords parted they glowed radiant white, as if covered in ice or light, it was a sight to behold and one Lia and the children had never witnessed before, as they looked down from the bell tower.

Now the Knights were ready to do what they did best; stamp out evil whatever its manifestation.

***

Dogran stepped out onto the street in-front of the forge as Hunter and those following him approached. He looked to the town behind them;

in places the sky was the colour of dark amber where buildings were put to the torch. It saddened him to see his town come to this, but he had to focus on the task ahead, this was not a time for reflection.

Bael saw the bodies scattered around the property. Even in the low light there was no mistaking the identity of the powerful figure heading towards him.

"How is the smith and his wife?" he asked.

"Koval is alive, sadly his wife is not," Dogran replied.

"I am truly sorry to hear that… Will Koval not join us?"

"I have tried to persuade him to leave, but his wish is to be by his wife."

"If he doesn't come with us…? There are still raiders in the town, if they should revisit this place he would most likely lose his life."

"He knows what he is doing, and knowing the man, there is no changing his mind."

"I understand, but these men need weapons," Bael finished.

"Take what you need," Dogran replied, addressing all the men behind Hunter.

Luckily, there were plenty to be had: swords, maces, flails, daggers and mauls. The fifty or so followers rummaged around and one by one re-emerged with his weapon of choice. Dogran kept his maul and picked up a steel buckler with a foot-long spike at its centre and then walked over to Vena.

"This is no place for a woman, you should go to the lake with the others," he said.

"I thank you for your concern Dogran, but you as much as anybody know I can handle myself."

"I don't deny it. But these men we face are not drunken fools to be put to the street with a boot up their ass. They are vicious killers the lot of 'em, and I would not see you hurt by them."

Vena was touched by his concern. He was one of the few in town she had a deep respect for and would in no way wish to appear arrogant in his eyes.

"You are a good man Dogran, but my choice is here," she replied lovingly.

He pressed the point no further understanding by her close proximity to Hunter why she chose such a perilous path.

"Then I would ask but one favour of you."

"Ask, and it is yours."

"Stay behind me and Hunter. And should either of us fall, make for safety."

"I will," she agreed, squeezing his arm affectionately. "If only others held my wellbeing in such high esteem." She glanced almost accusingly in Hunter's direction.

"The man would see himself to the afterlife before he saw harm come to you. This I know," Dogran returned. "I have come to see the honour in the man."

Even though she inwardly knew her comment was that of a woman seeking the attention of the man she loved, she found great comfort in Dogran's words.

Now that everyone was ready Bael and his Wolf took the lead, Dogran and Vena by his side at the front. As they walked towards the long stone causeway that led to the Keeps main gate, they could all smell the sweet scent of burning pitch pine, the mainstay of most of the buildings in town. As they got closer to the Keep the sound of combat within its confines overwhelmed the crackling sparks of the rendered timbers as buildings collapsed behind them. It was like wandering through a nightmare, ash fell like snow, smoke hung in the air like a fog ready to choke any who entered it. But as they all stepped onto the long stone causeway, that chaos was put behind them, now they faced another kind of chaos.

***

The initial assault on the Keep was easier than anticipated and for now it felt luck was with Yold this day. The surge through the town had gone mostly as he'd expected, for the main part anyway. Yes, he'd lost more men than he would have liked, but for his victims it was a slaughter; so, in his eyes it was a victory for that part at least. Entering the gates with his men behind him he was ready to finish what he started. He ordered the draw bridge raised and the portcullis dropped just in case any left in the Town capable of wielding a weapon might follow.

Bodies were scattered everywhere, some were Braxus' men but most were Farroth soldiers caught off guard by hardened killers who showed no mercy. He looked to the battlements for any sign of resistance, there was none. He ordered half his men to take the left side while he and the rest take the right, which was made up of tiered grounds accessed by stone steps to the area preceding the Keeps main tower at the top of the hill. The first area they passed housed a carpenter's workshop, it was almost burned to the ground. The house next door was left standing but the carpenter and his wife and two children were lay together as they'd died, still holding hands. The next tier held a bootmaker's, he and his family had seen a similar fate. Next came a blacksmith's, he was dead too but he had put up a fight because next to him lay three pit fighters.

The battle cries of Braxus and his men could be heard clearly as Yold turned to climb the last of the stone steps that led to the large open ground in front of the main Tower. The rest of his men joined him from the other side of the grounds, the farm they passed was put to the torch and all the livestock killed, but the farmer and his family were lucky enough to have made safe haven in the Tower.

The main body of the Farroth forces was making a final stand to protect whoever resided within. Archers had picked off quite a number of the arena fighters but not nearly enough to make a difference, and now they were within throwing distance of the Tower.

Yold could see the heavy doors were open to allow the remaining Farroth forces a safe retreat. This was an opportunity not to be missed. He and his soldiers joined the fray. The resistance was brave and bloody, but they were winning. He could see Braxus ahead of him he fought his way over to him taking a small wound to his arm. Braxus was focused on a knight cutting into his men like a demon blade. Half the man's face was covered by a strange purple disfigurement. Before he could cut his way through to face the knight the man bellowed for his soldiers to retreat back into the Tower. But the order came too late.

***

Lord Farroth discussed tactics with Fraene and his Captain of the guard as they looked to the open ground in front of the inner battlement that protected the main Tower of the Keep. Guards had been placed on the side and front outer walls with the orders to sound the horn should the enemy breach the battlements. Up until this point the alarm had not been raised, so Lord Farroth felt it was fair to assume that clear and present danger was not yet upon them. He looked to his side expecting Maccon to offer advice, but his friend was gone and even though his thoughts were taken up with the battle ahead, a sadness came upon him. It was times like these he would council his friend's advice, not just because he was a brilliant strategist but because he was the only true friend he had ever known or considered, and now he sought such advice from this relative stranger Fraene and Captain Gerrard who he'd brought out of retirement.

"My Lord I believe it would be prudent to hasten the main body of our forces to protect the front walls around the drawbridge" Fraene put forward. "We can see from the fires in the town that the enemy are close."

"I agree my Lord," Captain Gerrard added.

Lord Farroth stared down at his soldiers occupying the huge courtyard behind them. He screamed his orders to ready themselves and follow his chosen leaders.

Fraene and Captain Gerrard descended the stone steps to join their men below. Lord Farroth stayed where he was expecting his Knights of the Order to join him. Their duty as always to be the final wards of protection for the Tower itself and the safety of his family.

Arbar and Cirius were the first of the Order to join him. Arbar explained how they had placed the orphans high in the bell tower and that Osor and Garrus were charged with their protection. The rest of the Order weren't far behind, joining Lord Farroth and their fellow Knights as Fraene led the soldiers out of the doors below. Before even half the men were through, a horn sounded from one of the side walls. Lord Farroth couldn't hide his surprise and disbelief.

"How could they breach the walls so quickly?" he asked Arbar.

"They must have gotten in through the main gates. It is the only way they could get entry this quick," Arbar replied, as the last of the soldiers stepped into the open ground outside.

"I'll get the doors," Cirius offered. He ran down the steps closing one door then the other. Before the second one slammed shut he caught sight of the Northern fighters entering the clearing from the right. He looked to Emat who was last of his Order to join them.

"Emat! Get the door I am going outside," he shouted, ignoring his orders to stay within the confines of the Tower's battlements. Emat didn't even try to stop him. He wanted to do the same but he was always more of a traditionalist than his younger counterpart. He smiled and waved.

"Come back to us Cirius. May the Gods protect you?"

The fight was ferocious and bloody. Many of the Keeps soldiers! lay dead or dying all around their leaders. Cirius fought his way beside Fraene. Sadly, Gerrard was lying in his own blood his face obliterated by a cruel spiked maul. Fraene cut down one then another and another. Cirius had his back, using both shield and sword as weapons. He lost count of the enemy he saw to their deaths, but it was obvious even with his and Fraene's valiant efforts, that they were losing the battle. Archers were doing what they could from the battlements behind, but the advance of the enemy was so quick it took everyone by surprise and there weren't enough marksmen to make a big enough difference.

Fraene's attention was drawn to the figure smashing a path through his men to reach him. His armour was not that of a soldier or a Knight. It was leather, light, affording little protection as trade-off for greater freedom of movement. He had the presence of a leader and similarly dressed warriors rallied around him confirming his importance. Some of Fraene's soldiers did the same forming a protective circle around him, but the sheer brutality of the onslaught caused it to falter. Within seconds Fraene found himself ducking back from a lethal hammer blow that would have left him like poor Gerrard. He quickly retaliated parrying another blow as Braxus' sword glanced off his own, running its length and cutting his wrist where gauntlet met chain mail. Fraene almost lost the grip on his weapon. Cirius jumped between them to redirect another hammer blow with his shield that would surely have found its mark. Both men could see to carry on would certainly see all their deaths. Fraene shouted the retreat. Those of his men who were still standing and capable fought to break free of their enemy. Archers on the wall tried to force back the Northerners, long enough to allow Fraene and his men time enough to return through the now open doors. At first it appeared to be working. Arrows rained down on those below closest to the door. Fraene and Cirius got through and most of the thirty soldiers who were following. But as the last few made to enter and see the doors shut behind them, Braxus and his vanguard slaughtered them to get a foothold in the partially opened doorway.

***

Outside the Keep at the end of the stone causeway Bael and his group came to a halt. The Wolf had gone on ahead. Frustrated he turned to face them all, this was an unforeseen obstacle which for the present he saw no solution.

Dogran walked to the end of the bridge his gaze followed the full length of the walls.

"We need grappling hooks, as many as we can muster."

"But we can never scale these walls from this side of the moat," Bael added.

"No, but the walls at the rear of the Temple are much lower because they face the lake and there are rocks beneath those walls we can stand on."

"That is true, then where do we get these grappling hooks from?" Bael asked.

Before Dogran could answer Jack arrived with his fifty or so men, some carrying the hooks they needed. Vena scowled, still baring resentment for what the thug did to her.

"I can't believe we have allied ourselves to this scum," she mumbled, gritting her teeth on the unsavoury thought that they had no choice. Without saying a word, Hunter put his arm round her shoulder and gave her a reassuring hug; feeling the tension in her dissipate.

He let her go and made his way through the town's people to a chorus of mumbles and groans of disapproval, but that was as far as it went. None of those complaining had the courage of their convictions, and as Jack and his men pulled up, all went quiet.

As undesirable as his new companions were, Hunter couldn't help the feeling that they were a welcome addition to his group. He knew without them the task ahead would be far more difficult if not impossible. The crowd parted for him so he could greet his newfound allies.

"How did you know we….?

"When chaos abounds, who do you think benefits the most….? Jack interrupted. "The thieves. And these," he said holding up one of the grapplers, "are tools of the trade." He never took his eyes off Hunter's Wolf which had returned to his side. A sight that surprisingly gave great comfort to Vena.

Both Hunter and Dogran never thought the day would come when they welcomed the help of such a villain, but it had and they weren't about to question the morality of it. Vena on the other hand loathed every minute of it and stayed back until Hunter had finished discussing tactics.

By their very attire it was obvious that most of those following Jack were trained assassins. All but a few of them were covered from head to toe in dark brown leather garbs. Some had belts carrying three daggers and more, others were armed with picks and small razor-sharp hatchets. Jack as usual hefted Blood Bane over his shoulder. He looked at the raised drawbridge and smiled to himself.

"It would seem these hooks we brought are of no fuckin' use," he smirked.

"We believe we could get over the walls at the rear of the Temple," Dogran spoke up.

Jack mulled over the comment and by his expression rejected the idea as a viable approach.

"I have another idea. Follow me."

"Where are we going?" Hunter asked.

"There," he replied, pointing to a Farroth warehouse just to the left of the Keep's front wall. It was a large wooden building with no windows. A place he would have preferred to keep secret, but he had no alternative. It stood three stories high right by the lakeside. There was a small jetty to the side furthest from the Keep. At the front was a platform with a small wooden crane on it with open access to its interior behind. Directly beneath that were the double timber doors facing the street outside, the very doors Jack was leading them to. Dogran and Bael looked at one another in disbelief as the surly innkeep opened the door with his own key. Dogran was first to break the silence.

"How do you come to be in possession of a key for Lord Farroth's warehouse?" He asked incredulously.

Jack ushered everyone through. As Vena passed him, he smirked. In return she spat at the ground before her and carried on walking.

"Aw! Don't be like that," he jibed, winking as she passed him.

"You will get what you deserve, one-day you bastard."

"Don't we all," he whispered. The conviction of her words wiping the grin off his face.

The place was filled with uncut timber used in the upkeep of the town's buildings. There were large square bails of raw wool, wooden crates full of salt and dried herbs. All a legitimate front for Jacks illegal goings on after years of ill-gotten gains taken from wrecked ships and rich people's homes. Most of which were stored on the two floors above; a business arrangement shared with his unexpected partner in crime. Jack shut the door as the last man entered and faced up to Bael and Dogran, ignoring Vena's scowls.

"Where der yer think our Lord gets most of 'is wealth from?"

There was no answer forthcoming. "Well I can tell yer it isn't from the scraps of taxes 'e charges you town folk, an' that's for sure. How do yer think he can afford that fancy barge he likes to be seen paradin' around the lake?"

"You want us to believe Lord Farroth is in league with the likes of you?" Vena asked coldly.

Though she would never have guessed it Jack in his own twisted way admired Vena. In his experience she was a rogue by any other name, a quality in a woman that was rare indeed. In another world, he might very well have seen her in his employ or more. But he was under no illusion; in the here and now, that was a fantasy only a fool would court.

"Believe what yer fuckin' like. That Lord of yours isn't the man yer think 'e is."

"So, what are we doing here?" Dogran queried.

Jack made his way across the ground floor towards three massive wine barrels. He stood in front of the central one and twisted the wooden tap at the bottom. The sound of a latch releasing, preceded Jack pulling open what was for all intent and purpose a door and gestured for everyone to follow him. Before entering he removed a torch from a wooden pillar nearby and lit it. The tunnel beyond was high enough for most to pass through unhindered, but Dogran and Jack and a few others had to bow down to get through. Along the way, Jack lit lanterns hanging from tunnel supports.

It was damp with the constant sound of dripping water that collected in pools beneath their feet. The whole place reeked of damp earth and mildew, home to large black water rats scurrying inquisitively along the sides; stopping now and again to sniff out their unexpected guests. The floor was lined with long planks of wood, many rotten through years of use and covered in slippery green moss. It was obvious to all, that they were traveling directly beneath the lake making it feel even more claustrophobic. Some of the town's men had trouble controlling their panic, but they could see that Jack and his followers suffered no such problem.

The tunnel was wide enough to accommodate four abreast. Hunter and Dogran were at the front with Jack. Behind them came Vena and three of his most trusted cutthroats who seemed to be more than a little obsessed with her ass; but she had their measure and ignored the undesired attention. One of them sniffed the air as if to catch her sent. She answered the gesture by spitting in his face. The villain frowned and wiped the phlegm off his eye. The two beside him laughed.

"I think the whore loves yer," one of them joked. The one wiping his face put his hand to one of the three knives on his belt. The Wolf rolled a deep resonating growl around her throat and bared her huge teeth. The thug immediately released his hold on his weapon and cursed some obscenity under his breath. Vena ignored the outburst and disregarding caution stroked the beast as it walked alongside her, finding the longer she was in the animal's company the more she realized just how special the Wolf was.

Now they were almost at the Keep, Dogran took it upon himself to get a better handle on what was going on with this unsavoury ally they were all following.

"How did you know about this tunnel?" he asked.

For a moment it seemed Jack wasn't going to answer. Then he turned his head.

"The town harbours very few secrets for the likes o' me, and those it does I hold no interest. Knowledge is power, is it not?".

As Hunter listened, he could see that Jack was no ordinary thief. Even though his language was that of the street, it masked a highly intelligent mind. His words might be harsh and with his accent almost incoherent at times, but they were strung together in a very literal and educated manner. And for all his profanities he was not a man to be underestimated.

"You say Lord Farroth and you have an agreement, and this tunnel is part of that agreement?" Hunter ventured.

"Maybe, one day when we become friends, I will tell yer about my dealings with his Lordship, but for now we have more pressing matters to worry about. As for the tunnels, they were here long before you or I slipped into this world." He grinned.

"Tunnels? There's more?" Dogran followed on.

"One more. On the other side o' the Keep. But it collapsed a long time ago. They were made when the Keep was built, so those inside 'ad a way to escape should the need ever present itself. And today it has. Only, these fuckers we're about to fight, attacked the town as well, leavin' those inside the Keep with nowhere ter hide other than where they stand, trapped inside its walls."

"Where will this bring us out?" Hunter inquired.

"In the cellars beneath the main hall. Best you go in first. Only person in there knows 'bout me an' his Lordship is Farroth 'imself. So better you speak to 'im before me 'n my men step out of 'ere."

At the end of the tunnel a climb of well-worn steps leads to a single wooden door. Again, Jack used a key to open it. He and his men stayed back whilst Hunter and the rest made their way through the cellar to wooden stairs by the far wall. Then it hit him. The closer they got to the top of the stairs the louder it got. The sound of men fighting. Diplomacy was no longer an option. He turned to Dogran and Vena.

"Stay here."

"Where are you going?" Vena asked.

"The time for talk is over. Jack and his men must join us. Now." Hunter ran past the rest of his group; he could smell their fear. The Wolf joined him instinctively. He entered the tunnel and told Jack what was happening. There was no time for debate, Jack and his men readied themselves for battle and followed Hunter to join the others on the stairs. Then he, his Wolf and Dogran stepped through the door and into the chaos; the rest in quick pursuit. It was mayhem.

***

Yold fell as he entered the final door to the huge hall. The first arrow took him in the leg the next punched through his throat slowly killing him as he crawled along the floor, his life blood pumping from an opened jugular. Braxus and most of his fighters were inside, fighting their way through the few that remained in opposition. He had his eye on one target, the Knight with the purple birth mark. He relished the challenge of a worthy opponent as this man surely was. But there was a group of knights hampering his direct access to the man. They were all wearing the same emblem on their cloaks, a black orchid. Their swords seemed to be coated in ice, or something that resembled ice. They cut through armour as if it were cheese. But Braxus and his men had the numbers and with Yold's soldiers they were pressing the Keep's soldiers back.

Braxus was aware that the Knights with the orchid sigils were protecting one fighter in particular. *He must be Lord Farroth himself*, the pit fighter thought. These Knights were backing their way towards the wide stone stairway at the rear of the hall which spiralled off right and left to a wide gallery that ran the halls whole length on both sides. Braxus pushed forward. Instead of making directly for that retreating group he led his most trusted along one side of the hall where the opposition was weakest. As he hacked his way through soldier after soldier, he saw the Knight with the strange birth mark take a wound to the back. There was no time to get to him, he was now determined to stop the Lord's escape and to do so the fight with this marked Knight would have to wait. Though as the man dropped to one knee Braxus thought the fight may never eventuate anyway.

The strategy was working. The northerners had almost completely surrounded their enemy. Cutting off any chance that Lord Farroth and his protectors had of escaping to the upper floor. Braxus and twenty of his fighters were now at the base of that very stairway. On reaching his position the Northern leader noticed a beautiful young woman and an older one dressed like the Lady of the Keep appear above them, escorted by four of his fighters covered in the blood of the women's guards. Following Braxus' orders they had left the fight in the hall and sneaked their way along the upper gallery via a single stairway to the side. The prize, the Lady and her daughter, brought to the hall to witness the end of what must surely follow. Braxus felt a renewed surge of adrenalin, turning his attention once again to those ahead of him. The Farroth fighters had never faced men like his before, there was no martial discipline in the way they fought. It was both brutal and exotic in its execution. Fighting techniques that the Farroth men had never been trained to defend against.

***

Arbar and his Knights had fought bravely but the odds were just too overwhelming. Their only chance of survival was to get Lord Farroth up the stairway to where his wife and daughter were waiting. But that idea was soon crushed when they saw their retreat cut off by the brutal leader of their enemy. Cirius had taken a wound to his arm and he could hardly hold his shield. Emat was badly hurt, a sword had pierced his stomach and exited out of his back. Cirius could see it was only time now, there was nothing to be done with a wound like that, but still he fought on. They were being attacked from all sides, Cirius felt it was all but over. Then out of the corner of his eye he saw it. Hunter's Wolf leapt over several northern fighters ripping the groin out of one as he went to axe Fraene from behind. She turned on a coin and took out another two. Then he saw Hunter and his men burst into the hall to join the fray. Now there was a chance.

Hunter was like a whirlwind, his two swords slicing through fighter after fighter; Dogran by his side using shield and hammer to deadly effect. Vena stayed close as Bael and the innkeep had asked, her dagger opening the throat of one fighter as he came up behind them. Her stomach felt like a bowl of worms twisting and turning over each other, but her nerve held true. The Wolf killed another two pit fighters who were about to set upon Vena saving her from certain death. She looked at the beast finding it hard to believe that she could owe such an animal her life, more than this, that she actually cared for it. She quickly collected her thoughts and turned to stay with Hunter and Dogran who were cutting their way towards Lord Farroth and his protectors. Then, it happened so quickly she hardly had time to think: two pit fighters, one brandishing what looked like a meat cleaver the other a double-edged axe blindsided Dogran. Vena became suddenly nauseous as a pressure that felt like her head was about to explode increased to an almost unbearable intensity. A tiny trickle of blood dripped from her nose and onto her lip, through the throbbing her eyes rolled back and for a second the two fighters froze on the spot. It was like time itself had stopped. Everyone else around her moved as if they were wading through waves of sticky pitch. It was like she entered another realm; dead souls drifting in mindless chaos through black snow. Then, a shadow, tall and wisp like stopped and turned to look at her, its form neither male nor female and without a face. She felt a strange bond with the creature and it frightened her; she could feel its power, dark and malevolent, all consuming. Whatever it was it had seen her and as the connection to it got stronger the darkness was replaced by an all-encompassing bright light. Shimmering in its centre was the figure of an old woman. The image was too defused by the light to be recognizable, but as with the shade creature there was something familiar about her. The woman had her arms outstretched above her head, facing upwards as if warding something terrible back. As the image began to fade Vena heard a voice, a voice she hadn't heard for a long time, an echo, repeating itself growing ever fainter.

"Awaken the power within you. Awaken it, let it free."

As the figure dissolved into the light Vena reached out, but the figure and the light were gone. The whole experience had only lasted for a fraction of a second and now she was back in the hall with one word on her lips.

"Mother," she whispered. Then, involuntarily as if someone else possessed her, she glanced at the fighter with the cleaver. His eyes rolled back and he turned and cut deeply into the neck of his fellow fighter killing him in an instant, then time was once again as it should be. Dogran and those around him had no idea what just happened, but whatever it was it gave him time enough to impale the other pit fighter on the spike of his shield. The fighting continued.

Vena felt as though she had passed out for a split second and had no recollection of what just occurred. Both Dogran and Hunter thought it might be another manifestation of the Wolf's. But they were wrong: in that moment of peril Vena had unleashed a power that was denied her from early childhood. There was no controlling it, because she didn't know she was in possession of such magic, and from whence it came it returned to wait for the day it would be called upon again.

Bael moved to Vena's side to protect her as did Dogran; so too Fraene, who had seen her falter as if she was about to collapse. With the protective cauldron around her she felt the group surge forward towards the stairs. She couldn't see past them but felt as safe as was possible in such a terrible situation as this.

Because all their attention had been focused on the main bulk of the fighters forcing them back, Arbar and his Knights hadn't seen Braxus and his twenty fighters cutting their way towards them, leaving Lord Farroth exposed to their advance. Cirius turned but he was too late, Braxus held Lord Farroth from behind with his sword at his throat. The Northern leader bellowed for everyone to stop. He could see that since Hunter and his men had entered the fight the favour was now with them. But he was a psychopath with no fear of death and would make a spectacle of what was about to follow. A few carried on fighting after the order was given and some of those died. But slowly an eerie calm came over the hall and the fighting stopped.

Braxus in a final act of defiance slowly turned and pointed to four of his men at the top of the stairway, two holding Lady Farroth and her daughter with swords at their throats.

"Now what can we do? We are at a bit of an impasse are we not," Braxus said almost bragging. "I have your Lord and his family and you have us surrounded."

Something in this man's posture triggered a memory in Bael. The way he moved. The way he fought it was like those men in his dreams, fighting in those arena's; the young man and his father fighting for their freedom. In that moment he knew this enemy he now faced had no intention of leaving the Keep alive, he would see his mission to completion no matter the cost. He pressed his hand on the Wolf's neck as an indication for her to stay by Vena and Dogran's side. He stepped forward in the hope that Jack was about to execute a plan they had meted out before entering the hall. If he didn't then all would be lost.

Braxus watched the fighter brandishing two swords step forward to face him and his closest fighters. He like Hunter could recognize a fighter trained in the pit arenas of the North. Even the way they walked when carrying a weapon was unlike any other fighter.

"You are one of us, are you not?" Braxus asked, pointing his war hammer in Bael's direction.

Bael didn't answer he just kept moving forward.

"That's close enough," Braxus shouted, cutting a shallow red line across Lord Farroth's throat. Lord Farroth winced with the pain as little streams of blood ran down onto his chest from a wound that wasn't deep enough to be fatal. Bael had to keep talking until he saw his plan take effect.

"You are one of these fighters you speak about?"

"A champion. I earned my freedom," Braxus boasted.

Bael was surprised at how well-spoken the fighter was for someone that was once the slave of such a brutal profession.

"Your accent is not of the North?"

"It is not, I was a high-born child when they took me from my home in Alteria."

Bael could see he had reached the man for the moment at least.

"There is no honour in what you are about to do here. Fight me and should you win the prize is yours but should you lose you will die as a man like you should, with weapon in hand." When the last word left his lips, he saw a movement at the top of the stairs. The two pit fighters holding the women had their throats slit, as Jack buried Blood Bane into another's skull. The fourth died at the hand of the third assassin. As he dropped to the floor dead, Cailean screamed out.

"Father!" It was as if in that moment she realized that fate was about to raise its ugly head and rob her of ever getting close to the father she wanted all her life.

In an act of remorseless brutality Braxus' blade slid down his captive's face splitting it in half from forehead to chin. Both Alloria and Cailean screamed as husband and father fell to the ground in a pool of blood.

Bael sprang forward and in one move their weapons sang as steel kissed steel. Nobody else moved, this fight would see an end to it all no matter the outcome. It was vicious. Bael parried every blow made against him. He cut Braxus first on the leg then the side. The Alterian had never fought an opponent who harnessed such skills with the sword. Yet the cuts seemed to have no effect on the man. He stopped for a moment and began banging his weapons together in a taunt. There was madness in his eyes and not a hint of fear. He lunged ferociously hitting Bael's longer sword with such ferocity the blade should have shattered, but it held. They began to circle each other like predators gauging oneanother's strengths and weaknesses; waiting for that moment to strike. And it came. Hunter's Wolf moved as if to attack Braxus. For a split second the arena fighter's attention was drawn to the beast. That was all it needed. Hunter's short sword went clean through the man's sternum. Braxus' chest seemed to cave with the blow before his head parted his body as Hunter's long blade sliced through his neck; bone and tissue offering no resistance to its keen edge. The hall was silent. Now they were leaderless the will to fight on was gone. The remaining Northerners dropped their weapons and surrendered themselves to the mercy of their victors: for the soldiers such mercy was afforded them but Fraene had seen first-hand what cruelties these pit fighters had unleashed on those in their path. He ordered his men forward and was ready to execute each one of them where they stood, but Arbar and his Knights blocked his path.

"These bastards deserve to die," Fraene said, angrily.

"And so, they will, but not here. We've all seen enough death this day. If we do what you intend, we are no better than they are."

Fraene wanted the revenge most in the Hall also wished to see exacted, but the Order wanted justice served to a similar end but conducted in as civil a manner as all this chaos would allow.

Hunter moved to Fraene's side. He was of like mind and would see Arbar and his men move out of the way, then his attention was drawn to the stairs behind the priest knights. Alloria and her daughter Cailean broke away from Jack and his men's protection and ran crying towards the fallen body that all the rest in the Hall had forgotten about in this moment of madness. Alloria dropped to her knees to take her husband's bloodied head in her lap, the horror of what she held mercifully hidden from her through the blindness of grief. She rocked back and forth, cradling his head in hands slick with gore. Cailean dropped to the ground next to her. She took hold of her father's hand unable to look upon what was left of his face. She cried and cried. As much as their relationship had been less than she'd wished, her anger towards her father had only been fuelled by the pursuit of his love. A love he had shown before this terrible end and now any chance of building on that love was gone forever and it broke her heart.

The sight of the two women kneeling by the body of a father and husband dissolved all the tension in the Hall immediately. Fraene was the first to break the deadlock. He rushed to Lady Farroth and gently removed her bloodied hands from behind her husband's head and coaxed her to her feet.

Vena was now beside Hunter and was about to take his arm when, without even turning to acknowledge her presence he moved quickly towards Lord Farroth's body.

Bael followed Fraene's lead. He knelt down beside Cailean and placed his hand on her arm. At first, she made to resist, then she slowly stood up to collapse into his chest. He placed his arm around her and let her tears soak into his shirt. In that moment there was no one else around them. Neither of them was aware that all eyes were on them more from surprise than anything else. This was a side of Hunter that most in the Hall that knew him had never seen before. Though had he been aware of Vena's attentive glances he would have seen more than mere curiosity in her attention.

Arbar ordered Dorodir, Falon and Lonin to take Emat's body back to the Temple. As fortune would have it if it could be called fortune, the Order had only lost that one life. It could have been a lot, lot worse and in this thought Arbar was thankful for small mercies. He asked Hunter to let go of Cailean telling him he would escort her back to her parent's room where Fraene had taken her mother. Bael let his arms slip away but she held him tight, seemingly reluctant to leave his side. Arbar gently rested his hand on her arm. He moved in closer to whisper caringly.

"Please my lady. I will take you to your mother it is a time you should be together."

Bael was more than a little moved by her reluctance to leave him. This fragility was unexpected; she had only ever appeared arrogant, spoiled even, like most born of such privilege. He lowered his head and whispered something to her. Her tear-filled eyes met his and without any further resistance she gently parted from his embrace. She let Arbar take her weight. Clutching his arm tightly she ascended the stairs with him. On reaching the top she turned her head to look back down the stairs to the man whose comfort she found so welcome. He was staring right at her, and something in that gaze had changed, a warmth that in her moment of grief would have a profound influence on what she would do next.

Bael returned to Dogran and Vena. He noticed that Jack and his men were no longer amongst them. Like ghosts in the night they had vanished before any around them had realized they were gone. His lips curled into a wry smile. He placed his hands on Dogran's huge shoulders.

"Now the clean-up begins."

52
ALL THAT REMAINS

Thank the Gods the Temple was able to avoid the horrors the town and Keep had not, Cirius thought as he headed to the Lake with Dogran and the rest. The innkeep told him how his daughter and Lamia had taken refuge on the lake, such welcome news lifting his heart. Seeing Emat fall the way he did felt like he was losing a blood brother as Maccon was a father. The tonic of hearing that Emma was safe, made to soften the deep sense of anguish he felt and shared with his brothers at arms.

Cirius and Dogran hitched two horses to one of the Keeps open wagons and then the innkeep ushered Hunter and Vena onto the back of it whilst he and the young Knight sat up front. By the time the group arrived at Millers Landing the cold sun peeked above the forest canopy to bless the wisps of cloud with an orange corona. Nature had her way of ignoring all the horror beneath her casting her beauty once again on the new morning. A welcome sight indeed for all those troubled souls that greeted her display down there by the lake. And it wasn't waisted as Hunter stopped by the water's edge and filled his lungs with her crisp morning air.

Most of the town people who hid in the woods were already by the jetty waiting to greet them, their relief plain to see. Dogran looked about him to see who and who hadn't survived the siege. Thankfully there were enough familiar faces amongst the crowd to lighten his mood. But there was still Koval not accounted for, and by the looks of it Jered his baker friend was nowhere to be seen. He looked around the crowd some more until he spotted Sylda, Jered's wife and from the expression on her ashen face her husband would not be joining them. Dogran looked back to the lake saddened by the loss of his friend who had always been a regular source of entertainment at the tavern. But for now, he would allow himself the pleasure of meeting his daughter safe and sound; quietly thankful that neither he nor Emma would have to shoulder the same kind of grief many around him were suffering.

It wasn't long before the first of the boats arrived from the middle of the lake. Dogran waited anxiously for Emma and Lamia who were still some distance away. He could see Cirius was as eager as he was to get first glimpse of his daughter, and it warmed his heart that such a fine man should show such concern for his daughter's wellbeing like this. He looked then to Hunter and saw the same, and he smiled.

In the low light and morning mist that hugged the water like a veil, it was hard to distinguish who was in which boat. But after the first three of them landed on the shale beach Dogran saw her. He had to look twice, he was almost certain the man rowing them to shore was dressed in Northern armour.

Cirius was the first to move towards the end of the wooden jetty where the boat was just mooring up, Dogran on his heels.

Vena was surprised to find Hunter holding back. She took hold of his hand and squeezed.

"Why do you stay back? I know you have feelings for the woman."

Bael stayed quiet and watched contentedly as Emma's boat landed. He smiled to himself. It was obvious Cirius cared for her and that those feelings were returned in kind. This he believed should be their moment and theirs alone absent his distraction.

Emma stepped off the boat and into the welcoming arms of her father. He could see the blood all over her but before he could ask what had happened, she rushed into his arms and hugged and kissed him dearly. Then she turned her attention to Cirius who was waiting patiently behind her father. This time her hugs and kisses told another story as their lips searched each other, and she sank into his loving embrace. But as he released his arms from around her, she glanced across the water to see Hunter turn away and leave. Dogran helped Lamia ashore leaving Toran and the young soldier to fend for themselves. Blood was everywhere.

"What happened? Were any of you hurt?" he gestured to their appearance.

"No, we are all unharmed," Emma replied, "The rest we can discuss later father, Lamia is exhausted." Both Dogran and Cirius looked concerned at what they saw but agreed that the time for such explanation was better received in more appropriate surroundings. They all headed for the wagon hitched to a post at the entrance to the jetty. Dogran got everyone aboard but instead of joining them he held back.

"What are you doing?" Emma asked suspiciously.

"My young friend here will take you back to the Keep, most of the town's council are already making their way there. There are matters to be discussed that concern us all."

"Then why aren't you coming with us?" Emma frowned.

"I will explain later, now go, I will join you soon," he replied, his thoughts fixed on the wellbeing of one more person.

Bael could see that all was well in the Dogran household, and that of the old woman he'd become so fond of. He would look in on Lamia later and while Dogran was so pre-occupied he decided to take it upon himself to check whether Koval was still alive. Vena was still in shock and though she had tried unsuccessfully to appear otherwise, he could see uncertainty burn itself into her gaze.

Vena couldn't shake the strange feeling she was carrying with her since that incident in Farroth Keep. The more she tried to rationalize the moment those two men were stopped in their tracks as they went to kill Dogran, the more bizarre it became. Her memory was a blank, like a dream forgotten on wakening. But she kept having flashes of a shadow like image then a bright light and what appeared to be an old woman in its luminescence, none of which made the slightest bit of sense. She could only think, like Hunter, that it was some magical manifestation of the Wolf's. For there was no denying the fact that the beast possessed powers beyond her understanding, and that all these strange visions Hunter was having were almost certainly connected to the animal. Yet on reflection she couldn't dismiss the notion that something in her body had changed; exhaustion yes, but not just from the fight. It was her mind. She felt drained as if she had spent hours trying to solve an impossible puzzle. And all she wanted to do now was return to her home and sleep away the events of the night, but she sensed Hunter had other plans.

People began to part ways some returning to town to see if their houses were still standing. Others who had seen theirs burn made for the Keep to begin the mountainous task of collecting the dead and collating the head count. There were things to be done and they were all under no illusion, it was going to be tough.

Lamia was taken back to the Temple where she would find rest and convalesce under the watchful eyes of the men who used to follow the man she loved. Then, when the time was right, she would return home to the quiet of her lovely cottage. During the journey she stayed completely silent and was thankful that her traveling companions were so supportive.

The Northern Knight who shared their boat was held for the time being as a captive, though he was allowed his own guarded room within the confines of the main Keep. The rest of the Northern scum occupied every available cell in the lower reaches of the dungeons, many waiting to be tried and executed as the law demanded.

***

Bael and Vena approached the forge with caution, the Wolf showing no such restraint as it walked over the dead sniffing for any sign of life. From what Bael could remember there were no more bodies than he'd seen on his previous visit, giving him room for optimism at least. Vena on the other hand didn't really know the Smithy that well, but she was led to believe he was a goodly man, a family man.

Both of them entered the property leaving the Wolf behind to stand sentinel whilst they looked around.

Everywhere was in disarray. Furniture upturned with bloody footprints mapping the route of the killer within. There were even bloody handprints where doors were pushed open. It was an awful sight. Smoke hung in the air like a dark intruder of the open door casting its pungent odour about the place as the wooden skeletons of buildings nearby surrendered to the flames. Not a sound could be heard; nor sign of life, only the haunting silence that shadowed death.

Bael drew his short sword and Vena her dagger. Stealthily, they made their way through the house and up the stairs to the bedrooms above. Hunter waved for Vena to stay behind him as they passed one open door, then another until there was only the one remaining at the end of the hall. The door was closed. Vena felt those wriggling worms of tension course through her stomach as they got closer to that room. Hunter, she could see was more worried than nervous, she had no doubts he cared for this Smithy and his family and it moved her to see him this way. In fact, it almost drove her to tears for she had only ever been privy to this self-assured, some might call arrogant man, a loner comfortable in his own skin and intentionally distanced from the troubles of others. With each step it felt the door was moving further away. It was a trick of a mind that didn't want to face up to the reality of what lay beyond, and in truth it frightened her.

Hunter placed his hand firmly on the latch and pressed down carefully in an attempt to avoid its betraying click. But his efforts were fruitless, as the click sounded more exaggerated than ever; a victim of the unnatural silence surrounding it. Crouched and ready to attack should the need arise he slowly eased open the door. He straightened as he entered the room. Koval was slumped over beside the bed, his wife's cold dead hand in his. A sadness washed over Bael as he approached the bed. But as he got closer Koval turned his head in confirmation that he still lived. Relief carved itself across Bael's features after believing the Smithy dead.

Now, with Vena in the room Hunter sheathed his sword and made his way over to the bed. Vena shared in his relief and being the woman she was, knew it was her time to act. She eased Hunter to one side and knelt down by the bed next to Koval. She placed her hand on his and gently eased it from his wife's.

Koval found her gentleness comforting. He released his grip and leant back on his heels. His eyes were bloodshot and his cheeks were red sore with tears. He wiped the clear stuff running out of his nose on his sleeve and coughed several times to clear the phlegm from his throat.

"Let us help you," Vena offered in a whisper, guiding him to his feet. "There is nothing to be gained by waiting here…. From what I have been told about your wife, I am sure it would sadden her to see you this way. She would I am certain, like to see you move on from all this."

Koval found his answer choke in his restricted airways. His head bowed. Bael stayed silent. He felt Vena a far greater emissary for common sense and comforting support than he could ever be. He was moved by Koval's plight and found himself understanding such loss more than he would have believed possible.

Suddenly there came a shuffling noise from downstairs. Hunter slipped both his swords from their sheaths ready to face whoever might enter the room. Whoever it was, they didn't make any attempt to hide their approach. *And how did they get past the Wolf,* he thought. This made him relax a little, but he knew better than to drop his guard until all was proven. Vena looked really nervous, whilst Koval just stood at her side lost in grief. The footsteps got closer and closer. Bael readied himself, then to his great relief Dogran stepped boldly through the door. Hunter let his arms fall by his side. Vena was visibly pleased and for the first time during this brief gathering, life gave colour to Koval's cheeks.

Dogran ignored Hunter and Vena and made straight for his friend. The two giants hugged one another; sharing a bond that only men who have served for King and country understand. They embraced each other as brothers, their eyes awash with tears of mutual understanding.

"The gods are just my friend," Dogran choked. He stared down at Tyrna's cold remains, saddened yet also joyous to see his friend still drew breath.

"Come with us Koval. We can return here when you are rested and give Tyrna her rightful burial."

This time Koval offered no resistance. He followed his three companions down stairs. Dogran sat him in a large wooden chair by the fireside and asked Vena to fetch some cut logs from outside by the forge's furnace. Koval, exhausted and drained fell asleep almost immediately.

The three of them began to tidy the place and wash away the blood stains as best they could. Then the innkeep stepped over to the fire to check on his friend; it was a blessing to find him still sleeping. He threw a couple more logs into the flames and poked the ashes below with a rod of iron lying by the hearth.

"Thankyou. Both of you. I will not forget what you did here today," Dogran said, locking arms with Bael. "People in this town will know your worth, you can be sure of that my friend. But for now, there is nothing more for you to do. I am sure you have matters of your own to attend to," he finished.

Bael nodded his understanding and gripped his arm heartily. Vena waited for them both to part before kissing the big man dearly on the cheek; a tear dripping off her nose.

"What a pity there aren't more men like you in this town," she whispered, "you are a rare gem indeed."

Dogran returned the kiss, then saw them both to the door. The Wolf was sat just beyond, waiting patiently. The minute she saw Hunter the animal was on her feet her tail wagging excitedly. They all said their goodbyes, then Hunter, Vena and the Wolf set off for the Keep.

***

In the weeks that followed, carpenters and builders were brought in from nearby towns and villages to assist in its rebuild.

Within the first week all those from town and Keep who lost their lives were seen to proper burial. The bodies of the Northern invaders were placed in huge pits and burned before being covered in quicklime and soil. The arena fighters were quickly tried and executed in accordance with martial law; each losing his head on the executioner's block. It was a bloody but necessary affair and warranted another headman to be brought in from the near town of Eastmount.

The Northern soldiers were dealt with a little more leniently. Some of the youngest were given hard labour in the rebuilding of the town. And those that showed remorse for their actions and a willingness to help were shown a mercy they themselves would never have seen to purpose had the rolls been reversed.

The young officer who had helped Lamia and those in the boat was given amnesty for his willingness to surrender helpful information during arduous questioning by Arbar and his Order. After all that was done the head of the Order gave him work and lodgings within the Temple itself.

After returning to the Temple following the final battle for the Keep, Riayas, one of its members succumbed to a wound to his side. Poison had entered his blood stream and though for the following two days he seemed to make a recovery, on the third he tragically passed away.

After an intimate private ceremony Maccon, Emat and Rayias were laid to rest in the huge underground tomb beneath the Temple; other than members of the Order only the remainder of the Farroth household were allowed to attend. Though the ceremony was a solemn affair each member drew strength from the brotherhood. Lady Alloria and her daughter Cailean were quiet throughout. Following this they had the unenviable task of preparing with the help of Arbar and his knights, Lord Farroth's funeral that was to take place at the end of the week. His body would be laid in the family tomb at the rear of the Temple. There would be provisions made for those in the town who wished to attend, as unlike most stately funerals where attendance would be demanded, the people of Stonehaven were allowed their right to choose.

***

Razor, Cirius's falcon returned with a message from King Agramar after being sent to inform him of his brother's death. Agramar and his group were still on the road when he received the sad news and though they were more than half way to the Capitol he made the decision to return for his brother's funeral and was on his way back when Razor delivered the message to Cirius.

After discussions with Lady Farroth it was decided that the funeral be held back until the King arrived, a fact that gave her some comfort during this trying time. Cailean had for days wandered about the Keep like a lost soul, only finding respite from her misery by revisiting her sword lessons with Garrus; a distraction that seemed to benefit both teacher and pupil. What she hadn't noticed during these sessions was Hunter watching her from the arched entrance leading to the Keep.

On his visits to check on Lamia's recovery and his meetings with Lia and her brother Toran who was recovering from his wound in the bed that was once his sister's, he found his thoughts surprisingly filled with concern for the wellbeing of the young Lady of the Keep. On occasion he observed her progress with Garrus, not long enough to be noticed; though the Knight of the Order had seen him on two occasions and said nothing to his student. Throughout the days of that first week he made numerous visits to Farroth Woods to hunt fresh Venison for the arrival of the King. He like Fraene was looking forward to his reunion with those fighter's he'd got to know whilst protecting Agramar on his journey.

Lamia was given Maccon's old quarters which rekindled memories both good and bad of her time with her lost love. For the first two days her recovery was slow and for those around her, worrying. She just lay there, her eyes wide open staring upwards in a coma like state. If she did sleep you couldn't tell until on the third day her eyes closed and colour came flooding back into her cheeks. Dogran and Emma visited her every day bringing her fresh food and her favourite drink which until that third day remained untouched. Hunter always stayed back when others were visiting in the belief that the good intentions of the many could be tiring for someone trying to recover. But during those first two days when Lamia was in that trance like state there was another visitor who joined Hunter on those occasions. And, during those visits Vena looked sad and made sure her presence was undetected.

On the day following Koval's return home he buried Tyrna his wife. With the help of his old friend Dogran and Hunter he laid her body in a freshly dug grave at the rear of his property. Those in town who knew him held a candle light vigil around the forge as a demonstration of love and support for a family they held in high regard. The local stone mason made a headstone for no fee as return in kind for all those occasions when Koval supplied and maintained his tools without charge. The words simply read: –

TYRNA
MY HEART AND SOUL.

Dogran was one of the lucky ones. The Tavern was virtually unscathed. A few broken chairs and windows and missing casks of ale but nothing more. With the help of Emma and Cirius, who was visiting daily, he got the place up and running before weeks end. The clientele was slow to return, many, sadly his friend Jered the baker amongst them would never return; their bodies buried on the hill that is Stonehaven graveyard. But many of his regulars that did survive found solace in the company of friends and slowly but surely life in the town began to take on some semblance of normality they all thought would never be possible. But support from friends and family is a powerful healer and the tavern became the focus of that process. Emma got great comfort from Cirius' visits, the longer they were in each other's company the stronger the bond between them grew. But as people started to drift back into the Tavern, she was disappointed to see that Hunter wasn't one of them. But during her visits with her father to see Lamia at the Temple she was completely unaware that she was being watched by him from the shadows until she and her father left, allowing Hunter to visit undetected. The one thing she did know about Hunter though, was that he must have his reasons and for the time being that was enough. There were so many other problems that needed tending to, such thoughts seemed somewhat poultry and in the grand scheme of things there would be plenty of opportunity to revisit them should the occasion arise.

***

It didn't take long for Jack to drift back into his old ways. Chaos was his world and through grit and an uncompromising determination he was master navigator of that world. After the Keep he and his men took it upon themselves to relieve a number of rich merchants' houses of most of their valuables. With all the distractions the siege had presented the town, the pickings were simply too easy to resist. It wasn't long before his whores were back to entertaining the regulars, all in celebration of their participation in the downfall of an adversary who would have seen an end to all their subversive activities. Some of the celebrations got out of hand fuelled by over enthusiastic consumption of alcohol and opiates that were being bandied about like children's sweets. That first week Jack's pigs were kept very busy and his pies were particularly tasty.

Jack was kept informed of the comings and goings throughout the town as the re-build began. There was no doubt in his mind that things had changed. His silent partner Lord Farroth was out of the picture and what protection that relationship was able to afford his underworld activities was now a thing of the past. During the following weeks he knew he would have to rethink old ideals and come up with new strategies to maintain the growth and stability of his hard-built empire. In this endeavour his immediate priority was to surround himself with a crew he could trust by first replacing those who were lost during the siege. In this task Ayla and her girls would play no small part in weeding out the chaff from potential candidates; robbing them of their secrets with sex and sensual persuasion. Skills that Jack had helped them nurture to levels that could almost be classed as an art form.

The first night of the second week following the start of the towns re-build the giant of a man, Yorn Sharktooth walked through the doors of Jack's Tavern. It was rumoured that the jagged edged teeth he wore around his neck were trophies from a shark he bludgeoned to death with his bare hands after it locked its jaws around his waist whilst he was swimming by a coral reef close to where his boat was anchored. If the rumours were true it was said that he had to push his own guts back in before the ship's doctor could stitch him up. And though the story was hard to believe, he did have a huge crescent shaped scar disfiguring his left hip.

Jack welcomed him to a candle lit table in the farthest corner of the room. He greeted his new guest with a mug of his finest ale. From his pleasuring between Ayla's legs the night before, she had deduced that the giant wasn't the brightest of specimens but he was fiercely loyal and surprisingly gentle when he had to be. And though he had offered her a handsome payment for her services, she refused to take his coin and welcomed his unexpected respect of her womanhood and the almost protective way he made love to her: like she was this fragile thing lying beneath this hulking mass of muscle that must be protected from the hurt he could unwittingly inflict upon her. And though she had a job to do, she too was respectful in her execution of it. When the session was over, she had come to really like her unusual client and was quietly thankful that the size of his manhood was much smaller than his huge frame would outwardly suggest. After he left the Tavern, she told Jack what she had learned.

Now, with this information already in his hands he faced the giant across the table and tapped mugs in a toast. He didn't even have to interview the man; his mind was made up the moment the giant locked arms with him. Jack believed words could only tell you so much about a person; the real truth always lay in the eyes. And the moment the giant sat down opposite him; his eyes revealed the truth of Ayla's words.

Jack sat back and drank his ale in one long gulp with a look of satisfaction on his face having recruited his first new crew member. At last, his plan was underway.

53

LAMIA – A DAUGHTER - THE VISIT

Lamia's mind had gone into a meditative state of self-healing. The events on the lake had drained her both mentally and physically beyond anything she had to endure to date. No number of potions from well-wishing aids could speed her recovery. It had to come from within and for the first two days that's just what it did.

Even though her visitors didn't realize it, she was aware of each and every one who came to her bedside. She'd seen Vena visit with Hunter and for the first time in a long time it warmed her heart to see a daughter lost to her for so many years. On the third day when she awoke to that thought she broke down in tears with the knowledge that Maccon was never able to meet his own daughter, a daughter he never knew existed. And now all that Vena would have of her father's, was memories of a good man she had never exchanged words with during their lives together in the town, a man she only knew through opinions of others.

On the fourth day when Bael arrived alone following Dogran and Emma's visit earlier, she could see the darkness growing between the two-aura's surrounding his body was now a good foot taller than him. It was like his shadow, but unlike a shadow its movements were not mirrors of his, instead it moved randomly as if it possessed a life of its own; its form ever changing wisps of darkness that dissolved and reformed at will. One minute it would resemble smoke from a fire, tendrils flicking out of existence the next minute it would reform itself in the shape of a man, faceless and ever-changing. And as she watched it she felt had it got eyes it would be staring right at her. A chill ran through her bones like an icy wind causing her to visibly shudder.

"Are you alright?" Bael asked, seeing the colour drain from her cheeks. "Shall I fetch one of the Order."

"No, I will be fine, I just felt a chill," she lied.

"I will close the…" He gestured to the open window not far from her bed.

"No. please, leave it open, it's nice to get some fresh air. Come, sit here," she said tapping the side of the bed.

Acknowledging her request, he sat by her on the bed. She took his hand in hers and as she did the shadow following him disappeared completely.

"Tell me, why do you wait until Dogran and his daughter leave before you visit?"

He was momentarily caught off guard by the old woman's observation and just sat quietly, looking into her milky eyes.

"It is obvious you care for the girl, am I right?" She asked, breaking the silence.

"I care for her, yes. But it is better this way."

"For who?"

Bael stayed silent. He shifted uncomfortably but relaxed when Lamia placed her other hand over his.

"Ah? I sense your affections are focused on another. A beauty. Does Cailean know how you feel? I think not."

Bael could feel her inside his head and try as he may he could not block her out. And though he couldn't see it himself, his auras were testament to the truth of her comments. With a half smile she squeezed his hand; she enjoyed her time in his company as he did hers which to both was evident to the other.

"There are a few women in our town who vie for your affection, none less than the one you brought with you while I rested," she said, thinking of Vena her daughter.

"How…?" He asked.

"I was never asleep during those first days, my body was resting, but my mind was still active. There is nothing to be ashamed of, I know what this Vena does for a living but beyond that she is a good woman. You care for her also."

"I do."

"But not in the same way you care about Cailean," she said, watching his aura's change to the colour of uncertainty. "Listen to the words of an old woman who knows. Follow your heart. Let Cailean know how you feel. Believe me when I say this, do not regret choices made of indecision or worse, misguided stubbornness born of ignorance. For in my life I have made too many of these. You are a good man Hunter, you deserve the happiness only love from another can give, grab it with both hands before it is too late and hang on for all you are worth," she urged, as the sadness of regret washed over her.

Bael lifted her hand and kissed it gently, then let it down as he went to stand up. She sat up straighter with a look of deep concern; grabbing his wrist as the darkness between his auras took form, a shadowy hand grabbed her's. Her eyes rolled back as the entity revealed its secret.

VUL-SARH – a name only spoken in whispers, its very utterance filled most of Elven kind with dread and loathing: Most-but not all. It was a place created by the Ancients to trap forever the immortal souls of the Dark

Lords and their twisted minions; a place of perpetual storms where lightning was the only relief from the total darkness that covered a black foreboding landscape. A place mankind came to know as the Abyss, a place which existed somewhere between the living world and that of the dead.

The Dark Lords looked into the black shifting Pool of Seeing, their only access to what lay beyond the very walls that kept them imprisoned for an eternity; their bonds invisible chains forged of a magic only the Ancients could harness. The pool began to clear, in its centre images rippled into focus. Standing on a shelf of solid black marble high up in the Tower of the Damned was their creation and his six unholy pets. The Devourer of Souls. The dark tower which rose high into the storm filled skies was part of a huge Temple carved out of the solid black rock high above the endless Sea of the Dead, whose waves carried the souls of the fallen to shores of torment and despair. As the thirteen Wraiths stared into the swirling black pool, the apparition shifted to the horizon beyond the Temple where a circular light pulsated at regular intervals growing ever larger as time passed. The pool swirled into life again, this time they watched as a single rider on his demonic steed sped along the edge of a forest whose trees had grown to full maturity only to die, twisted and withered by shadow blight, leaving their bark blackened and lifeless. Again, the liquid rippled revealing the Devourer of Souls as he watched the single rider approach.

The messenger rode through the cavernous entrance of the Temple, which lay open and vulnerable to the elements. Once inside he had to ride a further league before reaching his destination so huge was the structure's interior, with only the blood red glow from strange crystal clusters to light the way. Waiting for him

In the oppressive gloom the Devourer of Souls moved from behind a massive stone alter that still dripped blood from its last sacrifice. The rider reined in his mount, its flared nostrils snorting vapour clouds into the chilled air of the interior. He bowed his head with a nervous courtesy and addressed his leader from the saddle.

"My Lord, you are summoned. The Dark Ones wish for your council on matters of the portal." The black stallion became jittery, throwing its head back almost unseating its rider as the six unholy pets shifted to their master's side. The Devourer of Souls slid his huge sword into its back scabbard, then nodded his head at the messenger who then quickly turned and galloped off; the sweat of fear dripping from his forehead.

The Chamber of Whispers was the largest and highest of three domed structures rising high into the ether, a sky of swirling souls spinning in the chaotic embrace of the violent storms: Souls trapped an eternity by the Dark Lords for their sick and twisted amusement. A single spiralling road stretched over three hundred feet up the side of the pillar island that supported the Chamber with nothing but a shear drop, either side. At the top, the Devourer's Soul hounds became skittish as they always did when crossing the unholy threshold. Entering the enormous cathedral like archway the master and his beasts began the arduous climb along the twisting path that led to the phantoms within. The hounds looked more agitated than usual. Maybe it was the metallic smell of the lightning charged air combined with something ancient and malevolent, but why their master thought? They had been here many times before. Yet he trusted their instincts and readied himself for the unexpected.

The Thirteen surrounded a circular stone platform at the top of a thousand stone steps in the middle of the

Chamber: Phantoms, Wraiths, they had many names but these were the Dark Lords, Demi-Gods ruling a godless realm where all within became corrupted by the shadow magic that bound all to this place. The largest amongst them towered some hundred feet taller than the platform and a head taller than all of the other wraiths in the Chamber; atop his head he wore a crown of blades, symbolic of his position as leader. Looking at each one by one he spoke in the tongue of the Ancients, his voice a prolonged snake like whisper; words that never left his lips, but ones that filled their minds.

"Our time has come; the portal is almost breached."

"Yes, time," the rest replied, like an eerie echo. Then one of the apparitions, slightly shorter and fatter than the rest, addressed him angrily.

"I tire of your plaything's impudence and growing arrogance. He dares to keep us waiting."

"Patience, our servant approaches. His purpose will be served as we have agreed, and when we are free of our shackles, he will then face his inevitable fate."

"We cannot underestimate this creature of death, he grows stronger when others would perish," the fat one replied.

"His power will never surpass ours, he was created to tame this terrible place and feed us with the souls we have needed to keep us strong, but when we return to our rightful lands we will no longer require what he has so freely provided."

The thirteen watched with disgust as the Devourer began his assent of the steps. Whispers filled the Chamber as he and his pets stepped onto the stone platform, one whisper stood out from the rest; 'you dishonour us with your arrogance, how dare you keep us waiting' it said. Then a burst of lightning forked around the interior sending the hounds into a fighting frenzy. The wraith King looked at the perpetrator of the sudden outburst with a look as threatening as it was unforgiving; the fat one shrank back a little and could see his display of power had not impressed the Devourer who now stood tall and unrepentant in front of his makers.

"I am ready to do your bidding. I can see the portal is ready for me to enter the old world and do what I do best," his thoughts linked to his creators.

"Then prepare yourself for the journey. The underlings who breached the gateway for our escape await your presence, so you can lay the foundations for our release and prevent a prophesy already set in motion. A prophesy written after our defeat at the battle of Sith-Ilyan."

It had only taken seconds for the whole vision to reveal itself and in that moment, she knew what was coming and it horrified her. Bael placed his hand over hers comfortingly.

"Are you alright?" He asked as her colour drained.

"If you could stay a little longer? I would be grateful. I just need a moment."

"Of course I will. Would you like some water?"

"Yes, that would be nice. Thankyou."

Bael poured her a cup of water and watched as the pink returned to her cheeks. Whatever it was that just happened, he could see she was shaken by it. He sat with her for a moment until she stopped trembling.

"You saw something? Something unsettling enough to see you to such a state."

Lamia took hold of his hand again and looked directly into his eyes. She had no explanation for what she saw but knew whatever that place represented it was somehow connected to the dark form that had manifested itself between Bael's auras. But for now, she didn't wish to burden him with anything else; he had enough on his mind already.

"I am alright, I had a turn, nothing more." She lay back down tired from the ordeal but had one last thing to tell him, then she would sleep.

"Before you leave, I have one more thing to say. I have come to love you like a son, please, this journey you are about to take is fraught with danger. This Raen you seek is in the company of a very dangerous man; he is like no one you have faced before. I know you two have already met and that he let you live but make no mistake he would see your end if he deemed it necessary."

"I underestimated him, I know, but never again, I have his measure," he replied, not with arrogance but from self-belief.

"If you are successful in finding your friend, bring him home then speak with me again and I will tell you about the Elders."

"The elders? What do they have to do with me?"

"Everything. But that must wait till later. Now go before you drive an old woman to tears, and please, please take care of yourself."

Bael moved back to the bed and kissed Lamia on the forehead then without uttering another word he left.

After convalescing in the Temple for a week Lamia returned to her cottage. Emma with the help of Dogran and Cirius had tidied everything up in preparation for her return. It was a welcome sight to enter her home and find fresh flowers displayed in vases by windows and table. Emma had made sure the pantry was full of food and Dogran had placed a flagon of her favourite tipple on the table next to the flowers. On seeing her, the young deer came springing out of the shadows to welcome her. Lamia picked her up and kissed her.

All of them sat for a while discussing how things were coming together in town. And after some debate Lamia convinced Emma that she would be alright on her own for the first night since leaving the Temple. Dogran respecting the old woman's wishes, ushered his daughter towards the door. They all kissed and said their goodbyes. Lamia sat back in her chair by the fire Dogran had lit for her and placing the fawn on her lap she fell asleep.

Not realizing several hours had passed she was awakened to a knock on the door. She wiped the sleep from her eyes and placed the fawn down on the floor. Shakily she stood up and walked over to the door, before she had even opened it she recognized the identity of the person beyond. She dropped the latch and slowly the door creaked open. She stepped forward surprised.

"Sister!"

54

PREPERATIONS

Before making his way home Bael thought he might pay Lia a visit and see how she was coping with life in the Keep. He passed the pigeon house where two of the girls were playing, they waved and shouted after him as he made his way to the door on the inner wall of the Keep. He waved back and smiled before disappearing into the grounds leading to the kitchens. He knocked on the door. Hilda, the head kitchen maid opened it to greet him. She was a goodly sized woman who obviously liked the taste of her own cooking. But she was a jolly sort with it and welcomed him inside.

"Now what can I do for you my lovely," she asked, with a hearty smile on her face.

"I have come to see Lia," he replied.

"A fine young girl that one. She's been a blessin' for mistress Cailean an' no mistake. In fact, I think she is watchin' the young mistress at this very moment. Yes, I'm almost sure you'll find them both in the training yard yonder."

Hunter took his leave and headed to the Farroth training grounds at the side of the main tower by the stables. Even before he reached the place, he could hear the sound of steel on steel. When he turned the West corner of the Tower he saw Cailean sparring vigorously with Garrus. Lia spotted him first and rushed over throwing herself against his chest. He wrapped his arms around her and hugged her dearly, for he knew this would be their last meeting for a long time.

"Where's your wolf?" She asked.

"I have left her at home so she can rest," he replied. He sat down on the bench close by, Lia by his side. He put his finger to his lips. "Ssh! We don't want to distract your mistress."

Cailean spotted Hunter whispering something to her young helper, causing her to momentarily drop her guard and feel the sting of Garrus' practice blade on her upper right thigh. Then, with a sudden burst of confidence she launched an attack on her teacher forcing him to make several skilful parrying moves. Bael could see she was a quick learner and was surprisingly not without her own martial skills. She still had plenty to learn but considering the privileged life she was used to, she was progressing in leaps and bounds. As he watched her, he couldn't help thinking of his time with Raen. He became thoughtful and remembered his promise to Koval and Tyrna. A promise yet unfulfilled but one that was going to be rectified, and soon.

"How fairs your brother?"

"Toran is much better. Lady Alloria lets him sleep in my old bed. He tells us all stories before we go to bed. Mistress Cailean lets me sit with the others, but then I have to go to my own room next to hers," Lia said with pride.

"That must be nice. How do you find mistress Cailean? Is she nice to you?"

"She is kind. Sometimes she will talk with me, long after I am supposed to go to sleep. She is very sad. I hear her crying in the night. Sometimes her mummy stays with her, and they both cry. It makes me sad."

"There is enough sadness in the world without a beautiful little girl like you being party to it. You are safe now. You have your brother close by. And even though it might not seem that way, things will eventually get back to normal. So, let's see that wonderful smile of yours," he coaxed, tickling the side of her mouth with the tip of his finger. A great beaming smile rewarded his kindness.

Garrus could see Cailean was distracted by the unexpected appearance of Hunter. He dropped his sword arm and stepped back as Cailean made one last thrust, not realizing the lesson was over. The move made her almost lose her balance causing her cheeks to blush with embarrassment.

"My Lady, I think we have done enough for today," he said, with a hint of humour in his voice as he realized the reason for her rosy cheeks. He took the sword off her and placed it back in the rack with his. "Same time tomorrow, he added before passing Hunter with a smug nod of acknowledgement.

Cailean couldn't help but notice the affection Hunter showed for her new-found chamber maid, and it warmed her to see it. Hot and sweating she made her way over to the bench where the two were sitting. Bael stood up as she approached, Lia following his lead.

"You progress well," he said, glancing at her sweat covered brow.

"Thankyou. I still have a lot to learn though."

"Yes. But what you have learned, you have learned well."

Cailean managed a half smile before her features took on a more solemn look.

"Would you mind if Lia and I went for a little walk before she returns to her duties?" Bael asked.

Cailean looked down at Lia.

"Would you like that?" The little girl nodded excitedly. "Alright then but on one condition," she added, turning to face Hunter. "That I be allowed to walk with you."

Bael ruffled Lia's hair with his fingers and nodded his acceptance to Cailean's proposal. The three of them set off around the grounds, heading for the gates and the lakeside beyond. Even though all the bodies were long removed, there was still dried blood everywhere as a constant reminder of the carnage that besieged the place. Once they were beyond the drawbridge they made their way along the bridle path by the water's edge. Up until this point none of them spoke, Lia, not too young to see there was an awkwardness between her two older companions, decided to break the ice.

"Hunter says that everything will be back to normal soon."

"I hope so," Cailean smiled.

"How is your mother?" Hunter asked.

Cailean's face saddened and for a moment it seemed she was reluctant to reply, then.

"She rarely comes out of her room. She won't eat, she barely sleeps and until the King arrives, I fear she will stay this way. If it wasn't for Arbar and the Order I wouldn't know what we'd do."

"They are good men."

"They are. Garrus and Dorodir have taken on the role of organising the rebuilding of the town. Cirius and Arbar have taken charge of my father's funeral arrangements and preparations for the Kings return," she finished, her lip quivering.

Bael did something unexpected, he put his arm around her and was offered no resistance.

"What will happen to us all?" she asked in the voice of desperation. Now Lia looked sad.

"All will be well. When the King arrives, you will have the best of men around you. The people of

Stonehaven are resilient, they will return the town to its former glory, I am sure of this."

"I wish I shared your optimism," she whispered, "but I'm sure you didn't come here to have to listen to *my* problems."

For the first time during their walk together, Hunter felt uncomfortable. What he had to say wasn't easy and if truth be known he would rather have spoken with Lia alone. He stopped walking and dropped down to Lia's height and as he did so the first snows of winter started to fall. The flakes were light and melted as soon as they touched anything solid. He blew into cupped hands as the temperature dropped and looked to the skies, feeling the snow kiss his cheeks and gently turn to water.

"I think we'd best be gettin' back. We don't want you to catch your death out here," he smiled, delaying explanation of the real reason for his being there until they were all back in the Keep. As they followed the edge of the lake, some of the snow was beginning to stick. Lia ran and jumped around deriving great pleasure in the making of little footprints that melted away almost as quickly as they appeared.

Once they arrived in the grounds of the Keep Cailean ignored the Hall's doors and led them to a stone bench that nestled under a large Oak tree in the gardens to the rear. She found comfort in watching the snow fall and was sure Lia would love the same. All of them were dressed for the cold so there was no resistance to the idea. The gardens had remained relatively unscathed by past events and especially with the snow falling they felt pleasantly tranquil.

Cailean was the first to sit and patted the bench next to her placing Lia in the middle. Instinctively the two adults snuggled closer wedging the little girl between them to help keep her warm. And again, all was quiet; the three just sat there staring at the snowflakes as they dusted bushes and trees with a fluffy white blanket. Cailean especially found it nice to just sit there quietly, without having to do or be anywhere. Bael shifted in his seat until his knees touched Lia's feet; he slicked her wet hair back, gently sliding it out of her eyes.

"I came here to tell you something…" He said awkwardly. "I will be leaving Stonehaven on the morrow."

"Why?" Lia replied, the smile on her face falling away sharply.

Before Bael can answer Cailean leaned forward so she could look directly into his troubled eyes.

"You are leaving?"

"I must. I promised someone I would find their son, and the longer I am delayed the harder it will be to do so."

"I know of who you speak. I too am sorry for their loss, but why should it be you who has to go and find him?" Her question filled with genuine concern. "Have you not done more than enough for the people of this town. Many of whom seemed not to like you."

For a moment Bael reflected on her comment and though true, let the thought pass.

"I gave Raen's mother my word. And had it not been for the attack on our town, I would have been well on my way by now."

Lia slid off the bench to stand right in front of Hunter. She seemed more anxious than sad as if she didn't fully believe the inevitability of his leaving. And also, that she had an idea.

"Can I go with you?" She asked with childish optimism. "Please Hunter? Please let me go?"

When she saw his expression, her little lips began to quiver in reaction to the answer she had already guessed was coming.

Bael lifted her chin up gently as those tiny jewels ran down her cheeks. He kissed her forehead and whispered.

"If only I could little one, nothing would please me more…. But the journey I must make will be dangerous and not a place for children."

"But I…." She began.

"I am sorry but I can't take you with me," he apologised, as she pulled away from him angrily.

"You told me you cared for me," she cried.

"And I do."

"Then how could you leave me?"

He took her little hand in his and cupped his other hand around it affectionately.

"Who would I be if I didn't keep my promise? And I have one for you," he said warmly. "I promise that when I have completed this task, I will return home and you will be the first person I seek."

"You promise?"

"I do. Now come here and let me wipe those tears from your eyes."

Cailean had stayed silent in the hope that Lia might change his mind, but it was only half a hope. It moved her to witness that unconditional love a child will reward a parent with when they too give the same, the very love she now showed Hunter. She stood up and lifted Lia into her arms. Stepping out from the protection of the tree she turned, shivering as the snow settled on her head. There was no holding Lia for long, she was heavier than she looked, so in one final attempt to change his mind, Cailean stepped back under the canopy of the tree.

"What if I ask my mother to organise a search party? I am certain she will agree…. What then? Would you stay?"

"I can't. As much as I would like to, I gave Koval my word. First, he lost his son and now he has no wife, that is more grief than any man should have to bear. So, I must do this. I want to do this."

There was an honour in his words she could not deny and though she wished otherwise she understood his unwavering sense of loyalty to see his promise through to fulfilment.

Cailean placed Lia back down on the ground, kissing her dearly as she did so. The little girl seemed more contented and it was obvious there was no changing Hunter's mind.

"One last kiss before I go," he said, throwing Lia into the air. As she dropped into his arms, she kissed him repeatedly on the cheek. He gave her one last hug then placed her back down.

"I love you," she whispered.

Bael knelt down and ran his finger along her cheek.

"I love you too, little one."

"You are a good man Hunter. I will pray to the Gods for your safe return." When the final word left Cailean's lips, she moved closer to him; her head leaned forward and almost involuntarily she kissed him. Instead of pulling away he returned the kiss, their tongues searching one another as passion welled in both their stomachs. Bael let her go somewhat surprised by the depth of feeling he now had for the young woman. She too looked surprised and as both parted ways Lia took hold of Cailean's hand.

"I must go now," Bael said with surprising reluctance.

Cailean just smiled awkwardly then turned and led Lia back to the kitchen entrance at the rear of the Keep. Before the pair disappeared around the corner of the building she turned, Hunter was gone and she couldn't ignore the empty feeling she felt in her stomach when she thought she might never see him again.

55

THE CITY OF THE FALLS - A WARNING – A QUEEN

The City of the Falls was the jewel of the Kingdom, its true name Freehaven, almost forgotten except for the songs of Bards and stories of well-travelled merchants. Its white stone buildings, flowered market places and picturesque narrow streets connected by an intricate network of fast flowing waterways added to its mystique. Two thirds of the City's perimeter are surrounded by mountains. Its collection of fast flowing waterfalls feeding currents that allow boats, barges and small ships to travel freely, carting goods of every description with far greater ease and less cost than could be achieved by road. Some of these waterways were narrowed to speed up the flow of the current and drive huge wooden water wheels which in turn powered massive circular grind stones for the production of ground wheat and barley. There were enough bakeries in the city to produce bread that could feed half the country. Massive granaries littered the Port ready for the city's main export, grain, there was no bigger producer in all the Kingdoms and its sale helped maintain the Royal coffers. Another thing that set the Capital apart from any other city was its sanitation system; a myriad of underground sluice ways that through the ever-moving waters were capable of carrying all the human waste beyond the city walls and out to the open sea. In fact, it could be argued that Freehaven was by far the most self-sufficient city anywhere in the known world and it was ruled over by Agramar and his Queen.

The King's messenger hawk circled around the bird tower of the Royal High-Castle, the city's natural beauty swirling around below. The Hall of Kings was the central Keep of a fortress that stood high on a rocky prominence that overlooked the mouth of the City Port and the open sea beyond. At the top level of that Keep the King's chambers played host to the Queen herself and someone else who was not the King.

As she lay atop the young man, Elena let her wet body relax into his, the night of unbridled passion leaving her exhausted but more importantly, satisfied. She had never thought the concept of loving two men, especially after uttering those sacred vows all those years ago, could be possible. Yet here she was, lying with a man twenty years her junior, in an affair that could see *her* beheaded and her lover's arms and legs shackled to four horses, and drawn until his limbless body bled away. But the fulfilment she felt at that very moment, blind as it might be, felt worth every bit of the risk she so unwisely set aside.

She let her fingers sift through her lover's long golden hair as he slept soundly; absent any sense of guilt regarding their age difference or that she was still married to the King.

It was one of those unexpected challenges life liked to throw at you; she still loved her husband dearly, but she had never felt this desirable in a very long time, and it felt wonderful.

Elena gently slid off her lover, sat up and cradled his head in her lap. She looked down at his boyishly pretty face, he was everything her husband was not. He was gentle and warm hearted, her husband strong and resolute, but a good provider. He was lean and tall, of simple birth, her husband powerful and of noble lineage dating back centuries. In fact, on reckoning, they were complete opposites, yet in her own unfathomable way she believed she did love them both. What she got from her lover was gratification in the bedroom, but most of all, a feeling once again that she was desirable. And not to put too finer point on it, it helped that he was hung like a Stallion.

Over their time together she was able to teach him the pleasures of the flesh, that her husband had so frequently denied her: his idea of passion was more in keeping with a man performing his god given duty, whereas Tommas more than anything wanted to please. What he lacked in experience he more than made up for, in youthful stamina and vigour. There was a selflessness about him she just adored, a quality that her husband lacked, totally.

She hadn't slept all night. Her loins ached, the flutters in her stomach felt as they did in her youth, exited, nervous, her skin tingling, alive; a feeling she wanted to hang onto for as long as she could.

Life with her husband was so rigidly structured, making emotional freedom of this kind that more alluring, if fraught with very real danger.

Tommas stirred, his throat dry from dehydration, he sat up placing his hand over his mouth in case his breath smelt like it tasted. He turned around to face his true first love, and with boyish exuberance, lifted the bedcovers to expose their nakedness: he loved the unique scent they created when their bodily fluids combined, a scent he would carry with him all day long, as a constant reminder of their night together.

"Behave yourself," she said, grabbing his hand and dropping the cover back over them.

"My lady," he replied playfully, sliding out of bed. Without a care in the world, he emptied his bladder into a piss pot not far from the bed. Elena slid across the bed and touched his testicles with her toes.

"You can be so disgusting sometimes," she said, not meaning a word of it.

He turned, smiled, then picked up the pot, opened the window and to her disbelief, poured its contents into the yard below. Luckily, most of the Palace staff were still asleep, the kitchen maids, who were always up at the crack of dawn were at the other side of the building and offered no threat.

"What are you doing? Close that window, if anyone were to see you," she said angrily.

Tommas, realizing he had gone too far, apologised for his childish behaviour and closed the window.

The affair had been going on all through the summer. Their paths first crossed when her husband hired his father's group of actors to perform at a garden party in celebration of her forty fifth name day. They performed a satire about a boy and girl whose forbidden love caused a family feud between neighbouring villages. After the show was over the troupe were introduced to her and her husband. The King liked his father and wandered off talking with him. She was left in the company of the handsome golden-haired young man with whom she felt an instant, inexplicable connection. The pair found they shared a refreshing commonality in their views on life. She was instantly smitten with his zest for life, *he*, by her witty banter and unpretentious, intelligent conversation. That she had a body to die for played no small part.

Then, one fine summers morning not two days past, she found the young man waiting below her window with a handful of freshly picked flowers. The King had told the young man's father that he would be away on state business over the coming week leaving a window of opportunity that was too good to miss. Agramar had invited them as guests to stay in the castle for as long as they liked before leaving for their home village of Mickerbrook not more than three leagues away.

The morning she looked from her window to find the handsome young actor waiting below, flowers in hand was the morning that would see her private life change forever.

Tommas could tell when the Queen was worrying, she would never stay still. She'd gotten herself dressed without the aid of her maid and busied herself with menial tasks that would not usually warrant her attention. She opened the window to see that the castle was awakening.

"Get dressed. You have to leave," she demanded quite sharply. In the distance she could see a figure heading towards the tower she was in. At first she couldn't make out who it was, but as he moved closer she saw it was the keeper of hawks and he was holding the message she had been waiting on these past two days. Her stomach turned over. There was no time to get Tommas out of the room, he was still only half dressed.

"Hide! Quickly."

He stumbled, his pants only half on he hopped over to the door of the huge closet; eventually pulling them on he hid amongst the Queen's gowns and closed himself in. He looked through the gap between the doors allowing just enough room to be able to see what was going on. One of the dresses fell off its hanger after his foot got entangled in the hem, followed shortly after by the hanger itself. It clattered against the wooden sides.

"Ssh! Be quiet," Elena shouted, "do you want us to get caught?"

Tommas pulled the dress over his bent knees, his face turning bright red in the dark. Seconds later there came a knock on the door. Elena brushed her dress straight, shook her hair free and opened it to let the messenger enter.

Roderic Stillwater was a simple man with only one passion in his life, his birds. He was keeper to the largest collection of Falcons in the known world and he loved every one of them. He was never married and had no children, his life dedicated to his job for the forty years he had lived within the castle grounds. Elena always referred to him as the grumpy old sod, she had never seen him with a smile on his face and he was forever mumbling to himself; sometimes she was sure he was a little touched but her husband wouldn't have any of it, for some obscure reason he seemed to like the man. Anyway, he was here and she wanted him gone as quickly as possible.

"You have a message for me?" She said as he began to dither about waving the parchment in his hand.

"I…." After a long pause. "I do my lady. From your husband the King."

"Let me have it then," she said frustratingly.

"Uhmm!" he muttered, as if chewing his lip. "Here you are." He handed her the parchment that still had the King's seal on it. She took it from him and expected him to leave of his own accord, but he didn't; he stood there as if waiting to hear what the letter contained.

"You may go now," she ordered.

The old man gave a short bow and left mumbling incoherently to himself, leaving the door ajar as he did so.

"Will you shut that door," she shouted after him. His hand appeared waving his understanding and then the door was slammed shut.

Tommas stepped out from the closet with her dress in his hands. He placed it back on the hanger and hung it back up. Elena was unravelling the note as he joined her by the window.

"I swear that bloody old fool tries my patience on purpose," she said before reading the message. She held it up to the light to make sense of some of the words that had faded during the journey. As she read it her features saddened. Tommas could see the message had clearly shaken her and though it wasn't his place to do so, he decided to ask what the letter contained.

"You seem troubled. What is it?" he asked sitting her back down on the side of the bed.

"It is the King's brother, my brother-in-law. He is dead."

"How?" Tommas asked, shocked by the news.

"All it says is that the Keep was attacked by Northern fighters and that he died in the attack. And now my husband is on his way back there." She dropped the paper on the floor and walked back over to the window. "I should be there with him, not here, not now. You must go. Please. I would like to be alone."

"As sad as that is, you can't surely contemplate going," he said with due concern. "Who knows what may still be lurking out there, it would be madness, nay frivolous to make such a journey after what you have just read."

"Please do not presume to tell me what I should or shouldn't do. Just leave, I need time to think. Now go. Please," her voice softened.

He'd made his point and could do no more. She was still his Queen as much as she was his lover and as such demanded his unquestioning loyalty and cooperation. With nothing more to say he collected his belongings and did as she asked. What would happen next, he had no idea, but he was sensible enough to realize that such matters were beyond his control. He just had to wait.

By the end of the day Elena with the help of Captain Nyal Mayford, chief military advisor to her husband's high council in the city, had organised a hundred-strong body guard of soldiers to escort her on the journey. All that remained to be done was the filling of the supply wagons with tents and food and all would be ready. She left all that in the capable hands of the Captain. The day passed quickly. She retired to her bed early to get as much sleep as she could, before leaving at the crack of dawn.

The Captain had worked through the night and finally all was ready. As expected the Queen arrived in the courtyard with the first sign of morning light. She was traveling in the Royal carriage, offering her as much comfort as was possible for such a long journey. She took the Captains hand and stepped into it, thanking him for his help. The man bowed graciously as the carriage pulled away.

Unseen in the shadows of the stables close by stood a lonely figure. As he watched his lover leave, he couldn't help wondering what the future had in store for him and without her his life would feel empty. But for now, there was nothing he could do to change all that, he just had to wait, and see.

***

Leonii Gallo had served in the Royal employ for a little over fifteen years. In not one of those years did she forget what the one she called master and King did to her family. Time, she was often told was a healer and in truth there were moments when her hatred for her captors softened but they were short lived.

Her father was a rich land owner, her mother like most mothers loved her children and though she had never worked a day in her life she was a house-proud woman who kept the family home spotless with the help of a few well-chosen house maidens.

She had two older brothers, Hanald who had been killed serving a local Warlord sympathetic to the King Malanon. Her other brother Hobard was only ten years old, well built for his age and ferociously protective of her.

As a child of five years old she had no concept of what her father's connection to this Warlord was. What she later discovered when she *was* old enough to understand, was that her family were behind the funding of foreign Sellswords; ruthless mercenaries used to disrupt King Agramar's holdings across lands he'd brought under the Royal Banner all those years back during the Northern Campaigns. They attacked wagon trains transporting crucial farm produce to Garrisons strategically located throughout the regions.

Agramar's spies had got wind of her father's treachery and not long after, the King led a small army of men to root out this troublesome Warlord and any found supporting him.

The battle that ensued saw the Warlord and his Sellswords retreat to her family home. What followed was a slaughter.

It seemed this Agramar wanted to make a statement to all others who might sympathize with her father and this Warlord. Every Sellsword was butchered without mercy, her mother killed by a stray arrow that was meant for the Sellsword next to her. Hobard like her was captured, though since that day she knew nothing of his fate after they were separated from one another.

Her father and the Warlord he served were taken to the Capital and beheaded in front of a jeering crowd.

The years of servitude that followed she spent perfecting the sweet innocent persona that all who knew her believed her to be. But hidden beneath that well-crafted mask lurked a highly intelligent and driven woman.

She began her journey of service in the King's kitchens as a child helper to a dozen scullery maids and a buxom cook whose temper was as fiery as her red cheeks. It was the ideal environment to begin honing her skills of survival.

At first, she suffered scolding after scolding from the great hulk of a cook, though most of that was verbal with the odd slap or two on the back of the leg and never hard enough to make a mark. In time the scolding stopped and through sheer grit and determination she eventually won the Cook over: but not before lacing her meal with the pollen of Lysilia, a rare flower found in the Castle gardens, causing the cook's bowels to become so badly irritated she couldn't even make it to the privy before they evacuated their contents down her legs. The stench was overpowering driving away all but one of the kitchen staff in close proximity to her. Leonii took it upon herself to escort the cook quickly back to her quarters where she performed the unsavoury task of removing the soiled clothing and procuring a hot bath that the big woman virtually leapt into.

Like all the staff that worked in the Royal household Leonii was taught to read under the welcome tutelage of the Royal Librarian. Unlike most of the other girls and women in the place, she was a willing pupil who had an insatiable appetite for learning. Whenever she could she would head to the Library and read. Books of bird life, books on trees and local fauna were her early favourites, while books about Dragons and Fae folk fulfilled the yearnings of a childish mind.

One of the tomes that was of particular interest to her was one called The Effects of Herbs in Procurement of Healing written by a scribe, three hundred years earlier in the Tower of Knowledge. The mild poison she mixed with the cook's meal it was said, used in the right amount it could alleviate the troublesome condition of a blocked bowel movement. Too little, no effect at all. Too much; well the cook could lay witness to that effect and the indignities it carried with it.

The antidote was a simple concoction made from leaves and roots of various other plants from the same garden. Leonii handed the cook the green coloured drink and after two days the symptoms had completely disappeared; during which time Leonii had achieved her well-orchestrated ruse to worm her way into the big woman's favour.

From then on life in the kitchens was better than tolerable and in her own uniquely disciplined way she saw a side of cook that she allowed only a chosen few to see. The other maids stopped goading her as well. Strangely and not coincidently those very women on numerous occasions found themselves suffering uncontrollable bouts of flatulence and vomiting.

It wasn't long before her willingness to work and her gentle nature got her noticed by the Queen.

Following her five years in the kitchens, she spent the next two under the watchful eye of Maester Elias, the head curator of the Royal library. His long hair was the silver of moonlight on water, stretching all the way down his back to the base of his spine. His face was weathered and old; old but kindly. Over their time together each grew a fondness for the other. She warmed to his kindness as a daughter would to a father or grandfather, *he* to her tireless spirit.

Out of all those she knew in the Castle he was her favourite and being in the cooks favour she liked to surprise him with baked delicacies that would otherwise grace the Royal table.

She enjoyed these years the most before fate once again raised its troublesome head.

Now eighteen, she had blossomed into a beautiful young woman a fact that hadn't gone unnoticed by the

King himself. It wasn't long before she was promoted to the Queen's personal handmaiden whose daily duties included such things as dressing her mistress, changing the bedding and keeping her living quarters tidy.

Over the years, she found that some of the resentment she harboured towards her captors had waned some, until the night the King visited her in her quarter's. The Queen was off somewhere visiting relatives it was rumoured; that night she lost her virginity and with it any respect she had developed for the King; lost in an instant of unwanted pleasure. She suffered no physical cruelty from the man inside her yet when she stared into those eyes as he mounted her, she saw something in them that frightened her.

The indignity only occurred three more times after that, maybe he'd found another flower to pluck she never knew, but whatever the reason it was a blessing. And she could only thank the Gods that she remained without child.

She told the one person she could about the Royal indiscretion, just to keep her sanity.

Elias took it upon himself to set up a meeting with a man he had known for many years; a man who worked for another Royal family. She trusted in her old friend and met up with this stranger in the back room of a small Inn on the docks.

After that meeting, she became the eyes and ears for another Queen, relaying any information she could no matter how small or irrelevant it might seem. In return she found favour and considerable coin from a woman she believed could change her life.

Now, as she stood in the shadows of an archway opposite the King's sleeping quarter's she watched patiently as she had done from the early hours of the morning. At last her patience was rewarded.

The bedroom window opened and a man she recognised emptied a piss pot onto the yard below. She'd had her suspicions for a while and now they were rewarded.

***

Queen Oreilia Graegor paced the deck of the Sea Dragon, the pride and joy of her personal fleet of ships, trying her utmost not to throw up again. Her ship, the biggest ever built by the renowned boat yards of the Western Isles carried one hundred of her elite guard, with one smaller ship either side carrying their horses and extra provisions for the long journey. In actual fact it was said to be the biggest ship of its kind in the known world.

It sailed from the Capital Port of Chaith more than two months past on its journey to the mainland Capital. It was so big it couldn't navigate the waters of the Capital's harbour because they were not deep enough; forcing it to anchor one league offshore.

As she looked beyond the bow, she saw the Royal barge approach her ship to escort her across the Port and on to the fortresses' own jetty where her own guards were armed and waiting.

Not far from the drop off point her thoughts drifted back to that moment she opened the message from King Agramar all those months ago, the day her heart was broken.

Now here she was, ready to seek out the truth surrounding her son's death that fateful day on his way to meet his bride to be, Cailean Farroth. Something no mother should have to endure; a matter that a simple message could not convey.

Standing beside her Knights was the leader of the King's guard Sur Edmond Longshank. He was a tall surly looking man with a bushy greying beard, ruddy complexion and a broken nose. He stepped forward with a dozen of his own men to greet her.

Eight young men of the King's carriage staff carried her in the Royal Palanquin through the streets of the city and on to the Castle.

It was here she discovered to her dismay that neither Agramar nor his wife were there to greet her. Arrangements had been organized for her arrival, but news of her hosts absence hadn't reached her during her time on the seas, leaving her feeling somewhat deflated.

After settling herself in, the visiting Queen took to wandering about the Castle taking in its architectural majesty. Two of her own Knight's followed her like a shadow but she couldn't help the feeling that other eyes were upon her.

It was a beautiful day outside, cold but clear blue skies posed as a backdrop for a silvery winter sun. Having seen as much as she wanted to see inside the Castle, she decided to visit the huge ornate gardens in the grounds. Most of the trees and flora had long shed their blossom except for the long corridor of Snow Willow whose gorgeous white flowers resembled a cathedral roof as she walked beneath them. Making her way along the covered path she noticed a pretty young woman feeding a white dove on a bench up ahead. As she got closer the woman stood up as if she wanted to talk to her.

The guards placed their hands on their swords and moved in front of her.

"Halt! Do not approach the Queen," one of them shouted.

"Please my Lady I mean you no harm, I have a message."

Sensing she was in no danger the Queen ordered her men to stand down. They both relaxed their hands on their swords and stepped out of the way.

"Come forward," she gestured. "What is it you want to tell me?"

"Night Owl."

The Queen immediately recognized the code only known to herself and her spymaster. She realized that the girl before her was the one he had employed on her behalf to supply what information she could about the Farroths.

"Please child, sit with me."

Leonii sat back down next to her mysterious employer and leant in close.

"It is not safe here my Lady the trees have ears," she whispered, looking around at the gardeners tending the plants. "I will call to your room later this evening with fresh linen for your bed. There is something you should know about Queen Farroth."

56
THE WEAVING AND THE NIGHTMARE

The room is shaped like the inside of a giant egg its walls and ceiling the gentle shade of pastel green. Sitting at a large oval table whose supports are the shape of elegant stags' heads are an Elder King and his shamen. Bael once again has no control of his environment, he just hangs there, motionless and unobserved by those he looks upon. On a perch made from the branch of an olive tree stands a white hawk, its piercing red eyes forever blinking as mirrors reflecting light from the candles close by. The bird turns its head and looks straight at him as he drifts over to the end of the table where he comes to a halt and listens.

"It is time. I have shown you what the gods have planned for the boy and his adopted father. Their fate is about to change as we speak."

The King stands up and walks around the table troubled by something. He passes right through Bael's ghostly form completely unaware he is being watched by the phantom intruder. He starts towards the Hawk and strokes the back of his head letting his fingers glide over its velveteen feathers.

"You believe this will help him?" he asks hoping for reassurance.

"I do sire. Frost Wing will be our eyes and ears and will be his protector and guide through the trials to

come," he hesitates, "he will need one as the circle has shown us."

"And should the bird fall he will be reborn as you say?" The King askes sceptically.

"He will. Less than he was but still a formidable companion to the one he serves. As you are aware, he was a gift from Auriel the spirit of sky and mountain, visiting us in Elven form as she takes the form of every race she visits in search of the preservation of the ancient magic that once flourished in the world."

Bael looks at the Hawk the very same creature that has been his friend for as long as he can remember. There is a bright flash of light.

Now he is back at the cottage in the mountains. Joran sits on a log bench at the back of the property watching his son Galas of ten years train with the White Hawk that mysteriously appeared some months earlier, one cold frosty evening as the first winter snow began to fall.

The sky turns rapidly from day to night and back again in the blink of an eye, over and over until it stops again in daylight. Galas is now a young man of eighteen, his father is training him in the way of the blade. The way Joran dances with the two curved swords tells Bael he is a master of his art and when Galas picks up those very same blades it is obvious he has learnt their secrets from a very early age.

Again, there is a bright light then all turns dark and menacing.

Bael finds himself in the rooms below the pit arena where Joren fought with his son for their freedom. The shadows feel oppressive as if they harbour darkly disturbing secrets that on closer scrutiny he might unravel. Sitting alone is Galas, covered in the blood of victory. Next to him lies the body of his father. Bael remembers the fight of his earlier dreams in which he saw Joran fall to the poisoned bite of a Grawl. As sadness washes over him.

There is a bright light.

Bael stands close to the funeral pyre on which the body of Joren rests. The body is dressed in the armour of his profession his face masked with the leather helm he lost his life wearing. Sitting with King Malanon and many of his close friends and councillors is Galas wearing the swords his father left him. He sits quietly as a high priest speaks in the old tongue and sets the pyre alight. As the flames engulf the body Bael finds himself looking down into the dead eyes below him. They are not the eyes of Joren, and as he turns to gaze upon Galas the young man begins to break up like black soot, leaving behind a dark black residue of what he once was; a shadow creature that wisped in and out of existence one moment shapeless the next the ever-changing form of a man.

There is a bright light.

It's odd how he can smell the blood and gore in the room that all fighters feared to look in. The massive figure of the butcher dressed in his blood encrusted leather apron stands over the thick wooden table with his huge meat cleaver in hand. As Bael drifts closer, the blade comes down and Joren's head falls into a wooden bucket on the floor. Next an arm then a leg until only the headless, limbless torso remains. The leather masked butcher puts down the cleaver and sorts through a row of razor-sharp knives on the stone table behind him. Then with the skill of his trade he opens Joren's body from stem to stern expertly removing first the heart, then the liver and kidneys, leaving what's left for the rats.

There is a bright light.

Malanon's kitchens are huge. What he finds strange as he looks upon those utilizing its space is that they are all men, not a kitchen maid or female cook between them. They seem almost mindless as they go about their duty. First the heart is cooked as it stands then sliced and herbed so as not to resemble its whole. The kidneys and liver are sliced and fill freshly made pastry. Finally, the limbs are ground into mince and with the bones and vegetables they are made into a cauldron of human stew. Bael is horrified with what he sees and tries unsuccessfully to pull away.

There is a bright light.

Now he finds himself in the dining hall of Malanon and his close council of shamen advisors. They are all feasting on the delicacy of the day, and only the King himself is served Joren's herb infused heart.

There is a flash of light.

Hunter woke up sweating, his head propped up against the side of his Wolf. She sleeps seemingly unaware of his visions, yet he couldn't dismiss the feeling that she was somehow connected to what he had just dreamt.

57

THE JOURNEY BEGINS

He walked over to the window and stretched away his weariness. A light dusting of snow covered the ground outside and it was cold enough inside the house that he could see his breath in front of him. Leaving the Wolf to rest, Hunter laid several dry logs in the hearth and lit a fire. It wasn't long before the room felt its warmth. It was more than a day's ride to the nearest port of Molehaven where he would seek passage to the White Isles.

He'd accrued quite a considerable amount of savings, only ever spending the money he earned from the Farroth's on Vena and whatever he consumed in the taverns. On top of this, both Koval and Vena contributed to his coffers, though for quite different reasons. Koval obviously wanted to help in the search for his son, whilst Vena just looked to his safe return, though, she did feel it was for a good cause also. As a way of carrying such an amount of coin that would fill a large saddle bag, he had the money converted into jewels of varying worth; mostly white pearls and a few of the rare black ones. Arbar had helped in this, arranging a meeting with jewellers from Stonehaven and nearby towns. The black pearls had come courtesy of Jack'and, for what he considered to be a fair price. And it was; for the surly innkeep found himself liking this man he'd set out to kill and though Hunter didn't know it Jack had slipped him a few extra pearls for good measure. This had all taken a few days of organising, but at last preparation for his journey was underway.

He layered his clothing for the cold. First cotton undergarments, then a dark brown woollen shirt. Finally, he slipped on a waxed leather jacket, matching britches and a pair of soft weathered boots. He'd prepared enough food for both him and his Wolf to see them to the Port well fed. The Hawk was to stay behind. This was no journey for the bird and Bael was well aware that the creature was more than capable of looking after itself. One lot of saddle bags he filled with lighter clothes for the temperate climate that was a constant in the White Isles whose shores had never seen snow or frost. The other bag was filled with food and the coin he did carry and the third contained the jewels, some of which he placed in a leather pouch on his belt. He was almost ready to leave. He donned his winter cloak of black wool with shoulders of long-haired sable, then warmed himself one last time by the fire until it became a mound of smouldering embers. It was time. He paced over to the Wolf and nudged her gently.

"Come, we must leave," he said, as she stood up. He picked up his swords that he had oiled earlier so they wouldn't freeze and stick in their scabbards. He slid them both home and picked up his bag of jewels.

The Wolf followed him outside where his horse was tethered and waiting, the top of its back already covered with a layer of snow that was replaced as quickly as it melted. As he slung the last bag over the saddle Hunter heard a crunching of footprints on the icy ground behind him. The Wolf's lips curled into a snarl exposing her huge canines then quickly returned to normal. He turned to find a hooded figure walking towards him carrying a small leather bag. The hood fell back as the woman got closer.

"Emma? What are you doing here?" Hunter asked, surprised.

"I have brought you these," she said holding up the bag. "Father thought you might find them useful on your journey."

"What are they?"

"Fresh chicken pie, and a skin of your favourite monks' ale."

"Tell your father he has my gratitude. But you needn't have come out on a morning like this, I have plenty of food already prepared." He watched her face drop and re-thought his response. "Thank you. It will be nice to eat food worth eating. It was kind of you to bring this to me," he said, taking the bag from her outstretched hand and see a smile return.

"I wouldn't have known you were leaving if father hadn't told me."

Through the veil of falling snow he lost himself in her large seductive blue eyes; there was a vulnerability about her he had come to love, as a cherished friend and someone he trusted without reservation. He was going to miss her friendly banter, there was no denying it. Tying the bag to the pommel of his saddle he stepped back in front of her. She was shivering with the cold. He pulled her into his chest and hugged her dearly. Before letting go of her he kissed her on the forehead. She looked up and kissed him on the cheek; a tear catching the snowflakes as they fell upon her lip.

"Please come back to us," she whispered.

"I will," he finished, giving her one last hug before returning to his horse. He jumped into his saddle and turned the horse around to face her. The snow was falling heavier and it was sticking.

"Can I ask one last thing of you? Could you look in on this place from time to time? I would be grateful," he shouted after her. She stopped walking and looked back.

"I will," she answered.

With that he healed his horse forward and as he faded away into the whiteness he shouted back.

"Thank you, you will be in my thoughts."

"And you mine," she whispered.

***

The Port of Molehaven was bustling with activity when Bael and his Wolf arrived. Warm sea currents from the West touched the shores of the market town leaving the area free from frost or snow all year round. Palm trees grew where they shouldn't because of the temperate climate giving the town a strange feel of the tropics: unfortunately, absent the glorious sunshine.

It took Bael two days to find a ship big enough to take his horse and accept his Wolf as extra cargo. What made the task even more difficult was the reluctance of legitimate vessels to make the trip to the Isles; an area renowned for its trade with pirates and worse. After a couple of nights trudging round the harbour inns he was finally introduced to a Captain that was to sail to the Isles two days hence.

The owner of The Sailor's Rest, a small drinking hole with a frontage built on stilts above the water, set up the meeting. She was the only female Captain to have ever graced the port with her presence. But she could never be called a shrinking violet. She was built like a man, broad of shoulder with battle scars across an unforgiving face that was as hard as it was ugly. Her ship the Sea Bitch was hers by birth right. She'd come from a family of traders and when her father died the ship that was originally called *Adventurer* became hers.

Her crew had been in the employ of her father for years and as she was an only child she was introduced to a life on the high seas from the age of six. During that time most of the present crew had gotten to know and respect her for the navel skills she so readily learned. The ship's quarter master, a rugged old sailor had on early journeys often affectionately called her little sea bitch with no sense of malice in its meaning, and so the name had stuck.

Milus the tavern owner and a close friend of her late father had set up a meeting place in a small room at the rear of the building. He'd asked Bael to leave the Wolf in the yard outside until all was agreed upon or not, whatever the outcome he felt it would be best. Bael obliged.

The Captain entered the room to find Hunter sitting at the table, ale in hand and more handsome than she'd expected.

As she approached the table he stood up.

"Don't stand fer me," she said in a thick tone for a woman. She banged her mug of mead down on the table spilling some of it on her lap. She brushed herself down nonchalantly. "So, you want a ship to take you to the White Isles?"

"I do."

"And you have a horse and a wolf that would travel with you?" She paused. "A Dire Wolf? Where is the beast? I would see it before I can agree to anything further."

Bael put down his drink and headed for the back door to the yard. He kept it open allowing his Wolf to step into the room. The minute she passed through the door he could see the fear written across the Captain's face.

"Please, don't be alarmed she won't hurt you," he said.

The Captain had seen wolves before but never one as big as this, yet there was something about this one that suggested she was safe in its company. She allowed herself to trust the stranger standing by what she believed was his pet and relaxed a little.

He, led the animal over to the woman who looked as if she'd fear nothing.

"Please trust me for a moment, stroke her. I promise she will not harm you."

At first it looked as though she was going to pass on the suggestion, then slowly she stretched out her hand, and began to stroke the back of the Wolf's neck, and to her surprise she found herself liking the experience.

"Does she have a name?"

"She hasn't."

"How strange, to have a pet like this and not name it."

"She is not my pet," Bael replied.

"I meant no disrespect, but if it isn't a pet then what is it?"

"A companion. A special companion."

"So, now we have cleared up what she is, how did you come by such a companion?"

"If you allow us passage on your ship I might one day tell you that story."

The Captain smiled. She was a great reader of people and she liked his pluck but something in his manner told her he was a man of honour. She stopped stroking the Wolf and sipped some of her mead.

"Then to business. I am Captain Jane Noble. Noble in neither name or nature. My ship is yours. On one condition. Your Wolf and horse are your responsibility. I will get what food you need for them on the journey. I want your word that should either fall foul of the voyage you will deal with them as the circumstance dictates."

"I will."

"That just leaves the matter of cost…?" But before she could voice her price.

Bael reached into the pouch on his belt and pulled out two large black pearls. He placed them down on the table in front of her.

"I think these should cover it."

Her eyes lit up. She knew in truth the value put before her could have paid for such passage twice over with some to spare. She picked up the gems, licked them and rattled them together like a set of dice. She dropped them deftly into a pocket of her blouson top and closed the button over it. She swigged down the rest of her drink, slammed the mug back down then stretched out her hand.

"Then, we have a deal. If you have a few loose ends to tie up before we leave then do so and I will see you aboard the day after tomorrow."

Bael shook her hand, nodding his agreement, he left to chat with the tavern owner who waited patiently outside the door for the meeting to come to conclusion.

The rest of the day he found himself wandering about the Port, soaking up its breath-taking Vista.

The following two nights, he spent in the tavern speaking with the innkeep to learn more about his ship's Captain, trying to gain some insight into the woman he was to put his trust in during the next month of sailing; and he liked what he heard.

The morning of the second day had arrived quicker than expected. Even though the Port was free from frost the wind coming in from the mountains was bracing especially as it was raining. First, he called at the stables to get his horse and then on to the ship at the end of the long dock. People along the harbour front couldn't help but stare as he passed them with his Wolf.

The Captain was organizing the final delivery of the ship's cargo, overseeing its positioning in the hold. There were large rolls of fine silks and large square bales of virgin wool. Barrels of various coloured fabric die were being rolled up a gang plank to be stored on deck by the side of the Captain's cabin. Members of the crew were busy lashing them down for the journey ahead.

Bael arrived at the bottom of the gang plank as the last of the barrels was tied down. The crew on that side of the boat looked uneasy when they saw the Wolf. Even though they had been told about it they like their Captain on first seeing, were shocked by the sheer size of the animal.

Captain Noble greeted him as he stepped on board guiding his horse by the bit in its mouth. She called over two deck hands who were just closing the hold door in the ship's midsection. She ordered them to take charge of the horse and have it placed between two large wooden screens by the stairs that led up to the ships steering wheel. It was a specially prepared area she'd enlisted carpenters to make for her to help facilitate the safe transportation of livestock, especially cattle and horses. Its wooden walls were covered in straw filled hessian as protective buffers in case of rough seas. The space between them could be adjusted so the horse could sleep and be put back should the horse need bracing during stormy weather. Not many ships possessed such a facility and it was all Captain Noble's design and she was proud of it.

Bael returned down the gang plank to get the Wolf that was lying patiently in the shadow of an upturned row boat by the dockside. As the pair stepped aboard, the Captain sensing the unease amongst her crew took the initiative to break the silence. Bravely she stroked the Wolf without Bael's permission and to her delight and nervous reservation the animal lifted her huge head in response to the kindness.

"Let me show you to your quarters. If you will follow me," she said, leading Bael to his cabin aft of the main deck. She opened the door and offered them entry. It was clean a little smaller than he'd expected but the bed looked comfortable and there was enough room for his Wolf without them falling over one another. There was a small wooden table by the bed with a single lit candle on it. A small square leaded window looked out to sea and could be opened to allow the fresh sea air to enter. There was a larger table under the window which he could use for writing should the need present itself. All in all, Bael felt it was at least cosy.

"Is it to your liking?" The Captain asked. "Not a palace, I know. But comfortable."

"It is fine. Thank you," he replied laying his saddle bags by the bed.

"Then I will leave you to settle in. Is the Wolf to stay in here with you?"

"She is."

"Then I will have one of my lads bring you some straw for her bed."

"Thankyou. You are kind," Bael added.

"Oh! And by the way, I have another passenger along for the journey. Strange that she wishes to go where ever you are going don't you think. Her cabin's right across from yours," she finished with a wry smile on her face. "Anyway, I should be going."

Bael waited until she was out of the cabin before placing his bag of jewels under his bed. He emptied the other of clothes and placed them in a single closet in the corner. He couldn't escape the intrigue of what the Captain had just told him. His curiosity peeked, he gestured for the Wolf to stay where she was and started for the door, but before he could reach it someone knocked on the other side of it. He dropped the latch and slowly opened it. Standing in the dark of the corridor her face covered by her hood was a woman. She lifted her head and let the hood slip away.

"You!" He said in total disbelief. "What are *you* doing here?"

EPILOGUE

VUL-SARH - THE VOID

DEATH-

The Lord of Whispers stared at his masters' new pet. A creature of darkness and shadow it stood a monster. Deformed in its painful creation it stood on two legs like a man but was more than ten feet tall. Its head and face a visage of twisted disfigurement; a result of the dark forces called upon in its inhuman transformation.

This was the first of many; many that would become an army. The Dark Ones had grown impatient with the Devourer's lack of progress. And leaving nothing to chance they had decided to set their plan in motion earlier than previously agreed.

Souls were gathered from the ether and introduced into the living bodies of those chosen by the Lord of Whispers and his minions for their physical prowess. All of them prisoners of the void for whatever crimes they had committed in the real world. Thousands were from the lands of men, different in race and culture. Not so many were from the realm of Elves, but thousands more were from the realms of unknown lands beyond the Great Maelstrom. Vicious, man like creatures of black skin, most close to ten feet tall, whose long muscular arms ended in three fingered hands each tipped with a long curved, razor sharp talon. Each face a unique disfigurement of nightmarish originality; twisted and grotesque.

The first of these creatures that now stood chained up in the Hall of Pain was of that very same species.

The Lord of Whispers incanted some words of an ancient tongue to bring this creature of death under his control. He had four of his minions unchain the beast only to have two of them torn in half for their trouble. The Lord stepped back quickly, but it had been an instinctive reaction that saw his followers mutilated as they were. The beast calmed down and dropped on all fours, using its knuckles to move forward. It turned to the other two minions who had released it from its chains and snarled in a deep feral growl. They stepped clear as it made a lunge for them, then the Lord of Whispers chanted something else and it stopped. It shook its head from side to side, snorting as it did so and followed him out of the Domed Tower.

It followed its master up the long stone steps to the Tower of Whispers, the largest and highest of the three Domed Towers. Once inside they made their way to the Hall of the Dark Lords. They entered and climbed their way up the thousand steps to the same stone platform that had seen the Devourer of Souls set to task before his journey through the portal.

Standing before the thirteen the Lord of Whispers ordered the creature to stand up straight in demonstration of its powerful build and monstrous visage.

"He was our first my Lords," he said in the ancient tongue. "Look to the Temple and see what we have done in your name."

The King of Thorns the tallest and leader of the unholy wraiths spoke through thought into the Pool of Seeing. Its black waters cleared. The Temple and shore beyond came into focus. Standing in front and along the black stone beach were at least another three thousand of the monster that now stood before them. The King waved his huge hand over the Pool causing the image to dissolve into blackness.

"You have done well, but it is just a beginning," his voice hissing snake like and echoing in the minds of all who occupied the space around him.

"Now it is time to speak with those beyond the Portal; our servant there has been summoned."

Again, the King waved his hand above the Pool. The ripples settled and in its smoothness the Devourer of Souls materialized, his pets by his side.

He was standing in the circle of ancient stones that was the portal. Before his mind could link with theirs, the air around him began to shimmer violently, then both he and his hounds vanished in a blink. Now they would once again face their makers.

The End

About the Author

My introduction to the Fantasy Genre was the Novel – King Beyond the Gate by David Gemmell. My son Christian who was studying English at University said, "dad you have to read this book. It was Sword in the Storm another Novel by David Gemmell. I loved this book so much I decided to write a screen play for it. The die was cast. I began toying with the idea of writing my own Fantasy Novel. In the mean time I carried on reading other Authors of the Genre, George R R Martin, Brandon Sanderson, Robert Jordan and many others. The afore mentioned were especially inspirational for what became a ten-year project writing short stories, another screen play and finally my first Novel Bael: Of King's Blood. This has been a labour of love and an undertaking that has put some worth back in my life. And if you are reading this you have hopefully taken and enjoyed the journey it has taken you on. For that you have my heartfelt thanks. And so, the Journey continues.

Printed in Great Britain
by Amazon